RUTHLESS KINGS MC

VOLUME 3

LIMITED EDITION

A RUTHLESS CHRISTMAS
KNIVES
TONGUE'S TARGET
BULLSEYE
ORBITING MARS

K.L. SAVAGE

K.L. SAVAGE
Ruthless Romance That Will RIP Your Heart Out

A RUTHLESS CHRISTMAS

RUTHLESS KINGS MC: BOOK NINE

COPYRIGHT© 2020 A RUTHLESS CHRISTMAS BY KL SAVAGE

All rights reserved. Except as permitted by U.S. Copyright Act of 1976, no part of this publication may be reproduced, distributed, or transmitted in any form or by any means, or stored in a database or retrieval system, without prior permission of the author. The scanning, uploading, and distribution of this book via the Internet or via other means without the permission of the publisher is illegal and punishable by law. Please purchase only authorized electronic editions and do not participate in or encourage electronic piracy of copyrighted materials. This book is a work of fiction. Names, characters, establishments, or organizations, and incidents are either products of the author's imagination or are used fictitiously to give a sense of authenticity. Any resemblance to actual persons, living or dead, events, or locales is entirely coincidental. A RUTHLESS CHIRSTMAS is intended for 18+ older, and for mature audiences only.

LCCN 9781952500268

PHOTOGRAPHY BY WANDER AGUIAR PHOTOGRAPHY
COVER MODEL: SONNY & JOLI
EBOOK COVER DESIGN: WANDER AGUIAR
EDITING: MASQUE OF THE RED PEN & INFINITE WELL
FORMATTING: CHAMPAGNE BOOK DESIGN

FIRST EDITION PRINT 2020

For everyone who believes in Christmas miracles. We hope we find yours this holiday season.

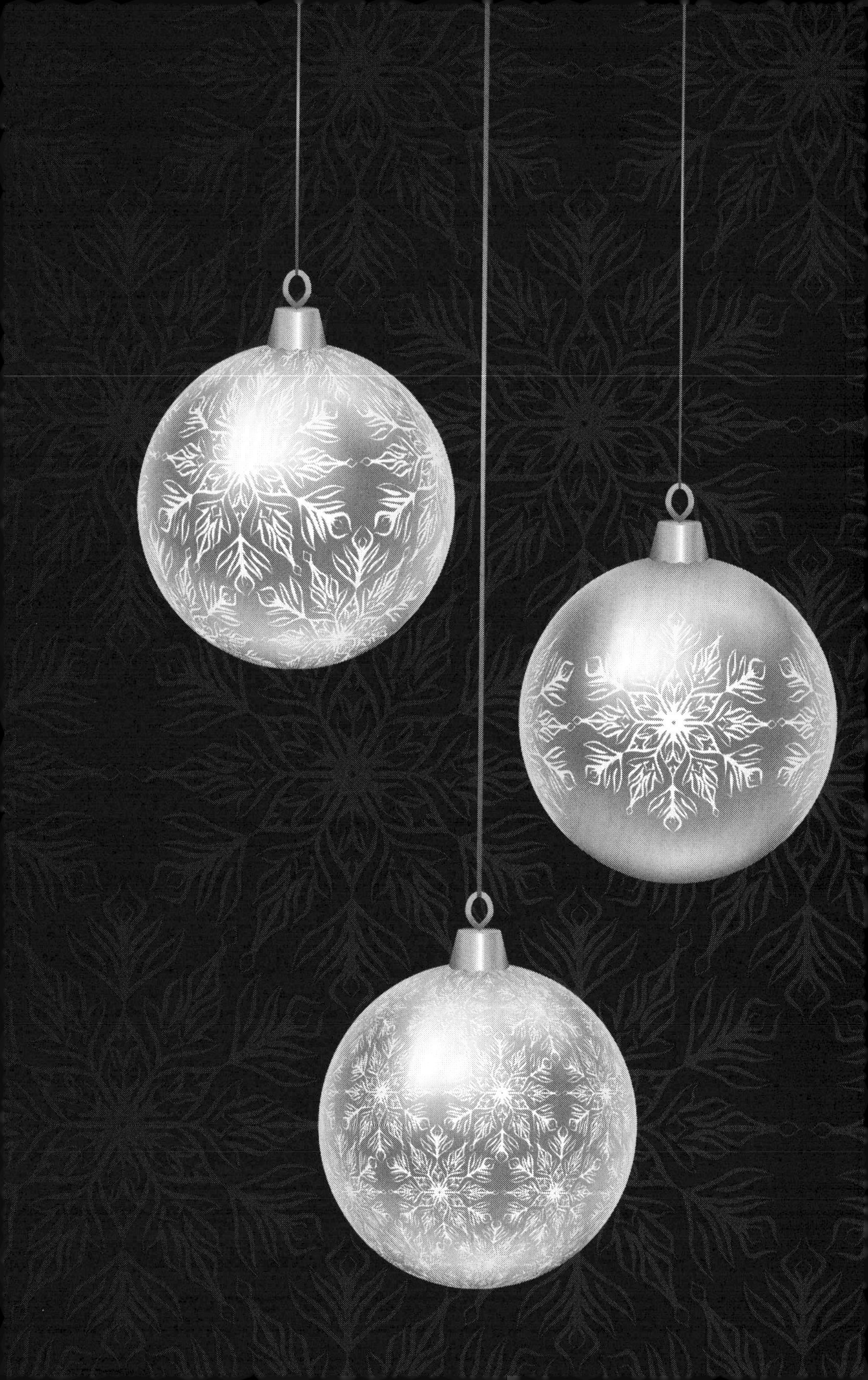

CHAPTER ONE

Reaper

One week until Christmas, and I haven't done any shopping, of any sorts, for anyone. That includes Sarah. I'm fucked. Santa is going to put fucking coals under the tree for me and burn my damn stocking. Who the hell waits this long? I don't know what to get her. I'm stressed the hell out.

Which means I'm hiding outside around back of the clubhouse because I need a damn smoke.

The damn Christmas carols, the jingle bells, the fucking Christmas movies; I'm about to drown in snow. And guess what?

It doesn't fucking snow in Vegas!

Well, it hasn't since I was a kid, but knowing my luck, this will be the year we get a record blizzard. And I can hear everyone now, "Let's go sledding! Let's make snow angels; let's build a snowman!"

Fucking shoot me.

But before any of that, I need a gift for Sarah, or so help me I'll never see another Christmas again.

I rub my temples, exhaling the stress of the holidays in a puff of air that clouds out in front of me because it's cold.

I hate being cold. I miss the heat. I miss the sun making me sweat and my skin turning pink.

I'm a damn scrooge.

Ho-ho-freaking-ho.

The pack of cigarettes in my cut pocket weigh against my right pec. I open the delicate leather and bury my hand inside, yanking the pack out. I pound the end of the box against my palm so I can tighten that tobacco. I take my time opening the container. Something about this moment is going to feel so fucking good, and I want to relish it. My fingers slide against the sleek, smooth stick. I glide out the cigarette and bring it to my nose, inhaling the rich, earthy scent.

"Oh god," I moan. It's been so long since I've had a smoke. I can't wait a second longer. I put the orange end between my lips, strike the lighter, cup my hand over the tip, and inhale. Ash starts to form, turning a beautiful shade of crimson. The smoke trickles down my throat, spreading over my lungs in the most toxic way.

I love it.

"Don't let Sarah see, or she'll think you're cheating," Poodle says as he comes around the corner of the clubhouse.

Taking another long drag, I blow the smoke in his face, not laughing at his joke. It isn't funny. I'd never fuck around on my doll. "Don't speak that way to me," I say, flicking the ashes from the tip. "I'm a little stressed. I needed a break from—"

"Christmas?"

"Christmas," I say on a tired sigh.

"We're supposed to go get a tree tonight. We've waited long enough. The kids are getting antsy."

"I'm not going."

"Are you pouting? Is Prez really throwing a tantrum?"

"Say that to me again and see what happens."

"Jesse!"

"Fuck, fuck, fuck." I throw the cigarette down and stomp on it. Poodle waves his arms through the air to get rid of the smoke. "Get rid of it!" I blow the rest out of my mouth, then start spitting. "Sarah's going to kill me."

"I'm trying to get rid of it," Poodle hisses. "It isn't my fault you're a damn chimney!"

"Do not make Santa Clause jokes right now," I snap in return, rubbing my tongue on my shirt sleeve to get the smoke out of my mouth.

"Oh, yeah. Real smooth Reaper. That's going to work. You need a freaking blow torch to get rid of the stench wafting off you."

"What's going on, guys?" Sarah's sweet voice comes from the left.

Poodle and I casually lean against the siding, pretending to talk about Christmas. "Hey, Doll. Don't come any further!" I stop her when she takes a step forward.

Her face falls when she sees she isn't welcome. "Why not? Maizey is asleep, Home Alone isn't on, and I thought we could—"

"Doll, I'm talking about your Christmas gifts. You can't know."

Her face brightens more than the damn sun when she hears the word 'gifts.' My Doll deserves all the gifts in the world.

If only I could figure out what the hell to get her.

"Really?" She rocks on her heels, cupping her hands in front of her. "What kind of gifts?"

I smirk, feeling like a real asshole for lying to her, but I don't want to tell her I've been smoking. I don't think she'll be too upset. She isn't controlling, but she's worried for my health. I only have one or two cigarettes a week, which is less than what I used to smoke.

"I can't tell you that, Doll. It would ruin the surprise. Now, let me brainstorm with Poodle. I'll catch you and Maizey in a few. Later, we'll go get that tree you want so bad."

"The biggest one they have?"

"Doll, I know how much you love big things," I purr, lowering my voice so she can't miss the sexual innuendo.

She blushes, looks over at Poodle, who is currently laughing, and then slides her eyes back to me. "Jesse, we aren't alone."

I love how bashful she gets sometimes.

"I know."

"Do I need to leave?" Poodle asks, pointing back and forth between me and Sarah. "Maybe give you a little privacy?"

I'm about to tell him to get out of fucking dodge when something bites my ankle. I immediately stumble away and hop on one foot in pain. "Ow, what the f—"

I look around to find the culprit, but it's dark. Then I hear a low hiss come from out of the darkness. "Son of a bitch! What was that?"

"Happy! Where'd you go?" Tongue yells out his pet gator's name.

I meet the eyes of my nemesis on the ground, its mouth wide open and baring its little fangs. He's still hissing at me. The damned thing swishes its tail, charges at me, and I do the only thing that enters my mind.

I hiss back.

"Oh my god!" Poodle falls over chuckling, and so does Sarah. Both of them are gripping their stomachs while I limp from a damn gator bite.

"This is not funny!" I snap. The wound isn't that bad. Tiny dots of blood, but that's not the point. That fucking gator is feral. "Tongue! Get your damn ... kitten." I can't believe he calls it that, but whatever makes Tongue mellow and grounded, then so be it.

Tongue comes around the corner and puts his hands on his thighs, relieved that he found his pet. "Oh, thank goodness. Maizey said she forgot to close the top to the tank; I was worried he would have gotten too far."

"Don't worry about him attacking people or anything." I roll my eyes, hobbling on one foot.

"He didn't attack you." Tongue rolls his eyes and claps his hands together. "Come here, Happy."

The little shit has the nerve to hiss at me again as he scurries over to Tongue, clicking up small clouds of dust with his paws. The talons click along the pebbles, and when I narrow my eyes, I notice something different about Happy's nails. They are painted red.

Is this some type of joke?

Poodle sees what I'm staring at and leans over to inspect the claws. "That's a nice shade," he observes.

"You like it? I picked it out. It reminded me of blood."

"No kidding?" Poodle says, clearly not surprised, but pretending to be. "I wouldn't have guessed, Tongue."

I bring the attention back to me. "Do you see the tear in my jeans?" I ask, turning to the left and kicking my leg out so he can see the gaping freaking hole. "He bit me."

Tongue bends over and picks up Happy, cradling him in one arm like a baby and starts tickling its belly. "It was a love bite. He didn't mean no harm, Prez."

"A love…" I say on a small breath that falls out of me when I hear such a thing. "A love bite? You cannot be serious. You better keep a freaking leash on him, Tongue. I won't have him hurting the kids."

"He loves the kids! Everyone's seen it. He loves playing fetch with Maizey."

"You're saying your gator doesn't like me? Is that it?" I ask, moving my eyes to Poodle who's whistling and staring at the sky as if it has painted him a pretty picture.

Sarah is filming the interaction on her phone, and I know I'm never going to live this down.

"Well, Prez … yeah, you need to earn his trust. You're the only one who pays him no mind."

"Tongue, I pay him no mind because he bites me!" I shout, then lower my voice when exhaustion hits. "All I wanted was two minutes of alone time. Two. Then, I get eaten by a damn gator," I start mumbling under my breath as I limp away. "All I wanted was a smoke. All I wanted was to figure out what to get Sarah." I make sure no one can hear what I'm saying except me.

"Where are you going, Prez?" Poodle calls out to me.

"Away from that damn thing!" I wave my arm back, hoping Happy gets the damn point.

"Reaper!" Sarah saying my road name has me stopping in my tracks. A droplet of blood runs down my leg when I put my weight on it. A small bead of blood, but I've killed for less, and I can't fucking kill a family pet. That's beneath me. "Give me your pack of cigarettes, right now."

Damn it. I was just about to go find a hiding spot to have a smoke. "Doll, just one," I beg. I flash her the biggest smile I can muster, but she holds her palm out and gestures her fingers for me to give up the goods.

I hate Christmas.

And Happy can go back to the damn swamp for all I care.

Bah-fucking-humbug.

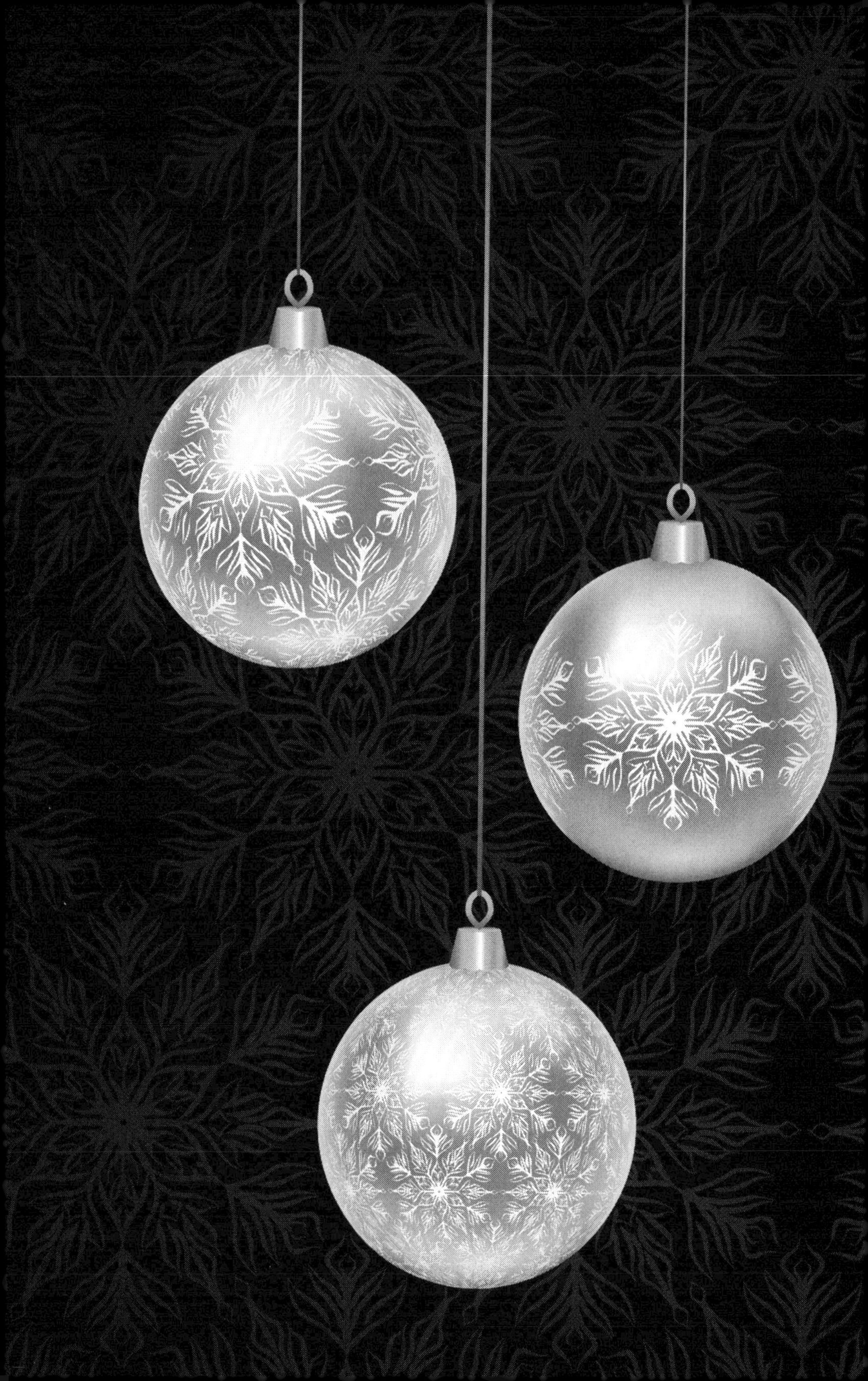

CHAPTER TWO
Sarah

REAPER HAS BEEN SO CRANKY LATELY. I KNOW EVERYTHING HAS BEEN TENSE. THERE'S still a lingering tension between me and Tongue, and Tongue and Reaper. Tongue accidentally stabbed me, thinking I was his uncle. He was upset, his mind racing as he went back in time to when his uncle did unspeakable things to him. The other members found his journals, journals I didn't even know about, and they looked through them without his permission.

Tongue broke.

He was only fighting for himself, and I don't blame him for that.

But we got into a fight. He said things, I said things, and now we don't say anything to each other.

I miss my best friend. Not that he needs me anymore; he has Daphne. Who is beyond perfect for him and so damn sweet that I don't even know how they work? No, that's not true. Tongue is sweet, kind, and fragile. No one would know that they have to handle him with ease because he's big, bad, and scary.

He's happy, and I miss him. I want to know how he's doing, but I'm too nervous to confront him. Our pride is getting in the way of making amends, and I don't know how to lower the wall that's been built between us.

All I can do is hope when the right time comes, everything will resolve itself.

Like my wound. It was deep, but it healed quicker than Doc thought, and now I'm back on my feet. I got cleared for sex weeks ago.

And I'm going to make Reaper's day and make him happier than a damn clam. I open the baby pink box I got downtown from the lingerie shop Juliette used to work at and grin when I see a handwritten note from Trixie.

"Go get'em, tiger."

Gosh, she's such a hoot. She doesn't hang around much; actually, she doesn't at all, and I don't understand why. Reaper says Trixie finds it too painful to be around the club because her brother Hawk died. Sometimes I forget Trixie is related to me and Boomer. We aren't close, but I think she does that intentionally. She must miss Hawk fiercely not to want to be around her family. I can't blame her. If Reaper ever died, I think I'd want to be alone too. Being around everyone that knew him and loved him would be too hard to handle.

Shaking my head to get out of the depressing thought, I peel back the tissue paper and pick up the red top. It's leather with white fuzzy cups for my breasts to mimic a Santa outfit. The panties are leather too, but there is something special about them I think he'll like.

They're crotchless.

My cheeks heat from the reaction I'm imagining in my head from Reaper. After everything we've shared in the bedroom, I can't believe I still blush. He makes me feel so innocent all the time, and the sex gets better with every thrust.

Oh wow, it just got hot in here. I fan myself and take a deep breath. I don't know why I get so nervous every time I dress up for him. I know he loves me mor than anything, but a small part of me always thinks he won't like it.

"Doll, you okay in there?" He knocks on the door, and my heart leaps up to my throat. I hold the top to my chest and close my eyes, taking a deep breath. "Is your stomach okay? Are you in pain?"

And then my heart drops back to my chest when I feel his love seep through the door. He's been worried sick about my wound healing. Every now and then I get a sharp pain, but I'm fine. There's no reason to tell anyone about it.

"I'm fine," I finally speak up. "Did Doc bandage you up from the wild swamp kitty attack?" I giggle at my joke. Reaper can be such a baby sometimes, which is hilarious, since he's the most badass man I've ever met in my life.

"I'm fine," he huffs. "'Tis but a flesh wound," he quotes in an accent from Monty Python and the Holy Grail movie we watched the other night.

He says the damn sentence every chance he gets now. It's adorable, but somehow, he relates it to everything.

"I'll be out in a minute," I say, taking off my top to get the show on the road.

"Okay, Doll, I'll be waiting for you. I thought we could go for a ride today? It'll be cold, but the day is pretty."

Oh, we're going for a ride alright. Just not the kind he's expecting. "Sure, baby. That's sounds good."

"I'll wait for you out here."

Yeah, we aren't going anywhere.

I slip the leather bra under my breasts, then spin it around and hook my arms through the straps. Wow, it's tight. My eyebrows reach my hairline in appreciation. My boobs are pushed up as high as they can go. Damn, they look good. I run my fingers through the white fuzz along the hem of the cups as the red leather shines in the light of the bathroom.

I slip off my pants and panties next, but before I can put on the second half of Reaper's surprise, a sharp pain ignites through the scar on my abdomen. I double over, catching myself on the edge of the sink. It's like Tongue's knife is stabbing me all over again. I breathe in through my nose and out through my mouth, then just like that, it's gone.

I finish dressing, then grab the pair of black thigh-high leather boots and pull them on. Thinking about Reaper already has me wet and aching. I fluff my hair by flipping it over and running my fingers through it. Next, I put on some cherry lip gloss and smirk at myself in the mirror.

Oh yeah, the only place we're going is the bed.

I open the door and see that he has his back to me. He's in briefs, changing his clothes to get ready for the bike ride he thinks we're going on, and his shoulders flex as he digs through the dresser drawers.

God, he's fucking sexy.

I lean against the wall, stick my leg out, and clear my throat.

"Have you seen my Ruthless Kings shirt? The one with the hole in the armpit? I know, I need to toss it, but it's my favorite."

"Yeah, I'm wearing it," I lie, but it has him turning around, showing off his impressive eight-pack abs. He's so sexy. I love that he's getting some more gray around his temples too. A gush of hot liquid leaves me as I stare at him, eating him up from head to toe.

I don't miss the noticeable bulge in his underwear. The big, thick, bulge that my pussy was made for.

He doesn't say a word. He is speechless.

"I was wondering, Jesse," I purr his name which has him gripping his cock. "Have you been naughty?" I rub my hands down my torso seductively, then up again, grabbing my breasts. "Or nice?"

He growls, then charges toward me in loud, pounding footsteps. He wraps a strong arm around my waist and picks me up. My legs wrap around his hips, and my crotchless panties rub against him, soaking his briefs with the lust he causes me to feel. He senses something different and slides one hand between us, dipping his fingers through my exposed folds.

"I've been real fucking naughty," he rumbles, sinking two fingers inside of me.

I moan, a jaw-dropping sensation taking over my body as he pumps into me, preparing me for the long, thick intrusion he's about to give me.

"You're never allowed to wear anything else ever again." He brings his hand from between my legs and stuffs the two fingers in my mouth. I let my tongue wrap around his thick digits, letting the sweet nectar slide down my throat. He loves it when I taste myself. "Looks like I'm not the only one who's been naughty," he says with hooded eyes as I suck his fingers like I would his cock.

He holds me by the meat of my ass and carries me to the bed in two steps. The soft comforter hits my back, and I sink into the soft pillowtop of the mattress. Reaper appreciates my body, slinking his hands up and down every curve before parting my legs. He closes his eyes when he sees me, then licks his lips. He takes my left ankle and places it on top of his shoulder, then does the same with my right.

His shaggy hair hangs in his face as he rubs his cheeks against the leather boots while staring at my pussy. Reaper slides up while wrapping my legs around his waist and finally kisses me. His lips always surprise me because they're so much softer than they look. Our tongues meet and lick one another before he takes my bottom lip into his mouth, then he runs his palms over my breasts. We groan into each other's mouths as my palms wraps around his scorching hot steel.

I push down his briefs just below his ass and guide him to my entrance. Every inch of me is on fire, and I need him to extinguish it.

"In a hurry?" I can feel the smirk of his lips stretching across mine just as the wide tip of his cock settles inside me.

"I need you," I moan. My clit throbs, my nipples are tight beads, and if he doesn't get inside me right now, I think I might die.

Is that possible? To die of not being fucked properly? It has to be.

He curls his hands around my shoulders, then pushes me down and thrusts forward at the same time. "Oh, yes!" I shout in relief as all of his thick, delicious inches fill me up.

"Fuck, Doll. So wet, so tight," he murmurs against the side of my neck. My nails drift down his shoulders, scratching down his back until I'm squeezing the firm globes of his ass. He pulls out, then thrusts inside again, leaving me gasping and that much closer to an orgasm.

He picks up the pace and lifts off me, staring at where we're connected. "This cunt is mine, Doll."

"All yours, Jesse. All yours." I drop my arms behind my head and stretch them out, getting lost in the sensations he's giving me. No one could ever make me feel as loved, appreciated, and sexy like Reaper does. He never makes me feel unwanted. If anything, sometimes I think his love for me hurts with how he looks at me and touches me. It's as if he can't get enough and that's what every woman in a relationship wants to feel.

"That's right," he growls, gripping the headboard behind us. He loves doing that. The more leverage he can get, the deeper and harder he can fill me. "My fucking pussy, my fucking body." He lays his hand over my heart and rocks his head back. "Mine."

"Yes," I moan as my orgasm approaches. "Yes!" A fever rushes in my veins as my belly flips and turns.

"Come for me, Doll. Come all over my cock," he orders.

I drop my hand between my legs to rub my clit, but he slaps it away, and the slight sting has me whimpering for more.

"You're going to come because of me and me alone. Understand?"

I nod, stretching my hands on either side of me and grip the sheets. I'm holding myself back. The pressure builds in the lower half of my body, and my breath catches in my ribcage.

"That's it. I feel that cunt wanting to release. Come on, Doll. Milk me," he says. Reaper brings his lips to my ear. "I want every drop of my seed inside you."

Thinking about finally having his baby tips me over the edge. "Jesse! Yes, so good," I shout, my entire body tensing as waves of sheer ecstasy pump through me at the same rhythm of his cock.

He groans, tossing his head back until the tendons are thick and protruding. His hands fall from the headboard and grab onto my tits with a painful squeeze, but I love it. I always love when he feels so good his pleasure brings pain.

In three rough thrusts of his hips, he plants himself inside me, trying to shove deeper inside me with every jet of cum. I milk him just like he told me to, hoping that one finally takes root. I want nothing more than to have his child.

Just one.

If I can have just one…

"Sarah," he grunts my name through a held breath and a red face as he pours everything he has into my womb.

Like he does every time.

He collapses on top of me but catches enough of his weight on his forearms, so he doesn't squish me to death. Reaper's cock spasms the last of his orgasm and he moans, capturing my mouth in a heated, yet gentle kiss.

His gigantic palm lands on my belly, and I know he's hoping something happens from this. I'm not holding my breath. It hasn't happened, and it will probably never happen, but no matter what, he's going to love me through it.

"I know what you're thinking," he says, breaking the kiss. We gasp for air, and the heat of his breath puffs against my chin. The room smells of sex, sweat, and cum.

And a hint of sadness.

"It's going to happen," he states with endless determination.

I wrap my arms around his neck and bring his head closer again to kiss the man I love. I don't want to get lost in despair right now. I want to be lost in Jesse, my heart's reaper. Our tongues intertwine tenderly, and he runs his fingers softly through my hair, pouring every ounce of love he has into it. I don't know how long we lay there kissing one another, but he slowly starts moving again.

It isn't rough.

It isn't hurried.

It isn't desperate.

He makes love to me, and I let him.

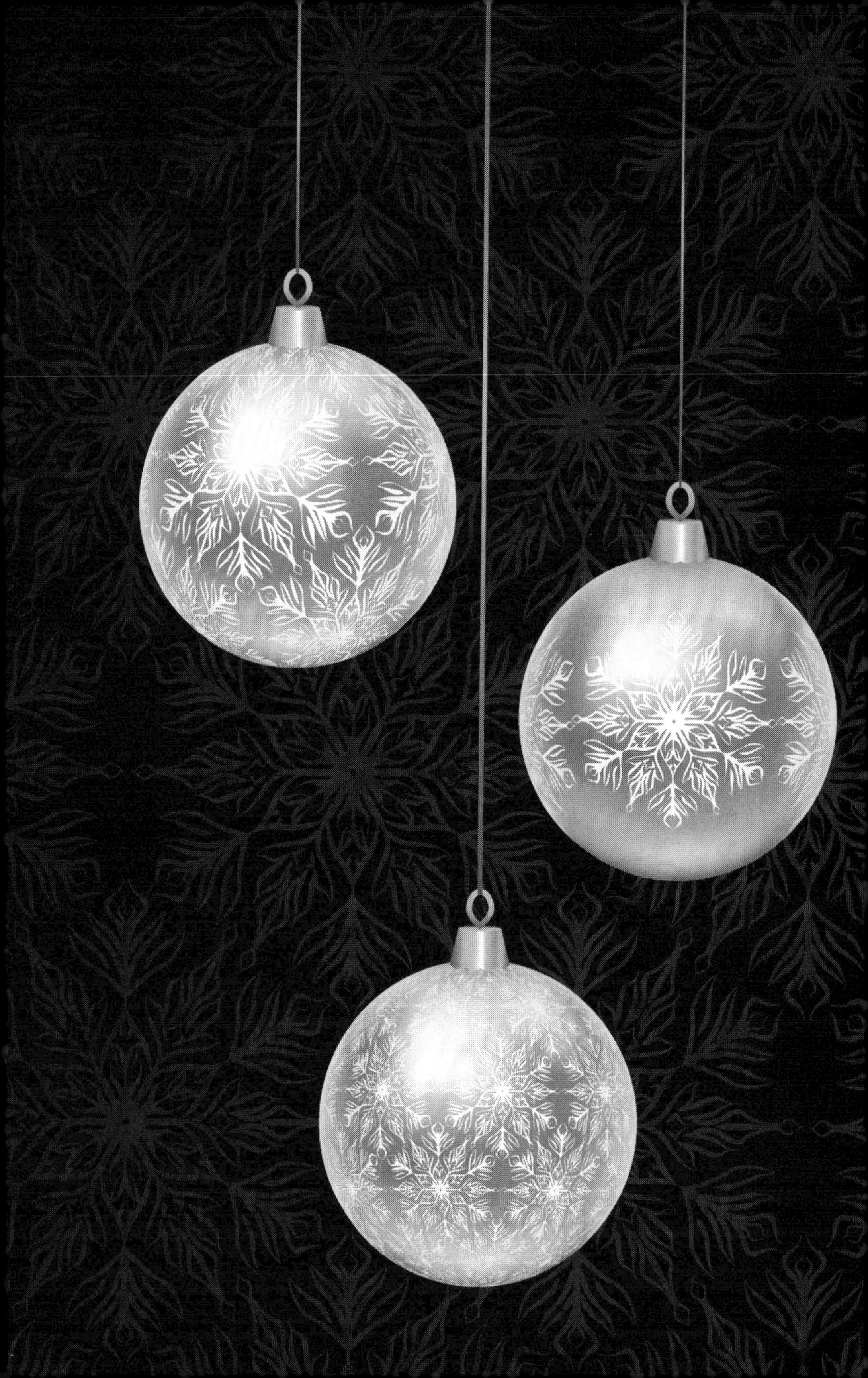

CHAPTER THREE

Juliette

We're only open for a few more days before we close for Christmas Day. We're debating staying open for Christmas Eve for all the lost souls that wander in off the streets, alone with no place to go. It sounds like a good thing to do, even if it is only one person, but we also want to be home with our Ruthless Kings family.

If I know Tool like I think I do, he's going to decide to keep Kings' Club open. On the inside, he's a big softy.

And he never stops being sexy.

"Damn it!" he shouts in pain for the hundredth time from across the stage. He's hanging mistletoe.

Everywhere.

He says if everyone has to stop and kiss every few feet, no one a reason to go home alone.

I think he's about to give up because it's the fourth time he's hit his thumb with the hammer. It isn't his tool of choice. My man is good with a screwdriver, but a hammer? He might end up killing himself if he isn't careful.

"You okay, sweetheart?" I yell, wrapping the garland around the vintage microphone.

"Fine," he grumbles. "'Tis but a flesh wound."

I roll my eyes from the quote. Him and Reaper can't seem to stop watching that damn movie. I'm about to call Boomer and have him blow up that damn DVD. Every single copy ever made. I'm sure he'd appreciate the challenge.

"Do you want me to kiss it to make it better?"

The hammer clatters to the ground, and his boots slam on the floor as he jumps down from the ladder. I don't even have to look away from what I'm doing to know he's on his way over. A black and blue thumb is shoved in front of me, and I gasp from how horrible it looks. I wrap my fingers around his wrist and gape. "Tool, I didn't know it was this bad. We might need to see Doc."

"I'm fine. It's just bruised."

"It looks broken." I twist and turn his hand, trying to look at it from every angle. I'm learning a lot about medicine from Doc, and I help out when I can because the poor man does so much for everyone when they're injured, and I know he gets overwhelmed.

"Well, it wouldn't be if you'd kiss it."

"Oh yeah?" I purr, adjusting my knees on the stage. I bring his abused thumb to my lips and press a kiss to it. "That better?"

His nostrils flare. "A little more."

The damn screwdriver behind his ear is getting the space between my legs wet. I love how he protects me with it, what he has done to make sure I'm here with him. There isn't anything hotter than a man, especially a man like Tool, defending you. He's muscular, tattooed from head to toe, and don't get me started on his cock.

It's huge, pierced, and always gets the job done.

And he needs to get to work on me because we're the only two here. The club doesn't open for another hour, and with how my eyes are level with the growing bulge in his pants, if I don't get a taste, my Christmas might be damned.

I roll my tongue over his thumb, licking it like I would his cock, and he grumbles. Wrapping my lips around the digit, I bob my head up and down, then stop. "Better?" I ask, my voice hoarse with arousal.

"Almost," he says, unzipping his pants. He's about to pull out that big, beautiful beast when an urgent knock on the door stops him. Tool's hand is inside his pants, most likely wrapped around his cock. "No! No, no, no. We can ignore them. They will go away."

But the pounding continues. It's desperate and fast.

"Son of a bitch," Tool gripes, zipping his pants in anger. He grabs my chin and forces me to meet his chocolate brown eyes. "You aren't going anywhere. I expect those lips around my cock to make my thumb better."

"I forgot your thumb was connected to your dick." I chuckle.

"Little sparrow, every part of my body is connected to my cock when it comes to you." He slams his mouth on mine and his new tongue piercing massages the inside of my mouth which has me whimpering with more need. That damn person at the door better be bleeding.

His tongue untangles itself from mine, leaving me wondering how the hell this is my life and how I have a man like Tool.

I watch his perky ass walk away from me, and I hurry to fix my hair, so I don't look like a sex fiend. I get back to wrapping the garland around the microphone. I'm hot all over. I knew I shouldn't have worn long sleeves today. Tool always makes my temperature rise.

"Juliette! Get some blankets from the back, now!" Tool yells, and I jump from the stage when I see him carrying a woman who is battered and bruised all over. Her lips are blue, and her skin is pale. I don't question him. I run through the club and dash through the purple velvet curtain. The pitter patter of my feet echo off the walls as I hurry to his office.

It's still the only part of the club that has yet to be renovated. We've been too busy to worry about it. I yank the door open and rush toward the closet in the back. I flip on the light and grab as many blankets as I can, including a heated one. If people aren't from Vegas, they don't know, or maybe consider how cold it can get in the desert. This girl looks like she's been in the cold for days.

And if the Ruthless Kings' history is anything to go by, it means bad shit is coming our way.

We will handle it. We always do.

Or maybe we will get lucky and this is some random girl, who just needs a little help getting on her feet, and is not lost, or getting abused, or homeless.

Christmas miracles happen, right?

I run out the door and down the hall, hugging the blankets to my chest. I push the curtain open, and Tool has her laid on the stage. He gently lifts her head up to tuck a pillow under her; he must have got it from one of the couches in the corner. "Here, I grabbed a heated blanket too."

"Perfect," he says, unfolding the electric blanket and throwing it over the frail woman. There's an outlet right beneath us, and he plugs in the cord and cranks the heat up to high. Luckily, we have outlets everywhere. We never thought they would be used for this though. Through the day, we serve brunch and coffee, and we get a lot of business from college kids and hungover partiers.

"My gosh, she's so cold." I touch her hand, then wrap my fingers around the side of her palm. Her entire body shivers, and her teeth clatter together. Her eyes are closed, but they're moving behind her eyelids quickly. "Miss?" I try to nudge her awake. "Miss, what happened to you? Can you hear me?" I try saying, knowing it's a longshot, but we have no idea what to do right now. Her clothes are thin, worn, and with plenty of holes. Her shoes are old, the soles barely hanging on, and she's filthy. Her hair is matted, her lips are chapped, and she's so damn skinny.

I can tell, even underneath all the mess and dirt, she's beautiful.

"Go get some water," I tell Tool, but he's already reaching for his phone in his pocket.

"We have to call 911. Maybe they can help her," Tool says, but her hand suddenly grips his wrist so tight, his skin turns white.

"No," she croaks, licking her dry lips. "No hospitals. Please," she wheezes. "Jesse. Get Jesse." She opens her eyes, and Tool inhales a sharp breath that sucks all the air out of the room. The woman's eyes flutter shut, and Tool just stares at her, open-mouthed and wide-eyed.

"What is it?" I ask, but he doesn't hear me. "Logan!" I make sure there is emphasis on his name, so it pulls him out of the trance he's in. "What's going on?"

He blinks, his lush black lashes fanning over his face as he prepares for what he's about to say. The damn anticipation is killing me. "What?" I ask again, getting impatient. He knows something. "Logan, out with it. We have an hour before we open, and we have a half dead woman on the stage."

"I think..." He runs his fingers through his hair. "I think she's asking for Reaper."

"Okay?" I say, not understanding where he's going with this. "A lot of people come to the Kings if they need help, right?"

"Yeah, but most of it is money situations. People owe us a lot of money, but Reaper stays on top of it."

"I didn't know that."

"It isn't that important compared to all the other things that have happened."

"So what, you think she owes money?"

"No. She doesn't need that kind of help. I think she's asking for Reaper because this woman, whoever she is, is his daughter."

"Shut the hell up!" I squeal so loud my voice echoes, and Tool throws his hands over his ears. "Are you sure?"

"Not completely, but they look so much alike; it's hard to deny the facts."

"I don't think they look that much alike," I say, tilting my head as I examine her face. Same nose, but she has bigger lips, sharp jawline like Reaper, brown eyes, dirty blonde hair, but that isn't evidence. "Plenty of people have similar features."

"And the people who have similar features don't just go around asking for someone who looks a lot like them."

That's a valid point.

"She's young."

"So is Sarah," he argues.

Another valid point.

"If that's true, things are about to get awkward."

"I just hope I'm wrong because if he has a daughter while Reaper and Sarah are trying to get pregnant, Sarah will feel like he doesn't need her anymore."

I hope Logan is wrong, but the more I look at the woman on stage, the more I think he's right.

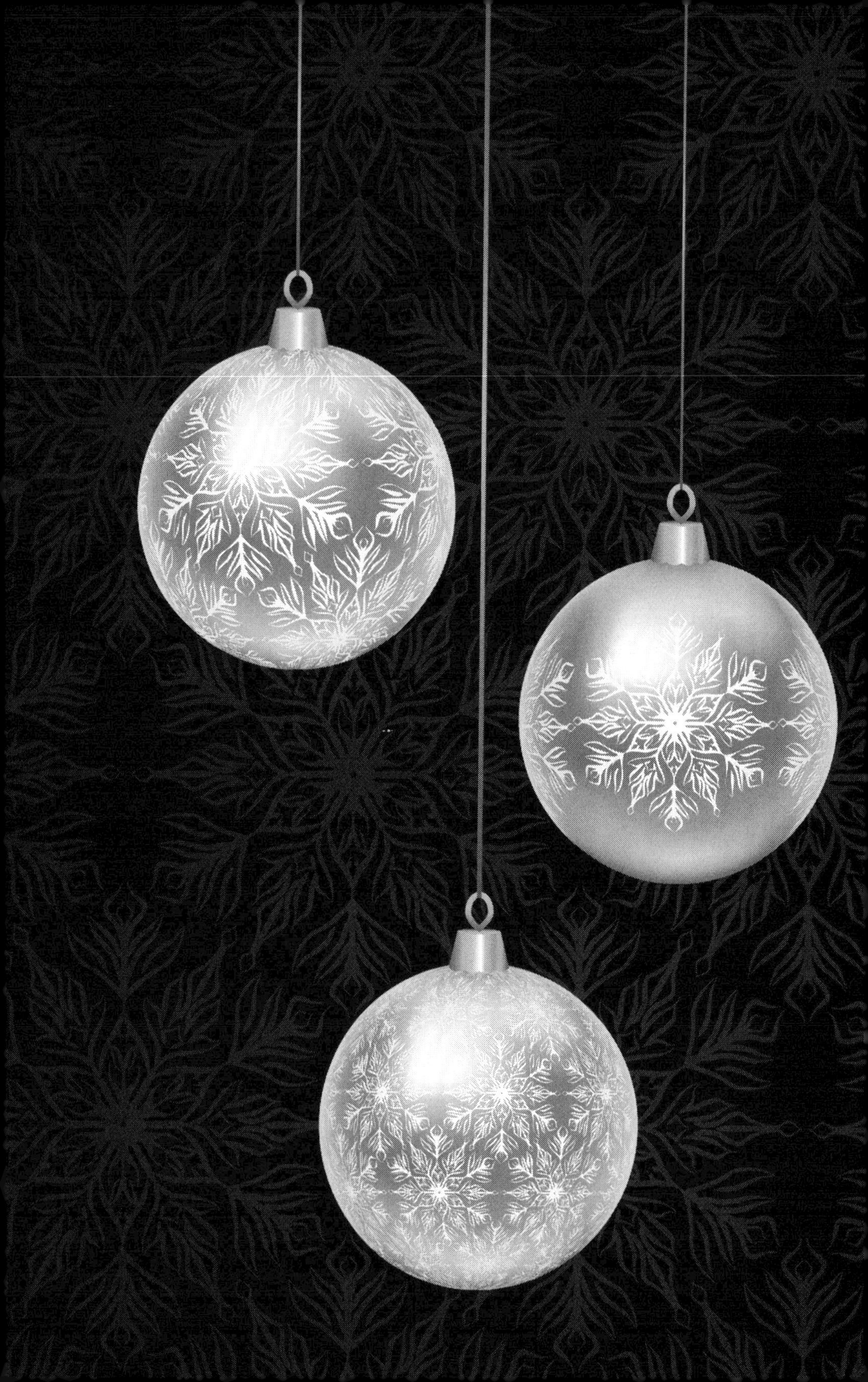

CHAPTER FOUR
Reaper

"My Maze, wake up." I nudge my little girl's arm gently as she sleeps. It's kind of late, but I'll be damned if I miss one more day to make her excited for Christmas. I've been a bad dad; I haven't tried hard enough to make Christmas special for her. That changes now, though, because it's the first holiday she's spent here since she was rescued, and she deserves to feel all the Christmas cheer.

I also shouldn't think of her as my daughter. Nothing is finalized. If anyone ever found out we had her, we would probably be charged with kidnapping. Badge dug into the missing persons database, but since we don't know her last name, there was only a few hundred pictures to look through because her name is so unique.

What we found had me begging to kill her father, who is currently in prison for sexually assaulting her younger brother. I don't know where he is; we have looked everywhere. I just hope her father didn't sell him to the same people that had my Maze. Her mother is dead, so we are the only real family she has.

Are we fucking dipped in gold?

No.

But we don't hurt innocent people. We don't fucking hurt kids. She's safe here. I'll fucking climb all the mountains, kill all the people, and slay all of the dragons if it means keeping her safe. Someone hadn't tried hard enough before, but that's not the case now.

She has more than a dozen men at her side, her army, and nothing is going to get in the way of us fighting all of her battles. Even when she's grown. And I don't care what I need to do, what laws I need to break—Maze will be here with us. She will have my last name, and she will be my little girl.

It's the only way I know she will be protected. We can give her the love she deserves. She's so different from me and Sarah. It's obvious she isn't our biological child, but it feels like it. Maze has long dark hair and big brown doe eyes with long lashes that nearly touch her brow. When she's older, she's going to be gorgeous.

You know how many souls I'm going to have to reap then? Stupid fucking boys. I know what they want, and they sure as hell aren't going to come near my Maze trying to get it.

Her lashes flutter, and those beautiful brown irises blink at me. "Dadd—

I mean, Reaper," she corrects herself, and I have to hold my breath to stop the pure fucking joy and emotion coursing through me right now.

I clear my throat and hold back the burn behind my eyes, so I don't lose it. I'm the Prez. I can't lose it. I have to be strong for everyone a hundred times over because that's what Presidents do—they find strength when none is left.

"Hey, Maze. Just letting you know, you can call me Daddy, or Reaper, or Jesse. I'm happy with any of them." I try to play it cool, but I really want her to call me Daddy. I never once thought I'd have the chance, but yet, here I am.

And I've never wanted it more.

"Okay," she whispers and stretches her arms up and over her head as she yawns, showing her two front teeth that are missing.

Shut the fuck up! No kid is allowed to be this fucking cute.

"You want to go get that tree we've been talking about?" I ask her.

I've never seen anyone move so fast in my life. She bolts out of bed, tripping on the comforter that's wrapped around her foot, but I catch her so she doesn't fall. She's wearing a onesie that has those Disney Frozen princesses all over it. She puts on her bunny slippers, then her Trolls beanie and grabs her puffy white jacket that makes her look like a marshmallow. Maze is ready in less than a minute.

It's impressive, but getting the girl to brush her teeth ... that can take an eternity.

"You sure you want to go?" I ask her, and she grabs my hand to drag me out the door.

"I'm sure. I'm sure. I'm sure! Let's go, Daddy. Let's go!"

She decided to call me Daddy.

I wipe my right eye on my shirt sleeve. Allergies. Presidents of a badass MC do not cry.

"Anything you fucking want, Maze." I smile, lifting her up by her arms and hitching her to my side.

"You said a bad word," she calls me out. "I'm gonna tell Mommy."

She's got to stop. I can't take it anymore. Maybe it's because Sarah and I have been trying so hard to have kids, and hearing the title hits home. "Badge, watch Maze for a second; I need to go find Sarah," I say, handing Maze off to the guy who can't stand children but loves Maze.

He holds her out in front of him, hands under her armpits, and looking unsure of what to do. "Um, okay. I can do it. I got it."

"I'm not an *it*!" Maze harrumphs, crossing her arms over her chest.

"You're something," Badge comments as I walk away, which makes me smile to myself.

She really is something.

Before I find Sarah, I need a minute. Right now, I don't want to be Reaper. I don't want to be the President of the Ruthless Kings.

I want to be a dad. For the first time in my life, I'm a fucking dad. I slink into the kitchen without bothering to turn on any lights and grab the edge of the table to stop myself from falling over.

In happiness.

In exhaustion.

In relief.

And I allow myself to tear up. I knock my knuckles on the table, harder than I intended, and let myself feel the immense joy in my heart right now. No one can relate except Sarah. God, we've been trying and trying and fucking trying to get pregnant. I don't have the strength to tell Sarah that I don't think it will happen. We lost the one we were meant to have, and for a long time I held out hope, but every time she takes a pregnancy test and she cries, I lose a little bit of that hope I've been clinging onto.

But now, I swear to God, my heart is fucking full.

"Ye alright, Prez? I swear, I hear sniffles," Skirt says from behind me, carrying his newborn daughter, Joey, named after Doc's ol' lady, Joanna after she tried to save Skirt's life from a fire.

"I'm fine." That sounds like a lie. My voice cracks, completely giving away how I'm doing.

"Shite, Prez. What the fuck happened? Is Sarah okay? Is Maizey okay? Did someone die? Damn it, don't tell me someone died."

I push Skirt by the shoulder until we are safe in the hallway where my office is. "Maizey called me Daddy," I say proudly, nearly puffing out my chest. "I'm a Dad."

Skirt's eyes soften around the edges as he stares at me. In a flash of understanding, he knows that right now I'm not trying to be tough. I'm not trying to be the man everyone needs me to be all the time. I'm fucking human at the end of the day, and I won't blink an eye when it comes to killing necessary evil. But when it comes to the ones I love, I have a soft spot in my heart. An area of quicksand that I get lost in when I'm around Sarah or Maizey.

"Aye, Reaper. Yer a dad. Bring it in, big fella. Congratulations." He gives me a quick hug and pats me on the back, and we're careful not to squish Joey between us.

"Thank you." Being soft, I place my arm on his throat and push him against the wall, so quick, yet gentle so I don't wake his daughter. "If you tell anyone about this, I'll be fucking furious."

"Ye don't want to tell people yer a dad?"

"No one knows I teared up. Got it?"

"Ah, aye, got it. Don't worry, Reaper. I don't think less of ye for dropping a few tears. Being a dad does that. I can't go anywhere without my Joey. I feel fucking lost when she isn't attached to me. I got to feel her little breaths and hear those tiny sighs. Her fist likes to grip on to me beard and yank it. It hurts, and I'll forever have a few bald patches, but I wouldn't trade her for the world."

I let go of his neck, and he brings Joey up to his shoulder, burying his nose in her bright red hair. She's Skirt's daughter, that's for sure.

"That's so sweet," Tongue's drawl comes from a nearby corner, but I don't know which.

It has me and Skirt jumping, and I don't find it to be a coincidence that Joey starts to cry. "Damn it, Tongue."

"Congratulations, Reaper. I'm happy for you." And just like that, the scary bastard is gone.

I reach my hand into the corner and grab nothing but air. He was here, though. He was right here.

"Shhh, it's okay. Tongue isn't going to get ye, baby. I got ye." Skirt bounces to hush his little girl to keep her from crying, but she isn't letting up anytime soon. She gets louder. "Damn it, Tongue."

"I plan on getting the tree. Do you, Dawn, Aidan, and little miss thing here want to go?"

"Aye. Let me tell Dawn and Aidan."

"Reaper! Reaper!" Tool's voice is urgent as he yells out my name.

I turn to look over my shoulder to see him dart through the kitchen, searching for me. I step out of the hallway and flip on the light. He stops in his tracks, and shakes his head at me as I start unsheathing the knife I keep tucked away in the back of my pants. "What happened?"

"No, you don't need that," he gasps, the light shining against the sweat on his forehead. "A woman came into the club. She's in bad shape. She's in the main room, and Doc is looking her over."

"Oh." I put my knife away and start toward the main room. "Is she okay? What's her name?"

"I don't know, but she asked for you."

"Uh, interesting. Okay, I'll go check it out."

Tool's hand stops me by gripping my bicep. "Prez, I have to warn you. She looks a lot like you. And she's young."

I think about what he's saying and hope like hell Tool doesn't mean what I think he means. "You might want to cut to the chase before you piss me off and ruin my good mood."

"Just go see for yourself. I'm probably wrong."

My heart thumps as I stomp my way down the hallway. When I come through, Badge is there, still holding Maizey as if she has a disease.

"I can do this all day, buddy," Maizey says, poking Badge in the cheek.

"I hope not," he mumbles under his breath.

I don't have time to deal with that right now. I have to go see what the fuss is about. I get to the living room, and Doc is listening to the stranger's heartbeat, while the guys hover around as close as they can.

The expression on their faces tells me I need to be worried. When Poodle's eyes meet mine, and he swallows. I look to Slingshot next to him, who pops a skittle in his mouth, but won't even meet my eyes. Knives is spinning his ninja start in his hand while Mary is on the other side of him, sitting in a chair, still healing from a piece of wood impaling her leg. She kicks Knives, and he drops his ninja star on the ground, which rolls to the tip of my boot.

Clink.

The steel-toe of my boot meets the silver star, and it causes it to tip over.

"You made me drop my star, Mary!"

"Maybe you aren't as slick with your weapon as you thought."

"Want to find out?" he challenges her, and even though I'm in the room, they won't look at me either.

Fuck.

My phone vibrates in my pocket, and I pull it out; it's Boomer calling. Damn it, he probably wants to talk about Christmas plans.

But there's always something, isn't there? Can't we have a fucking month where nothing happens? I'd love for the only thing I need to be worried about is Tongue blindly making people mute and Slingshot's taco disorder because it sure as fuck is not an addiction.

I ignore his call and squat next to Doc in front of the couch. I analyze the woman. She's skinny. Her clothes are old, and she smells like she hasn't bathed in weeks. "What've we got?"

"I wish I knew more, but I don't. She's coming out of hypothermia, which is odd. It's cold, but it isn't that cold. It's like she walked out of a freezer to get to this state. She's skinny, and the poor girl has been through it. She's bruised all over, a few cuts, fractured orbital socket. I'd put her in her early twenties, maybe nineteen? She's young."

"Jesse," she whispers my name, and I fall onto my ass in surprise.

I point at her. "I've never met this woman in my life. She can't be going around saying my name like that. Sarah will kill her."

The girl starts to come to, pinching her brows in pain before her eyes open, and they're the same color as mine. She searches her surroundings, and our eyes lock, and something snaps into place. I don't know what it is, but I have this need to take care of her. "Jesse," she says my name again, but it's weighed down with so much pain. Her eyes water, and the first of her tears fall. "I found you."

I knee-walk to her and take her hand in mine. "Listen, you've got to tell me how we know each other because I can't remember. I'm an asshole like that," I state, which causes her to smile. It's watery and tired, but it's there.

"What's going on?" Sarah asks as she walks around the couch. When she sees me holding the hand of another woman, she doesn't think twice or doubt me. She knows I would never set my eyes on anyone else, and I love her for it. She lays her hand on top of mine and the person she doesn't know. "Are you okay? Oh my God. What happened?"

"What's your name?" I ask her, squeezing her hand to keep her awake. "How do you know me?"

"My mom said." Her teeth clatter against one another, and she gives a full body shiver.

"Give me another damn blanket!" I bark.

Not two seconds later, the guest in our house is covered in ten of them. I'm going to leave them there. She seems like she needs all the heat.

She tries again, stammering through the shivers. "My mom … said if anything … bad ever happened to … to find you, Jesse. Vegas. Ruthless Kings." She repeats the last three as if reading from a list in her mind. "Jesse. Vegas. Ruthless Kings," she says again.

"Hey, you're here," I say, cupping her jaw with my hand, but she flinches away. "I'm sorry. I didn't mean to hurt you."

"Delilah," she stammers. "My name is Delilah."

"That's a pretty name," I say, staring into her eyes that are eerily similar to mine. "Are you my daughter? I swear to God, I didn't know about you," I blurt.

She chuckles before painfully groaning, then shakes her head. "Sister," she corrects me.

"Sister? That's … no. That's impossible." It isn't. My dad wasn't a saint. He fucked around with club sluts every single day until the day he died.

But the longer I stare into her eyes, the more I know she's right. They're too familiar. The structure of her face, her mouth, the color of her hair; even the way she smiles is too much like me. I don't need details when the facts are staring me in the face.

I have a sister.

And she's under the Kings protection now.

Until death.

And after.

It's the Ruthless way.

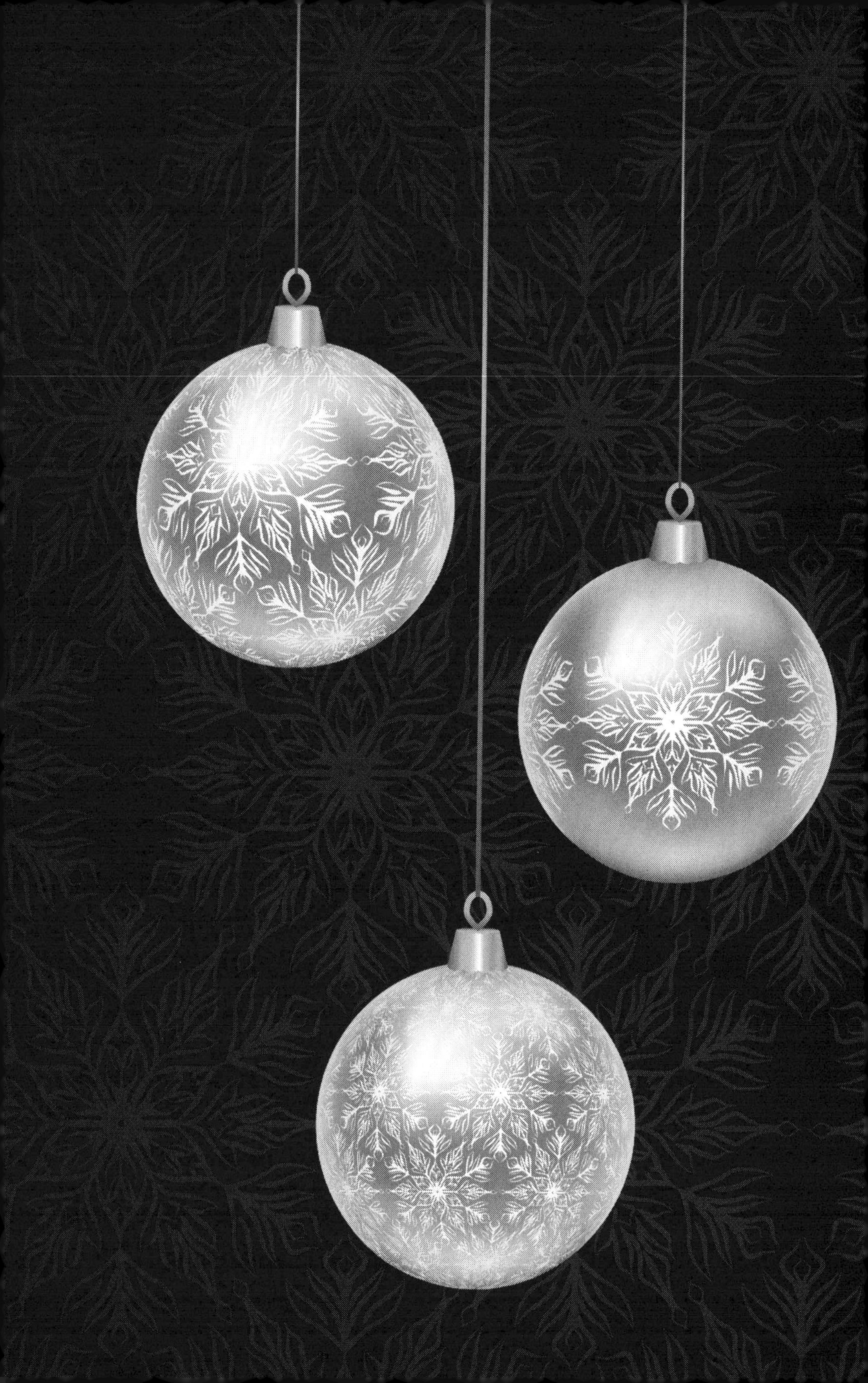

CHAPTER FIVE
Sarah

DELILAH IS ASLEEP. MAIZEY FELL ASLEEP IN BADGE'S ARMS RIGHT THERE ON THE FLOOR. They finally gave up whatever power trip they were on. Everyone might be asleep, but Jesse is wide awake. We haven't made our way home yet. The clubhouse isn't where we sleep anymore. We have a cabin on the property, but we've somehow been staying here more since everything has happened. I wouldn't be surprised if Reaper moved us back in temporarily.

He's sitting in Church at the head of the table on his throne. The chair is new, made up of black leather and hand-carved skulls surrounding the frame. The power he has in that chair vibrates my body. He's holding the gavel, staring at it as if he's waiting for it to grow the body it used to belong to. It's old, older than him and his father, along with this table.

Bad things happen in this room.

Deadly decisions are made, but sometimes, Reaper needs the room to think.

He isn't sitting in the chair normally. He's leaned against the side, one leg up and bent. One elbow is on his knee while the other is on the arm of the chair, rolling the human bone in his hand.

"You okay?" I ask him, knocking slightly on the door to let him know I'm here.

He gives an easy shake of the head, then lifts his eyes to look at me. I hate seeing him in so much pain. I'm the only one who ever gets to see it, and it kills me every time. "How did I not know about her, Doll?" he asks, hoping that I hold all the answers in the world. "She can't be older than you."

"Does…" I'm trying to untwist the knife in my gut from how his tone sounds. "Does that bother you?"

"What? No, it has nothing to do with that, Doll. You little maniac. You know I don't give a damn about our age difference."

"Anymore," I tease him.

"You were jailbait."

"Yeah, I was, wasn't I?" I giggle. "I was such a brat."

"Was?"

"You better watch it." I'm hoping our teasing back and forth helps his mood. I close the door behind me, taking one last look at Maizey and Badge on the floor.

His arms are tucked behind his head, and she's curled up in a ball next to him. The dogs surround them too. Yeti, Tyrant, Chaos, and Lady. Lady isn't as healthy as she used to be. Poodle is worried this will be her last Christmas, which will fucking kill him and everyone else. Lady means the world to everyone.

Once the door clicks shut, I make my way over to Reaper and take the gavel from him, setting it on the table that has the Ruthless Kings MC emblem carved in the middle of it. "Then what is it?" I say, keeping my voice almost as low as a whisper. I run my hands through his shaggy hair, which is a bit oily from the day, and it makes the strands slide between my fingers easier. Plus, the unkempt greasy look is sexy on him. When he is fresh out of the Kings' Garage? He can't get me off him.

"She's around your age, Doll. If what Doc said is true, how did I go nearly twenty years without knowing she existed? What's happened to her wouldn't have happened if she would've been here with me. I never expected to know how Boomer felt after meeting you, and now I do. I feel like I've been punched in the gut, and I'm angry at the world for not telling me about Delilah. She's hurt. She's scared. She was nearly frozen to death. Who did that to her?" He curls his lip in and slams his fist on the table, the gavel teetering on its end. "I want to find them, rip their hearts from their chest, and let her watch the worthless organ pump in my fist. I want her to know she's safe."

I straddle his waist, and he moves his legs down between mine so I can be more comfortable. There's one thing that can never be argued when it comes to Reaper, and that is how passionate he is. He takes his title very seriously. This isn't a job to him; this is his family. There isn't a better man to be President of the Ruthless Kings.

"You're going to keep her safe. She's only been here for an hour. She's home now. She's never been more protected than she is now."

"I know that ... I know. I'm just..." He sighs and tightens a hand around my waist. I snuggle against his chest, laying my cheek against his defined pec as I rub up and down his arms. "I'm shocked. God, I thought she was my daughter. What would you have done if you'd found out I had a daughter your age?"

I sit up and cup the side of his face. His beard scratches the palm of my hand, and his skin is softer than anyone would expect. He has a few wrinkles around his eyes from squinting so much, and the gray around his temples checks all my damn boxes. I make sure his browns meet mine. His are darker, nearly obsidian and blending into his pupils. It's hard to tell what's what some days depending on how the light hits them.

"I would have loved you just as much and probably more than I do today, Jesse. It wouldn't have bothered me if you had a daughter. I'm not oblivious to the life you lived before me. I know with our age difference comes experiences you have that I don't. I would have loved you, and I would have loved her."

"I just thought with us trying so hard, maybe it would take away from us, and I didn't want you to feel slighted."

"Baby," I exhale. "Never would anything take away from that. Nothing. If you have a sister today and three daughters walk through the door tomorrow, I'd still want you to lay me down at night and make love to me because I would still want to have your baby."

He hums in agreement, rubbing his hand over my stomach. His eyebrows do that worrying frown in the middle. I know exactly what he's thinking right now, but I don't want to talk about that. "I don't know how to be a brother," he says after a few minutes of silence.

"I'm sure she doesn't know how to be a sister either, but she came here knowing her brother would protect her. That means something, doesn't it? Already, there's a bond."

He slithers his hands between mine and places each palm on either side of my neck. His thumbs stroke down the curve of my neck, and I close my eyes, tilting back to give him more access. "I fucking love you, you know that?" he asks, skimming his hands down my front and cupping my breasts.

"Reaper, we can't do it here," I moan, rocking my hips against his erection pressing against my center.

"Your support turns me the fuck on. I need you now, Doll."

"We can't." I gasp when his lips land on the side of my neck, sucking one of his famous marks he likes to leave on me.

"I'm the President. I get to do whatever the fuck I want, when I want, where the hell I want." He unbuttons my jeans and dips his hand under my panties, his fingers brushing through the trimmed blonde tuft. My jaw drops when his index finger presses against my swollen clit. "I get to touch my ol' lady's cunt whenever I want; isn't that right?" he asks, nibbling down my neck. He licks the edge of my collarbone, and my skin pebbles with excitement.

"Yes," I hiss, rocking my hips for more friction.

"Prez!" Patrick knocks.

I sag against Reaper's body and bite the muscle of his shoulder into my mouth. I have to do my best not to cry out in rage; I'm so worked up.

"This better be fucking good, Patrick. Speak," Reaper barks, still rolling my clit slowly, and with every complete circle, my body jerks and my teeth dig further into his shoulder.

"Remember that guy I met in rehab? Loch? Him and his sister are here."

"Sisters are dropping from the sky today," Reaper mumbles, pulling his hand out of my pants with disappointment. He drops his forehead on my shoulder. "Sorry, Doll. I got to go."

"I know." I claw my nails into his shoulder as I try to gain control of myself. "I want you so bad."

He growls, picking me up and placing me on the table. "You're testing every ounce of my control. You have no idea how much I want to lay you down and fuck you right here."

"Real quick. Make them wait," I beg, pulling off my shirt and throwing it against the wall. I unhook my bra, which luckily snaps in front, and the material falls to the side.

I know I have Reaper hook, line, and sinker when he sees me half naked.

He takes his time dragging his hands over my flat, scarred stomach. He tweaks my nipples, poking his tongue from between his lips as he tugs on the red peaks. I bend my back and dig my nails into the old wood grain of the table from the sensations.

"You're nothing but trouble," Reaper growls, giving the beads a hard twist, which has me gasping for air.

"What are you going to do about it?" I fire back, challenging him, hoping that he makes them wait outside because I need him so much it hurts.

He unbuttons my jeans, unzips my pants, then tugs them down to my knees. "I'm going to fill you with my cock, use that sweet cunt, leave my cum in you, and then go take care of business." He slaps my ass as he takes a leg in each hand and flips me onto my stomach.

"Yes," I hiss, pushing my cheek into the table.

I hear the delicious sound of his zipper and then the cool air breezing over my wet heat. His finger pushes the annoying material of the panties aside, and then in one thrust, he's settled inside me. He wraps my hair around his wrist and yanks me up, so my back is flush with his front. Reaper nibbles on my ear, pushing another inch inside me, and I pulsate around him, already close to the edge.

"I love how wet you get for me. This is going to be quick, Doll. I want to fill you so bad." His dirty whispered words have my clit throbbing between my legs.

I place two fingers on the swollen bundle and quake as the sensitivity overflows through every nerve of my body..

"Hold on tight, Doll," he warns me as one hand grips my left hip and the other stays locked in my hair. His cock stretches me as he pulls out, then roughly shoves back in. His pace is quick, hard, and unrelenting. He shoves me face-first into the table, pressing me against the wood, and gives me the ride of my life.

The noises that leave me let everyone know what's happening inside Church, and isn't that just sinful?

I love it.

"I'm going to come, Doll. And you. Will. Take. Every. Drop." He punctuates his hips with every word, moaning his pleasure as he comes. I can feel the flex and jerk of his cock, knowing he's orgasming because I made him feel that good.

"Jesse!" I shout his name as one last circle against my clit has me clenching around him, trying to pull him deeper.

He collapses against me, kisses the back of my neck, and we groan when he pulls out. He hurries to slip my panties into place and grabs my shirt while I pull my pants back up. "You do know that everyone probably heard us." He gives a slight pat to my ass, and I shrug my shoulder, uncaring.

I needed that.

I re-hook my bra and pull on my shirt. I fluff my hair and try to look like I wasn't just fucked on the table. "How do I look?"

He grips the edge of the table on either side of me, his taut muscles bulging with the desire to grab me and have his way with me again. "You look like you need my cock again." His hands caress my backside and squeezes. "I don't know what's gotten into you lately, but I fucking love it." He smashes his mouth against me, burying his tongue in my throat and stealing the breath from my lungs as he owns me. He breaks the kiss, and he's right—I'm ready to go another round.

I must be ovulating. I hate that I know my cycle to the nearest second, but I always feel extra rowdy around that time of mouth.

"Now, you need to go to bed, and wait for me naked. When I'm done, I'm going to be inside you—" he blows cold air against my neck, and I whimper "—all night."

The space in front of me loses warmth, and then the door creaks open from his departure. "What the fuck are you looking at? Didn't you say someone is here to see me?" Reaper barks.

"Come and sex! You fucked her good in the pussy!"

I hold a hand over my mouth to stifle a laugh.

"Hi, Loch. How are you doing?" Reaper sighs.

"Not as good as you, sex machine, but I bet you have a little dick!"

This is going to be a long night.

Crap.

We didn't get the damn tree.

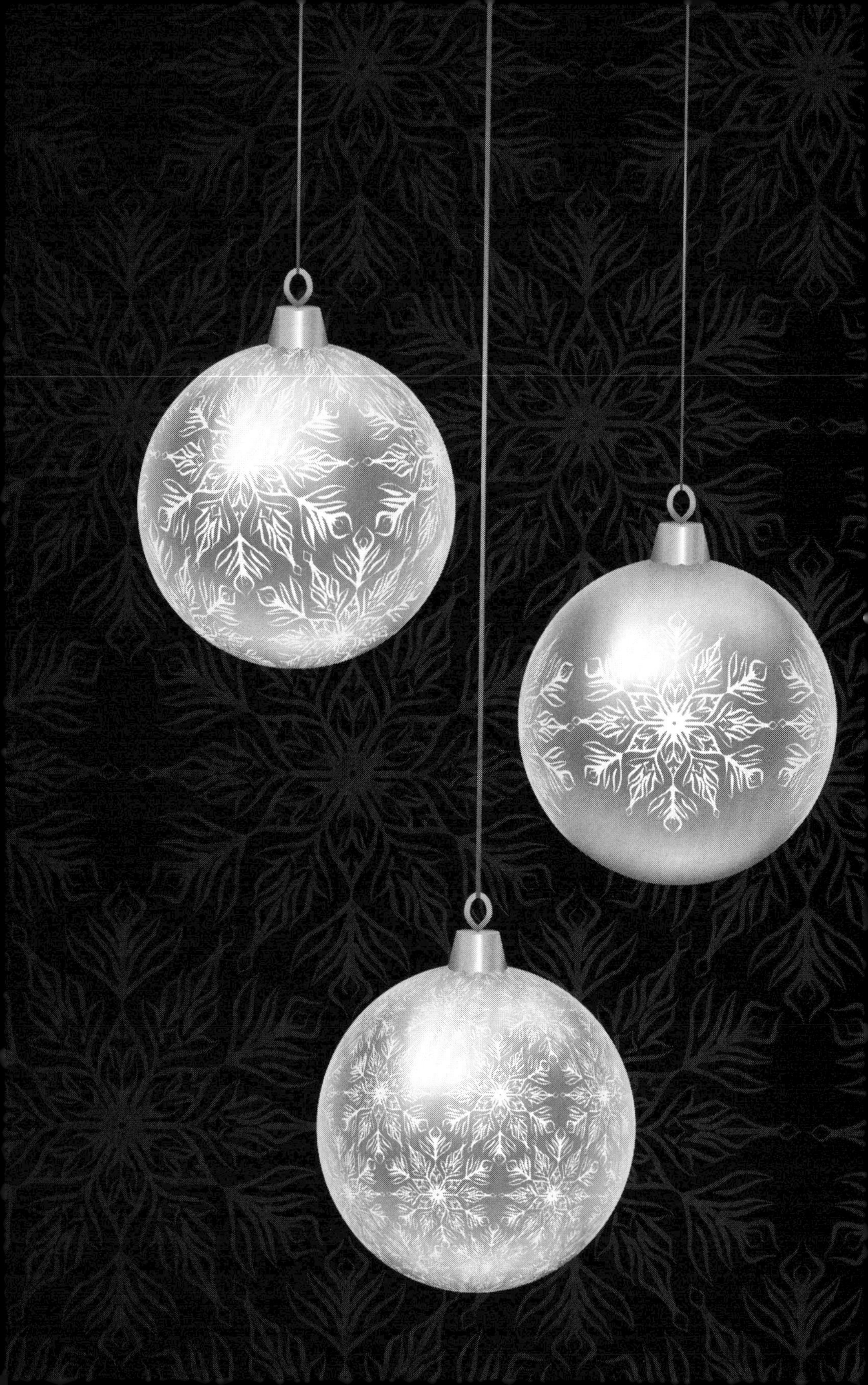

CHAPTER SIX

The Groundskeeper

Look at them.

Their festive Christmas spirit makes me sick. There's one hanging up lights right now, wrapping the red, blue, white, green, and yellow lights around the porch. If I remember him correctly, I believe he is the one with the drinking problem.

Maybe it's time I plan my next attack.

If I leave him alone in a room with a shot of whiskey or any alcohol, how long would it take for him to break? A grin stretches my lips as I think about him relapsing. He seems so happy, but I'd bet anything he craves for a drink to slide down his throat even still.

I watch him from the distance with my binoculars as he gets tangled in the lights. They wrap around his legs, and he nearly trips and falls when he pulls tight. Damn, he catches himself.

The tree branch sways from the wind, and I grasp onto it tightly so I don't fall. The Kings think they can beat me with these walls to keep me out? I will always find a way to hurt them, to try to make them weak. They might have beaten me these few times, but someone will fall.

And all of them will break.

"What are you doing?"

"Shit!" I slip off the branch, and the binoculars fall the ground. The lenses cracks, and anger boils because I know they are ruined. It's my third pair.

The bark scratches against my fingers as I look down to see Zain, the leader of our little misfit loony bin we have created; only I'm not crazy. I know what the hell needs to happen in this world to make it better, and biker scum—along with prostitutes and drug dealers—do not make it a better place. I'm cleaning the place up. People should be thanking me!

I'm not fucking crazy.

"Zain, what are you doing here?"

He crosses his huge arms over his chest. "It's good to see you too, Porter."

"Don't call me that," I seethe. I hate my name.

He rolls his eyes. "The Groundskeeper. That's ridiculous. I'm not calling you that." He rubs a hand over his bald head, then drags it down his face. "Also, I need you to lay off the Ruthless Kings. Okay?"

I let go of the branch and hit the ground. My knees soak up the vibrations as I straighten. "Why?"

"Because no thanks to you and your fucking stupidity, they are our new landlords."

"What? No, that's impossible. I scared them from that place!"

"No, you don't scare a King. You only dare them. Plus, I'm related to one."

"You're..." I clench my fists, doing my best not to launch myself at him to wrap my hands around his throat. If he's related to bikers, he's just as bad as they are. Except me. It's not like I asked to be related to Tongue. He's my half-brother.

That doesn't even count.

Plus, I haven't told anyone.

"Which one?" I ask.

"Reaper. He's my nephew."

"I'm so sorry." It disgusts me. How did I not know this when we were all in Riverside Mental Institution together before we broke out? If I would have known, I wouldn't have agreed to live with him.

"Why? It's going to be because of me that we have a home. I'm going to introduce myself, pay rent, and then we can move into the old asylum. You should be thankful."

"I'd rather live on the side of the road than live in a building they own," I spit.

"Then have fun dodging cars, fucker." He flicks me off as he walks away.

"Wait, you're doing it now?" I run after him and shove my hands in my pockets. I can't walk to the front door with him considering Daphne knows my face. Sweet little thing. She's got fight in her that I want to see again. I lift my hand to my head and feel the indentation left from the bar she smacked me with. I wasn't expecting such a hard hit from such a small woman.

It's beautiful.

"Um, yeah, I have to do it now if we want a place to sleep tonight. The others want a home too, Porter. Not everything is about you." His chest rises and falls, then he snaps his neck from left to right, an audible pop telling me to tread lightly.

I hate treading lightly.

But Zain has this disorder called mania, and when he's in one of his episodes, I know he could kill me if he wanted. A part of me wants to see him try. His mania is triggered when he feels like he has to prove himself. He gets a surge of energy and lashes out, becoming out of focus, desperate, irritable, and he gets an overload of confidence. When he crashes, he enters a depressive episode that can last days, maybe weeks.

Blah, blah, blah. We all have our problems, don't we?

"Stop calling me Porter."

"Realize you have an identity disorder, and maybe I will," he sneers. "Now, go back to the asylum. The others are there." He spins on his cowboy boots and kicks up the desert dust. His lumbering body turns the edge of the wall, and I don't tell him I'm not going back to the asylum. I'm going to watch this unfold.

I grab my broken binoculars from the ground, accidentally getting sand embedded underneath my nails, and climb up the tree again. I lay across the branch like a panther and get into position. "Yes," I cheer when I see only the left lens is broken.

The right is crystal clear.

I peep through the lens and watch Zain get to the front gate. Immediately, a scrawny guy appears from the gate, holding a gun at his head. The guy is brave; I'll give him that. Zain is holding on to the last ounce of strength he has not to release the mania building up inside him. I swing the binoculars to the right and see Reaper standing on the porch. He passes a tangled-up Patrick on his way down the steps to confront Zain.

Oh, this is going to be good; only, someone on the porch has me backtracking, and my breath catches when I see the most beautiful woman I've ever seen. She's helping Patrick untangle himself, laughing at him because he was dumb enough to get twisted up in Christmas lights. Her blonde hair hangs over her shoulders, and her body has parts of me awakening that rubs against the tree branch.

This must be Sarah, Reaper's ol' lady. Isn't that what the bikers call their bitches?

I want her to be mine.

"What a vision," I whisper with awe, just as she bends over to help pick up the lights off the porch. Her ass is fucking perfect. I rock against the tree branch, needing some type of friction as I watch her every move.

I knew she was beautiful. I really did, but my god, I'm seeing her in a new light since the last time I paid a visit here without any of them knowing. She isn't like Daphne. I was only trying to help Daphne when I kidnapped her because we are so much alike. People should stay with their kind of people, you know?

But Sarah might be the exception.

Merry Christmas to me. It looks like I've been a better boy than I thought this year.

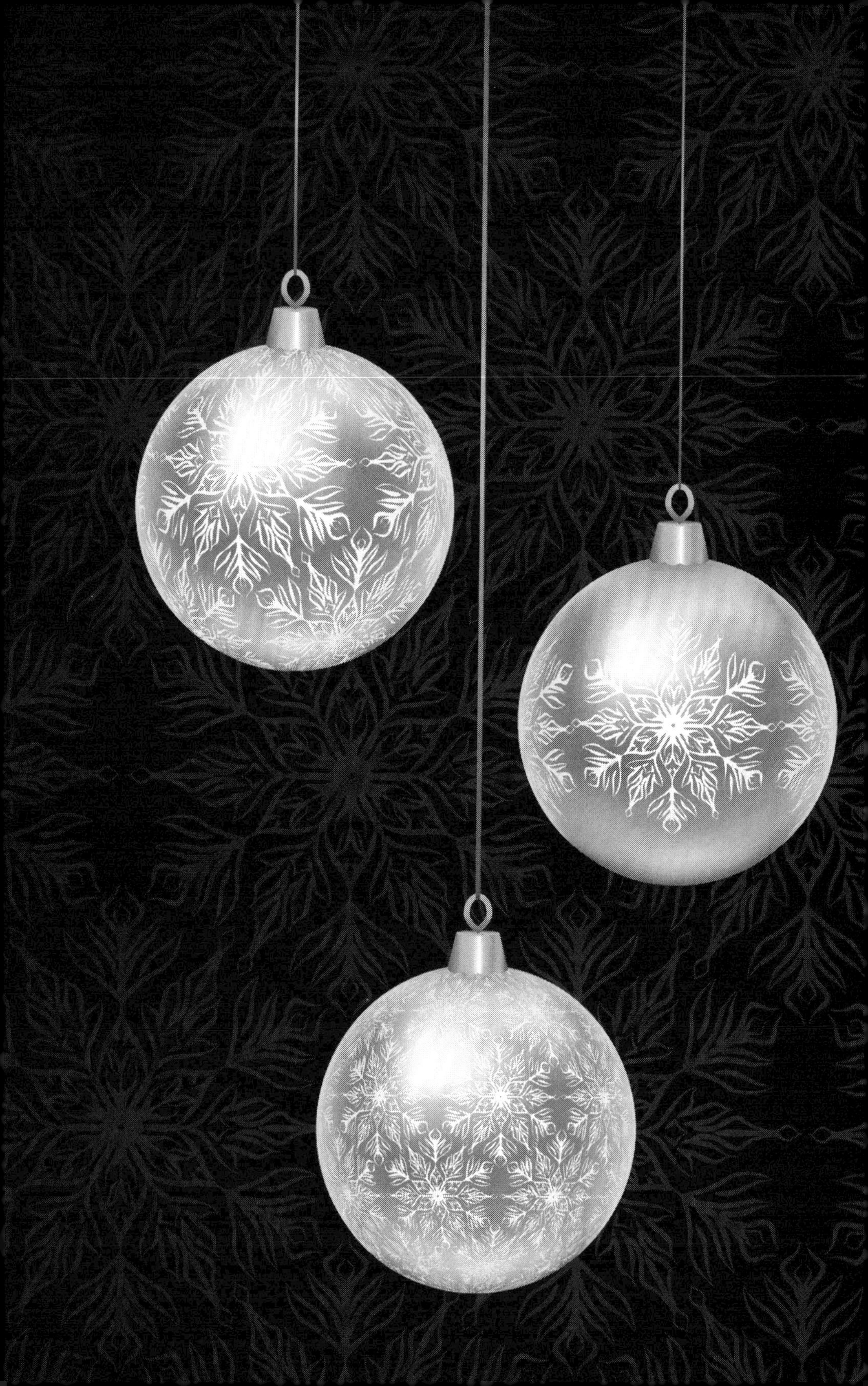

CHAPTER SEVEN

Slingshot

So much happened last night. I thought Reaper's head was going to pop off his body and explode. Not only did we find out his dad got a club whore pregnant, but that he has a sister! A hot sister. Not that I'd ever do anything about the fact that I find her hot. I like that my heart beats in my chest and not Reaper's palm.

So besides that madness, he finds out he has an uncle named Zain, a man he's never met, who was his dad's brother.

Damn, Reaper's getting hit left and right with all the surprises for Christmas.

All I want for Christmas is tacos.

Preferably an all-you-can-eat taco buffet.

I'm not picky, but if I know the guys, they aren't going to get me tacos.

A guy can dream.

There's officially five days left until Christmas, and while there are decorations everywhere, there's still no tree. My little Miss Avocado is bummed about it. I'm sitting at the kitchen table, waiting to see if Reaper has a brother that's about to walk through the door to stir the pot. I sip my coffee and see Maizey swirl her fork around in her scrambled eggs. It's more like ketchup with eggs, but to each their own, I guess.

It looks disgusting.

She lets out a big dramatic sigh, waiting for me to say something.

I grin around the rim of my mug and nod at Knives when he walks into the kitchen and heads for the coffee pot. His hair is a mess, and he seems like he's still asleep since I can't see his eyes. The man has gotten so many tattoos lately that he hardly looks like the same guy. My favorite one he has is simple. It says 'Judge Me' right where his neck meets his chest.

Maizey lets out another long exhale and taps her fork against the plate, creating that awful fucking sound I hate, so I give in. "What's got your unicorns lacking color, squirt?" I ask her, hating to see her so down.

She sits up and shrugs her tiny shoulders.

"Oh, no, come on. Tell ol' Uncle Slingshot what's wrong." I steal a piece of toast off her plate and bite into it.

"We don't have a tree, and if we don't have a tree, Santa won't come and make my Christmas wishes come true."

"You mean leave presents?" I question.

"No!" she shakes her head, and her dark brown frizzy hair poufs around her shoulders. "If we don't have a tree, then Santa won't know to give Mommy and Daddy a baby. They really want one. I wrote Santa about it and everything, but he hasn't answered. It's because we don't have a tree." Her bottom lip starts to wiggle, and those damn brown eyes get big, but I know what she's doing.

Nope. It isn't going to work. "The puppy eyes aren't going to work on me." I find myself saying that every time because when it comes to Maizey, I seem to be the one to give in the quickest.

Knives snorts, then pretends to clear his throat.

Ass.

"Did you really write Santa a letter for Sarah and Reaper?" My heart melts at the thought. What a sweet kid. And she's calling them Mom and Dad? They must be over the moon.

She nods like a bobblehead. "I did. I did. I even made a copy. Want to see?"

"You made a copy?" Knives repeats her question. His voice is rough with sleep still, tinged with gravel and morning time.

"Just in case Santa didn't get it, duh," she sasses, then leans in and whispers, blocking Knives from reading her lips by placing her hand next to her mouth. "Does he know anything?"

"'Fraid not. Poor guy. He still counts on his fingers."

"Everyone counts on their fingers, Slingshot! If not, you're a liar." He slams his mug down on the table, then picks it back up and stomps out of the room.

"He is so not a morning person," Maizey grins, pinching her lips before scooping up some ketchup egg soup.

Bleh, gross.

"He really isn't." I lean back in the chair until it's balancing on its hind legs, then rock forward. "Okay, I'm not going to be the reason why my Prez and his ol' lady don't get their baby. You want to go get a tree today?"

"Sucker," Badge's voice booms from the back room where he hides away.

"Officer Butthead," Maizey grumbles, then giggles. "I said a bad word."

"I'll let it slide because he is a butthead," I shout the last word over my shoulder to make sure he hears it.

"Okay, go change. We're getting a tree."

"Really?" she squeals.

I point to her breakfast. "After you finish that mess you call food."

She bounces in her chair as she scoops the food into her mouth. Reaper and Sarah walk through the entryway. Neither of them look like they have gotten much sleep with the dark circles around their eyes. "What's all the excitement about,

Maze?" Reaper bends down and gives her a quick kiss on top of her head, followed by Sarah.

"Uncle Slingshot is going to take me to get a tree!"

"I want to take her to get a tree." Reaper narrows his eyes at me, pissed that I'd dare take this opportunity away from him.

Oh my God. I can feel him about to take my heart.

I gulp. "I was going to ask before we left."

"We can go together. And we're going to get the biggest tree. Everyone is going!" Reaper announces throughout the house. "Be ready in fifteen." Reaper pours himself some coffee in a white mug that says, 'President of the Unites States of Ruthless America,' a mug I got him as a joke last Christmas. Not to toot my own horn, but he uses it every morning, so…

Toot-toot.

"I'm going to get us the biggest damn tree there is," he grumbles.

"I know you are, baby." Sarah soothes him by rubbing his shoulder.

"Stupid trees. You know, I could go out and chop one down and bring it in here. I'll cut a hole in the roof if I have to."

"I know you would, baby." She continues to be supportive while he vents.

Maizey giggles, and it always makes me laugh because she's so infectious.

"Don't laugh. I'm serious. The biggest tree."

"I know, Daddy," Maizey says with ketchup around her mouth.

"Any tree you want, Maze. You pick, it's yours. Nothing is going to stop me from getting this damn thing!" he bellows, then marches down the hallway and opens his office door. "The biggest fucking tree, got it? We leave in ten minutes, and for the ones who don't show, I'll have you acting like Santa Clause for the next three years!" He slams the door so hard the floor shakes.

"Mommy, Daddy said a bad word."

Sarah gasps and drops the mug she has in her hands, shattering on the floor. Hot coffee and ceramic pieces fly everywhere, but I'm up and out of my seat to get Sarah out of the way.

"Are you okay? Are you hurt?" I ask, just as the office door slams again.

"Doll? What happened?" Reaper says from behind me. "Are you hurt?" Reaper echoes my question and runs to her side, swinging her into his arms, but she fights him.

"I'm fine; put me down. Maze called me Mommy, and it's the first time I heard it." Sarah runs around the other side of the table where it's coffee and mug free, then kneels. "You sure, Maizey? Is that what you want?"

Maizey nods. "Is that okay?"

"Yeah…" She chokes and pulls Maizey in for a hug. "It's more than okay. I'm so happy to be your mommy."

Reaper makes his way over to his family, and I decide this is a good moment to give them some privacy. They've been wanting a child for a long time. We found the families of most of the other kids who were rescued. And it took a while longer to get two more of them back to their families because they were from Mexico. Now all that's left is Maizey and two more who haven't found their homes. They aren't like Maizey, though. They didn't bounce back from being kidnapped. Hell, I forget they are here half the time because I never see them. They stay in a room downstairs. We don't want to put them in foster care, but what do we do? They're too scared to be here.

They should be where they want to be.

I knock on Tongue's door since it's the closest room to escape to and try the knob. I open it and allow myself in, taking a deep breath of relief to be away from the special moment.

"Hi, Slingshot."

Tongue's voice startles me, which it shouldn't because it's his room.

My eyes land on the bed, and Daphne is reading while Tongue is placing a Santa hat on his baby gator, Happy. What blows my mind is how Happy is allowing this to happen. "Did you make Happy a Santa hat, Tongue?" I ask, taking a step closer to see if what I'm seeing is real.

"Ain't he cute?" Tongue says with a big smile on his face as he holds up his gator like a proud momma.

The gator opens his mouth wide, and I swear, Happy smiles at me. And damn it, if somehow that reptile doesn't look adorable with that Santa hat on. "He looks very cute, Tongue."

"Oh, that's not all."

It never is when it comes to Tongue.

"Look!" Tongue pulls out a wide red leather collar that has Happy engraved on it in gold. "I got him a matching leash too. For walks."

"Because gators walk. Obviously," I note. Daphne winks at me.

She knows.

"Well, are you going to bring him to get the Christmas tree?" I ask, sitting on the edge of the bed. I reach for Happy to pet the top of his head, but he hisses at me.

"Sorry; he only likes us," Daphne says, patting me on the shoulder before going back to reading her book.

"That's not true." Tongue strokes the spine of his 'swamp kitty' as he calls it. He's such an interesting person. "He likes Patrick and Poodle."

"He almost bit Patrick's finger off," Daphne says, licking her fingers and flipping the page of the book she's reading. Now that I'm looking around their room for the first time, it's exactly the same as it was before Daphne moved in, only there are books everywhere. In every corner, on top of the dresser, beside the bed, stacked behind the bed to create a headboard. Tongue is the happiest I've ever seen him.

"Patrick insulted him. Happy was defending himself. Isn't that right, good boy?" Tongue scratches under Happy's chin, and the gator shows his teeth and closes his eyes, nearly purring with contentedness.

What the fuck kind of twilight zone is this?

"Let's go! We're getting that damn tree, now!" Reaper bellows.

"Oh, hold on; I need to get his emotional support vest."

I freeze mid-stand. I know I did not hear what I think I just heard. A gator is not an emotional support animal. That can't even be legal.

The proof is right there before my eyes, though. He slips the vest over Happy's body, and on the side in white block letters it reads, 'Emotional support animal in training.'

"Oh, such a good boy, Happy." Tongue places Happy on the ground and reaches into a red jar, pulling out pink chunks of... something. He tosses the treat in the air, and Happy's jaws smack together.

I have a feeling those were bite-sized pieces of tongue.

And he keeps them in a Mason jar.

Next to his bed.

I need to get out of here.

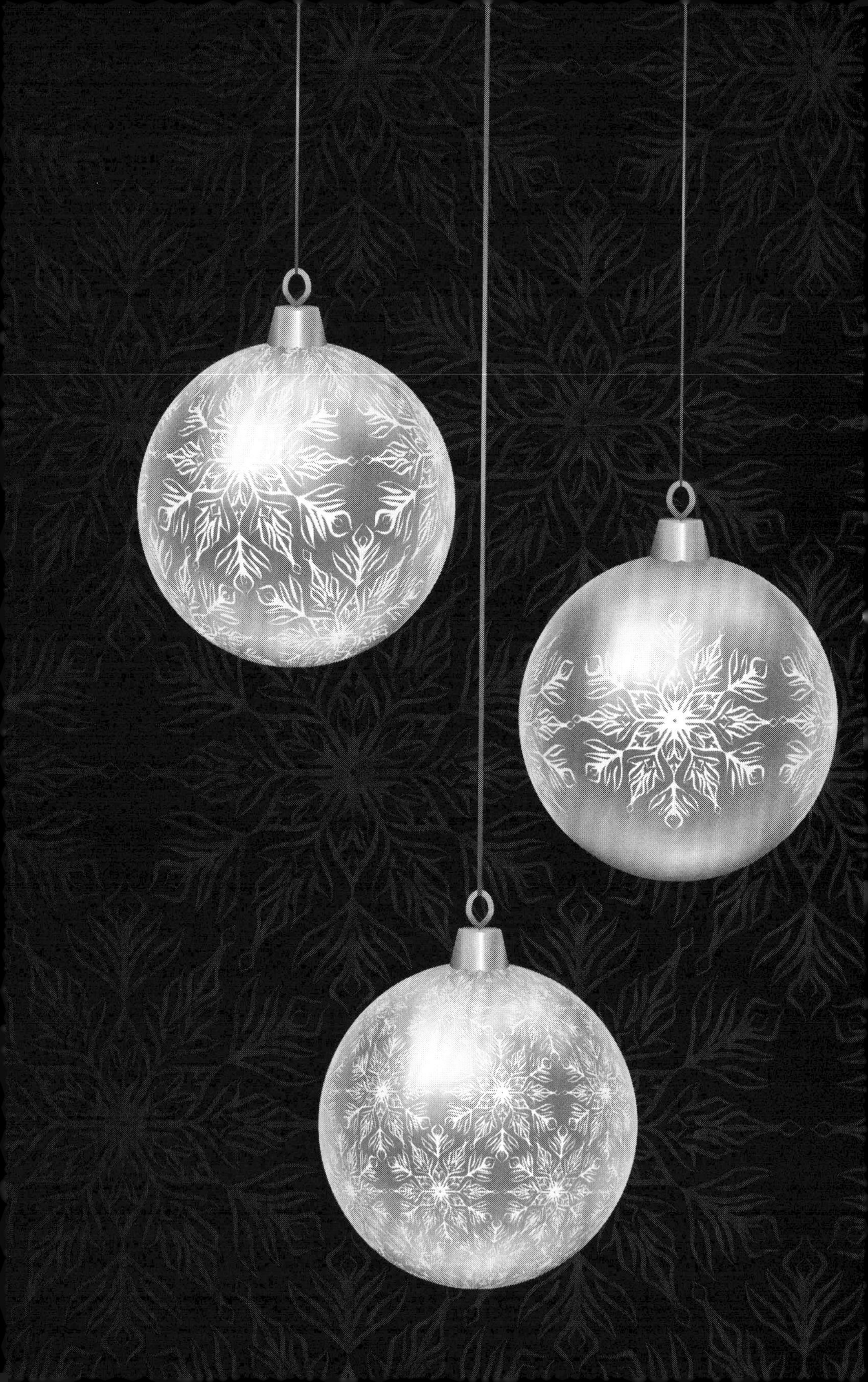

CHAPTER EIGHT

Poodle

"**W**HAT DO YOU MEAN, CANCER? I DON'T UNDERSTAND," I SAY TO THE VET, stroking Lady's side as she pants. My heart is hammering in my chest. "She's only been tired, maybe a little lethargic. I got her new food; maybe it's that?"

"James, she's extremely sick. It isn't the food. It's bone cancer."

"No," I frown, shaking my head. "It isn't bone cancer. She's fine. I only changed her food."

"Have you noticed that she isn't moving around as much? Not eating as much?"

"She's older; that's all," I whisper, my vision blurring with sudden heat. "She's old," I repeat, then envelope my best friend in my arms. I bury my nose in her fluffy fur and squeeze my eyes shut.

Melissa's hand lands on top of mine, sliding through Lady's fur to bring me comfort. I don't think anything could ever bring me comfort.

"I know this is a hard decision and not the right time, but I suggest putting her to sleep. The longer you wait, the more pain she will be in. Her cancer has spread to her kidneys and lungs."

"I'm not putting her to sleep. I can't. No!" I yell at Dr. Adamson, the woman who has been Lady's vet since she was just a pup. "I can't. Not right now." A tear falls from my eye. I don't even care who sees me in my cut, crying over my dog.

She isn't just my dog. She's my family.

"This cannot be real. She had puppies late in life. Was that the reason she's sick?"

"No, that's not the reason, James. She's old. That's all. Her health is declining. This is the day we have both feared ever since you got her as a puppy."

"But I didn't think the end would come so fast," I say, and Lady lifts her head up, giving me kisses along my palm. "Not before Christmas."

"We can wait until after Christmas, but, James, if you wait any longer, you'll be prolonging a massive amount of pain. I'll make sure to send home pain killers too."

"I should have brought her in earlier." I wipe my cheek on my sleeve. "When she started getting so tired. I should have known, but I didn't. I just thought she was getting old, and it was normal. I could have saved her."

"No, you can't think like that," Dr. Adamson tells me softly. "Even if you had brought her in sooner, her age wouldn't have given her a good chance."

"Such a good girl, Lady." I scratch the place behind her ear that she likes so much. "You have been my best friend for so long, and I promise, I'm going to give you the best Christmas of your life." Since she has issues walking, I slide my hands under her and pick her up, cradling her to my chest. Melissa lifts her phone and takes a picture of us and I lean forward, placing a kiss on her lips. She knows I'm going to want all the pictures of me and Lady before she passes away.

I can't even think about it. I'm a strong man. I'm not afraid to admit that I've done awful fucking things that will drag me to Hell. Animals are so much better than people in my opinion. People are assholes, but animals are loyal no matter what. The human race is vile, and we sure as hell don't deserve something as pure as an animal's love.

"Dad?" Ellie, my daughter, whispers my name outside the door as I walk through it. Ellie didn't want to be in the exam room because she said all she'd do is cry, but looking at her face, it seems that's all she's been doing anyway. "What did the vet say?"

"I'll tell you in the truck," I say, burying Lady's head in my shoulder as we stroll down the beige hallway toward the front door. The walls are lined with Christmas crap, red bows, cotton to mimic snow, and then wish-lists from other animal owners lined throughout.

When I get to the door, I turn around and push it open with my back. The winter air bursts over my heated face. I feel like I'm about to fall over. I hold Lady tighter and lean my weight against the truck, taking a minute to myself.

Melissa and Ellie are about to come outside, and I need to be strong for them, even if I'm falling apart on the inside. "Lady, I love you. I need you to know that, okay?"

She whines and licks my cheek. I know she can understand me. We've spent too much time together over the years. She knows what love feels like, and that makes me so happy that I gave her a good life. I want more. I expected her to live forever, which is ridiculous, but it's the truth.

"Dad, what did the vet say?" Ellie asks as soon as she opens the door. God, every time I look at her, my heart hurts just a little because I see the shadow of her mother.

Do I lie to her? I can't. I need to prepare her too. It wouldn't be fair. "She has cancer, Ellie. After Christmas we have to say goodbye."

"What! No," Ellie cries. "It's Lady. Lady can't... No! The vet is wrong."

Ah, she might look like her mother, but her denial is all me, isn't it?

"I wish she was, baby, but Lady is old, and it's showing."

Melissa comes through the door last, and the mascara under her eyes is smudged from crying too. It feels like I'm losing a child. Lady is everything to me. Especially before Melissa and Ellie came into my life. What the hell am I going to do?

"Um..." Melissa wipes under her eyes. "Reaper messaged and said everyone is going to get a Christmas tree. Do you want to meet them or go home? I'm sure he'll understand if we don't meet them there."

"No, we should go. It's Lady's last Christmas. She deserves to see everything." It breaks my heart that this will be the last time she experiences it. I open the door to the truck and gently place Lady in her dog seat and buckle her in. Another tear falls as her cold nose presses against my cheek, and a whimper escapes her when she senses my sadness. I reach up and scratch her neck, then kiss her snout. "Best fucking dog in the world, Lady. Best fucking dog." I shut her door, and I'm immediately engulfed in a hug from Ellie.

I wrap my arms tight around Ellie. She hasn't been in my life long because I thought she died when she was a baby. I don't know what I'd do without her. My life is rich with her and Melissa in it. I'm a wealthy man, and it isn't because of money.

It's because of love.

The one thing my old self never would have thought I'd have.

"Are you okay?" Melissa asks me as Ellie lets go of me and climbs in the passenger seat.

"No," I answer honestly. I grab the passenger door and close it behind Ellie. I need to get out of this parking lot. "I know Lady is just a dog—"

Melissa places her finger over my mouth, and the waves of her dark hair flow over her shoulders. She recently got bangs, which was an accident because she got bored one night, but I fucking love them. They frame her face and make her emerald eyes seem brighter. She stands on her tiptoes and places a soft kiss against on my lips. "She isn't just a dog. She's never been just a dog. You don't have to explain your heartache because I feel it too. She's our family, James. She was there for me during the worst time of my life and brought me comfort. She helped find Dawn; she has saved so many of us. She deserves peace."

My forehead falls on Melissa's, her skin surprisingly warm with how cold it is outside. Even in winter, she smells like a summer's day. "Let's go get that tree. I'm sure Reaper is ready to chop a cactus down at this point because we've waited so long." I want to change the subject. I don't want to talk about Lady anymore. I don't want to dwell on the fact that in five days, I'm going to lose my oldest friend.

It's Christmastime.

We deserve to feel happiness, and so does Lady. She isn't dead yet, and we aren't going to act like she is. I take Melissa's chin in my hand and place another kiss against her lips before we walk hand-in-hand around the truck. I open the back door for her, and she slides next to Lady, buckling herself in, then petting our loyal guardian.

Nope, can't do it. I won't fucking cry.

I'll let go when she closes her eyes one last time.

Telling myself that, my eyes dry up, and I compartmentalize my emotions so I can make it through the next week. I click the seatbelt over my chest, check to make sure everyone I love is safe and secure too, and check the mirrors. My eyes meet Melissa's, the love of my damn life, and I put the truck in reverse.

The further away I get from the vet's office, the better. We get on Loneliest Road, and drive past the exit we would take to go to the strip. About ten minutes later, we're in front of a pop-up Christmas tree sale.

And it doesn't look promising.

A line of bikes is parked along with a few trucks to hold the bigger families of the club, like Reaper and Sarah who have Maizey.

"Oh, no," I say when I see Tongue standing there with his gator in a baby sling on his chest. It's the most ridiculous thing I've ever seen. I pound my forehead against the wheel and Melissa starts to giggle, along with Ellie when they see Tongue. "Well, I guess I can't get too close to Tongue or Happy will attack Lady, and we can't have that."

Lady barks twice in agreement.

"I know, right?" I tell her, opening the truck door and jumping out into the cold desert night.

"What the fuck do you mean you don't have any eight-foot trees? Give me a ten-foot tree then," Reaper bellows, and the baritone of his voice bounces off the mountain.

"Someone is going to die tonight," Ellie singsongs.

"Ellie!" Melissa scolds.

"She isn't wrong, Sunflower," I snort, opening the back door to get Lady. I gather her in my arms and then hold her like I would Melissa. I wrap her back legs around my waist and put her front paws on my shoulder. "Good girl."

Lady lays her chin on my shoulder, her energy drained. She's exhausted.

My baby.

Melissa, Ellie, Lady, and I walk toward our big, weird, crazy family. Dawn is next to Skirt, cuddled against him with her hair in some sort of knot on top of her head while Skirt rocks the stroller back and forth. Aidan is hooked to Dawn's leg, who is actually Skirt's nephew; that was a shocker. They make a beautiful family too. I'm happy for the fighter.

There is Tool and Juliette, who are completely night and day. As far as I know, kids aren't in the plan yet just like with Patrick and Sunnie; they aren't ready yet.

Then there is Tongue and Daphne.

There are no words to explain how they work. Tongue is as dark as the horror stories people warn their kids about, and Daphne is the innocent book nerd who wears glasses. Yet, I'm watching them, and she has her head leaned against his shoulder, and she pecks the tip of Happy's snout.

Who. Kisses. A. Gator?

A crazy person.

"I don't give a fuck if your men have to go out and chop down my tree. You're going to do it."

Hearing Reaper get heated yanks me from my judgy thoughts, and I watch the scene unfold. There is one tree left, and it's dead. It's nothing but twigs. One good gust of wind and that thing is going to blow to pathetic pieces.

"How much are you willing to pay?" The salesmen smirks.

Oh, he has no idea who the hell he's talking to.

Right before Reaper can say anything, Maizey stands in front of her dad and pushes the salesman. "Listen, I have an uncle who will cut your tongue out and feed it to his kitty, so you better pay up!"

Her childish, high-pitched voice is adorable when she tries to sound threatening. She's so little, but she's sassy. I feel bad for Reaper when she becomes a teenager. She's going to be impossible to argue with.

"Is that right?" The salesman leers as he grins his nasty yellow teeth at her, then scratches his crotch. Reaper reaches behind him and pulls out the knife he always keeps on him, but Tongue beats him to it.

"Oh, the princess is spot on." Tongue's ghoulish tone matches the evil intent shining against the black tungsten of his knife as he holds it against the man's neck. He tilts his head, and Happy tilts his too, then opens his mouth and lets out a hiss. "The kitty she talks about is a gator, and he loves a good tongue. I should cut yours out for how you just talked to Maizey."

Tongue's arm has finally regained some motion again after being shot, but he isn't listening to Doc. It isn't going to heal, and he might not ever get full motion if he doesn't stop pushing himself. Only time will tell, but it doesn't look too promising.

"Let him have it, Tongue!"

"Maizey," Sarah says her name in a way that tells her to hush and be quiet. Sarah steps in front of Maizey to protect her from the man.

The man starts to sweat, and I glance down at his nametag and roll my eyes when I see that his name is Frank. I feel like all assholes are named Frank for some reason.

"Let's go for a walk. I want a tree for my princess. I want it now. If you're lucky I won't filet you like a fish and feed you to Happy."

The smell of piss fills the air, and Tongue smirks while the stench wakes the baby, causing Joey to cry.

"I love the smell of fear." Tongue buries his nose in the back of the man's head and trembles, as if he's turned on.

Curious, I glance toward Daphne, who's biting her lips as she checks Tongue out while he sniffs the tree salesman.

How did men like us end up with perfect partners?

Christmas miracle.

If only that applied to my Lady.

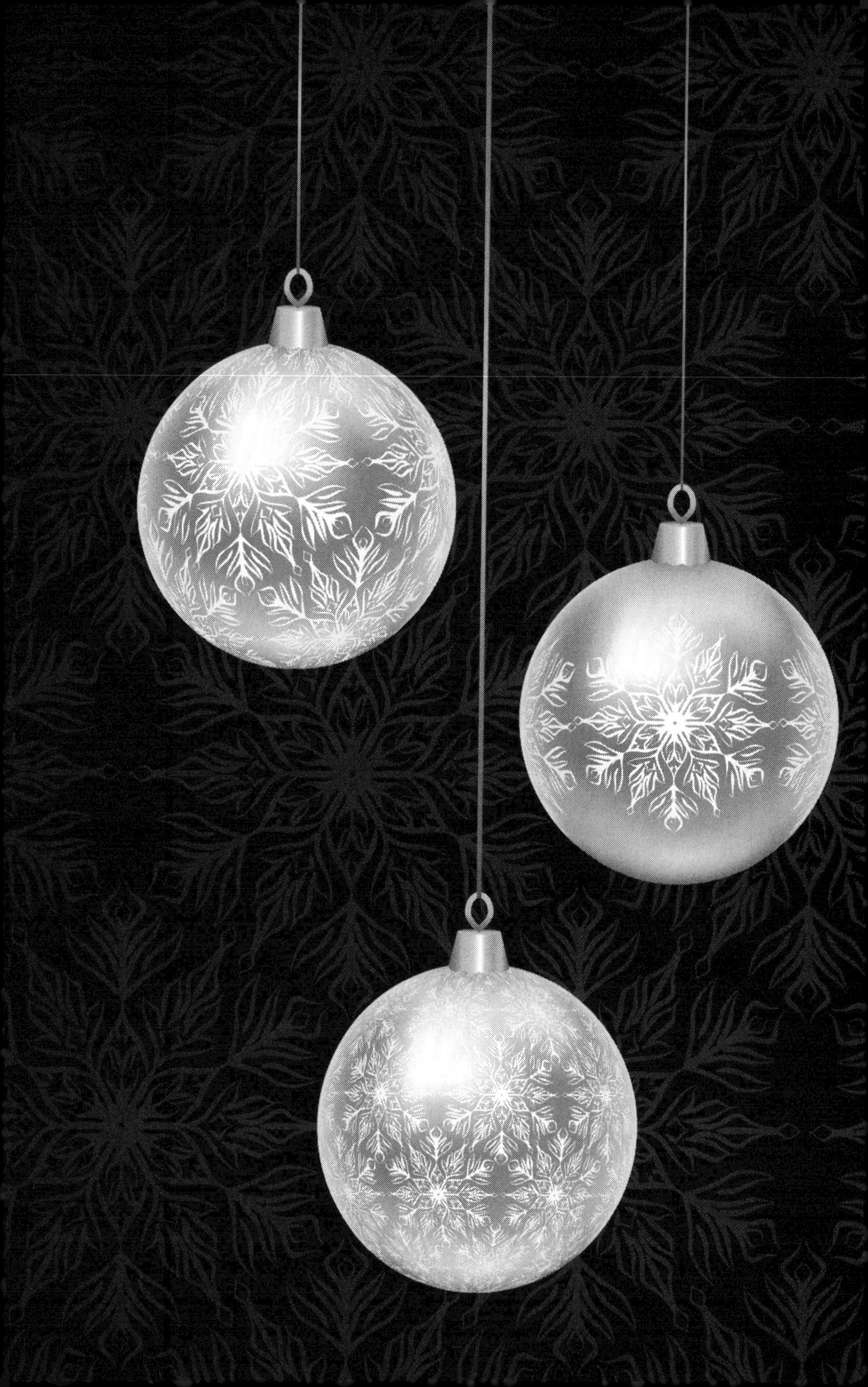

CHAPTER NINE
Sarah

"I CAN'T BELIEVE WE'RE DECORATING A CACTUS." I GIGGLE WHILE DOC PLUCKS NEEDLES out of Reaper's arm. He really did go chop down the biggest tree he could find, but he only found a cactus. The guys are around the cactus, wearing gloves and plucking the needles out one by one so no one hurts themselves. We will leave a few needles up top for decorations, but the bottom will be bare.

And it's taking so long.

"Well, if Tongue hadn't been so quick to kill the salesman, maybe we wouldn't be here right now. Ow, Doc!" Reaper jerks his arm back, and Doc rolls his eyes. There has to be a hundred different pinpricks along his arms beading blood.

"You survived an explosion, Reaper. You can deal," Doc says dryly, plucking another needle from his arm.

"Well, if I didn't have to put the Harley Davidson star on the cactus, by myself, I wouldn't have had so many needles. Ow! Doc, Jesus. Don't pluck my fucking arm off."

No one would put the Harley Davidson star on the cactus because of all the sharp pinpoints sticking out all over the place and Reaper was a few inches too short to miss a few needles. He will be okay. He's just cranky.

The tree topper is cute. When it plugs into the wall, a white light shines from it and a cut out piece of metal that says Harley Davidson is across the front. The light shines through the cutout letters in the metal and casts them on the wall.

"You. Survived. An. Explosion," Doc punctuates every word, taking his tweezers and yanking another needle out.

"Yes, Reaper. You survived an explosion. Hurray," Moretti fake cheers, then plucks a needle from the cactus and purposely stabs Bullseye in the arm.

"What the fuck, Moretti!" Bullseye bellows.

"Don't you need to check your blood sugar?" Moretti says matter-of-factly.

"I don't need to check it! I'm fine."

"Is that why you aren't waking up until the day is nearly over?"

Color me shocked, but it sounds like Moretti cares. We've all been worried about Bullseye's denial about his type-2 diabetes. It's serious. He needs insulin, but he's living like nothing ever happened. No matter how many times Doc tells him, or we plead our concerns for his health, nothing we say gets through his head.

"I'm tired. I've been going on long runs for Reaper; everyone knows that."

"You haven't enjoyed your fun with your favorite couple. That's a big deal. Don't you have a weekly meeting with them?"

I gasp, hanging a candy cane on one of the needles. Moretti might have just signed his death warrant. Everyone knows what Skirt, Bullseye, and Dawn do together. Granted, not much has happened since she's had the baby because she can't have sex yet, but it's only a matter of time. No one talks about it. It isn't our business. They are happy, and that's all that matters.

"What the fuck did ye just say?" Skirt comes around from the other side of the Christmas cactus, clenching his scarred fists in preparation for a fight. "Yer going to want to make sure of what ye say next or I'll make sure ye don't breathe again."

"Like that scares me," Moretti rolls his eyes, unimpressed with Skirt's threat as he hangs a sleigh ornament on the cactus. "I'm pointing out facts. It isn't a secret what you three do behind closed doors. Hell, I don't care." He laughs gently, placing his hand against his chest. "I wish I could join. I can't remember what I like, but I have a feeling I'd like that. I think I love a man in a kilt. Everyone here is tiptoeing around Bullseye because of his diabetes, yet no one is holding him accountable. Don't you think it's time he isn't treated like a baby?"

Skirt punches Moretti before any of us can blink again. I move out of the way before Moretti falls against me. Reaper wraps his arm around me, pulling me to his side for safety. If I had to bet who would win this fight, it would be Skirt. He's a professional fighter and blood thirsty. Skirt raises his fist again, and my eyes land on his knuckles. The living room light shines against the red wetness splattering across his fingers from Moretti's busted lip.

Blood has never bothered me.

But it does today.

I yank myself out of Reaper's arms and run to the closest bathroom. It's the one Poodle uses, and the lavender scent from his shampoo is everywhere, which usually smells good, but not this time. It heightens my gag reflex, and I barely have time to lift the lid and puke. Then the smell of the bathroom just makes it worse. That ... toilet water smell slams into my nostrils and I throw up again.

"Doll! Damn it, what's wrong? Are you okay?" Reaper's hand lands in the middle of my back, and the heat radiating from him feels good.

"I'm sorry, Sarah. I didn't mean to make you sick," Moretti says over Reaper's shoulder, next to Skirt.

Are they friends now? Did they just need a good scuffle? I don't understand men.

"Doll, what's wrong? Talk to me," Reaper rubs soothing circles between my shoulder blades, and it helps with the nausea.

"I don't know. I saw the blood on Skirt's knuckles." I gag again, not wanting to talk about it. "Then the bathroom smells terrible."

"It smells like my shampoo. That does not smell terrible," Poodle defends.

"Well, it does to me!" Another spasm twists my stomach, and I shoo everyone away with my hand. "Please, go away. This isn't a show." All I want to do is decorate the Christmas cactus. Is it perfect? No, but it seems pretty fitting considering we're all imperfect. I think the cactus needs to be a tradition in the Ruthless household.

I hear a hiss, and I lift my head from the toilet to see Tongue standing there, Happy strapped to his chest, and there's red along Happy's sharp teeth.

The tree salesman.

Oh, I'm going to throw up again.

"Here, take him." He lifts Happy from the sling and hands him over to Poodle, who holds him out like Badge did to Maizey last night.

"Uh," Poodle says cautiously as Happy hisses.

Tongue squats on the other side of me and flushes the toilet, tears off a few sheets of TP, and wipes my mouth. "Do you think you could be pregnant?" Tongue asks.

"Yes! Hell yes, she can!" Reaper announces with a clap of his hands. "You hear that, Doll? You're pregnant."

"We don't know that," I say, slowly lifting myself off the floor. I want to go lay down.

"You're sick. Smells are bothering you. It makes sense." Reaper's hand lands on my arm, and I shrug him off.

I'm getting angry. "I'm not pregnant! I'm just sick. God, just stop! Everyone just stop. It hasn't happened. It won't happen, and giving me hope is just fucking cruel! Let it go, Reaper. Everyone just…" I cover my face with my hands and catch a sob. "Just stop, please. Just stop."

I run between the members who crowded outside the bathroom and head toward the room we've been staying in. I slam the door, then lock it for good measure. I need to be alone. I need time to think.

I flip on the fan to help with the sweat building on my skin and throw myself on the bed. I grab Reaper's pillow and hug it to my chest. Slow, painful sobs shake my body, and I can hardly breathe. I want to be pregnant.

I don't want to be pregnant.

I'm scared.

"Sarah?" Doc calls out my name from behind the door. Right now it's muted and soft, but I know once the door opens, it will be loud and reassuring.

I can't handle that right now.

I don't answer him. I inhale Reaper's scent and let myself get lost in the comfort he brings me. If I am pregnant, what then? Doc told me once a woman has one miscarriage, it's probable she will have another. I can't go through that again.

"Sarah? Open the door, Doll."

I feel awful for acting this way. After all the trying, we might finally have what we want, and I'm terrified. I don't want them to give me hope. I don't want to talk about me being pregnant because if I'm not, I'll be crushed.

If I am, I'll be crushed. What if I can't protect him or her? The safest place for a baby is inside it's mother's womb, and I don't have that ability.

I'll lose it again.

"Sarah, open the door, or I'm going to break it down," Reaper threatens.

"Go away," I say, burying my face in the pillow.

I hear his deep sigh on the other side of the door, and the wood creaks, probably from him leaning against it. "Never, Doll. I'm never going anywhere. Open up this door and talk to me. Talk to Doc. I know you're scared, but I'm here. You know I'm going to fight every ounce of your fear like it's my own. Open the door so we can get answers and see what we need to do. Come on, Doll."

"Mommy? What did you do, Daddy?" Maizey accuses him.

"I only did what she wanted me to," Reaper says as innocently as he can, which makes me smile.

He did. I asked for a baby, and now I might have one.

I sit up and wipe the tears off my cheeks, still hugging his pillow. I glance toward the door and sniffle, unsure if I want to go down this road. If I'm pregnant, what steps can we take to make sure I'm able to carry the baby to full term?

Fresh water brimming my eyes, I stand and twist my hands together. When I get to the door, I unlock it without opening it, then hurry back to bed to lay down. I'm not feeling well, and I don't know if it's because of panic or the stomach flu.

The knob turns, and light spills in from the hallway into the dark room. "Sarah, Doll, what's going on?" Reaper sits next me, and the bed dips so low from his weight, I grip the side of the mattress to prevent myself from rolling off. He takes my hand and intertwines our fingers while Maizey climbs up and sits next me, laying her head on my shoulder.

"We got a tree, and Santa brought you a baby just like I asked," Maizey states cheerfully.

"What do you mean?" I ask her.

"I wrote Santa. Told him to give you a baby, but we didn't have a tree, so I knew it wouldn't happen unless we had a tree."

"Oh, Maze." I hold her against me and place my chin on top of her head.

"You don't want this anymore?" Reaper asks, his hope broken, but he holds my hand anyway.

"What? No, that's not it!" I sit up and lay our hands over my belly. "I'm so scared. If I am, I will be equally as happy and terrified. I'll be afraid to move, to breathe, to do anything to risk losing our baby."

"Anything you do won't be the reason why. These things, they just..." He sighs, blinking toward the ceiling as he takes a deep breath and exhales. "They happen."

"He's right, Sarah," Doc sets his medical kit on the floor beside the vintage nightstand I bought from a local antique store. "You can walk, breathe, eat, laugh, but even just laying here can put you at risk for a miscarriage. Let's take a test."

"But the stabbing..."

"I know," Doc says with a grimace twitching his mouth. "I'm not going to bite off more than I can chew right now. The first step is to see if you are pregnant. I'm going to take a blood test; it's quicker and will tell us if your hCG levels are elevated."

"Okay." I nod, holding out my arm for him to wrap the rubber band around my bicep to plump the vein. I squeeze Reaper's arm, holding onto him as if I'm about to drift away. He's my anchor, the strength that keeps me still in the storm that rages around us.

Doc cleans the inside of my elbow, sanitizes it, then draws a few vials of blood. "Okay, I'll get this downstairs right now and test them. You'll know by the end of the day. Everything is going to be okay."

Doc gives us a parting smile before exiting the room and closing the door behind him. Joanna is pregnant too, and Skirt and Dawn's daughter Joey is barely a few months old. If I am too, our kids will grow up close in age. How exciting would that be?

"Do you want to come decorate the tree?" Reaper asks. "We can stay in here if you want."

"No. I want to enjoy the night with my family." Maybe this will be the last Christmas it will be the three of us.

One can only hope.

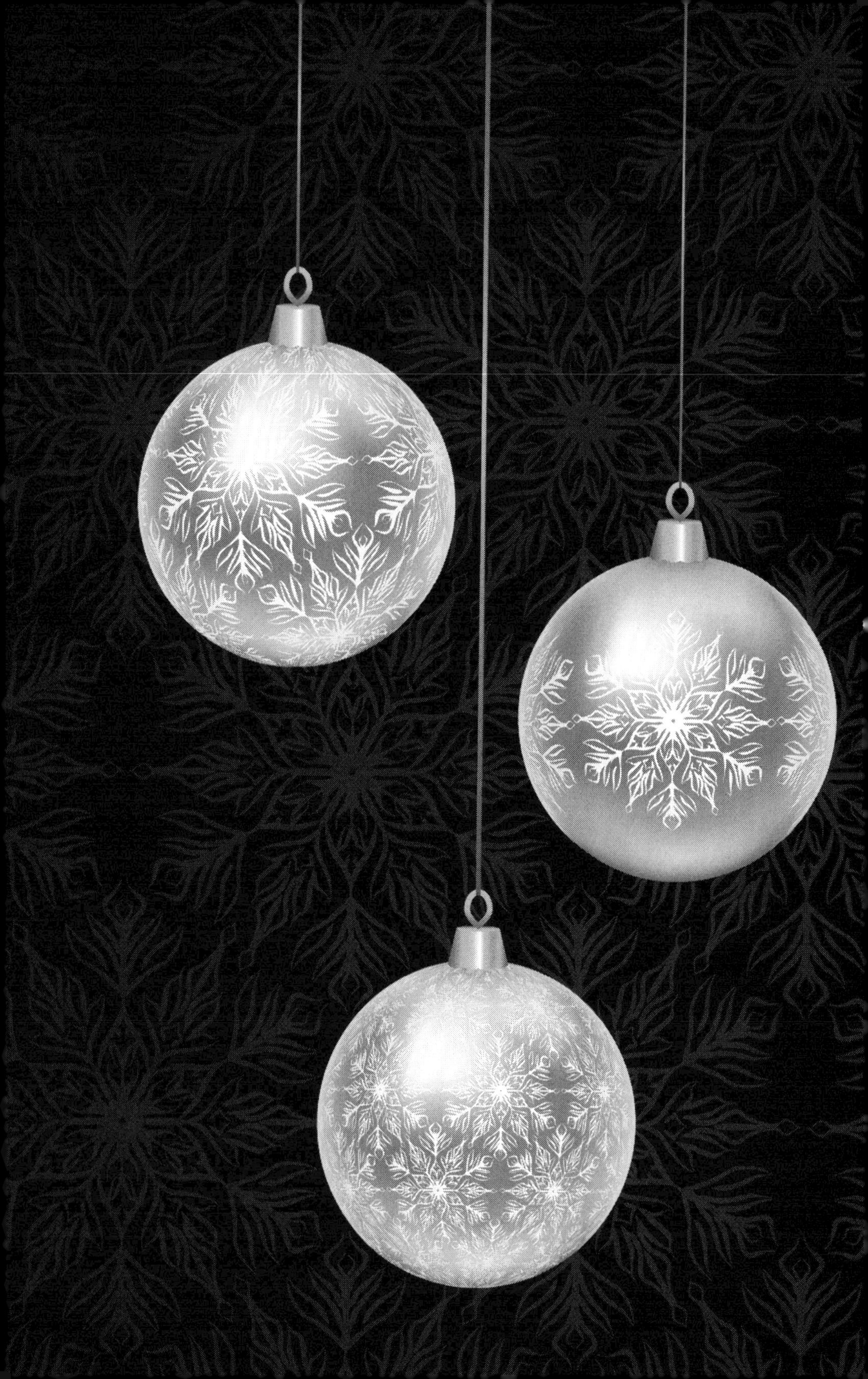

CHAPTER TEN

Tongue

FOUR DAYS UNTIL CHRISTMAS.
I got my comet the only thing in the world she's ever wanted.
A bookstore.

Andrew's bookstore, which I know will hold some meaning for her. I don't know why. The guy was a complete waste of space, but just because I can't understand her feelings doesn't mean they aren't valid. I'll love her through them, even if I disagree.

Plus, the bookstore has this really old book she likes, and I want her to have it. I want her to have everything.

I can't wait until Christmas. I got the keys to the place yesterday. The bookstore was supposed to go to next of kin if something happened to Andrew, and since something did happen, I had to threaten the lawyer that I'd kill him and feed him to Happy for that not to happen.

I won, and the lawyer still speaks.

How do I want to surprise her? Women like that, right? She deserves it. She's been teaching me how to read, but since I'm a fucking idiot, it's taking a long time. I'm lucky to read three words before I get frustrated and throw the book across the room.

"Tongue? I need your help. I can't—" Daphne grunts as she stretches her arm to grab a book on the shelf I just installed, "—I can't reach it."

Of course, she can't. What would make her think she could? It's an entire foot above her. Sometimes, I don't understand her efforts. I like watching her try, though. Her ass jiggles every time she loses her balance, and my cock hardens. I growl as her sleek body moves. A body that's mine. I was just inside her this morning, but I want her again.

I can't because there's no time. I need to take her to the bookstore, and then we're going to do some last-minute Christmas shopping for everyone. All I want to do is stay in bed, deep inside her tight cunt, rubbing her body with my knife that I had engraved with her. I want her to beg me to cut her, to carve my name into her chest like she wanted before.

"Wayne," she gasps as I pick her up and throw her on the bed.

Christmas can wait. It isn't like it's going anywhere. It will be there next year, and the year after, and then the year after that. And since me and Daphne are going to be together for all eternity and in death, I think it's safe to say we will have plenty of holidays.

Daphne's tits bounce as she settles on our mattress. Her nipples are hard, tenting the shirt she's wearing. "We have to go shopping. We can't," she moans as I strip off my shirt.

She loves my body for some fucked up reason, but it's why we're meant to be together. She loves me, and only the Devil knows why.

I'm about to unzip my jeans so her plump lips can wrap around my cock and suck me down her throat, when someone who has a death wish knocks on the door. I curl my lips, grab my knife from on top of the dresser, and lick it. I'm ready to kill somebody for interrupting me.

"Be nice," Daphne says with a giggle.

"I am nice," I grouse.

I open the door and place the tip of the blade under the visitor's chin. "Boomer," I greet with zero excitement. Maybe I would've been if he didn't interrupt me. "I didn't know you were coming. You and your members here?" If they are, I'll have to take Daphne away from here. I don't know Boomer's guys like I know the Vegas members. They will want her. I'm not afraid to cut out their tongues. I don't care if they are brothers by the Ruthless name. I'll kill.

I'll bathe in their blood victoriously, and you know what Daphne will do?

She'll join me.

Oh, now that would be the perfect Christmas gift. Maybe we can find someone walking down the strip again and do a little hunting, have some fun, let our hair   down.

"It's good to see you too, Tongue. Merry Christmas."

"I would say it's good to see you too, but I'm busy."

He peers around my shoulder, not doubt seeing my beautiful comet laying in bed. His eyes widen. "Well, how are you doing? I'm Boom—Ow!"

I drop my knife from his chin and slice it across is arm. "Don't." I wave the blade in front of him.

"I should've known that even after you found someone, you'd still be a psychopath."

"Don't call him that!" Daphne comes to my defense and loops her arm through mine. I tilt my head down and notice her glasses are crooked, so I straighten them and push the frames up the bridge of her nose.

Damn, I'm a lucky man.

"Does anyone know you're here? Reaper didn't mention you coming."

"I tried calling him, but he hasn't been answering, so no, I don't think anyone knows we're here. I'm excited to see everyone, meet all the new members we have—"

"We have. Not you. You left, remember?" I didn't know it bothered me that he left until this moment. "Don't say we. You picked a new family."

"Tongue, you're still my family. That hasn't changed. You know why I had to leave."

Daphne's body sinks into mine as she leans against me. She got new shampoo that reminds me of the beach. Coconut and some type of flower. I love it. I concentrate on her, her curves, her scent, the softness of her hair, and breathe out. "Everyone is actually downstairs to see if Sarah is pregnant. Everyone is excited," I finally say.

"Why aren't you?" His misfit market of members come from down the hallway, and the twins look Daphne up and down like she's candy.

"Mine," I sneer at them while they bump knuckles.

"Lay off, guys. Daphne is taken, and you do not want to fuck with Tongue, got it?" Boomer says over his shoulder, but he never stops looking me in the eye.

"Got it, Prez." The one that has the name patch 'Warden' on his cut, nods his head and turns into the kitchen across the hall.

Wolf is next to him, a guy I never thought I'd like because of what happened with the Jersey Chapter, but I do. He's a good guy who was trying to save his sister. Arrow, One-Eye, and Kansas drag the chairs out from the table and get comfortable. Wolf seems bored, so he finds the coffee pot instead of standing here and talking to me. He rinses it out and stares out the window. He slushes the water around in the pot, washing out all the flavor.

Doesn't he know that's a cardinal sin?

He tilts his head and pauses what he's doing, almost as if he's lost in thought. The faucet runs, and water flows down the sink, gurgling through the pipes. Wolf releases the handle, and the glass pot breaks in the sink, ruining any chance for coffee.

But he has a reason.

He dashes down the hall, toward the main room, and out the front door, leaving it wide open so the dusty air can get in.

Curious, Boomer and his men head out the door, but I don't follow.

"What the fuck is the racket about, Tongue?" Reaper opens the basement door, which jingles since Maizey put a bell on it. "I'm trying to see if my wife is pregnant."

"Boomer is here," I drawl.

His face lights up like our Christmas Cactus in the living room. "Doc! Wait. Sarah, Boomer is here!"

A high-pitched squeal has my ears ringing.

You know what follows Boomer? Explosions. I want a quiet Christmas. Maybe a little blood, a lot of sex, maybe at the same time, but I do not feel like getting blown up.

"Is there a story I'm missing?" Daphne asks me, tugging on my cut.

I shut the bedroom door and grin. "Oh, yeah."

She jumps on the bed, excited like a teenage girl about to gossip. "Tell me, tell me, tell me," she begs.

I mock her, jumping on the bed too, but my weight breaks it. One side of the mattress falls to the floor when a metal rod snaps, and I grab onto Daphne to make sure she's okay.

But she's laughing so hard she can't breathe. "You ... you ... can't jump on beds. You're ... too big," she gasps, her face turning red.

I'm getting worried. Do I need to breathe for her? Blow into her mouth? I will.

"I was excited to tell you the story."

"Tell me. I'm listening, Comet," she smiles.

Bed broken, books scattered, the remainder of the bed's frame moaning from having to support the weight.

My arm hurts, but I don't care. If I can be here with Daphne, what more could I want for Christmas? I have my swamp kitty, my knives, my tongues, and love. The only thing I need to fix is my relationship with Sarah. Boomer asked why I wasn't excited.

I am.

I just don't think she wants me there when she gets the news.

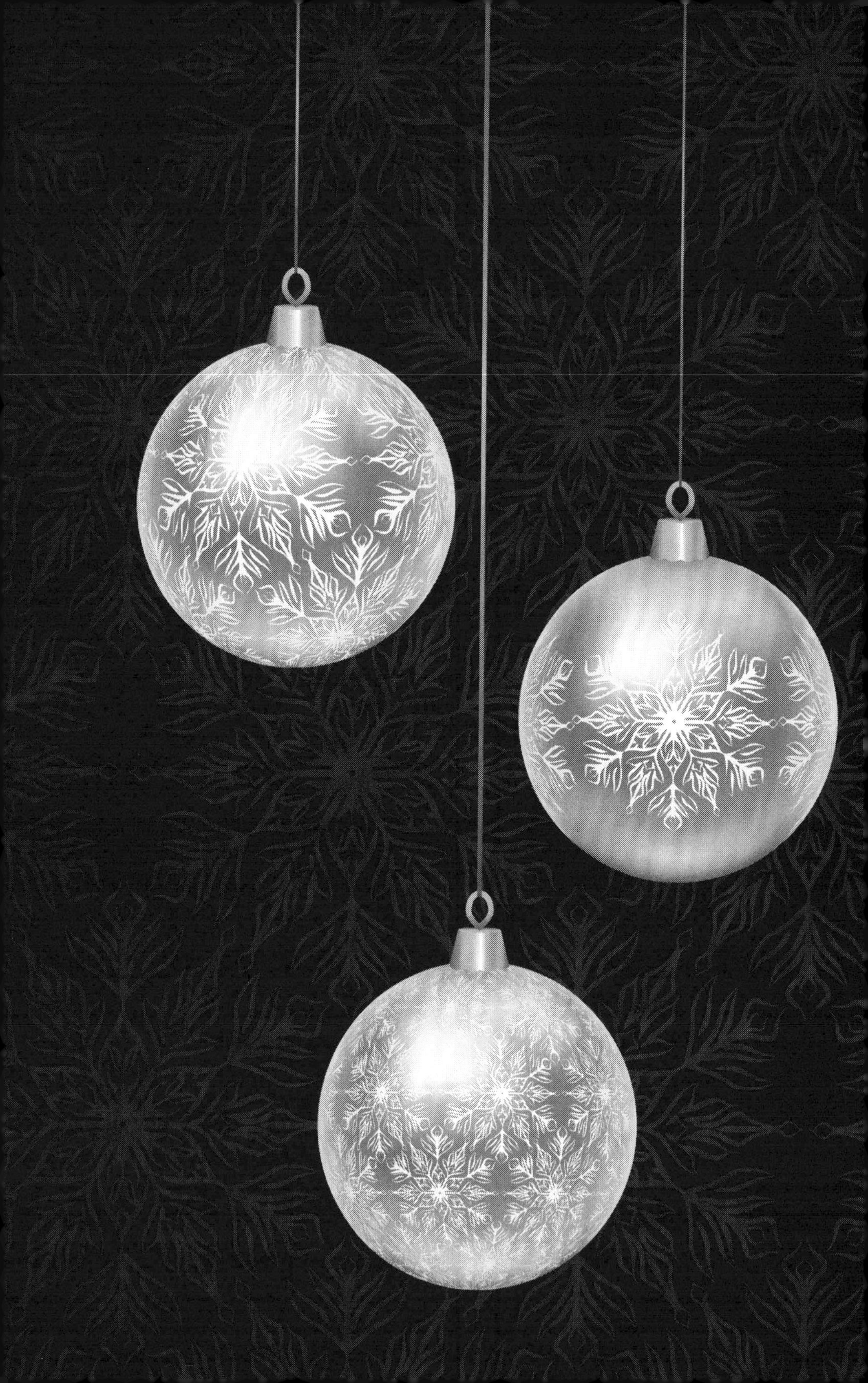

CHAPTER ELEVEN

DOC

EVERYONE IS GIVING BOOMER HUGS AND PATS ON THE BACK FOR HIS SURPRISE Christmas visit. At this rate, I expect everyone we know to show up, like the NOLA chapter, which I kind of hope happens. I want to see Tool creeped out by Seer.

"Doc, how are you, man?" Boomer comes in for a hug. Damn, I can't believe this is the same brat who used to set trash can fires at school. He's really grown up. His hair is longer, and it looks like he has a few more tattoos. His cut is still blank, but that doesn't seem to matter to the guys who follow him. After what a few members have been through, they're probably relieved to be able to breathe for a minute.

"I'm alright. It's good to see you, Boomer. I'm happy you came. Where's Scarlett?"

"Ah, she stayed back with Homer. He isn't feeling too well lately, and since he's older than dirt, she didn't feel right leaving him alone."

"Scarlett's sweet like that," I say, leaning against the porch beam and casting a glance at Boomer's VP, Wolf, as he traipses around outside. Right as I was about to tell Sarah and Reaper their results, Boomer interrupted us. "What's your boy doing, Boomer?"

"I don't know. He thinks he saw someone up in the tree. He's going to check it out, but he's a paranoid motherfucker. I doubt someone is going to climb up that tree to look over the wall. That's a bit much," Boomer says. He pulls out a flask, and I snag his wrist, stopping him before he can even think about taking a swig of it. "What?" he asks.

"You better put that shit away. Patrick is around. Have some respect."

"Fuck, I can't believe I forgot that. I'm sorry." Boomer tucks the flask in his cut pocket and catches a glimpse of Wolf headed back to us. "I know that look," he says, pushing off the wall with his boot. He jumps off the porch instead of taking the steps.

I know that tone of voice he used, and it isn't a good one.

Not wanting him to walk by himself, I'm at his side, ready to take on the news Wolf is about to deliver. "So is Sarah pregnant? Have you told her?"

"I can't talk about that with you. You know that."

"I know. I hope she is. They deserve it after everything that's happened." Boomer eyes where Skirt's house used to be. It's nothing but flat land now, covered in sand.

"Yeah, I think all of us needs a break, don't you?"

"You guys should come to Jersey. Clubhouse is being built, no cut-slut drama—"

"Yet," I finish for him.

"Doesn't mean I have to be happy about it. I don't miss cut-sluts, man."

"Neither do we. See any of them here? After Candy and Jasmine died, the rest of the sluts skipped town."

"Becks too? I mean, she isn't a slut, but she's usually hanging around."

"She's off pursuing her dream or whatever," I say just as we come face-to-face with Wolf. His nose ring catches the light of the sun, and he holds out a few pieces of glass.

"Someone was here. I know I saw them."

"Fucking hell, does this shit ever stop?" I flip the glass in my hand, noticing the curve of the lens. It's thick and has a bit of weight to it.

"You guys have bad omens," Wolf says, glancing around the clubhouse as if he can see the evil encasing us.

"Not you too! Do not bring that voodoo shit here!" Tool yells from where he's propped up against his bike.

Nothing ever gets better than hearing Tool get freaked out about the supernatural.

"We need to call a meeting," Boomer informs me as he lifts a piece of glass toward the sun.

"We call a meeting for everything these days." I just want to sit on my ass with my pregnant ol' lady with my hand on her belly as we watch B-rated movies on Netflix. People ask me what I want for the holidays? I say, 'nothing.' The truth, though? I want silence.

Quiet.

I want a day where, for once, things aren't complete chaos here at the clubhouse. I don't want danger surrounding us. I don't want another family member showing up out of the blue, and I don't want to find fucking glass littering the property. I don't want Poodle's dog to die of cancer.

One day. All I'm asking is one day for us to fucking *be*.

No threats. No medical emergencies. No panic.

Just happiness. I want us to sit around our Christmas cactus and open gifts. I want bad Christmas music on, and I want to hear all of us laugh at the dumb gifts we get each other.

There's always something going on, and I just want there to be nothing. I want our only worry to be cleaning up wrapping paper.

But that would be too easy.

Just like it would be easy to tell Sarah her tests came back, and it's positive—she's pregnant—but that isn't the Ruthless way, is it?

How do I tell a woman who has been wanting nothing more than to get pregnant, that her tests are inconclusive? What I do know is I'm telling Reaper and Sarah away from knowing eyes. This has to be done in private.

It's going to be a hopeless Christmas if these pieces of glass have any say in it.

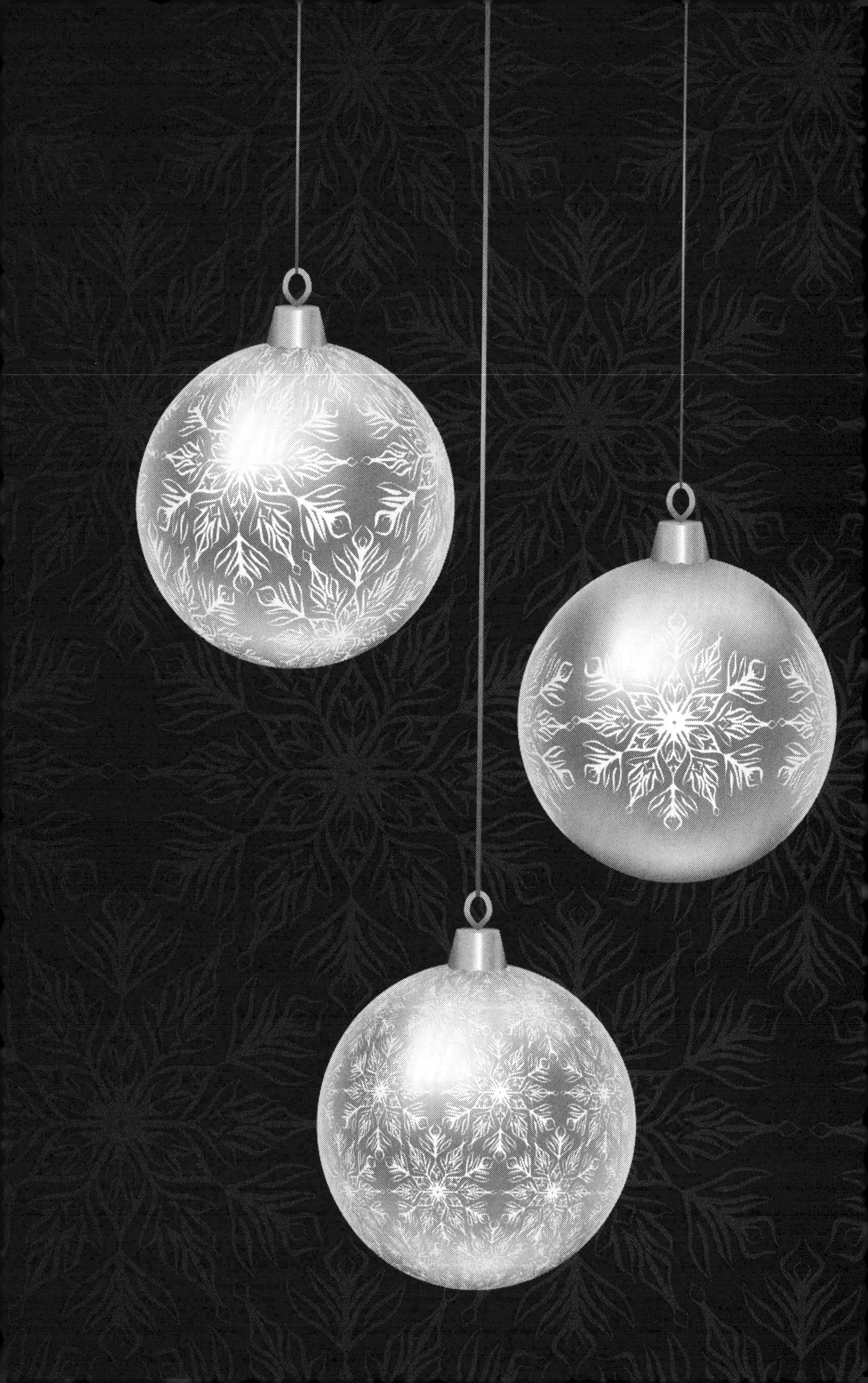

CHAPTER TWELVE
The Groundskeeper

So, what? I almost got caught. No big deal.

I found a new tree. It's more shaded than the last and bonus, it looks like the electric box to the gate is right below me. "Oh, now what do we have here?" I say to myself, leaning forward when I notice movement coming from the front door. I bring my new binoculars to my eyes

"Oh, the days love blessing me with opportunity, don't they?" I see the woman of my dreams leaving the house, Sarah, followed by Patrick.

Hmmm, now that is an interesting combination. Neither of them goes anywhere together unless they're all going somewhere in a big group. She's wearing a beautiful burgundy sweater dress that highlights her blonde hair with black leggings and boots, but the outfit is ruined with that damn 'Property of Reaper' cut. They climb into a new Ford Bronco SUV with Patrick in the front seat.

Tsk. Tsk.

Alcoholics should never be allowed to drive. Even the ones who are 'on a journey' to sobriety. Let's face it. They're never really sober. They're a disaster waiting to happen. He's probably fighting the urge to pour a bottle down his throat. He'd probably eat the glass if given the opportunity.

Pathetic.

And I am not going to let his addiction hurt Sarah.

The bark of the tree bites against my palms as I climb down the trunk. There are a few notches for me to place my feet. When I'm halfway down, I jump, then roll on the ground so I don't make any noise. A few twigs snap, but I could be an animal for all they know.

Who am I kidding? I am an animal.

I slither through the bare bones of trees, ducking under the long fingers of the branches, and bypassing large rocks. I need to figure out a plan. I only wanted Sarah, but Patrick would be fun to torment. This will be one of the only times I will get her alone. She's always with Reaper and surrounded by protection.

Why isn't she now?

I snort and laugh at myself, stretching out my arms, and my hands glide across the body of the tree trunks. Why am I questioning this? This is what I wanted.

Only I'm going to make her see just what kind of people she surrounds herself with and how they aren't good for her. I thought Daphne was better, but I had made a mistake. She's just as rotten as Tongue is on the inside.

Can no one see how horrible these bikers are? What do I need to do to take the blinders off their eyes?

One by one, I'll take them out. It's only a matter of time.

I finally get to my car that I pulled into the woods and pull out my bolt cutters. I make my way back to the box just in time to see them pull through the gate. I cut the wire coming from the bottom and the buzz of electricity hums to a slow stop.

I smirk.

Good luck getting to us in time, Kings.

Turning, I run for my car again. I have to get there fast if I'm going to get there before Pirate and Sarah drive by. I'm rounding the front when my foot slips on the sand. I catch myself on the hood of the car, and my forehead smacks against the bumper when my foot keeps slipping. "Son of a bitch!" I groan and hold my hand against the aching spot throbbing in the middle of my forehead.

No, I have to hurry, so I still have time. Time to do, what? I have no idea, but I'll figure it out.

My phone dings, and I see it's a message from Zain.

We're going out for supplies. When you get home, don't be surprised if no one is there. We'll be back soon.

A catlike grin sweeps over my face as I read the message just as another comes through.

You better not be at the Ruthless compound. Reaper is letting me rent this place for a great deal because it needs work. He doesn't know I know you, the guy who nearly killed his members. I won't keep covering for you. Stop with the obsession.

"Stop with the obsession," I mock him as I open the door to the old Lincoln car that someone's grandma used to drive. She's dead. It isn't like she needs it anymore. I punch the dice hanging on the rearview mirror and start the car. They are pink and fuzzy. Cute.

I bet Sarah would like them.

Inserting the silver key in the car, the 1970s radio plays static through the busted speakers, but then the hint of a Christmas song comes sneaking through the white noise.

Oh, the weather outside is certainly very frightful.

And the fire rushing through my veins is, well…

It's delightful

Smirking at the convenient tune, I press my foot on the gas and inch forward. I turn the wheel so I'm facing the long stretch of empty road. I whistle, waiting to see the Ford Bronco pass me. I roll down my window and patiently wait. I stay far enough in the woods where they can't see me, and since I'm less than a half-mile down the road and across the street, they aren't going to expect me.

The grumble of the Bronco engine comes close as I whistle the tune on the radio. There's not much in the desert we can do to make it snow, but the melody brightens my spirits anyway. When the Bronco passes, I put the car in drive and creep out of the woods. The tires dip before getting onto the road, burning some of the rubber when I punch the gas too quick as I crank the wheel.

"Oops," I say when I run over a cactus.

It isn't like we don't have plenty of them in Vegas.

I trail behind the Bronco for a couple of minutes before I decide I'm bored. I want to get the show on the road. I hate being incognito. I've never been good at it. When I want something, I tend to get it.

Even if it means burying my own brother on Halloween, torturing his lover to see what a big mistake she's making, or showing Sarah that she's the sun and the moon, and she deserves the stars. I'll do whatever it takes to take what's mine.

I gas the car, putting the pedal to the metal and cackle when the speedometer reaches the red lines. I quickly catch up with the Bronco and slam the front end of the Lincoln into the back. I laugh uncontrollably, bouncing in my seat when I see Patrick look in the rearview mirror.

They're going to wish that what I have in store for them meant being buried six feet under, but it isn't.

It's going to be more self-destructive, more of a lesson I hope they learn from.

I slam the against the back end again, and the Bronco fishtails as Patrick loses control of the SUV. Tires burn as the Bronco tries to stay on the ground, but the momentum is too much. They flip in the air twice, then the Bronco lands on its side, slamming against a group of trees with a sickening, thrilling crunch.

I come to a stop and get out of the car, casually. "My goodness, I hope everyone is okay," I fawn in a pretend caring, southern accent. "Whatever shall we do?"

"Kill them," the other side of me sneers.

"Not her," the better part of me pleads.

I watch as smoke comes from the engine and the tires spin, still reeling from the speed they were going on the road. The Christmas song still plays in the Lincoln, and I sing it as I strut over to the passenger side.

"The fire is slowly dying, and my dear..." I whistle the rest of the tune and open the door, seeing Sarah passed out with blood trickling down her forehead. "We're still goodbying."

Patrick is out cold too, a piece of glass embedded in his thigh and blood trickling from some part of his head. I can't tell since I don't care.

I push a piece of Sarah's blonde hair behind her ear, so silky and soft. "It really is the most wonderful time of the year," I say, marveling the beauty in front of me.

She's going to get the best present of them all.

Me.

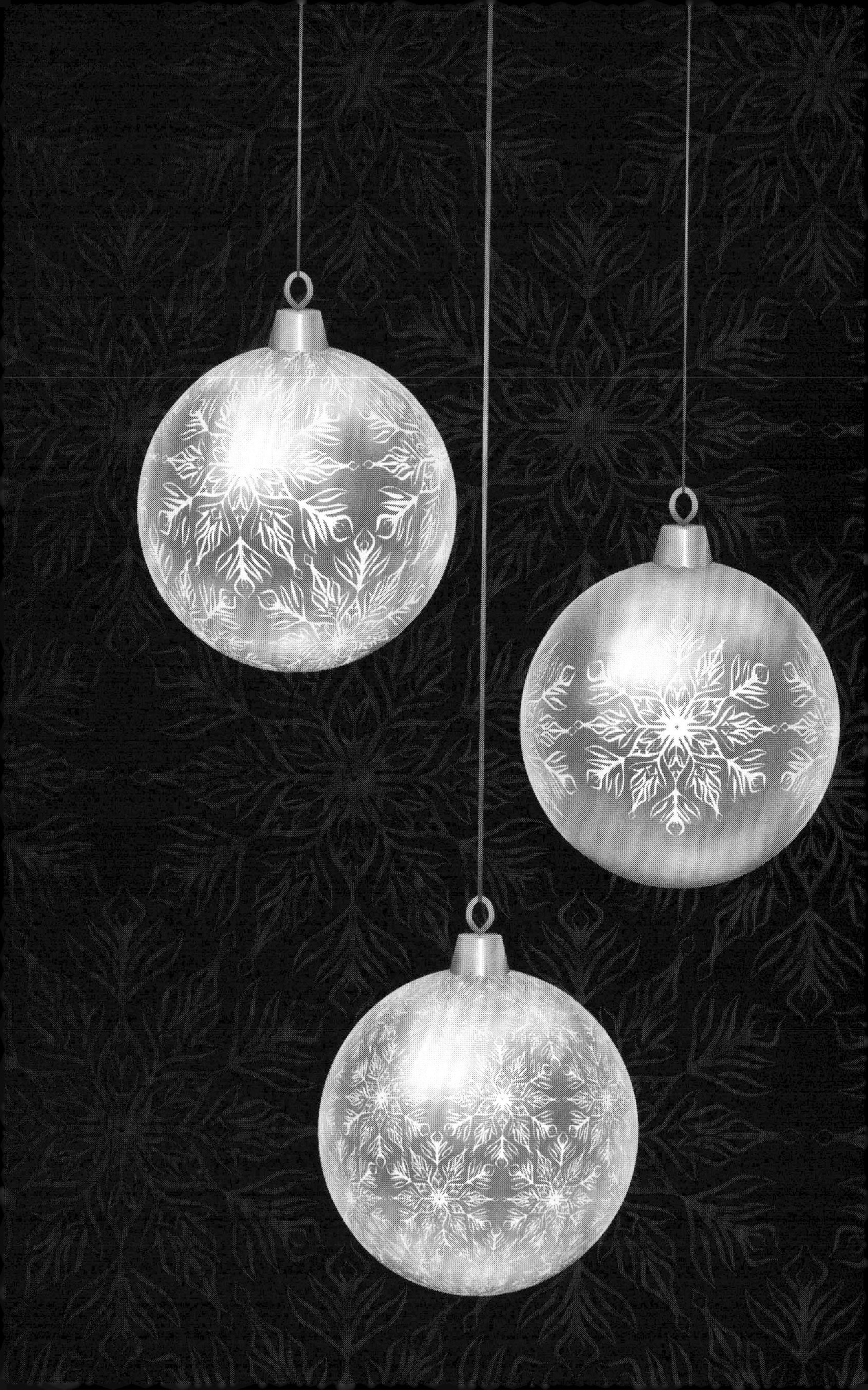

CHAPTER THIRTEEN

Reaper

I KNOW WHEN I HEAR IT.

The sickening sound of metal grinding against metal. The bang and crash of a vehicle rolling. The smell of burning rubber. Time slows when someone hears something like that. It's like the brain can't compute what it heard. It takes a minute to fully understand, to grasp. You have to ask yourself, 'What did I just hear? Is it what I think it is?'

And then comes the sudden silence.

There's no more squealing of tires or shattering glass. There isn't the screech of metal crunching.

Then that's how you know.

And what's worse is when you're running toward the chaos, you don't think there's a chance that someone you love is in the accident.

That's not the case for me.

I know. I know it's Sarah and Patrick. They'd just left, and that loud sound came all too soon. Time is sluggish as I run. I jump down the stairs, Boomer and Tongue at my side, Tool, Knives, Tank, and everyone else following. I pump my arms, trying to move as fast as I can. Fear and panic grip me. My heart can't pump. My lungs are freezing with every ragged breath. My skin is clammy and pale. I trip while I'm running, but Tongue catches me by the back of my cut, saving me from eating dirt. I don't have time to thank him.

My mind is on one thing and one thing only.

Sarah.

We all stop at the gate and grip the iron rods. "Open the fucking gate, Braveheart!" I roar. He presses all sorts of buttons, but it won't open. "Open it!"

"I'm trying, Prez. I swear, I'm trying. It isn't opening," Braveheart explains. He pulls the emergency lever, but even that isn't working. "I don't know why it isn't working! It was fine just a few minutes ago. It opened for them when they left." He runs his hands over his pale face, completely lost on what to do.

I bang my fist against the iron and growl. "Fucking open the goddamn gate, Braveheart!"

"I can't. It won't open, Prez."

My eyes burn with wild hot flames as I grip the rods in my hands and push with all my might. Everyone catches on, and they stand beside me, grabbing the iron rods and grunting as we dig our feet into the ground.

The gate groans in protest, but inch by inch our feet move as the barrier between me and Sarah finally gives. Sweat drips from my temple, tickling the side of my cheek. I narrow my eyes down the driveway. The dusty road seeming longer than usual, the potholes deeper, the sand thicker.

When one of the hinges snaps, the gate swings away. All of us break free, racing down the road. "No, please, no," I whisper a silent prayer to myself and whatever power there is bigger than me. I'm not the religious type, but right now, I'd get on my knees and pray to God.

It's Christmas. This isn't supposed to happen.

When we finally get to the road, all of us come to an abrupt halt. I nearly double over when I look to see the SUV about a half-mile down the road and on its side, smoking. "Sarah!" I yell her name, sprinting down the road. My boots clobber the pavement, and the closer I get to the wreckage, the further away she seems.

"Patrick!" Tongue yells for our brother. I feel like an ass for forgetting that he was with Sarah.

My main concern is her.

The engine is making an awful ticking noise as if it's about to blow.

Fuck.

"Get back!" Boomer screams at us. He turns on his heel and launches in the opposite direction of the car.

I'm the only one who doesn't listen to a man who blows things up for fun. Everyone bolts in the opposite direction. Everyone besides me runs away.

No. I run straight for it.

If Sarah is in that car, I want to die too.

"Come on!" Boomer and someone else grabs me by the shoulders and yanks me back.

"No!" I cry out as they drag me back. I fight against them to throw myself onto the wreckage to be with her.

Through life and death our love will survive.

The boom of fire and force fling us backward. The heat is almost too much to bear as it cloaks my body. The power of the explosion slams us against the ground. I land on my back and hit my head against the pavement. My ears ring, my eyes sting from the fire igniting the SUV, and it's hard to breathe from the smoke lingering in the air. I crawl to my hands and knees and scream.

"No! Sarah! Doll! Sarah!"

I scream for her, my voice hoarse and ragged, hoping she can hear me through the blaring blaze.

"Reaper." Boomer holds me back again from getting closer to the SUV.

I turn, sneering at him to let me go, but he has tears in his eyes too.

"She's gone."

"No! No, she isn't. She isn't gone," I yell, stumbling away from him. How can he give up so easy? Boomer's tears are silent as they fall down his cheek. The orange of the fire flickers in his eyes, a wicked reflection that shows my hell.

"I've never hated fire so much in my entire life," he mutters just before a sob reaches his throat.

This time, it's my heart that's been yanked from my chest. It's my soul that's been reaped.

We were a family. What am I going to tell Maizey? What am I going to do? I can't raise another kid on my own. My chest tightens, and I can't breathe. My left arm tingles, and my heart feels like it's about to explode. I fall to my knees, clutching my chest, where I no doubt believe the organ I harvest from others is being harvested from me.

"Reaper! Hey, Reaper? Call Doc! Call 911, fucking something!" Boomer yells at the guys surrounding us. "Reaper, what's going on? What the fuck is happening!" he screams the last sentence so loud his voice cracks.

Sirens churn the air somewhere in the distance. The scalding torch from the fire feels like it's melting my skin, but I can't seem to care.

Sarah's dead.

And if she's dead, then I don't give a fuck about living. Let me burn, let me turn to ash—let me be nothing but a memory.

But damn it, just let me be with her.

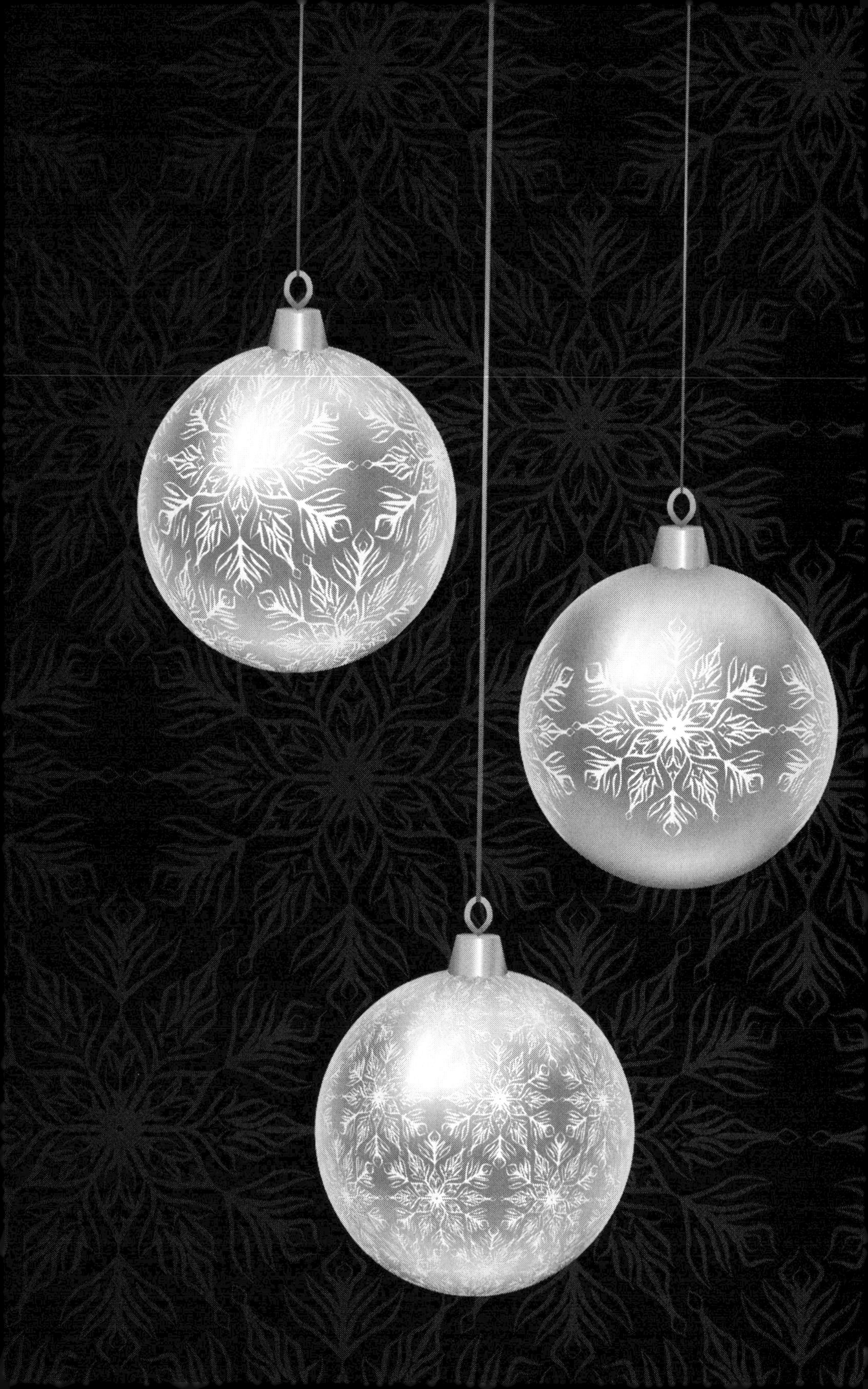

CHAPTER FOURTEEN
Sarah

I'M DROWSY. MY HEAD IS SPINNING, AND NO MATTER HOW HARD I TRY, I CAN'T OPEN MY eyes. I groan when I notice every part of me is in pain. What happened? I manage to pry my lids open, blinking to clear the blur. I can't see anything.

Squeezing my eyes closed, I take a deep breath and try again. I can see clearer this time. I don't know where I am. It isn't the basement or a hospital. It's run down and old. The walls are cracked, the paint is chipping, and the floor is cold, gray, and hard like stone.

Cement.

It's also cracked, with stains. I can only imagine what they are.

A painful moan comes from my left, and that's when I see Patrick. He has a piece of glass in his thigh, blood staining his blue jeans.

The accident.

Someone rear ended us, and Patrick lost control of the vehicle.

"Patrick!" I call out his name and try to run to him, but a thick, clear glass barrier is between us, stopping me. I bang on it with my fists, then squat to get to his level since he's still lying on the floor. "Patrick, get up. Get up. Come on."

He groans again and finally rolls to his uninjured side, leaving the leg straight that has the glass shard in it. "Sarah?"

"I'm here. I'm here, Patrick. Are you okay?"

"I've been better," he jokes, then staggers to his feet. Dragging his leg behind him, he comes to the other side of the wall and presses his hand against it. "Where are we?"

"I don't know. It looks abandoned."

"It's the asylum," Patrick recognizes.

"You're sure?"

"No, but it's the only place I can think of," Patrick says. "It's old, rundown, and the rusty wheelchair in the corner is giving me creepy vibes."

A sad chuckle bubbles in my throat. "I'll have to agree."

"Are you okay? You're bleeding. Prez is going to kill me."

"You're in worse shape than me."

"I've dealt with worse."

The sound of a door opening to the room has us turning. Patrick tries to get as close as he can to the glass to protect me, but he can't. While he takes a step forward to challenge whoever brought us here, I take a step back. The further away from this freak, the better.

He comes into a front area just outside of both of our cells. And he's wearing a baby mask. It's clear, showing the flesh colored tone of his skin, but the design camouflages what he looks like. "Can't even show your face?" I spit. "Coward."

"Oh, so feisty," he says, lacing his hands behind his back as he steps forward. "And so beautiful. Sarah, Sarah, Sarah."

I don't like that he knows my name. And the way he says it sounds like he's finding pleasure in saying it.

"So young and beautiful to be with men like the Kings. I'm here to show you the fault of your ways. To show you that the good in these people you surround yourself with is fake. I'm as real as it gets, Sarah."

His words lodge a weight of fear in my belly, causing the nausea to churn tenfold. "And you think, what? That I'm better off with you? I'd never be with you. I'd rather—"

Our kidnapper slams his hands against the door. "You'd rather what?" His spit sprays against the rectangular window. "You'd rather die than be with someone like me? You're surrounded by people like me. I mean, look at the man next to you. He's a drunk."

"He is not!"

"It's okay, Sarah. He's taunting you," Patrick says, trying to get me to calm down.

"I'm telling her the truth!" The man bangs his fist against the door, and I jump. Bile creeps its way up my throat. I want to throw up. All the horrible smells are getting to me. The dust clinging to the air, the mold along the walls, the rotten stench surrounding us; I can't handle it. "She deserves truth, not constant lies."

"Who are you?" My voice trembles. "What do you want? Money? We have plenty of money."

He tosses his head back and laughs. The column of his throat is thick, and his large Adam's apple bobs. He is in shape. His arms bulge and his chest is wide, which tells me he's strong. "I want you to see the truth," he says. "I don't want money. Money isn't important to me." His hand splays against the window. "But you are. The biker life isn't for a woman like you, Sarah. I've tried so hard to kill a few of them off, to better the world, but no on will fucking die!"

"Oh my god," I stumble backward. "You buried Tongue! You tried to drown Knives! And Daphne…"

"I'm going to fucking kill you!" Patrick slams his body against the metal door, but the metal doesn't even creak or give from the weight of him.

"You'll never be able to get me. You know what these rooms are? These are the insanity rooms. It's what I call them." He starts to pace, slowly, dragging his finger along the walls. "These are the rooms the crazies go in, the ones who constantly scream, the ones who cry, who hurt themselves. The ones who have to get strapped down. The ones who wear the straitjacket." He turns around and walks toward me.

Patrick watches him like a hawk, following The Groundskeeper's every step.

"So many evil things happened in these rooms," he continues, lowering is voice. The octave sends shivers down my spine. "I read one man banged his head against the glass so many times, he killed himself." He tsks, as if he cares. "Shame."

But he doesn't.

"If you look, you'll see the crack. Right there." He points in my cell, and I follow where he's pointing his finger.

When I see the point of impact, I lose any control I had over my stomach and vomit.

"Sarah, are you okay?"

"I'm fine," I say to Patrick.

"The baby?" Patrick asks, and I know it's to see if I feel any pain. I don't. Yet.

"Baby? You're pregnant?" The Groundskeeper bangs his fist against the door. "I'll get it out of you. Don't worry. You won't ever have to deliver a biker's baby."

I scoot back until I hit the wall, holding my stomach protectively. If I am pregnant, there is no way in hell I'm going to let this man touch me. What scares me even more is how sincere he looks as he stares at me, like he genuinely cares and believes in this mission that he's on.

"First things first," he says, lifting up a bottle of whiskey.

"No!" I shake my head, realizing what he's about to do. I turn to look at Patrick, who's watching The Groundskeeper unscrew the cap to the bottle, fingers clenched in his palm and chest heaving. He's already fighting himself. "Don't do this. I'll go with you. Okay? I'll go, just leave Patrick alone."

"Don't you mean, Pirate? I'm sure after all of this, he's thirsty." The Groundskeeper walks in front of Patrick's door and pours some whiskey on the floor. "You can't be a pirate without a nice swig of whiskey. Isn't that right, Pirate?"

Patrick's reaction is immediate. His nostrils flare, and he falls forward, catching himself on his fists as he tries to control the disease swirling inside him.

"Patrick, don't give in. You can do this. Think about Sunnie. Think about her. Hold onto that."

"This smells so good," The Groundskeeper says, almost with a sexual gratification. His eyes close as he inhales, and Patrick's eyes stare at the bottle with want and need. "Watch him fall apart, Sarah. Watch him and let him so you know just how weak the Kings really are." He places the bottle in the middle of the room and walks out the door, locking it behind him.

The buzzer sounds, and automatically Patrick's door swings open to allow him in the main room where the bottle waits for him.

"Sarah…" whispers Patrick, a desperate hinge to his voice that's begging me to save him.

Patrick finds the furthest corner in his cell and sits. His shirt is drench in sweat, and he licks his lips as if he can taste the alcohol. He buries his hand in his jean pocket and pulls out his sobriety chip, bringing it to his mouth and holding it against his lips. I hope he can taste the victory on the small token because it's the only thing keeping him grounded.

I thought the biggest villain was The Groundskeeper, but he isn't.

It's the square bottle with a narrow neck sitting on the floor, the burning smell of whiskey hanging in the air, and the temptation to get drunk. Patrick's damnation is only a few feet away, and the only thing stopping him from giving in is control.

And it's fragile enough that it can break at any moment.

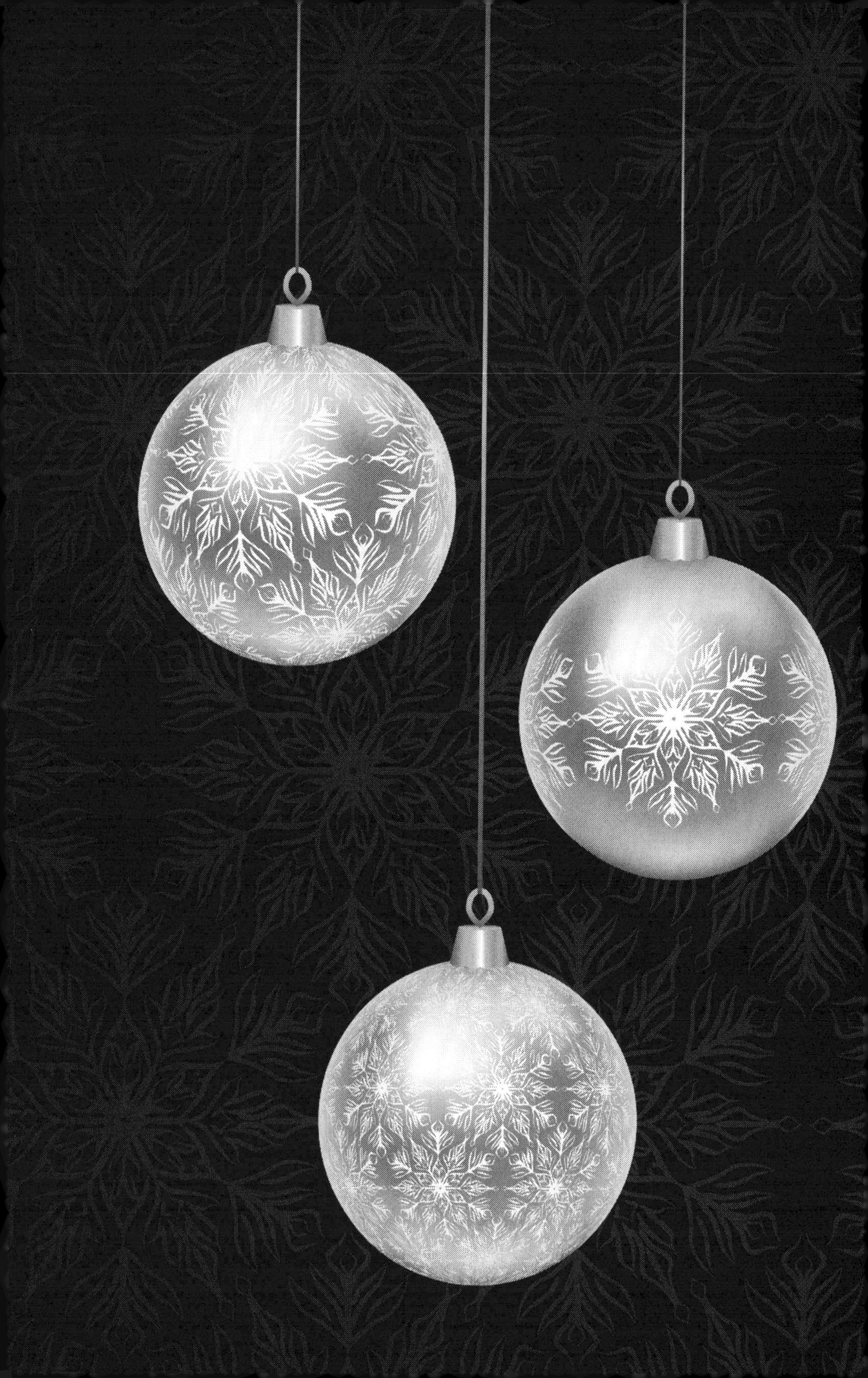

CHAPTER FIFTEEN

Zain

WHAT DID PORTER DO?
I know he needs help. I do. He has an identity issue that he has yet to be able to come to terms with. He isn't all there upstairs, but I guess that's the story for all of us here at the asylum. We're all fucked up in the head. Some are worse than others, like me. My mania controls who I am half the time. The battle inside me is loud, a constant bomb ready to blow, until I'm left gasping for air.

Peeking around the corner of the wall, I see him watching through the window of the door that used to allow doctors and nurses to check in on their patients without having to interact. This part of the house, this wing, it's closed off for a reason. It's too far away from the main branch of the house because this is where the doctors ran all of their illegal experiments.

Why did I choose to live here?

Because this house is unwanted just like the rest of us. When Porter reached out to me about this place, all of us were homeless, and we banded together to make sure we were protected. Then I found out where it was and who owned it, and I thought there would be no hope.

Jesse is my nephew, the President of the Ruthless Kings. He never got to meet me, and I never got to meet him. My brother had nothing to do with me because of my mental state. I was too much to deal with, too much of a hassle for my family. I've always been on my own, and when I explained all of that to Reaper, he graciously had me sign a contract, handed me the keys to the house, and invited me over for Christmas.

I could have a family, one with blood. I want that. I crave that. I'm a lunatic, a havoc, a broken soul, and I've found the birds of my flock. That doesn't mean I don't yearn for more.

If I'm not honest with Reaper, if I let Porter keep doing this, we'll end up homeless again. Or we'll be dead. I have a feeling Reaper isn't the forgiving type.

"It's just a matter of time," Porter says to himself before walking away. His footsteps echo down the hall. When he's far enough away to where I can't hear them anymore, I peek inside to see what he was looking at, and my mania roars its ugly head.

I swing my head back and forth, gripping the trim of the door. He kidnapped Sarah. I don't know the other guy, but this isn't right. This isn't right!

I can't open it because I don't know if I can trust myself once I'm in there. I might destroy anything and everything in my path.

Including Sarah.

I push off the wall and know exactly what I have to do. Like a pissed off bull, I charge down the hallway until I'm at the front of the house where the others are. They're sitting on the floor since we don't have furniture.

"Where are you going, Zain?" Apollo asks. I don't know if that's his real name, but I know he's delusional. He believes he is Apollo, a divinity, a God. He doesn't believe he is God, but a Greek God.

And honestly, I'm not sure which one is more dangerous.

"Porter."

"Again?" He stands, wiping off his jeans. "Want me to come with you?"

"No. There are two people he kidnapped in the forbidden wing. Two people who belong to the Kings. I'm telling Reaper. I don't care what you have to do—you put Porter in a room he cannot get out of; do you hear me?" I don't say another word. I know Apollo won't let me down.

I dig for the car keys in my pocket and notice how damaged the Lincoln is. "Damn it, Porter. Damn it!" I punch the hood of the car with both hands, denting it further, and try to take deep breaths like my therapist said. As long as I can control the outrage, I might not experience a full-blown episode, which I can hardly remember when it happens.

Porter is trying to ruin everything we want for ourselves, but I'm not going to let him. I climb into the Lincoln Continental, and the engine clicks as if it's about to die, but I pull out of the driveway and take the road leading to the compound. All I can hope is I don't get killed by my nephew.

The miles of desert on either side get my heart racing. I don't like to be in big spaces; they make me feel lost and alone. I swallow, keeping my eyes forward on the road. I tighten my fingers around the wheel until the leather squeaks.

A Christmas song tries to play through the busted speakers, but all it does is grate my nerves, so I turn down the volume until all I hear is the scrap of the bumper on the road and the hum of the tires.

Ten minutes later I get to the Ruthless Kings clubhouse, but an ambulance is there, along with firetrucks and cop cars. I park on the side of the road and open the driver's side door. Immediately, I'm hit with the smell of smoke, and I see Reaper shoving the paramedics off him. It's chaos, something Porter loves to create.

"What did you do?" I ask, knowing Porter can't answer me. I can't protect him from this. I'm not sure what his obsession with the Kings is, but it has to come to an end.

"Get off me! I'm fucking fine."

"Sir, you had a mild heart attack. We need to get you to the hospital," the paramedic yells and when I hear that, I run toward the wreck. Water splashes under my feet from the firefighters putting out the flames coming from the car. The smoke makes me cough, but the sorrow on my nephew's face makes me want to kill Porter.

As much as I want to kill him, I've seen Porter on medication, and he can be a good man. He needs help. I won't give up on him, even if he does deserve it.

"I don't give a fuck. Get off me!" Reaper shoves the medic again and staggers to his feet.

"The car is empty," the firefighter informs everyone at once.

Reaper turns around, hope on his face as he stares at the firefighter. "It's empty. You're sure?"

"Positive. There are no crispy skeletons in there," the guy says casually as he walks to the firetruck.

"Guys, they might be alive." Reaper grins, tears shining in his eyes. "Alive."

This is my chance. I step forward, cutting through the men in leather until Reaper can see me. "They're alive, and I know where they are."

In a second, Reaper has his hand wrapped around my throat. I expect the cops to do something, to aim their guns and to order Reaper to stop choking me, but no one does anything. Reaper has Vegas in his pocket for good reason.

I don't want to be the outsider.

"Tell me," he sneers. "Uncle or not, I'll fucking kill you."

I gasp, my face heating from the trapped blood. "They're at the asylum. It's Porter. He did it."

Reaper lets go, and I gasp, clawing at my throat and coughing to try to breathe. He holds a hand against his heart, and the medics come to his side again, but he pushes them away. "Get the fucking point. I am refusing medical treatment."

"Your funeral, dude," a small man with a feminine voice says to Reaper as he shuts the doors to the back of the ambulance.

"You need us, Reaper?" a cop asks, just as another member, Badge, hands him a stack of cash.

"No, this is club business," Reaper growls, his eyes like slits as he stares at me.

If I don't make this right, I'm a dead man.

"Okay. Call if you need us." The cop whistles and rounds up his officers. They climb in their patrol cars, turn off their sirens, and drive away. Badge hands over a stack of cash to the firefighters too and then to the medics.

"Are you buying my silence?" The gay medic sounds insulted; at least, I'm assuming he's gay.

"You can pay with your life if you want?" Badge suggests, slapping the cash against the guy's chest.

"It's been a pleasure doing business with you."

"It means you're who we call. You work for us now," Badge says.

"Honey, I work for the hospital. Until my paycheck says big bad bikers on it in the left-hand corner, I do not work for you." The guy struts toward the driver's side door, hops in, and waves goodbye as he drives off.

Little man has big balls. Good for him. I think.

You can kill him. Release it and you can kill all of them.

I scratch my fingers against the bumpy road, letting the skin peel and blood drip. Inflicting pain reminds me that I'm just as human as anyone else. I can control me. I am the control.

"Who the fuck is Porter?" Reaper snarls, his boots blocking my line of sight as I lay on the ground.

"You know him as The Groundskeeper. He has an identity disorder—" I don't get to finish my explanation because my tongue is being pulled from my mouth, and a knife is threatening to cut it off.

"Tongue, don't. He has answers, and he won't be able to give us information if he has no tongue."

The metallic taste of blood bursts across my taste buds. I can tell the man isn't happy with his Prez's order, but I'm appreciative because it causes him to pull away. "That man buried me, nearly killed Knives, kidnapped Daphne, and now Patrick and Sarah? We've killed for less."

"You knew? About Porter, you know him?"

I swallow, the cut on my tongue stinging with pain. "I've known him since we broke out of the mental institution we were in. He's a good guy on the right meds. We're all fucked up, Reaper."

"I want retribution," Reaper growls. "No one takes Sarah and lives to tell the tale."

"He's sick, Reaper. He's sick."

"Once I rip his heart out, he won't have to worry about it anymore. Take me to the asylum. Now."

"Reaper, I need to make sure your heart is okay," a blond guy with looks that tells me he isn't meant to be here warns Reaper.

"Later Doc. If Sarah isn't okay, then you'll have your answer."

Porter better hope he hasn't harmed a hair on their heads. The only way I can save Porter is if Sarah and Patrick are okay.

"Reaper, I don't know if she's pregnant. The test came back inconclusive."

The blood drains from my face when I hear that bit of news. Sarah could be pregnant.

"Let's hope she isn't, or this stress will cause another miscarriage," Reaper mutters. A few trucks pull out of the compound's driveway, coming to pick us up to go to the asylum. Tongue grips me by my shirt and lifts me to my feet.

Another?

Porter, what did you do?

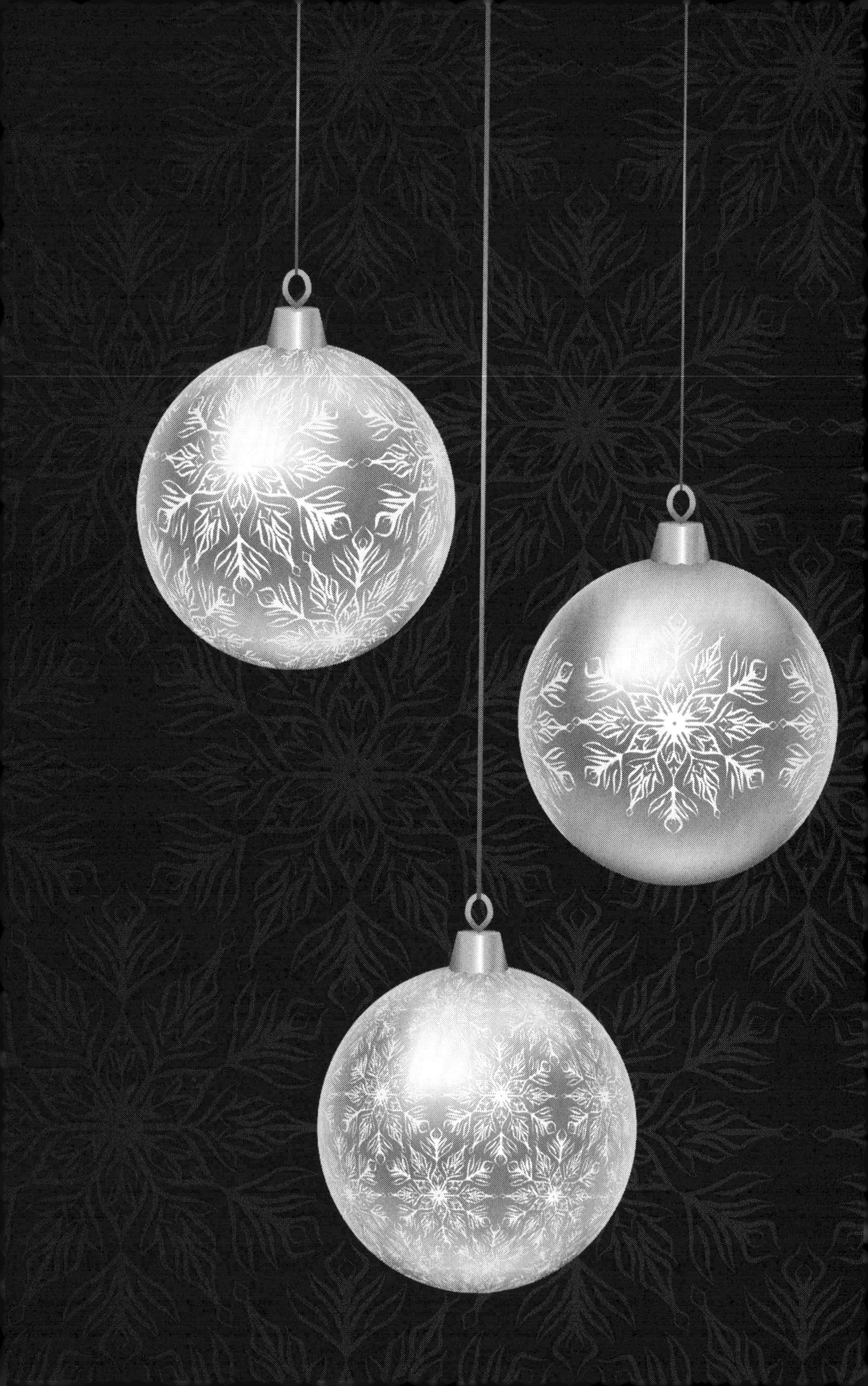

CHAPTER SIXTEEN

Patrick

THE WHISKEY SMELLS SO GOOD. I CAN ALMOST FEEL IT SLIDING DOWN MY THROAT. I can almost feel the burn, feel it pool like a puddle of gasoline in my stomach. I'm shaking, trembling, and my mouth won't stop watering. I really thought I was stronger than this, but I haven't been tested since I got out of rehab. Everyone has been so supportive by keeping the alcohol away from me that my will hasn't been tried.

Well, it is now.

And it feels like my skin is burning, crawling with need. There's a voice inside my head, encouraging me to take one sip. Only one. The last one ever. The chance to say goodbye. I can do that. There's no harm in one more taste. If I think about it, I never really got to have one last drink because I didn't know it would be 'the last' one.

"Patrick, talk to me. Tell me what you're feeling. Don't give in," Sarah says, placing her hand against the glass.

I bury my head between my knees and my fingers along the cold cement I'm sitting on. I need Sunnie. I need her so bad right now. "I forgot how good it smells," I admit, unable to look Sarah in the eye after saying the words. "I wish Sunnie was here." I tilt my head back until I hit the wall, closing my eyes so I don't have a constant view of the bottle sitting in the middle of the room outside my door.

Grabbing the bottom of my shirt, I lift it and wipe the sweat off my face. I almost feel like I'm in rehab again, only this time I'm not detoxing; I'm holding myself back from relapsing.

"Think about her. Think about how worried she is about you, Patrick. Think about rehab and everything you've been through, okay? You're stronger than the temptation. You're stronger than the whiskey."

I try to listen to Sarah and take a few deep breaths in, but that backfires because I can nearly taste the whiskey in the air. I hit my knuckles against the ground, over and over until I feel the skin split. With every slam, the pain becomes worse.

The pain might be the only thing stopping me from giving in and chugging the entire bottle.

So much for having a nice Christmas with everyone. I should have known. It's always something.

Right about now, when I'm craving a shot and the high only alcohol can give me, Sunnie reads that ridiculous romance novel to me. Samuel and Elizabeth. I almost know the damn thing by heart, word for word, but it's my safety net. A symbol of faith, love, and hope. Sunnie read that to me when I was at my lowest. When I hated everything in the world, even her.

She never gave up on me. She read that damn novel to me, and honestly, it wasn't the story that calmed me but the sound of Sunnie's voice. It was the way she read, her tone, and how effortless she spoke. She's my sun on a fucking stormy day, and I need her now more than ever.

The need to drink is clawing at my gut.

"What would Sunnie do?" Sarah asks.

For some reason it makes me laugh because I think of the 'What would Jesus do?' slogan.

WWSD.

I need that tattooed on my damn body.

"She'd read to me," I say.

"I don't have a book."

"It's okay. There's only one that will work anyway, and Sunnie has it. She takes it everywhere. I know the first few chapters by heart."

"Stop hitting the ground and tell me the story, Patrick."

I open my eyes and stare at her like she's crazy, but she has fear written all over her face. Her mouth is pinched, her brows are furrowed, and she plasters herself against the glass to try to get as close as possible to me.

"Tell me the story," she says again.

My cheeks flame with embarrassment. It's my secret with Sunnie. I suppose secrets don't matter anymore. Not when it comes to health. I tighten the sobriety chip in my palm and nod. I can do this. I can win.

"Elizabeth hated wearing a corset under her dress. The last thing she believed women should do was hurt themselves for beauty. Making a smaller waistline was not for her; it was for them—for men. Her lungs protested all day. Her breasts were pushed so high she was surprised they didn't touch her chin, but she had to deal with the fashions of a lady. Even if she didn't consider herself one."

Sarah giggles. "I'm sorry; I don't mean to laugh. It never thought you were the type to read regency romance."

"I don't read it. Only one story is read to me. It's different." Plus, it helps curve the urge, and isn't that all that matters? Thinking about reciting the next few sentences already has me calming down, the thirst dissipating. I think about rehab and laying in bed, hallucinating that I saw my sister Macy. I screamed, I begged, I cried. I constantly asked for a drink, and all Sunnie did was hold my hand and read me the silly novel she stole from Patricia, an evil bitch I later killed.

I stand on my feet, staggering because of the piece of glass in my thigh. I yank it out. "Fuck, that hurts."

"Where are you going? Stop, Patrick." Sarah bangs her hands against the wall to stop me, but I have a goal. "Patrick, tell me more of the story. Skip to your favorite part!"

I limp through the whiskey spilled on the floor, staring at the bottle standing all alone in the middle of the room. Light shines through the hole in the roof. The glass and liquid amber glimmers beautifully, casting a kaleidoscope of colors along the floor.

If no one thought whiskey in a bottle could be pretty, they were wrong.

"Patrick, please, tell me your favorite part. Do not pick up that whiskey." Sarah is at her door now, staring at me with glassy eyes.

I think about the book, and there was always one part I really liked more than the others. "Samuel is lost in her love and in Elizabeth's fierce independence. She takes on the world with strength he had never seen before with any other woman. She's a rebel, the kind of woman others would deem 'unworthy' of marriage, but Samuel couldn't disagree more. Elizabeth hasn't found a man who is strong enough to match her strength. Until now." I bend over and pick up the open bottle, watching the liquid swish on the inside like an angry sea.

I need to match Sunnie's strength, the kind she's placed in me. She counts on me. I bring the bottle to my nose and inhale. Clutching onto the chip, thinking about Samuel and Elizabeth, and Sunnie's love, I launch the bottle across the room. The glass hits the wall, shattering with the impact, and the whiskey is a tsunami after being released. The wave tries to get to me, but I'm too far away.

I'm safe.

The door kicks in right as I collapse. A pair of arms wrap around me to hold me up. "I got you, Patrick. Sunnie is waiting for you at home," comes Doc's voice. I am still a little lightheaded. But I did it. I didn't drink the whiskey. "Did you—"

"No," I say with a smile. "No."

"So fucking proud of you," Doc informs me and carries me out of the alcohol-infused space. "Sunnie will be too."

"I think I need a meeting, Doc."

"You don't say?" He tilts his lips in a smile as he leans me against the broken desk that's been here since the place was built.

I lean all of my weight on my other leg and watch as Reaper carries Sarah out of the room. When he feels like he has her in a safe space, he falls to his knees and cups the back of her head. He buries his face in her neck, and I know he's either crying or fighting the tears.

"I thought you died. I thought you were fucking dead," he says, wrapping his arms around her so tight, I worry he may to cut off her air supply. "I love you. You can't do that to me. You can't... You just can't." Reaper slams his lips against hers, and all the guys look at me to give Reaper and Sarah their moment.

"I'm glad you're okay," Boomer says.

"Thanks, Boomer. Glad to see you." All of his members are here too, which means he has come for Christmas.

Hell of a ride that's been. I can't wait for the holiday to be over.

"You can't keep me here!" I hear from down the hallway, followed by loud bangs.

"It's the only way your life can be spared, Porter. You have to stay in here until you're better." I limp down the hallway, but an arm helps support my weight.

It's Tongue.

We stand next to Zain, and another bang sounds as Porter keeps smashing his shoulder against the glass. He sees Tongue and becomes angrier. "You! I fucking hate you. I'm going to kill you; you hear me? I'm going to kill you. My dad might have fucked your mom, but we are far from family."

Holy shit.

Tongue's brother is this psychopath?

Christmas gifts keeping flying at us, don't they?

Tongue doesn't seem too surprised. "What are you doing?" Zain asks as Tongue enters the room his brother is in. Now that I see them side by side, there are a few similarities physically, but mentally, both of them are fucked up.

"You know what?" Tongue's voice is slow with gravel and a Southern accent. "I don't give a fuck if you're my blood because all my life you've been nothing to me." Tongue punches Porter across the face, then pulls out his brother's tongue. "You hurt my Comet." Porter tries to get away, but Tongue holds on tighter and grabs his homemade knife.

He places it against the pink appendage and right as he's about to cut, Reaper stops him. "Tongue, don't! He's your family."

"He's no family of mine."

"That's an order."

Tongue slides the knife across the wet muscle until he gets to the middle. "I've never really cared for orders," Tongue snarls and stabs through the middle of his brother's tongue. Blood spills, and Porter screams. He'll still be able to talk, but it will be awhile. Tongue listened to Prez, technically.

He bends over and wipes his knife clean on Porter's pants. Porter spits blood, yelling in agony, but Tongue isn't fazed. "Merry Christmas. Don't say I never gave you anything." Tongue slams the door as he exits the room, then slides the lock bar in place.

"Let's go home," Reaper announces to all of us.

"Yeah, I need to check on your heart."

"Your heart?!" Sarah screeches. "Why? What happened?"

"I thought you died. My heart couldn't handle it. I had a heart attack."

That's the thing about falling in love while you're a Ruthless King. When we fall, we fall fucking hard. And if we ever lose the one thing that gives our dark, fucked up lives meaning, we fall too.

"Promise you'll let Doc check you out?" Sarah begs, worry etched on her young face.

"I'm not coughing."

"That isn't how I check your heart, Reaper."

Tongue and Boomer help me walk out of this hellhole asylum, a psychotic estate I hope to never find myself in again, and everyone laughs at Doc and Reaper's banter. It lightens the mood.

There's still a grey cloud hanging over us, and Christmas won't be what it needs to be until it's gone.

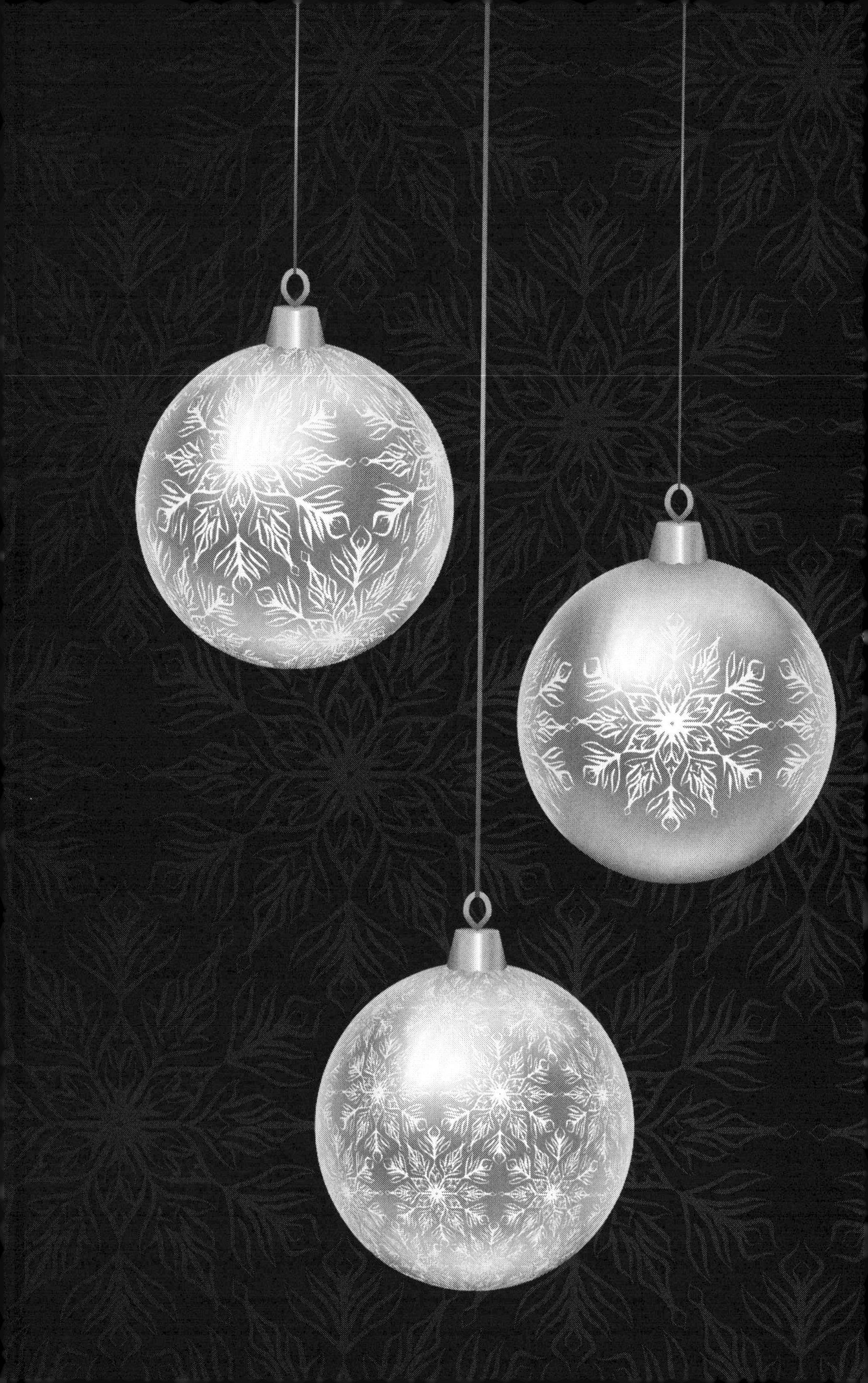

CHAPTER SEVENTEEN

Badge

Christmas Eve

"**N**o glitter, Maizey. You know the rules."

"Badge! Come on; it's Christmas. Glitter will make you look like a snowflake."

I cross my arms over my chest and glare at her. "I don't want to look like a snowflake."

"Putting glitter on you is on my Christmas wish list. See!" She shoves the paper so far in my face that I can't even read it.

Kids are so annoying, but Maizey is okay. I can deal with her. I never want kids of my own, though. Hell no. "I don't want glitter. That's just a wish you're never going to be able to get."

"I'm telling Reaper," Maizey huffs.

"Telling Reaper, what?" Slingshot asks, shoving a taco in his mouth as he stands in the doorway.

"Did you take your pill?" Maizey and I ask in unison as we watch him unwrap another taco from his bag.

"Yes, I took my pill. God, get off my back."

"Ew, Uncle Slingshot. Your back is stinky, 'member?" Maizey curls her nose in disgust, and I can't stop laughing at how serious she looks.

"It is not. You two are mean. I was going to let you put glitter on my face, but forget it. Be that way," Slingshot sharply spins on his heel and walks away, head held high.

Maizey lets out this scream that has my toes curling as my ear drums rumble. She throws her makeup brush down and runs after Slingshot in her princess gown. "Come back, come back, Uncle Slingshot. I didn't mean it."

"You did!" Slingshot argues with a seven-year-old girl.

I shake my head and grab the pink bedazzled mirror to see what Maizey has done to me this time. "Oh God," I groan when I see bright blue eye shadow, pink lipstick, and my hair in small piggy-tails on top of my head.

"You look so pretty," Sarah compliments me, chuckling when she sees my appearance.

She has a bandage on the side of her head still from the accident, but other than that, she looks great. "Do not," I grumble and stand, stretching my arms over my head.

"You're good with her, you know. I know you say you don't like kids but, Badge, you're a natural at it."

"Where's Reaper?" I ask her, wanting to change the subject. I don't like talking about kids. It makes me feel awful, like something is wrong with me when I say I don't want to have a baby. It's just how I feel. Maizey is cute and fun, but at the end of the day, I can give her back when I'm sick of her.

Not that I'm ever sick of her, but if I ever was, I could give her back.

Sarah's blonde hair falls in her face as she straightens her body from being perched against the wall. "He went to go pick up the rest of the gifts since Patrick and I were interrupted."

"How are you doing?" I ask softly, and her face falls. She lays her hand on her stomach and takes a minute to compose herself, but the emotion is written all over her face.

Doc told them about the inconclusive test, and Sarah cried for hours. We didn't see her the rest of the night when we brought her home from the asylum.

"I'm okay."

"I know." I bring her in for a hug, and Boomer comes over behind her. He's wearing a Santa hat and has a grenade in his hand. "Boomer?" I draw out his name, wondering what plan he has conjured up.

"Who wants to go blow holes in the sand?"

"Oh, oh, I do! Let me get my shoes on." Sarah claps her hands in excitement. I often wonder how the hell they're related, but then I see shit like this, and it all clicks. "I'm so glad you're here. I love you," she says, giving him a quick hug before she runs to get her shoes.

"Damn, Badge. You look hot."

"Fuck you, Boomer."

"Want to go out sometime? Can I get to second base?"

I push him out of the way, and he slams against the wall, laughing his ass off.

I walk into the living room, catcalls ringing through the air, and I find myself under a mistletoe. Before I can make my escape, a small hand tugs on mine.

It's Maizey.

"What?"

"Pick me up," she orders.

I pick her up by her arms and saddle her to my hip. "No glitter," I warn.

"No glitter," she agrees and gives me a quick peck on the cheek. "Mistletoe kisses instead." Maizey gives me another kiss, and my heart warms from her thoughtfulness.

I place a kiss on her forehead, then set her down on the floor before she's off running again. Everyone's eyes are on me, and I curl my lip, annoyed they saw me vulnerable. "What the hell are you guys looking at?"

"Nothing."

"Not a thing."

"Nice rack," Skirt says, giving me a wink.

I flick Skirt off, and he covers his daughter's eyes with his hand, so she doesn't see. She's five minutes old or something like that. She can't fucking see anyway.

I have to wear the makeup until I go to bed. That's the deal every time. I always have to hear jokes from everyone else. I make my way to the couch and sit next to Poodle, who's petting Lady as she sleeps.

"I'm sorry about Lady." I've must have said that fifty times since he told us about the cancer. Poodle doesn't even look up to see how ridiculous I am with makeup on; he stares at Lady, trying to make her feel better by loving on her with gentle strokes across her belly.

It's going to be a sad day when Lady dies.

I hope Christmas day is filled with joy. It's a day the club really needs. With Lady on her last few days, Sarah maybe not being pregnant, Reaper finding out he has an uncle he doesn't know and a sister he didn't know existed, and Tongue being related to a psycho—which is not surprising—tomorrow needs to be a good day.

It *has* to be.

It's why I've fucking volunteered to be Santa for some damn reason.

What the hell is wrong with me? Why do I do this to myself?

Right. At least I get cookies and milk. That will be worth it.

Because I don't even like kids. I can't stand them.

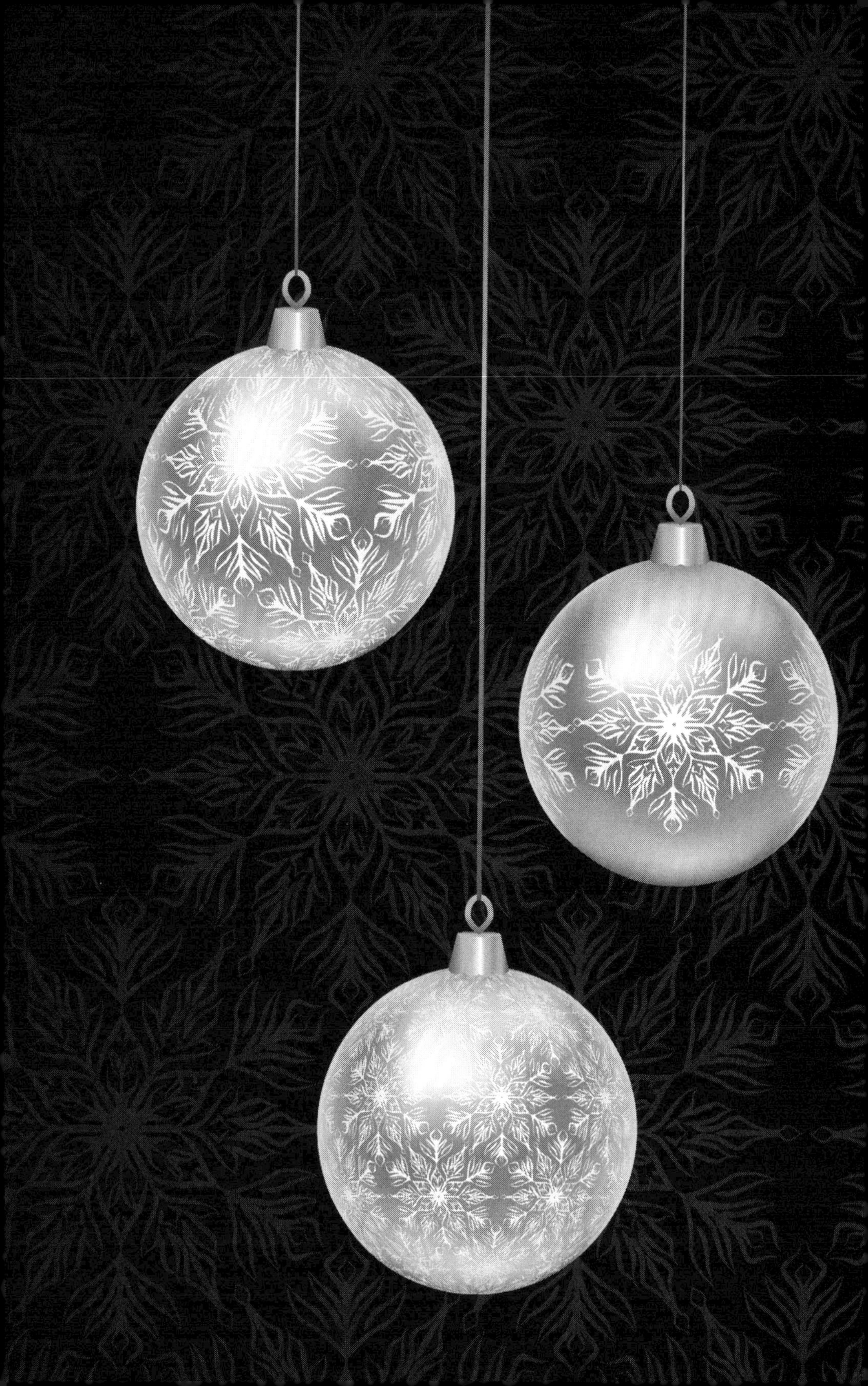

CHAPTER EIGHTEEN

Reaper

It's two in the morning, and Badge looks ridiculous. All the adults are awake, drinking, laughing, and blowing off steam. Sarah is trying to stuff one last pillow in the Santa outfit for Badge's fake belly, but it won't go in.

Oh, wait, never mind. She got it.

She grunts as she pulls the black belt tight and slaps his round belly when she's done. The outfit is complete. "There. You're all done."

"How do I look?" Badge asks everyone in the kitchen. Even my sister is here instead of downstairs. She has stayed next to me all day and night, and that makes me feel good; like she can trust me.

The last few days have been horrible. I never want to experience the horrors I went through thinking Sarah was dead. Doc ran some tests on my heart and come to find out, I didn't have a heart attack, but I did experience broken heart syndrome.

I didn't know that was a thing until Doc told me. My heart was literally broken; the tendons inside were under so much stress from the grief I felt that they snapped.

"You look like a fake Santa," Tongue says, placing Happy on the table.

Everyone scoots back, chairs fall to the floor, and Happy swishes his tail, which has a bell on it, so it jingles every time he moves. Let's not forget the Santa hat and the matching red nails. Daphne isn't scared like the rest of the guys. She's sitting on Tongue's lap and kisses Happy on the snout.

There really is someone out there for everyone.

"Tongue, you do know all Santas are fake," Badge points out, and Tongue whips out his knife and flings it through the air. It takes off Badge's Santa hat and pins it to the wall.

"I'll take that as a 'yes,'" Badge tugs the knife from the wall and readjusts his hat. "Okay, give me the bag. I can't believe I'm doing this," he grumbles as I hand him the heaviest bag of fucking gifts in the world. He grips the red bag and throws it over his shoulder, and Sarah sneaks a picture.

"Sorry, I had to," Sarah says. "Okay, remember, Maizey is going to wake up. She wants proof you're real. Be ready."

"Aidan too. They will work together as a team."

"I'm not scared of kids," Badge stays, shoving a cookie in his mouth. "Kids are dumb. In a good way, you know, innocent and 'growing' and all that." He finger quotes it, which only makes us think he's truly terrified of what's about to happen. Kids are smart, resilient, and clever.

And he has no idea what he's signed up for. "Okay, everyone, quiet down. Not one noise. Badge is going to put the gifts under the tree," I say, flipping the light off, so we're all in the dark. The kitchen is warm with so many bodies in it. On top of the Kings, Boomer and his crew are here too.

Patrick ad Sunnie aren't here. They're in their room. After the emotional ordeal with Patrick fighting off his urge to drink, he's been asleep since. Sunnie hasn't left his side and has read that damn book front to back three times for him, but Sarah told me that's what stopped Patrick from taking a drink. I'll be forever in her debt for saving my friend.

I peek around the corner to see Badge drop the bag on the floor and lay his hands on his stomach. He ho-ho-ho's like Santa does, and I have to cover my mouth to keep quiet. Badge is such an asshole; he loves this shit, no matter how much he says he hates it.

He finds the cookies and milk on the mantel and ignores the gifts for a few minutes. He stuffs the chocolate chip cookies in his mouth, then chugs the milk. When he's done, he grabs the plate of carrots for the reindeer, turns over his shoulder, and points to it. "What the fuck do I do with this?"

"Eat it," I whisper loudly.

"I hate carrots," Badge grumbles his dissatisfaction and tosses the carrots in the fireplace instead. "There. Problem solved."

I rub my hand down my face, wondering why we didn't get Tank to be Santa. He's much more pleasant to deal with.

Badge places the plate on the mantle, ignoring the already stuffed stockings, and opens the bag. "I can't believe we have a fucking cactus and not a real tree," he says under his breath, but if I can hear him, the kids can too.

"For the love of all things vile, shut up!" I warn him, and Sarah pinches my butt. "Ow." I rub the tender spot. She lays her finger over her lips, telling me to shut up.

I'll show her how to shut up by stuffing my co—

"Get him!" Maizey warrior cries, and Aidan follows suit.

Everyone in the kitchen does their best to stay quiet when they hear the tiny squeals.

"You go right, I go left," Maizey orders.

"Oh no," I chuckle, watching as Maizey wraps a string of Christmas lights around Badge.

Aidan goes the other way, making sure Santa is stuck in the string of lights.

Maizey high kicks Badge in the belly, and he falls in a perfectly placed chair. Aidan wraps more lights around him and the chair, so Badge has nowhere to go. He's yelling at the top of his lungs, mouth open, chestnut colored hair glowing almost red against the Christmas lights. When he runs out of light, he does the only thing he knows to do with them.

Aidan plugs it in.

And Badge lights up in blues, oranges, yellows, reds, and greens. I see the annoyance in Santa's eyes, staring daggers right at me.

"We caught Santa!" Maizey squeals, and she and Aidan high five one another.

"Mommy, Daddy!" Maizey calls out for us, and Sarah intertwines her fingers with mine.

"I think that's our cue," Sarah says.

"Do we unwrap, Badge?" Skirt asks, peeking over my shoulder.

"Nah, leave him like that for a while. It will be good for him," I say.

"This is the best Christmas ever," Warden says with a big smile on his face. Everyone gives him a hard glare, and he backtracks. "I don't mean the bad shit. I just mean now."

Bane throws his arm around his twin's shoulder. "I know what you meant."

"Mommy! I caught Santa. I caught Santa. Hurry, come see before he poofs away!" Maizey says with urgency.

Maybe Warden is right, maybe this is, right now, the best Christmas ever.

"We're going to take pictures of Badge like this, right? Blackmail him for the rest of time?" Poodle asks.

"Oh yeah, definitely."

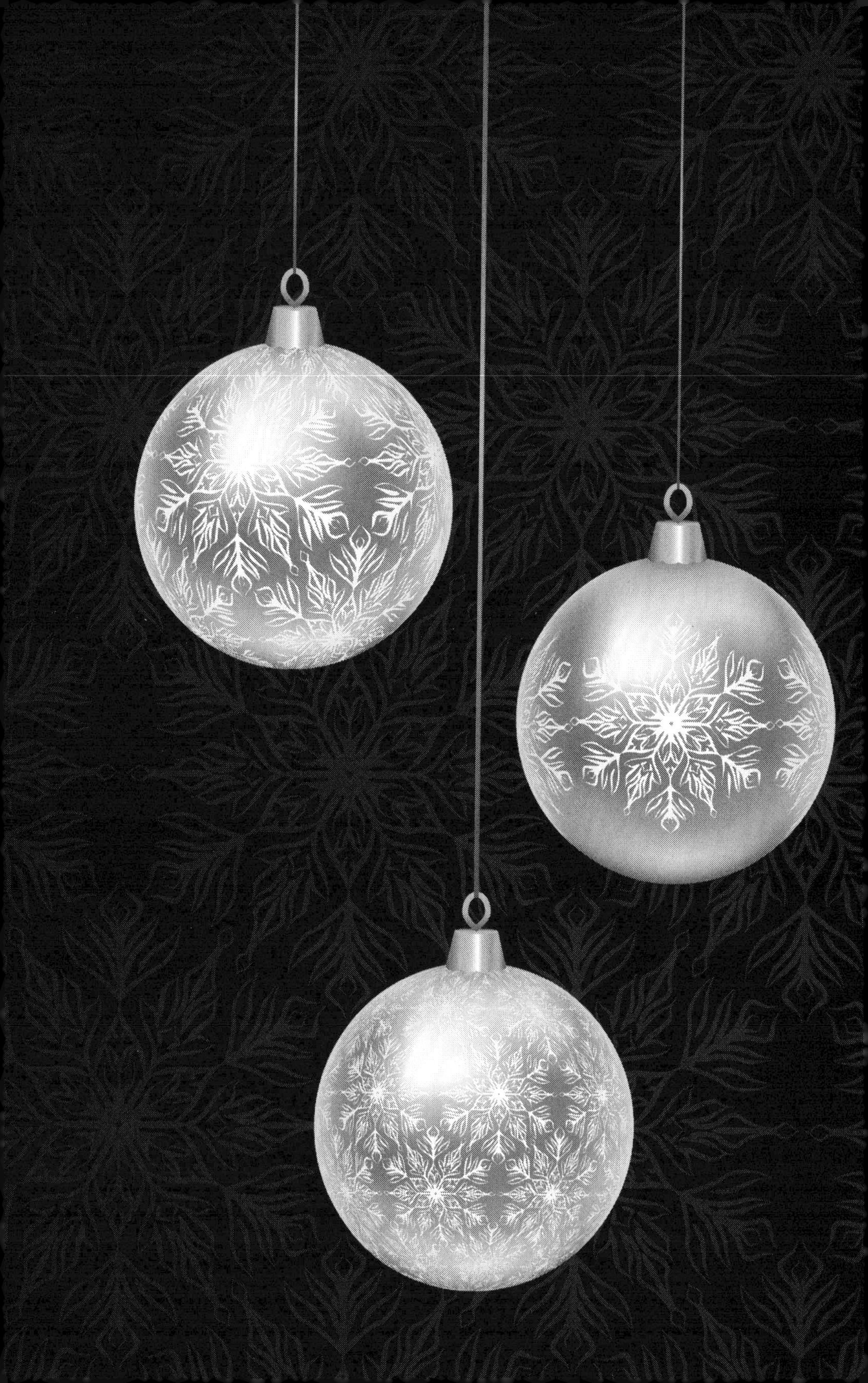

CHAPTER NINETEEN
Sarah

Christmas Day

"Can you untie me now?" Badge asks, wiggling around in his chair. Aidan and Maizey crashed and fell asleep around his chair a few hours ago, but now it's about time to wake them up for presents. "I really need to take a piss."

"Badge, Santa does not say those words," I chuckle, then smell the sweet scent of coffee. "Yeah, I'll untie you." I unplug him and unwrap one string, going in a hundred circles before starting on the other.

"Good thing I'm not Santa. Ever again." Once he's free, he runs toward his room to get undressed and do his business. My cheeks still hurt from laughing at what the kids did. Scrubbing my eyes, I yawn and step over Aidan, who has his hand on top of Maizey's. Oh my God, what if they grow up and fall in love?

A mother can hope.

I throw my hair up in a quick, messy bun and head to the kitchen. Reaper, Patrick, Poodle, Warden, Bane, Wolf, and Boomer are there making Christmas breakfast.

"Is everyone ready for presents? The cactus is overflowing. Santa really outdid himself," I say, greeted by Reaper's kiss.

"Eat first, then we will."

"Aye, the kids will sleep for another half hour. Let's dig in before the little spawns wake up," Skirt says, biting into a piece of bacon.

Delilah comes up the steps of the basement next, holding the hands of the two kids we haven't seen much since we rescued them. Micah and Delaney, brothers.

Everyone stops what they're doing, looking up as they enter the kitchen, and the siblings hide behind Delilah's legs.

"Well, good morning, you two! Guess what? It's Christmas! Do you want to go open your gifts?" I ask them, wanting them to feel like part of the family.

Micah blinks at me and steps away from Delilah. "We have gifts?"

My heart breaks when I hear those words. "Of course, you do! Santa brings presents to everyone. Come on, everyone. Looks like we're moving to the living room early. Grab your coffee," I say, guiding the kids to the living room.

When they see the cactus, they're astounded. "Woah, that's the coolest tree ever."

"It's a cactus," Delaney says. "Stupid."

"You're stupid!" Micah pushes his brother, and he pushes back.

"Okay, that's enough. Everyone, calm down. You're both right. It's a Christmas cactus," I say with pride.

"Maizey," Micah pokes her side. "Wake up. Christmas is here."

"We caught Santa!" She bolts into a sitting position, but then she sees the empty chair. "But he was right there! We caught him."

"He poofed. I saw it," I say, wanting her to know I believe her.

A knock at the door interrupts everyone getting settled, but Tank gets up as soon as he sits down. "I got it."

He opens the door, and Zain is there, holding a bottle of wine with a bow on it. "I … uh … I don't know if I'm still wanted here, but I wanted to bring something by. I didn't know what to get."

"I'm sorry, we don't allow alcohol in the main room," I tell him.

"Oh, it's non-alcoholic. I saw what Porter did to your friend," Zain says, and to know he was so thoughtful has Tank swinging the door open for him to come in.

"Come on in," I invite him in, and he gives me the biggest smile, one that is remarkably similar to Reaper's.

Reaper comes in the room and gives Zain a nod, which is better than a knife to the chest, so hopefully he understands that.

Everyone gets settled in the main room, and I can't help but feel overwhelmed with love. This is my family, my home, my people. There are so many here, so many who would risk their lives for another. I'm so lucky.

Poodle and Melissa are on the couch, feeding Lady pancakes. They have given her everything she wasn't allowed to have before since she isn't doing so well. Patrick and Sunnie are next to them, Tool and Juliette are sitting next to Reaper on the floor to be close to the action. Doc and Joanna are on the other side of the cactus, Skirt and Dawn are on the loveseat, Joey on Skirt's lap. Aidan is in front of the tree, looking like he's about to tear into the gifts any minute now.

Tongue and Daphne are in the corner, watching from the dark as they like to do. Badge, Slingshot, Knives, Tank, Bullseye, and Braveheart are on the new sectional we just purchased. It's huge, an L-shape, to fit everyone.

That doesn't even include Boomer and his guys, who are lined up against the wall since there's no room.

Maybe we should have had Christmas in the gym…

"Okay, here we go," Reaper says, grabbing the first gift. "Slingshot, it's you, buddy," Reaper tosses it to him, and Slingshot catches the red gift with a silver bow.

He tears into it, opens the box, and jumps up and down when he sees what it is. "It's a three-hundred-dollar gift card to my favorite taco stand!"

No one is happy about it.

"Who did that?" Reaper asks, but no admits a thing.

"Duh, Daddy. Santa." Maizey pats Reaper's arm. "It's okay. It only means Slingshot deserved it."

"I'll have to write a letter to Santa and tell him my complaints then." Reaper shoots me a glance and winks, and my body flushes in response. He knows it too because his eyes darken to molten lava.

"Thanks, Santa!" Slingshot nudges Badge, and Badge slaps him on the back of the head.

"Bullseye!" Reaper throws him a gift, and we hope it lightens Bullseye's spirit. He's been quiet and down. We miss him.

Bullseye tears into the black wrapping paper and grins, smiling for the first time in months. "A dart maker. I love it! Thank you, Reap—Santa," he corrects himself quickly. "Really, thank you."

"Daphne, this one is from Tongue. You have two," Reaper says, and Daphne manages to pry herself away from Tongue's hold to take the boxes.

One is wrapped in pink, and the other is wrapped in green. She gently unfolds each side of the paper instead of tearing into it. The box is long; maybe a necklace? No. That's too basic for Tongue.

"I love it!" she announces, sliding out a blade that looks a lot like Tongue's, but when the light hits it, I notice it has his name engraved in the steel. Not his road name, his real one.

"I got mine engraved too, Comet," Tongue says, unsheathing his knife to show her. "It's got your name on it."

Daphne kisses him, deep and long, and the guys whistle at them for putting on a show. She pulls away, flushed, and her eyes are glittering with lust. Tongue growls, and Reaper has to snap his fingers to get the couple to focus.

"What's this?" Daphne holds up a key, analyzing it by twisting the ribbon which causes it to spin in circles.

"It's the key to your new bookstore," Tongue says, kissing her on the cheek.

This time, there is no stopping them. Daphne jumps on Tongue, wraps her legs around him, and his hands move to her ass. I move my palm in front of Maizey's eyes, and Reaper does the same with Aidan. A few of Boomer's men take note and go to hide Micah and Delaney's eyes when Tongue walks backward to their room.

"I love it. I love you," Daphne says between kisses. "I want you so much."

"Okay, kids in the house. Kids!" Reaper calls after them just as their door slams. "Bunch of rowdy teenagers." Reaper shakes his head and gets up to grab the big box against the far wall.

"Boomer, here." Reaper hands him a box that isn't wrapped. "Sorry, I ran out of paper."

Boomer gives Reaper a bepuzzled look and yanks the box open. "Fireworks!" he gasps, then giggles. "Big ones. Holy crap, Reaper, Sarah, thank you. Can I go shoot one off now?"

"It isn't nighttime, Boomer," I deadpan.

"So..." he murmurs.

Everyone laughs, and Reaper continues handing out gifts until there is only one left. Even Boomer's men have a little something, cash to gift cards; something simple since we don't know them too well. Zain even has one, a small album full of pictures of Reaper and everyone here throughout the years so Zain can feel like part of the family. Tool has a new screwdriver set from Juliette, and Juliette has a new microphone, and Reaper and I got them new sex toys.

Skirt, Dawn, and Bullseye got a new room for their escapades. A real watch room. There's a private section where Bullseye can watch without Skirt and Dawn knowing, or he can join. We do know Skirt doesn't allow Bullseye to touch, but we wanted them to have a nicer room to share their desires besides the rooms the cut-sluts were in.

Gross.

Reaper hands me a gift next. "I thought we agreed we wouldn't buy each other anything? I took that literally. I didn't get you a present."

"It's for both of us," he says.

"Okay." I lift a brow and pucker my lips as I carefully open the envelope. I pull out two plane tickets and a brochure. "Oh my God." I read the itinerary. "A week's vacation in Alaska! You're serious? How ... when? You need to be here?"

"Tool can handle it. Maizey is going to hang out with Dawn and Skirt. Everything will be fine. Tool is VP for a reason. I want time with my wife. Me and you, Doll. Do you want that?"

Pinpricks sting my eyes as I try not to cry, but it's a losing battle. "Are you kidding? I'll go anywhere with you." This time, it's my turn to kiss him senseless. I can understand why Daphne took Tongue to the bedroom. I'm ready to tear his pants off and mount him standing.

"I have a gift for you two," Doc says, handing us a small package.

"You're under the mistletoe!" Maizey points to Knives and Mary.

They're arguing because Mary got him coal for Christmas, and he got her a pegged leg. A fake one, but she's currently beating him upside the head with it.

"I'd rather kiss a freaking toad then kiss Knives!" Mary slams the leg down on Knives' shoulder.

Knives wraps an arm around her waist and tugs her head back by her hair. "If it gets you to shut up, I'm willing to do anything!" He smashes his lips against her, and I'm nearly bursting at the seems with excitement. Finally.

They act like they hate each other, but they don't.

The kiss turns from angry to soft, and Mary pulls back, trying to blink away her daze. She shoves the wooden leg into Knives' stomach and stomps away.

"That woman is crazy!" Knives groans.

"Anyway," Doc clears his throat and offers us the gift again. It's cute, wrapped in a metallic green paper with a red satin bow. "You have to open it together."

Reaper and I tug the ends of each side of the bow, and the ribbon floats to the ground. We tear the paper off to reveal a piece of plastic. I'm staring at a positive sign right in the middle. "What is it?" I ask him. "Is it a life alert for Reaper?" I chuckle at my own joke, and everyone laughs with me.

I can be funny.

"Maybe. In about nine months. You're pregnant, Sarah. I re-ran the test. It's positive."

"It's—" I gasp, my words failing me. "It's p-p-pos… positive?" I whisper, and my hand trembles. "Really?" My voice becomes high-pitched as I cry.

"Really, Sarah. Merry Christmas," Doc grins.

Reaper and I stare at one another, not believing what we're seeing. Reaper falls to his knees in front of everyone and kisses my stomach. "Thank you, thank you, thank you," he chants.

"We're pregnant."

Reaper wraps his arms around me and lays his cheek against my stomach. "I love you."

"I love you too." I run my hands through his hair, and he jumps to his feet. I stand back, stunned by the sudden movement.

He takes my hand and lifts it in the air. "We're pregnant!" he announces to everyone, and the entire MC cheers and claps.

It really is the best Christmas ever.

Because only the best miracles happen on Christmas.

A RUTHLESS CHRISTMAS PLAYLIST

HAPPY HOLIDAYS, YOU BASTARD BY BLINK-182
SANTA STOLE MY GIRLFRIEND BY THE MAINE
FOOL'S HOLIDAY BY ALL TIME LOW
MERRY CHRISTMAS, KISS MY ASS BY ALL TIME LOW
DON'T SHOOT ME SANTA BY THE KILLERS
DASHER BY GERARD WAY
YULE SHOOT YOUR EYE OUT BY FALL OUT BOY
GRANDMA GOT RUN OVER BY A REINDEER BY REEL BIG FISH
THIS CHRISTMAS (I'LL BURN IT TO THE GROUND) BY SET IT OFF
CHRISTMAS DRAG BY I DON'T KNOW HOW BUT THEY FOUND ME

ACKNOWLEDGMENTS

To my greedy Ruthless Readers thank you for being so supportive and helping us have a great first year.

To Give Me Books we owe you so much this year, you have been so supportive and helpful. Thanks for all you do.

To Wander and Andrey as always thanks for being our rock, words will never express just how much you mean to us.

Donna thanks for all you do, you are everything, my voice of reason, my ear when I need to vent, our biggest supporter and for that I'm so grateful. #BOOMERISDONNAS

To all the bloggers and reviewers, we appreciate the hell out of you, thanks for sticking by us.

Lynn thanks for being my other half and knowing when I need you before I do.

To the Instigator you make this possible, love you.

Harloe thanks for being you.

Silla thanks for all you do.

Stacey thanks for your amazing formatting.

Austin thanks for always being there and pushing me to be the best.

Mom thanks for believing in me.

Jeff FIVE LITTLE WORDS

KNIVES

RUTHLESS KINGS MC™
BOOK NINE

COPYRIGHT© 2020 KNIVES BY KL SAVAGE

All rights reserved. Except as permitted by U.S. Copyright Act of 1976, no part of this publication may be reproduced, distributed, or transmitted in any form or by any means, or stored in a database or retrieval system, without prior permission of the author. The scanning, uploading, and distribution of this book via the Internet or via other means without the permission of the publisher is illegal and punishable by law. Please purchase only authorized electronic editions and do not participate in or encourage electronic piracy of copyrighted materials. This book is a work of fiction. Names, characters, establishments, or organizations, and incidents are either products of the author's imagination or are used fictitiously to give a sense of authenticity. Any resemblance to actual persons, living or dead, events, or locales is entirely coincidental. KNIVES is intended for 18+ older, and for mature audiences only.

PHOTOGRAPHY BY WANDER AGUIAR PHOTOGRAPHY
COVER MODEL: GABE LADUKE
COVER DESIGN: LORI JACKSON DESIGN
EDITING: INFINITE WELL
FORMATTING: CHAMPAGNE BOOK DESIGN

FIRST EDITION PRINT 2020

To all the outsiders, the runts, the lonely souls,
our Ruthless Readers,
We know what it's like to be the ones looking in. We know what it's like to feel isolated, hopeless, and so alone you don't know where to go or how to get out of the bubble you've found yourself in.
There is always love. There are always people willing to welcome you with open arms. We are those people. You have us.
Pop. That. Bubble.
It feels good to be set free.

PROLOGUE

Knives

Fifteen Years old

SILENCE IS THE CLEAREST SPEAKER OF ALL. ITS WORDS RING LOUD AND TRUE.

I read that somewhere a few years ago etched in a bookshelf in a library. I ignored it at the time because I didn't understand what the statement meant. Silence doesn't speak. Silence doesn't make noise.

But silence spoke volumes when I started high school last year, and that's when the understanding clicked in my mind.

It's what happens in the quiet that means the most.

Teenagers are brutal. Physically, mentally, and emotionally. They are bullies, plain and simple. And even worse are the ones who stick around to watch me get my ass beat. Every damn day. No one says a word. They laugh, they point, they watch.

It's because I'm a nobody.

I'm scrawny, I'm short for my age, I have long hair that's dirty because I have no money to get it cut. I'm only allowed to shower once a week to save on the water bill because everyone else in the house has to bathe too.

I'm a natural target.

I'm the kid everyone avoids. I'm the kid no one trusts. It's easy to be an outsider when I've never fit into any group, made friends with any kids, or have had a home to call my own. I don't have parents, and the kids love to remind me every day that I don't have a mom and dad.

As if I could ever forget that I've been on my own for a long time.

My caseworker found me living on the streets a few years back after running away and sent me back to another foster home. It's my tenth one since I was eight. It used to bother me, not having that sense of family, but I've learned not even family is all that cracked up to be. My foster home has ten kids. Our clothes are always dirty. We go days without eating a proper meal. We get slapped around some, so it has skewed my idea of what family is. The foster parents are only in this for the paycheck.

I've learned to trust no one because everyone disappoints.

Well, I take that back. There is one person. My foster brother, Mason. He is a year older than me and takes the 'big brother' role seriously. He's a protector. He's always standing up for me when the kids at school call me a loser, a freak, a creep, a bastard. Other kids don't make fun of Mason. They wouldn't dare. Mason is already over six feet tall, and muscular, while I'm pathetic and weak.

It's not like the kids at school are wrong about me. I'm all of those things because I don't know how to be anything else, but it's time for me to learn. Mason won't be around forever to save my ass, so it's up to me to make the change, to be my own protector. When Mason turns eighteen, he is going to be out on his ass because the system doesn't keep adults, and where will that leave me?

Alone.

Vulnerable.

And with no one in my corner.

It's why I need to find a way to protect myself. A weapon of some sort. Something that's quick, agile, and fierce. I want my weapon to say, 'don't fuck with me'.

Maybe then the bullies will see how serious I am.

I'm tired of always looking over my shoulder. It's exhausting, and I want to be done being afraid.

Like right now.

"Hey, loser!"

I keep my head down and shrug the raggedy blue backpack up my shoulder. It's torn, stained, and the straps are barely hanging on to the last bit of thread. I stuff my hands in the hoodie pockets and walk faster. The sooner I get off this back road and onto the main road, the better.

"Hey, freak, I'm talking to you."

"Yeah, we're talking to you. It's rude to ignore us."

"I bet he's scared."

The three of them taunt me, but I know better than to pay them any attention. I'm damned if I do, and I'm damned if I don't.

My breaths come out quicker. Sweat starts to bead across my neck. I knew I should have taken the other way, but it adds on another twenty minutes. The back road is abandoned, and everyone dumps what they don't want back here along the sides of the fence that block the road off from someone's property. Tall weeds stand tall among a few silver trash tins, rusted bikes, and old sewing machines strewn all over the ground. This road is a homeless person's dream, but horrible things happen here because of the weapons laying around.

This road always has a massive amount of random trash all over it. It's why everyone in town calls it Miscellaneous Way, because anything and everything can be found. Even bodies.

And I don't want to be one of them.

If I only had a weapon that could go the distance, that could protect me from a few yards away; then I'd have a chance at escaping these guys.

"Thomas," Murray singsongs my name, then hits one of the trashcans with the bat he always has in his hand.

The loud clatter startles me. I trip over my own feet, which only draws a big, ugly laugh from the three bullies. I hate this life. Everyone says it gets better, but when? I'm face down in the dirt, rocks are digging into my hands, and I can hear their footsteps getting closer. Nothing about this is *better*.

I'm a dead man.

I look around for something to protect myself with, but all I see are some rusted knives on the ground next to a busted-up kitchen sink. It's probably not rust; it's probably blood that's been there for far too long. But they are the only thing within reach.

I dig my elbows in the ground and scurry toward the knives hiding in the grass and reach for the closest one. It's a useless steak knife.

You've got to be kidding me. Why couldn't it be a butcher knife? Something big and scary?

I get to my feet and throw the one in my hand, launching it with a panicked grunt, but the blade comes detached from the black handle, and the threat falls short.

"Oh my god, you're so stupid. Did you honestly think that would work?" Louis says. He's shorter than the others, only around my height. I'm sure if he was all alone, he'd turn into a scared dog like me.

Falling to the ground, I gather the last four knives in my hand, ready to use them if I have to. A spider crawls around the blade, then scrambles to my hand. Its legs are light on my skin, a tickle. In a way, I feel like it's good luck. Unlike most people, I'm not afraid of spiders.

Insects, reptiles, and animals only attack when they feel threatened. Humans attack whoever the hell they want to, when they want to. Or just because they feel like it. It's why I think out of everything this world has to offer, humans are the most dangerous.

The spider falls off my arm and disappears into the grass, leaving me alone against my enemies.

"What are you going to do with that, Thomas?" Murray asks in a mocking tone, digging the baseball bat into the ground as he takes a step. "Are you going to stab me?"

My hands shake as I slice the knife through the air. "I... I might if you come any c-closer," I stutter, then lick the sweat off my top lip. The backpack slides down my shoulder into the crease of my elbow, and I drop my hand to let it fall to the ground.

"You think you can kill someone?" Murray tosses his head back and laughs, placing a hand in the middle of his chest. He abruptly stops laughing and taps the aluminum bat against his left foot. "I could kill you," he sneers at me, then spits. "You are worthless. You take up too much space. You breathe my fucking air. You don't deserve to breathe my air!" He swings the bat, and I hear the swoosh of it as it barely misses my face.

Stumbling back, I trip over my backpack, and when Murray goes to hit me in the face, I roll away and stab his leg, then yank out so I can still have my weapon.

"Mother fucker!" he screams, adding most of his weight to his other leg. He points the bat at me, red-faced with anger. "You're a dead man, you hear me? Dead."

Louis tries to attack me next by taking the bat from Murray, but I move to the side and bring the knife down on his back, slicing directly into his shoulder blade. Louis pitches forward with a pained grunt, and his grip loosens, causing the bat to clink to the ground. The blood spreads across his shirt and drips down until it's soaking into his jeans.

I'm waiting for guilt, for the voice in my head to tell me to run, but only adrenaline is speaking to me, and it's telling me not to stop until all of these assholes are bleeding. For good measure, I kick Louis in the stomach, and he cries out in agony.

"How does that fucking feel? Huh? How does it feel?" I scream, then pick up the bat and slam it against the stab wound on his back.

"Stop! Stop, no more. Please," he sobs.

"Stop?" I ask, barking out a chilling laugh. My eyes fall on Murray, who is currently backing away from me. "You want me to stop? That's rich coming from the lot of you! You didn't stop beating me last month when I asked you to. I pissed blood for a week!" I yell, tears blurring my eyes as I slowly make my way toward Murray and Pete. Pete is the quiet one, the one that follows but never says or does anything because deep down, he knows he is just as weak as I am. "I'm going to—"

A hand pulls me back and yanks the bat from my hand along with the knives.

I whip around to punch whoever it is in the face. I'm done. I'm fucking done with the constant bullying, the pain, the crying. I'm sick of it. I lift my arm and clench a fist, preparing to fight again, when a hand grips around my knuckles.

"It's me, Thomas. It's Mason. You're okay. You aren't alone."

"They were attacking me. I didn't know what else to do. I...I..."

"You did the right thing." He grips my shoulders and tugs me behind his oversized body and hands me back the knives.

Why can't I be more like him? Why do I have to be stuck in this body?

"Problem, Murray?" Mason asks him, swaying the bat left to right.

Louis groans from my left and somehow manages to get to his feet. He stumbles back over to his friends and sags against Pete. I stare down at the knives in my hands, speckled with blood, and I still don't feel guilt.

I feel like the job isn't finished.

"Yeah, your fucking boyfriend here is a psycho!" Murray pulls up his pant leg and shows Mason the wound on his leg. "Look what he did to me."

I hate it when they call us boyfriends. All because we aren't blood related, and Mason is always coming to my rescue.

"And what were you going to do to him?" Mason slams the bat against the trashcan next to him, denting it.

"Nothing he didn't deserve," Murray hisses.

And that's when Mason surprises me. His hand disappears behind his back, and lifts his red shirt, grabbing the handle of a gun. I gasp and take a few steps back. This isn't like Mason. Where the hell did he get that?

"You have two seconds to get the fuck away from my brother before I put a bullet in your head. You've been warned a hundred times from me. I'm done giving out chances." Mason cocks the silver gun, the cylinder spins to lodge the bullet in place, and the three boys that have been picking on me instantly freeze.

"Woah, Mason. Just hold on a second," Murray says, trying to calm Mason down.

I tug on Mason's sleeve, but he doesn't look my way. He's bound and determined to stare at them on the other end of the barrel. "Mason, what are you doing? Let's go home."

"We won't pick on him anymore, I swear. Let us go," Murray holds his arms wide and steps back. "We'll go. No more trouble."

"I think I need to go to the doctor," Louis moans.

"Shut up, Louis," Murray snaps, staring at the gun as the sun shines against the sweat dripping down his temple.

"Mason, let's go home. Please," I beg him. I don't want any more trouble. Mason has come to my rescue one last time. He's risking himself for me, and I don't want to be responsible for ruining his life too.

"I'm going to call the cops if you don't put the gun down," Louis warns us, fumbling for his pocket.

Mason's jaw ticks, and his chest rises and falls in a burst of anger. He's really holding himself back. His body is shaking, and his face is red.

"Mason, put the gun down," I beg him. "They aren't worth it."

"Yes, they are," he says, taking his eyes off the trio for a moment. He stares at me. Mason seems a lot older than seventeen years old right now. "You don't deserve the treatment they give you. It's up to me. I'm your brother. Me. I protect you."

Okay, so he's a year and three months older than me. Same difference.

"And I protect you too," I say, wrapping my hand around the barrel of the gun to get Mason to drop it.

"They aren't going to stop until you're dead, Thomas." Mason jumps when he hears sirens in the background, and with every second that passes, they get closer.

Mason lifts his gun again, pinching his lips with determination as he aims at

Pete. Time slows as I turn my head and grab onto his arm to stop him. "Let go, Thomas! Let me do this," Mason grunts, fighting me.

"No. We can't—" My ears ring, and the heat from the bullet leaving its home is hot on my palm, burning me. I hiss and yank my hand away.

"Murray!" Pete yells, and that's when my stomach churns as I peer over my shoulder, seeing Murray with a gunshot wound in the middle of his chest.

"Oh my god," I mumble.

Mason doesn't hesitate. He lifts the gun again and aims it at Pete, letting another bullet fly. My mouth falls open, and I'm on the verge of puking. Pete's neck snaps back when the bullet lodges between his eyes. Mason swings his arm and lands on an injured Louis, but he is on the ground, gasping for air and blood bubbling out of his mouth.

I must have nicked his lung somehow when I stabbed him.

The sirens are anxiously close now.

"Mason, we need to go. We need to get out of here." Oh my god, what did he do? How can we get out of this?

"We have to tie up all the loose ends, Thomas." Mason squats next to Louis. A fifteen-year-old kid who sat in the back in Biology class today is going to die.

I didn't want this. Did I? I only wanted to go home, to get away, I wanted them to let me be, but they couldn't. They had to keep pushing. I stood up for myself and maybe I got carried away. I was protecting myself.

I never thought Mason would find me and commit murder.

Mason slides the gun between Louis's lips and pushing it down his throat until Louis gags. When he coughs, he spits up blood. Tears trickle down his cheeks, and he slides his eyes to me, silently begging me to help him.

"You aren't ever going to hurt anyone again," Mason says to Louis.

Louis grips Mason's bicep with a bloody hand, squeezing it, but doesn't have the energy to push him off.

I can't have Mason kill someone else for me. I'm not worth it. I run to him, and right as I'm about to launch myself at my foster brother, my feet digging in the sand to push me off the ground, he pulls the trigger.

The breath is knocked out of me when blood splashes against my face, warm and wet. I close my eyes, not wanting to see the raw scene in front of me. I can't figure out how to breathe. I'm panicking. The sirens are getting closer, the world is caving in, and the only person I could count on just ruined his life for me.

How am I going to live life without Mason? He's the only reason I'm alive.

"Thomas, open your eyes and look at me. Look at me!" He shakes my shoulders until my eyes snap open. "Breathe."

I manage to pry my wet kids back and peer into the eyes of the only person that's ever given a shit about me. I'm trembling.

"The cops are going to come, and they are going to arrest me."

I shake my head back and forth, dislodging the pools of water filling my vision.

The droplets drip down my cheeks, and when I look away from Mason, I see three dead bodies. Blood is everywhere.

So much blood.

"Thomas, I need you to run."

I'm so confused as to how we got here. My stomach is rolling. I think I'm in shock, or maybe I'm dreaming. "We need to get out of here Mason. Let's go."

"There isn't time. You need to hide. They are going to be here any minute. I want you to go to that biker bar we pass all the time, okay? Tell them I sent you. Tell them you don't have anywhere to go."

"What?" This makes no sense. Why the hell would he know any bikers? "Bikers? Mason, you aren't making any sense. Come on, we can cut through here—" I point over the fence where the mountains are "—We can keep running until we are far away from here, and we can start our lives."

"No. Someone has to take responsibility for what happened here, and it's going to be me. I shot them. I do the time. You always take responsibility. For everything you do, you hear me, Thomas?"

"Mason, please. You're all I have. This was all my fault. Let me take the blame. This is my fault. If I had taken the other route, you wouldn't have looked for me and grabbed that gun from... where did you get it?"

"That doesn't matter."

The sirens are only a block or so away. I turn around to look down the road to make sure we are still alone. "Please, we don't have much time. Mason, let's go. Let's go now." I tug on his hand and try to pull him to the fence, but he stays in one spot, unmoving, the blood spreading across the ground and touching his sneakers.

"Let's go. Why aren't you coming!" I yell. "Damn it, Mason. You're the only person in the world who has my back. I need you. If you do this, I'll never see you again. Please."

"I will always have your back. Always." His head jerks when the sound of squealing tires comes ripping across the road. He pushes me toward the abandoned building. "Go. Go, Thomas. Now!"

I stumble when I see the rolls of dusty clouds from the police cars speeding down the road getting closer and closer. The sirens are ear-splittingly loud. The hints of red and blue lights are already filling the distance. I don't want to leave him. I open the wooden door to the rundown shed. It's dark, musky, and cobwebs are all over me. The only light that spills through is from the window that's clouded with dust and grim. The bottom right square is broken, but I can see Mason from this spot.

The wet, humid air sticks to my skin, and when I grab onto the ledge of the window, beads of sweat mixed with blood drip down my lips. I almost lick them.

Almost.

Until I remember it isn't my blood I'm about to lick. I wipe my mouth on my shirt sleeve and hope Mason makes it out of this situation okay.

"Put your hands behind your head!"

I inhale a sharp breath, staring at a cop who has his weapon drawn, pointing it directly at Mason.

"He's armed!" the cop announces, and three other officers flank each other, pointing their guns at Mason.

Four cops.

Four guns.

One Mason.

No hope.

"Please," I beg, someone, anyone, to not take Mason away from me.

"Put down the weapon," the cop barks at Mason.

"Okay," Mason says, giving me a quick parting glance. He has no fear, at least none that is showing, which only makes me admire him more. But I know the look he gives me, and it isn't one filled with hope.

It's one that says goodbye.

He leans down to place the gun on the ground, but the barrel is pointed at the police officers, and the first gunshot sounds.

Then the next.

And the next.

I place a hand over my mouth to stifle my sobs when I see Mason's body jerk until he is boneless on top of Murray, Louis, and Peter.

I flip to my back and slide against the wall, unable to look out the window a second longer and cry silently. My best friend is dead. For some fucked up reason, he decided I was worth it.

Worth what? I have no idea.

"Fuck, Ripley. He was putting the gun down," one officer says.

"Like it matters." One snorts. "Look at the kids he killed."

"We didn't know the story. He was just a kid himself. You never pull that shit again; do you understand?"

"Yeah, Nolan. I got it."

"Call it in. Let's get this crime scene taped off and these bodies bagged."

I cup my hands over my ears and begin to rock back and forth. I don't know how long I sit there, but the zippers of the body bags are so loud they break me open. The sirens come and go.

And soon, the only thing left is silence.

The wind blows through the broken piece of the glass, blowing against the sweat on my neck. All I can see every time I blink are the bullets piercing through Mason's body. I stand on unstable legs and open the wooden door that leads outside. It's colder outside. The night sky reminds me of the night I lost my entire family.

My real family.

My sister. My mom. My dad.

It's only fitting I lose Mason on a night that feels so similar. Cold, beautiful, star-filled, and the crickets… yeah, the crickets were just as loud as the night of the accident. Life goes on even when you don't want it to.

Taking a lungful of air, I make my way to the left, and the door behind me slams shut. My nerves are shot, and I jump from the loud boom it brings over the empty pastures on either side of the road. My heart thumps in my chest as I stare at where Mason was shot hours ago.

Four people died today, right here, right in the middle of the road, but it's like it didn't even happen. The road is clear, disappearing into the edge of the sky. The silence, the world around me, the crickets… everything is as it was, but I'm changed forever.

There are only the puddles of blood drying in the sand of the road. It's the only proof to let me know it wasn't a dream.

It's evidence to reassure me that I'm alone.

I wipe my cheek on my shirt sleeve again, dragging the material across the dried blood and wet tears. I place my hands on my hips and start walking, because what else am I supposed to do? I see my backpack out of the corner of my eye behind a trashcan, and I debate if I want to take it.

If it's up to me, I'll never go back to school. I'll never get close to anyone again.

I remember the biker bar Mason brought up to me and told me to go to. It's a place we used to pass every day walking to and from school to go home. The place scared me, but he loved it. He loved the tough and rough look, the bikes, the women, the leather. Mason was always badass like that though, and if he wanted me to go there, then I'm going to go.

Picking up my backpack, I toss it in the trashcan and cover it with a lid. I give one last look to where I saw Mason's body fall.

What am I going to do without him? In the last two homes, he protected me from perverted dads, handsy moms, and disturbed kids. When he could, he protected me at school.

And he died doing the one thing he always did.

What can I do to return the favor?

Go to the bar.

Where the badass bikers are going to kill me, probably.

I tuck my hands into my pockets, my fingers brushing over a ball of lint, and hunch my shoulders as a rare howl bursts through the air. A coyote. They probably smell the blood in the road, hoping to feast.

When the highway comes to view, it's empty, nearly as abandoned as I am. I take a left, the soles of my shoes scuffing against the asphalt. I'm not afraid to admit I'm crying. I know I shouldn't. My foster dad says, 'Men don't cry. Men aren't allowed to cry.'

But I've lost the only person that's mattered to me in a long time.

I don't know how long I walk. I keep my head down, eyes glued to the road, watching the bumps of rocks in the pavement vanish from my footsteps.

A grumble of bikes comes from up ahead, and it has me jerking my head up, seeing a headlight float in the night as it turns left, the opposite direction of where I am coming from.

I stop at the edge of the fence where the road turns to gravel, and the old, beat-up bar looks like it's about to fall apart. It's made of wood planks, and there isn't a sign to tell me if the bar has a name. Loud music spills from the inside, and all the chrome of the bikes lined up out front shine against the red neon skull sign hanging on the inside of the window.

My feet drag against the gravel, the rocks crunching under my converses. I thought I'd be afraid, but after everything I've just been through, what I've seen, what's the worst these guys can do to me? Kill me?

I dare them.

I pause at the door, which is wide open, and decide to walk in. The air is warmer in here from all the bodies moving around. Smoke hangs heavily in the air, and the floor is sticky against my shoes. My adrenaline is crashing. My body is starting to shake, and my eyes are pooling again. I'm hoping I'm in a safe place because I think I'm about to lose it.

No one notices me yet in the dark room. I don't blame them. Men are watching women strip on the poles; some men are having sex, screwing right here in front of everyone. I look over my shoulder, wrapping my arms around myself when I slam into something solid.

"Who the fuck are you, slim?" a raspy dark voice asks me.

When I turn to him, his eyes widen in surprise. It must be the blood all over me.

"Slim, what the fuck happened to you?"

I'm too distracted. The lights, the music, the conversations, everything is so loud.

"Hey." The man lays his big paw on my shoulder, shaking me. "Slim, you okay? Hey," he snaps his fingers in front of my face, and I know he can see how scared I am. I don't hide my emotions well. "Come here. Follow me." He lights a cigarette and throws an arm around my shoulders, forcing me to walk as he does.

There are a few other men by his side, huge guys. They remind me of Mason, in a way. Like grown-up badass versions of him.

But he'll never be able to become them now.

The music dies down as we walk to the back. The lights are brighter, and the music is a dull thump against the walls. The guy opens a door, revealing a huge table with a skull engraved in it. He pulls out a chair and drops his arm from my shoulder. "Sit," he says.

Like I'd ever disrespect a man eight-times my size.

I sit down quickly as he takes a seat in the chair at the front of the table while the other two men flank either side of him. They are wearing the same leather vests, but his says Prez, while the other two say VP and SGT at Arms, respectively.

Whatever that means.

KNIVES

"Want a drink?" he asks.

I nod eagerly. I'd love some water.

The VP opens a mini-fridge in the corner and pulls out a brown bottle, opens it with his forearm, and sets it in front of me.

"I'm... I'm... not old enough to drink," I say, my voice shaking.

The three of them laugh. "Kid, we know that. You look like you need it, though. Go ahead; it'll be our secret," says the VP.

I wrap the bottle in my hand and bring it to my lips. I've never had beer before. It's cold, and it tastes like shit, but it feels good. Half the bottle is gone by the time I place it on the table.

The man that calls himself the Prez leans forward, crossing his arms on the table. "Now that you look like you aren't about to pass out—"

"—He might throw up," the VP jokes.

It isn't funny. I might.

"Slim, do you know where you're at?"

"Biker bar," I mumble, wiping my lips of beer foam. "I..." I start to rock again, pressing the palms of my hands against my eyes. "He told me to come here. I don't know where else to go."

"This is Ruthless Kings territory you're in. What happened to you? I need you to tell me everything. Are you bringing bad shit to my club?"

I shake my head and yank the knives out of my pockets, slamming them on the table. "Mason. Mason saved me. These kids followed me, but he was my foster brother, and he saved me—"

"You're Mason's brother? You must be Thomas."

I lock eyes with the Prez, a hundred emotions suddenly swirling in me. How do these guys know about me and Mason?

"Yeah."

The Prez's eyes soften. "He's said a lot about you. Says you're smart. That true?"

I shrug my shoulders at the Prez. "I know how to survive. Barely. Mason..." My eyes start to water again. "He's dead. He died. He killed the guys following me, and the cops killed him. Before it happened, he made me hide and told me to come here. I don't know where else to go. Where do I go? I'm sorry. I don't want to cause trouble, but I don't have anyone else. Mason was all I had. I tried to protect myself with these knives, but Mason had a gun."

"Fuck. I was wondering where it went." The man who calls himself Prez slides his fingers through his beard and tugs on the silver strands on his chin. "I need you to tell me everything, from start to finish, and don't leave shit out, okay?" Prez says.

"Mason died, you sure, Slim?" the VP asks. "He had real promise in becoming a prospect. Damn it. Damn it!" he shouts, kicking the mini-fridge so hard, the door breaks off the hinge.

"Let's all calm down," Prez states, and the two men surrounding him take a seat, the VP breathing heavily like a raged bull. "Start from the beginning, and the more you can tell me about those cops, the better, okay?"

"Yeah," I nod, swigging my beer. "Yeah, okay."

The man across the table reaches in the middle and grabs the only weapons I have. I try to steal them away from him, but he is quicker, lifting them up in the air so I can't get them. "I think I can teach you how to make a pretty cool weapon out of these knives."

His patch says SGT at Arms, and the guy's arms are the size of my head. "They are old, rusted to hell, but we can shape them up and make a badass ninja star. We'll break the blades, then weld them together in the middle. After all this is settled, of course. It will be easier for you to learn since you're so small."

I hate being small. I blush and glance away, twiddling my fingers together. A rag is placed down in front of me. "Clean yourself up, Slim. Get that blood off you. And there ain't nothin' wrong with being small. It's here that matters," the VP taps my chest, "and here." Then presses his finger against my temple.

"That's really fucking sweet, but I need information. You two keep getting off track. Slim, fucking speak before these assholes start going on about something else. I want retribution for what happened to Mason," Prez states.

I take another swig of beer to gather some sort of courage and meet the eyes of the Sergeant at Arms. He gives me an encouraging nod, and I take a deep breath before returning the Prez's gaze.

"I'm the kid that gets bullied, and there were these three kids that always liked to give me a hard time. I don't have family and neither did Mason. We lived in a shit foster home, but he took it upon himself to always save me. He was my brother. My best friend. I owe him everything."

"Mason was good like that," Prez nods, a genuinely sympathetic tone in his voice. "Go on."

I do. From start to finish until I'm sobbing like a damn baby, because I feel like it's all my fault. Mason would be alive if it weren't for me. I have to prove myself to him now, so he didn't die for nothing. I need to be more than I've ever been.

"We will have our lawyer draw up some adoption papers. We're going to send you to a new school. When you turn eighteen, it's up to you on what you want to do. Prospect or get the hell out of dodge, but I think you'll like it here. I got a kid about your age named Jesse. Relax, Slim. You're with us now, but that's the only beer you're getting from me until you're a man. Got it?"

I nod eagerly, wondering if I'm dreaming, but when I rubbed the damp towel over my face and see red, I know this is reality.

Mason sent me to a place where I'd be safe. Even in death, he is protecting me. I'm not going to let him down. This place, if they will allow it, will be my home, and I'll be everything Mason wanted to be.

It's the least I can do after everything he has done for me.

CHAPTER ONE
Knives

Present day

"NINETY-EIGHT. NINETY-NINE. ONE-HUNDRED." I LIFT MY CHIN OVER THE PULL-UP bar one last time and drop to my feet, then fall to the floor and get into a push-up position. I place one hand behind my back and grunt as I push down. I do three sets of ten, alternate my hands, then do three more sets of ten on the other side. A bead of sweat drops from my forehead, rolling down my nose, and splashes against the floor.

I don't work out because I want to. I work out because I have to. I refuse to be weak. I refuse to not be at my strongest. I refuse to be that small, scrawny kid that didn't know how to hold his own.

Dropping to my back, I call out for Yeti, our resident white pitbull, and I hear the clobber of his paws against the wooden floors. When he is at the door, I point to my feet, and his pink tongue is out of his mouth as his stocky frame comes and sits on my feet.

"Good boy," I praise him, placing my hands across my chest to begin my sit-ups. Every time I hit my elbows to my knees, Yeti gives me a big wet kiss on my cheek, which gives me that much more motivation, because who doesn't love kisses from dogs? My abs begin to ache and tighten. I do five sets of twenty sit ups, only taking a few seconds between sets to catch my breath. By the fifth set, my body is shaking, and when I fall to the floor to stop, Yeti barks at me, slobbering all over my legs.

"Yeti, I don't want to. God, I'm tired."

He barks at me again to finish the last twenty. He always knows when I want to quit, and he always gives me fucking lip when I want to stop.

"Okay, okay. I'll do it. Just give me a second to breathe."

He growls, showing his teeth, threatening me that I better get off my ass or he'll do something about it

"You're a ballbuster," I mutter, taking a deep breath and sit up, exhaling the breath. Yeti licks me before I fall back, only to come up again. My stomach cramps as I crank out the first half. I have ten more.

My muscles protest, and I start to slow. "I can't, Yeti." Every sit-up, every crunch of my abs, and every time my elbows hit my knees, I let out a painful groan.

Five more.

Inhale. Exhale. Inhale. Exhale.

Three.

Two.

I think I'm going to puke.

One.

"Damn it!" I collapse on the floor; arms spread out as I gasp for air and sweat my body weight. Yeti's weight leaves my feet, and he cuddles up next to me, shoving his nose under my dead arm. "You kick my ass, Yeti. Ever heard of giving a guy a break?"

He lifts his nose and snorts, spraying fucking dog snot all over me. "Thanks for that. I appreciate it." I groan as I sit up and sling my shirt off, then wipe the sweat off my face with it.

I walk towards the kitchen and lift my arms to grab the trim of the door and stretch, leaning my body out of the entryway. It's quiet here since Boomer and his members left. They only came for Christmas, and since that was a complete shitshow, just like everything else is around here, I'm sure he was excited to get home. Especially since he missed Christmas with his ol' lady Scarlett. She decided to stay back with Homer, the old man who is officially part of the MC, according to Boomer.

Now, there are just a bunch of us assholes and a few kids to fill the noise.

I'm not going to lie; I'm one of the few that likes the ruckus.

Chaos, strife, and pain are the only mistresses I need to keep me awake at night. And you know who checks all those boxes?

Mary St. James.

She's far from a damn saint and reaps nothing but pure havoc on me. I swear the only reason for her existence is to get under my skin and piss me off. Well, mission fucking accomplished. She's sassy. She's wild. She's fucking fierce.

And all that adds up to one hell of a dynamite package that I want to ignite if I could get over how fucking crazy she drives me. I swear to god, if there was a cliff every time she cocked an attitude with me, I'd fucking jump off it.

She's maddening, but I know underneath the red lipstick that is supposed to make a statement, and the black leather jacket that hugs her breasts when she zips it up, Mary is scared.

With what happened to her, she has every reason to be. She's one of the girls that we rescued in Atlantic City; the chapter Boomer is taking over. The so-called Ruthless Kings that didn't deserve the name bought and sold women. Doc's ol' lady, Joanna, she was a part of it too, along with Boomer's ol' lady, Scarlett.

Hell, I would think having Joanna here would help Mary, but she's bound and determined to lose herself in the pit of the hell created by the Atlantic City members. She did her best to join the cut sluts on their mission to suck and fuck every member in the clubhouse, but no matter how hard she tried, none of us would touch her.

We might be bastards in some way, shape, and form, but we don't use women who are only looking to feel something other than fear. When a woman wants to be a cut slut, she does it because she wants to; she wants to be used in every hole, in every way. And if that's their choice, more power to 'em. All of us know Mary isn't like that. She's a good girl. When we found her, she had on pearls and a fucking cardigan.

And now she's dressed for a rock and roll concert.

Don't get me wrong; some of those leather pants she wears has me watching her walk away longer than I should. Her new look fits her behavior. I'd be sad to see it go, especially since getting to know her. I don't know much about her past; she doesn't talk about it, but pearls and cardigans? They don't match the hellraiser simmering beneath her skin.

Does it mean I want to touch her flames?

Abso-fucking-lutely.

Does mean I'm going to?

No.

She annoys me too damn much, and I know she can't stand me either. She got me coal for Christmas. Coal! As if I've been naughty this year! Please. I'm a fucking angel wrapped in a damn bow, and my halo shines brighter than the damn horns she has on her head, I can say that much. She got mad at me for getting her a fake leg because she still walks with a limp after getting impaled by a piece of wood. I thought it was funny.

And she hates me for it.

But it's the kiss I hate her for.

Maizey pointed out at Christmas that Mary and I were under a mistletoe when we were arguing, and I just got fucking tired of always fighting with her, so I pulled her in by her hair and kissed her to shut her up.

I didn't think I'd actually like it.

And goddamn it, I hate her for giving me the best damn kiss I've ever experienced in my entire life. That chaos, strife, and pain I live for, that's constantly roaring inside of me, came to an abrupt halt as our mouths became one. Time slowed. Sounds ceased. And when our tongues slid together, we forgot we were enemies, and we gave in to one another.

Her lips were velvet, and her breaths were sweet like candy. I was getting lost in those flames I should always stay away from.

Until she hit me in the gut with that peg-leg I bought her. Then, she stomped off in a hissy fit, leaving me fucking harder than nails and confused.

Confused because all I wanted to do was run after her, slam her against the wall, and own her mouth again.

It's been two weeks, and every single night I'm waking up from a wet dream, cock in hand, and cum coating my stomach. I have never had that happen, even when I was sixteen and getting erections because the fucking breeze blew.

Mary has inserted her havoc in my veins, mixing herself in with the other three mistresses constantly whirling around inside me.

I'm wound up tight, and I'm ready to sling a few of my ninja stars, maybe draw some blood. But now that things are quiet at the club, I'll just go get another tattoo to help take the edge off. The more I have to be around that damn woman, the tighter she winds me, and the more I want to remind her that when we kiss, the last thing we do is hate each other.

We *want* each other. I know she feels it too.

"You want to take a picture? It lasts longer," Badge grumbles with a slight curl of his lip as he pulls out a chair at the table. He doesn't take his eyes off me as he sips the plain black coffee from his mug. Badge is a prickly guy, and on a good day, he might not bite your damn head off.

"Let me grab my camera. There's nothing I want more than your ugly mug framed next to my nightstand. I'll kiss it every night before I go to bed."

"You're so fucking weird, Knives."

It's true. I never joke about anything. Why bother, when the truth can make people that much more uncomfortable?

That's the only rule I have always made sure applies to me, until recently.

The truth is a wicked bitch, and everywhere I turn, she's roaring her ugly head at me. For instance, I'm starting to wonder if I actually like Mary, and that truth makes me uncomfortable. I'm going to ignore it.

Nothing good can come out of her and I being together. Two people that don't like each other. That's like a hurricane and a tornado finding their way into each other's paths, ready to destroy.

But the whisper of truth is still there, telling me I want Mary more with every second that passes. I want to kiss her again to see if what I feel is the same or if it was a fluke, but there is no way she's going to let me near her again.

And she shouldn't.

I've done too many bad things, and even though she pretends to want the cruel side of temptation the MC offers, she isn't ready for it or me.

Like Tongue, I'm a bit fucked in the head, but not in a crazy sense like Tongue is. I'm not going to be bringing home a fucking swamp kitty and calling it 'Happy.'

I'm crazy in the sense that I don't feel grief for what I do. I cut, I draw blood, I inflict pain, and I never want the pain to stop.

I want to keep cutting, keep them pleading for help. I want to hear the victims begging me to stop. I love making them bleed so much they pass out, so I wait until they wake up, maybe give them a transfusion, and I do it all over again.

And I'll keep going until there is almost nothing left.

Give them hope that they will be able to live, and when I see their smile, their thankful, relieved smile with blissful tears raining down their cheeks, that's when I'll sling my ninja star across the room and lodge it directly in their foreheads.

And even after all of that, I'll still feel nothing.

Yet I think of Mary and I feel everything.

"Jesus fucking Christ, Knives. Stop looking at me." Badge slides the chair back and stomps away toward his office, where all the fancy gadgets are.

I wasn't looking at him. I zoned out.

See what she's doing to me? I need to get with Tongue. He and I like to sharpen our blades together, or sometimes he helps me make a new ninja star. I have one I haven't used since it's been made, and it's the one made of the knives I found the night Mason died. I should use it.

And I almost did on the cop who pulled the trigger first. I waited and waited, and then he became Chief of Police, but then he died of a fucking heart attack, and now the man that replaced him is my friend.

Well, ish.

We do each other favors, like when Sarah's SUV got blown up, and we wanted to make sure a report wasn't filed? I called him. Paid him. And we are in the clear.

It's good to have the law on your side, which is why I'll never understand why Reaper gave Badge the ultimatum.

The other cops involved in Mason's murder moved away right after, and I haven't been able to find them since. But I will.

And when I do, I'll use the knives from that night, and I'll bring myself some sort of peace.

Sarah comes into the kitchen, and the dark memories fade, replaced by a grin as I watch her tiptoe. She's holding her stomach, which is still flat, and slowly, gently, and quietly walks to the coffee pot. Sarah is pregnant. After what seems like forever, Prez and his ol' lady finally get their happy ending, but Sarah isn't fully excited just yet. She's afraid of every move she makes because she doesn't want to miscarry again.

She's isn't that far along. Eight weeks, maybe? Twelve weeks is usually the safe space for women not to worry about miscarriages, at least, that's what Doc told us.

"What are you doing?" I ask, crossing my arms over my chest.

Sarah yelps, holding her hand to her chest and taking deep breaths. Then, she lets out a gasp, sliding her hand to her stomach to make sure nothing happens. Her hand being there won't stop a miscarriage, and I think she knows that. It's only about comfort at this point. "Knives, you can't do that. You scared me," she says, taking a second to gather her breath. She tucks a strand of hair behind her ear and starts tiptoeing again to the coffee pot.

Even though Doc said she can have one cup of coffee a day, she doesn't want to risk it, so Reaper bought a decaf coffee machine for her instead. She stares up at the cabinet above her and opens it, but the mug is just out of reach.

And she won't reach for it. She's too nervous to stretch her body. I'm worried about her. I understand she's scared, but she needs to realize that normal, everyday things she always does aren't going to hurt the baby.

"Here, why don't you sit down, and I'll get it for you?" I walk out of the hallway between the kitchen and the gym, and Yeti follows behind me. When Sarah sits down, Yeti falls at her feet, then stares at all the entrances to the kitchen. He's protecting her.

"Thanks, Knives. I know, I'm crazy for acting this way, but I'm so nervous."

I grab the mug, set it on the counter, and pour the decaf coffee to the rim. God, I can't imagine the withdrawals she must be experiencing. I have to have caffeine every day. "Here you go." I place the mug in front of her, and she uses her hands to cup each side. I bet it's nice and warm. "It's okay to be afraid, but don't be so afraid that you stop living your life. Okay?"

"We've wanted this for so long, and if we lose another… Knives, I don't know what we would do."

She tries to hold it in, but soon enough, the tears spill right out of her.

I don't know what to say. I haven't experienced this situation before. I want to say, 'you'll try again.' It's the logical answer, but kind of heartless, because I'm not being sympathetic. I used to be. The teenage me would have cried right along with Sarah, but I haven't cried since that night.

Tears dropped are energy wasted.

"Why the hell is Sarah crying?" Reaper barges into the kitchen, and I lean back in the chair, crossing my hands over my chest to protect my heart.

If there is one thing I am afraid of, it's Reaper's ability to yank someone's heart out of their chest and not blink twice as he watches it beat to a slow, irreversible stop.

"I'm hormonal, Jesse! And I'm afraid of everything I do. Knives was trying to encourage me! Don't be mean to him."

My brows raise to my hairline as Sarah buries her face in her hands and sobs. Reaper wraps his arms around her, and then gives me the stink eye when he notices my shirt is off. "You could have covered your hairy chest," he says. "You're a goddamn werewolf."

I rub my hands down the fur, and Sarah turns around just in time to see me do it, which has me stopping, but her cheeks turn red. Something flashes in her eyes, and I stop rubbing down my chest, because she whispers something to Reaper and runs toward his office, leaving me wondering what the hell I did.

I know I'm hairy, but I'm not hairy enough to clear a room.

Reaper points a finger at me. "I'm saying this once. Walk around with a shirt on after this. Sarah is hormonal and the sex… is fucking amazing. She's always needing sex, and apparently, men shirtless really get her revved up, but I don't need my woman revved up over anyone but me, got it?"

"This has happened more than once?" I raise an eyebrow, trying not to laugh.

"Knives."

"Oh, okay. I wouldn't call it a pattern, Prez. Just a coincidence. Hormones are like that."

"And Slingshot, Patrick, Badge, and Tank. One second with their shirts off and she comes running to me—" his eyes widen when he realizes what he is saying. "You have my permission to always be shirtless until she has the baby." Reaper runs down the hall after his ol' lady, whipping his shirt off to get down to business before he enters his office.

"You're welcome!" I shout after him, which earns me the middle finger. This won't be the last time I'm half-naked in front of Sarah. I have to listen to my President, right? I snort, taking Sarah's coffee in my hand and taking a sip, only to spit it right back out when I taste the lack of caffeine.

How do people drink this?

My cell phone ringing from my bedroom has me getting up, pouring the coffee down the drain, and getting a new cup of coffee. I sit back down, letting the ringing come to an end. I don't feel like talking to anyone. They can leave a voicemail.

I'm thinking about how everyone around me is finding their ol' lady and being happy, but I don't know if I'm capable of feeling happiness like that. My soul was damaged a long time ago, and there is no way it can be repaired.

Then the kiss I shared with Mary plays in my mind, and I remember a sliver of healing that started to thread the gaping hole in my spirit together again.

No, who am I kidding?

I'm beyond repair.

CHAPTER TWO

Mary

CRAP.

This is the second time in a week I've been pulled over. The first time, I got out of it because I flashed the cop a pretty smile, but it didn't work this time. Probably didn't help that I was apparently "rude", and "uncooperative", and "being booked for wanton disregard for safety".

So sue me, I'm not perfect.

The cell door slides shut, the metal clanking as it slams against the wall, locking into place. It smells like piss in here. I know I'm a bit reckless, but landing in jail for a speeding ticket, of all things, is a new low for me.

Even if it was kind of fun for a moment.

When I'm speeding down the road, the rush is almost too hard to explain. My foot against the pedal, pressing it against the floor as the needle on the speedometer climbs to the red lines. The engine roars, and when I hit 110 miles per hour, I feel like I'm flying, like I'm free.

Then a damn cop had to flip on his lights and ruin everything.

I grab the metal bars and push my face against them. "Hey, come on. Let me out of here. I don't belong here. My speedometer is broken, honest." It's a lie, but I need to try something. The one phone call they gave me was useless, since Knives didn't answer.

I don't know why I called him. When they read me my rights and said I get one phone call, the first person that entered my mind was him. He is a pain in my ass ninety-nine percent of the time, but if there is one thing about that damn annoying man is it's he's dependable. When the men call him, he drops everything, and he is there for them.

And for some stupid reason, I thought he'd be there for me, even though we don't like one another. Even though we fight more than we talk, I stupidly thought he'd come to get me out of this hell hole. After what happened at Christmas... oh, who am I kidding? I can't even recall what happened because it made no sense.

Because someone's first real kiss shouldn't be that good, right? Toe-curling, body aching, leaving my skin in a fever, good. A first kiss is supposed to be messy and gross, with too much tongue and too wet, wondering why people kiss to begin with, but no, that was not the case with Knives.

When he smashed his lips against mine, I knew what he was doing. He wanted to shut me up, but the firm grip on my hair loosened, and he sighed into my mouth as we both relaxed.

I bang my head against the bars, and the thud echoes in the small space. Am I hitting myself with the metal rods to help me forget the kiss or to remind me how stupid I am for speeding and then mouthing off to the cop to land me in here? Or to remind me how dumb I am for having a flicker of hope that maybe Knives and I like one another, and falling for that Christmas kiss?

All of it.

I'm just full of bad ideas lately.

"You aren't going anywhere, Miss St. James. Not until your bail is posted. This time you have a court date," Officer Daniels says as he bites into a donut and flips the page of the newspaper.

"Court? Come on! I was barely speeding."

"You're right. At first, your speed wasn't too far above the legal limit, but your *choice* to engage officers in a high-speed chase for nearly five miles was. Maybe think about that next time."

Oh, right. So I may have put pedal to the metal on the highway, attracted a bunch of cop cars, swerved off the road to try to escape, and cut across the lanes headlong into traffic to throw them off before finally getting pulled over.

Like I said, I'm not perfect.

He takes another bite of the donut, and my stomach grumbles, reminding me I haven't eaten since last night. I'm not going to ask for food. I just want another phone call. I let out a long sigh, push off the bars, and take three steps back.

My knees hit the metal cot, and I sit down, running my fingers through the inky strands of my hair. I hate sitting here. It gives me time to think about the things I'm doing and why I'm going them, and the answer is, I don't know.

For the longest time, I was the perfect daughter. Straight A's and fake smiles, along with fake happiness and a fake family.

The only real experiences I've ever had are the ones the Ruthless Kings have given me, good and bad. I know how I got to the Atlantic City chapter. I know it was my own doing. It's my own fault, but I don't care to go back to that old life.

It was stale, lacking in love and life, and any type of excitement. Is that a reason not to go home? Probably not, but I know my family, and I doubt they are worried. They never were before, and Reaper says Badge checked for missing persons and found nothing. He found more, but I stopped him before he could tell me.

I don't want to know.

All that matters is what led me here, to now, to the present.

The past doesn't matter, and what happened to me is irrelevant because I didn't experience abuse from the bikers like the other girls. I have no reason to be afraid.

But you are.

I just don't know what I'm afraid of.

I like it here with the Kings, even if they barely give me the time of day because I tried to be a cut slut. I'm going to go ahead and mark that off my to-do list, because there aren't any sluts there now since two of them died.

I prefer to stay alive. Thank you very much.

Then why am I still with the motorcycle club? I should leave, get the hell away as far and as fast as I can, yet I'm rooted here.

And I have no idea why.

"Well, well, well."

I grit my teeth when I hear his mocking tone. I knew I should have called someone else.

"Looks like the little hellraiser is off doing what she does best, isn't she?"

I sigh when I see Knives standing in front of my cell, waving his phone in the air. "I got your message. Why am I not surprised to find you here?" he asks. He tucks his phone in his pocket and whips out a ninja star, scratching a spot under his chin. The cops see it and they don't even blink.

"He has a weapon!" I cry out, pointing at the man who drives me freaking bonkers. "Hello," I singsong. "He has a ninja star. He might kill me." I wave my arms in the air like I'm a person trapped on an island, waving my hands in the air, hoping the only helicopter I've seen in weeks saves me.

Freaking crickets. What good is law enforcement if they can't save me from Knives?

"It helps when you have the entire department in your pocket, Hellraiser."

"Stop calling me that," I seethe and then bolt to the bars, gripping them tight until my knuckles turn white. "I swear, you better be glad I'm in here, or I'd—"

"—You'd what?" He inches forward, and his nose touches mine between the bars. "Tell me."

The muscles in my cheek jump as I squeeze my jaws together. "I'd freaking choke you."

He chuckles; the sound is dark and delicious and travels down my spine like a shiver. When the tension has nowhere else to go, it seeps into the surface of my skin, creating goosebumps. "Oh, don't make promises you can't keep. You know how much I love a good time," he says, a teasing glint in his eyes.

I cross my arms to hide my hard nipples that his response created. I don't have control over my body. It's not like I want to be attracted to him. "Are you going to get me out of here or not?"

"Nah. I just wanted to come by and see you in here. Maybe being stuck in jail might give you a little perspective."

"Perspective! You can't be serious. Like you've never been in jail before?"

"Actually, I haven't. See, I'm a good boy, no matter what the lump of coal you got me says."

I'm fuming at this point. He is such a dick. I should have called Reaper or Sarah, someone that actually gives a damn and doesn't want to see me in here. "Just because I made a mistake—"

He slams his fist against the bars, but I don't flinch, even if my heart is drumming against my chest. "It isn't just this mistake, Mary. It's all of them. It's your reckless behavior. TJ here says it's the second time this week you've been recklessly driving. Fourth or fifth time this winter." He slices the ninja star across the bars, and sparks fly when metal grinds against metal. "You're going down a dangerous fucking road, and you expect me or other members to pick you up along the way? To adhere to your carelessness?"

"Adhere? That's a fancy word for a guy like you," I nearly spit, rage shaking my body the longer I stare into his sky-blue eyes. They are cold and calculating.

I've heard people say the eyes are the window to the soul, but that doesn't apply to Knives. When I look into his eyes, I see nothing. His soul turned to stone eons ago.

"Hey, TJ. What is Miss St. James' bail?" Knives asks, never taking his gaze off me.

"A few thousand," the cop answers.

Knives hums as he thinks about what he wants to do; the right side of his mouth tilts up in a conniving smirk. "Perfect. Let her stew for a few days, will ya, TJ?"

"Anything for the Kings, you know that," he says to Knives, which leaves me baffled.

This can't be legal.

"Knives, you can't be serious? You're going to leave me here?"

"Guess you're going to have to see me walk away from you to realize that, aren't you?"

"Knives, don't you fucking dare leave me here," I growl low in my throat so he can hear the frustration. I grip the bars and try to shake them, which is pointless, because they don't ever move. It's called a jail cell for a reason.

He backs away slowly, flicking the ninja star over his fingers. His knuckles are so scarred from that trick, but he doesn't seem to care. He lifts his other hand and gives me a finger wave goodbye. "Hey, TJ, can I have a donut?" Knives asks, ignoring me.

"Knives!" I pound my fist against the bar. "Don't you fucking leave me here. I swear to god!"

"Mmmm, chocolate covered ones are my favorite. Thanks, TJ. I appreciate ya."

He stabs the donut with his ninja star and takes a big bite of it as he watches me. "The real world is so much better, Mary. Oh—" he bonks his forehead with his hand, "—but you know that. Later, Hellraiser. See ya on the other side."

He really is walking away from me. He is going to leave me here. "I will never forgive you for this, Knives! Get your hairy ass back here!" I scream, slamming my fist against the cell bars one last time as I yell for him. The bastard only lifts his donut in the air and walks out the door.

I don't know if he has a hairy ass; I only said that because he has a hairy chest that I dream about running my fingers through. It's why they call them dreams. I'm not liable for what my brain likes to think about while I'm unconscious.

The exit door slams shut, and I'm left alone.

He really left me here.

This has to be some sort of joke, but as I'm standing here waiting for Knives to walk back through the door, the seconds turn to minutes. I pinch my lips together and try and control the anger. The members have done worse things in life, and Knives has their back; why can't he have mine?

"Looks like you pissed off the wrong guy, Miss St. James," Officer Daniels polishes off another donut and wipes his hand on his uniform, leaving chocolate smears on the khaki.

"Mind your own business," I mumble. Mouthing off to an officer, while I still can't make bail, probably isn't the best idea, but I'm shocked right now and disappointed. I can't believe Knives left me here.

If there is one thing I know more than ever right now, it's that the kiss we shared meant nothing to him. I had this bread crumb of hope that the dislike we shared toward one another was really passion just bursting at the seams to be released, but now that he left without giving me one last look, I know better.

If people really care when they walk away, they usually pause and give a parting glance over their shoulder, but I guess when dealing with a man whose soul is stone, I shouldn't expect much else.

But if that's the case, why am I so mad?

CHAPTER THREE
Knives

I PAID HER BAIL, AND THERE ISN'T GOING TO BE A COURT DATE BECAUSE I PAID THE NEW Chief of Police off too. He seemed very happy to be in business with us. Nothing like a large stack of cash to help pay for his daughter's college to get him on my side.

She's in there because the cops are following my orders. Mary needs to learn that what she is doing to herself isn't okay. I read the report. She was going 90mph in a 65mph zone, and then when she got pulled over, she veered off-road, nearly slammed into a bunch of cactuses, then gunned it to 110 mph while weaving in and out of traffic and crossing over into the other lane. Took a dozen cop cars to chase her down in the end. I don't know why the girl has a death wish, but I'm not going to let her die easily on my watch.

So she's going to sit there in jail and think about what she's done.

Oh, she's fuming.

Good. Let her boil in her mistakes, and maybe she'll come out of the slammer having learned something about herself.

I lift my leg over my bike and sit down, then pop a piece of bubble gum in my mouth. I chew it, letting the cherry flavor roll around, and blow a bubble. When it pops, I'm reminded of when I was around thirteen years old and Mason got us two packs of gum. He said we had to chew all the pieces, and whoever blew the biggest bubble won.

That's it.

We just won. There was no prize. It was just the ability to have bragging rights.

I rub a hand over my heart when it begins the ache. I swear, the only time I feel pain is when I think about my brother. I lean against the backrest on my back, watching the front doors of the police station. A lot of riders don't like backrests because it doesn't make the Harley look badass.

Listen, my bike is awesome, and I'm badass, so if I know that, then everyone else can go fuck themselves. I like to be comfortable, and when we're on long runs, I can relax while everyone else has a sore back.

I tap my fingers against the handlebars and debate if I want to go in the police station and get her. She can ride bitch behind me, but there is one problem: I've never had a woman on my bike, and I don't want the guys getting any ideas. Ol' ladies only on a member's motorcycle, and Mary is not my ol' lady.

No, she can't get off easy. Fuck that. She got herself into this mess; the least she can do is do a few days in jail.

I crank my bike and hit the throttle, waving to a few police cars as I drive by. It's a good day for a ride. It's cold, but the sun is out, and I need to clear my head. Mary fucks me all up. I'm a one-track-mind kind of guy. I know my duties and what I can bring to the table when Reaper needs me, yet Mary gets in my head, and I'm wondering if I'm a little more complex than I originally thought.

Maybe it isn't her I want; maybe I just want someone. All the guys are finding their ol' ladies, and it is making me want what they have. No one likes being alone. People choose to be because they feel like they don't deserve the love and happiness that comes with being with someone. Honestly, I think it all starts with yourself.

If I can't be happy and alone with myself, how can I be happy and alone with someone I love? It starts with the individual. I'm more than content with myself and being alone, I just know no one deserves to be pulled into my life. The MC life isn't for everyone.

And it isn't for Mary.

I don't know where she's from or why she doesn't want to go back, but someone out there has to be looking for her. She's too damn beautiful, too damn smart, too damn proper to be abandoned. There's a story behind how she got to Atlantic City before she came to Vegas, and I want to find out what it was, even if she doesn't.

"It's none of my damn business," I say to the wind as it blows in my face. "I need to stay away from her and let her figure out her own shit." I'm talking to myself, great. Isn't that what they say when you're going crazy?

She's made me insane. Perfect. The last thing I need is to be like Tongue, fucking stalking her with a damn gator strapped to my chest.

My phone vibrates in my pocket just as I come to a stop outside the tattoo parlor. A ride is what I need, but a different kind. I want to feel pain. I want to remind myself why I choose to stay alone, because anyone that enjoys pain can't enjoy love.

When I look at the screen, I see Seer's name flashing on the screen. "Oh, that's a big fuck no and fuck you, Seer. Sorry," I ignore the call and tuck my phone back in my pocket.

And then it rings again.

I groan and tilt my head back, staring up at the blue sky. "Why is this day fucking with me?" Just to make sure Reaper isn't calling, I bring my phone out again and see Seer's name. "I don't know what information you've got for me today, but I don't want to hear it, man." I ignore the call again, muting the vibration. Seer is one of a kind. He's good people, odd, but in the sense, he has sight.

He can see things before they happen. It doesn't bother me when it comes to someone else, but me? I'm not interested in what the future has in store. I'd rather take the punches as they come instead of dodging them, and if that means I die, then that's when I'm meant to leave this world.

My phone rings again, and this time it pisses me off. I throw the phone on the ground and step on it with my boot.

Again.

Again.

And again.

Until it's nothing but broken pieces and wires.

And the bastard still has the nerve to ring even if it does sound drawn out like a piece of machinery shutting down.

"You have got to be kidding me." I stomp the phone again, then dig my heel into the cracked screen, grinning when the ringer starts to die. "Yeah, take that, fucker."

"Tough day?" Luci's amused tone comes from the side of the building, as does cigarette smoke. He spins around the corner and stares at me with a playful grin, pulling the cigarette out of his mouth.

"You could say that." For good measure, I kick the pieces of the cell phone across the parking lot and breathe easier when it's out of my line of sight. I really don't mind Seer, but I don't want to know shit about something happening to me. His gift doesn't scare me; it's the truth of his visions.

"You shouldn't have done that. Reaper might need to get a hold of you," he says. "And you crush your phone too many times for the man to remain patient."

"Shut up." Damn, if Luci ain't right. I'm going to get my ass handed to me if the club needs me and I'm not available. "Come on—" I slap his shoulder and do my best not to inhale the cloud of smoke he blows from his mouth, "—I need a tattoo."

Luci flicks his cigarette to the ground and steps on it. "Let's do it, then. You caught me at a good time. I don't have an appointment for a few hours."

When I walk inside, my nerves settle, and the buzz of the tattoo gun eases me. The shop is nice, but what I love most about it is how classic Luci keeps it. It has American traditional flashes framed over the walls, and every artist has their own private room to tattoo their clients, but it's simple. There aren't any gimmicks. It's just a place where people come for tattoos and piercings, then get the fuck out. The walls are painted a simple color, beige because Luci doesn't like to make things complicated. He likes to keep things simple, but decoration is where simplicity ends.

He's the best fucking artist I've ever come across, besides Tongue. Actually, now that I think about it, Tongue would be a great tattoo artist. He can draw and make people bleed. Two things he loves most. I make a mental note to tell him my idea later.

"Well, well, if it isn't my favorite cock I pierced," Bobby-Jane greets me as she dries off her hands and snaps on a pair of gloves. The artwork on her body is more delicate, flowy, and feminine.

"Hey Bobby-Jane," I say and lean in to kiss the side of her temple. I've known her for a few years now before she became a tattoo artist. "How's it hanging?"

She cocks her head and stares at my crotch. "If I remember correctly, a little to the left."

I have a Jacob's Ladder, bars pierced right through my cock and two hoops on the crown, like horns, and Bobby-Jane is the one that pierced me. "You want to come find out again?" I ask her, remembering the few times we hooked up. The sex was good, but we both knew the deal.

It was just sex.

Maybe that's what I need. It's been a while because I've been so caught up with Mary that I've forgotten that I'm a single man. Mary drives me nuts, Bobby-Jane tugs my nuts. See the difference?

"Maybe, I'll call you later," she gives me a wink and heads into the room where her client is.

"Yeah, too bad she can't call you," Luci says, sitting down on a stool and pushes his feet against the ground to roll in front of me.

"Why not?"

"You destroyed your phone, remember?" he smirks, grabbing his notepad and a red pen.

"Fuck." I cover my face and let out a painful groan. A beautiful, missed opportunity, gone because I can't keep my head on straight.

"Your dick will live, but the time is ticking, Knives. What are we doing?"

"I want a pinup on my arm, a woman with long black hair and red lipstick." Once the words come out of my mouth, I nearly choke on my tongue and wish my swamp kitty carrying MC brother was around to cut it out of me. I just described Mary.

"How do you want her body?" Luci asks as he starts to draw on the paper in delicate lines.

I imagine Mary; she has fuller breasts and an ass shaped like a peach that I want nothing more than to sink my damn teeth into. My cock jumps, and I clear my throat and take a deep breath to get myself under control. How awkward would it be to get an erection while Luci tattoos me?

"Medium size tits and ass," I say to him, which he just nods as he starts creating the outline of her tits, and it's almost like he has seen Mary naked, because the body on the paper is everything I dream about.

I shouldn't be doing this, but as he draws her hair, long and wavy behind her back, I want nothing more than to finally close the distance between me and Mary. I think somehow… in some way; the little hellraiser wiggled her way into my heart.

I don't know when that happened, but as Luci places the stencil on my forearm and pulls it away, I know it's the only way I'm really ever going to have her. This picture is the only way I'll be able to have her close to me. "Can you add a leather jacket? Keep it unzipped."

"Yeah, I can freehand that on with a marker," Luci states as he starts putting the tattoo gun together and unwrapping a clean, sterile needle. "Come on. Come sit on my throne of pain," He laughs at his own joke, but all I do is roll my eyes. I flop onto the red leather chair, flip my arm over, and Luci shines the light on it.

I dig into my pocket for my ninja star and roll it over my fingers as the gun buzzes, and the needle hits my skin. Euphoria takes over as the pain hits. It's sweet, it stings, and it burns.

Just. Like. Mary.

CHAPTER FOUR

Mary

I'M GOING TO KILL HIM.
    I cannot believe I've had to stay in jail for two days. I haven't showered. I have had to hover when I pee because there is no way in hell I am sitting on a stainless steel toilet that's probably never been cleaned.

When I see him, I'm going to wrap my hands around his throat, punch him in the gut again with that damn leg he bought me for Christmas, then scream in his face.

"Well, looks like you're a free woman," Officer Daniels slides the key in the cell and slides the door open.

Don't get sassy, Mary.

"You look familiar," another cop says, his blue eyes narrowing as he evaluates me.

I swallow, hoping he doesn't stare at me too long. Not a lot of people know who I am, but there are a few sprinkled about who recognize me. I zip up my leather jacket, and that's when he shakes his head clear, scoffing at himself. "Never mind, you can't be her. That's impossible." He tilts his head down and goes back to what he was doing.

Blowing out a breath, I start walking the green mile toward the exit when I remember I have a court date. "Officer Daniels? When will I know about the court date?"

"Oh, you don't have to worry about that. Knives took care of it when he paid your bail."

I freeze. His words encase me like an iceberg, and if snow could fall right about now, I'd be making snowballs and launching them at the cop. "You're going to have to repeat that. What?" I say with a bit of a bite.

"Oh yeah. You could have left days ago, but Knives wanted you to stay. We listen to the Kings. We know who really pays our bills." He walks around his desk, picks up a file, and doesn't pay me any mind as if what he just said doesn't make me plan Knives' murder.

"He's a dead man," I say through tight teeth. I cannot believe the bail was paid days ago. My fingers twitch, and the fury inside me is boiling over. I'm about ready to take his ninja star and stab him with it. I stomp toward the door and slam the bar against it, opening it with so much force it bounces off the brick wall and nearly hits me again.

The sun is too bright after being locked inside for two days. I lift my hand and block the yellow light out of my eyes.

"Hey, Hellraiser. Damn, you look like shit."

I scan the parking lot for the bane of my existence, and when I see him, I fly down the steps. He looks cocky sitting on his motorcycle, all leather cut, muscles, trimmed beard, the sides of his heads shaved with a bit of hair on top, and a mischievous smile to wreck my heart. "You! Why would you do that?" I poke a finger against his chest.

His hard, broad, muscular chest. A real man's chest. It isn't shaved, not baby smooth, but hairy, all the way down his abs, and I itch to run my fingers through it.

Not that I'd ever admit that out loud to anyone.

"Here. Put this on," Knives says, completely ignoring the anger and the poke against the chest. My eyes land on the tattoo below his neck that says 'Judge Me.'

Oh, I'm judging. He doesn't have to worry about that.

"Did you hear me? Why would you do that, Knives? I am not a person you can fuck with whenever you want. I have feelings. Everyone makes mistakes, and you walked out on me when I needed you. You wouldn't have done that to one of your MC brothers."

"Don't for a second compare yourself to them," he says. "My brothers know when they make a mistake, but you don't. That's the difference, Mary. You're doing it for the good to fuck yourself over. My brothers land in jail because they are breaking laws for the better good. What the hell are you doing to better yourself or the world? Nothing."

"I—"

He stops me from saying anything else by pushing the helmet against my chest. "You, nothing. You have no reason to defend yourself. You're putting yourself in harm's way, and guess what? You were safer there in that jail cell than you were in your car. And guess who could sleep at night? Me. The club. The people that care about you. Shut the hell up, Mary. Put the helmet on and get on my bike."

If my ass wasn't burning from the spanking he just gave me, I'd sass him and tell him I'd rather walk, but the hard glint in his eyes tells me there is no room for discussion. With a nod, I slide the helmet on my head and swing my leg over to mount the bike. I'm squeezed tight between Knives and the backrest, my tits snug against his back. I inhale a sharp breath as my nipples harden from the contact. I dig my fingernails into my thighs to stop myself from wrapping my arms around his waist.

He revs the engine, but we don't move forward. He reaches behind his back and grips my hands, pulling my arms around his waist.

Just like I didn't want.

"You're going to have to hold on a lot tighter, Hellraiser. Lean when I lean, and don't distract me. You want freedom? You're about to experience it."

I have no idea what Knives means about freedom, but if it feels anything like his abs do clenching under my fingers, I want it. Once he feels like I have a good hold on him, he punches forward, and the bikes jerks, which pushes me against his backrest more. I hold on tighter, my fingers toying with this shirt, and the motion, along with the air breezing by us, has his shirt inching up his torso. My fingers graze against his bare stomach, and the coarse hairs I love so much tickle my palm. I gasp and do my best not to move or explore, but being this close to him without fighting feels different.

It's just like that moment we kissed. Seems like we only ever get along when we're touching each other.

That's not a good thing.

The bike vibrates between my legs and tickles my swollen clit. Every bounce of the bike, every vibration from the bike speeding up, nearly makes me whimper and fall apart. With the throbbing between my legs, it is hard to figure out if the rumbling is actually coming from the bike or the man in front of me.

We zigzag through the parking lot until we are at the stop sign that takes us to the main road. He takes a right, passing the strip where all the fun is. Even though I've been in Vegas for almost a year, I have never been to the strip. Maybe I'll go and get a job; there are plenty of jobs I can do to put distance between me and Knives. Eventually, I'll move out of the clubhouse, and they won't ever have to worry about me again.

It hurts to think about, but I feel like the Kings got stuck with me. They aren't. I can take care of myself. It might not seem like it, but I can if I have to.

And I really think I have to, because something is changing between me and Knives. I'm not sure what it is, but it can't be good.

Nothing good can be built from hate.

And Knives hates me, that much I know.

We make our way to Loneliest Road, a long stretch of narrow pavement that cuts through four-hundred miles of the United States. There is desert on either side of us, mountains and forests. It's beautiful. Getting lost in the desert, the horizons of the sun, and the sand disappearing between my toes.

It sounds like heaven. A real break from life. I have been running from the truth for so long that I don't know what it's like to stop and think about what I want. I haven't pressed reset on my life since I've been here. I think maybe it's time I move on, somewhere, and do something.

I don't know what, but it's got to feel better than being a burden.

I hold onto Knives tighter when he speeds up, and the grumbling of the engine whips through the air.

I expect for him to slow down, but he doesn't.

The bike goes faster, quickly gaining more speed until I'm worried Knives is going to lose control and we're going to wreck. I squeeze his waist and raise my voice, "Stop it, Knives! Stop. You're going too fast!" I try to yell over the rush of wind we are slicing through as we fly down the road.

Most of my hair is flattened by the helmet, but the ends are slashing, dancing, stinging my arms. His hand twists the throttle again, and the bike lurches forward, gaining more speed, going even faster. "Stop! Knives, please!" I nearly sob. I'm scared. Everything is blurring past us. I can't see anything.

He slams on the brakes, and the bike fishtails. The smell of burnt rubber surrounds us, along with a cloud of smoke. He pulls off to the shoulder, the bike dipping from pavement to sand. I jerk off the helmet and toss it on the ground. I'm breathing heavily, inhaling dust and smoke from the tires. "What the fuck, Knives? What was that?"

He hops off his Harley, and his cold eyes hit me like daggers. "Isn't that what you wanted, Mary? Didn't you want to be free? Don't you like speed? Don't you crave the adrenaline pumping in your veins the faster you go? What, you didn't like it? Was it too much for you to handle? Is it so different from bursting past the cops at 110 mph, feeling the wind in your hair? When you aren't cozied up in a box of a car."

"Stop it," I sound pathetic with the emotion clogging my throat.

He kicks his helmet, and it flies across the desert, landing with a loud smack before it bounces again, this time stopping next to a dead bush. "Goddamn it, Mary!" he roars so loud, I can hear the gravel in his throat as he stresses his vocal cords. His voice carries, and a few crows down the road stop picking at a dead animal and fly away. "I won't stop it. I won't stop. You can't be doing shit like this; do you understand me?"

"I'm not a child. Don't talk to me like a child, Knives."

"Then stop acting like one. What the hell is your problem? Why are you doing this? Why act out? Why with the rebellion? Why do you have a death wish?"

"Why do you suddenly care?" I hiss, swinging my legs over the bike and sliding off. "Why do you care what I do? I'm a goddamn adult, Knives. I can do whatever I want. Stop acting like you give a damn when you'd be perfectly happy if I swerved off the side of the road and—"

Before I can say another word, he takes four long strides over to me and shoves his hand over my mouth. "Don't you dare say another word. Don't you dare sit there and say what I think you're about to say. I swear—" He removes his hand and screams in the air, takes out a ninja star, and scratches his beard with it. It's like the ninja star is his comfort. "You drive me fucking nuts, you know that? You drive me... insane."

"That's why you should be happy that—"

He flings the ninja star at me, and I jump. The metal lodges in the metal of his motorcycle right as I flinch. "I said, don't say another word. God, you think I'm that kind of man? To want you dead? Do you really think I hate you that much? Is that how much you hate me?"

"What? No, I don't think you want me dead, I care—" I catch myself before I say I care about him. "I would never want you, me, or anyone dead."

"Well, you know that isn't the case with me, right? You know that there are plenty of people I want dead, but you aren't one of them, Mary. Do you want to know why I don't want you speeding down the road? You want to know why I care?" He stomps toward me again and places his hand on the back of the neck. "This."

He slams our lips together in a fiery kiss, not giving me a second to think, a second to breathe, a second to figure out what the hell is going on. His palm is so wide, his fingers nearly touch as they wrap around my throat. Knives is telling me he is in control, the way he guides my head, moves his mouth, flicks his tongue.

I'm transported back to Christmas, where I felt his lips for the first time, and I can hardly breathe.

We are horrible to one another, though. I pull back to let him know I want to bring the kiss to an end. I don't, but I need to. The more I kiss him, the deeper I'm going to feel about a man that isn't good for me.

I'm not good for him either.

We're snakes coiling around each other, and the more we fight, the tighter we grip each other. And we are both too stubborn to let go. If we don't stop, one of us will get hurt beyond repair.

He pulls away and puts space between us, enough to where I can catch my breath without breathing the same air he is. Our chests are in sync as we grovel to breathe. My entire body is hot, his eyes are locked on my face, and his chin is nearly touching his chest. He's staring at me through ill intentions, wicked eyes, and long brown lashes. His shapely brows are drawn together, and his fists clench at his sides. The pinkness of his lips is heightened from our kiss.

I check out his entire body, slowly dropping my attention to his chest. His nipples are hard, and every time his lungs expand, the shirt stretches over the brute strength of his pecs. I swallow, coating my mouth with saliva as I notice things I tried not to notice before on his body.

Like how tall he really is. And how built and defined his muscles are. And how every time I see him, there's a new tattoo. And how about the erection tenting his black jeans right now? His cock is traveling down his left thigh, nearly poking out of the tear he has in his jeans. I can see the pale flesh of his leg, the coarse hair that is also on his torso.

"Why did you do that?" I find my voice, but it doesn't sound like me. It's hoarse with desire and uncertainty. I lick my lips, and I make my way up his body, but pause on his forearm. There's a tattoo there that wasn't there a few days ago. It's glistening in the sun from ointment, but the further I inspect it, the more I see a pin-up girl.

She's wearing my leather jacket and my red lipstick.

That has to be a coincidence. No way would he get me tattooed on his body when we can't figure out how to have a conversation with one another.

"Did you feel it?" he asks. "That moment where everything else faded away. All there was, was me and you."

I shake my head. I don't want to admit that I felt the exact same thing, just like I did at Christmas.

"You're lying," he says with a smile on his face, as if it doesn't bother him that I'm denying whatever… this is between us.

It's hate.

It's lust.

It's like.

But it isn't love.

And if it isn't love, if it can't be love, then I don't want anything to do with it. Nursing a broken heart isn't worth the tears over a man that can't commit himself to you, but you knew damn well he wouldn't be able to.

Yeah, I'm not about to fall down that hole.

There isn't much I know about Knives, but I know this, he isn't boyfriend material.

He isn't husband material.

But if I'm honest with myself, I'm not wife material either.

And what happens when the two clash?

Arguments. Fights. Yelling. He'll start drinking and call me a no-good, worthless whore. I'll tell him he doesn't know how to keep his dick in his pants.

What will we be left with?

Misery.

And my misery does not like company.

CHAPTER FIVE
Knives

I WAIT FOR HER TO SAY SOMETHING, ANYTHING, BUT SHE STARES AT ME WITH ROUND LIGHT brown eyes, frozen next to my bike. She's a pretty fucking picture standing next to my motorcycle, wind blowing her already fucked up hair from not being brushed over the last few days. The cascading strands fall to her ass, and the breeze picks them up, and they flow to the right, then left. Her lips aren't red from her lipstick since she isn't wearing any; they are swollen from our kiss.

She's lying if she says she doesn't feel anything between us. Because I see the emotion clear as fucking day as she stares at me. Don't get me wrong, I don't expect us to go skipping hand in hand across the desert any time soon, but damn it, she has to know there is something other than the constant arguing.

No, you know what? It isn't even arguing. It's bickering over little pointless shit because we get on each other's nerves.

"Knives, we don't even like being around one another—" she pauses, lifts her nose in the air, "—I smell gas."

"Don't change the subject, Mary. Slingshot isn't even here."

"Not... gross, no, not that gas. Like...gasoline," she coughs and fans her face.

"Jesus, okay, I should have known talking to you would be impossible. Maybe you're right. Maybe we just need to get each other out of our systems or something," I say, placing my hands on my hips.

"No, Knives—"

"—I'm going to go get the helmet. Let's just not talk for a minute, okay? I need to think." I need to find someone to throw my ninja star at, and since it can't be Mary, I need to figure out something, because I'm itching to fuck shit up. Maybe I can get with Tongue, and we can go to the Asylum. His brother is there; it's only fair that we pay a visit. Maybe draw a pound of flesh or two as revenge for all the shit he pulled on us this year.

I shield the upper half of my face with my hand as I look out along the endless amount of sand. The helmet is a good thirty yards away, not too bad, but enough to annoy me because I had to lose my temper. Stopping here was a bad idea. I shouldn't have tried to teach her a lesson because the only thing I learned is how I want my lips on hers again.

It's easier than fucking fighting all the time and for no damn reason. I don't want anyone else. I try to think of Bobby-Jane, her fake tits, and perky ass, but not even thinking of her hands on my cock does anything for me.

She doesn't have the sass, attitude, or the ability to piss me off like Mary does, and as much as that shit drives me crazy…

I fucking like it.

I want to bend her over my knee and spank her ass every time she gets mouthy.

I stop when I'm about halfway to the helmet and peer back over my shoulder to see Mary standing there, hands tucked in her pockets as she kicks the ground.

The woman is a damn mess, and because I'm an idiot, I want her to be my mess.

A red truck drives by, the window down, and I watch as the passenger flicks a cigarette out the window, which isn't a big deal.

Until a line of fire starts from the road and makes its way to my bike.

I've felt true fear a time or two. And right now is one of those times.

"Mary! Mary! Run!" I yell, but I don't know if she can hear me. She's fucking walking in a straight line and doing spins and twists, not paying attention to her surroundings. I pat my pockets for another ninja star because if I can throw one in the air and nail her in the shoulder, she'll fucking listen then.

Holy shit.

I check every pocket, but I don't feel another star. I always carry extra.

I pick up my feet and run, the sand making it difficult as my boots sink with every step. My heart is thundering under my bones as I pump my arms. I feel like I'm in damn quicksand with how much effort it's taking me to run.

"Mary!" I call out her name, hauling ass toward her. She finally hears her name, and when she jerks her head in my direction, the flames engulf my bike.

She gasps, jumping back, but the flames get higher. The hot red and orange fingers dance as they climb into the sky, black smoke billowing quickly.

Mary screams as her shoes catch fire.

Fuck. She said she smelled gas. Of course my bike was leaking. It was probably from the ninja star I threw. I punctured the damn tank.

She's probably been standing in gasoline, but the sand soaked it up and made the liquid hard to see.

When I get close enough to her, I tackle her to the ground and whip off my cut, patting her shoes until the flames are gone. When they are, luckily, her boots are a bit burnt, but I don't see her skin. That's good.

The roar of the fire is too loud. We need to get away before the bike blows up. I pick her up in my arms and begin to run anywhere that isn't here. We get far enough away right as the gas tank explodes, sending more fire into the air.

I should care more than I do about losing my baby. A man's bike is his treasure, but a bike can be replaced.

This headache of a woman can't be.

And I know I can never replace her.

"Are you okay? Are you hurt?" I check her over to make sure she doesn't have any burns. "How are your feet?"

"Warm, but I think I'm okay. Thank you." She tucks her hair behind her ear, and her mouth drops open when she sees the bike burning. "I'm so sorry—"

"What is it with you and not paying attention to your surroundings, huh? Are you fucking kidding me? Are you so reckless with your life you couldn't see a fire?"

She struggles as she gets to her feet since I'm sure they are sore, and I help her by grabbing onto her arms and stabilizing her, but she shrugs me away. "There wouldn't have been a fire if you didn't throw your damn ninja star and pierce the gas tank. I told you I smelled gasoline, and you didn't listen to me."

"Oh, so this is all my fault? All because I was trying to teach you not to kill yourself driving."

"Says the guy who threw a damn ninja star at me!"

"I missed you on purpose! I know what the fuck I'm doing with my ninja stars," I yell, needing to get the last word in.

"So you knew what the fuck you were doing when you aimed at the goddamn gas tank? Trying to teach me a lesson by nearly killing us both?"

"It was an accident!"

She throws her arms in the air and shakes her head. "You're impossible. Regardless of whose fault is—it's yours, by the way—we need to call for help."

I grind my teeth together when she blames me. "Okay, get your phone out."

"My phone is dead since *someone*," she glares at me, "left me in jail."

"You should blame yourself for that one, Hellraiser. You got yourself into that mess."

"Fine, whatever. I just want to get home. Get your phone out and call 911."

I squeeze my eyes shut because I know we are about to get into another fight. "I don't have it."

Besides the screeching of melting metal in the background, she doesn't say a word. "What?" she questions. "Don't joke right now, Knives. I'm not in the mood."

"I'm not kidding. I broke my phone days ago. I'm waiting on a replacement to come in the mail." It's been nice to get away from technology. It's put things in perspective. I've liked not having it in my hand constantly. I've read more, hung out with my friends more, and—

"Are you kidding me! I swear, you constantly pull this shit just to piss me off."

"Oh, right. I planned to blow up my bike for you, just so you can give me a migraine. Yeah, that's the dream, Mary. Nice one."

"Did you leave it at the poor girl's house?"

Do I hear jealousy? I should tell her I fucked someone. That would crush any... odd, slim, next to nothing chance she and I have together.

"I broke it when I got a call I didn't want to get." I'm starting to wonder if I should have answered that call from Seer. I wonder if this was what he was going to warn me about. There aren't many times I want to know my future, but I would have wanted to know this.

The last thing I want is to be stuck out here with Mary.

"Okay, someone will come. It's impossible not to see that fire from a distance," she sighs, sitting down on the desert floor again. "We wait."

I don't have the heart to tell her that there have been plenty of people on the side of Loneliest Road that never get helped. They eventually wander the desert for help, only to never been seen again. As long as we stick to the road and follow it, we will be fine.

Not many people travel this road at once. It could be hours before another car comes. I sit down on the desert floor too, wondering how the hell I ended up here.

It's not like this can get any worse.

Thunder rolls above us, and out of the corner of my eye, I see Mary's head tilt back on her shoulders to look at the sky just like I am. When did storm clouds roll through? Out of all the times it never rains, the weather has to choose today out of all days to show itself?

This is a cruel joke.

"Karma, for leaving me in jail."

I wish I had tape to keep her mouth shut. All of my torture supplies were in my saddlebag, which is currently roasting.

Stay. Calm.

Don't. Kill. Her.

Thunder vibrates the ground floor, and the first droplet falls on my face. "If it rains and puts out the fire, no one will come," she points out.

"Well, let's not sit here then, let's go home. We just have to follow the road." I hold out my hand to help her up, and she decides not to take it.

Independent woman and all that. Good for her.

Or she's as stubborn as a mule and needs a good smack on the ass.

From my hand.

Because even though she drives me crazy, her body makes me crazier.

In the next blink, heavy blankets of rain come billowing down, stinging my skin and soaking my hair. "You've got to be kidding me!" I roar to the sky, and in return, lightning cracks in the middle of the road in reply.

Mary grips my hand, then immediately lets go of me when she realizes what she did. My shirt is soaked, the water is flowing into my mouth, and I want to curse myself for not paying attention to the damn weather.

My damn bike is ash, and I'm stuck with a woman that pisses me off as much as she turns me on.

Another bolt of lightning strikes the middle of the road, and the clouds start to spin. "Oh, no." Whether she likes it or not, I grab her hand and start to run in the opposite direction toward the mountains. If I know one thing about tornados, it's that they need flat land to gain strength. "Come on. We need to go. Now." How can all of this happen in one day?

I'm starting to wonder if the Ruthless Kings are cursed. There is always fucking something we have to deal with.

Always.

"Hurry up," I tell her, dragging her behind me as we haul ass to the mountains.

"I'm hurrying as much as I can! My feet were on fire a minute ago, if you don't remember."

Damn it, she's right. Instead, I stop and swing her into my arms. "What are you doing?" she squeaks.

"Hurrying like I fucking want to." I throw her over my shoulder, wrap an arm around her legs, and check behind me to see if the funnel is being formed. My heart aches when I see the burnt pieces of my bike and the flames dwindling from the fire. The smoke will be there for a while. It's just as black as the sky is turning. I glance up to see the beginning of a funnel starting. The clouds are spinning, and I swallow, wondering if we are going to be able to get away in time.

"Why did we stop? Is everything okay?" she asks.

No. We are about to be tornado fodder. I turn around and look into the woods. The mountains are right behind them, and I know there are plenty of nooks and crannies we can hide in. I start sprinting toward the forest again, through the wind and rain. My eyes sting as the water bullets them. I don't have a free hand, so I can't wipe my face.

Small beads of hail start to fall next. The black clouds light up above us, and a second later, the thunder follows. I hiss when they pepper my skin, and as I enter the canopy of the trees, the only thing I can feel is the danger of the storm surrounding us and the whistling through the wind.

"Knives, I'm freaking out."

"Everything is fine. I just want to make sure we're away from the threat." I don't want to tell her that I'm freaking out too. Bad fucking omens everywhere. Maybe this is the universe telling me that if Mary and I get together, the world will explode.

Because not a damn thing has gone right since I've kissed her.

Damn, I should've answered Seer's call. I'll have to apologize to him.

Suddenly, the wind calms. The rain stops. I can't hear the hail against the leaves or falling against the ground.

"Fuck," I hiss when a realization hits me.

"What? What is it? I can't see anything other than your ass."

"Like that's a bad thing. I have a great ass," I say, trying to keep things light as I run away from the tornado.

Silence.

Even nature speaks the loudest when it's quiet.

I burst through the other side of the woods, and my feet dig into the rocks to stabilize us as we try to get to the top.

"I've seen better asses," she grumbles, and I know she's joking.

She better be joking.

I don't like the idea of her looking at another man, even if I can't stand her.

I want to be the only man she stares at in anger, frustration, annoyance, and love.

Love. Let's not get crazy. Let's start with like.

"Will you shut up? I'm trying to save our lives."

"You're doing a heck of a job."

The sarcasm. I want to spank her ass. "Yeah, I don't see you doing anything, fire toes," I say, digging my feet into the mud as I start to climb. My boots slide, unable to maintain a decent grip.

"Well, put me down, and I'll show you what I can do."

Yeah, I'm not stupid. She's going to punch me across the face. I ignore her because I have better things to do, like trying to find us shelter in two minutes before we are sucked up in a funnel. When I'm high enough up the mountain, I look over the desert to see the small bonfire created by my motorcycle just as the funnel touches the ground. It's slow-moving, barely spinning, but the funnel itself is growing.

I set Mary down and spin her around, pointing to the tornado. "Do you see that? Do you see why I'm trying to get us the hell out of here now? If you want to help, help look for a place to hide."

"Oh my god. I've never seen a tornado before," she whispers, her face losing all amounts of color.

"We are going to be fine," I say, wanting to give her hope. Desert storms are intense, sometimes quick, and come out of nowhere. Just like this one. A few miles away, I can see blue skies, but right now, that beautiful blue color is hidden by darkness. "Come on, let's go around." I take her hand in mine again and pull her toward the direction I want to go in. I'm keeping my eyes on our surroundings while also trying to keep an eye on the tornado. It's inching down the road, but tornados have a mind of their own. Any moment, they can change direction and shift.

When I get to the other side of the mountain, I let out a breath of relief when I see a farm about a half-mile ahead. I'd rather be in a barn than be out here in the open. "Okay, up ya go," I tell her as I swing her into my arms again.

She squeals, and her arms hook around my neck. This time, I'm carrying her like I would my bride, and something about holding her that way feels right. It's difficult to run down an incline with her in my arms, but I'd rather be in control and know she's safe than wonder if she is able to keep up.

Plus, her boots are still smoking. I bet her feet are hot, and the skin is sensitive.

My leg twinges where I got shot a few months back, and my knee buckles, slamming against a very well-placed rock. I groan, grinding my teeth together as pain shoots up my thigh.

"Are you okay? I can walk—" she says, placing a hand against my cheek.

"No, it's okay. It's the gunshot wound. I thought I was healed for the most part, but this incline sucks." I find myself leaning against her hand for a split second before I push myself back to my feet.

Mary buries her head in my chest as the rain starts to pour again. The wind gusts, sending water and sand against us in a whirlwind of fury. Alarms ring throughout the city, which tells everyone to take cover because a tornado has been spotted.

When we get to the fence, I lift her over the wooden post, exhausted, cold, drenched in sweat and mud. I place her down on the ground and hop over in one leap, then pick her up again. If I was that scrawny kid I used to be, I wouldn't be able to do this.

This is why I refuse to be weak. I wouldn't be able to protect the people I care about.

I run toward the rundown barn, and now when I see it, it isn't a farm, but an abandoned building. When we get to the barn door, the wood is nearly rotten, the lock rusted, but it's the best we have right now.

Right as I try to open the door, the wind decides to push against me. I lift my head to see the swirling of clouds, the rain blinding me, and I grunt, digging my feet in the sand. I would run over a damn mountain to escape a tornado just to have another one form on this side too, but I won't let this fucking storm beat me. I refuse to be defeated again.

I won't let any situation get the best of me.

Mary grips the edge and puts her back into it. With her help, we open the door, and I'm surprised. I didn't expect her to help me.

"Why are you standing out there? Get in here, you fucking mad man," she grips me by my shirt and yanks me inside where it's nice and dry.

I turn around, hiding the shock on my face, and close the door, sliding the wooden slab across the width to lock it in place. The inside is spacious, but there is hay and a few old saddle blankets for horses. I survey the room, looking for anything else we can use when I see a section of the barn where there is a white tarp covering something.

"Stay away from sharp objects."

"So I should stay away from you, since you always carry sharp objects, right?"

I don't say anything because I don't have the energy to argue with her or bitch about semantics. She knows what I mean.

The tin roof dings with the hail and rain pounding against it. The old bones of the barn shake from the wind, and Mary wraps her arms around herself. She's scared. I don't blame her. Storms like this aren't fun.

KNIVES

Before I walk over to the white tarp, I tilt her chin up with my finger, doing everything I can not to kiss her. Kissing her is a bad idea. Things turn to shit when our lips meet, and if that isn't a sign to stay away from her, I don't know what is.

"Everything is going to be okay," I tell her, locking our eyes so she can see the truth in mine. "I'm not going to let anything happen to you."

"You can't promise that. Anything can happen. We don't know how long this storm will last, and this barn is being held up by hopes and freaking dreams."

I smirk at her silly words and wipe a drop of water hanging off her bottom lip. I've tasted those lips, and they are just as delicious as they look. "I can promise I won't let anything happen to you, Hellraiser."

"I am not."

I snort and slide my thumb off her lip as I walk away. "You're a fucking train wreck, but that's okay. I wouldn't have you any other way." When I get to the corner where the tarp is, I grip the corner of the crinkled material and yank it off. Dust flies and my dumb ass inhales, causing me to cough. I wave my hand in front of my face and see what goodies we have here. I want to know if there is anything to get us warm.

Standing before me is a vintage bike, but the beauty is gone. It's rusted from the inside out, and the tires are flat. There is an iron bedframe that needs some TLC. There is a black chest with gold hinges, but it's locked, and if there is a key, it's somewhere in here. I don't care to look.

"I'll be damned," I mutter, wondering if I'm seeing what I'm really seeing. There is a wood-burning stove in the corner. It's small, but it's enough to warm up us. I know I won't be able to pick it up. These things are made out of pure iron.

"What is it?" Mary asks.

"Salvation," I say, cleaning the cobwebs off. I wipe my hands against my jeans and start pushing against the stove, but it isn't moving.

Looks like if we are going to get warm, we are going to come to the oven instead of the other way around. I grab the handle and open the mouth of it to see if anything is inside. It's too dark to tell.

I grab some hay and stuff it in there, then take the closest nightstand and break it into pieces.

"What are you doing! Those are antiques."

"Are you cold?" I ask, but don't bother looking at her. I keep two pieces of wood out and stuff the rest in the oven.

"I'm freezing," she shivers.

"Then hush your mouth and let me get a fire going."

"You're so—"

"Amazing? Handsome? Brilliant? Strong? Smart? I'm all ears." Do I think I'm all of those things? No, but I know when I sound cocky, it pisses her off.

"You wish," she says, then yelps when lightning flashes between the wooden slats of the barn. The loud crack makes her jump, and the howling of the wind gets stronger. I'm sure we are safe here, but I'm not sure for how long. All I can do is hope.

I place hay between the sticks of wood and start to rub. I learned how to make a fire when I was thirteen. I spent plenty of time in the streets, cold, and the only thing I had was survival skills.

"Holy shit," Mary says as the kindling starts to smoke.

"It's okay to be impressed by me." I roll my lips together to keep my smile hidden.

"I actually am impressed. I've never seen someone make a fire like that before."

I'm glad it's dark, because I can feel her watching me, and for some damn reason, the blood rushes to my face, and I blush. "Well, when you're on your own like I've been, you learn some things." I shouldn't have said that. I don't usually talk about my past, but luckily, she doesn't ask about it.

I carefully lift the kindling and place it in the oven, then blow, giving the fire the oxygen it needs to thrive. After a few seconds, I open the chute, and the smoke billows out the top.

Mary sits down next to me just as I whip off my shirt. "What are you doing?" she squeaks.

"I'm getting warm." I twist my shirt and wring the water out of it. I lay the shirt on the oven and hear it sizzle. Next, I stand, unzip my pants, and slide them down my legs. "And I'm getting my clothes dry." I throw them on the oven too, then sit down on the scratchy hay. I'm still in my briefs. They are soaked, but I'm not about to let my cock hang out right now.

She might cut it off.

I lean back on my elbows and enjoy the warmth. The rain against the roof would be soothing if it wasn't for the thunder shaking the barn.

"Come on, Hellraiser. You scared? Don't worry, it's nothing I haven't seen before."

"You have never seen me," she says with a bite of anger.

She's right. I haven't.

And if I do, I know hers will be the best body I've ever seen.

She loves to call my bluff.

CHAPTER SIX

Mary

THE MAN REALLY LIKES TO TEST ME, DOESN'T HE?

Well, joke's on him.

I sling off my leather jacket and hang it on the iron headboard. The barn shakes as another crack of lightning flashes outside, and the rain is hitting the tin roof so hard that I can't tell if it's raining or hailing. The sirens outside have stopped, but that doesn't mean the storm is over. Knives and I don't have a choice. We have to stay here unless we want to get caught in the rain.

I flip my hair over next, gathering the thick, unmanageable strands that I don't have the heart to cut, and squeeze out the water. Next, I twist, then wrap my hair in a bun, tying the strand in a way that keeps it up high and tight on my head, since I don't have a hairband with me. That's the benefit of having long hair. I can pretty much do whatever I want with it.

My heart hammers in my chest. I'm so nervous that I'm wondering if I'm about to have a heart attack. I've never been naked in front of a guy I've wanted to be naked in front of. I've never even really kissed a guy until Knives. Maybe that's why I'm so defensive about myself when it comes to him. He isn't the guy I imagined myself with. Knives is a biker. A killer. Tattooed and hot.

Crazy fucking hot.

And actually crazy.

When he gets in his violent streak, everything else around him fades. Something flips in his brain and a red haze takes over. He isn't the same guy. Does it scare me? No.

I've been in the clutches of bad men before, and I know Knives isn't one, no matter how much he likes to say he is.

He's a beautiful, unique man. The kind of guy I can't seem to wrap my head around, but he isn't hard to understand. I've never been allowed to like people like him, not with how I grew up. My household was religious. My father is a preacher.

And I don't mean a preacher of a little tiny church in the middle of nowhere.

He's The Preacher. He's on TV, in newspapers, and he even baptizes celebrities' kids.

But a religious man, my father is not.

He likes to put on a show every Sunday and puts on a smile for the camera, but behind closed doors? He's a monster.

My own personal brand of hell.

I've had bad shit happen to me my entire life. Underneath the cardigans and pearls that Knives likes to bring up is a girl afraid of the dark and what lurks in it.

"Hey, you don't have to do anything. I'm not trying to get you naked; I swear. Honestly, wet clothes—"

"—I know that, Knives." I take off my shirt next and lay it on the back of the oven, then wiggle out of my pants, but I forget about my boots. I unzip the backs and fling them off along with my socks. I have to dance a bit since my jeans are stuck to my skin, but I manage and lay them next to my shirt.

I got so lucky. Knives tackled me in time before the fire could eat through my boots and cause real damage. My skin is a bit sensitive, but it's not burned.

Knives doesn't hide how he checks out my body. His eyes linger on my chest, almost as if he is memorizing the lace detailing of my bra. When he is done, his eyes drop to my stomach, then legs, and then his eyes wander up again, pausing on my face.

Do you know what I like about Knives?

He doesn't try to hide anything.

I hate people that hide themselves, their true selves. I think when someone tries to hide their bad intentions, that's what makes a monster.

I should know; I lived with one for twenty-four years.

And he touched me for twelve of them.

I should be afraid of men after what my dad did to me, but having to stay quiet about what happened brought other things into perspective. I know not all men are cruel, but I know a lot of bad people are in the world.

Bad things don't happen to good people.

Bad people do.

And it's made me love and appreciate good people more. Maybe I'm different. Maybe I'm not crying every night or having nightmares. Maybe I'm not losing myself in drinks or drugs, but I have lost something about myself.

I'm just trying to find it.

"You give me a headaches twenty-three out of twenty-four hours a day, but I can't sit here and lie to you and say you aren't beautiful," Knives says, honestly, meeting my eyes and keeping his hands to himself.

The flames dance in his cornflower blue eyes, and they are so damn bright. I've never seen irises like his before. They are unique, just like him.

"And the other hour?" I tease when I sit down on the hay, which scratches my ass and is very uncomfortable.

"I'm sleeping. It's the only damn peace I get."

"Shut up," I giggle, nudging his side with my arm. I lean forward and lay my elbows against my knees, watching the fire as it pops. The rain is slamming against the barn, and the door shakes when the wind carries around us.

"It's not letting up, is it?"

"No, it isn't. I can't believe it turned so ugly so fast."

"The way of the world is bittersweet, ain't it?" he asks, he stands and when I go to ask him where he is going, my eyes land on his package.

His very big, very long, very in my face, package. He has a tattoo above the waistband of his underwear, right above where I assume his pubic hair is, and it says 666.

What's that mean?

If a woman hops on top, does that mean she gets possessed by the devil?

Why does a part of me want to find out?

"You might give me a headache twenty-three out of twenty-four hours in the day, but I can't sit here right now and not tell you that you're beautiful too," I sling his words back at him as I take my turn to check him out. He is a hairy man with thick hair on his chest and legs. His tattoos decorate parts of him that enhance his body, something I tell he works hard at keeping in the best condition. Strong shoulders, a thick neck, and while he is lean, he has just the right amount of bulk to his body.

"What about the other hour?" he grins, being cheeky.

"I'm cursing you."

He tosses his head back and laughs at the same time a loud burst of thunder rolls, trembling the barn and everything inside it. "Look at that," he sighs. "We just complimented one another. Looks like we can be civilized after all. I'm going to go get those blankets for our asses. I'll be back." His hand falls to my shoulder and grazes my back as he walks away, awakening my skin in goosebumps and leaving me shivering.

Only I'm not cold.

What the hell is happening between us? Figuring that out causes me a damn headache.

"Alright, stand up. Let's get comfortable." He lays the blankets on the chest and unfolds the first, then shakes it out on the other side of him. Knives lays the blanket down, then does the same to the other. "There," he says.

Gosh, if I didn't know any better, I would think this moment was romantic, but that would be ridiculous because the series of events that led us here were not.

I sit down and do my best not to think about the last time these were washed. We are lucky to be alive. "Thank you," I tell him, feeling warm and flushed.

I don't think it's from the fire, either.

Knives being so close, and how the shadows curve the muscle of his arms, abs, and legs make him seem like he is from another world.

"I wonder if there is anything to drink in this place," he muses, looking around in the dark.

"You're kidding, right? Whatever is here would be deadly."

He plops down on the blanket and covers his legs. "You're probably right," he says, just as the alarm bells sound again.

I hold my breath and wrap my arms around my legs, hoping the tornado is nowhere near us. I hope the clubhouse is okay. I hope everyone is safe. Knives throws his body over mine when the walls start to shake violently, and I hold onto him, ready for us to get sucked up in the tunnel of the tornado.

And then it stops, and Knives pulls away from me, taking the cloak of bravery and strength with him.

"I think we are fine," he tries to reassure me, rubbing soothing circles on my back. "But I'm going to try to look for some alcohol in this place. Farmers always hide booze, and I'll be damned, if we are going to be stuck here, we are going to do it right." He pops up again, and he seems jittery and restless, like he has to be doing something. I mean, now that I think about it, he always is. He's always working out, always making ninja stars, always practicing his aim, or he is in the garage or at Kings' Club helping Tool.

He's always doing something, and I'm sure resting isn't something he is used to.

"I'll be back," he says again, grazing those calloused fingers along my back again. My skin prickles again, moving down the knots of my spine.

"Sure," I whisper, watching him dart into the darkness. I can see the outline of his figure every time lightning bursts outside. It's like a show. When I do see him, he is standing somewhere else in a new position. And with a flash, the outline of his body appears again, and even from here, I can see the square, cut jawline slicing through the sudden night.

"Ah-ha!" he cheers, holding up a bottle. "Told you." He runs back over to me and sits on the blanket, wiping the dust off the label to see what it is. He whistles. "Damn, this is fifty-year-old whiskey."

My nose scrunches at how horrible that sounds.

"Not a whiskey drinker, huh? Could have fooled me before we got rid of the booze at the clubhouse. I saw you turn up a few bottles."

"—Of vodka, or tequila, but not whiskey. Bleh." I shake my entire body as if just the word grosses me out.

"Do me a favor and try it," he says, twisting off the cap and taking a swallow. He doesn't flinch, but my eyes are burning from here from the strength of the whiskey.

I bet this whiskey could start a lawnmower. Makes me wonder what the hell it will do to my body. The bottle is heavy in my hand, and I can still feel the grime on the glass from years of being in this barn. "I have a feeling I'm going to hate you for this," I say to him.

"You already hate me, remember?" There is a teasing note in his tone, but in the depths, there is this breach of pain that makes his words crack.

I turn the bottle up like I have a dozen others and wince, cough, then somehow manage to swallow. The liquid burns, just like I thought it would. My stomach warms, and my eyes water, but the after taste isn't that bad.

"Hair on your chest?" he asks, taking another swing.

"Well, I'm sure I'm sprouting hairs, but nothing like yours." I wipe my mouth and chuckle when he falls to the side, grabs his stomach, and laughs. It's deep, like it's stuck in his gut and can't seem to find a way out. It's raspy, a larger than life kind of laugh, which is curious to me, because when he is around the guys, he's more serious.

He hands me the bottle, wiping his eyes as he gains control of himself. "Well, don't let me stop you from being a man."

I snort, and the air rushes inside the glass, causing a whistle. "I'm better than a man," I inform him, taking another large gulp. After the first one, the second isn't so bad.

"Oh yeah? How might that be?"

"I'm a woman." I take another drink for dramatic effect.

"A pain in my damn ass is what you are," he jokes, taking the bottle away from me.

Out of habit, I tuck my hair behind my ear, forgetting that I have it up in a bun. Knives and I fall into a comfortable silence, the white noise of rain comforting instead of threatening. The worst part of the storm must be over.

"I'm sorry about your bike," I say, playing with one straw of hay. I repeatedly tie a knot in it until it's nothing but a ball, toss it into the fire, and grab another.

"Yeah, me too. Shit happens, right?"

"Today it does," I grumble, stealing the whiskey from him

"Yeah, today was a shit show. I can't help but wonder if that's why Seer called me the other day."

"You didn't answer?"

"No. I'm not the kind of person that wants to know their future. I want it to happen when it happens."

"I don't know. If someone would have told me I would be chained in a basement before it happened, I would have wanted to know." I keep my voice light and playful, but Knives doesn't find it funny at all.

"Don't do that. Don't joke about what happened to you like it doesn't matter. It matters."

"I'm not saying it didn't. I'm saying if someone had the ability to tell me something horrible was going to happen to me, I would want to know, but that doesn't stop other terrible things from happening, does it?" The fire in front of me mirrors how angry I am.

Maybe that's why I'm so reckless. Because I have this rage inside me burning away at my humanity every moment I'm awake.

"Want to know something?" I ask right after, not really giving him an option to say no. "When I found myself chained up in that basement in Atlantic City, a damn collar wrapped around my throat and my hands bound, you know what I finally thought?" My eyes begin to water, but the last thing I wanted to do was cry in front of Knives.

Must be the whiskey.

I take another drink and sigh, swirling the bottle until the amber liquor creates its own funnel. "I thought, finally, a break. I went from the hands of one monster to another, but what's even more disgusting is when I looked at the bikers that wanted to use me, I didn't care. I was happy to be away from home, away from the man that numbed the part of me that's supposed to care. The Atlantic City chapter were assholes and horrible people, but at least they weren't family. Isn't that sad? I almost looked forward to their touch, Knives. A part of me welcomed it. I'm not like the other women Boomer saved. I'm more haunted over what happened to me before I ended up in that basement."

He steals the bottle from me, twists the cap on it, and sets it to the side. "I'm going to need you to clarify that, Mary. What do you mean you didn't care? You knew what they were going to do to you, right? They weren't the kind of men that were going to tell you they loved you or fluff your goddamn pillow at night."

"I know. They were going to drug me, keep me loopy, use me up, and spit me out. I know. Yeah, that didn't scare me. Like I said, it would have been a good change to the norm."

"And what was the norm?" he asks.

I turn to him when I hear the murderous rage. His jaw ticks, and the Knives that is about to flip the switch and disappear from this moment is close to the surface.

"It doesn't matter."

"It matters to me. No one knows anything about you."

"I don't know anything about you either," I point out, then reach out to steal the whiskey from the side of him, but he snatches it away from me in time.

"I'm an open book."

"With a damn lock on it that no one has the key to," I sass, and my words take him by surprise, so I hurry to grab the bottle. "Got to be faster than that!"

And then he jerks it away from me right as I take the cap off. "Gotta have a tighter grip than that!" he winks, and the way his lashes curl at the tip and fan over his cheek, heat floods me.

My nipples bead, and I pull my legs up to my chest to hide the traitors. The way he says, 'I need a tighter grip' sounds like there are implications in it, like he is giving me a dirty secret.

Maybe he likes a tight grip?

"So, what's the story with Mary St. James, Hellraiser? What has her wild?" he asks, eyes glittering with humor.

Being wild isn't new.

My wild just isn't being suffocated.

I'm free.

The moment I could, I unleashed what's been hidden inside me for so long. It isn't about being untamed or a rebel.

It's about living, and that's all I've ever really wanted.

I've only ever want to feel alive.

Not just to wake up every day, thankful for the heartbeat in my chest, but the electricity in my veins and the wild thump of my heart when something exciting happens, *that* kind of alive.

I've been searching for it, and I've found it.

And I fight with him every day.

CHAPTER SEVEN
Knives

I WANT TO KILL THE MAN THAT MADE THAT KIND OF ABUSE A NORM FOR HER. HOW THE fuck can she sit there and tell me she was looking forward to what the Atlantic City chapter had in store? They were monsters. A girl like her with the pearls, the class, the riches, she isn't supposed to know the hardships of life.

I guess it doesn't matter what walks of life people come from; shit happens that will change you forever.

"I feel like all we are doing is talking about me," she says, her voice smooth with a hint of vintage. Like if I asked for whiskey on the rocks, her beauty would be the whiskey, and her voice would be the ice.

It's the only way I know how to describe it

"What do you want to know?" I look up just as another piercing crack rings through the night.

"I want to know your real name."

"You don't? It isn't like it's a secret. I'm not like the other guys. A name is a name."

"I don't know it," she answers.

"Thomas."

She blows a raspberry with her lips as she cackles, nearly falling backward in fits of fucking giggles. I can't help but smile. "What?"

"Thomas? I don't know what I expected. Tyron or Zeke, maybe Loch or something badass, not something nerdy."

"Knives is badass," I protest, shocked and almost offended. Almost

"Exactly. You're this badass guy. You have tattoos and muscles. You're a biker. But to call you Thomas, I can't," she snickers. "Thomas is a frat boy who wears khakis."

"I fucking hate khaki," I mumble, remembering the time when my mom made me wear them. I only wore them once, and that was the day I lost my entire family.

"I didn't mean to make you mad; I'm sorry."

I grab her hand, and it's warm from the fire. "You didn't. It's me. Bad memory."

"A penny for your thoughts?" she asks, scooting over to inch closer to me. I expect her to move her hand away, but she doesn't. I should move my hand away.

I don't know if I can. Fighting her is too exhausting.

My entire life has been a fight. There comes a point where someone in my position has to accept that something I thought might be bad for me will be the best thing for me. I'm not used to good things. I'm used to pain, marveling in it, soaking in it.

I don't want Mary to turn to pain. I can't handle the idea of something happening to her to add any more agony to the loss I've already experienced. What if I fall for her, which, as crazy as it sounds, I can see myself falling fucking hard, and something bad happens? I'm left with picking up the shadow of myself again.

I've done that too many times, and I don't think I can do it again.

I don't talk about my past, but since she's shared a little bit of herself with me, and since we are stuck in this barn for who knows how long, getting to know one another seems to be the only option. We could fuck, but I need to earn getting between those legs, and I'm not going to do that on a stack of hay in the middle of a storm.

First off, it's cliché, and second, we aren't fighting, and that needs to be last more than a damn day.

I want to earn her trust. I want... hell, I want her.

I must want a headache for a damn lifetime.

"What do you want to know?" I lean back, prop myself up on my elbows, and hope I don't have to dig too deep.

"Where are you from?"

"Here. Vegas."

"Mom? Dad? Family?"

Damn, she has to hit all the spots I don't want to talk about, doesn't she? Makes sense, since she loves to drive me crazy.

I shake my head. "No, my family died when I was a kid. I grew up in foster care." I took another swig of whiskey, but it isn't enough to burn the pain from my chest.

"I'm so sorry, Knives." She squeezes her hand around mine. "Can I ask what happened?"

"Car accident," I whisper, thinking back to the best memory I had. "Remember Halloween? When I nearly drowned because of Tongue's brother?"

"Yeah, I still can't get over that detail," she says. "And yeah, I remember. That was terrible. I was so worried about you."

"Oh, I bet."

"Hey, we might fight, but I care. I don't ever want to see you hurt."

"I don't want to see you hurt either." My voice deepens, and the air between us sparks, crackling just like the lightning outside.

I trace her knuckles with my index finger, loving how soft she is and wondering how anyone could hurt someone like Mary. "People say that your life flashes before your eyes when you die, but I didn't have that experience. I relived one day." I smile when I think about my sister running after me, me running after her, and mom yelling at us to stop. "It was a regular day, beautiful, and the sun was out. Dad was grilling, and my sister and I were as thick as thieves. Mom was watching us to make sure we didn't hurt ourselves, but I remember laughing. We decided to go to a movie that night, and out of nowhere, a truck ran a red light and smashed right into us."

She gasps, holding a hand over her lips. "Oh god," she says, squeezing my hand even tighter.

"My parents died on the spot, but my sister…" my throat clogs up when I remember the moment as if it happened yesterday. "She had this piece of metal, right here—" I rub the side of my neck, a spit right under my ear. "She couldn't breathe. There was so much blood. I was the only one that came out with no injuries, can you believe that? I was safe. What crock of shit is that?"

My eyes blur, thinking of my sister's young face and her long hair coated in blood. "She looked at me, unable to speak. She tried. She kept trying to talk to me, but her throat was crushed. I held her hand and waited for help to arrive, but by the time they did, she had already died."

Mary is crying, big tears wetting the sharp edges of her cheeks. "Knives, I'm so sorry. I'm so sorry that happened to you." She throws her arms around my neck and buries her face in my shoulder. It takes a second for me to react, because I can't remember the last time someone hugged me.

I wrap my arms around her, too, pulling her tight and enjoying the way she feels against me. I inhale her scent, getting lost in her comfort, and a tear falls, dripping down my cheek until it lands on her shoulder. I haven't cried in a long time, but Mary brings me to my knees. She opens me up, and I think she always has. It's one of the reasons why we fight so much. She makes me vulnerable.

I hate being vulnerable.

I hate… feeling. I'm not used to it. With Mary around, it's like the walls I built around me crumble and welcome her home to heal me.

But I miss what my life could have been. I miss my family. I miss my best friend. I hate what my life turned into after my parents died, but now, my life isn't so bad. It took too long to get here, though. Way too long, and I've pushed the pain away, locked it inside, thrown away the key, and lost hope that my beat-up heart can be anything other than rundown and tired.

Mary is breathing life into me, and it terrifies me more than death itself.

Death is easy.

And I think I've been waiting for it to come back around for me.

I'm not afraid of a lot of things. I love making people afraid of me, but emotions bring even the strongest men to their knees.

She pulls away and sits back down in her spot, sooner than I was ready to let go, but I don't want to make her stay in my arms. I want her to *want* to be there. "I need a drink," she says, taking the bottle and taking a gulp. "No one should have to experience that."

"It didn't stop there," I say in a small whisper, hoping she doesn't hear me, but at the same time, hoping she does. "Foster care sucked. I bounced around a lot. I wasn't the kid that everyone liked. I was a loner, a weirdo, scrawny—"

"—You were scrawny? No way, I don't believe that for a second."

"Believe it. I was short too. And the damn butt to everyone's joke. I ran away for a bit when I was thirteen. That's when I learned to build fires." I can't believe I'm telling her this. No one knows this about me, but she makes me want to talk. She makes me want to heal. "Most of the foster parents I had, they were in it for the paycheck. They would have so many kids and all of us shared a room sometimes. We could only bathe once a week, eat certain times during the day, so I was skinny and smelled a lot of the time."

"That should be illegal. The system shouldn't allow that to happen."

"System fails everyone all the time, but there was one good thing that came out of it." I smile when I remember his face. "Mason. Reaper knows about Mason, but only because Mason hung around the club when we were teenagers. When he aged out of the system, he was going to prospect, but that never happened."

"Why?"

"Because of me," I admit, hanging my head. I deserve the shame and guilt to wash over me. "I wasn't always fit. I wasn't always six-foot-three. And there was this group of kids, three of them, and they loved to beat the hell out of me every chance they got. Mason, even though he was a foster kid, no one gave him shit. He was big for his age, strong, nearly looked like a man, and was only a year older than me. He was my protector. My brother, when I had no one else."

Her hand slides over my thigh and squeezes, telling me that she's here and listening. How long has it been since I talked to someone and they willingly listened? I can't even remember.

"He was all I had, and at fifteen, that's a big deal. Especially when it seemed like the entire world was against you. He tried to protect me all the time, but he couldn't always be there, and I'd get the shit kicked out of me."

"If they only saw you now..." she says, letting it be known that I'd be their worst fucking nightmare.

Rain continues to pound the tin roof, and I open the oven to shove another piece of the nightstand in there, along with hay, to keep the fire roaring. "I was walking home from school one day, and I decided to take a short cut. It was this old back road, I'm sure it's still there, but I haven't checked. I haven't been able to go back. They called it Miscellaneous Way because that's where people dumped anything and everything. If I had just gone the other way home, everything would have been fine, but I didn't, so Mason came looking for me." I let out a big exhale until I have no air left in my lungs and wrap my arms around her again and pull her close. Our knees touch, and her hands fall to my legs. It probably isn't comfortable for her, but I need to be close to her. I fought it before by fighting with her, and I hope tonight gets us past it.

"I protected myself with a few old knives, stabbed one kid, and right as I was about to attack the others, Mason was there, saving me like he always did. Only this time, he didn't use threats to scare off the kids. He had a gun, and he shot all of them. He told me to run, but I wanted to take responsibility, yet, he wouldn't let me. He said, 'always take responsibility for your actions,' and the police came. I ran into a shed and watched as the officers drew their guns. When they asked him to drop the weapon, the barrel was pointed to them, and they fired."

Pow. Pow. Pow. Pow.

I can almost hear the ringing in my ears still.

"I watched him die and fall on the guys he killed. For me. It was always for me, and that pissed me off. Before he died, he told me to go to the biker bar we always passed by, and that's where I met Reaper's dad, who was the President, and Reaper was only a few years older than me. They've been my family ever since, but it still hurts like hell thinking about the family I've lost."

Her hands lay on my chest. My heart thumps with the sad memories coursing through me and the way the warmth of her soaks into me, wrapping around the ache in my soul like the fire coming from the stove or a blanket.

I never thought sorrow could be thawed and warmed until it reached relief, but here we are. I lay my hand on top of hers and rub the top. I'm cut open, raw, and I feel weak.

A feeling I never wanted to feel again, but she's here, and the weakness isn't so bad when she's touching me.

"That shouldn't have happened to you," she whispers, lifting her eyes from the middle of my chest to meet mine. She's trying not to cry, but tears spill anyway. "Bad shit happens to everyone."

"And what about you? What made you think the Atlantic City Chapter was a fresh start?" She shakes her head, and the tears reflect off the glow of the fire beside us. One falls, then another, and I'm trying to catch them and wipe them away, but I'm not quick enough.

"I'm from a very religious family," she whispers, cutting her eyes to me. "My dad is a preacher."

"I know," I say, thinking back to when Reaper called for Church and Badge gave an update on the girls we rescued. Mary St. James was a preacher's daughter, a famous preacher who makes a ton of money, but Mary doesn't seem like the religious type to me. Now that I'm getting to know her, I'm starting to realize her rebellion isn't new but hidden.

"You knew? And all the times we fought, you didn't try taking a dig at me?"

"I'm an asshole, but that was your family; I wasn't going to slap that in your face. Especially since you're so adamant about not going back to them, so I kept quiet. As did everyone else. Pretty funny though, the Preacher's daughter hanging out with bikers. I bet your dad would have a heart attack."

"I doubt it," she says, a flat, monotone grip to her throat. "He isn't very religious either. He's a fake. He's horrible." Her fingers dig into my chest, her nails pinching my skin like she wishes he were in front of her so she could rip his heart out. "He's the reason why Atlantic City wasn't so bad." Her gaze meets mine, and hatred, holy hell, hatred unlike anything I've ever seen before, flashes in her eyes.

I thought she didn't like me, but that wasn't the case at all. Now that I see what her hate looks like, it is safe to say I'm on her good side.

"For twelve years, he molested me. Twelve. Long. Torturous. Years."

And just like that, the peace I felt disappears. I lift her off me because somehow, she found her way to my lap. I start to pace, feeling the need for blood pumping through my veins. I pop my neck, grab the sides of my head, and snarl.

I'm breaking.

"Knives?"

"He did what? For how long? I'm going to kill him. I'm going to fucking kill him!" I yell so loud, someone up above must hear me, because thunder grumbles the ground and lightning booms overhead. I'm fucking pissed.

Twelve years of being caged.

Twelve years of being in her own prison.

Twelve years of being silent.

Twelve years of acting normal.

No wonder she is how she is.

She's free now. It's no wonder she's a fucking hellraiser when praying got her nowhere.

And then I've been kissing her, throwing my lips on her because I couldn't wait another second. Did she even want it? "I'm sorry, Mary. I didn't know. I wouldn't have... I would have respected your space and not kissed you."

"Don't do that; don't take that away from me. I'm not someone who is ruined by her past. The only thing I don't want is to go home. I never want to go there again, but I want to move on with my life. I want more than what I had. That's why I was okay with Atlantic City; at least there would have been variety—"

Hearing her talk like that, about being raped and abused by different men, has a possessive beast swelling inside me that I've never felt before. Barely breathing, I cup her face and hope she can see the cold in my eyes as I make a promise, "I swear, I promise, I'll kill him. He won't even have to be in the back of your mind anymore. I'll hunt him down. I'll—"

She hushes me by kissing me this time, and her lips are lava soaking into my veins, warming me from head to toe in the middle of this desert winter. My hands go from soft to hard along her jaw as I take control, slipping my tongue between her lips. This isn't good. We're nearly naked, her breasts are rubbing against my chest, my cock is hard and leaking, but I know the last thing I want to do is have sex with her here.

Mary deserves more than some haystack fuck.

No, she doesn't even deserve to get fucked; she deserves better than that.

How the hell do I give it to her? I've never experienced anything like that before. I've never felt like this for anyone before. It's consuming me.

Her hands slide down my chest as mine drift down her back; the smooth lines and the curve of her delicate spine have me growling low in my gut. Her fingers tease the waistband of my briefs, but they don't slip under, so I take her lead.

I don't grip her ass, I don't cup her tits like I really want, because I want her to be able to call the shots.

And I'm not going to lie, having her fingers tease me like this is the hottest fucking thing I've ever experienced. My stomach clenches, and the touch feels… intimate. My brows pinch together, trying to understand what intimacy is.

I don't love.

I break people.

I'm not a person someone takes a chance, on because I don't let them.

I suck her lip into my mouth and groan as her nails sink into my hip bones. This is a bad idea. Just because we are getting along now doesn't mean we always will. What if we aren't constructed to love the way other people do?

Then I'll deconstruct myself and find a way to build the foundation of who I am again. She deserves the effort for me to try.

"Knives," she gasps, saying the only name that I've ever really felt like matched my soul. My cock jerks from how wispy my name sounds, falling off her lips. I lay us down on the blanket, fall to the side, so I'm not nestled between her legs like I want to be and keep my hands on her waist.

My balls pull against my body when she sucks my tongue into her mouth and strokes me like I'd imagined she would my cock. My eyes roll to the back of my head and a dollop of precum slides down my shaft.

"Mary," I rumble her name, laying my forehead against hers as I try to bring this to a stop. "You have no idea what I want to do to you." I slap my hands on either side of her head and grip the blanket in my fists, trying to squeeze out all the desire into the hay under us. My entire body shakes from roping in the control, nearly smothering me.

"I…we can…" she tries to find the words, but I interrupt her.

"I don't want us to be here in this barn for the first time, Mary. I'm a fucking asshole, and I've done a lot of questionable things, but I won't take you and claim you before you're ready."

"Claim me?" She lifts a curved brow at me, a questioning and challenging tone. She doesn't like the idea of being owned.

That's too fucking bad.

"Claim you," I lower my voice. "Fucking show you who owns you and this body, show you that the only fight you're going to give me from now on is the one you relent when I'm ten inches deep."

Her mouth drops open, and the flames allow me to see the blush staining her cheeks. "Knives... I—"

"—Not now, or tomorrow, but when you're ready. You can act like the cut sluts all you want, Mary, but I know better. You aren't the kind of woman to give yourself up like that."

"Maybe I don't want to be claimed. Or owned. Ever think about that?"

Her sudden reversal has me defensive.

"Mary, it's not—"

"Maybe I should be the one claiming you. Maybe I want to make you mine."

That throws me for a loop. I look down at her, then look back up, totally at a loss for what to respond.

"Does that bother you?" she asks, crossing her arms over her chest to hide herself. I haven't seen her like this before, naïve, but I guess she is. The only person she's been with is her father, and that makes me fucking sick.

I wrap my fingers around her wrists and gently lay them on either side of her body so I can see the mounds of her tits hiding behind that bra. "No, Hellraiser. You're making me learn a lot, that's all."

"Is this a joke? How can we be at each other's throat one minute and laying here the next? I want nothing but to kiss you again, but if we are going to fight all the time again, maybe we shouldn't do this."

"I'm not going to let it stop me." I don't care if we fight, if she screams, or if she punches me in the stomach with the fake leg I got her for Christmas. Headache and all, temper and all, fights, screams, and everything else in between.

I don't care what comes with this.

I realize what I want—no—what I need is her.

CHAPTER EIGHT

Mary

I HAVE NO IDEA WHAT I'M DOING OR WHY.

All I know is Knives is more than I thought he was. No, that isn't true. I always thought there was more to him than meets the eye, but he hid behind his ice-cold demeanor, the frozen tundras of his eyes, and his ninja stars.

We fought each other because we were fighting what we felt for one another. Things still might not be perfect. From the sounds of it, we don't know how to have a good thing when we have been surrounded by bad.

He grew up poor and lost everything.

I grew up rich and had nothing.

We are cut from the same cloth.

"Can I watch you and you watch me? Because I need to take the edge off, Knives."

I barely have the question out of my mouth before he seals his lips on me again. He slides between my legs, his hard cock rubbing against my clit, and his hands slide down my shoulders, cupping my breasts, and he groans into my mouth. Every inch of me is lost in the touch he gives. I've never been touched like this.

My dad stole from me.

I've never been explored, and Knives wants to. I can tell he is trying to respect me at the same time, and it only has my heart falling for him even more. I whimper and cry out when something hard like metal slides over my bundle of nerves again. My eyes widen, and my entire body tenses. Knives backpedals and sits on his knees, staring down at me. His chest booms with every breath he takes, and he inches his briefs down until his cock bobs free.

"Holy mother of...." I pinch my lips together and sit up on my elbows, a gush of heat leaving my center and wetting my panties when I see the beautiful, erotic sight in front of me. Of course, his cock is magnificent, just like the rest of his.

Long.

Thick.

And pierced.

He has a Jacob's Ladder and two hoops on his crown, reminding me of horns. My eyes drift to the 666 tattoo, and it makes sense.

The plum-colored head is nearly purple with how hard he is and how much blood is pumping through. I can't tear my eyes off him. He has a slight curve to the left, and I have to dig my fingers in the blanket to stop myself from reaching out.

I lick my lips, watching the palm of his hand wrap tight around the thick shaft and pump. My breaths leave me in tiny bursts. I lift my hand, trickle my fingers down the middle of my chest, slide down the bumps of my ribs, and tease the edge of my panties. "Kiss me," I tell him, but he shakes his head.

Does he not want to do this anymore? Disappoint slams through me, and I look away from him, tearing my eyes off a man I'll never be able to forget.

"If I kiss you, and I want to, I'm going to push those panties to the side and slide into that hot cunt, because I'll be able to feel the cushion of your lips against me. I'm only so strong, Mary."

"Oh," I say, locking our eyes together again.

"Oh, is right," he says as he tugs on the rings attached to the crown of his cock. He groans, continuing the tease. A bead of precum leaks off the tip and drips down the vein protruding along the ten inches. "Do you know how beautiful you are, my little Hellraiser?" he asks, using not one but both of his hands to grip his cock and jack it. "What you do to me, what you've always done to me?"

I shake my head, keeping quiet as I dip my finger below the waistband of my panties. My fingers slide through my wet folds, and I moan in my throat, dropping my jaw when I feel how hot I am.

"That fucking mouth, that temper, every time you fought me, you have no idea how bad I wanted to bend you over..." he can't finish his sentence because he speeds up his thrusts, moving his hips, so he fucks his palms. He tosses his head back, the tendons on his neck tensing, and just like the rest of him, his cock seems so mad, so intense, and all I want to do is show him how fucking unique he is.

Unique because I'm going to assume there are not a lot of men with so many piercings in their dick.

Knives must like the pain, which also helps me understand him a bit more. The scars on his knuckles because of how much he plays with his stars, the tattoos all over him, the piercings... does he truly like pain, or does he think he deserves it?

His chin drops to his chest as he looks at me. "I thought we were going to watch each other?"

"Sorry, I got caught up in watching you," I say and sit up, becoming eye level with the intimidation of his cock. I don't have the courage to take him in my mouth. I've never done that before, but I also don't want us to do things we aren't ready for, only for me to be disappointed when we walk out of this barn to the real world and go back to who we used to be?

What if this barn is all there is? What if when we are home, the bickering and slight frustration comes roaring back? The last thing I want is to have sex with a guy who winds up treating me like everyone else he has ever been with.

I trust Knives with my life. I know he'll protect me, but my heart? The heart is another matter, a delicate one, something that can break without being put back together again.

Life has room for fault, but the heart does not, or the fault line makes it fracture.

I purse my lips and blow on his throbbing cock, getting a good view of the piercings decorating his length. I'm in awe that I like it so much. I never thought I'd be into something like that, but my tongue twitches to flick out and tug on the silver loops, then lick the ladder.

His knees buckle as I tease him. My nails scratch along his legs as I move up his body and grip his hips. Knives has a V-shape of muscle on either side, leading to the thick patch of hair settling around the base of his cock. He is more than I could have imagined.

I lean down, staying away from his cock, but I can feel the heat of it as I lay my lips on the delicate skin of his V, right along the V. I move to the other side, kissing him there too, grabbing onto the lust I've been feeling for him all this time. It feels good to let go of the anger and just be.

Keeping my nails stroking his thighs, I blow air on his cockhead again, watching a bead of precum drip from the slit. I want to lick up and taste him. Does he taste sweet? Salty? Maybe he tastes like nothing. I kiss my way up his ribs, and he is panting, his stomach rising and falling as he struggles to take in a lungful of air.

"Jesus Christ, if you keep doing this, I might come," he admits, taking me by complete surprise. He acts as if no one has explored him either. What kind of woman would do that when a man like Knives is with her?

"Good," I tell him, making sure to keep a distance from his groin. I graze my nails up his sides and around his back, staying away from his ass as I drag them up his spine. I move around his shoulders, dragging the blunt edges of my fingers down his chest. I kiss his right nipple, lick it, then blow on the bead too. I watch as the pink bud tightens, reacting to the wet and cold. Grinning, I move to the other one and do the same before I kiss my way down his other side, loving the scratch of his hair against my palm.

I'm level with his cock again, staring at the beast before me. I can't help but wonder how he will fit in my mouth when the day comes. His hands land on my shoulders, and as a quick goodbye, I kiss the head, letting the bead of precum drop onto my lower lip before I lay back down on the blanket.

Licking him off me so I can taste his flavor, I moan as my taste buds awaken.

I tug my panties down, remembering what I said about watching each other, and spread my legs so he can see me.

All of me.

Sitting back, his eyes hood when he watches me slide through my folds, the wet sounds mixing with the rain falling to the ground outside. Like Knives, I use two hands. One to plunge two fingers inside me, while I use the other to circle my engorged clit.

My back bows as my thighs tremble, and Knives growls. "Fuck, you're killing me. No one has ever teased me like that before. You're going to be the goddamn death of me, Hellraiser. I knew you were fucking trouble."

I remember that I need to watch him, so I bring my head down to see him furiously fucking his fist, his stare locked onto my cunt. "Knives, it feels so good." I want to tell him to touch me, but I'm already addicted to his kiss. I'm afraid if I give in, then I'll always want more from him. Reality is different than being locked away alone.

I should know.

For too long, my mind was bent and shaped by my father, a man who made sure he was alone with me every chance he got.

No, I can't think about him right now. I don't want him ruining this.

"I'm close," I say to Knives, feeling the trembling warmth of an orgasm brewing in my body. "I'm so close." My toes curl, and Knives tugs on the horns again, stretching the tip of his cock in rhythm with his strokes.

"That pussy looks delicious. You have no idea how bad I want to taste you; how bad I want to slide in and fill that cunt to the fucking brim until you're dripping with me. I'm close. Goddamn it, I'm so close." His hand jerks faster, and I move my fingers at the same speed, circling my clit in desperation, so we fall over the edge together.

"Knives," I breathe. "Oh—oh, yes!" I shove my fingers as far as they can go until my knuckles stop me from going deeper. My body ignites in an array of fireworks and sweat. I'm rocking against my hand, hoping the friction will prolong the sensation.

"The death of me," he whispers before grunting my name, "Mary!" And hot streams of cream land on my stomach. I don't know what to expect, but I don't expect so much. I gasp when a sixth line coats me, landing on my inner thigh.

I don't know what's gotten into me, but he said he wanted a taste. I sit up, get to my knees, swipe his cum off my stomach with one hand, and at the same time, shove one hand in his mouth and the other in mine.

His salty seed slides down my throat, and Knives grips my wrist in a tight lock with his fingers, keeping my fingers in his mouth for as long as he can. He sucks and licks, moaning when he tastes me. He makes me sound like a five-star meal, a gourmet dish he can never get enough of.

I fall backward, exhausted, and high. I never thought it could be like that, sex without the sex. Well, was this sex? I don't know. Foreplay might be a better word for it, but it was better than anything I've ever experienced.

"Holy shit," he huffs, falling to his side.

We chuckle at the same time as we notice how hard we are breathing. He turns my head and traces my jaw as he stares at me with…I don't know… adoration?

"You're pretty fucking amazing, you know that? I've never experienced that. I usually…" he stops himself, and I roll over, tucking my hands under my cheek, and I stare at the tattoo on his chest.

"I know you've been with plenty of other women, Knives. You don't have to stop yourself with me. You aren't going to insult me or anything. Just because I don't have much to compare it to doesn't mean you don't. I know that. You probably are used to just having sex and—" I'm about to launch into why I didn't want to compare, but he kisses me, it's quick with no tongue, but his lips are soft and passionate against mine.

"You're right. I am used to it. I'm used to fucking whoever I want, whenever I want. I bend them over and get down to business, but there is no comparison, Mary. What we just did, it's number one for me."

"Yeah?" I ask, not wanting to sound so damn hopeful, but I can't help it. The way the annoyance for Knives morphed makes me hope.

"Yeah, Hellraiser." He wipes my stomach off with the edge of the blanket, then folds it, tucking it under the sheet, so we don't roll in wet goop. "Come on, let's get some sleep, and tomorrow we can see if we can get home." He kisses the top of my shoulder before pulling the blanket up.

I expect us to roll over and go to bed, but Knives surprises me again by yanking me against his chest and spooning me. His chin is on my shoulder, and his leg is thrown over mine.

He likes to cuddle!

I bite my lip to stop the squeal of excitement. It's right there, bubbling in my throat, needing to be released. I swallow it down and let the beat of his heart against my shoulder lull me to sleep. The fire has died down, just a few crackles and pops every now and then, but I'm warm since Knives is against me.

Right as I'm about to be dead to the world, a hand falls over my mouth. I snap my eyes open, and it's Knives. He lays a finger against his lips, brows drawn in concern as we remain as quiet as possible. The barn door opens up, and two masculine voices are arguing.

"No, I don't know, okay? You have to let Natalia go. I'll give you money. I want my niece back."

"Not until I get what I want!"

"I don't know where your daughter is, Mr. St. James. I swear, but I want Natalia. I did what you asked last time—"

I grip onto Knives as hard as I can, knowing I'm leaving bruises, but it's the only thing stopping me from screaming when I hear my dad's voice. What the hell is he doing here?

"And look how well that turned out. You're useless."

Bang. Bang. Bang.

Knives covers me with his body, just like he did when he thought the tornado was about to take us, and when the barn door slams shut, he lifts his head. "Are you okay?"

I'm shaking. I can't form words. "That was my dad. I..."

"I know. I know. Fuck. Okay, this is a mess. I need to go check on the guy he shot."

"No! Knives, please," I whisper and try to hold onto him, but he kisses my inner wrist before running to the middle of the barn.

"Holy shit, Maximo. What the fuck did you get yourself into?"

There isn't a reply.

I should have known my dad would come back for me. I should have known he would come back to ruin my life the moment I found happiness. And if I know my father, I know he will kill anyone and everyone in his way to get what he wants.

I've brought the Kings more trouble, something they don't deserve. Knives will be a target now; everyone will be in danger because of me.

Maybe I should disappear, but the thought of leaving hurts more than death. I'd rather my father kill me than take me away from the home I've built here.

And just when I thought I was living the dream...

My monster had to come emerge from the dark.

CHAPTER NINE
Knives

NOTHING CAN SURPRISE ME MUCH. I'VE EXPERIENCED PRETTY MUCH EVERYTHING THERE is to see and feel that would drive a man to kill himself, but being in a remote, abandoned barn with Mary and having the best night of my life? That surprised me.

Drinking with her surprised me. The depth of how much I want her that surprises me.

Finding Maximo Moretti in an abandoned barn, shot twice in the shoulder and once in the thigh? That surprises me.

And knowing it was Mary's father who pulled the trigger? That fucking shocks me.

Two men that have a fucking death warrant on their heads.

"Maximo? Long time, no see." I pat his sweaty face, and his eyes open. "Yeah, your injuries aren't deadly, so don't play the dead card on me." I slap his face again, and a painful wheeze leaves his chest. "Where have you been, buddy? You know who has been looking for you?"

His eyes snap open then, and he gulps when he knows exactly who I am talking about. "I—I have my reasons. I swear, I'd never hurt any of the ladies who belong to the Kings. You have to understand—"

I wrap my hand around his throat and pull him up by his neck. Maximo fucking Moretti. The man Tongue has been salivating for after what he did, not only pinning Skirt and him in the same ring but for holding a knife to Daphne's throat. Tongue is a maniac, a fucking unstable, sick, and twisted man, but no one fucks with his woman

"We require payment for your actions," I whisper, letting my breath cross his face so hopefully he can smell the fucking threat in the air. Once I get him back to the clubhouse, I'm going to make sure we drain every bit of information from him.

He turned his back on the wrong men.

"Knives?" Mary asks from our dark corner, our spot, and disappointment rears its head when I realize our fucking moment is ruined because, for some reason, her father and Maximo decided to bust in here. Out of all places they could fucking ruin, they had to ruin this.

Mary and I already don't have the most stable relationship without jumping down each other's throats. We made progress. More than progress. I got to see her come, and I wanted to see that a hundred times over and more.

"Get dressed, Hellraiser."

"Mary? As in Mary St—"

I squeeze Maximo's throat and sneer, "You don't get to fucking ask questions about her. Do I make myself clear?"

"Crystal," Maximo says, groaning when I dig my knee into his shoulder.

On purpose.

Mary comes out from behind the old furniture, dressed in her tight jeans and T-shirt with her leather jacket in hand, then tosses me my clothes. They are dry, luckily, since it's been a few hours, and the storm has seemed to pass with just a mist of rain peppering the metal roof.

"I need a hospital," Maximo struggles to say.

I lift my knee off his shoulder and get dressed. Mary stays away from Maximo, leaning against the wall of the barn, right underneath a damn hook that looks like it held pigs or cows for someone to butcher. After I tug on my shirt, I walk over, move her to the left because all I can think about is the hook falling and slicing through her neck, just like my sister. I kiss the top of her head, hating that the happiness we shared is now gone.

I want to kill Maximo for ruining my goddamn night.

Her eyes are red and swollen, her cheeks flushed with fear, and tears fill her beautiful chocolate eyes. I want to kill Maximo for making her cry, too, and her dad.

Oh, I really want her dad's blood on my ninja stars.

"I'm going to fix this. You're going to be safe. I don't want you to be scared, okay?" I tell Mary, needing her to see that I'm going to protect her. She has nothing to worry about. Her father isn't going to lay his hands on her again, not as long as I am alive.

And history has proven, killing me is not easy.

Maximo tries to get up by placing his body on his hands and knees. "Oh, I don't fucking think so." I slam my foot into his back, and he shouts as his body bends, and he falls to the ground. "You don't get to try and get out of here. You're coming back with me." I grip him by the back of his hair and yank his head off the floor, hoping he is uncomfortable. I could break his neck right now if I really wanted to.

Tongue would cut out my tongue and feed it to Happy if I did. This is his retribution, but I'm allowed to be angry for my brother, and I'm allowed to be angry that Maximo is friends with Mary's father.

Nothing good can come out of that.

"What are you doing here?" I ask him.

"I live here."

I push his head against the ground, my fingers twitching for a ninja star, but I don't have any on me. I don't have my backup gun either.

What a fucking shitshow.

"You aren't exactly in the position to get smart with me. You have no idea how deep of shit you are in with the Kings. After everything we have done for you and Moretti, your own fucking brother, you turn your back on us."

"I'm doing this for my brother!" he hisses, but whimpers when I push my knee into the exit wound on his back.

I want to know everything, but it's pointless to get the story out of him now when I know he will go to the playroom at the clubhouse with a few of the guys, and they will get every drop of information out of him. "What's in this barn? Why is Preacher Man here, huh? Didn't know you were the religious type."

His eyes roll to the back of his head, and for a minute, I think he is pretending, so I kick him for the hell of it. But he doesn't make a sound. He's completely passed out. "Damn it. They always pass out right before I need information." I turn around to see Mary folding up the blankets and making sure the fire is out; she's still crying, and her hands are trembling, but she's trying to pull herself together.

I want her to fall apart.

I want her to realize she doesn't have to be strong anymore, or runaway, or feel caged. She can fall, and I'll catch her.

And I'll put her back together again

Mary isn't the kind of woman that can be hidden. She needs her freedom, and I can be that for her.

"How are we going to get back to the clubhouse?" Mary asks, looping her arms through her leather jacket when she shivers.

"Mafia boss has to have a phone on him, right?" I flip an unconscious Maximo over on his back and see blood spreading over his suit and dripping on the floor.

Uh.

He might be dying.

And I couldn't care less.

I search his pockets and pull out his phone and dial Reaper's number. As it rings, I glance around the barn and wish we didn't have to leave. This place was a little getaway for us; it healed me in some ways and opened me in others.

And it's ruined because if a man like Maximo and her father are here, it means this is a place that holds bad intent.

I won't bring Mary to a place that is a meeting ground for men like this.

"Maximo," Reaper answers with a dark growl. "You better hope I don't find you because when I do, I'm going to rip your heart from your chest, crush it with my fist, then shove it down your throat."

I'm really fucking glad I'm not Maximo right now. "It's me, Reaper. It's Knives."

"Knives?" he sounds shocked, and the threat in his voice vanishes and is replaced with confusion. "What the fuck are you doing with Maximo's phone? And where the hell have you been? The guys have been trying to call you."

I really need a phone. "I don't have my phone yet. It's been a hectic twenty-four hours. Mary is with me—"

"I thought she was in jail."

"I picked her up yesterday. My bike blew up. The tornado happened. We are in an abandoned barn off Route 50. Maximo is here."

A rumble comes from the other end, and there is a flurry of sounds in the background behind him. "You're going to have to tell me what happened in more detail later. We are coming to get you, don't fucking move, and don't you dare lose Maximo."

"We have more issues to worry about than him, Reaper. Shit is brewing, and I'll tell you everything later. Bring my ninja stars."

"Why?"

"Because I don't have them, and I feel naked," I say, suddenly feeling defensive. I crack my neck, annoyed that I even have to defend myself.

"I should have known something like this would happen. Seer called me and told me to tell you that you're an idiot. What's that deal with that?"

A loud bang pulls me away from the conversation, and I see the bedframe fell over, and Mary mouths, 'I'm sorry' to me.

"Another long story," I say, pinching the bridge of my nose. "Can you just get here, please?"

"Yeah. Be there in ten."

The line goes dead, and I stuff the phone in my back pocket. When I stand, I try and find something about this place that rubs me the wrong way, but it's just a barn. I stare into every corner, evaluating the stacks of hay, but nothing stands out to me besides a bunch of cobwebs and the musty smell of horse and rain.

Reins hang on the hook against the beam, and I step over Maximo, yanking the leather straps off. I flick the cobwebs away and flip Maximo on his stomach, pull his arms behind his back, and tie the reins around his wrists into a knot I know he can't get out of. When I'm satisfied, I take a step away.

"They are on their way," I say to Mary, who is still in the same spot as she was in before.

"Good."

I don't like how she said that. I don't like that she's putting distance between us. She won't even look at me in the eye. I'm about to show why we fit when a dozen Harleys grumble outside. This time, I do give her space, because I'm not sure how to be with her in front of the guys. Or maybe I do.

I shouldn't care.

But I'm in unknown territory here. She doesn't seem like she wants me around, but if I act the same, I'm damned. If I out us to the world before she's ready, I'm damned.

What the fuck? Relationship business sucks.

I expect a knock on the door.

I should have known better.

The door is kicked down, and Tongue is standing there in the entryway, his shaggy hair hanging in front of his face and his fists clenched at his sides. He has a knife in his hand and the urge to kill in his eyes.

Hay particles and dust zoom around us, and Tongue looks from left to right, staring at Mary for a few seconds before stepping inside the barn, breaking the downed door even further as he walks across it. The wood creaks and splinters from his weight.

"Tongue! Don't you dare kill him. I want answers." Reaper comes into the doorway next, rubbing his chin when he sees Maximo tied up on the ground.

"I want his tongue."

"That isn't shocking." I pat Tongue's shoulder with my hand, and heat is radiating off him in waves.

Tongue kneels on the ground, snarling like a beast, ready to rip the man's head off. He digs his knife into the ground and drags it in the dirt and straw. His fingers hold the blade tightly, and he doesn't look away from Maximo. He doesn't blink.

He barely even breathes as he holds onto Reaper's order. Tongue wants more than Maximo's ability to speak.

He wants his life.

"Load him up, Bullseye," Reaper says, turning his cheek to his shoulder as if he is talking to someone behind him.

Bullseye comes through the doorway next, twirling a dart in his hand, which makes me wish for my stars. Bullseye must have seen the longing on my face because he pulls two stars out of his pocket, and they gleam in the early morning light.

So pretty.

He flings them in the air, and I catch them without hesitation. One star is one of my newer ones, but the other is one I haven't touched since I made it.

"Sorry, we were in a hurry, and I grabbed what I could," Bullseye says, jerking Maximo up to his feet. "What did you do?"

"He passed out. That's not my fault."

"The bullets. Doc needs to—"

"Leave them. His pain is far from over." Reaper steps out of the way when Bullseye throws Maximo over his shoulder with a grunt and walks outside.

"Maybe tie him to the back of the truck and drag his ass home," Tongue says, perking up when he mentions the options. His eyes stop frowning, and the darkness in his head spins with the idea. He is probably imagining what Maximo would look like rolling around on the ground, losing limbs, becoming bloody. He groans, closing his eyes and licking his lips. He grips his cock, which is hard, and I jerk my eyes away to stare at the ceiling, then drop them to Mary. For the first time in an hour, she has a smile on her face because my discomfort amuses her.

"Stop getting off on getting your revenge, Tongue," I mutter and stalk my way toward Mary. I need to close this distance between us. Now that I've had her, I don't want us to go back to the way we were before.

Why fight something that comes so easy and feels so good?

"I can't help it. The thought of him dying is turning me on. I need Daphne," he says without shame, without blinking that he just admitted that death makes his cock hard.

"Well, stop your moaning, literally, and let's go home. I have a feeling it is going to be a long night. Bullseye? Tie him up in the playroom. Knives and Mary, you're going to Church when we get home."

Ah, what a horrible choice of words.

"I hate church," Mary says low, so only I can hear.

"You can worship the ground I walk on later, then," I tease her, hoping to make her smile.

"Like I'd even want to get near your feet. Gross," she jokes back, and my chest flickers with happiness. I had hoped the teasing nature wouldn't go away in our relationship, just the fighting.

When everyone walks out the door, Reaper backtracks and tosses me a set of keys. "Bullseye is leaving his bike for you to take back. I'll call up Pocus and Seer and see if they can't get a price on a customized one down in NOLA for you. Their hogs are beauts," he says, just as I catch the keys in the air. "We saw your bike. It's fucking toasted. Nothing was salvageable, Knives. I'm sorry."

"It's all good, Prez. Shit happens."

"Story of our fucking lives," he says, stomping outside in the muck the rain left behind.

Before we leave, I lay my hand on Mary's shoulders and notice she is looking away from me again. Her lip is trembling, and she keeps wiping the tears that fall on her cheeks. I want to fix this. I don't want her to cry again. It... it makes me feel things I haven't felt in a very long time. I doubt this will be the last time too.

I bet every day I'll wake up and experience an emotion that has been in hibernation for twenty years. She's awakening me from a coma, and I nearly don't recognize the world I'm seeing or myself, but I like it.

That's new to me too. Liking something. I've been so focused on rage and harm, so lost in violence, that I've forgotten how to *be*.

"You okay?"

"I don't know," she answers honestly. "It's not a good thing if my dad is here, Knives. He isn't here to talk about God."

"I know." I wrap my arms around her and pull her close, kissing her forehead as if I do it every day. The other day, I wanted to tape her mouth shut, and now the thought of silence brings pressure to my chest.

But if Preacher Man wants to talk about God, I'll make sure that before he leaves Vegas, he gets a one on one meeting with the man upstairs.

No one is going to take what's mine.

And if they do, it's nothing a ninja star to the throat can't fix.

CHAPTER TEN

Mary

"Tell me everything, start to finish. I don't want you to leave anything out. Mary, sit down, please."

My ass hits the seat so hard, I slide backward. I would have hit the wall if Knives' arm didn't stop me. Reaper makes me nervous. He always has. He can be the reason why I stay or go. He holds the power.

Power can be a scary thing when it is in the wrong hands.

"You're okay, Mary. No one is in trouble. I need details before we go downstairs."

"Down..."

"Don't worry; you don't have to go and see what is about to be done—"

"—I know that Knives, but I can handle it," I snap.

"I didn't say you couldn't," he defends himself, digging his fingers into the table.

"I'm sorry. I'm stressed out. I shouldn't take it out on you. I don't want us to fight." I find his hand and grab onto it.

"Aw, you two kissed and made up. I knew that would happen after what happened at Christmas. Bullseye and Tank owe me fifty bucks."

"You've been betting on us?" Knives pulls out a ninja star and slams it into the table. I think he is about to throw one at Reaper he is so mad. "No one could have told me what was happening between us? I figured she was just a pain in my ass—"

"—Hey," I say, pretending to take offense. He's right. And for all I know, he is still going to be a pain in my ass.

"You know I'm right," he says, tugging the star from the table.

"We figured you two would figure it out. Glad you did, I'm a hundred bucks richer." Reaper leans back in his chair and lays his hands on the armrest. "Catch me up. What the fuck happened?"

"Well…" Knives starts. "I went to go pick up Hellraiser here from lock up—"

"—After you left me there for two days!"

"Anyway," he drawls. "We were on our way back when I tried to teach her a lesson about speeding…"

"Nearly killing me."

"Did you die?" he grins.

"Might as well have," I huff, crossing my arms.

"I pulled over, and we fought…"

"You yelled at me, and then you flung a ninja star at me."

"Semantics," he says.

"Semantics!" I nearly come out of the chair I'm sitting in and strangle him.

"She wasn't listening."

"Oh, you want to talk about listening. He hit the gas tank to the bike with the star, trying to prove a point, and guess what? A man tossed a cigarette out the window."

"And you wouldn't move," Knives drones, slamming his head against the table.

"Yeah, keep doing that. Maybe it will knock some sense into your head."

"Like how you would have been knocked on your ass if I wouldn't have gotten you away from the explosion," Knives counters. "You were kicking fucking rocks."

"Pretending they were your head at the time."

Knives growls at me, and if it were possible, I know steam would be rising from his body with how angry he is getting. He flips the star over his knuckles, something he does when he has something on his mind.

"And the tornado happened," he grits out. "We had to hightail it out of there. I carried her because her shoes were on fire. We found the barn. Maximo came into the barn a while later, early morning, I guess. We were waiting out the storm, and that's when her dad came in."

Reaper is rubbing his temples and taking deep breaths. "You two are going to give me an aneurysm with your bickering. So much damn bickering."

"Sorry," Knives says at the same time I do. "I guess there are a few things that won't change."

The words cut deeper than they are supposed to. I set my jaw, reminding myself that this is why I didn't take it further with him in the barn. "My dad came in next and shot Maximo. I didn't hear much. Something about a woman named Natalia. My dad was looking for me."

"Do you want to go back with him—"

"No!" Knives throws both of the stars against the wall, then slams his fist on the table. "She cannot go back with him."

"That isn't up to you, Knives."

"The hell it isn't," he sneers at his Prez, and then realizes his mistake when Reaper stands tall.

"Watch yourself. You don't control her. Sit your fucking ass down before I tie you up next to Maximo."

Knives lowers himself into the chair, then grabs mine and rolls it closer to him. His hand falls on my knee, his fingers playing with the frayed hole in my jeans. "Sorry, Prez. She can't go back."

"He's right, Reaper. Please, the last thing I ever want to do is go back home. My dad isn't who he says he is, and I think Maximo knows more."

"Why don't you want to go home?"

"Prez—"

Reaper lifts his hand in the air, silencing Knives on the spot. "I won't ask again."

"Um…" the table blurs as I stare at it, and I realize I'm on the verge of tears. I don't want to say this again. Knives' hand finds mine, and he locks us together by intertwining our fingers.

His hold on me grounds me.

"He molested her for twelve years, Prez. He isn't a man of God," Knives speaks for me, and I'm relieved just as much as I am disappointed that I couldn't find the strength to say it to a man that wants to help. When I talk to Knives, it's easy.

Anyone else, I want my secrets to stay my own.

"Is that right?"

I can see Reaper's fingers folding around the gavel and the bone creaks.

"I think we need to go see what Maximo wants. We will find your dad and take care of him, then figure out what the hell Moretti's daughter has to do with this too."

Take care of.

I'm not stupid. I know exactly what that means.

And I don't care.

"I won't let him take her, Prez. No way in hell."

"I'm sorry," I say to Reaper. I stare at the stone-cold expression masking his face. He looks so mad, and this time, I can't stop the tears falling onto the table. "I didn't want to bring you trouble. I don't know how he found me. I thought I got away when I ran—" I gasp and zip my lips shut. I have never, ever been that close to saying those words.

A chair creaks when Knives leans forward. He spins my chair, and his eyes analyze me, confused, but then his brows do a little jiggle as they reach his hairline, and the blue irises become even brighter. It's like a light bulb turned on in his head as he stared at me.

"You ran away," Knives says in horror. "And you ran right to them, didn't you? You wanted to be with the Atlantic City chapter. They didn't steal you, no one sold you, no one trafficked you, you went to them willingly."

Words catch in my throat, and shame crawls up my neck. I trace the groove in the table with my finger and try to think of an excuse, a lie, something that didn't make the truth sound so bad, but nothing came to mind.

"Yes."

"Why? Why would you do that? Out of all places, you could have picked to save yourself, and you picked them? It was as if you were asking to die."

Reaper clears his throat when the awkward tension heightens.

"You...you went there to die?" Knives whispers in realization. "You knew exactly what you were doing when you ran away."

"I couldn't do it myself," I admit. I rub my palms on my thighs when they start to sweat. "I wanted to die, but I knew I needed someone else to do it."

Knives stands, picks up the chair, and with an agonizing cry, he throws it over the table. It crashes against the wall, and I jump, closing my eyes as the chair falls to the ground. "How could you do that?" he yells at me. "How could you give up on yourself? How could you?"

"Knives, that's enough," Reaper says.

"No. It isn't. It's far from being enough. How could you do that? What about me? You were just... you were going to leave me? You would have left me. Everyone always fucking leaves," he continues to scream at the top of his lungs, which starts to gather a crowd outside. "You would have chosen to give up on me."

"I didn't even know you," I say to him. "All I knew was what I felt, and after what my dad did, I heard about the Atlantic City chapter, and I knew that life had to be better, and if I died, I died," I shrug.

"Death. Is. Not. That. Simple," he bites out each word and pulls his ninja stars free. "Death leaves behind everyone that loves you."

"Don't you get it, Knives?" I asks. "No one loved me."

He hangs his head, flipping the ninja star over his knuckles as he thinks. Bullseye comes into the room and tries to guide Knives out of the room, but Knives pushes him away.

Knives throws his star, and it whooshes by me, landing so hard against the wall, it disappears into the crack. "I would have missed out on you," he says, patting his chest. "I never want to miss out on anything again. I've lost, and I've lost, and damn it, Mary, I would have missed you if I never met you." Knives starts to walk out the door and slams into Bullseye's shoulder. "Get out of my way."

The guys part to let Knives through, and I want to go after him, but the stomps of his feet going down the stairs tell me he does not want to be bothered since Maximo is down there.

"I didn't know," I sob, whipping my head to Reaper. "I didn't know about him. I just... I felt useless after what my father did to me and... I wouldn't do it now. I'm sorry. I didn't mean to bring you trouble. It's always on your doorstep. It's the last thing I wanted." I bury my face in my hands and sob. Knives' heartbroken face is all I see.

I would have missed you if I never met you.

The words play on repeat in my mind, dissecting what he meant and didn't mean. I need to know more, but I decide to give him space instead.

"Listen, I've known Knives for a long time. He doesn't handle emotion well. He's had a lot happen, and he tends to put his feelings in a box and shove them away.

You kind of open that box for him. He hasn't felt in a long time; let him have his space." Reaper pushes on the table to help him stand, and he gives my shoulder a comforting squeeze as he walks behind me to make his way out.

"Yeah, okay," I nod, staring at the ninja star embedded in the wall. I wipe the tears and decide to sit in the room alone to gather my thoughts.

This church is so much better than the other kind. Truth is spoken here, love is here, pain is here.

The Ruthless Kings are a religion.

Or at least, they have the qualities that religion is made up of. The right qualities.

Like my father, a lot of people use religion to fuel their hate.

After everything that has happened, I don't know what I believe in. I find it hard to believe that my path in life has always been set in stone to lead me here.

"You okay?" a soft voice comes from the doorway, and Reaper's sister Delilah is standing there, tapping on the trim with her knuckles. She surprised everyone when she showed up a few weeks ago. They look so much alike, but it is obvious Reaper is older.

"I don't know."

"Been there," she sighs, slinking into the room. She's so small, like if a stiff breeze blows, she'll float away. Her dirty blonde hair is in a Dutch braid hanging over her shoulder. We don't know much about her. Her stories are hers to tell when she's ready, which I can relate to. Everyone knows my truth now, and I don't want to see how they will look at me now.

"Everything will be okay. It might not seem like it now, but it will be. Knives cares about you. That's been obvious since I've been here, and I'm sure it's been obvious before that too."

"We bicker a lot. I don't know. Maybe it's just sex." The words don't sound right as they leave my mouth. They leave a bad taste, because I know it isn't just sex. It's more.

"Maybe you're bickering to stop what you really want to do. Maybe you're bickering because that's what you two have been doing for so long, you don't know how else to be. It takes time to learn. Or maybe it is sex. Would that be so bad?"

My body turns to fire when I think about what happened in the barn. Sex with Knives wouldn't be bad; it would be out of this world.

And it could never be just sex, because I know I'd fall in love with him if I'm not already there.

Maybe that's why we fight

It's because we might love each other after all.

Except he doesn't want love. And I don't know how to love.

CHAPTER ELEVEN

Knives

"Tell me!" I swing the star and cut a gash on Maximo's cheek. I'm fucking pissed off. Ever since Mary told me the truth, I've had this burning in my veins to kill someone. I need to inflict pain. I need to figure out where her father is so I can throw a dozen stars into his body.

Maximo groans in pain, but not once has he tried to beg for his life or pull on the straps in the chair. It's like he has given up. "I swear," his Italian accent slurs. "I swear, I don't know much. Preacher St. James isn't the kind of man that drops by for a visit. I've never met him before tonight."

"It sure seemed like you knew each other," I spit, wondering why we are prolonging this mother fucker's death.

"I say you let me slice his tongue out and feed it to Happy," Tongue says from the corner. "I want payback for what you did. You touched Daphne!" Tongue unsheathes his knife, and Reaper blocks him from trying to come closer.

"This is bigger than you. Stand down," Reaper orders, and Tongue blows out a breath through his nose. He's barely hanging on to his restraint, and he starts to pace, never taking his eyes off Maximo.

Reaper sighs and stretches his arms before coming over and pressing his finger in one of the gunshot wounds on Maximo's shoulder. "I suggest you tell us everything there is to know about this Preacher Man and why he wants Mary."

Maximo's entire body trembles from the pain Reaper is inflicting by digging his finger inside the wound. "It has everything to do with Natalia. I swear, I'm not trying to get involved in his plan. He wanted information. His people came to the casino. They asked questions. I said I hadn't seen Mary, but then Natalia was gone, and he sent me a picture of her. It isn't a prostitution ring. It's an auction. I would do anything for my niece, and I'm not about to let her get sold to some fucking asshole! So if it means throwing Daphne or Mary under the bus for my own flesh and blood, then I will!"

I throw a ninja star at him, and it lands between his ribs. He tosses his head back, gritting his teeth through the pain. "You act like you wouldn't do the same," he says, spittle flying from his mouth. The veins in his neck jump as he gathers himself. "I know all of you, and there isn't anything you wouldn't do for one another."

He has me there. I'd trade Natalia for Mary in a heartbeat.

"How did his men find you? How did he know to come here?" Reaper digs his index finger in the bullet wound again, and Maximo shouts, tugging on the straps at last.

I pluck a freshly made star from its packaging and roll it over my knuckles. It's one of the reasons why I'm so scarred along my hands. It took a lot of practice to throw, catch, and play with them like I do, and I messed up.

A lot.

And now I'm a fucking pro, and it all started with my first one made of knives.

"I don't know, Reaper. I swear I don't know."

"That isn't good enough," Prez says.

"It's all I've got. Natalia is all I have. My brother, he doesn't even know me. I can't let his daughter disappear. You've met her, Reaper. This is Natalia."

So Preacher Man auctions women off. I guess praying doesn't pay the bills. My stomach rolls when I think of Mary and what her father did to her. Was he grooming her for future auctions? Or was she his own deviant secret that he always wanted to keep?

For the hell of it, I throw another star, and it lands right under the one lodged in his ribs. Fuck, that feels good. I roll my shoulders, then wipe the sweat off my mouth and forehead. "He's here, though. In Vegas? For how long?"

"Until he gets Mary." Maximo's normally perfectly styled hair is messy, dripping with sweat. His shoulder rises as he wheezes. There is no doubt he is in pain.

I grip his jaw and squeeze as hard as I can, wishing I could break every bone in his fucking body. "There is no way he is getting her. You hear me? Sorry to disappoint you."

"What did Daphne have to do with it?"

"He said he wanted a brunette. Daphne was perfect—" a blood-curling scream fills the room and leaves the open abyss of his mouth.

Tongue has cut three fingers from Maximo's hand. He stares at them in disgust as he examines them and plucks the gold ring off the pinky that's still twitching. Damn, Tongue moved quickly. I didn't even see him bring down his knife across Maximo's hand.

Reaper doesn't reprimand him because, at the end of the day, you fuck us, you get fucked in return. An eye for an eye.

"I'm feeding these to Happy. No way in hell you're getting these back. Be glad you have your tongue." With that, Tongue scoops up the fingers and leaves the room, kicking the door open with his foot. It slams against the wall, and in his departure, he didn't close it.

And Moretti steps inside.

"What are you doing to my brother?" Moretti asks, his accent just as thick as his brother's. Something about him feels familiar like he is in business mode. "I suggest you stop."

"Why do you care?" Maximo heaves, blood dripping onto the floor from where his fingers used to be. "You don't remember me anyway."

Moretti comes out of the dark, and the burns on his arm aren't as bad as I thought they were going to be. "But I feel it. What did you do?"

"I betrayed them, for good reason, just believe me. Okay? Fuck! He took my fingers. That crazy bastard!" Maximo tries to get out of the restraints again, but it's pointless. He is at our mercy until we say otherwise.

"Why?" Moretti presses. "Why would you do that to them?"

Bullseye interrupts by throwing a dart, and it lands right in the muscle of Maximo's calf. Everyone turns to him when Maximo curses. The dart isn't as bad as getting your fingers cut off, but I'm sure it's uncomfortable. "Oops," Bullseye says, shrugging his shoulders. "My fingers slipped."

Moretti pulls out a gun and aims it at Bullseye's head.

The only sound in the room is the drip of blood coming from Maximo's hand.

"I'd think twice if I were you," Tool growls, pressing his screwdriver against Moretti's neck.

"I'd get a bullet between his eyes before you had that shoved in my throat."

I reach around and pull out a new gun, aiming it at Moretti's head. I cock it, and the click of the bullet sliding into place always gives me the same feeling a ninja star does.

Almost.

"Mine's bigger," I say with a smirk, noticing the small handgun he has. Mine will blow his head off and paint the fucking walls with his brains.

"Drop it," I say to him, and when he doesn't listen, I move the aim from him to Maximo. "I said drop it, Moretti. You know we aren't afraid to make you both gator food."

"What did you do, Maximo?" Moretti has a desperate edge to his voice. "What did you do?"

"It's Natalia. Your daughter. She's been taken as collateral."

Moretti drops the gun and backtracks. "No," he says, shaking his head. "No! Not Natalia. Why? For what? Give the man whatever he fucking wants!"

"He can't." I lower my gun next, pointing it directly to the floor. "What her captor wants is something he will never have again." If he is in Vegas, I'm going to search every hotel, every corner, every house, apartment, shack, and whatever else I can find. I'll look under every rock, look in every hole in the ground, have Badge look into his credit cards, his life, and I'll fucking ruin him.

"But Natalia—" Moretti asks, rubbing the middle of his chest.

"I'm sorry, Moretti. I can't risk Mary for you. I won't. This your problem, you fucking figure it out." I step forward and yank the five stars out of Maximo's body. I have no idea what to do with him. If this had been anyone else, he would be dead. I almost don't understand why we don't kill him. Sure, we have a working relationship, but he ruined that when this shit happened.

I believe that Maximo doesn't have all the answers that I'm looking for. For instance, how did Mary's father find her? Why did they go to Maximo? And how the hell can I make sure they never come here again? I want answers. Maybe Mary has them, by some off chance.

"I'm sorry," Maximo whispers. "I was only doing what I needed to do for my family."

I get that. I've done a lot for my family, been through a lot, seen a lot, and I think that's why I'm so mad. In a sense, I thought Maximo and Moretti were a part of this fucked up family. I thought we could count on them.

"Why didn't you come to us, Maximo?"

"Because he asked me not to," he says.

Reaper, Tool, Bullseye, and I all share a look. "So he knows about us?" I ask, the hairs on the back of my neck standing up.

Maximo closes his eyes, sweat dripping down his temple, and there is a smear of blood on his lip from when I punched him in the face about twenty times.

The man has taken his beating like a champ, I'll give him that.

"A lot of bad men know about you. How can you be surprised?" he mumbles through a wince as he tries to readjust himself to get comfortable.

Yeah, that's not happening.

"How can a Preacher know so much about us?" Bullseye asks, plucking his dart from Maximo's leg, which earns a sudden pained shout. Bullseye lifts the dart and clicks his tongue when he sees a chunk of flesh on the fingers of the dart. "It hurts more coming out. I should have warned you."

Maximo doesn't miss the sarcasm dripping in Bullseye's voice and curls his lip to show his teeth that are glistening with blood.

Thanks to me.

"Maybe he didn't know about Vegas, but he knew about Atlantic City," I say as information starts clicking into place.

How did Mary know about the Atlantic City chapter? Maybe her father knew what happened, and he didn't care, and now that he wants her back, he has gone and examined all resources—including other chapters.

Which led him here.

Reaper's phone rings, and when he pulls it out of his pocket, he sighs. "It's Seer."

And I bet he saw everything the day he fucking called me. All of this could have been avoided.

Reaper slides his finger across the touchscreen. "You're on speaker, Seer."

Tool digs his screwdriver into Moretti's neck but doesn't break skin before tucking the Phillip's head behind his ear. It clearly was a warning not to make any sudden movements.

Seer's cajun accent fills the room, and I smile, forgetting how much I enjoy listening to him. "Mon Amie, it's about time one of ya'll answer my fucking phone calls. I'm going to assume now isn't the best time considering Maximo is tied to a chair, three fingers less. Hi, Maximo," Seer greets.

Maximo stays quiet.

"You have any new information now that we are listening?" I ask, needing every detail I can to keep Mary safe.

"Oui. You've got the fight of your life ahead of ya.' I wish I had better—" but it sounds like betta' coming from Seer "—news. But the man you're at war with, he ain't a good man. A son of God, he is not, more like the Devil's spawn. His Preachin' is a set-up, a cover. He's in Vegas. A tall hotel."

"They are all tall, Seer," Reaper sounds exasperated.

"Oui, but this one has an M on it."

"That's better detail, thank you. That it, Seer?" Reaper rubs his eyes, no doubt exhausted and annoyed that all this shit keeps happening.

"Knives, I know ya' ain't one to want to know what happens with your future. It's why you kept breaking ya phone when I called."

Tattletale.

"Ya gonna lose Mary, Knives."

Everyone sucks in a breath, even Maximo, but that's probably because he can't breathe.

And I can't either. I shake my head, dropping the stars in my hand, and they clatter against the floor. The rings of them trying to fall to their sides goes on and on; they twirl, like a penny spinning until it finally loses momentum.

"No," I mutter. "No. I just got her, Seer. I just realized—" I rub the ache in my heart, the one I've felt twice before when I've lost someone I've loved. It's why I'm so closed off from everyone and everything. It hurts too damn bad to feel anything other than what I need to be for the club. "No. I can't lose her too, Seer. Your visions, you said they can change, right? They change. They aren't set in stone."

"Most of the time, they are."

"Not this time. I've waited too long. I've lost too much. I won't lose her too. You hear me, you sight-seeing sonofabitch! She's mine. I finally have something that's fucking mine, and none of you fucking assholes are going to take her from me. I don't care what I have to do, where I have to go, she'll be safe."

"That's not how it works, Knives, and ya know it," he says sadly. "I'm sorry, Knives."

"When?" I place my hand on my hips and tilt my head up, staring at the ceiling as if it has all the answers, but it clearly doesn't. Only Seer does.

"Two weeks from today."

"What happens?"

"Ya really want to know?"

"Yes." Because I'll do everything in my power to save her.

"She saves you." Seer takes that moment to hang up the phone, leaving me staring at a blank screen and a dial tone.

She saves me.

I now understand why I didn't want to talk to him, because nothing he has to say to us is a good thing. I'm sick of it. I'm sick of always fucking fighting. I'm getting tired. How much bullshit can a club take before it falls apart?

"Knives—" Reaper starts to say, but before he can get a word out, I turn on my heel and walk out the door.

I need to clear my head. I need to go for a ride; only I don't have a fucking bike because it exploded.

I have to be cursed. The universe loves to take everything from me. Why not just kill me? Why torture me consistently? I slam the door behind me and run up the steps, getting away from Maximo, Moretti, and Reaper. I'm getting away from the pain they want to inflict.

I'm the one that came out inflicted. My heart is in tattered pieces. When I get to the top of the stairs, I lean against the door and take a minute to myself. I feel dizzy. Memories bombard me: the sound of metal crunching, bullets flying, blood, fear. Before I know it, I'm that little kid again, wondering how I'm going to make it through life without my person at my side.

I'm not meant to be with someone.

I'm meant to be alone.

I'm always alone.

CHAPTER TWELVE

Mary

I CREEP OUT OF MY BEDROOM IN THE CORNER OF THE CLUBHOUSE. IT'S IN THE BACK. A newly renovated room near the gym. I think Reaper wanted to give me space from the guys, but I want to be close to everyone else. As much as I wanted my father to leave me alone, I hate being alone. Sometimes, he would sneak into my room and hold me, and I was so afraid; I didn't want his touch, but I wanted the company.

How sick is that?

It's why I'm on the couch right now, sleeping with Tyrant at my feet and Chaos by my head. Tyrant is Juliette's dog, and Chaos is Skirt's. I fell asleep watching reruns of Friends, but the sound of the front door opening and closing has me stirring. I glance out the window right as the motion light comes on outside, and that's when I see Knives. He is leaning against the porch rail, the puffs of breath fogging in front of him as he breathes in the cold air, and he hangs his head.

Something is wrong.

I rub my eyes and get up. The dogs groan, not too happy to be jostled and roll to their backs at the same time. The only dog missing is Lady. She's been hanging on to life, and the vet doesn't understand why. It's killing Poodle. He barely leaves his room so he can be with her. It's sad.

"Good boys," I say to them, patting their heads, so they know they are loved. I wrap the fluffy blanket around me and make my way to the front door. I open it and carefully close it behind me.

Knives hears the door click and turns around. My breath catches from how beautiful he is. The scalding blue eyes sear a brand on my heart in the shape of his name. The mug he has in his hand drops to his crotch to cover the bulge, and that's when I notice he is wearing a black onesie.

That hugs everything.

Yeah, the mug doesn't hide a thing. And as funny as it should be that this badass biker is in a onesie, I find myself wishing I could unclasp the white buttons to reveal the hair on this chest.

"I... uh... it's laundry day. This is what I wear when I need to wash clothes," he says, bringing his fist to his mouth as he coughs. "No one usually sees me in this."

"I like it," I smile, keeping my hand clutched on the blanket. My feet are freezing, and the deck is just as cold as the air. I sit down in a rocking chair, and he forgets that he is covering his bulge when he brings his mug to his lips, taking a long sip.

My eyes drop to his crotch and widen. It's impressive. I can see the outline of his piercings too.

"Knives—"

"—No, let me." He sets his cup down on the rail and kneels. It's funny to see him in something other than his cut and jeans, but something about this onesie brings out his vulnerable side that he keeps hidden away. Like he is dying to feel comfort, so he does this because no one can see it.

He thinks no one can see him, but I do. I see him.

I see right through him.

Knives isn't made of ninja stars and blood. He's made of onesies and aches to feel the warmth of being secure.

I won't ever say it out loud, but I'll be his onesie if he allows me to be.

"I can't... I don't know how to do this." There is a pain in his eyes, the same pain that was in them when he threw the chair. "I don't do this. And Seer..."

"What?"

"Nothing," he says, but I know it's something. He is hiding it from me. Seer told him something that spooked him.

"Tell me."

He takes my face in his hands and shakes his head. "No. There isn't a time that's more important than right now, and I want to enjoy every moment I have with you." He presses his lips to mine, soft, slow, and deliberate. He takes his time prying my mouth open to make room for his tongue. I deepen the kiss and lean forward, wrapping my arms around his back and pulling him into the warmth of my blanket.

The cold hasn't affected him. His skin is warm, but his tongue is cold. I don't know how long we sit there and kiss, but the crickets are in the background, and heat lightning flashes across the sky.

I'm starting to wonder if Knives is the reason why I didn't die. There were so many chances for me, but none ever came, no matter how hard I tried.

And he was there every time.

At first, I thought he was a nuisance, but he was the saving grace I had no idea I needed.

"I want you," he says against my lips, not breaking the kiss or breaking us apart. "I want all of you." He slides his hand down my jaw, caresses the curve of my neck, and lays his hand in the middle of my chest. "I've never had it before."

I've never freely given it before.

Not that I ever planned on giving it to him. Knives kind of wiggled his way in and stole it without me noticing. He's had my heart for a while now, and I've fought him to get it back; I just didn't know what I was fighting so hard for until now.

The heart is fickle.

It breaks, it mends, but it is never the same after being welded together.

I don't want to have to weld myself together. I don't want Knives to wreck me. I don't have the energy to pick myself up after that.

And I don't think he does either.

"Take me then," I say.

We pull away from each other, but not by much, just so we can look each other in the eyes. I could look at his eyes forever and not once get tired of their depths. He holds so much behind those blue prisons. I used to think he was cold, but really, he is an inmate in his own body, and he is begging to be released.

He lifts me up into his arms, the blanket dragging along the porch, and he takes the steps carefully. I don't know where we are going, but I trust him. He walks around the building and heads toward the back entrance to the gym. I almost want to stay outside, but we might get caught, and I don't want anyone seeing us.

"What's wrong? Change your mind?" he asks.

"Not when it comes to you." I drag my finger through his beard. It's thick and coarse, just like the rest of the fur on his body. "I just wish we could be outside for our first time. I loved being alone with you in the barn."

He nuzzles my cheek with his, and his breath ghosts over the shell of my ear. "I did too." He lifts up and stares out toward the back of the property. "I'll make sure to build us our own barn."

"You'd do that for me?"

"I'd give my life for you, Hellraiser. You want the barn? I'll bring it here. You want the stars? I'll fucking bottle them for you. You want the moon? I'll find a way to give it to you. I'll find a way to give you everything. I hate that we didn't realize what we felt for one another sooner. I lost out on so much time. I'm afraid I won't be able to give you all the things you deserve."

"Knives, I'm right here. I'm not going anywhere anytime soon."

The look in his eyes tells me he doesn't believe me. I'm not sure what has him spooked, but I'm sure it has something to do with Seer. I'm not going to ask because I don't want to know. I just want to be with Knives.

"Take me to bed," I say, tugging on his beard while snapping my fingers.

He smirks and opens the door. When it is cracked, he bumps it open with his hip so we can fit through. "So fucking sassy. You and that mouth."

"What are you going to do about it?"

"Tape it shut."

"I'd like to see you try." I lift my chin in a challenge, and when he steps foot on the gym floor, his boots echo.

That's another thing I love about him wearing this onesie. He has his damn boots on, and the laces are untied.

He's a mess, and he only lets it show through at moments like this.

Onesies and unlaced boots

My new favorite combination.

He stops in the middle of the gym and sits me down. He takes the blanket from me and lays it in the middle, fluffing it, so it's an even square along the slick floor. "Stay here. I'll be back." He brings his lips to the top of my head, and his boots scuff with every step he takes. He presses a few buttons, and that's when the roof opens.

I gasp. I had no idea it could do that. The stars are out by the millions, surrounded by black and blue hues.

"I know it isn't the barn, and I know I didn't bottle them, but maybe this can be a close second."

"It's perfect. Come here. Come look at the stars with me," I say, holding out my hand, telling him silently to come back to me.

His boots scuff again as he crosses the floor. When he gets to the blanket, he takes off his shoes and lays down. I nestle against his side, staring up at the vast sky that seems to hold more questions than answers.

"Seer told me you were going to die in two weeks. You die saving me, Mary. I can't... I can't lose you too."

I roll over on top of him, wishing he hadn't told me, but I'm not mad. I push my hair out of my face and stroke his cheek. "I can't think of a better way to die than protecting the person I—" Am I about to say love? It's too soon for that.

Is it? How long have I really been in love with him and denied it, fought it? Too long, but I'm too afraid to admit it. "If that's what he saw—"

"Death really doesn't scare you?" he asks.

"No, but just because he saw it doesn't mean it will happen."

"He said one of us."

"Let's prove him wrong, Knives. We've fought for so long, and now we have something to fight for. Let's not stop fighting now."

"As long as I'm fighting for you and not with you, I'll be a happy man," he says, bringing his lips to mine, kissing me under the stars. He brought me the outdoors, just like he said he would. He might not have bottled the constellations or brought me the moon, but he brought me a memory that will last forever.

He whips my shirt over my head, and he unhooks my bra with a flick of his fingers, freeing my breasts. He never breaks the kiss, and when he tugs the straps off my arms, Knives gathers my hair and lays the thick strands over my chest to hide my tits.

Leaning back, he admires his masterpiece. "I've been wanting to see this dark hair covering your tits for so long. You're so fucking gorgeous, Mary." He tweaks my nipples, and I gasp. "But I want to see you like this completely naked." He smooths his hands down my body until his fingers hook in the waistband of my shorts and tugs them down to my knees, taking my panties with them.

Time stands still as I'm laid bare before him.

And I get lost in the silence as he becomes speechless, staring at me so hard it is like he is burning me into his memory. He fluffs my hair just right, covering my tits, and the ends of my hair stop at my hip. I love how he looks at me like I'm the only star he sees.

CHAPTER THIRTEEN
Knives

I don't know how she can be so calm about death. I know I've killed dozens of people, but when death is close to home, it scares the hell out of me. When she said we had to keep fighting, I knew she was right.

No matter what, Seer's vision cannot come true.

I'll fight, tooth and nail, skin and bone, blood and guts, until I've given all of me to make sure she has breath in her lungs. I won't stay silent and watch her die. I won't be the guy on the outside looking in and watch his world pass him by.

She looks fucking hot with her hair cascading over her breasts. It's better than all the dreams I've ever had of her. My cock is throbbing, pulling against the thin material of my onesie. I should be embarrassed for her to see me like this, but for some odd reason, she likes it. She sits up, her long luscious strands of hair still covering her round tits, and her pink beads poke through, hard and waiting to be plucked. Her hands skim down my arms, tracing the outline of my tattoos, pausing on the one that looks exactly like her.

She doesn't ask.

She doesn't need to.

Her nails tickle as she gently rakes them up my arms before coming to the middle of my chest. A shiver runs down me. She works with the buttons, unclasping them one by one. With every inch of skin exposed, she kisses my chest. She works her way down, her lips getting lower and lower until she's at the last button.

My hand moves on its own accord, taking one side of her hair and throwing it over her left shoulder. I want to see her. All of her. When her breast is exposed, I have to hold back a groan. Of course, they are fucking perfect. Round, perky, nipples that are red and remind me of those candy Jolly Ranchers I love so much.

Her skin is soft, creamy, and flawless. The light from the stars is so bright, and the half-crescent moon hanging in the sky shines, giving Mary an ethereal glow.

Reaper spent a shit ton of money on the retractable roof because Sarah mentioned something about stargazing with him, and of course, he went all out.

I'm glad I get to use it for my benefit.

She traces the ridges of my abdomen, lifting her lashes so her eyes meet mine. She's turned me into a goddamn sap just like the rest of the guys that are in love with their ol' ladies. Her hands grip the lapels of my onesie and slide them down my arms. The material hangs on my hips, and Mary kisses her way up my stomach, my muscles bunching from the softness of her lips.

When she's almost eye-level with me, she tilts her chin up, so our gazes catch. It has me sucking in a stunned breath. She is so gorgeous.

I've only ever fucked before. It was only ever about getting in and out, a temporary relief for the permanent pain I felt, but I don't want that with Mary.

She's the permanent fix.

And I'll fight like hell to make sure this love isn't temporary. I won't let it die in two weeks. I finally have my chance at happiness. I'm no longer alone.

I grip her chin and bring my lips to hers. It's almost painful kissing someone so damn perfect because, at any moment, I know that I might not be able to feel perfection again. Our kiss is lazy and languid. We take our time exploring each other's mouths. Our tongues fight for dominance, which has me smiling against her mouth. I don't expect anything less from her.

My cock throbs painfully, keenly aware of what is about to happen. I push her down against the blanket, never once breaking the kiss. She pushes the onesie down my legs, and my cock slaps against her leg, heavy and dripping with precum.

"Do you have a condom?" she asks, making every fucking ounce of lust I'm feeling screech to a halt.

"Where would I put a condom? In my onesie pocket? I didn't know this was going to happen."

"You should always be prepared."

I pin her against the floor, the bickering turning me on more than it should, and I decide a condom would have never mattered. "I'm not fucking you with a condom, Mary. We've had a barrier between us for far too fucking long, and I'm not about to feel this cunt for the first time with latex. I'm going to own you, raw. And you know what you're going to do?" I press my hand between her legs and roll my thumb over her clit. I can't wait to bury my face between her legs.

"What?" She has a hard, defiant glint in her eyes as she meets my challenge.

"You're going to lay back and get the fuck over it." I plunge three fingers inside her channel, not bothering to stretch her or get her used to me.

She'll never be used to me.

And no amount of prep will change that.

Her nails dig in my shoulders, and she whimpers, relenting to me, giving me control. Fucking finally. Is that all it takes to get her to listen to me?

What a hardship.

"You're so tight, Hellraiser. I can't wait to feel you wrapped around my cock," I say, watching her tits bounce, and I continue to finger fuck her.

Her eyes squeeze shut as if she's in pain, and I stop. "Are you okay?" I should have thought about how sex with me would feel for her. I'll be the first after her father. "We don't have to—"

"—No, I want you so much. You feel so good. I've never felt so good before. Don't stop."

I pull my fingers out of her warmth and bring them to my mouth, licking the sweet nectar. I nearly fall on my ass when her hand wraps around me, giving me a tight pump. I groan, closing my eyes as she has her way with me. Her fingers slide up and down the Jacob's Ladder, and I'm trembling with how good it feels. Not a lot of women play with the piercings, which is a shame. The bars heighten the sensitivity. I get they can be intimidating, but Mary doesn't fucking hesitate. She tugs on the hoops, and the cry that leaves my mouth bounces off the gym walls, singing my pleasure back to me.

"Did this hurt?" she asks, rubbing me with one hand while pulling on the hoops with the other.

I can barely breathe. I think I could come just like this. "Yes," I answer.

"Do you like pain?"

"Yes."

She twists the hoops, and the skin screams for her to stop, but my balls pull tight. I grip her shoulder and hold my orgasm back. I don't want to come. Not yet.

"Do you think you deserve it?"

"Yes," I answer honestly, and her hand leaves my cock. "What? No, come back. Keep doing that." I grab her hand, but she yanks it away, and right as I look down, she's kissing the head, dipping her tongue through the hoops. "Oh, fuck." My head falls back onto my shoulders, and I stare at the starry night, enjoying her soft kissing on each bar she finds.

"You don't deserve pain, Knives." Her words are soft puffs of air that dance over the sensitive flesh. "If you want pain because you like it, that's one thing, but I won't give you pain because you think you deserve it. That's not pleasure, Knives. That's torture. I don't want to torture you."

"You are. Right now, you're torturing the hell outta me—" my words are cut short when she sucks the tip into her mouth, lapping her tongue along the slit. "Oh, fuck. Sweetheart, you feel so goddamn good." She's trepidatious as she takes me to the back of her throat. It's obvious she's never done this before, and hell, if that doesn't have me wanting to spill down her throat and watch my cum drip from her lips.

She gags, chokes, but them hums, then grips my ass to pull me closer. Her nose is buried in my trimmed patch of hair as she sucks me, her tongue licking and playing with the piercings like she's experimenting with a lollipop.

I'll be her goddamn sucker anytime she wants. "Fuck, Hellraiser. Is this what I've been missing out on this entire time? I thought the only thing this mouth could do was bitch." I bury a hand in her hair and close my eyes, enjoying the hot mouth taking me better than anyone ever has before.

She bites down in response to my words, and I grunt, getting the picture that it is her way of telling me to shut up. "Do that again," I say, surprised that I liked getting my cock bit.

I can tell she's confused by the wrinkle appearing in her forehead, but she does it anyway, and the bars rub together from the pressure, then her tongue twirls around me, and I'm fucking lost. Tingles spread down my spine, and the threat of pouring down her throat is becoming a real possibility.

But I want to be inside her.

I pull out of her mouth and shove her to the ground, covering her lips with mine. Her mouth is red, swollen, and spit is everywhere. It's a sloppy kiss, but knowing her mouth is wet from sucking me has me manic.

I nudge her legs apart and settle between them, pressing my cock between her folds, I rock. She cries out as the piercings rub over her clit. I can't help the smirk that appears on my lips. As much as I want to be inside her, I want to feel the slickness of her lips hugging me while I bring her to orgasm fucking her clit.

"Knives. Oh my god." Her body jerks, and her hands fly above her head. It's like she doesn't know what to do with her body.

I glance down, watching the tip peek from between her sheath with every rock. I speed up, needing her to orgasm before I slide inside.

I'm not ashamed to admit this, but I'm not going to last long. I've never felt this intensity before with someone. It's always been about sex, never about anything else, and with Mary, it's everything else.

"Knives!" My name reverberates in the room. It's music to my ears to hear her voice crying out for me over and over again while she comes. Her back arches, her mouth falls open, and her legs shake around me as the hold she has around my hips weakens.

"Fucking finally," I growl, and this time when I rock back, I thrust inside. The balls from the piercings rub against her velvety walls, and I have to give myself a minute to calm down. If I move, I'm going to come.

And there is no fucking way in hell I'm going to have this end that quick. I want this moment to last all fucking night. Or for the next two weeks. If she's in bed with me for fourteen days, then nothing can happen to her, right? Just mind-blowing orgasms.

"Move," she begs, her fingers digging into the flesh of my ass.

"Not yet." I lower myself onto my elbows and steal another kiss.

"I said move, damn it."

"And I said no," I huff.

"I want to feel you."

"I'm going to come. Do you want that? I don't want this to end so damn fast, but you seem to have a negative effect on me!"

"Then fuck me through it!"

God, she really pisses me off. "You want to be fucked?" I flip her over onto her stomach and hold her head down. "Then I'll fuck you." I pull out and slam home. Her ass shakes from the constant pounding. "You want to feel me fill you up? You want me to lose control?"

"Yes! Fuck yes, I do," she moans, thrusting her ass back.

Her pretty puckered hole winks at me, and without a second thought, while I'm driving into her vise of a cunt, I stick my finger into my mouth. I let it go with a pop, rim her hole with my fingertip, and her hips stutter.

I'm not going to give her time to give me any more of her mouth. She's going to shut the fuck up for once in her life and take what I give her. I shove my index finger knuckle deep. "I'm going to take this ass too. Every fucking hole, Hellraiser. I'm going to stretch you out and ruin you for everyone else." Sweat drips into my eyes, and my hair falls over my forehead. I stare down at where we are connected and love how my dick is shining with her juices.

She rises up and hooks her arm around my neck. "You feel so good. I love your cock. I love the piercings," she gasps on a heavy breath.

She's out to kill me.

I spin her around, keeping us locked together, and bite her bottom lip. I'm fucking angry with how much I want her. I'm not close enough. This isn't enough. I growl as I let go, then, like a savage, seal our lips. I fall to my haunches, grip the meat of her ass, and use the new leverage to grind her against me.

She whimpers, and I moan; her sounds are a symphony playing down my throat. She groans with every rock, every thrust.

And I come.

My body becomes rigid, and I toss my head back and shout, relishing in every spurt coating her insides. She falls against me just as her inner muscles spasm, and her teeth lock onto my shoulder as she stifles her own cries while she orgasms.

I don't stop either.

I fuck her through it and hold onto her tightly, letting my forehead fall against her chest with every up and down motion of her pussy.

I can't lose this. I can't lose her.

CHAPTER FOURTEEN

Mary

I WAKE UP IN MY BED, AND IF IT WASN'T FOR THE SORENESS BETWEEN MY LEGS, I WOULD have thought last night was a dream. I can't remember how I got here, but I'm not going to question it because the night I had with Knives is something that can never be explained, just felt. The intensity we shared, the passion, the sweat…

I've never been so slick in my entire life

I yawn, stretching my arms over my head, and groan when certain spots on my body hit me with a pinch of pain. I'm definitely bruised.

It was worth it.

I sit up and notice I'm alone. His side of the bed is cold as I lay my hand against the pillow. He's been gone a while, then. I'm not too sure how I feel about that. Waking up alone after the night we shared, I don't want it to be devastating, but it is. Maybe I was just another girl to him, after all?

"So stupid." I fall backward and sink into the pad of my mattress. My eyes burn, and I press my palms against my eyes to hold back the tears. I should have known better. A biker like Knives doesn't do relationships. He has club whores and anyone he wants, really. Not that the club whores are something to be worried about right now, since none of them are around. It's been too dangerous, and they don't want to risk getting killed like their friends.

I thought they were my friends too, but the moment things got rough, they bolted, and I realized I'm nothing like that. Sure, I ran away after dealing with my dad, but that's different. I would never run away from my family. My *real* family. Whores aren't family, are they? That's why none of the guys ever touched me. I was more to them than that, and it makes me happy knowing I had a place to call home this entire time I was trying to find a home.

The only person that's been missing is Becks. She has been gone a while now, but at this point, I'm starting to wonder if she's ever coming back. She seems like the nomad type, not to stay in place for too long because she gets restless. I miss her, and I hope she's doing well since I haven't heard from her.

"Hey, what's wrong?"

I put my arm down from my eyes and gape at Knives, who is holding a tray of food. The smell of coffee and bacon has me sitting up, clutching the blanket to my chest. "I thought you left."

"I did leave," he says, tilting his head in confusion. "I wanted to make you breakfast. I can't say it will be good. There might be an eggshell in the eggs, but I tried."

I love him. He's so different from what I thought he was. "You didn't have to do that," I say, scooting over to make room for him on the bed.

"I wanted to," he says, placing the tray on my lap. "You deserve breakfast in bed." He pushes my hair off my shoulder, then tucks it behind my ear before tapping the tip of my nose with his finger.

"Well, if I eat an eggshell, I'm sure it will taste so good."

"Aw, I hope you choke on it."

I gasp, taking the fork and pretending to stab him in the arm. "Brat."

"I'm kidding. There is only one thing I want you to choke on, and it sure as hell isn't breakfast," he lowers his voice.

I shove his shoulder, and he slips off the bed, landing on the floor with a hard thump. "Oh my god, Knives. Are you okay?" I move the tray to the side and slip off the edge of the mattress. I land on his lap, straddling him, and lean down to give him a kiss. "I'm so sorry. I didn't mean to shove you off."

"Sure you didn't," he grunts, laying his tattooed hands on my hips.

"I really didn't. What can I do to make it up to you?"

He opens one eye, the intense color of ice freezing my veins as he deliberates. "Well," he starts to say, before rocking against my sore center. I moan suggestively when I feel his erection, right as my damn stomach grumbles.

"That's embarrassing. Way to ruin the moment, right?"

"No. My woman needs to be fed. I think we might have skipped dinner last night, but make no mistake, when you're done, I'm fucking you, Hellraiser."

I bite my lip, then slide off his lap and climb back on the bed, swaying my ass in the air to drive him crazy.

"Don't tempt me," he growls, slapping my ass to get me to sit down, but that only makes me hotter. "You're going to be the death of me. Eat your food." He picks up a piece of bacon and shoves it in my mouth. I moan in appreciation as the salt bursts over my tongue, along with a hint of maple.

"There you go again, making those fucking noises. Is the bacon really that good?" He takes a bite and nods. "Okay, it's debatable."

I laugh, scooping up a spoonful of eggs, and just swallow. I don't want to risk biting into an eggshell. If I do, I might not be able to eat the rest of my breakfast. We fall into a comfortable silence, eating our food, and enjoying small touches between each other. Every now and then, he will place his hand on my knee or feed me a grape, and those little gestures, the small ones that everyone overlooks, are everything to me.

A man like Knives doesn't give his touch away to anyone, not like this.

"When you said you thought I left, you really meant that you *thought I left*."

I take that moment to bite down on a damn eggshell. But I don't make a face, I don't gag, I hold my breath and swallow, because he took time out of his morning to make me food. I grab the coffee and sip, washing down the hard bits and pieces of the shell. I nod, then push the eggs around the plate. "I know, I shouldn't have, but I woke up, sore and happy, then I felt for you, and you weren't there."

He places two fingers under my chin and forces me to turn my head. "Listen to me," he says, his hair wet from a shower. He is out of his onesie now, dressed in faded blue jeans, a t-shirt, and his cut. "I'm not going anywhere. I need you to believe that." He slides his hand over mine, and I love the differences. My skin is naked compared to his. He has a large red flower on one hand; his knuckles are decorated in traditional stars and letters.

He's so different from me on the outside, but we are the same on the inside, and that's all that matters.

"You're used to a certain kind of woman, Knives," I tell him.

"No, I'm not. I'm not used to any kind of woman, because I never got to know a woman like I've gotten to know you over the last few months. No woman drives me crazy the way you do, and no woman turns me on like you do. No woman has ever brought me to my knees so fast. I'm not someone who gets scared, Mary, but what Seer said scared the hell out of me."

"Nothing is going to happen to me."

"Everything he said has come true so far."

"Remember what we said last night," I say. I want to change the subject. I don't want to talk about this anymore. If I die saving Knives, then I died for someone that matters. What better way is there to die? "How is Maximo?"

"He's still strapped to the chair. His brother, Moretti, is there too. Even if Moretti doesn't remember Maximo and his daughter, he says he remembers how he feels, so they are talking about Natalia."

"Is it really necessary to keep him down there? He is three fingers less," I point out. "And it isn't like he is truly the bad guy. He isn't my father. I feel like that's where the attention needs to be."

"He turned his back on the club. Reaper isn't sure what to do with him."

I hand him the tray, and Knives places the empty plate and tray on the dresser. "I know what to do with you," I say in a low purr, rubbing my hand over the bulge behind his zipper.

"Is that right?" His hands fall to my ass and grip the cheeks. "How are you feeling?"

"Sore," I whisper, licking up his neck. "But in the best way."

"You want me again? Is your pussy greedy for my cock, Hellraiser?"

My aching hole flutters with need, wanting nothing more than to be stretched by his cock. I want to feel the piercings rub against that spot inside me. I want to feel him pour inside me again. I rock my bare pussy against his jeans, wetting them with the liquid lust he causes to erupt from me.

"Fuck. This is going to be quick. I need you too fucking much," he says, dipping his hands between us to free himself. The heavy head slaps against my clit the moment he is free, and the hoops leave a slight sting behind. I toss my head back and moan and rub my slit over his flesh, similar to what he did to me last night.

I don't know what it is about it but feeling him against me like this turns me on so much that I know if we only did this, I could climax. "Oh, you feel so good, baby." I quicken my speed, chasing every spark that ignites through my body after his cock rubs over my clit.

"I need more. Fuck this," he growls, and when I'm about to slide down, he shoves himself inside me, pushing in to the hilt, sending an electric surge all the way up my entire body.

"Look at you," he admires me by sliding his hands over my breasts and stomach. Every scratch of his hands, every glide of his cock, every breath heating the skin of my neck from his lips, I fall.

I fall into him.

I fall in love with him.

I fall for him.

"I'm going to come, Hellraiser," he growls, fucking me so hard the bed slides across the floor and the mattress groans. "Come with me." His fingers twist and pluck my clit, electrifying me, and my arms spread out just as my back bows and my orgasm possesses me.

He groans deep in his throat, a sound of pure pleasure as he feels my release dripping down his shaft. In three more thrusts, he plants himself inside me, emptying his warmth as deep as biology allows him to go.

"Nothing feels better than you. You've fucked me up, Mary. You got me all tangled up in your web."

"I understand your demon dick now," I gasp, shoving my hair off my sweaty face as I fall onto the bed.

My body shakes as he laughs. "My what?"

"Your demon dick. 666. It possesses me," I gasp, swallowing to coat my dry throat.

His laugh his louder, shaking my breasts as he lays his head on my chest, his fingers digging into my sides. "Demon dick, huh? I've never heard it called that before."

"I thought you named it that because of the tattoo."

"I just wanted the tattoo, but now that I think about it, it makes sense, and you're inflating my ego, so please don't stop talking."

"Shut up."

"You shut up," he says with a smile, then starts tickling my sides. "You."

"No! No!" I scream, shouting with laughter as he tickles me from my armpits to my hips. His cock is still inside me, and every time I try to get away, he hardens again. "Oh my god, I give. I give."

"Tell me you love me, and I'll stop."

"Wh—" my words are broken as I come down from the tickle high. "What?"

"Tell me you love me, and I'll stop." His face gets serious, the fun expression is gone, and the serious mask falls over him. His blue eyes aren't as inviting. Like if he doesn't hear the answer he wants, he might kill me instead.

Loving him might kill me anyway.

"I love you," I say to him, pressing my hand to his cheek.

"Really? You aren't just saying that because I asked you to say it?"

"Well, yeah," I pluck a few hairs on his chest when the excitement falls from his face. "Hey, you know I do. I think I have for a long time. Why?"

"I've never been loved before, so I wanted to know if you did. I love you too, you know. And if you didn't, I'd make you love me."

"You wouldn't ever have to make me. I simply, just... do."

A knock comes from the door, ruining the sweet moment we are having. I was ready to jump on that demon dick again and go for another ride after he admitted he loved me.

"Go away!" Knives says, licking his lips as he pulls out of me, only to slide back in, which steals my ability to breathe.

"Knives, Mary, you're going to want to come out here."

Knives' head falls on my stomach and mutters something I can't understand.

"Slingshot, we will be out in a minute," I holler.

"Knives, you're going to want to load up," Slingshot warns, and that gets Knives' attention.

He lifts up and pulls out, grumbling in discontent, and if I'm not mistaken, whimpers when he stares at my pussy. "One of these days, we are going to stay in bed all day. I'm going to fuck this mouth—" he rubs his fingers over my lips, "—this pussy," he slaps between my legs and my legs tremble, "—and this ass." His finger rims the forbidden hole, teasing me. "I want to own every inch of you."

"You do, Knives. You do. More than anyone ever has."

He brings my knuckles to his mouth and gives me a kiss. "Come on, let's go see what is in store for us and why I need to pack heat."

"Oh, you're packing heat."

He swats my ass as I get up, and my cheeks hurt from grinning so much. He stands up and tucks himself in his jeans, careful as he zips. "Why don't you go without me? I'll catch up," I say, opening a drawer to pull out a simple yet sexy black pair of panties.

"You are not wearing those out there."

"I wouldn't just be wearing these," I say with a roll of my eyes. "I'll be wearing pants."

"Yes, but then I'd know you're wearing them, and then I won't be able to focus on being the big bad man they want me to be, because all I'll be able to think about is the sexy underwear you have on."

"You'll live."

He crosses his arms and watches me get dressed. His eyes stay heated as I slide on a pair of jeans, taking my sweet time, so I torture him. I throw on a shirt, then my leather jacket, put my hair up, and go brush my teeth. When I'm in the restroom, I spray on perfume and apply my red lipstick. I'm not sure what it is about it, but it makes me feel empowered.

I walk out of the bathroom, and Knives' fists clench. "You do this just to test me."

I rub a finger down his chest as I strut away from him and head toward the bedroom door. "I have no idea what you're talking about."

Oh, but I do.

I love testing him.

CHAPTER FIFTEEN
Knives

I stop by my bedroom and grab a few ninja stars per Slingshot's request. Mary is behind me, safe and alive, and it's hard not to think about what waits for us in 13 days. She's so nonchalant about it, and it irks me.

I don't care what we have to do. I don't care if I have to lock her in jail 13 days from now; she isn't going to be anywhere near me. I'll make damn sure of that. "You ready to go see what the fuss is about?" I ask her, noticing how I don't like that her leather jacket doesn't have my property patch on it

Holy shit.

The pain in my ass is the love of life.

Go fucking figure.

I want my name tattooed on her too. I want there to be no doubt who she belongs to. Everyone here knows, but everyone out there in the world doesn't. One look at the woman tattooed on my arm, and then one look at the woman by my side, makes it obvious I belong to her. I want it to be obvious that she belongs to me.

"Yeah, the voices are getting louder, so that can't be good," she says.

I wrap my arm around her shoulder as we walk down the hallway to the main room, and saying the voices are getting louder is an understatement.

Reaper and Mercy are going at each other's throats.

Whistler is behind Mercy, gripping someone by the back of the neck that has seen much better days. One, Whistler's righthand man, has a gun aimed at the stranger's head.

"Go in the room with the other girls, Mary. I'll get you when it's safe."

KNIVES

She nods at me, giving me big round Hershey's kiss eyes when Reaper turns around and points at her. "She stays!" His booming voice has her flinching.

Mercy shakes his head and says something, but I can't hear it since Tool shoves him from behind, which starts a fucking brawl. Mercy rears his fist back and punches Tool, which dislodges the screwdriver from his ear, and it clatters to the floor. Tyrant latches onto Whistler's arm, and Yeti is in front of Tool, growling so deep, drool starts to drip off his canines.

Another one of Whistler's men, Socks, according to his patch, gets a hard hit from Skirt. Socks stumbles back, and before I can pull Mary back, he slams into her, knocking her off her feet. Her head bounces against the wall, and her eyes roll back.

"Mary!" I dive for her, gathering her in my arms before she can hit the floor.

Okay. Now I'm fucking pissed. "Enough!" I yell, flinging a star across the room until it lands right in Whistler's shoulder. I throw another before anyone can think, making sure the next one lands in Socks. The fucker.

Everyone stops yelling, and Doc comes from the kitchen, wiping his hands off after dealing with Maximo, and squats down to check on Mary. "I've got her," he whispers.

I stand slowly, wanting to kill everyone in the room. "What the fuck is going on?"

Something hits me on the forehead, and I see Slingshot across the room, hiding the slingshot behind his back, pointing at Patrick, who then throws a bag of skittles in his face. One annoying MC brother at a time.

"You fucking got me with a ninja star," Whistler groans, leaning against the couch. "I knew you were good with them, but holy shit." He cups the star and has to let go of the guy he has a hold of, but he stays right where he is, so he isn't a prisoner. "Someone get this fucking thing out of me."

"Not a chance in hell," Bullseye says from behind him, then moves to the side and flicks the star, pulling a hiss from Whistler. "Whoops."

"Knives, Mary is fine. She's just knocked out," Doc informs me.

"Just knocked out? She wouldn't be knocked out if everyone in the room could act civil."

"Knives, that was before Mercy came to our doorstep and said he had information on Mary's father. Apparently, the FBI has been investigating him for a while now," Reaper says.

I stomp forward and press a star under Mercy's chin before he can blink. "Are you even good at your job? He abused her for twelve years. Twelve. Where were you and your agents?"

"I'm sorry, I didn't know that," he says, the crinkles around his eyes not only showing age, but sorrow. I hate that I know he is sincere. "I hope we can take him down. He has really built a name for himself over the years." Mercy looks toward the guy they brought in, who has a black hood over his head. "He can help."

"Why is he hooded?" Patrick asks, popping a peanut in his mouth. Ever since he stopped drinking, Patrick has been eating his weight in peanuts. I think it helps him stay off the bottle.

"That's One's doing. He said he didn't like how 'sad' the guy looked."

"I don't like sad people. They freak me out," One says, shrugging a shoulder as he holsters his weapon.

"This fucking star hurts! Get it out," Socks yells.

"No one help him. He is the reason why Mary is knocked out," I say.

"Yeah, suffer, asshole," Bullseye grumbles, and he and I tap knuckles.

Mercy rips the star from Whistler's shoulder, and the guy's knees buckle while he rolls his lips together to hold in the pain. "Thanks," he says on a held breath.

Mercy side-eyes me and tosses my star to me, then rips off the black hood from the guy. "I believe you know each other," Mercy states. "Thomas, this is your brother. Mason."

Blood rushes to my head. My heart beats so fast; I'm positive it is about to pump right out of my chest. "That's impossible." I stumble, and Reaper catches me. My world tilts as I become dizzy, memories flood my mind, and his death plays over and over again in my head at the speed of light in this very moment.

"Thomas," Mason says my name with a familiarity that only a brother would. He struggles to get out of One's hold, but he can't. "Let go of me. Thomas, it's me. It's Mason. I swear to god, it's me."

"No," I shake my head. "No!" I yell. I can't breathe. I can't fucking breathe. I gasp for air, pressing my hands to my head when the pressure becomes too unbearable. "You can't be. You can't. I watched you die! I saw it."

"It's me. You always take responsibility for your actions," he says, tilting my crooked world back into place.

Only Mason would know the very last words we ever said to one another.

"You can't be real," I whisper, my hands shaking. I glance over to Mary, needing her more than ever right now, but she's still unconscious. "You died."

"Yeah, that's a long story," Mercy says. "He's been an FBI agent for a while now. He's been undercover for Mary's father."

There are so many questions.

"Who is Mason?" Slingshot asks, popping a skittle in his mouth. Everyone turns to him and stares from his poorly timed question. "What? What'd I say? Oh, please. As if no one else is curious?"

"Mason was my foster brother. I watched him die when I was fifteen, after he killed three guys that constantly bullied me. That's how I know this is wrong." I point to the man calling himself Mason, then to Mercy. "You have it wrong. This man no longer exists. And if he was safe, why is he zip-tied?"

"That's Zip-tie's doing," Mercy says. "No one trusts anyone." He snatches my ninja star from my hand and sliced the thick plastic, so the stranger's hands are free. The guy that says he is Mason.

"I need to go. I need to clear my head."

KNIVES

"Thomas—"

I silence Mason with a quick punch to the jaw, then another, and once he is off-balance, I slip a star into my hand from my cut pocket—the one I made out of the knives I found on the road all those years ago—and throw it as hard as I possibly can through the air. I've never thrown a star so hard in my life, but I'm so fucking mad.

So fucking hurt.

The star veers to the right, away from harming his heart, which is too fucking bad. It lodges deep into the muscle of his shoulder. Mason stumbles back and holds his hand to the wound. Blood is spilling, but he'll live.

"I deserve that," he says, as if we haven't gone years without talking. As if I haven't gone every day without mourning my brother. As if I didn't visit his grave every single fucking day and wish like hell I had been in his place instead.

"You deserve that?" I ask, taking a step toward him, then back, because I don't want to be anywhere near him right now. I still don't believe it's really him. "This is a fucking joke, right? You expect me to believe my dead brother has worked for the FBI all these years? What... he faked his death and wasn't allowed to tell anyone? And then, boom, coincidence, he works for my ol' lady's father? Get the fuck out of here."

"It's all true. Every last bit of it," Mercy says. "It's a long story about how we found him, but—"

"—There are no buts," my throat burns as I yell. "And I don't give a fucking shit. You've been dead to me twenty years. You can be dead for another twenty." I stalk forward and yank the star from his shoulder and start to walk out the door, then pause. I turn back to Mercy. "How long have you known? Have you known the entire time?"

"No, just recently. When I got put on the case, they gave me the file," he says. "I'm sorry you had to find out like this, but Mason is our best lead to bring down her father."

"No, Seer is."

"We checked all the hotels with the letter M, and he wasn't there Knives. Mason might be our best bet," Reaper acknowledges.

"I would rather die than ever ask for his help. A person that would lie to his brother about being alive... all this time, knowing he was all I had, and still chose to leave me alone?" I lock stares with him, and Mason steps forward, holding his hand to his shoulder.

I hold up my hand and shake my head. "Don't. Nothing you say will ever make me forgive you. Any information you have for Mary and about her father, tell Reaper. They will update me. I don't want to hear a thing from you. And fuck you, Mercy," I add for the hell of it.

Fucking, fuck everyone.

"Doc, call me when she wakes up, and I'll come right back. I need to clear my head. I don't want her to think I left her. I'd *never* leave anyone I care about. I'll always be back." I run out the front door, ashamed to admit that not only am I angry, but I have tears in my eyes. I am feeling a hundred emotions.

A part of me is happy that he is alive. Holy shit, my brother is alive, but a part of me feels stupid. I feel like that little boy again who knew nothing about the world, and I hate it. I have worked my ass off to not be that boy, yet here I am. Once again, Mason is showing up to be the knight in fucking shining armor, and I'm left to watch him save the day from a distance.

I pause at where I usually park my bike to see the spot empty. I'm confused for a second, wondering where the hell my bike went, only to remember it's burnt to a crisp on the side of the road, so I can't go for a ride.

"Sonofabitch!" I scream at the top of my lungs. I don't need to ride like this anyway. Riding angry is never a good thing; that's how accidents happen. You become more careless and not as aware of your surroundings. I need to be here for Mary when she wakes up anyway.

"Everything okay, Knives?" Braveheart pops his head from the security shed where he controls the gate.

"Does it sound like everything is okay, Braveheart?" I snap at the kid, feeling bad. None of this is his fault. I rub a hand over my face, trying to get my bearings. "I'm sorry, Braveheart. I didn't mean to snap."

"It's okay," he says, his large Adam's apple bobbing as he gulps. He is wearing his glasses today, which reminds me of when he first started to prospect for the club. He usually wears contacts these days, so seeing him wearing the black frames makes me remember a doofy kid who had no idea what his strengths were.

He is a lot like Skirt, more of a scrapper than a professional fighter, but holy hell, Braveheart has the heart of a lion. It surprises me because he is tall and lean, a bit awkward too.

"Well, if you ever want to talk..." He lets the words hang out as bait, and I wonder if I should take him up on it. I'm still riled up from the tension in the clubhouse. It might be good to talk to someone who isn't pissed off either. "I have hooch," he says, holding out a bottle of whiskey.

"You dog. What the hell are you doing with that?" Warmth firing down my throat is just what I need.

"We can't have any near Patrick, which is fine, but out here, I get bored and cold. Whiskey helps."

"You know you don't have to stay out here, right? Please, tell me someone told you that."

"Um..." he pushes his glasses up the bridge of his nose and twists the cap off the whiskey. He gulps it down and coughs from the spice of the whiskey. "No..." he admits, and his blatant oblivion has me tossing my head back and laughing. Oh my god, the poor bastard.

I take the whiskey from him and shake the bottle at him before sighing and take a swallow. "I needed that. Braveheart, man, you don't have to protect the gate at all times."

"Yes, I do. Too much shit has happened. Too many people have hurt us. I'm here. Night and day. I watch the road. I watch the gate. I don't want anyone to hurt my family again."

He feels guilty. He doesn't look at me. He doesn't have to. I see it in his profile as he stares down the road. Braveheart's jaw is tight, and he stuffs his hands in his jacket pocket. It's cold out here, lonely, and he feels obligated to protect us.

"You haven't done anything wrong," I tell him, setting the bottle on the shelf in front of him. "These people, they come at us from all angles, from every aspect. Whatever happens here, it is not your fault. You should be inside with everyone. Believe me when I say, there is no obligation here to waste your life away in a fucking shed when there are people who care about you inside, Braveheart. Tank is in there, bless his damn teddy bear soul, he jumps when Happy is near. He doesn't have a brave bone in his body."

That makes Braveheart smile. "And what about you?" he asks. "Why aren't you inside?"

"Because someone is in there that's been dead to me for a long time. I need a minute to wrap my head around it."

"Oh, the guy Mercy brought in?"

"Yeah. He has information on Mary's dad, but how can I trust him? How did he get into the FBI? Why didn't he tell me? What if he wasn't on our side? Does he know anything about Maximo and why the hell he is working for Preacher Man?"

Braveheart blows out a breath, and frozen particles fill the air as he thinks about what to say. He lifts his feet up, placing them on the shelf to get comfortable. "Those are a lot of questions, Knives. Questions only he knows the answers to."

"I don't want to talk to him, Braveheart. I don't think I can."

"For Mary?" he asks me. "Maybe don't do it for you. Do it for her. After all this is said and done, you don't have to talk to him again."

And the thought of that hurts like hell too. "Give me that." I steal the bottle away from him again and take another swig. "Don't let Patrick see this."

"No, I keep it locked up like Prez says to do. If Maximo went behind our backs, if he's as slimy as I think he is, what would happen?"

"War," I say, the word causing my stomach to turn. A lot of lives would be lost. "Moretti needs to remember. If he can get his memory back, I think we would know a lot more than what we do. Right after our partnership solidified, the hotel explosion happened, and we weren't able to grow like we wanted to. Maximo came and changed everything."

"Something is up with him, Knives. I'll be honest, and I've never said this out loud, but I don't think he can be trusted. Every move he makes, every time he speaks, I don't understand how Reaper can look past the obvious. He has to know Maximo is not on our side. He has to."

"Reaper has a lot to think about right now. He is trying to keep the peace. We have families here."

"Either way, they are in danger until the threat is neutralized."

"Yeah," I agree. The more I think about his words, the more they resonate with Mary. The club isn't my only family anymore; Mary is too. Until her threat is taken care of, she will always be in danger.

"Oh, before I forget." Braveheart ducks back into his shed and grabs a package, handing it over to me. "This came in the mail for you."

I raise an eyebrow in curiosity and rip open the package. It's my new phone. Finally. With everything going on, at least something went right today.

"Thanks, Braveheart." I don't just mean for the phone, but by the look we give each other, I'm sure he understands what I mean.

"Anytime, Knives."

I turn on my heel and head to the clubhouse, sucking up all my pride and all my pain to go take care of Mary.

Mason is dead. My past has no say here.

It's all about Mary and how I can make sure she's safe.

CHAPTER SIXTEEN

Mary

O^{w.} "Holy crap," I say on a held breath as I start to rouse. My head is killing me. I feel like I got hit with a bat.

I did see Whistler…

But no, that's not what happened.

"Hellraiser."

I wince as I look left to see Knives sitting in a chair, and he looks so relieved to see me awake. "What happened?"

"Someone ran you over, and you tripped and hit your head."

"You worried us," Sarah says from the bed next to me. "Sorry, I'm down here for monitoring for the little chipmunk, since I've been having some pain."

"Oh no, is everything okay? Is the baby okay?" I ask her in a hurry.

"I'm fine. I have to take it easy. The muscles in my stomach never healed properly after being shanked—"

"—Don't say it like that. It isn't funny," Tongue says out of the darkness… somewhere. And his statement is followed by a hiss.

That is terrifying. I'm glad I woke up to Knives next to me.

"Anyway, he might be hard to carry to term because I won't have the muscle strength for my stomach to grow, and it will mess with my hips and pelvis."

Tongue comes out from the far corner and walks by us, head down, and heads upstairs with Happy strapped to his chest.

"Tongue! I'm going to be—" but Tongue shuts the door before she can finish her sentence. "Okay." She lays her hand on her stomach, which is still flat. If I remember correctly, she isn't that far along, and she's already having issues. I'm sure she's scared.

"Okay, Sarah. Everything looks good. No exercise," says Doc.

Sarah purses her lips and narrows her eyes. "Define exercise."

Doc rubs his temples and then places his hands in a steepled position under his nose. "No rough sex. Nothing that will strain the muscle in your stomach. Keep it vanilla. Extra vanilla. I'll have a talk with Reaper."

Sarah groans dramatically and falls back on the bed. "Vanilla? No one likes vanilla here, Doc."

"Oh, me so sad for you," Doc pouts.

"You're mean."

"You'll thank me when you're holding your baby for the first time."

Sarah gets this wistful look in her eye as she lays her hand on her belly, but the moment is ruined when loud, pounding steps hurry down the basement stairs. It's Reaper. His eyes are wide, and he seems scared. "Doll? What's wrong? Why are you down here? What happened? Is the baby okay? Are you okay? Why didn't anyone come and get me!" he roars, and the stainless steel walls vibrate from the loud boom.

"Oh my god, no," Reaper leans against the wall, defeated, broken, and his eyes water. "We lost the baby? Sarah…" He turns around and punches a hole in the wall, and everyone is so shocked from the quick conclusion that he made that no one speaks up to calm him down.

"Reaper, no. Oh my god, no. The baby is okay," Sarah says, swinging her legs over the bed to stand. She pulls the stickers that connect to the monitors off her stomach and tugs her shirt down and runs over to him. Her hand lands in the middle of his back, and he pulls her in front of him to where we can't see her anymore because his body covers hers.

"You're okay. The baby is okay?"

I turn away from them, my heart breaking for Reaper and Sarah. The relief, fear, and tremble in his throat has my eyes burning.

"I was having some pain, and you were in a meeting. It wasn't the same kind of pain as before," Sarah explains. "The muscles in my stomach didn't heal like they should have and carrying can be complicated and dangerous. Doc wants to keep a close eye on me. Very close. But the baby is healthy. And… Doc found something I think you'll really like. Want to hear it?"

Reaper doesn't say anything, and I watch as Sarah drags him to the bed where she was sitting moments ago. I squeeze Knives' hand, and for some reason, I feel really lucky to be a part of this moment with them. Knives kisses my temple and brings his lips to my ear, "I want that with you."

"Really?" I say, holding back from tackling him to the ground and getting to work on a family. I never thought this would happen. I thought I'd always be at my dad's mercy, but I ran, thinking I was running toward death, when really it led me right here, to freedom.

"Really."

I'm about to ask what changed when Doc squirts the jelly on her stomach and rolls over an ultrasound machine.

Reaper is holding her hand, his entire body shaking. It's hard to see this big bad man, the President of the Ruthless Kings, become emotional and afraid. Knives leans over and slaps Reaper on the back, giving him an encouraging nod.

A gesture that everything will be okay, but I can tell Reaper doesn't believe it.

Doc places the wand on Sarah's stomach and points. "Okay, Reaper. Do you see this area? It's grey."

"Yeah," he chokes.

"That's the muscle. It's fragile, but it isn't in the worst shape. Down here—" Doc sides the wand further down and searches for something specific. "Where is it..." he continues to try, and then a fast whoosh takes over the speakers.

Thumpthumpthumpthump.

"That's your baby's heartbeat, Reaper. Strong and healthy."

Reaper stares at Doc with watery eyes, and his cheeks turn red. "Yeah?"

"Yeah, Reaper. You want me to record it for you?"

Reaper nods, squeezing Sarah's hand so hard, I'm afraid he is going to break it. "Please, please, please. I want to hear it every day."

Even Doc is getting emotional.

"Sure thing," he says, pressing a few buttons. "And that little bean right there is your baby." He points to a little blob on the screen, and I can't tell it's a baby, but I believe Doc.

Reaper can't stop staring at the computer. He lifts his finger, grazing it over the white dot. He peers down at Sarah and lays his hand on her belly, cupping it with protection. The width of his palm covers her midsection, but it makes me hold my breath.

"Thank you," Reaper's voice breaks. "I love you so much, Doll." He pulls himself forward and kisses her senseless.

I can't help it. I'm a crying mess, and I start clapping. "Congratulations. I'm so happy for you guys."

"Mary," Knives rolls his eyes but keeps a smile on his face as he tries to lower my hands, but I shrug away and keep clapping. "They don't want a round of applause."

"Don't tell me what to do," I say out of the corner of my mouth, and Reaper takes a bow. "Yay! You did it."

"Yeah, we did." He doesn't say it in a cocky way, but a proud reassuring way. "Hey, Doc. Do you care if we stay down here for a while and watch the screen? I just... I'm not ready to leave yet."

"I'll say you two deserve it. Take as long as you need."

"When can we find out the sex?"

"I don't want to know," Reaper says. "It doesn't matter. Happy and healthy, that's all I want the two of you to be."

"Aw."

"Okay, Doc. I think she is having concussion symptoms," Knives says about me.

"I'm allowed to be happy for them. And aren't you supposed to be…" A pain shoots through my head when I think about the fight upstairs. "Isn't there something important you need to be doing? I can't remember what it is…"

"You missed all the important stuff," Doc says, flashing a light in my eyes to check my pupils. "You wouldn't have remembered it, so don't strain yourself. Knives' brother came back from the dead, and apparently, he worked with your dad because he is undercover FBI."

"What?" I stare at Knives, who is flipping a star across his knuckles. I snag it from him and hide it under my butt. "Mason is back? I thought you said—"

"He is. He was. I didn't know he was alive. I don't know if it is him."

"Would I know him?" I ask. "If he worked for my father?"

Knives' eyes go dark, and the clear crystal color replaces the bright blue, something that happens when he is pissed. "He better hope like hell he never ran into you, because I'll kill him all over again."

"Why aren't you talking to him?"

"Because you're more important. He can wait. Your dad can wait. You were hurt, and I want to be by your side. I want to make sure you're okay. When I know you're safe, I'll talk to him."

Moretti walks out of the playroom, and as he walks to a nearby bed, he leaves bloody footprints behind him.

Doc closes the playroom door right as Maximo screams.

"I don't think my brother is a good man," Moretti says. "I can't remember why, but I don't believe him when he says Mary's father took Natalia. Something in my gut tells me, Reaper."

"We will find out. I think tonight, everyone settles. Relax. Tomorrow, we try and get everything out of the way. We'll make a plan. Mary will be safe, and maybe, we can save a few others from his clutches too. It won't be easy, but nothing worth it ever is." Reaper rubs Sarah's stomach and closes his eyes to listen to the song of the heartbeat on the monitor.

"Congratulations, Reaper. I am happy for you," Moretti says, trying to smile, but his eyes are sad.

"I'm not going to let anyone hurt my family, and that includes your brother. I think he is trying to play us. I'm starting to wonder what else he is behind if he has his hand in this."

"I wish I could tell you," Moretti says, dropping his elbows to his knees. "I wish I knew."

I can't imagine not being able to remember anything. Every memory Moretti makes is one of his firsts. We are all he knows, and I'm wondering if that is why he has stayed here. I know Doc said he could leave, but he chooses not to.

"I swear, Reaper. If I remember anything, one tiny thing, I will let you know, but my head is dark. There is nothing. I want to protect him. He is my flesh and blood. He's my brother."

"I know," Reaper says with understanding, not only for his MC brothers but for his sister that surprised everyone for Christmas. "It isn't you I doubt, Moretti. Okay?"

Moretti nods, stands, and leaves. He is light on his feet as he climbs the steps to head toward his room.

"Seems like all the issues revolve around family," Knives says, tracing the spot where a ring would sit on my left hand. "Family can be a real pain in the ass, can't it?"

"You need to talk to him before getting information out of him," I offer, hoping he chooses to be put next to his issues and make himself a priority. "Talk to your brother before you talk to the agent side of him. You won't be able to talk if you don't ask the questions I know are rolling around in your head."

"You come first."

"Knives—"

"You come first. End of discussion, Mary. I love you, but please, do not push this. Mason might not be dead to any of you, but he is to me. The sooner we figure this out, the sooner he can leave."

I know Knives doesn't mean that. He is angry, and he has every reason to be, but we won't be able to move on. Knives will regret having Mason leave his life again. I can't push him though.

"And don't get me started on if he knows you. What if he helped your dad get to you every night?" Knives shakes his head and gets up from the chair, then lays down next to me. "It's something unforgivable. I'll kill him myself if I find that out."

I want to say Mason had nothing to do with me, but I don't know that, and I can't comfort Knives if I don't have the whole truth. Instead, I run my fingers through his hair and take Reaper's advice.

Tomorrow is a new day, but a voice in the back of my head whispers: Only twelve more.

CHAPTER SEVENTEEN
Knives

It's eight in the morning. Everyone is in Church. I've never seen every chair taken up before, but here we are. I sip my coffee, unable to bring myself to look at Mason, who is sitting right across from me. He's staring at me too. I can feel it, that invisible cloak blanketing me and the energy warping the hair long my arms, taunting me to look.

But I won't.

I won't give in.

He left me hanging for twenty years; he can deal with the fact that I've moved on from his death.

"Thomas," he says my name to get my attention, but I ignore him. Is it childish? Maybe. I feel like I have the right to be fucking mad. No. Mad isn't the word.

Devastated.

He was my only friend in the world, a person I thought would never betray me. He did what he said he'd never do: he betrayed me.

"Thomas, please, you have to talk to me. I know—"

Tongue slams his knife between Mason's index and middle finger. "He doesn't have to do a damn thing, Mason-jar. Keep asking him to talk; I'll feed your tongue to Happy. Your voice is fucking annoying."

Tongue yanks the blade from the wood and sneers at Mason. "And I don't give a damn that you know Knives. I stabbed my own brother, right in his tongue. If I can do that to him, imagine what I'll do to you." Tongue rubs the onyx blade against Mason's cheek, but Mason doesn't flinch.

A few other members trickle into the room and shut the door. My thoughts are on Mary. She's still downstairs recovering from the concussion Socks gave her. I'm worried about her, but instead of being there with her, I have to be here, because somehow, someway, my formerly dead brother is connected to Mary's father.

Small fucking world.

Too small.

If Earth had a twin planet, I'd take Mary and get the hell out of dodge because the way people are connected here makes me unsettled.

The gavel made of one of our first enemies slams on the table as Reaper calls Church into session. Everyone has a cup of coffee in front of them; the room fills with the aroma. Sips are the only thing that fills the silence.

I hate the quiet anyway. It's too loud, with endless bouts of possibilities and leaves me alone with my thoughts.

Can't have that.

"Okay," Reaper says, already pinching the bridge of his nose. "Before we start. You bastards are going to listen to something, and hopefully, some of the tension will be gone." He pulls out his cell phone, and I smile around the rim of my mug.

I know what he is going to do, but I'm not going to say anything. This is his moment, and he is proud and excited. He presses play, and the biggest, cheesiest, happiest fucking smile blooms across his face as his baby's heartbeat sounds in the room.

"That's my fucking kid. It's beautiful, isn't it?"

Everyone sitting around the table bangs on the wood, then cheers, all except for Mason because he isn't a part of this life and doesn't know what to do.

Now who's the outsider?

"Reaper, congratulations, man," Mercy says, holding out his hand.

"Thanks, Mercy."

"Way to go, Reaper!"

"Happy for you, Prez."

"I hope it is a girl, so she drives ye nuts," Skirt says from the back. For the first time in weeks, he doesn't have Joey strapped to his chest, and he seems a bit lost. Out of habit, his hands go to his chest, as if he feels her there, but then when he feels air, he scratches his pecs to play it off.

"Don't you dare, Skirt. I can't handle a girl. I'll kill all the boys."

"Aye, the boys," Skirt's voice darkens, becoming threatening. "I'm going to make them fight me to take Joey out on a date."

"You'll kill them, Skirt. How is that fair?"

"Ye don't fight fair, ye fight to win, and if they are smart boys, they will figure that out."

"Jesus, okay," Reaper says, pressing the mute button on his phone. When the heartbeat stops, he frowns, plays it again, and takes a breath.

I think Reaper is more afraid than he lets on. Losing their first child in a miscarriage fucked with him. It would mess with anyone, but now that Sarah is pregnant again, if he isn't listening to that heartbeat, for a moment, it's like he thinks it will vanish.

It's how he was all night. I don't think he slept.

"We need to get on track. We should hear from the FBI agents. They're the reason why we are all here, right?"

Mercy stands beside Reaper and gestures for Mason to get up. Tongue snarls in Mason's ear as he stands, trying to scare him, but Mason still doesn't react. I know Tongue is on a mission now. He will have to scare Mason, or he will be a nightmare for us all.

"Thomas—"

"Don't fucking talk to him," Tongue says, pushing Mason forward.

None of my MC brothers correct Tongue for what he did. Mason has found himself in the wolves' den, and I don't know if he will make it out alive.

Mercy clears his throat. "Okay, I know there is a lot of tension in the air. There are a lot of issues that need to be addressed. The first place to start is with you, Knives."

I finish off my coffee and smack my lips together, then throw the mug right as Mason's head. He dodges it, green eyes wide with shock. "I'd rather not, Mercy. Let's talk about how to save Mary."

"No. You'll be too pissed off. This needs to be addressed," Mercy says, "in order for this to go smoothly. Mason, explain."

Mason pulls out an extra chair from the corner, turns it around, and straddles it. Looks like some things don't change at all. It's the only way he sat in a chair when we were kids. Always too cool for school. "My name is Mason Fletcher. Thomas Underwood is my foster brother."

"Was. This isn't a fucking soap opera, Mason. Get on with it so we can move on to more important business."

"This is important. You want to know what happened to me? Do you remember Louis? Well, he was a kid of a drug lord. The cops? They just shot me, but they didn't kill me like they thought. I survived. I was in a coma, but when I woke up, I was somewhere else. Witness protection, so no one could find me. I couldn't come to you, Thomas. I wasn't allowed to."

I slam my fist on the table. "Bullshit! Bull-fucking-shit. I would have come to you. You were all I fucking had, Mason." I hit my chest. "I was alone."

"You went to the Kings."

"Good thing, because they became my family."

"That's what I wanted for you. I really thought I was dead, but when I woke up, I wanted to reach out, but I wasn't allowed. When I turned eighteen, I decided to be an agent and—"

"And you decided to leave me alone anyway. The witness protection was an excuse, but after that? It's been twenty years, Mason. Your excuses mean nothing to me now. You've been dead to me since I was fifteen, and you're still dead to me now."

I sit down, trying to calm my racing heart, and Tongue gives me a nod, a silent way to support me. I'm with my brothers. This is my home. My real home. I'm not with people that will abandon me. "And my name isn't Thomas. It's Knives," I correct him. "What do you know about Mary's father?"

"I've seen Mary—"

Before I can blink or inhale, I have a star in each hand, and I throw them.

Bam.

One in each shoulder.

"What the fuck!" he cries out.

Mercy gives me an annoyed, exasperated look and plucks the metal out of Mason's shoulder.

"You knew her? You knew and you let that happen to her?"

"I didn't know. I made sure she was safe and that she never made it to the underground auction house her father had."

"And the other women? What the fuck took so long to get the information you needed?"

"His name was never anywhere. We needed evidence. We had suspicions. A ton of suspicions. But he never does anything himself."

"Except when it comes to Mary," I sneer.

"Yeah, it's what led me here. I followed him, and the agency told me of a contact. I met Mercy, and they put Mercy on the case."

"Okay, do you have any useful information?"

"He and Maximo have been working together for a while. Your ally is not your ally, Reaper."

Reaper doesn't seem surprised, but he also doesn't seem like he believes it. He swings back and forth in his chair by keeping his legs on the ground and using the ground as leverage.

"Daphne," Tongue's voice is dark, demeaning, and holds a vow of murder. His knife stabs the table again, and this time he drags it down to the edge. His shoulders rise in rapid beats, and his tongue flicks out over his lip. He is practically vibrating in his chair to go downstairs and kill Maximo.

"Tongue, deep breaths," Reaper says, giving Tool a warning glance to make sure we are prepared to stop Tongue from leaving.

Tongue doesn't have the ability to control himself, not really, and not when it comes to Daphne. He is... obsessed with her. I would argue it's borderline unhealthy. He watches her constantly, but when he isn't near her, I notice she looks for him.

But he is always there in the darkness.

He loves her more than anything. More than this club, that I know for sure.

I understand. I feel that way—a healthy way—about Mary.

"He was going to take Daphne from me," Tongue says. "No one takes Daphne."

"Tongue, Daphne is safe, remember? She's here. She's in your bedroom, reading, probably. She's always reading," Reaper reminds him, trying to get through the haze that has glassed his eyes over.

When he remembers that Daphne is in his bedroom, he relaxes. "Daphne," he repeats, then brings the knife to his nose and smells it, which turns him into a smiling fool.

Why would he smell it?

"Okay, you have Maximo here, right?" Mason asks me.

Me.

I don't answer him, and Reaper gives me a warning glare. "We have him."

"Fed Happy three of Maximo's fingers. Happy wasn't happy it wasn't a tongue, but he'll take any treats."

"What the fuck is a Happy?" Mason asks.

"My swamp kitty," Tongue says with a 'duh' tone.

Mason's brows pinch when he tries to think about what a swamp kitty is, but he stares at Reaper for more clarification.

At least he isn't staring at me.

"It's an alligator."

"You have an alligator here?" Mason straightens in his chair.

"Yep and if you try to do anything about it, I'll feed you to him," Tongue warns.

"Okay, we need a plan."

"Mary is the plan," Mason says. "She's bait. Use her, get her father, boom. Done."

I don't remember getting up. I don't remember walking to Mason.

All I know is right now, my hand is wrapped around his throat, and I slam the back of his head against the wall, kind of like how Mary hit her head last night. I lift Mason off the ground until his toes are barely touching the floor, and I hear a commotion behind me, but I'm too focused on Mason to give a damn. I tighten my grip, watching his face turn red, and the veins in his eyes pop. "I'm not that fucking kid anymore, Mason. I'm not weak, so let me be clear to you when I say using Mary in any way is not an option. If you try to use her, I will fucking rip your spine from your body. You might be used to running the show, but here, you don't fucking matter."

"Let go, Knives."

I turn around to see Mary at the door, her beautiful dark hair in a big nest on top of her head. She's sleepy. She's wearing sweatpants, a simple white tank top, and a grey zip-up jacket that hugs her curves.

"Mary, I won't risk you," I inform her in case she doesn't know.

"I'm offering."

I let go of Mason's throat, and the fucking silence in the room deafens me.

CHAPTER EIGHTEEN

Mary

DO I LIKE THE PLAN? NO.
    Should I have heard the plan? Also, no. No woman is allowed in Church unless they are invited, but I invited myself when I realized the meeting was mostly about me. I have a right to know, and I openedthe door at the perfect time because Knives was choking his brother.

"You can't be serious. You're not thinking straight. You hit your head last night," Knives says, trying to make excuses for why I want to go ahead with the plan. I understand he's scared; I am too. My dad is a horrible man, and what if he does get his hands on me? What if the Ruthless Kings can't find me and I'm lost forever?

It's a chance I have to take. This isn't only about me; it's about all the women my father has sold, auctioning them off like they are pieces of antique furniture.

How long did he keep me prisoner, only to keep other women prisoner too? How can a man like my father get up every day pretending to preach faith, yet steal faith from others?

Mason is gasping for air, rubbing his throat, and staring at Knives with sorrow. He isn't angry. He isn't trying to attack; he just looks… sad. He has missed his brother.

"I wasn't allowed to contact anyone from my past, Knives. Ever. You have to understand," he explains through a raspy, strained voice. "I was done with my past."

"And you're still done with it," Knives says to Mason, turning his head to his shoulder, but not looking behind him to stare at the person that used to be his best friend. Knives makes his way over to me, walking behind the men who are sitting in chairs, and Reaper's eyes harden as he stares at   me.

Probably because I entered the room when I wasn't allowed.

"You are not going. You will not be bait. Do I make myself clear?" Knives is stern, pointing a finger at me and setting his jaw. "I won't have you putting yourself in harm's way. I won't."

"Don't talk to me like that. Don't patronize me. Don't talk to me like I'm a child. I know what I'm doing."

"The answer is no, Mary."

"It isn't up to you," I say, noticing the shift in our arguing. This isn't bickering. This isn't to poke fun. This is a real make it or break it argument. I shift on my feet, never meeting the freezing temperature of his eyes.

He's pissed.

"The hell it isn't up to me. I don't care what I have to do. I'll throw your ass in jail again," he threatens.

I gasp, uncrossing my arms from my chest as if he slapped me in the face. "You wouldn't dare."

"I would. If it meant keeping you safe, I'd do anything. If it means you hate me and never talk to me again, I'll do it. Your life is more important than anything else. I'll risk you not loving me anymore if it means your heart is still pounding and your lungs are still breathing. Don't mistake it for one fucking minute, Mary. I'm that man you used to think you hated, remember? Hold onto that if you have to, because I will do anything—" He crowds my space, and I take a step back out of the room. He follows me, and the heat of his body warms mine. "—Anything to keep you safe. Don't raise hell with me about this, I'm begging you," he pleads with me

"Knives—"

"—Mary, please," his words break, like a dam holding in a river, the barrier cracks and threatens to spill. He's on the verge of breaking, because Knives is proving he is already fractured. "What do I need to do? I'll do it."

"We need to know what to do," Mason says from behind him.

Knives spins around and throws a star, slamming his foster brother in the arm again. "You can shut the fuck up before I decide to kill you. For good. You can wait. You waited all these years to show your face; you can wait a while longer."

"Twenty," Mason grunts in annoyance, holding his bicep against him as he yanks the silver out. "It's been twenty years."

"Semantics. All the years blend together when someone dies and goes missing from your life."

The moment he says the words, I know they aren't just meant for Mason, but they are meant for me too. He thinks that I'll go and never come back. In my mind and my heart, I hurt for Knives because of the mindset he has.

I intertwine our fingers together and pull him out the door. "We are going to go talk. We will be back later."

"No the hell we—" I slam the door before Knives can say anything else.

"You're so fucking bossy."

"I learn from the best."

"You—"

"Knives!" Maizey bursts from the kitchen in her princess dress, and she waves her wand in the air and bonks him in the leg with the glittery stick. "You will now be happy!"

Aw. She's so damn cute.

"Kid, not right now," he snaps, in a harsh tone he never uses with Maizey.

"Knives!" I scold him, and Maizey pouts her lip, her large brown eyes well with tears. There is no stopping it. She wails, throws her wand at Knives, and runs right toward Sarah, who is cutting up apples to make a pie.

Skirt will be happy.

Maizey wraps her arms around Sarah's thigh and buries her face to cry.

"Are you kidding me?" I say, the words a harsh hiss directed at Knives. "Apologize to her, right now."

Knives thinks about it for a minute and nods, realizing he fucked up in that moment with Maizey. Our issues can wait. Sarah lifts her chin when Knives stands in front of her, a stance only a mother takes to protect her child, and Knives kneels. "Maizey, I'm sorry. You didn't deserve that. I have a lot going on, and I took it out on you; I shouldn't have. I hope you can forgive me, squirt."

Maizey sniffles, rubbing her wet cheeks against Sarah's jeans before turning her chubby cheeks to Knives. "You mean it?"

"I swear it."

"Pinky promise," she says, lifting her tiny finger in the air.

Knives lifts his pinky, which is so much bigger than hers, and locks it around her tiny one. "Pinky promise."

"You gotta kiss it or it don't matter," she sniffles, waiting for Knives to give in to her demands.

He brings his face down and kisses his hand. The toothless smile beams across her face, and she does the same, plopping a wet kiss on their fingers. "I'm going to go dash Daddy's office with happiness. I need my wand." She runs to where her wand is on the ground, picks it up, and heads for the Church door.

"Oh, no. Maizey, sweetie, you can't bother your dad when he is in the office," Sarah calls out, but it's too late.

Maizey is gone, and the roar of laughter coming from Church can be heard from the kitchen, followed by a high-pitched squeal.

"If you make my daughter cry again, Knives, I'll kill you," Sarah says as if she is having a normal conversation while she cuts the apples with calm, controlled slices.

"Yes ma'am," Knives says, gulping.

"Knives! Get your ass back in here, right fucking now," Reaper bellows from Church.

Not if Reaper kills him first.

"We really need to talk," I tell Knives. "I'll go tell Reaper."

"No, I will," he says. "We will talk, but my stance isn't changing," he says defiantly, leaving no room for argument.

If I know anything about us, there is always room for argument.

I bite my tongue until he leaves the room, and I lift my hands to strangle the air, pretending it's his neck as I let out a frustrated growl. "He is so impossible. He won't listen to me. He doesn't understand that this needs to happen."

"He cares about you, Mary. Think about if it wasn't an issue, what would you think if he agreed with Reaper to put you in harm's way?"

"How do you know it has to do with that?"

"Those walls aren't as thick as Reaper likes to think. I can hear everything they talk about. Don't tell him that, or he will soundproof it," she winks.

I pull out a chair, plop down, and sigh. I don't look away from the hallway, so I know when he is coming back. The longer we wait to talk about this, the more I calm down and realize Sarah is right. It could be worse. Knives could just not give a shit at all about me and let me be dangled as bait.

I'm lucky, I know, but what else is there to do? If they can't find my dad in Vegas, we draw him out. I'm the best way to do that.

"I just want to help. I know the risk, and I know Knives has been through so much—"

"—Mary, all the guys have been through so much. These men, they are glued together by pure will alone. Everyone has their story. I don't know much about Knives, but I know enough to know, he has lost so much. He finally has you, a new story, don't you think he is afraid to see how it ends? Especially with what Seer said. He must be freaking out."

It makes me think about all the ol' ladies and what they have been through. I wish more of the girls were here right now. Juliette works with Tool, Joanna seems to need sleep all the time since she's pregnant, Dawn just had a baby, Sunnie...well, I don't know where Sunnie is, actually. All I know is that she isn't here.

"I want him to trust me."

Sarah puts the knife down and takes the seat next to me. "You think he doesn't? It isn't you that he doesn't trust, Mary. It's the world. It's everyone else around us. It's men like your father, men like the Groundskeeper, men like Maximo that make him realize he can never leave you alone or unprotected. After everything this club has been through in the last couple years, the only place trust exists is here."

"Damn it!" Knives roars just before slamming the door, and the slam has my hand falling to my chest.

I exhale and rub my temples. "I know. I know, you're right. I better go check on him. That doesn't sound good."

"It never does. Reaper probably called a vote."

Which means if Knives is mad, Reaper voted in favor of what I wanted.

I steal an apple slice off the counter as I get up and bite into the juicy crisp. The flavor bursts across my tongue, but the Granny Smith apples that are usually sour are muted. It doesn't taste the same when I know Knives is mad at me. Granny Smith apples are my favorite too. "I need to go check on him. I hate how upset he is," I say, throwing the other half of the apple in my mouth as I walk away and head toward the man that has my heart.

But he is also a ticking time bomb. His fuse is becoming shorter and shorter until I'm worried the man I've come to know and love will be gone because of the circumstances around him. Knives has hidden how he really feels for far too long now, and now that his past is back, I doubt he will ever be able to hide how he feels again

"He has a lot going on. Everything he thought he knew, he didn't know at all. Keep that in mind, okay? I'm sure he doesn't know how to process it all." Sarah gives me a warm smile. I appreciate it, but it does nothing to make me feel better.

I tuck my hands in my jacket pockets and give her the best smile I can and head toward the door; the light spilling in from outside shines from the crack.

I feel like I'm about to meet my maker walking toward the light. My dad used to preach that the light holds acceptance and peace, but I think he has it all wrong.

The same things that happen in the dark, happen in the light too. The only difference is that you can see what is happening rather than wonder.

CHAPTER NINETEEN
Knives

I've never felt like I've hated Reaper before, but right now, it is debatable. I can't believe they took a vote without me because he said I was too close to the issue. Too close? Too fucking close? What a joke. If that happened with Sarah, Reaper would have raised hell, but because he is Prez, he is able to do whatever he wants.

He has the best interest of the club at heart.

I have to keep telling myself that, even though I feel like no one is taking my heart into consideration. It sounds needy. It sounds like I'm a real fucking pussy when it comes to my feelings.

And maybe I am. I've kept them locked up for so long. I numbed myself, and it worked, for a very long time, until Mary happened.

Fucking Mary.

She reached inside me with her warmth and thawed my soul. Pandora's Box has opened, and now my feelings are spilling out, and I can't contain them. It's like poison, completely killing who I used to be and changing me into this... I don't even know what.

I don't recognize who I am.

"Hey. I've been looking for you."

"You found me." I hang my head and stare at the ground. Even though it rained the other day, the desert is still cracked and dry, as if it hasn't seen water in months.

When I left the clubhouse, I walked around toward the back where Skirt's house used to be. I'm sitting on a stack of cinderblocks that are sitting in the middle of the lot. We are going to try and rebuild it soon. The supplies are slowly coming in. It would be easier if we owned a hardware store. The building process would speed up, and Skirt and his family can have their own space. But right now, the clubhouse is safer for them to live, considering we don't really party anymore, and the whores aren't there. If we want to drink, we go to Kings' Club. And if we get too drunk, Tool has extra rooms in the back with cots where we can sleep it off.

I almost prefer it. I don't miss the sluts. I miss Becks though, even though she wasn't a whore. She was a damn good massage therapist. I could use a backrub right now.

Things at the clubhouse won't be like this forever. Cut sluts come and go all the time, but when they return, the drama between them and the ol' ladies will return, and with Mary's attitude, I have no doubt she would kill one of them.

Not that I'd ever give her a reason to. Ruthless Kings can be bastards, but we don't cheat. Once we find our ol' lady, no other pussy will do.

It's a harsh way of putting it, but it's true. It's because no other woman makes us fucking feel or makes us weak like our ol' ladies.

"Knives, I know you don't want this to happen, and I understand why. I love you. If the tables were turned, I wouldn't want you to do this either. You and the guys, you are always running into danger. Don't you think that bothered me before? You might have driven me crazy, but I worried every time you walked out that door to take care of club business."

"Yeah?" I ask, lifting a thick brow at her.

"Are you so surprised?"

"A little bit. You surprise me, that's all." I open my cut pocket and grab a star, but this one is different. It's old, handmade, and a bit rusted.

"I remember when I met Reaper's dad, and he said, 'I have a son about your age.' And Reaper is a few years older than me, but I think his dad was trying to make me feel better after everything that happened." I'm not sure why I'm telling her this, it doesn't make sense, but I feel like I have to. "His Sergeant at Arms, you don't know him, he died a few years later, took the knives I had in my hand when I arrived at the clubhouse and made me this. They are sharp, so be careful."

"These are the knives you defended yourself with the day you thought Mason died?"

"Yeah, these are it. It's ugly, right? Not smooth and pretty like my other ones, but they are jagged, almost more threatening, since they have that knife feel."

"Your name makes sense now," she teases, nudging me in the shoulder.

"I want you to have it," I tell her. I never thought it would be so emotional to give something to someone I love that was built because I missed someone I cared about.

"I can't take this."

"You need something to protect yourself. Please, if you're going to do this, I need to know you're okay."

"You aren't going to fight me?"

"I don't have the energy to fight you, Hellraiser. I can't go against Prez. He *will* kill me. Especially after I made Maizey cry." I feel fucking terrible about that. I can't believe I snapped at a little girl who was only trying to make me happy. "I don't want this to happen. I don't know what I'd do if I lost you too, Mary. You're everything I didn't know I needed. After my family died, after Mason, I don't have the heart to go through another loss."

"Mason is back. You didn't lose him," she says, laying her hand on my knee. "Why won't you see that?"

"Because I know eventually, I'll lose him anyway. It's easier to keep myself distant from him. You don't know how much I struggled in the foster homes. You don't know how much I wished I would have died in that car accident with my family. Mason made the little bit of love I had for life worth it."

She lays her head on my shoulder, and the breeze takes the moment to sweep by. Her long hair dances, and the smell of her shampoo hits my face. It's that cheap shit, Suave, but it smells so fucking good, like strawberries and cream. She could have the most expensive shampoo, and all she says is, "nothing makes my hair shine like this."

Good, because I'd miss the scent of her.

We sit there not saying a word to one another, just enjoying the peace and the sun against my face and my girl by my side

That's when it hits me.

It's quiet. There isn't a sound. It's just the wind picking up dust and a few vultures overhead.

The silence isn't bothering me, but it's still speaking volumes. It's still fucking loud.

And it's saying what a lucky sonofabitch I am.

I wrap my arm around Mary, my biggest pain in the ass ever, and pick her up to set her on my lap. "Just don't die, okay?"

"You deal with death every day," she says, pressing her lips against my cheek.

"Yeah, but I can get over those deaths." I close my eyes and relish in the feel of her red pouts against me, the softness of the plump flesh grazing against me. I know it won't be the last time I feel her, I'll make sure of that, but it feels like it.

With what Seer said, with the threat of her dad, it's hard for me to stay positive.

"You saying you won't be able to get over me, Thomas Underwood?"

I groan when she uses my full name. I haven't been called that since I was fifteen. "Come here." I turn her around so she can face me, the damn breeze taking another opportunity to blow her hair, so I catch it, holding it down so it doesn't get tangled. I want a picture of her like this. It reminds me that we have no pictures together, and if we do, it's with the rest of the club, and we are as far away as we can be from each other.

We always fought to stay away, but now we have to fight to stay together.

And one kiss changed everything.

"I'd never be able to get over you, Mary. You need to know that—"

"Knives…"

"Look at me." I grip her chin in my hand and force her to. "I can get over a lot of things. I have and I always will, but not you. When all this is over, and you're back right here where you're meant to be—" I grab her ass for good measure, making sure she understands me, "—You're going to be Mrs. Underwood."

She gasps and then slaps me across the face. Mary covers her mouth with her hand, and water sparkles in her eyes.

"Ow, Hellraiser." I lift my hand to my cheek and rub it.

Next, like the crazy ass woman she is, she smashes her lips against mine.

She's going to give me whiplash from not being able to make up her damn mind and what she wants to do to me. She rears back and slaps me again, my cheek blazing and my cock hard. I fucking love it when she makes me insane. "It isn't funny. Don't joke like that. Plus, you know it's too soon—"

"I'm not laughing, am I? I'm not kidding, and I don't give a fuck if it is too soon. We live in Vegas. I'll marry your ass on the strip, in front of Elvis and everybody. Tomorrow. I don't give a fuck."

"You're serious?"

"Deadly." It's way too soon according to society and normal people standards, but fuck society. They have never done a damn thing for me anyway. There is one thing I have in a drawer in my room. It's a plastic bag, pushed all the way in the back. It holds my parents' wedding rings. They're the only items I have from them. They're all I have left of them.

Oddly enough, my dad's ring fits me.

And I'm going to wear it.

Mom's engagement ring was simple, a teardrop diamond on a rose gold band, but I can see Mary wearing it. It suits her. I've saved the rings all these years, not having the heart to part with them, and this is why.

"I could slap you again."

"You better not unless you want to get bent over and fucked," I say, my cheek still tingling from her palm.

"I'm sorry, I was shocked, and I had to make sure I wasn't dreaming."

"You usually pinch yourself if you think you're dreaming, Hellraiser."

"Yeah, but what fun would that be?"

There she goes, checking all my damn boxes and driving me mad. I smash my lips against hers, diving my tongue inside her hot mouth, and this time the kiss is sweeter. My beard rubs against her chin, and my palm slides down her throat, getting a semi-hard hold, so she doesn't move.

I bring the kiss to an end and lay my forehead against hers, panting. "You going to marry me or what?"

"And if I say no?" She leans back, her lipstick smeared, so I bring my finger up and wipe it off from her chin. I like it when she's all fucked up and messy because I know I did it.

"Too fucking bad. You're going to marry me anyway. I was only asking to be nice."

She tosses her back and falls back in my arms, laughing at my response. I slide my hand up her spine and make her come back to me, chest against chest. Her arms wrap around my neck, and her laugh finally dies down. "I guess I have no choice in the matter, do I?"

"Nope," I state.

"Then marry me tonight." She ups my ante, trying to see if I'm bluffing.

"Tonight it is, Hellraiser."

No one will take my wife from me.

I'll claw tooth and nail, peel flesh from bone if someone dares.

She's my fucking Hellraiser, my Pandora's Box of fucking emotions.

This wedding has to happen now because in the back of my mind, in eleven days, I might not have that opportunity.

CHAPTER TWENTY

Mary

HOLY CRAP. HE ASKED ME TO MARRY HIM.

I think I said yes. I'm not sure. I wouldn't say no. I'm just surprised. We have known each other for a while, but we have only been lovers for a few days. If my parents knew what I was up to—well—I guess that doesn't matter, because they no longer matter.

This matters. Knives matters. The Ruthless Kings matter.

My home matters.

"We're getting married!" Knives hollers as we walk through the door of the clubhouse, and everyone, I mean everyone, including the dogs, stare at us with open mouths. It's comical.

And it's making me nervous, because no one looks happy, but no one is mad. Well, Reaper doesn't look too thrilled.

Crickets.

This is awkward. I know it isn't the best timing, but a little amount of support would go a long way right now. "Knives, maybe—"

"No," he cuts me off and grips my hand tighter. "I'm marrying her, and I know all of you assholes think it's a bad time, but what better time is there than right now? With all this fucking shit going on, all I want to be is happy. She makes me happy, and I want to live my fucking life before we do go after her father—"

"—Knives, we have a lot to plan. Getting married right now is not a good idea. Her father is here."

"Exactly, he is here, and he isn't going anywhere without her. If in eleven days something happens to her, I want to know I did everything I wanted with her."

"Nothing is going to happen to her, Knives. We will make sure of it."

"I promise, Thomas," Mason has the courage to pipe in.

Knives lose his patience, and his anger engulfs him instead. "You don't fucking know that! You. Don't. Know!" Spittle flies from his mouth as he yells. He points at Mason and sneers, "You have no right to promise me fucking anything. You're nothing but a fucking liar. Her dad, he can wait a day. He's waited nearly a year; he can wait one more day, can't he?"

"Fuck yea! Let's get ye fucking married, brother!" Skirt lifts his fist in the air and cheers.

"Let's do it!"

"I'm in. Oh, hey, can I be the best man? You know I'm your favorite," Slingshot says, taking a swig from his water bottle.

"Can Happy come?" Tongue drawls from the corner. "It would be his first wedding. He can be the flower boy." There is so much excitement in his words that I know Knives will say yes. I'm not sure if they allow alligators wherever we are going, but I'm sure they will figure it out.

"Did someone say they're getting married?" Sarah squeals from the kitchen. She rushes into the main room and pushes Reaper out of the way. "You're getting married?" she asks me and stops right in front of me and takes my hands in hers. "Really?"

"I… think so? Yes? As long as it is okay with everyone."

"Fuck everyone. If they don't want to see me get married, they aren't the family I thought they were," Knives says, staring down at his boots.

I squeeze his hand, and he returns it, but I think they are more surprised than they are against us.

"Hey, you're going to get married," Reaper says, and once his affirmation is heard, the energy changes in the room, and the buzz that I wanted when we walked in is there. I can sense the buzz of anticipation. There is a round of applause, and Knives lets out such a big breath and curses. He doesn't care about anyone else's opinion; he just wants his Prez's approval. "Well, that means all of our ugly asses need to go get cleaned up."

"And we need to get you a dress. Oh my god! You're getting married," Sarah screeches again and starts to prance in place.

"Doll, no bouncing," Reaper suggests, kindly.

If I didn't know why he told her that, I would think he was controlling, but I know he's worried.

"Let's go shopping. There is a little boutique by Daphne's bookstore that is so cute," Sarah says, looping her arm through mine as she guides me to the couch.

"Can I go?" Tongue asks as he sits down next to me. In his arms, he is holding Happy, petting the top of his head, and even though Happy is still somewhat small, his teeth are big.

Big, sharp, pointy teeth.

That can tear into my flesh without a second thought.

"You want to?" Sarah asks him, sitting up straighter and hopeful.

"I'd like to."

I know their relationship has been a bit rocky since they got into an argument and Tongue accidentally stabbed her, but they are slowly coming back together as best friends.

"I'd like that," Sarah whispers, playing with a piece of her hair. "You have great advice. I remember when you helped with my prom dress. I couldn't have done that without you."

"I couldn't have done a lot of things without you. Like live," he says, stroking Happy down his spine while he wears his 'emotional support animal' vest.

Apparently, Happy is a docile, soothing alligator that Tongue can take into shops; who knew?

"Well, we don't have much time," Sarah sniffles, slapping her thighs as she gets up. "I'm going to go get changed, and we should go shopping. Pick a place to get married and we will meet you there, Knives!" Sarah wipes her cheek as she walks away. Reaper places his hand on her shoulder as they disappear down the hallway to get to the bedroom they are staying in.

"I say we get married in Maximo's hotel. That's the biggest 'fuck you' I can think of," I say with bite, digging my nails into my forearms as I think about him partnering up with my father.

"Damn, you are a Hellraiser," Patrick says, throwing a peanut in the air and catching it in his mouth.

Knives' hand lands on the back of my neck, warm and calloused, sending arousal down my spine. It's how I respond every time he touches me. "Damn straight she is." He holds me tight and brings his lips down on mine.

"I'm going to marry the fuck out of you, Hellraiser."

"Yeah?"

"Yeah, and you're going to fucking like it."

Like it? I'm going to love it.

"Okay, I'm ready," Sarah chirps. She struts in much happier than she was before. Her neck is flushed, and her hair is in a messier bun now, resembling a nest of some sort. The front of her shirt is tucked in while the back isn't, and she has a hickey on her neck. Reaper comes out next, and his shirt is on backward, but no one is going to say anything to him. "Are you ready?" Sarah asks me.

"Are you? You're the one wearing two different shoes." I point down to her feet, one boot, one slipper.

I'm going to go out on a limb here and say she meant to put on the other boot.

"Oh. I'll… let me… just…" She twirls around and heads toward her room again.

At this rate, I won't be getting married until I'm dead.

Knives' phone rings, and when he pulls it out of his pocket, he bangs it against his forehead. "It's Seer."

"No!" Everyone in the room yells at the same time, not wanting him to answer it.

"Yeah, fuck you all. The last time I didn't answer, my bike exploded, and we nearly died in a freak tornado." His finger swipes across the screen, and he brings the smartphone to his ear. "Hey, Seer." He does not sound enthusiastic at all to talk to Seer. "What? Of course, I am happy to hear from you. I'm just a little nervous, is all." He doesn't say anything as he stops to listen. "Sure, yeah. Hold on." Knives brings the phone down and presses a button. "Okay, you're on speaker."

Seer's Cajun accent comes through the phone immediately. "I just wanted to call and say congratulations. You guys are taking me by surprise. You like to keep me on my toes."

"Thank you, Seer," I say. It's hard to be nice to a man that knows I'm going to die, but it isn't his fault he knows. I'm sure if he had it his way, he wouldn't want to know half of the information in his head because of what he sees.

"And go with the dress that makes you think of the future, Mary."

I almost ask why, but he hangs up the phone, leaving us wondering what that call was about.

"Okay, I'm sorry. Now, I'm ready," announces Sarah.

"I want Bullseye to go with you," Reaper says.

"Tongue is coming with us."

"Tongue is going as a friend, not a guard. I want someone there who will be focused on their surroundings, not tulle."

"I want to go. I want to go! Can I get a princess dress?" Maizey says, already wearing a princess dress. She wears it every day. Sarah is lucky to wash it, and when she does, Maizey throws a damn fit.

"You can get anything you fuc—fudging want, Maze," Reaper says, catching himself before he drops a curse word.

"Yay!" Maizey squeals. "I can walk with Happy down the aisle." Showing how fearless she is, she reaches up to pat Happy on the head, and the damn gator closes its eyes.

I swear, he is smiling, showing me all those teeth.

"Okay, let's go if we don't want to hurry. I might get a little something from Trixie's shop," Sarah says off-handedly, and Reaper's growl can be heard from across the room.

"Doll..." he warns.

"Okay, we are leaving, or we are never going to get out of here." Sarah takes my hand and drags me away from the couch.

"Bye," I say to Knives, blowing him a kiss.

"I'll see you down the aisle, Hellraiser."

This is really happening.

I give him my biggest, cheesiest grin I can before Sarah is opening the door. Tongue and Bullseye are right behind us, a low hiss coming from Happy.

"You just ate," Tongue tsks.

Happy snaps his jaws, and his teeth clank together, which has me flinching back and almost falling down the steps. I'm not sure if I'll ever warm up to the idea of a gator as a pet. I'm trying. I really, really am.

"One more," Tongue reaches into his pocket, and I almost throw up when I see a large tongue. "There you go," he says, dropping it from above his head. Happy catches it and gobbles it down until there is nothing left but a piece of flesh between his teeth.

"What was that?" I ask in horror, wondering how Tongue has tongues on such short notice.

"A bull's tongue. It's not all the time I can use human, so I order from the nearby butcher shop."

"Right," I say, almost in a daze.

Happy stops hissing though, so that's a plus.

"I love my new car," Sarah says as she digs into her purse for the keys.

Reaper bought her a brand new Range Rover. It's top of the line and safe. It's black, like all the other SUVs. The license plate on the front says 'DOLL' in gold block letters, and the windows are tinted black. They are bulletproof too, and I'm pretty sure the metal he had the car customize with is fireproof to a certain degree.

After what happened over Christmas, Reaper took no chances with protecting her when it came to cars.

"Listen, listen," Sarah giggles as she clicks the button that locks.

"Doll, get your ass in the car before I spank it."

"Why would Daddy spank you, Mommy? Are you in trouble?" Maizey says, tugging on her shirt.

Bullseye, Tongue, and I stifle a laugh. Sarah was all too excited to show us the Range Rover.

"I'm always in trouble, sweetie. Always," Sarah says, opening the back door. She holds Maizey's hand and helps her climb into her booster seat.

"I'm gonna have to talk to Daddy about that. That isn't nice."

"Oh my god, kids are the fucking best," Bullseye chuckles from the backseat.

"You said a bad word! Give me five bucks." Maizey holds out her hand and waits, kicking her short legs over the seat.

Bullseye looks astonished by her words, placing his hand on his chest in a dainty position. "Excuse me, what?"

"Daddy said to ask for five bucks from everyone who curses around me. I have fifty dollars. Fifty-five now, cause you cursed."

"Orders from Prez? That's some shit," Bullseye reaches into his pocket, then pauses when he realized what he did. "Damn it!"

"You owe me fifteen. Keep it coming, buddy," Maizey chirps and wiggles her pink painted fingers. Bullseye narrows his eyes at her, pulling out a twenty-dollar bill.

He slaps it in her hand as Sarah gets in the driver's seat. "You have change?"

"Let's call it good. We know you'll slip," Maizey states, and everyone in the car is laughing until they can't breathe.

"Kid, you know your business," Bullseye says.

"Everyone buckled up?" Sarah asks as she adjusts the review mirror.

"Yep," I say, turning around in the passenger seat to check on Bullseye and Maizey, then look toward the back to see Tongue buckled up too.

Happy has his own car seat.

How is this my life?

Sarah drops her sunglasses on her face from the top of her head and puts the car in drive. When we get to the gate, Braveheart is there and presses the button to open it. When the accident happened over Christmas and Reaper and the men tried to get out of the compound, the Groundskeeper snipped the wires on the electricity box, and the gate wouldn't move, so Reaper installed backup electrical boxes so that wouldn't happen again.

We wave and get on our way, driving down Route 50. When we pass the tree Sarah and Patrick crashed into, Sarah speeds up, and Bullseye reaches up to pat her shoulder. The tree is broken, the bark is missing, and the body of the trunk is burnt.

It's like it happened yesterday, but it's been weeks.

"I can't wait to see Daphne," Tongue says out of nowhere. "She's meeting with the painters today to paint the bookstore. She doesn't have a name for the store yet."

Tongue was never much of a talker before, but he could go on and on about Daphne. He's happy, which is why I'm assuming he named his gator—wait—his swamp kitty, Happy.

"We will have to help her think of a name," Sarah says.

"She's there with the painters? By herself?" Bullseye asks, and Sarah and I groan because we know what that will do to Tongue.

"She's okay. I installed cameras in every corner. I can see her." He lifts up his phone and shows us. "She's reading a book right now, but…I'm not liking how that guy keeps looking at her. Sarah, hurry up."

"I'm going the speed limit." Sarah scoffs and gives Bullseye the stink eye in her review mirror.

The rest of the ride is silent. I'm stuck looking out the window, wondering how I went from being a Preacher's daughter to a biker's wife.

The only thing I'd change is that I wish it'd happened sooner.

CHAPTER TWENTY-ONE

Mary

We pull up to the town next to Vegas, where Daphne works. It isn't a long drive, only about fifteen minutes. The town is one of those that you stop at to use the restroom before coming to Vegas. It's quaint, and there is a candy store named Paula's. It's painted different shades of pink, like bubblegum and hot pink. There is a cotton candy machine in the window, and my mouth waters; it's been forever since I've had cotton candy.

Next to the candy shop is a hardware store; there is a cranky man standing outside, mumbling nonsense to himself as he smokes a cigarette. He has on a tan apron, and when he sees me staring, he sneers at me before heading inside.

Nice guy.

There is one road cutting through the town, and on either side are brick buildings. The place is almost historical. Like it came out of the Wild West a hundred years ago. It's hard to find buildings that look like this anymore in Vegas. Everything is modern and sleek; there is no charm.

Maizey holds Sarah's hand, and Tongue holds Happy in his sling strapped to his chest. Happy's tail sways from side to side, and the people that walk by us give us a wide berth when they see an alligator.

Bullseye leans against a parking meter and sways. I reach out to steady him. His skin is clammy, and his face has lost all color. "Bullseye? Are you okay?"

"I think my sugar is low."

"Have you been checking it?" Sarah asks. "You know you have to check it."

"If it's low, this happens; if not, I feel great. Why bother checking it?"

"So this doesn't happen, or something worse, Bullseye," I say.

"I'll go run across the street and see if the candy shop has a coke or something. I'll be right back," Sarah tells me.

It's on the tip of my tongue to ask for cotton candy, but right now isn't a good time, considering Bullseye looks like he is about to pass out. He's sweating, and he loses his strength, his knees buckling as he falls to the ground. "I'm not feeling that well," he says. "I'm really dizzy."

"I know, I know," I start to panic. What if Sarah doesn't get back in time? What if he goes into shock? "She'll be back soon, Bullseye."

"Uncle Bullseye? You okay?" Maizey asks, waving her wand in the air. "You're going to be all better."

"You bet I am," he says, trying to sound happy and believable, but he doesn't.

A ding sounds in the distance, and I lift my head to see Sarah crossing the street, a bottle of orange juice in her hand along with cotton candy

I bet it's for Bullseye.

Lucky dog.

"Here." Sarah opens the bottle and hands it to Bullseye, who chugs it down; orange juice flows down either side of his mouth. Sarah grabs a chunk of cotton candy and shoves it between his lips. "There, maybe you'll see how important it is to take care of yourself."

Bullseye mumbles around the cotton candy. It's gone in a few seconds after it melts, and he takes another swig of orange juice. We sit there for a few minutes, Bullseye laying down on his back with his eyes shut as he waits for the sugar to kick in. "I'm sorry. I'll try to do better," he says, finishing off the orange juice.

"We just want you to be safe," Sarah says, pushing his dark brown hair back and off his forehead.

He nods, but I can tell he feels weak. Not physically, but mentally. He lifts his hand, and Tongue helps him to his feet. "Let's get you a wedding dress. Gosh, I can't believe Knives, that crazy fu—fudger is getting married."

"Good job, Uncle Bullseye," Maizey compliments him.

Tongue walks inside the bookstore first. The door is open, and the aroma of paint smacks me in the face.

"Hey, I'm going to go inside the boutique. You guys go and talk to Daphne. I want a minute to look alone. Say hi to her for me," I say.

"Yeah, we'll be there soon," Sarah replies.

I step over a piece of gum on the sidewalk, thankful I saw it just in time, so I didn't ruin my shoe. I stop outside the boutique, loving how cute it is. There are two mannequins in the display window. One is wearing a leather skirt with a red crop top, but the one next to it has my attention. It looks like a vintage dress, a soft peach color. The sleeves hang off the shoulders, wrapping around the biceps, and there is a silk slip underneath the beautiful lace detailing. It seems tight at the bust, but fans out on the hips.

I glance up at the name of the boutique, wanting nothing more than to try this dress on.

Ruby's Rarities.

That's adorable.

I skip one of the steps, since there are only three, and when I get to the top, I open the door. The bell jingles, and there is still a mistletoe hanging over the door from Christmas. With one look around the shop, I just know that this is the place where I'm going to get my dress.

"Hi, welcome to Ruby's! I'll be with you in just one minute." A short woman with a pixie cut says from a wobbly ladder as she changes a lightbulb.

"Are you safe up there?" I ask.

"Oh, yeah. I do this all—woah—" the ladder teeters, "—the time."

"Just let me know."

"Everything in the store is fifty-percent off. Have at it."

I want to ask her why everything is on sale, but I figure it isn't my business. "Actually, I'd love to try on the dress in the window, if that's okay. I'm getting married tonight, so I would love to see if that's the one."

"Congratulations!" she says, the metal of the ladder creaking. She isn't tall enough to reach the light with the ladder. She's on her tiptoes, stretching her arms, and is sticking out her tongue as the pads of her fingers graze the bulb. "Just one second," she grunts.

The door opens, and Bullseye walks in, followed by Tongue, Sarah, and everyone else. Bullseye stares at the disaster in the middle of the floor. He runs to the ladder just as it tilts to the side, and Ruby screams.

And witnessing Bullseye saving her is like something out of a movie. He catches her in the nick of time, cradling her in his arms.

"Oh, gosh. Thank you," she says in choppy breaths.

"You're welcome." Bullseye continues to stare at her, and Sarah bumps my hip with hers when we get the same idea.

Bullseye sets Ruby down, well, I think it's Ruby. She never said what her name was, but she has a big ruby ring on her finger, so it has to be her. Bullseye grins when he sees how short she is. Her forehead comes to his stomach, and she's skinny. "You're tiny," he says.

"My attitude is six-foot-six, so you better watch it with the short jokes." She waves a fist in the air. The scowl on her face falls when she turns away from Bullseye and stares at me. "The dress in the window, right? It's been there awhile. I've been waiting for the perfect person to ask for it. I think it's going to look great on you."

"The peach one?" Tongue asks. "That will look gorgeous with your hair up and your complexion. Good choice."

"Oh my god, what the fuck is that?" Ruby screeches when she sees the gator.

"You owe me five bucks," Maizey says. "Pay up."

"She doesn't count, sweetie," Sarah whispers, kissing her daughter on top of the head.

"This is Happy. He is allowed in here. He is my emotional support animal."

She points her finger to all of us and laughs. "You lot are a bit crazy, aren't you?" She side-steps away from Happy and climbs on the stage, then unzips the dress from the mannequin. "I've seen it all now. Damn, gators as emotional support animals. I need me a glass of wine after seeing that; I tell you what."

"Is she talking to us?" Maizey whispers loud enough for her to hear.

"Sorry, I do that." Ruby jump off the stage and stumble, running right into Bullseye again.

"We keep meeting like this. I'm going to need your name," he says, flashing his cocky smile.

"It's on the shop." She saunters by him and heads toward the dressing room. She slides the red curtain to the side and hangs the dress. "I'll grab some heels. Not stripper ones. Not that I have anything against strippers, but something classy," she tells me.

"Mommy, what's a stripper?"

"A woman who likes to dance and she makes money," Sarah explains with a questionable tone.

"I want to be a stripper!" Maizey cheers.

"Never sweetie, never. Daddy won't allow that ever."

I snicker as I head toward the fitting room. The floors are all shag carpet, but everything is clean. Nothing has been updated, which makes me like this store even more. I play with the material between my fingers, feeling the aged lace. I try to imagine the story this dress holds, but I know anything I think of won't do it justice. "Hey, Ruby? How old is this dress?" I ask.

"From the '50s. It's an original, a real classic." Her voice comes closer, and she places a closed toe, three-inch heel on the ground. The shoes are a nude color with a thin ankle strap and, she's right, the heel isn't a stripper heel.

"Okay, try it on. Let's see it," Tongue says, tickling the chin of his swamp kitty.

I close the curtain and get undressed, starting with my shoes. My toes dig into the harsh material of the carpet, and as I slide off my pants, the mirror exposes the bruises on my thighs from Knives. My heart thumps when I think of him, and it has me getting undressed faster. I can't wait to meet him down the aisle.

Stepping into the dress, I'm careful as I zip, since it's so old. I bend down, slipping my feet into the heels. Before I show my friends, I take a look in the mirror on the wall and gasp. I hardly recognize myself. It fits me just right. The dress stops just below my knee, hugging my curves and showing the delicate ridge of my collarbone since the sleeves hug my arms. I twist my hair up like Tongue suggests, tying it like I usually do without a hair tie. My eyes water.

There is a glow to me I can't explain as I look at myself. Maybe it's the slight sweetheart neckline of the dress or how the events of tonight happened so fast that I can't believe I'm here.

All I know is whatever led me here; I need to be the woman Knives deserves. I've been lost this past year, trying to find a way to live again. I've been doing odd jobs for Reaper, nothing special, which has to stop, and I need to try harder to find something I'm good at. For me. For Knives.

He'll help me find my way.

He has so far, and I know with him, I can do anything.

I open the curtain and look down, stepping out for all to see. I'm nervous. What if they hate it?

Everyone gasps in awe.

"That's it."

"I love it."

"So pretty!"

"Give us a twirl, Mary," Bullseye says.

"Oh, I knew it would find the perfect home," Ruby grins, dabbing the tears under her eyes. "Sorry, I'm a sucker for weddings. Don't mind me."

"Let's have the night of our lives before we can't," I say. "I'm going to keep it on, if you don't mind."

"Absolutely not," Ruby says, her ring glittering in the light. "It's all yours."

I want this to be the best night, since my life is on a timer, but my father is going to be in for a rude awakening.

I'm going to fight *for* the rest of my life

They say like father like daughter, but I don't think that's true. I'm nothing like him, unless you consider how much I want Knives, then I guess our greed is the same. We only apply it differently.

"Can you believe you're getting married?" Sarah asks with wobbly lips, her hormones getting the best of her. "You've been through so much."

I didn't before, but *I do* now.

CHAPTER TWENTY-TWO
Knives

HOLY SHIT.

I'm nervous.

I've trimmed my beard, shaved the sides of my head, and I'm wearing a suit.

I never wear a fucking suit. The last time any of us dressed up was for Sarah's prom. I look in the mirror, rub my beard with one hand, and make an impressed expression.

Damn, I clean up fucking good. I really do.

I dip my hand into the black silk lining of my inner pocket and pull out the plastic bag holding the rings. I know, it's supposed to be in a pretty box, but I don't have one.

"You okay? Are you getting cold feet?"

I don't have to look to see who it is. I'd know that voice anywhere. "What the hell are you doing in my room, Mason?" I straighten my tie and grab my cologne. I don't wear it often, just for special occasions, and I consider this the most important occasion of my fucking life.

"I'm checking in on you," he says, leaning against my bedroom door.

"Well don't. That isn't your job anymore, remember?" I place the cologne on the dresser and pick up four stars and slide them into my pants pocket.

"It will always be my job. You don't think I kept track of you? That... what? I forgot about you? You're my brother."

"I was your brother. Was." I grip the edge of the dresser before pushing off and facing him. "You left me behind just like everyone else."

"Thomas—"

"My name isn't fucking Thomas, okay? You don't get to call me by my name. There is one person in this world who can call me that, and I'm about to marry her. Stay out of my way tonight, Mason. Just stop," I beg of him. "Just. Stop. Don't ruin this day for me. Act like you don't exist. You seem to be good at it." I shove by him, slamming my shoulder into his as I walk out of the room, leaving my past and who I used to be behind me.

When I walk to the main room, I feel like there is a part of me missing, and it isn't because Mary isn't here. It's the fact that Mason has popped back into my life out of nowhere, and no matter how much I fight him to stay away from me, deep down, I'm fucking glad he is here. I'm happy he is alive, but I can't get over so many years of him being alive and me feeling like I'm drowning.

"Well, look at you. You aren't so ugly after all," Tank says, wearing a powder blue suit that is not easy on the eyes, but it matches him.

I don't know how or why, but he pulls off the look.

"Whatever, I look better than you do. I look better than all of you," I point out. Everyone is in their suit they wore to Sarah's prom.

It's probably the only one they own.

Except for Reaper.

He is wearing black on black, looking more like he is about to go fuck shit up than go to a wedding.

"Is everything set? Where are Moretti and Maximo?"

"Moretti is coming with. Me and Mercy are staying here to keep an eye on Maximo. I'm thinking he can give us more information than he has been saying," Mason says from behind me. "Go get married. We will be here to hold down the fort."

I nod, not having the energy or the heart to bite his head off again. Moretti comes from the basement, a crisp expensive suit on, something he used to wear all the time, and he is pulling at the collar. "I cannot believe I used to wear these all the time. Are you sure?" Moretti directs his question to Reaper.

"Just as sure as you saying you wanted Tool to suck your cock," Reaper laughs, rocking on his toes as he shoves his hands in his pockets.

"Did I really?" Moretti swings his gaze to Tool, who looks very uncomfortable. "I can see why. You are a marvelous looking man. You still don't suck cock?"

Juliette giggles, hiding her face in Tool's shoulder as he stares at the floor, white as a sheet. "Nope. No, cock. Sorry, Moretti. Juliette is my ol' lady."

"Well, we can all suck each other, I don't mind," Moretti says just as Tool takes a sip of water, which he promptly spews out in a massive spray

And now Patrick is soaked. "Oh, fuck, Patrick. I'm sorry."

Patrick takes out a handkerchief and wipes his face clean. Sunnie helps him too, grabbing a napkin from the shutdown bar in the corner of the main room.

I really miss that fucking bar, but I'd miss Patrick more if he weren't here, and if we had booze lined up everywhere, I don't think he'd have a chance in hell at making it out alive.

"It's fine. Just answer the man, okay?" Patrick gives Tool a sly smile, teasing him.

Tool spins on his chair as Moretti waits patiently, unbuttoning the top of his collar. "Sorry, Moretti. Juliette and I only suck each other. I'm flattered, though."

"It's okay, I don't remember liking men too, yet here we are." He fusses with the collar of his shirt again and curses something in Italian. "Are you sure I wore these? This makes no sense. They are fucking uncomfortable. Who would wear something like this?"

"A rich mafia man," I say, hoping he understands that the clothes he has on are the clothes that encompassed the reputation he earned.

"Well, that's not the case anymore, is it?" he says, sadly. "Okay, let's go get Knives married." He cocks his head as he studies me.

"No, sorry, Moretti. I don't either. I'm marrying Mary, remember?"

"None of you are any fun. You're so boring when it comes to your sex lives," he huffs. "Can we go? Being in this clubhouse is making me cranky." Moretti heads out the door, and for some reason, we all follow suit as if he is in charge of getting the show on the road.

When we all walk outside and shut the door, it hits me how serious the moment is. I never thought I'd be here or that I'd get married. I take the first step down the stairs, the first step to start the rest of my life, when my phone rings.

"Don't answer it," Slingshot says, launching a skittle at me. "It's time to marry Mary. See what I did there? Did you?" He laughs at his own joke. "I'm fucking funny."

"You're a fucking idiot, is what you are," Poodle says.

I do what they say. I ignore the call because there is nothing in this world that is going to stop me from enjoying my night unless it is Mary calling to say she doesn't want to get married. Or what if she doesn't show, and I'm standing there at the end of the aisle looking like a real bastard?

Shit. This is how people feel when they are in love? I hope the anxiety ends, because my stomach is in knots.

A bunch of the guys hop on their bikes, and my heart twists, reminding me I have to drive a fucking car. I hate driving a car. I'm not the best at it, but I do it if I have to.

My phone rings again as I walk to the Bronco, and when I stop at the driver's side door, my gut turns, and the hair on the back of my neck stands up. Something isn't right. I glance around to see what the issue is, but the guys are laughing and having a good time. It's been too long since we have all gotten together and have had fun. Too much shit has happened. Tonight is the night we deserve for ourselves.

But something is wrong; I feel it. It's like when you wake up one day, and you have that ache in your gut, the one that tells you not to get out of bed because you know something bad will happen. Then, you chalk it up to it being nothing, just stupid negative thoughts, but you walk out the door, drive to work, and get in a car accident, or you spill hot coffee all over you, or you see something you weren't supposed to see, and you tell yourself, 'I should have stayed in bed.'

I feel like we should have never left the clubhouse.

I'm doing my best to chalk it up to nerves and ignore it, but every time someone does that here, bad shit happens.

The sun is setting, the lower temperatures have kicked in, and while the horizon is beautiful on the edge of the desert, the beauty camouflages the ugliness that's being hidden right now.

I just have no idea what it is.

My phone rings again, vibrating more intensely than the last time, or maybe that's just how it feels, and I decide to answer it. My limbs are sluggish; my mind is fuzzy. A cold sweat drenches over me. I lean against the truck, staring at the name on my screen.

I know she's gone when I see Bullseye's name.

I can't say how I know, but I feel it, and that's how I know.

I try my best to answer, I do, but I'm frozen.

"You going to answer that, Knives? It keeps ringing over and over. Is it Seer?" Reaper places a cigarette between his lips and lights it, watching me out of the corner of his eye. When I don't answer him, he blows out the smoke, and the phone rings once more.

Then someone else's phone blares.

And someone else's.

Then Reaper's.

My new phone flashes Bullseye's name again, and with a deep, broken intake of air, I slide my finger across the screen and put it on speaker. "She's gone, isn't she?" I feel dead inside, like Reaper carved a hole in my chest and fucking ripped my heart out.

"Knives, fucking finally!" Bullseye panics as he speaks. He must be running because there is static in the background as if he is moving. "We don't know what happened. She walked out of the store. Dress on. We were walking to the car right behind her and climbed inside, and that's when we realized she wasn't with us. We checked inside the store again. I've run all over, Knives. She isn't here. She just disappeared. It's like she vanished. One minute, she's there, laughing and talking, happy. All she did was talk about the dress, and you know how much she loves you, and then it stopped. Mary isn't here. She isn't anywhere. Mary!" he yells out her name and hearing it without her answering kills something inside me.

Reaper rips the phone out of my hand. "No one fucking vanishes, Bullseye! I want everyone to look, except for Sarah. I'll be there to pick them up. I don't want you leaving that area until you have talked to everyone. Searched everywhere, even the dumpsters. Fucking look!" Reaper hangs up the phone and lets out a ferocious roar, tossing my new phone across the damn desert.

It can keep it.

"Knives, look at me," Reaper grabs my shoulders, but I'm limp all over. I can't seem to think, breathe, or move. "Knives? We will find her. We always find them. Always. She's going to be okay. Knives," he snaps his fingers in front of me.

I expect rage. I expect fury to take over, and I go on a warpath, but all I feel is this numbness again. My past is playing on repeat all over again. This is why I didn't want to get close.

Everyone always leaves.

And I'm always left hurting for everyone.

Reaper slaps me across the face, and all eyes are on me. "Fucking listen to me; you don't get to call it quits. Not now. Not when she needs you most." He slaps me again, but his words don't penetrate.

"Aye, Reaper. That isn't what he needs," Skirt says. The brass knuckles glimmer against the sun as he slips them on.

"I didn't want to bruise him on his wedding day."

"He ain't getting married, Reaper," Skirt says, launching his fist through the air and punching me right in the jaw. The pain shoots to my head, my heart, and wakes me up. I'm bloodthirsty.

I fall to the ground and cry out.

"That's it. Let it out, Knives. Let it out."

My ears ring from the hit, and blood pools in my mouth. The taste of it, the pain, it brings me back to the present.

Mary is missing.

I lift my head just as the blood drips down my chin.

"There he is," Skirt says, taking off his brass knuckles.

The sand grinds against my fingertips as I stand, a silent fury filling me as I stare at the clubhouse and head back inside. The scuffing of boots against the ground tells me my brothers are behind me.

There is one man that might know where she is.

And this time, I'm going to listen to my gut.

I'm not leaving this clubhouse, not until I have answers, and not until I've raised fucking hell.

CHAPTER TWENTY-THREE

Mary

OH NO, I'M GOING TO BE LATE FOR MY OWN WEDDING.
No, late isn't the right word
I'm not going to make it.

My head swims with dizziness, and nausea rips away inside my stomach like a storm swirling in the middle of the sea.

Don't throw up on the vintage dress, Mary. Whatever happens, whatever you do, keep the dress safe.

When I get out of here—at least, I hope I'll get out of here—I'm going to marry Knives as we planned. Reaper was right; we should have never left the clubhouse. Now was not the time to be selfish, but I wanted to be. The club never gets to be selfish, and I wanted more for myself, and so did Knives.

This is what we risked. We knew something bad would happen, but I thought we could have one night to ourselves.

What a joke. No one can ever get one night without something bad happening.

"Mary, it's good to see you again. Do you need anything, Sweetheart?"

The sound of my father's voice has me turning over in the silk sheets on the luxurious bed. There's a chandelier in the middle of the room and a chaise lounge in the corner that has gold trim and white cushions.

Turning to my left, I notice the view of Vegas. The flashing array of different lights has me mesmerized for a second. There is a large Ferris wheel in the distance. Reds, whites, greens, blues, neons, the hotels around us putting on a show to attract all the tourists.

My father's fingers graze down my neck as I look out the window, and it has my skin crawling like a thousand cockroaches. "I've missed you so much."

"Don't fucking touch me." I scoot away from him until my back hits the headboard.

"Mary," he tsks. "You know what happens when that pretty mouth leaves a curse in this world." He starts to unbuckle his pants. "I searched everywhere for you. And when Mr. Moretti said you were with a biker group; I knew I had to save you."

The belt cracks in the air as he walks around the corner, looking more threatening than ever. His white hair is combed back, and his beard is a few shades darker, a grey on its way to turning to snow. He has a gold chain around his neck with a gold cross hanging from it, settling in the middle of his chest.

And if I remember correctly, it has his favorite bible verse etched in the metal. Colossians 3:20.

Children, obey your parents in everything, for this pleases the Lord.

A crock of big fucking shit if you ask me.

I've never seen a more despicable man in my entire life. He doesn't serve God; he serves himself.

Instead of wrapping the belt around my wrist like he used to do, he wraps it around my neck, pulling the belt tight. My hands fly to my neck, and I gasp. I kick, and my back bends as I struggle to breathe. My fingers curl around the black belt to pull it away from my airway, but it's too tight.

The blood rushes to my face, and I choke, gasp, and cough.

"You thought you could get away from me? You thought you could run away from me? You can never get away from me. I fucking own you, Mary. You're mine. Wherever you think you can go, I'll follow. You will not disobey me again. You will serve me, you will get on your knees, and fucking worship me. It's what you are meant to do." He tugs tighter to drive home his words, and I'm worried that he isn't going to let up.

I'm going to die.

I know what he means when he says I need to get on my knees. It's something I've never done before with him.

Fear soaks into the marrow of my bones when I dissect his words.

The only man I've ever been on my knees for is Knives, and I don't care if my dad kills me; Knives is the only man I'll ever worship. My father can go to hell.

He rubs his erection against my arm, and tears prickle my eyes. From the pain of the belt against my neck, the terror of feeling him along my arm, my freedom is slowly slipping away. I'm back in his clutches, and I know this time, he will make sure he will never let me go.

He wraps the belt around the post of the headboard, which has me lifting to get the pressure off, but it doesn't work. I can't get a full breath of air. My windpipe is constricted, and it has me barely choking. My heart is racing, and my lungs are already burning. He fumbles with his zipper. The sound of it lowering has me kicking harder, struggling more to get away. I pull on the belt, tightening the constriction further.

Now I can't breathe at all.

"You're a gift from God, Mary. My gift. Your mother hated how much I wanted you. How much I loved you. Still love you. I think you were always supposed to be mine." He pulls out his cock, one I've seen one too many times, and I close my eyes.

His hand rubs up my leg, his fingers digging into the same spots Knives did, pressing against the bruises.

Bruises that were left from love and desire. Knives wanted me so much, he couldn't contain himself, and my father is ruining the passion Knives left for me to remember.

My father groans, fucking his fist as he lifts my dress further. "What's this?" he asks breathlessly, tracing the fingerprints Knives left behind. He knee-walks on the bed and settles between my legs. He tries to jerk them apart, his cock hard and leaking precum, angry that I dared to be with someone else.

"Were you a whore, Mary? Did you spread your legs for someone else?" His hands hook around my thighs to pull them apart, but I keep them shut, the edges of my vision turning black from the lack of air.

The more I struggle, the more I can't breathe.

If I don't struggle, he gets what he wants.

Me.

I refuse to let another man have me.

"Was it that fucking guy with you at the boutique? Was it him?" he roars, yanking my legs apart so hard that the muscles tighten and cramp. I cry out, the pain unbearable in my upper leg. I feel like it's pulled or strained, and in the moment of weakness to try and compose myself, my father bends his head down and inspects the bruises. "I'll forgive you," he says, kissing one of the marks.

A tear trickles down from the corner of my eye from his kiss. "I don't want your forgiveness," I croak, lifting my leg, damn the pain, and kick out again. My foot smacks against his face, but it isn't enough for him to get away from me.

He pins my legs down and crawls up my body, keeping his hands tight on my hips to keep me down. His bare cock rubs against my leg, and I sob, not wanting him anywhere near me. "Please, stop. Stop! I don't want you. I hate you. Get off me. Get off!" My voice is hoarse as I struggle to yell as loud as I can, but the strap around my neck makes it impossible.

He backhands me, drawing blood by splitting my bottom lip open. When he notices, he smashes his lips against mine and licks the droplet off.

I do the only thing I know to do. I bite down on his lip as hard as I can until I can feel the give of his flesh as my teeth sink in. His blood flows into my mouth, and he screams, pulling away from me. His cock is flaccid now, and he is holding his hands over his mouth. I spit, spewing his blood that's gathered on my tongue. A red haze covers his face, and when he drops his hands, the way he looks at me promises nothing but torture.

His brown eyes dance like devils as he looks up me and down. "You found fire while you were away."

I think about Knives' nickname for me: Hellraiser. I suppose I am.

I'm not about to let this monster put my flames out.

"That only makes it more fun for me." He reaches up to the post on the headboard and unwraps the belt, then loosens the clasp, and I gasp, welcoming the oxygen. It's all he gives me, though, before choking me again and wrapping the belt around the post. "I love you so much," he says, rubbing his nose against my cheek.

I stop struggling for a moment, needing to get as much air as I can. The more energy I have, the better chance I have of getting away.

"It's why it's going to hurt so much when someone else will own you."

I'm not perfect. I try to school my features, but the shock shakes me.

"Oh, yeah. Your beauty is money, sweetheart." He traces my jaw with his lips, inhaling as he licks the tears off my face. "Our time will come to an end. I think you're going to make someone very happy. There's an auction in ten days. So many other women, so many men wanting to buy."

"You'd sell me?" I choke.

"I love you. I don't want to, but there's an offer on the table for you that is too good to pass up." He checks his watch and sighs, placing a kiss on my cheek. "I have a sermon to give. I do virtual church now, and it's brought in so many new believers, Mary. You could be a part of it; you could be at my side instead, do you want that?"

He is giving me an option?

My tug on the belt around my neck, sneering at him. "You're giving me an option? I thought the money was too good to be true?"

"If you wanted to be with me, start a family, be at my side as my wife, I will not put you in that auction. I want to know if you'll be mine or if you want to be someone else's. Your faithfulness is priceless to me."

The bile creeps up my throat, helping the belt choke me further. A family? He wants his own daughter to have more children with him?

I can't hold back. Bile works its way out of my mouth, down the belt, and my chin. What would his followers think? He can't marry his own daughter. He is delusional.

"Our bloodline will remain pure and holy," he says, finally taking the belt off my neck. I bend over and throw up over the bed, stomach bile searing my throat. "I know it will take some getting used to, but I think you'll be happy. I can tell the buyer I'm no longer interested. It's up to you."

So my options are, get raped by my father for the rest of my life, or get raped by someone else. With my dad, at least, Knives would know how to look for me. What if I'm at the auction, and the man who buys me lives in Europe? Knives will never be able to find me then, but the thought of being with my father, for years, forced to have his children… I don't know if I can do that either.

"Where is Mom?" I ask, spitting out the remainder of spit in my mouth. "Is she okay with this?"

"I sold your mom a year ago, sweetheart. I have no idea where that bitch is. She wasn't a true believer." He tucks himself into his pants and zips up.

"No! You fucking bastard. How could you do that to her?" I launch myself across the bed to… I don't know, kill him? But with one backhand to the face, my head snaps to the side, and I fly to the floor, landing with a hard thud on my shoulder.

"If you don't choose correctly, maybe you'll see her." On that note, he walks away, shutting the hotel door behind him.

I'm slipping in my own puke, crying, and I know whatever choice I make, it will kill me. I used to want that, but now that I have something to live for, the last thing I want to do is die.

Putting my elbow on the mattress, I use it to lift myself up. I have to try my best to make sure not to look at the puke against my arm or leg. I need to call Knives, but as I look around the room, I notice there isn't a phone.

But there is a notepad.

Walking over to it, my heart broken because of my mom and what's she is going through, I pick up the thick pad of paper. My eyes widen when I see the name.

Maximo has to be behind this auction.

The notepad says, "Circus Circus." It's an old notepad, because the hotel and casino no longer have a name while he renovates.

I'm in a web full of lies and deceit.

And the more I struggle, the further I sink.

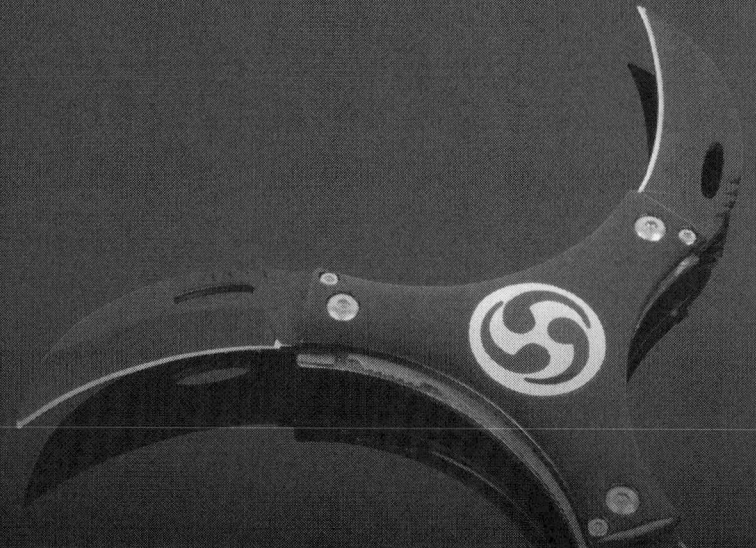

CHAPTER TWENTY-FOUR
Knives

It's been ten days since I've last seen Mary. Ten, long, depressing days. I've lost myself. All I do is search the city. Day in and day out. At night I torture Maximo, but the bastard has stayed quiet. His wounds are infected, and he fucking smells like shit. If he doesn't speak soon, I'm going to have his tongue cut out, and right in front of Maximo, I'll feed it to Happy.

Then I'll start taking from other body parts.

I haven't slept. I've drunk myself into a stupor.

And I wake up at night, crying out her name, fear gripping my heart when my dreams turn into nightmares. I'm always clutching the sheet, drenching the blankets with sweat and reaching out for her.

Only to find her side of the bed cold.

I miss her.

We were supposed to get married, and my job, my one job, was to protect her.

I'm running out of time.

Today is the day Seer said Mary was going to die. I have to make sure that does not happen. The last ten days have made me realize just how precious life is with Mary. I didn't understand it before, but now that I think about it, all the fighting we did before I kissed her, I wouldn't have been able to be without it.

"Knives, you need to go get some rest," Reaper says, standing by the sink. He leans against the counter, crosses his legs at the ankle, and sips his coffee. I'm not the only one tired. Everyone is.

We have searched every single hotel in Vegas. From top to fucking bottom.

She's vanished, and it's time for me to start thinking that maybe she isn't here anymore. I'll need to search the globe for her.

Every damn city, town, and abandoned building this damn world has to offer, I'll tear it down. I'll find her.

And if I find her in her grave, I'll join her.

I need my Hellraiser.

The bickering, the frustration, the madness she makes me feel, I need it. I've always needed it.

"Rest?" I laugh bitterly, rubbing my eyes with the palms of my hands to bring life back into them. "You wouldn't rest if this was Sarah, just like any of you wouldn't. You want me to rest? You want me to laugh too? Tell a joke? Dance? What the fuck do you want!" I slam my fist on the table, and everyone looks away from me. "She's gone."

"Our answers are downstairs, I know it," Mercy says. "Maximo knows a lot more than he is saying. I can feel it."

"Me too," Mason says, running a hand through his hair.

He's changed so much and hasn't changed at all. His hair is longer, and the scruff on his face isn't to grow a beard, but because he keeps forgetting to shave.

"I say we get a little more creative," Tongue adds, staring down at Happy, who is at his feet.

"You want us to threaten him with a baby gator? What's that going to do?"

"Torture. Happy is growing, but his bite is strong," Tongue says proudly, puffing out his chest as if his kid is the best there is.

I can only imagine Tongue as an actual dad. He would be so protective, so intense, and his kids would probably be just as fucked in the head.

I drop my head in my hands, and my stomach growls, but I ignore it. I can't even think about eating right now. I haven't been able to stomach anything. Not with the vivid images playing in my mind every second of every day.

What if she's been calling out for me? What if she's been crying every day? What if she's been fighting and it hasn't mattered? What if he has been using her? I can't get her eyes out of my head. They are pleading for me to save her, and I can't.

I'm fucking done with this. I'll kill Maximo for what he has done. I don't give a fuck if he is Moretti's brother or not.

No one deserves to live after what he has done, but as long as Natalia's life is in his hands, I can't go too crazy. We have to save Natalia too. Innocent lives cannot be sacrificed. I have to try and think smart.

We find Mary. We find Natalia.

We kill Maximo.

I will kill her father.

This bullshit is done, and Moretti can take over as the mafia boss again. At least with him, we didn't have to worry about shit like this.

I check to make sure I have my ninja stars and get up from the chair. My girl's life has a fucking time bomb on it. I'm not about to let it go off.

I swing the basement door open and hurry down the steps. I don't tell anyone what I'm doing. I'm not asking Reaper for permission for what I can and cannot do to Maximo.

I'm just going to fucking do it.

Opening the playroom door, the metal hits against the wall as I stomp in. Maximo's head is bent, his breathing is labored and choppy, and his suit is nothing but soggy scraps from the blood, cuts, and piss saturating him.

His days are fucking numbered.

I grab him by the thick of his hair and yank his head back, then slap him across the face. "Wake the hell up!" He doesn't move; he just groans. "I said, wake up!"

When he doesn't, I let go and move around him. Along the wall is a counter with various tools, but it's the gasoline I'm after.

I'll set him on fire and send his rotten soul back to hell.

Taking a page from Boomer's book, I grab the red jug of gasoline and head toward Maximo, circling him like a lion, a beast waiting to fucking kill.

It's amazing how I went from feeling nothing to feeling everything in just a few days of being with Mary.

I sit the jug down on the floor, the floor vibrating a high-pitched frequency from the weight, and slip a few ninja stars from my pocket.

Maybe this will wake him up.

Gripping the silver between my fingers, I admire the pointed hooks on the tips of the star, then fling it through the air. A whoosh of a blade spinning sounds before thudding against Maximo's eye. His left eye opens, and he beings to scream. Blood flows down his right cheek in thick streams, and my nostrils flare when I hear his pain.

I was taking it too easy on him before.

I fling another, landing right in his crotch, and another painful wail begs for me to stop.

Never.

"You took my fucking eye! You took my eye!" Maximo pulls on the restraints doing his best to get out of the trap he is in. "And my dick! My dick is bleeding."

"And you'll lose it if you don't start talking." I hold my star up to the light and let it shine. Maximo's reflection mirrors off the metal. His mouth is open, begging for mercy, begging for me to let him go because he can't handle the pain anymore.

Footsteps sound at the door, and I see Reaper, Tool, Bullseye, Tongue, and Happy. And that crazy fucker is off his leash, opening his mouth in a deadly hiss when he smells blood.

"What the hell is that? What is that!" Maximo rocks back and forth to get the chair loose, but it's pointless. It's welded to the floor, and it isn't going anywhere.

"That is the reptile that is going to eat you for dinner if you don't start talking, and you better tell me everything, Maximo. Or I'm going to skin the flesh from your cock with the very tip of my ninja star. I'll take my time. I'll make sure every second is you in complete agony." I yank the star from his dick, which was more in his groin, but the threat was close enough. "Do you take me seriously, yet? Do you understand? Moretti has already told us to do whatever we wanted to you, because even he doesn't trust you. The man that can't remember anything remembers how he feels about you. What's that say?"

I yank his head back again so I can get a better look at his face in the light. His good eye is watering, and the star is stuck deep in his other eye. To drill in how serious I am, I pull it out, and his eyeball comes with it.

He screams until he pukes. I barely have enough time to get out of the way, so it doesn't get on my boots. The eye is nearly sliced in two, the nerves red and dripping from the back, and the hole in his eye socket is about to become a home for gasoline. With two fingers, I pinch the eye and pluck it off my weapon. It's squishier than I thought it would be.

"Have at it, Happy," I say, tossing the gator the eye. He catches it quickly, snapping his jaws before he swallows it down.

"Good boy," Tongue says, praising him as he pats him on the head.

"I promise I'll feed you bit by bit to Happy, and then I'll burn your goddamn bones, but not before I make you watch Happy eat your dick. Then, my Prez will rip your heart from your chest, and you'll see it stop pumping. Happy will eat that too. I'm done fucking around, Maximo. Where is she!"

Silence.

This is so fucking frustrating. I hate silence.

I pick up the jug and start to pour gasoline over his body. I know it burns the open wounds, but I don't care. I don't care about anything right now. I shove the nozzle between his lips, and he coughs from the fumes he inhales from the gasoline. "I'll make you drink this. What is your role in this? What is her father's plan? Why the hell were you at the barn? Where is she? What's so special about today?"

He nods eagerly, wide brown eye dripping with tears while the abyss on the other side cries blood. I rip the nozzle from his lips and toss it to the side, then take the same star that blinded him and put it against his neck. "Talk," I say.

"He's a business partner. At first, it was just drugs. I didn't want to get into anything else. When you're in my line of work, it isn't hard to figure out who is who. Everyone knows about the Preacher who doesn't follow the bible, if you know what I mean. I heard he was looking for his daughter. I got a picture, and any information would have my network tripling. The fights would grow, money would grow, power. It's all about the power," he says, blood spraying from his lips when he speaks.

"I didn't know she was an ol' lady at first. When he came to the hotel, he saw Natalia, and he said until he got Mary, he would keep her. I met him at the barn, which is where all transactions, drug, human, and whatever else related goes down. He said there was going to be an auction. The last one of the year. Natalia would be in it if I didn't comply, but then I started thinking, what's the harm? Moretti doesn't remember her anyway, and she'll be alright. She's a smart girl. She can get out of this—"

I stop him from talking by grabbing his shoulders and shaking them "—Where is the auction? What time does it start?" I remember Mason warning us that her father was going to do something like this.

"It's at my hotel. Elevator, east side, takes you to a level no one has ever seen before."

"What about the attack on the club a few months ago?" Reaper asks. "I knew it was fucking fishy that that college kid happened to shoot us up after working your club. That was you, wasn't it?"

"Yes," Maximo says. "I wanted to be on top. I wanted to be the one that controlled Vegas. I told you the truth, please, let me go. Please. I'm sorry."

Reaper gets in Maximo's face. "When we get back, I'm going to soak in your fucking soul, Maximo. You better count down the hours of your life as a free man."

"Please. I'll work for you. I'll put all my men at your disposal. I'll give you money. Anything. Please, just let me go. I'm sorry. I'm so sorry."

"Save it," Reaper snaps. "I don't want your money. I don't want your apology. I don't want shit from you but your goddamn heart beating in my hands as I crush the life out of you."

"Please, just let me go. I'll do anything. I never meant for our alliance to end up like this."

"You should have thought about that before you decided to fuck with the Ruthless Kings."

We storm out of the playroom and lock the door.

Leaving him alive is hard, but there is no more time to waste.

I have to get to Mary before someone buys her.

They don't even know that what they bid would never be enough.

She's fucking priceless.

CHAPTER TWENTY-FIVE

Mary

My energy is gone. I've been starved, slapped, jerked-off on, but at least my dad hasn't had sex with me.

That's the one silver lining in all of this.

I told him I didn't want to marry him, because maybe when someone buys me, they won't be as cruel as he is. Maybe I'll get lucky.

He's kept me drugged with a tranquilizer to keep me in line over the last ten days. Not enough to knock me out, but enough to keep me loopy. I've taken a thousand pictures in lingerie. I'm sure they are posted on every website imaginable. My father even made a brochure, so when the buyers come in, they have something to reference while they hide behind tinted windows.

Right now, all of the women are in a room, shoulder to shoulder, shivering from the cold and shock of the situation. There are no windows, no fan; it's a basic, plain room with four walls and a door we can't go out of.

"Mary?" a familiar voice says from behind me.

I turn around and gasp when I see Natalia, Moretti's daughter. She's a little younger than me, and I can see the innocence in her red eyes and wet cheeks. "Natalia, what are you doing here?" This is the first time I've seen all the women. I didn't know if I was going to be the only one or what, but of course, I'm not.

Men always think they can do whatever they want to us.

"My Uncle, Maximo. He gave me up," Natalia cries.

I'm not surprised. Maximo has always rubbed me the wrong way.

"Everything is going to be okay." I wrap my arms around her and bring her in for a tight hug. "They are going to find us, okay? They will." I have to believe that, or I will be lost the moment I step out onto that stage. I'm wearing a sheer bra that crisscrosses in the front, black lace panties, and stockings. My hair is down, but I've been ordered to play with it and give the buyers a show.

Natalia is wearing a light blue teddy, a short sexy nightgown that showcases her small chest and flat stomach.

"Do I hear three million?" my father announces over the speaker that's attached in the right corner of the room. "Sold!"

I almost expect to hear a slam of a gavel, but it's quiet.

"Next up, we have a special guest," he says, quickening the pace of my heart.

The door opens, and a man I've never seen before surveys the room. He's tall and buff, reminding me of a bodybuilder, and his eyes fall on me. He doesn't ask; he doesn't gesture for me to come to him; instead, he reaches out and snags me by my hair.

"No!" Natalia screams, trying to hold my hands to keep me from being dragged out the door. "No, Mary! Please, don't do this," she begs while the other women cry along the back wall, away from the door.

The guy still doesn't say anything. The way he has my hair has my scalp burning. I reach up to grab his hands to take the pressure off, but he trips me with his big boot and proceeds to pull me across the floor.

The hallway turns into a long tunnel the further away I get from the room that holds a dozen women. The walls are grey, the floor is black, and it's like I'm sliding along pools of ink. I'm waiting to sink into the ground. The tile is so spotless, so shiny, that as the light shines against it, I know it's going to suck me under into the unknown.

My captor's boots pound against the floor, loud drums that strike fear into my soul. When he comes to a stop, a door opens, and he throws me into the room. I roll to the middle, and the carpet leaves burns across my skin. I'm too afraid to get up.

But I do.

I push myself up onto my hands, then again to get to my feet. I'm surrounded by black glass. I can't see what's on the other side, but I have no doubt it is sleazy men in expensive suits debating if they want me.

Lifting my chin, I do my best to show I'm not scared of what will happen to me. My heart is ripped out, and I know my fate. Anything these men do to me will be nothing to the pain I already feel.

"Gentlemen." My father's voice is heard over the speaker again. "This lovely lady is named Mary St. James. She's beautiful, feisty, and has hair you can grip for days while you pound into her from behind. She's only ever been with one man, and that's me. You're going to want to get your hands on this one."

I fling my hair over my shoulder and give every window the middle finger.

My father laughs over the intercom, and a red light flashes above one of the windows.

"Oh, we have a bet coming in already," he whistles. "The betting is starting at 5 million. We can do better than that. You'll never have a pussy like it. It's tight, hot, and wet."

The way my father talks about me makes me sick. I can barely stay on my own two feet, and he is lying to them.

He is not the only man I've ever been with, and I hate that I have twelve years of memories to prove he wasn't a dream, but—shudder—experience.

Another red light goes off, then another from the left, one more to the right. It's a light show, and they won't stop flickering.

"Twelve million," my dad's voice lowers in a sexual hue. "Can I get fifteen?" But as soon as he asks the question, the glass to my right shatters from a gunshot. I scream in surprise, and through the glass I can hear shocked gasps and murmurs.

I glance up to see Knives there, holding the neck of a stranger, a star to his throat.

My heart leaps into my throat.

"Sold," Knives says, slicing the blade across the man's neck until he is bleeding out.

I flinch when another glass wall breaks from another bullet, and Slingshot is standing there. I've never seen him use his weapon besides to launch skittles, but when he does use it, it's a sharpened rock that's thrown. It hits the guy against the temple, and when he falls backward unconscious, Slingshot snaps his neck.

Another window breaks.

And another.

Then another.

All the Kings are there, their boots crunching against glass as they kill every single threat. Bullseye's dart hits a man between the eyes, Tool shoves his screwdriver into a man's throat, Tongue cuts out another villain's tongue, then walks to every room to do the same to the others, and Reaper appears.

With my father in his clutches.

"Mary!" Knives drops down from the window, landing on his feet, and slowly standing like some sort of superhero. "You're okay? Did he hurt you? Christ, he did. Look at your neck, Hellraiser—" He swings me into his arms and kisses me all over my face until our lips meet. "I was so goddamn worried about you."

I suddenly realize I'm weeping. Big, heaving sobs rack my body. But he is here. He rescued me. He is keeping me safe. Knives' strong, muscular arms hold me tight, and I am able to calm down and lose myself in his grip again.

I finally gather the strength to open my eyes and look at him. He looks horrible. His hair has grown out, his beard is longer and scraggly, which is not like him, and he has dark circles under his eyes.

"My dad liked to use his belt on my neck every day and masturbate until he got off."

"Did he..."

I glance away, ashamed, but shake my head. "He only jacked off on me after watching me struggle against his belt," I say, lifting my fingers to my black and blue neck.

"Only?" Knives growls. "Only?"

"What do you want to do?" Reaper says. "A quick death is too easy."

My father is shaking. "No, no, wait! Wait! I have money. I have a lot of money. Mary, you won't let them do this to me, right? You love me. You love me!"

"I hate you!" I don't know what comes over me, but I steal Knives' star, which is the one he gave me, his original one. The one he made when he was just fifteen. He must have found my jacket in the chaos of all this. Before I move another inch, Knives throws his jacket over me, and I make my way to Reaper.

But I can't get up there.

Reaper grins, then pushes my father down. He hits the ground, lands on his back, and groans. Knives steps on his arms and Reaper jumps down, landing on his legs. One breaks from the force, and my father exhales a wail of pain.

"I hate you so much, it physically aches my bones," I tell him as I straddle his stomach. "You want to kiss me?" I pinch his lips together with tears burning my eyes and, with the star, start slicing his lips off. I toss them to the side until all I see are teeth and gums.

Tongue laughs, giddy and excited to add to his collection.

"You stole my innocence. You raped me." I slide back, unzip his pants, and squeeze his pathetic cock until I know it hurts.

"Please," he cries. "Don't." The words are hard to hear, since he has no lips to speak with.

"You never listened to me! You never stopped! Twelve years!" Hot, fat tears drip down my cheeks. I yank his pants down and use the serrated edge of the star to cut his dick off. My father screams in agony, and it is the most cathartic sound I have ever heard in my life. I throw the inches to Tongue, but he ignores it.

"I want Happy to eat it! I want nothing left of my father, you hear me? Nothing!" I scream, then with bloody hands, I stab him right in the heart, a tear falling from my chin to his exposed mouth. "You wanted me to love you. You sick, twisted bastard."

"I'll take it from here," Reaper tells me gently, and Knives grabs my shoulders to steer me away.

"I want him so far gone, Reaper. I want him erased from the planet." My entire body is shaking uncontrollably, and when I glance down at my hands, all I see is blood.

"You got it, Mary," Reaper says, using the star embedded in the Preacher's chest as he cuts to rips his heart out. "May the Devil chew you up and spit you out, and may God have no mercy on your soul."

Knives turns me away, and my father's screams sound eerily familiar to mine over the years. We walk out the door that I came in from, and the bodyguard that brought me to the stage is there, aiming a gun right in the middle of Knives' chest.

I guess this is it. This is where I die to save Knives. It was worth it.

I do the only thing that enters my mind. I jump in front of him to take the bullet as the barrel rings release, but nothing ever comes.

I finally open my eyes to see Mason jumping in front of us, taking the shot in the chest. A gun in his own hand, he aims it at the guard and fires.

The guard falls to the floor in a useless giant heap when the bullet catches between his eyes.

"Mason! Mason, no. No!" Knives drops to the ground next to his brother, and I do the same, taking Mason's hand in mine. "I just got you back. I was supposed to work out my feelings. You can't… no," Knives is full of denial as he presses his hand against the bloody wound on Mason's chest. "We were supposed to be brothers again. What were you thinking taking a bullet for me, again?" Knives lifts Mason's head onto his lap. "You're going to be fine. You'll be okay."

"I wanted you to have the life you always deserved. It was me or Mary," he wheezes, a hint of blood foaming his mouth. "It had to be me. You were right—" he coughs roughly, struggling to gain his breath, "—I shouldn't have left you alone. I should have found you. Consider this—" he coughs again, "—taking responsibility."

"You saved her for me," Knives cries. "Thank you."

"I never stopped having your six, Knives."

"Thomas. Call me Thomas."

Mason grins, his face white as death and sweat dripping down his temples. "Thomas. My brother."

"Your brother," Knives says. "It's okay. It's okay, Mason. You can go. I'll be okay. Thanks to you, I'll always be okay."

Mason locks eyes with me, another weak grin on his lips, and his hand falls on top of Knives' that is pressing against his chest. And then his chest deflates as he exhales his very last breath.

"No," Knives clutches his brother against him, hugging his dead body. "I'm sorry, I'm sorry, I'm sorry, I'm sorry," he whispers.

The guys from the other room pile in. Reaper is soaked in blood, but he kneels down next to Knives and uncurls his fingers from Mason's shirt. "It's time to let go, Knives. We have to get out of here. We will bring him with us and have a proper burial."

"Let go?" Knives asks with red eyes.

"Let go," Reaper affirms.

"I'm not good at that," Knives replies, holding out his arm for me. "I'm not good at letting go at all."

I take his hands immediately, and Knives pulls me into a tight hug. "I'll never be able to repay him. He always saved me, and now he gave me you."

Mason made sure Seer's prediction didn't come true.

"There are more girls in a room down the hall, on the left," I tell Reaper.

Reaper takes charge and grabs the keys off the dead guards' body before handing them to Skirt and telling him, "Go get the girls."

"Thank you for coming for me, and I'm so sorry about Mason." I begin to cry. The adrenaline is starting to wear off. I'm overwhelmed and exhausted.

"I'll always come for you, just like my brother always came for me. You'll never have to worry about that." Knives lays a kiss on my forehead.

A minute later, Natalia comes out of the other room with the girls.

Reaper bends over and picks up Mason's body. "Come on everyone; we are going home."

We follow Reaper out, the women covered by jackets from the guys as we all huddle in the trucks.

When we get home, we can tell something is wrong.

It's quiet.

"Moretti and Maximo are gone!" Sarah screams out the front door as Reaper jumps out of the driver's side of the Ford Raptor.

And nothing good ever happens in silence.

EPILOGUE

Knives

One month later

"YOU MAY NOW KISS THE BRIDE," REAPER OFFICIATES, FINALLY TELLING ME TO KISS my bride. And I'm not going to half-ass this either. I dip her down over my leg, hold the back of her head, and kiss her until I know her knees are weak, and her pussy is wet.

Whistles and catcalls sound, and when I bring the kiss to an end, she nips my lip. "You put on a show on purpose."

"As if you don't like being the center of attention," I wink, lifting her up until she's standing straight again. I clasp her hand in mine and lift it in the air as another round of cheers sound.

I only wish my brother could have been here to see it.

I spent too much time being mad at him, too much time holding on to the past and the anger I felt, that I could have built new memories over his last few days on earth. We could have had a beer as men, talked as men, laughed as men, and not some silly little boys.

But I'm stubborn, and I know how to hold a fucking grudge, but I'll never do it again.

We left a seat open for him, and Mercy is sitting next to it, my brother's badge lying flat on the chair.

I'll never be able to thank him enough for saving Mary's life.

We decided to get married at the clubhouse. With friends and family around us. Yeti, Tyrant, and Chaos are on the ground.

Lady is in Poodle's arms. She's lasted so long, but we don't know why she's holding on. I'm glad she's here, though. I'm happy everyone I love is here to see me move on with my life.

Mary leans over and whispers, "I'm pregnant, and if it's a boy, I want to name him Mason."

My head whips to the side so damn hard and fast, I nearly lose my balance. I can't find the words. My mind is jumbled. I grab her hand, the one with my mom's ring on it, and hold on tight. "Are you serious? Don't play with me, Hellraiser. That's a cruel joke."

"No joking. I found out this morning," she says, laying her hand against my cheek. "Are you happy?" she asks, her long lashes shadowing her cheeks as she blinks.

The gold band that belonged to my father now sits on my hand, and as I stare at the wedding rings, the emotion bubbling up in my chest almost stops my heart.

There was a time when I thought happiness was something earned, but it isn't.

Happiness is something someone waits for.

And I couldn't be happier.

"Sonofabitch! She's pregnant!" I cheer, smiling from ear to ear, then swing her up in my arms.

"You owe me five bucks!" Maizey says, the little hustler wearing a purple princess dress.

I grin and lay another kiss on my wife. When her lips touch mine, everything fades away. It's her. It's me.

It's our baby.

And as my world rights itself, I realize it's quiet. The background noise is muted by love and happiness.

This. This is the silence I can live in, because I'm no longer alone.

I have a family.

And my ninja stars, of course.

THE END.

KNIVES PLAYLIST

HELLRAISER BY: MOTORHEAD

MAGIC BY: THE BLUE STONES

I WANT A LOVE LIKE JOHNNY AND JUNE BY: HEIDI NEWFIELD

MUTHAFUCKA BY: BEWARE OF DARKNESS

WALKING DISASTER BY: SAYWECANFLY

TOGETHER, WE'RE ALONE BY: SAYWECANFLY

CHASING HIGHS BY: TOO CLOSE TOO TOUCH

SCUMBAG BY: GOODY GRACE

AS ABOVE, SO BELOW BY: IN THIS MOMENT

HEADSPACE BY: FAME ON FIRE

ACKNOWLEDGEMENTS

To our Ruthless Readers thanks for sticking with us another year!
Give Me Books here's to another great year.
To all the bloggers and reviewed and shared Knives thanks y'all are the best.
To Wander and Andrey here's to another PHENOMENIAL YEAR.
Donna we love you! #BOOMERISDONNAS
Stacey at Champagne Book Design thanks for all your amazing work.
To my Instigator you're the best decision I've made.
Lynn as always thanks for being my rock all these years
Silla here's to another great year!
Carolina your enthusiasm is infectious
Harloe you are amazing
Mom love you
Jeff 5 LITTLE WORDS
Austin as always y'all are such a blessing
David Cowboys are gonna still suck this year!!

TONGUE'S TARGET

RUTHLESS KINGS MC
BOOK ELEVEN

COPYRIGHT© 2021 TONGUE'S TARGET BY KL SAVAGE

All rights reserved. Except as permitted by U.S. Copyright Act of 1976, no part of this publication may be reproduced, distributed, or transmitted in any form or by any means, or stored in a database or retrieval system, without prior permission of the author. The scanning, uploading, and distribution of this book via the Internet or via other means without the permission of the publisher is illegal and punishable by law. Please purchase only authorized electronic editions and do not participate in or encourage electronic piracy of copyrighted materials. This book is a work of fiction. Names, characters, establishments, or organizations, and incidents are either products of the author's imagination or are used fictitiously to give a sense of authenticity. Any resemblance to actual persons, living or dead, events, or locales is entirely coincidental. TONGUE'S TARGET is intended for 18+ older, and for mature audiences only.

PHOTOGRAPHY BY WANDER AGUIAR PHOTOGRAPHY
COVER MODEL: JONNY JAMES
COVER DESIGN: LORI JACKSON DESIGN
EDITING: INFINITE WELL
FORMATTING: CHAMPAGNE BOOK DESIGN

FIRST EDITION PRINT 2021

This book is for everyone who kept Tongue alive with their love for him and Daphne. Their story continues because of YOU. All the stories are written for our readers, but Tongue is special. For some reason, our lurking, dangerous, corner-loving killer became everyone's favorite. His story seems never-ending and we are so happy to be able to tell their journey.

Thank you everyone. I know Tongue and Daphne appreciate it and we do too.

Love is a journey that you never give up on, just as Tongue.

PROLOGUE

Daphne

Eight years old

My Barbie doll never gets mad at me, not like Daddy. Daddy is always screaming and yelling and his breath smells like that nasty stuff he drinks out of a silver can. He has always been mean but lately it has gotten worse. Mommy tries to calm him down, but every time she tries, he gets angrier.

"Are you fucking listening to me, you little brat?" He bends down and slams his drink on the table. He snatches the Barbie out of my hand, and I reach for it to get it back, but he lifts it in the air so I can't reach it. I shrink away from him and start to cry.

"You cry baby," he hisses. "Maybe you wouldn't get in trouble so much if you stopped playing with your damn dolls and fucking did what I told you to." Daddy throws the doll against the wall and the sound of her falling to the floor has me crying louder.

"Daddy, stop it. Leave her alone, please," I beg him. Mommy got me that doll. It's the only toy I have. I know that Mommy works really hard while Daddy sits in the chair and watches TV all day. She always comes home smelling like French fries and Daddy says she stinks and makes her shower.

He stinks too, but he doesn't allow anyone to tell him that.

"I said to go get me another beer."

"Daddy, I don't want to," I cry. "You don't need any more. Can't we watch a movie?"

"Can't we watch a movie?" he repeats what I say like my friends do on the bus

"Stop it!" I jump off the chair and land on the dirty floor with my bare feet.

He reaches out and grabs me by the hair when I squat down to pick up my Barbie. "Stop it!" He makes fun of me again and grabs the doll from my hands again. "You're spoiled. When I was growing up, I had to earn my toys. What the fuck have you done besides be a pain in my ass?" I try to get away from him, but he tightens his fingers in my hair and pulls harder. It hurts.

"You're hurting me, Daddy!" I cry when he throws me to the ground. I curl in a ball and press a palm against the spot on my head where it hurts the most. It burns.

"Maybe you'd learn to listen to me if you got your ass whooped," he says, undoing his black leather belt that's hit me so many times, I've lost count.

"No! No, please, don't. Please." I crawl away until I'm able to get to my feet and run toward my bedroom.

"Come back here, you little shit," he sneers, cracking the belt in the air in warning of what will happen if I don't stop running away.

It doesn't matter if I stop or not.

The end result is the same.

I run into my bedroom and slam the door, then lock it.

The number one rule in the house is to never lock the doors, but Daddy scares me. I don't want to be here anymore. I want Mommy to take me away and never look back. Daddy can keep the rundown trailer and the nasty drinks he likes. It's all he cares about anyway.

A loud *bang* crashing against the door yanks a scream from me. I push against the wall and look around for any kind of weapon that I think will stop him from hurting me. The only thing I have is the book my mommy reads me every night. It's an old copy of Little Women. I don't understand a lot of it, but the sound of Mommy's voice always puts me to sleep.

"You better unlock this door, Daphne, or so help me, I beat your ass until you can't sit for a week."

I'm frozen in place, staring at the door while my legs tremble. The door handle shakes while he pounds against the wood. I can't get out either. The only window in my room is nailed shut from the last time I tried to run away. Daddy hit me across the face while Mommy was sleeping. When I was pretending to be asleep, I waited until I heard the loud snores coming from the living room and opened the window, but I wasn't quiet enough. Daddy caught me just as I was about to close the window and escape. He yanked me back inside, locked me in the closest, and I wasn't allowed to come out until he was done.

It felt like forever, hearing the hammer hit the nails and him cursing underneath his breath before he opened the door to allow me to crawl back to bed.

He's going to get me.

I jump on the bed and lift the torn comforter and throw it over me to hide.

If I can't see the monsters, they can't see me.

"I swear I should have fucking left you and your mom before it was too late." He kicks the door with his boot, and I bury my face in the pillow to muffle my cries.

I wish Mommy were here. She always knows how to stop him.

"Fucking bitch," he swears, and in one last try, he kicks the door again. This time the wood cracks. I hear pieces of wood fly and hit the blanket covering me. I curl into myself tighter and squeeze my eyes shut. "How many times do I have to tell you," he says between broken breaths. "Not to lock the door." His hand wraps around my ankle and yanks me out of bed. "How many fucking times, Daphne?" he screams in my face and his spit hits my face.

"I'm sorry. I'm sorry," I say again, even if I know it doesn't matter.

He never stops.

"Is this what you want?" he asks, waving the Barbie in my face. "Look at me," he demands, slapping me across the cheek.

I cry out from the hard slap, which only burns more than usual because of the tears wetting my face. I raise my legs to kick him off, but he straddles my hips to keep me still.

He places the head of the doll between his teeth and rips it from her neck. "No!" I cry, slapping him against the chest. I hate him so much. It was the only doll I had. Mommy got it for me for my birthday last year. I don't get many gifts. Daddy takes all of her money and spends it on those nasty drinks.

I don't care that it was a toy. I care about it because it was from Mommy.

He spits the head out and it hits me in the face, tumbling to the floor. Then he throws the plastic body across the room. It hits something breakable, maybe the lamp, because in the next instant, it falls to the floor and shatters.

He flips me over and I try to get away from him again, kicking his stomach with my feet, but he's too strong. "Fucking sick of you and your momma disobeying all the damn time." He yanks down my pants and holds my head down into the carpet. I brace myself for what's to come and shut my eyes, a single tear falling down my cheek.

The belt cracks in the air like lightning and rakes sharply across my skin, like fire burning wood.

I keep my mouth shut, like I always do for the first few strikes. He always likes to hear me scream. He likes to hear that he thinks he is getting through to me, but he isn't. The only thing it does is make me hate him more.

After five lashes, I can't keep the pain inside anymore. My screams ring in the room and Daddy laughs when I try to get away from him again.

"You get your hands off my daughter!" Glass breaks behind me and Daddy falls to the side groaning.

I scurry away, my butt burning with every inch I move, and I pull up my pants. Daddy is on his stomach, a hand pressed against the back of his head, and an alcohol bottle is shattered all over the room. At least, it smells like alcohol.

"Come on, Daphne, we are getting out of here," Mommy says, taking my hand in a tight grip and dragging me out the door.

She still has her work uniform on. It's checkered blue with a white collar, and her apron is black. A groan comes from behind us and we are nearly to the front door when Daddy stumbles against the wall.

"Listen to me," Mommy squats to the floor so she's eye level with me. I'm happy that I look like her. We have the same blue eyes and brown hair. "You are going to take this money—" she digs into her apron and takes out a wad of money "—and you're going to go to the neighbors and call your Aunt Tina, okay?"

The closest neighbor lives through the woods on the other side. My bottom lip wobbles. I'm trying to stop crying, but I can't. The tears keep falling. "You're scaring me, Mommy."

"It's going to be just fine, baby. I'm going to stay here and take care of your dad."

"What about you? Come with me, please!" I beg her and take her hand, tugging her to the door. "We can run away, Mommy. We can be together. We can get away from him." I cry for her, for me, for us. I want us out of this house.

"Come here, you bitches! Don't try to take my daughter from me!" Daddy stumbles again, falling to the floor. "You two better come here." He opens the drawer on the coffee table and Mommy opens the front door to push me out.

I dive to the left so she can't get to me, but she grabs me by the shirt when she hears something click. Her eyes widen and she begins to cry too. "We need to go. Daphne, come on!" She drags me away from the front door just in time before a gunshot rigs out.

I scream when realize what Daddy was looking for in the coffee table.

"You two get back here and I'll think about forgiving you," he says, sounding more stable than he did when Mommy hit him in the head with a glass bottle.

"I'm scared," I whisper as Mommy has us running through the kitchen to get to the back door.

"I know, but everything is going to be just fine, baby. I promise." She opens the sliding glass door and shoves the money in my hand. "Now, tell me what you're going to do."

"Mommy—"

"Daphne, what are you going to do?" she says, frustrated.

"I'm going to go to the neighbors and call Aunt Tina," I sob.

"You aren't going to look back here, do you hear me? You swear?"

I nod and rub my nose across my arm. "I swear."

"Where the fuck are you?" Daddy yells in the house.

Mommy wraps her arms around me and gives me a kiss on the head. "I love you, baby. I love you so much. Don't you ever forget that."

"This is your last chance!"

Mommy turns around and sees Daddy behind her, shirt off, belly hanging out.

"Get your ass back inside, Daphne, or I'm going to kill your momma," he says.

I panic. I don't want Mommy to get hurt. I take a step inside, but she blocks me and slams her hands against my chest, shoving me backward. I lose my footing and fall backward, hitting against the porch rail. She slams the sliding glass door in my face and her hand touches the glass. "I love you," she mouths. "Go," she says just as another gunshot rings out. Blood spreads across her shoulder and the air is forced out of my lungs. "Run!" she yells, her hand landing on the glass again.

Only this time, it's bloody.

"Mommy," I choke her name out as I trip down the steps.

Go to the neighbors. Call Aunt Tina.

I sprint into the woods and hide behind a tree trunk, staring at what is happening through the sliding glass door. Her back is to the door and Daddy is facing her, aiming the gun at her head. I cover my mouth, my tears flowing freely now.

Another shot fires, sending blood all over the door. It drips down just as Mommy falls to the ground.

Daddy opens the door and shoots the gun in the air, sending birds flying off the trees. "Come back here, Daphne! I won't hurt you; I promise." His feet pound down the steps, banging against the wood. I hear the gun click again, and I remember my mommy's panic when she heard it.

I do what she tells me to.

I run, and I don't look back.

And I don't want to remember anything about this night.

Ever.

CHAPTER ONE

Daphne

Present

I GASP AWAKE. The sheets stick to my skin from the sweat beading across my body. I haven't had a dream like that in a long time. I don't know what happened to my mom, but I know Dad didn't kill her. He was an asshole, but a killer? No.

At least, I don't think...

I press my palms against my eyes and take a few deep breaths.

"What's wrong, Comet?" Tongue asks me, flipping on the lamp on the nightstand. "You're sweating." His hand lands on my cheek and turns my head to look at him. His touch settles the wave of uneasiness inside me. "Do I need to kill someone? Has someone scared you?" He reaches for his knife that is sitting next to the lamp.

I know he is telling the truth. Tongue would do anything for me, and that brings me comfort too. "No, I'm okay. I promise. It was a dream. I think it was a dream. I don't know if my mind is playing tricks on me or not."

He places the knife down on the nightstand and slides his arms under me, holding me to his chest. "I think you're perfect the way you are," he says, sliding a finger down my cheek.

I can't help but believe him, especially when he looks at me like I'm the only person in the world. I lean my head against his chest and sigh, replaying the dream over and over again in my head. I jump when the gunshot rings throughout my mind, as if it just happened in front of me.

"You're okay," Tongue whispers, gliding his hand through my long brown hair. "I'm not ever going to let anything happen to you, Comet. Not ever. You're safe with me."

The deep tone of his voice vibrates his chest, slightly tickling my cheek. I let out a deep exhale and snuggle into him further. I wish I could crawl inside him and stay safe forever.

"Want to talk about it?" he asks after a few minutes of being in silence.

I'm staring at the stacks of books all around the room and smile when I think about how Tongue only has these books because of me. He doesn't care that he can't read or write, he just wants the books because I like them. How lucky am I?

He will know how to read soon, though. Every night we sit in bed and I teach him how to pronounce certain words and write. We are starting small and working our way up. It's hard to learn things like this when you're an adult. As a child, you're introduced to it your entire life through school. As an adult, there isn't that same structure, so it becomes more difficult.

You couldn't tell with Tongue. He's so brilliant, and he doesn't even know it. But I do.

He is catching on quick; it won't be long before he is reading by himself or writing letters. No one gives him the credit he deserves, but I always will. He is everything and so much more.

"I think I need to see Doc," I whisper to him as my heart pounds in my chest.

"Hey, why do you think that?" He flips me around without effort until I'm straddling his lap. My hands land on his bare chest, his skin warm under my palms.

He's beautiful.

I look down and with my fingers trace the tattoo on his stomach that says, 'Unscarred'. It makes me shake my head. He's one of the most scarred people I know. "What's this tattoo mean?" I ask, not wanting to talk about me just yet.

"I want to believe that every time I look in the mirror, I'm not completely fucked up," he states with a shrug of his left shoulder. "I know it's a contradiction, because look at me—" he says, spreading his arms wide. "I'm scarred all over."

I lay one hand on his heart and the other on his cheek. "I'll have to disagree. You have the purest form of love I've ever seen. This," I press against his chest, the beat drumming against my palm steady and strong. "This managed to survive untouched." I stare into his rich brown eyes and watch as he tilts his head. The expression on his face softens, the wrinkles around his eyes disappear, and a faint pink blush tints his cheeks.

He doesn't take praise well. He isn't used to it.

"We know that isn't true," he says, glancing away from me, suddenly shy.

Tongue is a contradiction. There is no doubt about that. He's a brutal killer. Obsessive. Intense. But in intimate moments like this, I manage to see the glimpse of the innocence inside him.

"I've lived to experience your love, Wayne. I think out of all people, I'd know."

It isn't often I call him by his first name, but sometimes when I want what I'm saying to really stick, I make sure not to call him Tongue.

He wipes above the top of my brow, then brings his thumb to his mouth and sucks it between his lips. Tongue moans as his eyes flutter shut. "Even your sweat is sweet, Comet."

"Now I know you're lying." I play with the strands of hair curling along his nape with my fingers.

His eyes snap open. The abyss of those chocolate eyes swirls with anger as his nostrils flare. He pops his thumb out of his mouth and the skin shines with his saliva. Before I can blink, his hands are around my neck and his wet thumb presses under my chin. I gasp, trying not to get turned on by his dominance and rage.

"And when have you ever known me to lie to you?" He sits forward and hovers his lips over mine. "I'm livid that you think I would." He nips at my chin, gliding his thumbs to my mouth and tracing my lips. "I should punish you for saying such a thing."

"I was only kidding." I stretch my neck back to give him more room to explore.

"I don't like jokes like that. They aren't funny."

Tongue isn't the kind to find amusement in jokes. He doesn't seem to understand what is funny or what causes laughter. I don't hear him laugh or see him smile much, hardly ever; but every now and then I'll catch him looking at me and the slightest of grins will tilt his full lips.

And then, poof. It's gone.

But I get to be the lucky one to witness it.

"Tongue."

"Yeah, Comet?"

"Kiss me," I beg him, since he is the reason why my body is on fire right now.

"Not until you tell me about your dream and why you think you need to see Doc."

"That's blackmail." I lift my hand and caress his bare chest and over to the puckered scar from where he got shot a few months back. "How's your arm?"

"Don't change the subject."

He knows me too well, but I am worried about him. Even with physical therapy, he hasn't gained all the strength back in his arm. The heaviest thing he can lift right now is a gallon of milk, and even then, his bicep shakes. Some days, he is fine, because everyone has good days, but there are days where it's limp at his side. Doc says it's normal, but I can't help but worry. A part of Tongue's persona that I know he needs is his strength. He acts like it isn't affecting him, but I know better. I see him looking at himself in the mirror, flexing his hand and trying to lift his arm above his head, but he can't manage just yet. He's struggling and he won't let me help.

"Tongue, I don't want to talk about it because it scares me, and I don't know what's real anymore. And when I don't know what's real, I start to look at everything like it's a symptom of my psychosis." I tilt my head down, the desire on pause as I fiddle with the frayed edge of the blanket. "I need to know that everything around me isn't a version of something morphed and completely—"

"—Fucked up?" he finishes for me, rubbing his hands down my sides until they land on my hips. He gives a quick squeeze before roaming up my body again and pushes the long brown strands of my hair behind my shoulders.

"We're all fucked up here, Comet." He wraps his fingers around my wrists and drags my hands down his chest. His abs ripple under my touch and the 'Unscarred' tattoo comes to life as if it is trying to jump off his skin.

"You feel that? I'm real, Comet. This is real. And whatever you have to tell me," his voice is a rasp after speaking so much. Talking isn't one of Tongue's favorite things to do. He has scars all over his tongue; sometimes when he speaks his words slur from overuse. "Whatever you tell me, I'll tell you what's real or not. You can always count on me for that, okay?"

"Yeah?"

"Yeah, Comet. You know you can always count on me to tell you the truth. Please, talk to me. I don't like that you're having nightmares and waking up sweaty the last few nights."

"I want to see Doc because I don't know what my dreams mean. I keep having the same nightmare."

Tongue presses a kiss against my collarbone, causing sparks to scatter along my skin. "Yeah?"

I nod, pinching my brows together as I piece together what I remember from the dream. "It always starts off with me holding the only Barbie I ever had. My mom got it for me. She worked long hours at the diner, and we could hardly afford anything growing up. In my dream, dad was an alcoholic and mean, so damn cruel and—"

"What makes you think he wasn't those things?"

I scoff. "He couldn't have been. I never remember him being mean to me. Impatient, yes, but mean? No. And he would drink but it never made him a bastard like he was in my dream. He even stopped drinking before I moved out here."

"What happened in your dream?" Tongue asks gently. "What's got you so shaken up, Comet?"

Anxiety clenches my chest when I remember the hatred in my dad's eyes as he looked at me. "He would call me worthless and stupid. He ripped my doll from my hand, and he threatened that if I didn't get him another beer, I'd never see the doll again. He got louder and he kept spewing these words that made me scared of him, so I ran to my room and locked the door." I quickly wipe my cheek when a tear slips free. "My window was nailed shut. I had nowhere to go. I hid under the covers because when you're a kid, monsters didn't exist if you hid under the covers."

"Monsters always exist, no matter where you hide. I don't understand," Tongue says. I know he is doing his best to understand, but he isn't like most people, and I doubt he was like most kids.

"It's just something I thought," I say simply. "Anyway, Dad kicked the door down and he yanked me out of the bed, tore the head off my doll, pulled my pants down and started to spank me because I was so ungrateful."

"He touched you?" Tongue growls, digging his fingertips into my thighs. "He fucking touched you?"

"In my dream," I remind him since I don't know if my dream was real. "Breathe, Tongue. Like I said, I don't know if it's real." I place my head on his shoulder and kiss the side of his neck where his scruff tickles my lips. "My mom came home and hit him in the head, picked me up, and we ran. She told me to run through the woods and go to the neighbors house to call Aunt Tina, her younger sister. Dad came after us with a gun and we ran to the sliding glass door. My mom tossed me outside and told me to run, slammed the door, and my dad shot her. I was so shocked I just stood there, but she begged me to go, so I jumped down the steps and ran to hide behind a tree. I made the mistake of peeking around the trunk to see my dad aim the gun at mom's head and shoot. Blood went everywhere. And that's when I ran and then that's when I wake up every time."

Tongue's chest is heaving, and a growl is constant in his throat. "I'm going to kill him. I'm going to fucking murder him."

"No, Tongue, my dream can't be real, because I lived with him, remember? Was he the world's best dad? No. I came here to prove I didn't need him. My dreams can't be real."

"Why not?"

"Well, for one… my Aunt Tina would have never agreed to send me back to Dad after he killed my mom."

"What if she doesn't know?" Tongue says distantly. "What you're dreaming, those aren't normal dreams, Comet. It's like something deep inside you is trying to tell you the truth. Remember when you were at the asylum with…" he sneers in disgust before he says his brother's name, "Porter? You said you saw your mom. Then, your dad showed up and shot her. Comet, what makes you think your dreams aren't real? Trauma caused your psychosis, and for the longest time you thought your mom killed herself. What if that isn't the case?" He reaches for the bottle of water next to the bed, unscrews the top, and drinks half of it. The plastic crunches in his hand. "And I'm going to relish in killing him."

"No," I shake my head as I fight the urge to sob. "Promise me, Tongue. Promise me you won't do anything until we know the facts." I stare at him dead in the eye and lay my hands on either side of his face. "Promise."

He wraps his arms around me and hauls me to his chest. "Only until we know more," he states. "After that, I can't promise anything."

"I know, and I wouldn't want you to."

His palm cups the side of my neck and his thumb is on my cheek, wiping away the tears. "I think your dreams are real and I think you need to start cutting yourself some slack. You aren't insane, not in the way you think you are."

"And in what ways am I insane?" I ask, setting my arms on his shoulders.

He bites his lower lip as he brings his face closer to mine. "You're crazy about me," he says. "Downright mad for me." His nose brushes along mine.

"What makes you say that?"

"Because the only way a woman like you could love a man like me is if you're fucked up in the head in some way."

The way he views himself absolutely shatters me. "You know how you said I needed to cut myself some slack?"

A hesitant nod bobs his head, and he isn't able to look at me. "I need you to be able to do the same. There is nothing wrong with you, Tongue. Nothing. You are perfect for me and what this world needs you to be. When you give yourself a break, that's when I'll give me a break," I say to him, enjoying the feel of his chest pressed against mine.

Tongue is the epitome of darkness, a long dark tunnel that leads to the middle of nowhere.

At least, I know that's what people think.

What others fail to recognize is someone's nowhere, is someone else's somewhere. And wherever the darkness leads Tongue, that's my somewhere, because wherever he is, is where I'm meant to be.

There it is. The rare tilt of the lips, a crooked grin that could hardly be classified as happiness or a real smile. Again, that's what others would think, but I know Tongue. This is as real as it gets for him. I trace the outline of his mouth, trying to memorize the small change to his face.

He has such beautiful teeth too. Smiling takes the hard edge off from his face.

Tongue surprises me when he swings his legs over the bed and lifts me into his arms. "Where are we going?" I ask, but he doesn't say a word.

He walks into the direction of the bathroom, stepping over mounds of books. "Open," he states when he gets to the door.

I reach a hand out and twist the knob, then he steps inside the large en suite bathroom. I turn on the light, and he plops me on the counter. The cold surface against my bare butt has me shivering. "Holy Moly, it's cold in here," I say, wrapping my arms around my midsection.

"Not for long," Tongue informs me as he turns the shower on. Steam fills the room and fogs the mirror. I'm left with the view of his back flexing as he dips inside the shower to check the temperature of the water. My eyes travel down the impressive canvas of his body, mapping the geometric tattoos across his shoulders that lead halfway down his back.

With every bend and twist he makes, the ropes of muscle tense. As he shifts his feet, his plump bubble butt flexes too, then leads down to his thick thighs that have my mouth watering.

"I can feel your eyes on me," he tells me, keeping his back to me. "I can always feel your eyes on me, Comet."

"I can't help it. You're a sight no woman in their right mind would ever look away from." Even his scars hypnotize me. He hates them and tries to cover them with tattoos, but they will always be there, and I'll do my best every day to reassure him that his scars are beautiful.

When he turns around, his cock sways left to right, hard and long, thick with a livid red tip. His sack is heavy, hanging between his legs. His abs ripple and his pecs jump as he struts over to me like a peacock showing his feathers.

My eyes land on the small lines on his upper chest from our knife play. The memory of feeling the sting of pain as he plunges his thickness between my legs has stolen my ability to breathe.

"And what are you thinking about?" he growls, caging his arms on either side of me.

My folds slide together from the liquid heat dripping out of me, and I moan when he drags his hand up my leg. He stops when he gets to my inner thigh, his fingers brushing the spot just below my pussy.

"No need to tell me. I can feel what you are thinking about." He drags his fingers long my seam, gathering the juices but not applying pressure. He's a tease. "You want me?"

"I always want you." I hold my breath as he sucks his fingers into his mouth. He tilts his chin down and a strand of dark hair falls across the left side of his face.

He picks me up and takes us into the shower stall. Since we live in the clubhouse as our home is being built on the property, the bathroom is your typical one. Plain white tiles, plain ceramic tub, shower, and sink. It's nothing special. But Tongue is making sure that the bathroom in our new home will be what dreams are made of.

Tongue pushes the blue curtain to the side and steps into the tub. The hot water sprays against my back, but not for long, because he presses me against the wall. His cock is nestled against my entrance. His shoulders hunch. His teeth dig into my skin of my neck.

"Yes," I whimper, clawing my nails into his back.

But then he steps away, leaving me hot and bothered. "What... what the fuck, Tongue?" I don't curse often, but when I do, it's usually when I'm overly frustrated.

He holds out his hand for me to take, and I pout my lips as I slide my palm into his. "I want you, you know that. You can see that, but right now, I want to take care of you." He tips my head back so the water soaks my hair. "I've realized that maybe I haven't like I should be. "

"Don't say that. You know that isn't true. You take better care of me than anyone."

He grunts in reply, not believing what I say. He massages my scalp as the floral scent of my shampoo invades my senses. I close my eyes and let him do what he wants. If this is what he thinks I need, then I'm going to let him do whatever he wants.

"That feels good," I slur as sleepiness hits me from waking up in the middle of the night. I could go back to bed right now.

Mmm, he's right. I needed this.

He tilts my head back again, careful to keep the soap out of my eyes as he languidly rubs his palm over the curve of my head to get my hair free of shampoo.

"You're mine."

"I am, Tongue."

"All mine," he growls, rubbing the sudsy loofah over my breasts.

The scratchy material glides over my hard nipples. The sleepiness that weighed on my body moments ago is gone, replaced with lust he seems to love to stir inside me. I open my eyes to see him staring at the space between my legs as he drops the loofah between them. Inhaling, I stand on my tiptoes and dig my nails into his shoulders. He rubs back and forth, cleaning my most delicate area; it shouldn't be such a turn on, but it is.

His cock is still hard, curling up and over his belly button, the vein pronounced with the blood pumping through it. Right as I think he is going to do more than clean me, he pulls the loofah away and drops it to the bottom of the tub.

"Tongue, please," I beg of him, needing him to do something, anything to alleviate the pressure inside me. I wrap my palm around his cock and squeeze, needing him to snap out of this idea that the way he can make me feel better is to handle me like glass.

He growls low in his throat and unhooks the showerhead from above us, switches the settings, and washes me off.

I stroke him just as he changes the settings again on the showerhead until it is a quick, pulsing rhythm. Tongue doesn't leave me guessing with what he is about to do, he just does it. He inserts the showerhead between my legs until the constant flow of water is cascading on my swollen, sensitive clit.

"Tongue, oh god," I moan, trying to remember to stroke him as I get taken higher with every hard beat of water against me.

He rocks his cock in and out of my fist to bring himself to orgasm along with me. It doesn't take long for the showerhead to do its job. My toes curl along the floor of the tub and my stomach flips with warmth. I have to rip my face away from his and take in a much-needed breath as my orgasm shatters me from the inside out.

I cry out his name, clawing at his chest as waves of ecstasy course through me. There is a distant voice in the back of my head telling me that I let go of his cock too soon, but it doesn't seem to matter. Tongue drops the showerhead and forces me to my knees, pries my mouth open, and thrusts himself between my lips.

I gag and choke but let him use me anyway because he deserves it. I love it when he does this.

Holy Moly, he has a big dick. I can't take it all, but it never stops me from trying. He grabs the side of my head and his sack slaps underneath my chin. My eyes lock onto the sharp edge of his jaw. The water is a river flowing down his chin as he stares down at me. His hair from this angle looks like wet branches hanging down his face. His piercing eyes are black as evil as he uses me.

He plunges his cock as far as he can down my throat, grunting as warm creamy streams fill my mouth. I do my best to swallow, but instead of holding himself still, he ruts through his orgasm and continues to fuck my mouth until he is satisfied.

When he is done, his come is dripping down my chin, and I'm licking my lips trying to get it all. His right hand grips my face and hauls me to my feet, slamming his lips down on mine to help clean himself off me.

"I fucking love you," he snarls into my mouth.

And to be the woman that's somehow earned this man's love, a man that had no idea he was capable of it makes me feel like one in a million.

Who am I kidding?

Tongue and I are one in a million.

CHAPTER TWO

Tongue

SOMETIMES I WONDER IF I'M TOO ROUGH WITH DAPHNE, MY BRIGHT RARE COMET. I tend to lose control with her sometimes. Lose my sense of mind. But then I see the dazed look in her eyes whenever we have sex, and I know I could never lose my way with her, because she's meant to be mine. She's meant to love whatever we do together because she was made for me.

I'm dangerously obsessed with this woman. She has no idea just how threatening that is, or maybe she does. Maybe I know nothing.

No, that's not true.

I know she's taught me that I'm capable of an endless number of things. Daphne has taught me that there are infinite amounts of possibilities I can do and the only person that stops me from accomplishing anything, is me.

Daphne is my reason for change. Don't get me wrong, I'll never be like Doc or Juliette. I don't know if I'll ever have a different purpose than being a stone-cold killer. Maybe the only purpose I'm meant to have in this life is Daphne. I'm okay with that. I'm a better man in some ways, but I'll never change in others.

I'm dead set in most of my ways, but I'm more alive in more ways than one.

I turn over in bed and see her next to me. Her dark hair lies across the blue pillowcase and the blanket has fallen to her hips, leaving her torso exposed. Her hand is tucked under her cheek, her elbow bent right over her breasts, hiding them from me.

I don't like it when her body is hidden from me.

She's so small, so delicate, it's hard to believe I haven't broken her yet.

I press a kiss to her shoulder, and she rouses but doesn't wake. I want her to rest since she hasn't been sleeping well and our late shower scene didn't help matters any, but I don't regret it. I love fucking her face and seeing those big blue eyes stare at me, her mouth split wide open with my cock. It only happened a few hours ago and I'm ready to do it again.

Her lips are swollen and red and nothing looks prettier.

Which gives me an idea. I roll out of bed and grab my jeans off the floor. I slide them on and leave them unzipped and unbuttoned because I want to be comfortable. I walk around the bed, stepping over books so I don't ruin them. I'd be so upset. These are one of our most prize possessions. I can't read good—well, I mean. I can't read well. But that doesn't matter. Daphne has a huge love for them and that means I do too. In our new house, I'm building her a library. She doesn't know it yet, but I can't wait to show her. She's going to be so happy, and then every day I won't have to dance around stacks of books.

Each one has different colored post-its. She has her own system. Blue for her favorite sex scene, which we have played out a few. I never want to stop doing that. Red for a violent scene. Yellow for ones that made her smile. Orange for the ones that made her cry. And if you open up a book—any book, it doesn't matter—there is always a sentence highlighted on every page. It's as if she dissects the words and stores them in her brilliant mind, and I'm envious of her ability to do that.

I hope one day I can do the same. The only thing I can do right now is struggle with kid's picture books and write my name and Daphne's. It's hard not to be embarrassed by it, but she reads books that are four hundred pages and then she somehow has the ability not to judge me but treat me with compassion as she teaches me how to read.

I sound like an idiot sounding out those simple words. But when I get frustrated, she's there to soothe me. She has all the patience in the world and that's the only reason I'm able to get through our daily sessions.

"Good Morning, Happy." I tap the glass of his tank that he is nearly too big for, which reminds me that I need to start Happy's Haven. He is getting too big. He gives me a wide smile, showing me all of his teeth. People think he wants to eat me, but I know better. Happy and I have a connection. I bring my nose to the cold glass and Happy turns around and presses his nose against it too. "Who's a good boy? You are. You want a treat?" I keep my voice low, so I don't wake Daphne. It's important that she sleeps.

I'm going to have to look into the truth of her father. I believe in my gut that her dreams are a way for her mind to tell her what really happened, and I swear to God, I'm going to be that man's worst nightmare.

He thinks he can inflict fear? He doesn't know true fear. When I get my hands on him—not if but when—he's going to pray for a quick death. And you know what I'm going to do?

Tell him I'm agnostic so his prayers don't mean anything to me. And then I'm going to take my time slicing him. I only believe in what I can kill and Daphne.

That's all I'll ever need.

What's belief if you can't see it? What is faith if you can't touch it? Those concepts are too complex. I'm too simple of a man to try to understand them.

Taking a deep breath, I calm myself so I don't fly out of the clubhouse and take matters into my own hands. I unscrew the treat jar and dig my fingers inside to grab a piece of bull tongue, then toss it in the tank. Happy hisses, flinging his tail back and forth through the water, then snaps his jaws shut after he catches the treat.

"Good boy," I say to him, wishing I had his haven ready. I'll feed him live animals then, and he can hunt. He'll like that. I know I like it when I hunt, so it only makes sense that he would too.

I give a tap to the tank before turning around and walking toward the closet. I swing the doors open and stare at the filing cabinet. A lot of emotions are coursing through me right now as I stare at it, but the biggest thing I feel is betrayal. I'm not over what the guys did, breaking into my privacy and opening wounds all over again. Maybe in time I will, but right now? I have the urge to kill every single one of them who saw what is in these journals. I haven't drawn since.

I've been too scared, which is something I don't like to admit. I never get scared, but those journals hold nightmares that create the torture in hell. I don't want to see what used to exist, but I want to start drawing the good things in my life now that I have them.

I have good things.

That's so hard for me to understand.

"Good things," I mutter to myself as I reach for the gray drawer and open it, seeing dozens of black books. Some are worn and tattered, the edges curled up and wrinkled, while some are new and barely opened. I bend down and grab a new journal, one that is still in the plastic wrapping, then grab my charcoal pencils Daphne got me.

She wants me to really focus on my art, but I don't know how, not when chaos is constantly living in my mind.

I don't know how to focus on something I want without ruining it. Daphne is different. I've ruined her in ways that can never be erased, but I don't regret them. I want to learn how to want something like I want Daphne. I want to focus on something like I focus on her.

How?

Daphne has been the only thing in the world that's been able to grab my focus and keep it.

I guess that's why she's about to be my muse.

I head around the bed, stepping over those damn books without looking because their location is seared into my memory. I know this room like the back of my hand. Even the headboard is made out of books, something she fucking loves, and I never plan on changing that. In the new house, the bed is going to bigger and higher.

Sighing when I plop in the chair in the corner, I turn on the lamp, which casts a soft yellow glow on my side of the room. It lets me see her better. I take off the plastic wrap and drop it the floor, the crinkling louder than what I wanted it to be. I hold my breath in hopes it doesn't wake my Comet up. After a few seconds of her lying in the same position, I open the journal.

Like with any new book, the binding is smooth as it opens, and the first page has a 'this journal belongs to' section. I never do this, but I'm going to this time. I write my name on the designated line. The black charcoal makes one line down and I smile to myself because I know what I'm doing.

Oh, wait. I need to make it capitalized. First letters in names are always capitalized. That's what Daphne said.

I make another line on top of the other to create a T, then finish writing the rest of my name. Hmm, maybe I should have written my real name. Oh well, maybe next time. When I get done, I hold my journal out in front of me and while my handwriting looks a lot like Maizey's, it's mine and it's there, on paper.

On. Paper.

And I did it all by myself. It seems ridiculous to be so proud, since I'm a grown man learning to write, but I am so damn happy.

With new excitement, I lay the journal on my lap and flip a white page, then analyze the love of my life while she sleeps soundly.

Damn it, I can't get over her beauty. A man like me and a woman like her don't make sense, but I'm glad the universe made an exception, because I need her.

The navy blue blanket is still hugged around her hips. Instead of being on her side, she twisted her back to be flat on the bed and her hips are still on their side. Her arm is angled above her head, and now I can see her breasts. My cock takes notice and begins to plump in my jeans. All I want to do is ravish her right now, but I'm trying to think about her and what she needs.

And with everything going on inside her head, she needs rest.

With a disappointed growl at myself, I begin to sketch.

I ease a line down the page, curving it where her waist is, then stop, since the blanket covers the rest of her body. I can count five-hundred places on her body that need to have my mark or name on it. We still haven't gotten married or gotten tattoos of each other's names. I'll need to think of a remedy to that soon.

Ignoring the throb in my cock and the desire in my veins, I drag the pencil over the page, getting lost in the lines and shading to bring her image to life. I take a peek every now and then to make sure I'm doing her justice, which I'm not, because nothing compares to the real thing.

The faint golden hue of her skin, her small perky breasts with tight dark pink nipples, her small waist, and the memories of my hands exploring every inch of her…

"Damn it, what was I doing?" I mutter to myself, forgetting the next part of the picture I was going to focus on. See? I can only focus on her.

All the time.

She consumes me.

"Oh," I say when I realize her right breast isn't finished. I drag my pinky finger under the curve, giving her body a natural contour, then make my way to the other.

When her body is done, I make my way to her face. I draw the slim column of her neck, the delicate soft jaw I've dragged my lips across, and her pouted lips I've kissed and fucked.

I growl again when my cock fully hardens, and I can't lay the book flat on my lap because my erection is in the way. I can't blame myself. Of course I'm going to get turned on when the woman I love is naked in front of me.

Lifting my leg, I cross an ankle over my knee and prop the journal against my thigh. She's so serene and calm in this moment. I try to think back to when I ever looked like that, but I can't think of a time or place.

The charcoal scratches along the paper as create long strokes for her hair. When I'm done sketching her, I begin to work on her surroundings, like the bed and books, the nightstand, the closet behind her, and just... draw what I see.

I've always been better at this then I have been at writing anyway.

I do something I've never done again. I write my name in the bottom right corner of the page. Not that anyone will ever see this. If they did, I'd fucking feed them to Happy. The only person who can ever see Daphne naked is me.

"Are you done?" she whispers, her voice light and full of sleep, but her eyes don't open so I can't see the monumental shade of blue staring at me.

"You know what I'm doing?"

She smirks. "I hear your pencil against the page. It didn't take long to figure out."

"Are you mad?" I ask, wondering if I should have asked. "I couldn't help it. You're so beautiful and peaceful, I wanted to capture it."

This time, her eyes do open, and she shakes her head and scoots to the edge of the mattress, holding out her hand. "I could never be mad at you for finally drawing. And I'm honored that you chose me."

"You're the only one I want to draw," I admit. "You told me to focus my talents, so I'm focusing them on you."

She blushes and makes room for me by sliding across the sheets. "Can I see?"

I inhale a painful breath as I think about her request. It feels... personal, for some reason, to show her. What if she doesn't like it? What if she decides I'm bad and wants nothing to do with me because I hold no promise for myself?

A bead of sweat breaks along my temple, and I lift my shoulder, bending my head to wipe it away.

"You don't have to," she says, quiet and sleepy. "I know I'll love it because you did it."

"I haven't drawn in a while and when I woke up, seeing you asleep made me want to draw, and—"

"—And nothing, Tongue. You don't have to explain yourself to me. I support you always in everything you do. You might have a mean bone in your body for other things in your life, but I know when it comes to me, there isn't a mean bone in your body. I know you didn't draw me in an evil way or ugly way."

"How?" I question, slipping off these damn jeans because there is no way in hell I want to leave this room yet. I lie down in the same spot I got up from about a half hour ago and keep the journal laid flat against my chest so she can't see it.

"Because..." she trails off, trying to find the right words. "It's how you always look at me, Tongue. I know I'm beautiful in your eyes. You let how you feel about me show when I'm near you. It's one of the many reasons why I love you so much." She tugs the blanket up her body, hiding all of those sleek lines. She shivers, going as far as her teeth chattering but it isn't even that cold in the room.

My brows dip in the middle. "You're cold?"

"A little bit," she says through clinking teeth. "Can you get me pajamas? Well, after you show me the drawing?"

"The drawing can wait until you're warm." I get up again and bend over, reaching across from the bed to my dresser. I open it, reach inside to grab a pair of my sweatpants, then a second time for a shirt. "Here you go, Comet." I flip around and help her into a sitting position. I tug my Ruthless Kings shirt over her head, and the faded red shirt swallows her body. I throw the blankets off her and tug the pants up her legs.

She lies down again, and I throw the comforter over her and tuck her in. Daphne reaches for the journal that I laid on the pillow before I got the pajamas. I notice a few things in that moment. I notice she's pale, which seems sudden.

"Can I?"

I nod, sliding a hand up her body as I lay down next to her.

"Oh, Wayne."

I close my eyes when she says my birth name, a name I don't hear unless it falls from her lips. It's the only time I like to hear it. Usually, I get flashes of my past, but when Daphne says it, a comforting balm spreads across my heart, like she's healing me from the inside out.

"You're so talented. Oh my god, I've never seen you draw a portrait before. This is...this is gallery level, Comet."

I roll on top of her and snatch the journal out of her hand, close it, and lay it on the table. "No way in hell I'd ever put a picture of you in a gallery where everyone can see your body."

Her hands cup my cheeks. The way she's looking at me, it's like all the answers in the world live inside me. "I believe you can do anything, Tongue." She turns her head to the left and coughs. It's dry and shallow, as if it's just starting out.

I press my palm against her forehead and frown when I feel how hot she is. "Comet, why didn't you tell me you weren't feeling well?"

"It kind of hit me suddenly. I need to get up though. The contractors are coming to the bookstore."

"No."

"No?"

"No," I say again. "You aren't going anywhere sick. You're going to stay here and rest. I'll call the contractors and cancel."

"But I really want to go. I'm so excited about the bookstore you got me for Christmas because you're so thoughtful, and I want to do well for you."

I tuck a piece of hair behind her ear and kiss the apple of her cheek. "Comet, you could decide to be at home forever, locked in this room, and you'd be the most successful person I've ever met. I'm profoundly in love with you."

"You're so sweet with me." Her voice has gone from normal to hoarse in the matter of minutes.

"Don't tell anyone," I say, attempting one of my first jokes. I don't know if I did it right.

A smile as bright as the sun takes over her face. "Did you just try to tell a joke?"

"Yeah, I don't like that you feel sick. I want to make you feel better. How did I do?"

"You don't need to make jokes to make me feel better, but it was a step in the right joke direction. See? Quick learner," she struggles to say as her eyes start to hood.

"Go to sleep, Comet. I'm not going to go anywhere, but I am going to have Doc come in here and check on you, okay?"

"Okay," she whispers, curling into a ball. "Can I get another blanket?"

"I'll get you a blanket and space heater." I kiss her temple and force myself to get out of bed and get dressed. All I want to do is stay with her. A second away and she might need me. I pause mid-push off the bed and remember I have a phone. All I need to do is text Doc and ask him to come and to bring a space heater.

The blankets I have in the closet.

I don't have to leave after all, and I'm relieved, because I don't think I'm capable of not being around her while she's ill. What if something happens? What if she calls out for me? I need to protect her.

Grabbing a blanket off the shelf in the closet, I fluff it over her and crawl into bed, and wrap my arm around her waist.

Yeah, I don't have it in me to leave, not when she needs me most.

I'll never say I'm scared, but I know being sick means she can get worse, and if that happens, there will be no saving me from the downward spiral.

I am, after all, attempting to find light in my dark, unforgiving hole.

CHAPTER THREE

Daphne

"She's got the flu."

"Okay, well, take it from her. Isn't that what you doctors do?"

"Tongue, it isn't as simple as that. I can't just take a virus from her body. It has to work itself out of her system. She has to be sick and feel like crap."

"Well, what good are you?" Tongue huffs, and the familiar creak of the bedroom door sounds. I pry my eyes open, forcing the lashes through the gunk that's built in my lash line. Well, Doc is right on one thing. I do feel like crap.

"Since you can't take it from her, you can go," Tongue says matter-of-factly.

"Tongue, buddy," Doc places his hand on Tongue's shoulder before he steps out of the room. "It isn't a big deal. She's young, she's healthy, especially after what happened with your brother in December—"

"—He is not my brother. Don't you ever call him that again. Do you understand me?" Tongue shrugs out of Doc's hold and pushes him out the door. "He is nothing to me. He is lucky he is still alive, but time might change that."

Doc holds his hands in the air, showing defeat. "I know that, but brother, I'm worried about you. You've been on edge since Mary got taken outside of Ruby's Rarities, and I understand because it's so close to the bookstore. You're worried about Daphne's every step, but what about you? When are you going to give yourself a break? When will you see that Daphne's flu is random? People get sick and people get better. She isn't dying. Nothing is going to happen to her."

"Nothing?" Tongue sneers. "She's sick. Something has already happened to her. The flu kills people."

I sniffle, but they don't hear me as I watch them have their little pow-wow.

"Tongue, the chances of that happening to a young, healthy woman is slim. Is it impossible? No, but slim. She has a mild case with a low-grade fever. She will be better in no time. She probably got it from the bookstore, with how many contractors are in and out stirring up the dust in there." Doc realizes his mistake as soon as the words leave his mouth.

"They did this to her? I'm going to fucking kill them. I'll do the renovations myself."

"No one did anything to anybody. Tongue, things just happen sometimes. You're going to have to learn how to accept that. You can't stop the world from touching her in some way, brother," Doc says sweetly, keeping his tone soft as he tries to calm Tongue down.

"The world has touched her enough. It's my job," he hits his chest with his fist, "It's my job to keep her safe from the world."

"Sometimes, you can't stop everything. Plenty of fluids and sleep, that's all that will help." Doc opens up his bag and digs through it. "Ah, here it is." He shows Tongue an orange bottle and shakes it, causing the pills to clank around. "Sleep, Tongue. I know you haven't. The circles around your eyes tell me you need rest. Don't make me tell Reaper to force you to go to sleep, okay? Just do it and stop worrying so much. Things are good here at the club. Everyone is safe. It's time you start taking care of yourself. Feel better, Daphne."

Oh, he must have seen me wake up. "Thank you, Doc." I sound so stuffy and my eyes are already getting heavy again. Tongue stares down at the bottle in his palm and closes the door, blocking out the outside world. "Tongue, he's right."

"I just want you to be safe."

I cough into my fist and he rushes to my side, placing his palm on my forehead again. "You feel like you're on fire. I don't like this. I can't do anything. I don't know what to do. Tell me what to do," he says in desperation.

My comet, he seems so lost when things are beyond his control.

"Take one of those pills and sleep."

"But there is so much to do. I need to start on the swamp for Happy and I need to check on the bookstore. I need to—"

"Sleep. That is what I want, Tongue. Please, stop worrying about everything so much and just be."

"Just be," he mumbles and then exhales a haunted breath. "I don't know how to do that."

"I know, but please, sleep. I know you get maybe two hours a night. The more you rest, the more you will see that I'm okay. It's a silly cold."

"Flu. It's worse than a cold."

"Take the damn pill," I snap at him, which is then followed by a nasty sneeze. "Gross." My nose is red and raw from blowing it so much. I take another tissue and wipe my face. He must think I'm disgusting.

"I hate that you feel so bad. I want to fix it and take it away." Tongue lies down next to me and wraps an arm around me, tugging me to his chest. My cheek presses against his chest, right between each pec and his heart beats against my ear.

"I know," I yawn, then pat his stomach as my eyes start to droop. "Take the pill, for me."

An unhappy sound escapes him. "Fine," he grumbles, popping the lid off and shaking a pill from the bottle. "I'm only doing this once and that's it."

No he isn't, because I know if I ask him again, he will do it. "I know, Comet. I know." I wipe my nose on his shirt and he starts to laugh after he takes a drink of water.

I sniffle.

"Did you just wipe your nose on my shirt?" he asks, sounding amused for the first time since I've been awake.

I shake my head. "No?" I make sure to sound unsure and his stomach starts to shake. I lift up on my elbows and peer up at him to see his hands over his face as he laughs.

A full blown, deep, raspy laugh. It's like every chuckle gets rid of a bit of rust as he learns to embrace laughter.

Even sick and possibly seeing double, I take his hands from his face and see an actual smile. It's so big, his eyes crinkle and his cheeks are plump and red. I can see his teeth. The front rows are straight and white, equally the same size. He got gifted in the teeth department. I climb onto his body until I'm straddling his chest and hypnotized by his face.

And what's even better is I'm getting to see two of him, since the flu is getting the best of me. I grab my phone from under the pillow, swipe the camera up, and take a picture of the rare moment before he can protest.

"How is me wiping my nose on your shirt so funny?" I start to lie down again when my head starts to swim. I'm getting lightheaded. I collapse to his side and stare at the picture on my phone for a minute.

"Because it's disgusting and yet, I don't care. I want you to do it again because I like that we are comfortable enough with one another that we can do things like that." As quickly as his smile is there, it's gone, and he is yawning. "I'm already getting sleepy," he says, rubbing his hand up and down my arm. "I'm sorry I've been worried, but I won't be sorry for trying to keep you safe. I'll never apologize for that."

"I know and I love you more for it," I say. "You're unlike any man I've ever known, and I'll never forget how you make me feel, and if I do you'll have to make sure you remind me."

I wait for him to say something, to say anything, and a pit starts to form in my stomach when he doesn't say anything back. Tongue is surly and grumpy most days. Deep inside, down burrowed under my heart, I'm afraid he'll get tired of me and that anger will win. So I need him to answer me because it reassures that he loves me.

"Tongue?" I sniffle again and groan when I get a hot flash, getting dizzier by the second when I try to look up at him.

He's already asleep.

And now I feel guilty for thinking he might be getting tired of me.

I cuddle up as close as I can and pull the blanket over us to make sure he stays warm. He might be able to fool himself into thinking he is indestructible, but he can't fool everyone else. There might be no rest for the wicked, but there is rest for the dead, and if he keeps going like this, I'm afraid I'll lose him before I get the chance to have the experience we deserve together.

Living is for the wicked, sleep is for the living, and everything in between deserves a gallon of Redbull.

That is... until you need sleep so you can survive the next brutal round the world has to offer.

I close my eyes, trying to get myself to fall back asleep and debate if I want to take one of those pills that Tongue just took. My eyes feel so swollen, they could glue themselves shut, but my mind is racing, thinking about the dream I had the other night.

When dreams and reality clash, how does someone decipher the difference between the two? If it came down to having to choose, how will I pick the right one? It scares me because I know my psychosis is getting worse.

My dreams chain me down and life isn't strong enough to break the shackles. I don't know how to win, but there are only two ways this is going to end for me: insanity or death.

Or maybe one will have to do with the other.

A soft knock on the door grabs my attention and the hinges squeak as it opens. Sarah pokes her head in and smiles. She's about to say something when her gaze falls to Tongue, who is fast asleep and snoring every few seconds.

She chuckles from the sound, and I have the urge to defend him. I know their relationship has been less than stellar lately, but I won't allow her to laugh at him.

"Sorry to interrupt," she whispers, inviting herself in. Her hand is on her belly, something I've noticed every pregnant woman does. Her stomach isn't as big as Joanne's, but it's bigger than Mary's since Mary is hitting twelve weeks, I think. "Doc said you had the flu, I was wondering if you wanted anything. Tea? Soup? I'll be happy to bring it in for you."

Well, now that she is being nice, my defenses fall a bit.

"Actually, tea sounds great." I rub my dry, aching throat at the thought of sipping tea with honey in it.

She turns to leave, grabbing the knob of the door to close it on her way out when she stops in the middle of the doorway. "Is Tongue okay? I know he's been restless."

"He'll be fine. If there is Church, can you tell Reaper Tongue is finally getting some sleep?"

She nods and a piece of her blonde hair falls from her ponytail. "Yeah, of course. Reaper's been worried too. I'll pass the message along."

"Thank you," I say, turning to my side and pressing against Tongue's body. He's warm and hard, strong in all the right places which has me feeling safe.

"Daphne, I want to let you know, just because Tongue and I are still figuring things out, doesn't mean I don't consider you my friend."

"Sarah, I'm on his side. I'm always on his side. And if his relationship is rocky with you, then it's rocky with me. I do my best to tell him to talk to you, but you know how he is. Even if I want to be best friends with you, I can't. Tongue is first. I won't betray him because you offered to bring me tea. Sorry," I wince, reaching for another tissue to blow my nose, "I sound so bitchy and my patience is thin since I'm sick, but my words are true. Just like you'd stick to Reaper, I'm going to stick to Tongue. I hope one day the dynamic between everyone changes, and I appreciate your offer for tea, but I don't want you to get sick, so I'll get up and get it."

"Nonsense." She blinks steadily at the ceiling and her eyes are glassy. "I'll have Doc bring it to you."

Damn, I've made a pregnant lady cry. I'm an asshole. I don't like that. I sit up, clutching the blanket to my chest, and lean against the headboard. "I'm sorry, Sarah." I press a palm against my forehead when it starts to build with pressure, threatening to explode from my sinuses being clogged. "I don't mean to hurt you. Tongue is my best friend, lover, soulmate, so he comes first."

"No, I get it. I understand. There's no need to explain yourself. I'll make that tea for you now." She closes the door behind her, but not before I hear a hiccup from her crying.

"I'm terrible," I say to myself.

With a regretful sigh and the wheels turning in my head to form another apology, I swing my legs over the bed. I'm not going to fall asleep any time soon, especially with how bad I feel about hurting Sarah's feelings. I know our relationship has no bearing on her and Tongue, but I can't form a close bond with her when their relationship is hanging by a thread. It isn't fair to him, for me to get close to Sarah. Tongue misses her. It would be like rubbing salt in a large bleeding wound.

I stand, giving myself a minute before walking, when my head spins again. When the world stops spinning, I head toward the bathroom and plug the tub with the stopper. When I inhale, there's a rattle in my chest followed by a quick cough. Flipping the nozzle, hot water starts to fill the tub and I open the cabinet to grab the lavender bath salts.

"Holy Moly." I stare at the empty package and ball it up, then throw it in the wastebin. I didn't mean to pour the entire packet in the tub. It just kind of happened.

Tap. Tap. Tap.

Three little knocks tell me someone is at the bedroom door. Mumbling incoherent words to myself that I can't even understand, I take a look at myself in the mirror and gasp, horrified at what I'm seeing. "Oh my god, how can he love me when I look like this?" My hair is a rat's nest, completely tangled on one side, and sticking to my scalp.

Probably from sweat...

Another reason why I need to bathe.

My face is pale, black circles sag under my eyes, and the tip of my nose is red. Don't get me started on the constant wetness dripping from my nostrils. I look and feel disgusting.

But I don't have the energy to care about how I look for someone that isn't Tongue right now. I meander to the bedroom door, open it, then lean my head against the cool wood.

Oh, that's nice.

Doc's face comes to view. He gives me a sad, sympathetic filled smile as he hands me a big mug of tea. On the side it says, 'Property of Tongue.' All the ol' ladies have their own mug. Mine is red with black lettering and there is a small black heart under Tongue's name. It's my favorite. "Hey, Daphne," Doc greets, then sees Tongue asleep on the bed. "Wow, he took my advice."

"Only because I asked him to."

"You look... better."

"Liar," I call him out and take the mug from his hands. The heat warms my cold hands. "Thank you, for this. After I take a bath, I think I might take one of those pills too and sleep. I tried, but I'm so congested. How is it possible to have a runny and stuffy nose at the same time? What sense does that make?"

"Sickness never does. If you need anything, let me know, okay? You look like you might need an IV bag soon if you don't start getting color to your face."

"I'm fine. Don't worry about me. Nothing can keep me down." I take a sip of the hot tea and moan when the honey flavored liquid heats my sore raw throat. "I'm going to take a bath. I'll see everyone later."

"Later, Daphne," Doc says as he shuts the door.

I keep the mug tightly wrapped in my hands and inhale the steam billowing from the top. For a second, I'm actually able to breathe. I scoot my feet across the floor, not having enough strength to walk normally, and step in the bathroom.

The white ceramic tub is almost full, so I hurry to turn it off so it doesn't overflow. I'm already tired from walking so much. I reach across the tub and set the tea in the inner corner so I can sip on it when I'm soaking. I undress, sliding off Tongue's shirt and sweatpants, then step into the water and sit down.

The water splashes against the sides, almost rocking out of the tub and onto the floor. My aching body is appreciative for the heat engulfing me and the steam filling my lungs. My skin turns light pink from the temperature and the congestion in my chest lightens. My butt slides across the bottom of the tub as I sink lower. My chin hits the surface of the water and I tilt my head back, shutting my eyes as the lavender scent of the bath salts seep into my lungs.

"Daphne!" Tongue suddenly screams for me, the urgency and fear startling.

This time, water does hit the floor. "Daphne," he cries out for me again. The pain in his voice has me hurrying out of the tub, dripping water everywhere, and rushing to the bedroom.

He isn't awake.

"Daphne," he twists in the sheets, the tendons in his neck tensed, and his knuckles are white as he grips the comforter.

Soaking wet, I jump on the bed, bounce, and place my hand on his chest. "I'm here, Wayne. It's okay. I'm here."

"Daphne," he mutters my name again, his hand grabbing onto mine, pressing it harder against his sternum. His heart is running wild, bumping against his breastbone with terror and adrenaline. Sweat beads across his brows and his face pinches as if he is in pain.

"I'm here, Comet." I cup his face next, dripping water all over him and the blanket. "Wake up, Wayne. Wake up. I'm right here." A coughing fits hits me, and I turn my head over my shoulder, so I don't spew spit all over him. "I'm right here."

"I don't want to. Uncle—" he screams at the top of his lungs. A tear drips from the corner of his eye, and I know the door is about to burst open, so I crawl under the covers to hide my naked body. I take ahold of Tongue's shoulders and shake him, but he won't wake up.

That pill is keeping him in a nightmare.

"Please, wake up." I begin to cry, because I hate seeing him relive something he has already put behind him.

"It hurts. Please, don't Justine. I can't take anymore." His mouth opens on a silent shout, as if his voice is being held captive. The door flings open, smashing against the wall. Reaper is there, with Doc just a step behind him.

"What's wrong?" he asks.

"It must be the sleeping pill. Side effects are different for everyone. He must have night terrors. You can't wake him up. You have to let him sleep or he could wake up violent," Doc says, sorrow lilting his voice as he squeezes by and checks Tongue's pulse.

"But what he is going through is violent," I argue, then drape myself over Tongue when he cries out again. I hold him as tight as I can as he quakes in his sleep. "I'm here. I'm not going anywhere. I'm here."

So is every member of this club, apparently. The room is rapidly filling up with all the others coming by from the commotion.

"Justine, the red dress. No! I don't want to."

"Everyone get out!" I yell at every member in the room. They are watching Tongue like he is some sort of sideshow, and I won't allow it. "He isn't some sick enjoyment for you. Get out!" A warm tear slips free at the same time another cough grips my chest.

"It hurts. It hurts. Stop it! Get off me. Get off! I don't want it." Tongue's arms are glued to his side, as if he is unable to use them.

"I think it's best if I stay, to make sure he doesn't hurt himself or you," Doc states.

"I'm going to stay," Sarah says, sitting down in the chair in the corner that Tongue always sits in when he watches me. "He needs us."

"Me too," Slingshot agrees.

"Aye," Skirt nods.

"I'm not going anywhere." Badge crosses his arms and leans against the wall. "He is family. Family doesn't suffer alone."

"This isn't a sideshow, Daphne." Reaper's fingers slide under my chin and tilt my head back, so I have no choice but to meet his eyes. "He is family, and out of everyone, we worry about him most."

"I'm going to come so far in your ass, you'll leak me for weeks, Wayne." His voice is deep, as if his memory is having him role play what's happened to him.

I hold my breath and stare down at him in horror, crying for him, crying for the boy that lost his innocence way too young. "Oh, Comet." I lean down a kiss his cheek. "You aren't there anymore. He can't hurt you."

"No, Justine. I'm sorry. I'm sorry!" he sobs and starts to fight me in his sleep. I grab the blanket just in time before he throws me off him. I fly off the bed and slam against the floor. Pain radiates up my spine, and my head hits the wall with a hard thud.

"Daphne!" Badge drops to my side and touches the back of my head. "Fuck, Doc. She's bleeding."

"I fucking hate you! Get off me, you bastard. I'm going to fucking kill you!" Tongue roars and swings his fist through the air, connecting with Reaper's cheek.

Doc kneels at my side and shines a light in my eyes. "She has a concussion."

"Help me hold him down." Reaper tries to gather the troops, but Doc is quick with his order.

"Fuck no. You can't. If you do, he could feel that in his dream. He could hurt you or hurt himself. He can break his bones or bite his tongue off. You have to let him work through it." Doc gives his attention to me again and tucks the blanket around me to make sure I'm covered. "Do you have a robe?"

"Bathroom," I wince when sharp pains spreads across the back of my head. "He didn't mean to. He'd never hurt me." I fist Doc's cut and use it as leverage to help myself sit up. "He wouldn't."

"I know. This is no one's fault."

"Go to your bedroom. I have no use for you." Tongue's voice takes on another and the bed finally stops shaking. There are books scattered along the floor, open and face down, pages bent from him shaking the bed and knocking them loose from under the mattress.

His body relaxes and everyone in the room exhales.

Not me.

I want to lie next to him and tell him everything is going to be okay. "Can I be with him?"

"No, I have to get you downstairs. You hit your head pretty good on the edge of the wall. You need stiches."

"I'm not leaving him!" I yell, placing one hand against the wall to steady myself as I stand. "You can fix me here because I am not fucking going anywhere." I forget I'm naked under the blanket. Cold air hits my butt as the cover parts. Badge, despite being able to see me, doesn't say anything. He holds out the robe, keeping his eyes fixed upon my face, and I slide one arm through it while clutching the blanket with the other, so no one sees the front of my body. I turn to the wall and drop the blanket, then sling my arm through the other sleeve, and tie the belt in the middle. The robe is soft and warm, but my body is cold and in pain.

Not because I hit my head or the floor. Not because I'm sick.

But because Tongue will always suffer. When he is awake, when he sleeps, when he breathes or fucks, the innocence inside him is twisted and burnt, stained with hate that love cannot clean.

I'll always comfort his innocence, cradle it, and cherish it because no one ever has. No one believes it's there, but it's all I see when I look into his eyes: the tarnished, innocent boy that needs to be held.

And until the breath is stolen from lungs, I'll grip on with every ounce of strength I have. Even if Tongue tells me to let go, I won't.

It will be in that moment he'll need me most.

CHAPTER FOUR

Tongue

RIGHT WHEN I THINK I'M DONE HATING MYSELF, I'M SHOVED THREE STEPS BACK, RUINING any progress I've made at finding some sort of self-love.

It's why I'm outside in the chilly weather, manually digging the start of Happy's Haven. I don't deserve help. I deserve to sweat and hurt and think about what I've done. It's going to take me months, maybe years to dig this hole for Happy, but I deserve it.

I hurt Daphne.

I made her bleed.

I threw her off the bed.

I'll never forgive myself.

I don't care that I was asleep and having a bad dream. I don't care that I was fighting my Uncle, fearing for my life, and I don't care that I had no idea what I was doing.

I simply do not care because I should have known. I should have woken up. I'll never take that damn sleeping pill again. I'd rather stay awake for days, starve, and die of thirst then to ever risk hurting her again.

Forcing the shovel into the ground, I step on the metal lip with my boot. The dry dirt cracks only the surface, the fissure stopping near a small cactus. Dust kicks in the air, and I wipe the sweat off the side of my temple against my shoulder before throwing the dirt to the side to add to the growing pile.

I'm a real bastard. I'm no good. How can I take care of her when every time I turn around, I do something wrong? With another angry shove, the metal point burrows into the desert as I gather another round of dirt.

"What do I do, Happy?" I ask him as he swims in the pink kiddie pool I got him. Pink was the only color they had left. "I can't let her go, but how can I hold onto her when all I do, all I've ever ended up doing, is hurting her?"

His paws scratches along the edges and his head pops up from the side. His snout rests on the edge of the pool, staring at me with those big reptilian eyes as he waits for me to say something else. "I love her so much, Happy. It's tearing me apart what I did. When I look at my hands, all I see is her blood. Even though it never got near me, I made her bleed. Therefore, her blood is on my hands." I toss another scoop of dirt to the side and stare at the small hole I've managed to make.

I deserve to be out here thinking about what I've done, just like a child.

Happy hisses as he lifts himself over the edge of the pool and then walks over to me, wiggling his body across the ground. His talons sink into the sand, scraping along the hard surface rather than sinking into it. His tail swishes. His black, tan, and green coloring are stark against the red desert. He stops at my feet, purring as he rubs his reptilian skin against my leg.

"I love you too, Happy." I bend down and scratch the top of his head. I don't know how Seer found a gator so damn friendly toward me, but I'll forever be thankful. Besides Daphne, he's the only friend I have who seems to understand me.

I'm lucky, but I don't know if that's sad or not. I'm surrounded by a dozen men that claim to be my brothers, my friends, and I know they would risk their life for mine, but would it be for our code? The law we live by? Or because they are truly my friends?

I don't know. I only know Daphne actually cares and Happy cares as much as a swamp kitty can.

"Go on. Go swim. I'll be okay. I need to start digging," I say to Happy, pointing to the kiddie pool. He brushes against me one last time and scurries over to the pool. It always surprises me how quick he can move. He isn't full grown just yet, but he's still fast. In the water, alligators can travel up to twenty miles an hour, but on land, around eleven miles per hour.

It doesn't seem fast, but their bodies are so awkward, it's impressive.

He slides into the pool and floats, spreading out his legs.

"Man, you live the life, you know that?" There's a heat lamp next to the pool to make sure he stays warm, since this isn't his ideal environment. I plan to fix that for him. In our house, he is going to have his own room, heated, but I'm sure he will hang out with us throughout the house. He'll be able to go back and forth to the swamp I'm going to build him too. And eventually, I'll get him some friends.

"At the rate you're going, you aren't going to get that hole dug until 2034. And that's being generous."

My foot lands on the shovel, and I grip the handle, tightening it to the point I think it's about to break. "What the hell do you want, Slingshot?" I throw another scoop of dirt to the pile and begin working again.

"I brought you lunch. I used my gift card I got for Christmas and I got the family pack. There are fifty steak tacos in here. It's going to be so good."

"I'm busy."

"A man has got to eat, you know," Slingshot says, sitting on his ass on the pile of dirt I've made.

"You didn't come out here to share your lunch. And besides, I doubt you—"

"I took my pill, damn it. Sit down, shut up, and eat the tacos or I'll never offer them again."

"No." Slingshot is a good man, a bit naïve, and thinks tacos are god, but he doesn't want to get caught up in the likes of me.

"Come on, Tongue. I have an update on Daphne."

I never thought he'd play that card. I toss the shovel on the ground and take a seat next to him just as he...

"Are you kidding me?"

"I'm sorry. I just took the pill..." he slurps on his coke and kicks the ground with the tip of his foot, an innocent action by a very guilty man.

"You know, you better hope you don't always smell like ass, or no girl is going to want to be with you."

He shrugs. "As long as I have my tacos, I'll be a happy man."

I lift a disbelieving brow at him and watch as he digs through the simple white bag with grease spots on it. One by one, he takes out different sauces. "We have my favorite, salsa verde, which has this tangy kinda sweet flavor with a tiny kick of heat. There is the pico de gallo, which is good, but I always get extra of the verde. Extra sour cream, because duh, sour cream is the best. And then we have jalapeños. Voila," he spreads his arms out over the buffet of sauces and then hands me an aluminum foil wrapped taco. "Bon Appetit." He claps his hands and rubs them together evilly before diving in the bag and pulling out one for himself.

"You said you had an update on Daphne?" I ask, turning around to stare at the clubhouse where she is resting. She's downstairs in the medical room where Doc can keep an eye on her, because not only does she have the flu, but she has a concussion. Thanks to me.

I've been checking on her every few hours. The last time I went down there, she was finally allowed to go to sleep, so Doc sedated her because apparently, she kept asking for me.

Not that I deserve her to want me. I deserve the desert and being alone.

"She's doing good, Tongue." Slingshot groans when he bites into the taco. A chunk of sour cream, steak, and salsa verde drips from the end of his lover—at least it sounds like a lover with how he is moaning—and falls on to the foil laid across his lap. "Her fever is still there, a little higher than where Doc wants it, but with the concussion and fighting the flu, he isn't surprised. She's going to be fine. His words."

My stomach turns knowing she is still sick, worse with what Slingshot is saying. Her fever is higher and it's all my fault.

"Hey," the playful demeanor of his voice changes. His hand claps me on the shoulder and whether he knows it or not, he has smeared sour cream all over the sleeve of my shirt. "You can't blame yourself."

I dress the taco in the sauces I want. I'm not hungry but doing something with my hands helps my mind ease.

"Tongue, I'm serious. You couldn't help what happened to you last night. Doc knows that you need a different kind of sleeping pill—"

"I'm never taking them again, and no one can make me. What I did last night was inexcusable." I bite into the tortilla and the flavors burst across my tongue. On any other day, this would have been an amazing meal, but right now, it tastes just like the dirt I'm digging up.

"What you did last night was survive. You were lost." He taps the side of his head with his finger. "Here. You were gripped by a nightmare, a bad horrible nightmare, and from what I heard from you, I'm sorry you had to go through that. I saw the journals… but… they were nothing like this. Daphne doesn't blame you. No one blames you for what happened."

"I do. I blame me. I should have felt her there. I always feel her. I always know where she is, whether it's dark or I'm asleep. I know when she's near. But last night I felt nothing."

"It was the medication, Tongue. Any other night, do you think you ever would have pushed Daphne off the bed?"

I tear into the taco with a vicious snarl, like a primitive animal feasting on his kill. "No, absolutely not."

"Then there's your answer, man. You don't deserve to kill yourself out here. Whose hole are you really digging?"

"What do you mean?" I finish off the first taco and dip my hand in the bag to grab another.

"Well, you say it's a Happy Haven, but it looks more like a grave to me."

I analyze the hole and realize for the first time it's a long, deep shape. It does look like a rectangle.

"Looks like you're punishing yourself, digging your own grave to plan your own funeral for something that was beyond your control. Tongue, there are things in this life that you cannot hold onto with both hands. You can't take care of every problem by cutting someone's tongue out, and you can't work yourself to death as penance." He dives in for another foil wrapped taco and sighs, staring off across the desert. "Can I tell you something? It just stays between you and me."

Something… different blooms in my stomach. I don't know what it is, but if I had to guess it would be happiness. No one chooses me to tell their secret.

I am the secret. I'm what the corners hold, and the shadows keep. I'm the monster no one talks about until he is seen, until he is believed.

That's who I am. The ghost story people tell around a fire to scare each other, but in my case, the ghost is real, and I haunt people every chance I get.

Yes, I think I'm feeling excitement. Someone wants to tell me a something about themselves that maybe not many others know about. "Sure," I keep my answer short and keep the impatience out of my voice. *I want to know. I want to know!*

"So only a few people know this here because I don't go broadcasting it, but my mom died of the same cancer I had in my twenties."

"Your mom died from cancer?" I didn't know that. "I'm sorry." I don't know what else to say. I'm slowly learning how to empathize, but it's taking time.

"Stomach cancer. It's why I'm so big on tacos. 'Cause for the longest time I didn't think I'd ever be able to eat them again. When my mom died, I blamed myself. I thought, 'you know, maybe if she didn't have me and could focus on herself, maybe she wouldn't have died.'"

"You had nothing to do with it. It was the cancer."

He gives me a knowing look, then winks. "See what I did there?"

"No." I shake my head. "Why are you looking at me like that?"

"You don't get the point?"

"Not unless you say it," I state obviously.

"You just said cancer was the reason my mom died, not me. Just like you aren't the reason Daphne got hurt, but Justine is. The sleeping pill is. Medication doesn't mix well with people sometimes, man. Take it from me. I've nearly been on all of them."

I think about what he says and let it roll around in my thick skull. It's hard not to take blame when the woman I love got hurt because of me, but maybe Slingshot is right. Maybe there were circumstances beyond my control.

And I need control just like I need air in my lungs and Daphne's lips on mine. I need it to keep the tiniest edge of sanity sharp in my mind or without it, innocent people will get hurt.

"I see," I say, finally understanding the point he tried to make. "So, is that why you are so damn gassy?"

He tosses his head back and laughs so loud it booms across the desert. Buzzards fly away in the distance and ignore the roadkill. Even Happy jumps out of the pool, a bit startled, before jumping back in. "Between us?"

I nod, feeling way too damn giddy about this secret sharing.

"Yeah. I had a portion of my intestine removed. We weren't as close when I was a prospect so I'm sure you don't remember. I had to work up to foods like this, but now that I can eat them, unfortunately, gas is a part of it. And the pill I take? It isn't the only one I take."

I frown. "Why do you let us give you a hard time? It isn't…" I think of the right word. "Nice."

"I don't care. I lived through something I shouldn't have. I'm okay with joking about it. I like that you guys tend to forget about it. Makes me feel normal. Besides, it could be worse."

"How?"

"I could be in a grave like the one you just dug for yourself, Tongue. And honestly, I'm real fucking glad I'm not."

I bite into the taco again and stare at Slingshot in a whole new light. I always thought he was this annoying guy with a childish personality. He does have a childish personality, but in a way that I'm still somewhat a kid too. He never got a chance to be a child, not a real one, and I can relate to that. I feel bad for not knowing or not trying to get to know Slingshot as well. I stayed in the shadows too much for this to be new to me.

"Thanks for the tacos, Slingshot. I appreciate it."

"No problemo, amigo." He balls up the foil and the sun reflects off of the silver wrapping before he places the garbage in the bag, only to fish out yet another damn taco. "So, after tacos you want to see Daphne and then get an excavator to dig this swamp instead of shoveling?"

"You want to build it with me?"

"Hells yeah. I'm not going to let my buddy do this alone. Come on, eat up and let's turn this grave into a swamp sanctuary."

"I plan on getting Happy friends, too."

"He'll like that. Everyone needs a friend, including people."

I didn't understand friendship before Daphne. She's opened my mind to new possibilities, and she's made me see the world differently. Don't get me wrong, the world is jaded and cold with more bad than good. I didn't always pay attention to the good because I didn't believe in it, but I'm seeing more of it now. I'm not sure if I believe in it because the concept of belief is foreign to me, but if anyone can make me see the light in anything it's her. And right now, I think… I mean… I might be starting to feel something.

Joy.

I have a friend to add to the list.

A list I didn't have before Daphne. For some reason, Slingshot decided to take a chance and be the one to come out here. No one else has. Before, I chalked it up to them being afraid of me. Now, I know it's because no one understands me. This loneliness I feel isn't only my fault, but theirs.

The sun is still high in the blue sky, shining without a cloud in sight. The mountains surround us, and the sound of a bike grumbling grows from the distance. I get up from the dirt mound and stand, wiping my ass off with my hand. "Yeah, that sounds good." I take another taco out of the bag as we walk to the clubhouse. "Happy, stay. I'll be right back."

"Good tacos, right? I swear, they are the best in the country, and I should know, remember? I took a bike trip around the Unites States and tried tacos everywhere. This little taco stand has my heart, man."

"They are good."

"See, stick with me and I'll feed ya good."

I rub my chest when that funny feeling returns. Friendship is a hard concept for me to swallow, but I won't choke on it like I used to.

Not anymore.

Everything I am and everything I'm able to recognize now is because of my Comet, my rarity.

Only something so damn special and more powerful than the stars and moon aligned, could change a devil like me—the devil *in* me.

CHAPTER FIVE

Daphne

HOLY MOLY.

I am so glad to be out of that basement. It's so dark and cold. If anything, it makes me feel worse. It's so sterile, lifeless, and don't get me started on what happens behind the door they called 'the playroom.' The basement is full of nightmares, pain, sickness, and tears. How anyone can heal when they are surrounded by depression like that is beyond me. I'm one to believe that if someone surrounds themselves with what they love and what makes them happy, they will get better.

"Well, rise and shine, Daphne." Reaper is huddled near the sink, pouring himself a cup of black coffee in his 'President of the Unites States of Ruthless America' mug. He uses it every day. "How are you feeling?"

"Better." The first thing I notice is Tongue's not here. My sadness must show all over my face and Knives reaches across the table and takes my hand.

His scarred thumb rubs across my knuckles. "He's been checking on you. He's outside working on the swamp for Happy. He had a tough time seeing you because—"

"He blamed himself. I know," I say. "I figured as much. Is he okay?"

"Yeah, him and Slingshot are out there digging a giant hole in the ground," Bullseye's voice comes from down the hall. He's holding gauze over his finger as he enters the kitchen. Pulling out one of the old wooden chairs, he takes a seat beside me and Doc comes in next. Bullseye shoots him a mean sneer and Doc rolls his eyes.

"You need to get over it, Bullseye. It's a prick to the finger. It isn't the end of the world. How do you think people feel when you throw darts at them? Not only does it penetrate their skin, but the metal spikes under the muscle to latch on. You can't handle one tiny needle?" Doc asks, placing a small glass bottle of insulin on the table with a new syringe. "You need your shot. You still aren't regulating your sugar well enough."

"I'm fine."

It isn't often I see Doc get angry. He is always calm and composed. A man of rational thinking, but not right now. He slings his arm across the table and the insulin flies against the wall, shattering. The liquid wets the paint and drips onto the floor, good medicine gone to waste.

If there is one thing I know about insulin, it's how expensive it is.

"You're a goddamn idiot!" Doc yells, getting right in Bullseye's pale face.

Knives, Reaper, and I share an uncomfortable glance. No one likes to witness an argument when they aren't a part of it.

"I'm so fucking sick of you denying, denying, denying, Bullseye. You want to fucking pass out? You want to go into a diabetic shock or worse, a coma? Go ahead. Don't let me stop you. When you need my help, when you realize the incompetence and stupidity of your choices—" Doc hits Bullseye's forehead with the palm of his hand and Bullseye's head snaps back. "Don't fucking come to me. Go to the damn hospital or urgent care, because I am done with your stubborn ass to last me a lifetime."

Doc pushes Bullseye in the chest so hard, Bullseye rocks back and the chair balances itself on its rear legs. He stays up right and then tips over, hitting the floor so hard the rods that support the lumbar of the chair snap in half. Bullseye slams his head on the ground, but Doc doesn't do what he usually does, which is drop on the floor and check on his friend.

Doc stomps by Reaper, who is casually sipping on his coffee. He backtracks, opens the cabinet, grabs a coffee mug, jerks the pot out from the coffee maker, and pours himself a cup of morning java. I've never seen someone make an angry cup of coffee, but I guess there is a first for everything. Reaper smirks over the rim of his coffee and Knives puckers his lips as he shines his ninja star, acting like nothing is happening.

Typical.

"I'm going to go help Tongue and Slingshot," Doc gripes, then hauls ass down the hallway before kicking the door open. I press a hand over my heart when the loud shudder of the door slamming startles me. Jeez, everything does these days.

"I'm going to go see Ruby," Bullseye says as he pushes himself off the ground and dusts himself off.

"Has she even let ye inside the store?" Skirt asks, scratching his stomach as he yawns and opens the fridge. "Oh my god, look at all the pie. Oh, Sarah must really love me."

"She's been craving apple pie," Reaper says. "Sorry, Skirt. I'm afraid she made them for selfish reasons."

"Does that mean I can't eat 'em because they are for baby cravings?" Skirt's face is pure agony as he holds a pie to his face and inhales. "Not even a wee little nibble?"

Bullseye tugs on his cut and fishes out his bike keys. "I'll have you know I got as far as opening the door before Ruby pushed me out and locked it. I call that progress."

"Sounds romantic, Bullseye. Yer making ye way into her heart."

"Eat your pie, Skirt." Bullseye grabs his leather jacket off the chair and makes his way to the front door. Tyrant and Yeti run by him as they run to their food bowls. Poodle is next, but he is carrying Lady, since she doesn't have the strength to walk.

She's getting worse every day that passes, and I think he's realizing that keeping her alive at this point is cruel. Melissa told me he made an appointment with the vet next week to put her to sleep and Poodle hasn't put her down for more than a few minutes since. I think it's his way of saying goodbye. It's sad.

Everyone falls quiet when Poodle takes a seat. No one knows what to say when Poodle is in a constant state of depression, which is odd, because he is a lot like Slingshot in the sense that he is the person everyone can count on to make them feel better.

Boots scuff down the hallway, and the closer they get, I know who it is.

I sit up straighter as my heart starts to pound. I'd know those footsteps from anywhere.

"Anyone got an update on Daphne?" Tongue shouts from the middle of the hallway.

I feel coy, suddenly. Tongue specifically asking for me is making me feel like a schoolgirl.

"Come ask her yourself," Reaper shouts. "Damn, I'm not everyone's messenger."

"You said a bad word. You owe me five bucks."

"Maizey, get out from under the table." Reaper tells her, without even looking under the table to see if she is there.

The boots rushing down the hallway match the anticipation beating in my heart. When Tongue comes to view he slides to a stop, nearly running into Skirt who is clutching his pie like he does his daughter Joey.

"Christ, Tongue. Ye nearly made me drop me pie."

"Comet." The gravel in his voice has me closing my eyes as it smooths over me like a healing balm.

His hair is wet from sweat and a few pieces of the dark stands are plastered to his forehead. Several splotches of dirt cover his blue jeans, especially near the pockets where he cleans his hands off. He doesn't have a shirt on, and his abs are glistening in the light of the kitchen. He has a smear of dirt on his cheek and all I want to do is clean it off.

We don't speak. We just stare and the room charges with our sexual tension that tends to make others uncomfortable.

"There is a child in the room," Reaper advises us under his breath while also clearing his throat after, so Maizey hopefully can't hear the warning.

"Damn, yer making me want more than apple pie."

"Skirt," Reaper scolds, but doesn't have a serious look on his face.

"I need to... uh... go check on Dawn."

"I'm going to go see Melissa."

"Yeah, Sarah might need her belly rubbed or something..." Reaper throws it in the pot along with everyone else since they are getting affected by Tongue and I. Well, not us as people, but what we are creating in the air.

Sexual need.

Desire.

Lust.

It's been too long since I've felt him inside me, and I need that to change. I know some people's love language revolves around hand holding or small gestures, but not mine.

I find reconnection in Tongue with sex because we give each other what we need. Often times, what we need is so much darker than anyone else could ever give. It's because he's my soulmate. I never believed in soulmates before him. I believed everyone could love as many people as they wanted. The heart heals when love is taken away and eventually the person learns to love again.

That's the story I told myself. Since I had never been in love before Tongue, I just thought love was an easy notion. I told myself love was a choice, because there was no such thing as two souls being destined to be together. Even reading all the books I do about love and loss and one true loves, I was skeptical, but it never stopped my curiosity. There was always a part of me that wondered if it was real.

And then the experience with Tongue let me know that love isn't a choice. We don't choose love.

It's decided for us.

Tongue is my fate. The one destiny wrote my life for. When I met him, my life made sense and found purpose.

My soul is linked to his. I know in my heart; I was born to die being loved by him.

If something happened to him, if fate took him away from me, I have no doubt that's when my journey in this world would come to an end. I was created for his hands, for his heart, and for the wicked side of love people don't like to experience.

Our love is blackened and burned by the trials of this world. No one can tell me different, but underneath the soot is a diamond. The gem is black, but it shines just as bright as one that isn't tarnished.

When we die, cover me in our blood so I can become one with the love that's made its home in the marrow of my bones after I decompose into nothing. But even then, I'll be something, because I'll have him embedded in my dust.

People might think they are above us because of how Tongue and I show love is beneath them, but they're wrong. It's in the black, in the void, in the places no one wants to go where the deepest, craziest, most intense love exists.

And if you can't touch that place, have you ever really loved?

Tongue stares at me, watches me, cocking his head as he evaluates. When he looks at me like this, it sends a trickle a fear down my spine. His eyes are dark, promising the darkness we make love in. He takes three steps until he is beside the table and holds his weight by pressing his hands against the table. His knuckles turn white and his fingers turn pink.

I slide my eyes around the room to find us alone.

"How do you feel?" he murmurs, reaching across the table until his fingers slide through my hair. He probes the small cut along my scalp that's being held together by two stitches. I can't feel the pain; Tongue's presence numbs me with arousal.

"Better."

"Good. You've been asleep for three days. I've been getting worried about you."

"Three?" I yelp, shocked. I don't remember it being three days. It was yesterday that I hit the wall… I thought.

His finger slides from the side of my head, dragging his calloused fingers down my cheek. His wide palm wraps around my throat. "You sure you're better?" his voice deepens, taking on a supernatural tremble that makes him sound demonic.

"Yes."

He doesn't say another word. He pulls me across the table by my neck. The chair slides back and hits the stove, and his mouth crashes down on mine, bruising my mouth in painful kiss. I taste blood and Tongue must too, because he shoves his tongue in my mouth and licks the metallic taste clean. His growls fill my belly, making me whimper into his mouth.

Half my body is across the table while my feet dangle off the other side, the tips of my toes scratching across the floor.

Breaking the kiss, he keeps me locked in his hold, and he flicks his tongue out to gather the smear of blood across his lip. "I'm going to fuck you whether you feel better or not, because I need to feel you."

"I want that. I need that too."

A normal person would let me get off the coffee table by way of placing my feet on the floor, and then I'd walk around the table.

But Tongue isn't normal.

And I don't want my feet on the ground.

He drags me the rest of the way across the tabletop with a burst of strength I wasn't ready for, but welcome. It doesn't stop there. Tongue doesn't let me stand; he continues to pull me to our room. My knees slide across the hardwood floor and when he opens the door and that is when he picks me up. The bedroom is as clean as it will ever be with all the books littered across the floor.

He slams it shut behind us and clicks the lock. He carries me to the bed and lays me down, his chest heaving as he takes deep breaths. His cock is tenting his jeans and he closes his eyes. "I'm sorry. I'm trying not to be rough with you. I know you need time."

I sit up quickly and grab his cock, squeezing hard until I know it hurts.

Just how he likes it.

His biceps shake as he growls, still holding himself back from doing what he really wants.

"You better be as rough as we like, Tongue, or I'll have to tie you down and fuck you how I want," I threaten, knowing he hates the idea of losing control in the bedroom unless he willingly gives it up.

The words are enough to break him out of the ridiculous notion that he needs to be easy on me. He shoves me back and curls his fingers in the waistband of my pajama shorts and yanks them down along with my panties. He doesn't take my shirt off, he doesn't lean down and kiss me.

He unbuttons and unzips his jeans, fishing out his fat cock. He pulls his jeans down the curve of his sculpted hips and gives the beast three strokes before he spreads my legs and comes. Tongue isn't a quick trigger, so when I feel the warm splashes of his seed coating my pussy, I moan, shocked and turned on by feeling it drip down my sensitive seam. He grunts, watching himself come all over my fold.

My legs tremble from being held open.

"I won't apologize for needing you."

Needing me. Not wanting me.

Because he always wants me and that is never in question.

"You look so fucking good covered in my come," he says, pressing his thumb against my clit and using his come as hot lubricant.

A bead of his white cream gathers at the tip of his cock. It's about to drip onto the bed, and the only thing I can think about is how it's about to go to waste. I try to sit up to wrap my mouth around him, but he doesn't allow me to move. His hand is pressed against the middle of my chest and his other hand slices through the air before landing on my aching fire.

My clit breaks, shattering in a fireworks kaleidoscope reminding how fragile my glass heart really is. My legs jerk on instinct. I want to get away, but I want him to do it again.

"I'll never forgive myself for hurting you," he says, slapping his palm on my clit again. "And there's only one way for me to feel better." He lashes me again, and I toss my head back as the fires spread below.

Tongue is making me burn, and the only way I'll find peace is if he extinguishes the desire blazing in my veins.

CHAPTER SIX

Tongue

I'M TRYING TO CALM DOWN. I'M TRYING TO REIN IN MY DESIRE, BECAUSE I KNOW SHE'S healing and she's been through a lot, but the desire ripples over my skin. My entire body is stretched tight. I feel like an animal is about to shred me apart from the inside out if I don't get inside her, claim her all over again, and show her how much I need her.

Even after I've come, my cock is pissed off and rock solid. I grip it in my fist and rub the head against her wet, come-covered folds. Her pinkness glistens with our fluids, and I want nothing more than to drive into her, but I have this urge to hear her beg for me.

I have to hear that she needs me just as much as I need her.

I roll off the bed and kick my pants off. I'm filthy. She's filthy. What's the point of getting clean when we're just going to make ourselves dirty all over again? Some people would find it disgusting, I'm sure. I'm covered in sweat and sand and she hasn't had a proper bath in three days, but I've given her a sponge bath in her sleep. She just doesn't know it.

My boots stop my pants from coming off and I growl in frustration. There is dirt on the floor surrounding my shoes and I bend over and angrily unlace them. I kick them off and they hit a stack of books, causing them to crumble to the ground. My jeans are next, and when I'm done, I climb back on the bed and unwrap her panties from her ankle, where they lie in a useless puddle.

Her glassy eyes are locked on mine and her legs are spread open, shaking along with her breaths. Her pussy is swollen from just a few slaps of my palm. A dollop of her nectar seeps from her tight hole that has only ever known my cock.

And only I will ever know her.

I grab the hem of her shirt. There is a spot that has a small tear where the stitching has come undone. Deciding I want her shirt off, I tear it in half by gripping each tattered side with my hands and ripping it down the middle until her small, perky breasts bounce out. She moans as the cool air wraps around her tight nipples.

"I liked that shirt." She's breathless as the jagged edges of the material drag over her beaded peaks.

"I don't care." I run my hands up her body, closing my eyes when her ribcage expands with each inhale. I let my palms linger there, getting turned on by feeling her breathe.

That's all it takes.

Knowing she's alive, knowing I can feel her life in my hands, knowing she's under me willingly, and knowing she loves me.

Me.

How could I not be turned on by that?

The ridges of her ribs slide against my palm. I make a mental note to get her to eat a little more. I don't want my Comet hungry. She's perfect as is, but I want her as healthy as she can be so she can be by my side for as long as we live.

Fuck that. I want more than life.

I want her in death, too. And in every life we live after this one.

She's mine.

Until the end of time.

I open my eyes and find her watching me, and my hands move, gliding up and over the mounds. The callouses on my hands scratch along her beaded twin peaks and she inhales a sharp breath. I linger there for a second and move my hands in small circular motions. She bites her bottom lip into her mouth. Those spine-tingling noises escape her lips, driving me fucking crazy.

Here I am wanting to ravage her, but now I find myself wanting to take my time.

I roam down her body until I dip between her legs and force her legs apart again. I love seeing the mess I made down there. My come is dripping on the sheets and sticking to her thighs. My fingers twitch with the desire to spank her clit again. I get a flash of sudden desire to make her come from it.

I want to use something else though.

Something more intense. Something harder.

I reach into the nightstand and pull out my knife, remembering how much she loves it when I bring the blade out to play. I grab the sheath too. Don't get me wrong, we like to cut, but I don't want to cut her down there. It would bring her too much pain, and like I said before, I never want to hurt her.

Sliding the sheath onto the black, sharp blade, I clip it into place. She follows my hand with her eyes, and when I lay the protected blade between her legs, her hand snags around my wrist. "Why is the sheath on it? You know I like it when we—"

I let the action speak for itself. I lift the blade and smack it against her swollen bundle, getting come over the sleek protectant of my knife.

Her lips make a large O, and I'm imagining my cock plummeting her throat again, which causes it to jerk another drop of come out of the slit. I want to be inside of her, but I want her to fall apart like this first. I want to cherish the way she makes me fall apart every second of every day by destroying what I've known and teaching me all the things I don't.

I smack her again. The loud *slap* of the hard plastic of the sheath against her sweet candy echoes into the room, playing a new favorite song I want to listen to on repeat.

I don't ask her if she wants it harder, I just apply more pressure with my swing.

"Oh god, Tongue. Yes, feels so good," she mumbles, high on the pain and pleasure only I can give her.

Only. Me.

My come acts as a sticky barrier that causes each smack to feel more intense than the last. The V between her legs is swollen and red. Her clit is erect and poking between her folds; the sensitive flesh of her thighs is trembling uncontrollably.

Fucking gorgeous.

"It hurts so much," she cries, a tear drips down her face, and I bend over to lick it off her cheek. *Delicious.* "Don't stop. Please, don't stop," she cries.

Like I'd ever stop.

I'm a strong man, but I'm not that strong. Her cries fuel my sick need to inflict more pain. Another hot tear escapes her, and I drink her up before it goes to waste. "Tastes so good, Comet."

"Tongue, I need you inside me. Please, please." The desperation. The pleading. The tears. The irritated skin between her legs has me giving in. I give her clit one more slap and place the knife to her lips. She knows what I want her to do. She sniffles, the whites of her eyes red from crying, and she hums in satisfaction as she licks my come off the sheath. She slowly runs that beautiful tongue of hers all over her lips, relishing my taste.

I toss the knife to the side, crawl over her body, and shove myself inside in one deep thrust.

"Tongue!" she screams my name as she convulses around me.

"Is that all you needed, Comet? My cock inside you for you to come?" I slowly slide out until all that's left is the tip. I look down, watching myself being coated in her juices. Her pussy is hot from the knife slapping and her legs are still shaking as they hook around my hips.

"That's always what I need." There is a sheen of sweat gathering between her breasts. My mouth waters to drink her up.

I thrust in again, squeezing her tits tight in my palms to show her how good she makes me feel. She's grabbing at my chest, clawing at the skin from the punishing rhythm. Her body scoots up the bed and the books that support our mattress start falling onto the floor.

It's something I have to fix every time we have sex.

"All you'll ever need is me," I growl to her, pressing my pelvis against her hips. I lift her legs and push them together, laying them against my torso, then I wrap my arm around the silky-smooth limbs as I gain momentum. I lay my cheek against her calf, moaning her name. "Daphne," I utter in the back of my throat as the wet sounds of us bring me closer to filling her.

She isn't just tight and hot. She doesn't just squeeze me until I can't think straight. She doesn't just make all of my wet dreams come true.

When we are tangled in one another like this; when she gives herself to me—not just by spreading her legs, but by giving me her trust—that's when I understand what love is.

She trusts me to take care of her. To only bring her pleasure. The same pleasure I equate with pain.

Daphne trusts me.

The thought has me slowing down, positioning her legs on either side of my waist, and curling my body over hers. I tuck my arms under her back, then hook my hands around her shoulders to drive in with long languid strokes until my sack is pressed against the crease of her ass.

I think about her struggle, how I hurt her the other night, how she deserves better. I clutch on tighter. I don't ever want to let go. If I do, she might realize she's better off. She can't leave me. She isn't ever allowed to leave. I would die.

Death would be welcome after losing someone so full of life.

I feel….

I clutch onto her tighter, burying my head into the nook of her neck and inhaling. She's here. She's safe. She's okay.

I feel…

The blunt head of my cock pierces her again and again. She's whimpering sweet songs in my ear that make me want to slam her against the wall or chain her to the bed to have my way with her.

Her arms wrap around me in return, her hands gentle as she coasts down my back. "Oh, Tongue. I'm here. I love you. We were made for one another, Tongue. Can you feel it?"

Her whimpers and whines are broken with how much deeper I become with every thrust.

I feel…

Exposed.

This isn't how it's supposed to be with us. We fuck hard. Messy. Bloody. That's how we show each other we know what we need.

Not understanding the burning behind my eyes, I pick her up, swing us over the bed, and walk to the nearest wall to prove my point. I keep my hand behind her head, so she doesn't hurt the wound I caused. The bang of her body hitting the wall has me humming down her throat in satisfaction.

That's better.

Her hands cup my face, and she arches her back, giving me the perfect view of her silken throat. I bend down to bite the flesh, to show her that pain is who I am. It's the only way I can function.

But I kiss her pulsing vein instead. I watch the beautiful pearl-colored flesh pebble from the simple brush of my lips. Why does she react to me like this? I don't deserve such an exquisite reaction.

I'm so confused.

Why is this happening?

I stumble back and the bed hits the back of my knees. I flip us again, pinning her on her back; I'm prepared to fuck her hard and fast, but I'm curling over again, pressing my lips against hers in a slow, sensual kiss.

This pace, this place with her, in her embrace and between her legs, makes me feel her love. My body is rejecting the rage in my mind. I'm screaming at my body to do what it knows, but the thrusts are slowing, and I'm holding onto her so tight I'm worried she can't breathe.

"Comet..."

Her name sounds more like a question as I drive into her, slow with most of my inches, and then I thrust my hips at the last minute. She likes that because a loud moan always leaves her. "Comet..." I try to explain myself again and the damn burning is back in my eyes.

Images of what my uncle did slam against the front of my mind. His hate burns across my back with every cigarette he puts out against my useless flesh. I rub my forehead against the crook of her neck, wanting the memories scrubbed. They don't have a place here. He doesn't have a place here. It's only Daphne. It's only me.

Us.

"It's okay," my Comet whispers in my ear, clenching her fingers into the mess of my hair. "I love you," she says. "Let go." The fragile tickle of her hand presses against my heart. "I have you. I'll always have you."

Holding the side of her neck to keep her head in place, I kiss her, driving my tongue into her mouth as my other hand migrates down. I hold her hips still, rolling in and out from between her legs, and try not to lose myself completely the more I allow myself to let go like she says.

I can't let go more than I have, or I don't think I'll recognize myself.

Would that be such a bad thing?

The voice inside my head sounds like reason. A fickle bitch I'm not familiar with.

"Wayne." She pushes against my chest to lift me off her and she kisses each cheek. "Your tears are safe with me." Her thumb brushes under my eye and my uncle's voice fades into the distance as my eyes focus onto her face, her beauty. The more her blue irises shine with understanding, the more I hate the kind of man I am. She needs me to be stronger, but the more she breaks me open, the more I see just how weak of a man I really am.

She squeezes around me just as another book clatters to the ground. Her broken puffs of air barreling out of her tickle the side of my jaw as she climaxes, whispering my name.

My given name.

And the rest of me that refuses to let go breaks free. I push to the hilt, trying to get deeper, trying to get as far as her body and mine allow. I orgasm, holding my breath and seeing double from the intensity. Strong jets leave me and bathe her womb.

I hope it does.

Bound to me in sickness and health isn't enough. That will happen in time, but I want more.

I don't leave her as we come down from our high. Instead, I kiss her senseless, locking my come inside her. We don't speak, we just lose ourselves in the kiss, and I start smaller thrusts as my cock hardens again.

I'm going to be between these long legs all night.

The haunted images of my uncle are long gone. My chest is open and bared to her as she reaches inside, clutches the agony I carry in her hands, and squeezes it until it dies.

Madness created me.

Abuse broke me.

But it's Daphne is who is stitching me back together.

CHAPTER SEVEN

Daphne

I'M FINALLY INSIDE THE BOOKSTORE AFTER ANOTHER TWO DAYS OF RESTING. WELL... TWO days of amazing, passionate sex with Tongue. I don't think we ever left the room unless he got up to get food and water, well, and bathe. Even when we were bathing, we got dirty.

He has been an emotional rollercoaster ever since I hit my head. The monster inside him has been dormant. Almost like it curled up hibernating in the back of his mind, safe and sound tucked underneath a wool blanket. I thought I saw him for a minute when he sheathed the knife and slapped me with it, but it was fleeting, and then something big happened.

I don't know what it was. I don't know what made him recoil into his skin again. As much as I miss the monster (because I do, I fell in love with the monster first), I'm so happy I got to see the reluctant bunny instead.

Bunny is a bad word. Tongue could never be an actual rabbit. He's more the type to skin it, cook it, and eat it, then save the fur for a pelt or something. A bunny is the only animal I can think of at the moment to describe his hesitancy to bring his softness forward. Bunnies are timid, and as soon as they experience something out of nowhere that scares them, they bolt.

Now, while Tongue doesn't run, he clams up when it comes to feelings, because he is learning what they mean.

While his beast sleeps, the bunny comes out to play.

Until the beast wakes up of course and eats the bunny... well, that's a bridge I'll cross when we get there. It's my job to protect the bunny when he emerges, so

I can only make sure that's what I do when Tongue decides to push the soft and cuddly to the side.

And his soft and cuddy is like something walking over the tip of nails, but he is learning.

"Ma'am? Excuse me?"

I blink my eyes and stare at the contractor, who is snapping his fingers in front of my face. His blue overalls are splashed with paint ranging from white, red, black, and green. He has drywall in his brown hair, and he seems annoyed as he waits for me to answer him.

"Where do you want this?"

He holds a book in his hand and waves it around the air. I am horrified and insulted that someone would treat a book with such carelessness. The pages act as an accordion as he swings the delicate, vintage, classic, historical novel in the air. As if it's being used to help paint dry. I'm so stunned that I'm barely able to say and do anything.

"I'm sorry, ma'am. It's in the way of us knocking down the wall. It was in a weird glass case, but the case broke when we tried to move it. Cracked right down the side. I really do apologize. I'll cover the cost of the damage."

My mouth hangs open as dust flies in the air. The pages are hanging on by… by… sheer will!

"Holy Moly, Mister. What are you doing!" I shriek, launching over the makeshift countertop that must be made out of plywood and hopes and dreams, because I don't know how it's standing. I rip the book out of his hand, the first edition copy of Wuthering Heights.

The first. Edition.

How dare he treat a book with such malice. "Do you know how valuable this book is? Do you know how old it is? Do you know the damage you've done by manhandling it the way you have? Just the oil from your nasty, dirty, unwashed fingers that have paint and dust all over them have probably compromised the integrity of the pages. The binding is delicate, and I think you ruined it." I double check the pages and let out a sigh of relief when they seem to be intact, but the binding is weaker. "This is… this…"

"You're cute all flustered, lady." The workman leans against the plywood and smirks, creasing the lines in his cheeks as he tries to flirt.

Oh, he is an idiot, isn't he?

I ignore him with a shake of my head and find an empty box under my fake desk. I kneel on the ground and lay it in the box, closing the four cardboard sides as gently as I can. I'll need to get another container and have a velvet lining added in it. This book can only be handled with gloves.

It was the only good thing that came from Andrew, the man who owned this store and employed me before he decided he wanted me and wanted to fight Tongue.

He ended up dying for his stupid decision and Tongue did something amazing. He bought the store for me, and now I get to live my dream.

Tongue is making my dreams come true, but I can't help but wonder what his dreams are. He hasn't even shared them. Wouldn't he want to do more than be at the beck and call of Reaper? Or fix cars in the garage? He has to have some type of goal, but then again, maybe he doesn't. He's never had the opportunity to think about himself.

And his art, the way he draws, is not just a random talent that won't get him anywhere in life. He has a real gift. I want to show him he is more than the tasks everyone has him doing.

The man kneels on the ground and peeks his head underneath the desk. "So, your name is Daphne, right? You own the place?"

I nod, not wanting to give him any satisfaction of giving him my attention by speaking.

"I've seen you around here before. It's been a while. You're pretty, you know that? You want to go out sometime? I'll take you to this local diner, maybe catch a movie. How's that sound?" His green eyes meet mine when I whip my head up in shock. I've never been asked out on a date before.

And I don't like it.

I like when a man just takes, not asks, and that's why Tongue is the perfect man for me.

The contractor has a buzzed haircut, short to the scalp, which makes the ridges in his skull appear. I don't like short hair, something I've had to tell Tongue a hundred times, especially since he cut off his beautiful long locks with his knife.

It was such a sad day.

"Um, no thank you. I have a…" Boyfriend? That sounds ridiculous when Tongue and I are so much more. "I have a husband," I lie, kind of. My heart is married. That is what matters.

"I don't see a ring," he notices, laying his hand on mine and rubbing his index finger across the blank space where a ring should be.

"I… I didn't wear it today because I knew I'd be working. I didn't want it to slip off." I slide my hand away and pick up the box. "Anyway, I really need that wall knocked down today." My voice comes out low and slightly panicked. Anxiety is forming in the pits of my throat. The man walks around the plain wooden desk that has made me pluck splinters out of my palm.

"I'm Zed." He holds out his hand. There isn't anything about him that screams for me to get away. Even though he treated my book badly, he seems nice. Nice for some other girl who doesn't get off on being cut with a knife or cutting the man she loves and licking the blood off the wound. He's being a little pushy since he isn't taking no for an answer, but he's only calling me out on my lie.

"Listen, Zed. You seem nice, but I am with someone and it is serious. Very serious." The words are out of my mouth, but the determination on his face doesn't disappear.

"We can be friends. You're allowed to have friends, right?"

I'm about to say yes, but not friends who are interested in me, when the glint of a black blade suddenly presses against Zed's throat. It's the same blade that's made me orgasm. The same blade that makes me yearn for Tongue to carve his name into my chest.

"Hey man, I don't have any cash on me. Don't hurt the girl," Zed says. "She doesn't have any either."

"She has me," Tongue sneers, pressing the sharp edge against Zed's Adam's apple. "And to answer your question, no. She isn't allowed to have friends. Not when the person wants more than friendship." Tongue flings Zed against the wall, and I look for fear in Zed's eyes, but all I see is understanding and realization.

"Sorry, man. I thought she just didn't want to take the leap, but I get that she is truly taken."

"She's taken. Off-limits. And fucking mine. I don't want to see you around here again." Tongue lashes the knife against Zed's cheek, opening a three-inch wound.

Zed hisses and holds his hands against the bleeding mark. "Fuck. I said I was going to stay away from her."

I need to speak up. I need to stop Tongue from doing what he does best but seeing him in his element has me barely able to breathe. He's strong, imposing, and in Alpha mode right now. If Zed wasn't here, I'd lock the door and jump him.

"I don't know if that's enough." Tongue takes a step in the man's space. He lifts the knife and digs the tip in the man's throat, but not hard enough to kill him.

But enough to want to.

"You weren't kidding when you said you were with someone," Zed stammers, his head tilted back to relieve the pressure from Tongue's knife.

"She's mine," Tongue growls.

"And that's crystal clear. I will just get back to work. No harm, no foul. I swear. It won't happen again."

"I think I'll kill you instead." Tongue's hand is quick, his fingers dipping into Zed's mouth and pinching the red appendage tight.

Zed cries out, eyes wide, and his tries to push Tongue away, but the more he tries, the more his tongue is stretched out, so he stops the struggle.

Until the knife glides up his neck, the tip cutting another bleeding line in his skin. He tries to mumble something, probably a plea for Tongue to stop.

I finally push the lust aside and unglue my feet from the floorboard to stand between them. Tongue's hardened gaze flickers from Zed to me.

And just like that, the anger flees, and the edges of his eyes where life has created wrinkles softens.

"He's okay, Tongue. Let him go."

"I never let a threat go," Tongue replies, transitioning his attention from me to Zed.

I look over my shoulder to see Zed nodding, hoping Tongue listens to me. Now that he is in this position, he looks a little pathetic, cornered by a man so much more dangerous than he is. It would be fun to watch Tongue do what he wants. It's been too long since Tongue and I had a little fun. Like those two guys in the alley when we were walking in downtown Vegas. He tore those men apart and seeing him in his element made me want him even more.

But it's daytime. There are other workers here. Now isn't the time or the place. "Let him go, Tongue. He won't be an issue again."

"That's what you want?" he asks, and he does that curious tilt of his head when he is trying to understand me, because he wants to give me what I want.

"Yes, Tongue. It's what I want. He won't be a bother again."

"He can't work here. I don't trust him around you."

"That's fine. He doesn't have to be here. You can take his honest day's work."

Tongue grunts with a slow chin tilt. He likes that idea. It means he can be here with me. "Whatever Comet wants, she gets." With that, Tongue lets go of Zed's tongue and the guy dashes to the door.

He touches the blood dripping down his face and points a red finger at us. "You two are fucking nuts. Jesus Christ. You're crazy."

"You have two seconds to get out of here before I decide to change my mind and kill you anyway." Tongue steps forward and spins the knife in his fingers.

"Fuck this. Crazy fucking people," Zed opens the door, then slams it, the bronze bell ringing from his departure, but also ringing in old memories.

The days that this place wasn't mine. The days that I knew Tongue watched me outside through the window. An admission he had no shame in telling me.

"I might kill him later because I feel like it."

I giggle, patting the middle of his back. I know he wants to kill Zed, but unlike Tongue, I know when someone is good or bad. Zed isn't so bad. He deserves to keep his tongue. "I love you for wanting to do that."

He turns around and bites the air when another man passes by too close. "I don't like you here with these men. I don't trust them. Can I kill them all? I'll build the bookstore for you."

"You can't kill everyone you don't like, Tongue."

"Why?" He's pouting now. Bottom lip poking out in distress.

"Because that's how you go to prison."

"I'll just kill everyone there too. No one can keep me from you. I won't allow it."

Now that is something I believe wholeheartedly.

"Hey, Daphne. You want the same dimensions for the new door?" another worker asks. His name is Zack if I remember correctly. "Just want to make sure before we get started."

"Yes, I do. Thank you."

"He likes you too," Tongue growls, watching Zack like a hawk.

Zack lifts a sledgehammer, typical oak handle and black rubber end, and Tongue breathes heavy, huffing like a bull who is hoofing the ground. He wants to charge. "They all fucking like you."

"No, they don't. Tongue, come here." I take his hand and lead him toward a corner, a place where he feels most comfortable. "What's going on? You're atypically growly today."

The beast ate the bunny.

Crap.

"I miss you. I don't like others looking at you." He rubs the back of his neck and stretches, as if he is trying to get a kink out. "I want to lock you in the room again where the world can't admire you. I only want to admire you. It isn't fair, but I don't care. I want you to myself." He darts his eyes above, staring at the unfinished ceiling.

Can he not look at me? His hands scrub along his scalp and then then brush down his chest.

"Tongue—"

"I love you too much to have someone else come in and love you too and to take your love from me. I won't allow it. I can't. I can't…" his chest rises and falls, and he continues to shake his head.

"Look at me."

He won't.

"Look. At. Me."

He hears the biting edge to my voice and finally lands his eyes on me, and the pain… my god, the pain I see, no wonder he can't breathe. His heart is racing, and his shirt is hot and damp. His neck is red, and beads of sweat are traveling down his neck.

I do the only thing I know to do.

I grab his face with my hands and kiss him. In the background, the men whistle and cheer, but I don't care about them. I only care about the man in front of me. The very controlling, temperamental, possessive, dangerous, frightening, loving, caring, and kindest man. The man who's mine.

Mine.

He somehow learned how to love me while thirsting to kill everyone around me.

His breathing changes. The thundering heart beneath his chest evens out, and when we break apart, his forehead lands on mine and his coffee laden breath puffs across my nose. "I'm sorry I'm so much to deal with. You're the only good thing I've ever had. And it makes me crazy. It makes me… the thought of losing you makes me crazy."

"Why are you thinking like that? Why would you ever lose me? Does this still have to do with me bumping my head?"

His silence is the only confirmation I need. "Tongue," I brush the scruff along his face with the back of my hand. "You can't do that to yourself. I don't blame you. I blame your uncle."

"It isn't about that. Well, it's not just about that," he corrects himself. "It's about all of me. How fucked up I am. My fucked-up way of thinking and feeling, and that isn't going to change. I want you to myself. The world can burn in hell for all I care. That's who I am."

"And I love you for who you are. Because I don't want the world, Tongue. I only want you. I want the most fucked-up parts of you because that's what I love most. You think I care if others want me or look at me? The only attention I want is yours."

"Yeah?" he questions on a relieved exhale. "Why?"

"Why?"

He taps his head and then his heart. "I'm not right, Comet. You don't think I don't see that? I'm not like everyone else. I need blood on my hands to sleep most nights. How does that make me worthy of you? How do I know next time won't just be a bump on the head? But worse?"

My hands move up and over his arms, feeling the hard muscle of his biceps flex under my touch. His forearms are strong, and his veins are protruding all the way down to the wrist. My fingers make their way home between his and hold onto him tight.

"I'll get my hands bloody with you and when we get home, I'll help wash it off. Blood doesn't scare me, but not having you? That does. You have to stop running with the ideas you think of, Tongue. That if I'm hurt, it's your fault, or someone is going to come and love me in ways you can't. You love me in all the ways that matter to me. Get out of your head, or you're going to drive yourself crazy."

He takes my hand in his and brings it to his lips, kissing me softly. I stare at the hands that have caused so much pain and torment and been drenched in so much blood. They are the same hands that have caressed me in bed as he makes love to me, the same hands that protect me, and the same hands that hold me.

"Knock, knock! Sorry to interrupt."

I turn to see an older man standing in the doorway. Tongue immediately clears his throat and masks the emotions on his face. Those emotions are for my eyes only. Only I get to see the side the world will never have the privilege to see.

"Mercy, what are you doing here?" Tongue asks, his shoulders thrusting back and his tone suspicious.

Oh, Mercy. Right. I've seen him briefly, but we have never met.

I step around Tongue and kiss the side of his cheek. "I'm going to go in the other room to look at paint samples. I'll leave you to it."

"Wait," Mercy says, lifting a finger to gesture 'one minute' as he dashes out the door. "This was wrapped and ready at the clubhouse. I was going to the hardware store across the street anyway, so I told Reaper I'd bring it. He said you wanted it to come here." Mercy's eyes flicker to me. His black brows pinch together, which are such a contrast to his silver hair. He leans the package against the primed wall and eyes the room. "Place is looking good."

"Thank you," I say, Mercy's eyes falling to me again.

I lower my sight to the floor and stare at my feet, watching my toes wiggle under the material of my Converse sneakers. He's making me uneasy.

"You're Daphne, right? I only saw you briefly one time, quick, you were on you way out somewhere."

"Yeah. Hi," I greet, and he holds out his hand to me for me to shake.

Tongue slaps it down and growls. "No touching."

"Right," he says. "I'm not trying to step on your toes, man, or cross lines. I wanted to check out the place and properly introduce myself since I'm going to be around more. Daphne and I don't see each other much—"

"Good," Tongue states. "You don't need to see her a lot."

I hide my smile, but Mercy doesn't get the picture. He continues to stare at me, and not only is it making me uncomfortable, Tongue is getting edgy.

"I'll go. I'm meeting Whistler and One. If you need any extra hands, let me know. See you." Mercy pushes the door open and Tongue watches him walk down the sidewalk and pass the window in the front of the store.

But before Mercy is out of my sight, he gives me one last look, and it isn't with want. It's with another intention. I can't place my finger on it.

"Everyone is looking at you today," Tongue slams his fist on my fake countertop and cracks it in half.

Great. Now, I need another one.

"I don't know why. I'm just me…" I push my glasses up the bridge of my nose and then tug the long purple sleeves down my wrists.

Tongue lifts my chin with his fingers. "That's why. You're too beautiful for anyone to miss."

Feeling uncomfortable with all the attention, I try to put Mercy's odd interest out of my head and bounce over to the package he delivered. "What's this?"

Tongue gives that small tilt of his lips as his cheeks turn pink. "It's something I made you. For your store."

A loud drill digs into the wall, followed by another loud bang of a hammer somewhere.

"You made me something? Can I see?"

"What if you don't like it? I don't know—"

"It's from you. I'm going to love it."

Unless it's bones. I have no idea what I'd do with them. Maybe it's a real human skeleton. I could put it in a corner.

Well, now that I've thought of it, I hope that's what it is.

Tongue steps over a few two-by-fours and glides his knife down the package. I wait for it to bleed or moan, but nothing happens.

What in the world is in this box that doesn't leak red?

Tongue's just full of surprises lately, which goes to show, no matter how much time you spend with someone, there is always something to be learned about them.

And I just learned, Tongue loves surprises. Not getting them but giving. He's chomping at the bit with excitement, giving me side-eye glances and tiny grins.

I see more of him peeking through his damaged exterior lately. He's a lesson that will never be finished. A subject I can forever learn about.

What will I learn next?

I don't know.

But I can hardly wait.

CHAPTER EIGHT

Tongue

I'M NERVOUS.

I've made this in secret for the last few weeks. The only person who knows about it is Slingshot, since he's been the one outside helping me build the swamp for Happy. I swore him to secrecy. I didn't want anyone to know what I was up to. Lately, I've felt like more of an outsider at the clubhouse. They watch me like I'm planning some hideous crime.

I thought I was one of them, but Daphne has made me think about life in a new way. Maybe I'm not one of them. The thought has put me in the corner again, only the shadows feel lonelier than ever. I don't say anything, because speaking up about it would make me seem weak. So I hold back and let them stare, let them see if I'm about to go on a killing spree.

Which I haven't done in a while. I've been calmer since Daphne came into my life, but that doesn't mean to I don't crave it sometimes.

Reaper's been cautious about everyone, especially since Moretti and Maximo are still M.I.A. It's like they disappeared off the face of the earth. No one knows how they managed to get over the gates. Braveheart wouldn't let them go.

Moretti figured out a way, and as curious as I am, I find myself not caring.

It's hard to care when no one seems to care what happens to me. I've dedicated my life to the club, but I'm starting to wonder if the club would do the same for me. They are good guys, but whatever notion they have about me, it's pushing me away.

I shouldn't care, but I do.

They don't trust me, and if I don't have the trust of my brothers at my back, then when the time comes that I'll need them most, it will be too late.

I don't know how to redeem myself. I always thought redemption was weak, a pointless goal to achieve for someone who isn't being themselves. Redemption? No such thing. People are who they are. They don't change.

If someone actually wants to get something done, they should try justification for their actions. What type of man are you to do what needs to be done?

And then everyone can go back to the way things are because redemption is a façade.

"Well, when am I allowed to see it?" Daphne bounces on her heels and has a giant smile on her face.

"What's it that you tell me sometimes? Something about waiting makes good things worth it?" I say, trying to throw her words at her, but it fails.

She shakes her finger at me. "Someone is getting sassy." She tugs the lapels of my cut and having her near almost makes me forget about Mercy staring at her. Almost. It's one thing for strangers to look at Daphne, but a… friend? I guess that's what he is, to the club at least. It's crossing the line. I won't have him lusting after her.

Killing someone for betrayal leaves a sweet taste in my mouth. I'm not afraid to kill Mercy. I don't know what he was thinking, but I'll need to keep a close eye on him. Daphne was uncomfortable too.

"Stop it," Daphne says, wrapping her arms around my waist and tilting her head back. "You're thinking too hard. Stop it or I'll have to take you down so I can unwrap this gift myself."

"Take me down where?" I kiss along her jaw. "The floor? In front of everyone? I won't like them seeing you come on my cock, Comet."

"Tongue." She tilts her head back more and lets me have my way with her throat. So soft, so creamy, so slender. I can see the blue tint under her skin from the delicate vein. Daphne read to me once that the jugular veins, when severed, can drain blood from the human body in 5 to 15 seconds.

How beautiful is that?

It's important for people to protect themselves, or something as sharp as a knife could end their life with one quick swipe.

I press a kiss to the nearly exposed vein, vowing to protect it from such evils.

Like me.

Those feelings bubble in my chest again. I feel exposed.

Nothing scares me, but that does. Because it means someone can see my weakness and use it against me.

"Okay, I've tortured you long enough. Just… keep an open mind okay? I've never made anything for anyone before."

"It's big," she rasps, her cheeks painted a brilliant shade of pink, and the tint turns darker when she realizes how her words sound. "That too." She grinds herself down on my leg against my shaft.

I glance up to see a few guys watching us, but they hurry back to their tasks when I narrow my eyes at them. One grabs the wheelbarrow and the other starts cleaning up the sheets of broken drywall. "Not here, Comet." I kiss her one last time before I'm pulling myself back, reluctantly dropping my arms at my sides. If we keep touching one another, I'm afraid we will say 'fuck it' and not care about everyone else around us. I'll bend her over and fuck her on all fours while the contractors watch. Maybe then, they will stop looking at her.

"Then stop staring at me like that," she says.

"Never. I'll never stop staring you like this." Trying to rein in some control, I take a full step away from her and land on a board, which rocks from the awkward placement of my foot. I have to put space between us or this damn gift will never get unwrapped.

"Okay," I blow out a nervous breath and continue to cut around the packaging. It's just a bunch of random cardboard pieces I put together. Daphne has a habit of sneaking home new shipments of books she orders for the store. Every single day, a new box shows up, and she insists she has to read every book before putting it up on the shelves. She's horrible with breaking down boxes and putting them in the recycling bin. She gets too excited about the damn books.

After the different sized boxes accumulated against the wall of our bedroom, I decided they would be perfect to use to wrap her gift.

"Tongue, whatever it is. I'm going to love it."

I nod absentmindedly as I run the tip of the knife through the black tape. It's a big box, and heavy. It's impressive Mercy got it in here all by himself. Probably showing off for Daphne.

Strike two.

And when strike three comes, I'm going to rip his tongue out of his mouth and let him watch while I feed it to Happy.

"You're getting lost in your head again."

"Am not," I argue.

"Are too."

"Am not." My lips twitch to smile, but they don't. Happiness is a learning process and the muscles in my face aren't used to being used. When I smile, my cheeks hurt. I don't want my cheeks to hurt, so I don't grin.

Problem solved.

"I can do this all day."

"I know. It's fun." I open the top of the box and lay it against the wall. The gift itself is wrapped in pictures of tongues I printed out. It isn't hard to sit at a computer, type 'tongue' in the search box since it's one of the few words I know how to spell, and then have Slingshot press 'print'.

Daphne giggles, covering her mouth with her hands as she stares at the atrocity of the wrapping job. It's hideous.

"Come on, come, open it."

She flies toward the box and grabs the middle, crumbling the paper with her fist. She tosses it to the floor and then goes at it with both hands, tearing at it like it's Christmas. Shredded paper tongues scatter across the floor.

Since the gift is so big, she starts working on the other side. She grins as she unwraps, making tongues snow around her feet. It takes a few minutes, but she finally takes the last scrap of paper off. Before her is a large wooden beam, nearly the size of her. It's made of a redwood tree I imported from California.

Redwood roots are shallow on the ground, but they never stop growing toward the sky, and that's how I feel about us.

My roots are shallow, but my love for her constantly grows.

"So," I clear my throat. I'm nervous. I have never done anything like this before. Giving gifts is all too new for me. "You don't have to use it. Don't feel pressured or obligated to. I... I... I wanted to do something nice for you." There I go, stuttering and sounding like an idiot because of how nervous I am. If she doesn't like it, that's okay. I can break it down and use it as firewood. We can have a big bonfire. My feelings won't be hurt.

My feelings are few and far between, and the only ones I have are for Daphne.

She runs her hand down the beam, her fingers stroking the polished wood. "What is it?"

Before I lose my nerve, I grab each side of the heavy wood. Grunting from the amount of strength I have to use, I turn the damn thing around. When it's turned, I lay it on its side against the ground so she can see it level, not up and down.

She gasps, her lips parting and her eyes watering.

"I... um. I kn-know th-that..." God, you fucking idiot, just speak. It's Daphne. Everything will be okay.

"Deep breaths, Comet. It's me and you," she says. "No judgement. Take your time."

I inhale, my chest rising all the way before releasing. "I-I know you were struggling with a name for the bookstore. I wanted to surprise you. I drew the image and was going to give you the paper but decided maybe..."

She finally tears her eyes away from the gift and looks at me.

"Maybe this could be your store sign."

She clasps her hands to her mouth in a gasp.

I try to keep going. "So I or-ordered the wood and carved it in. Slingshot taught me to read 'Once Upon a Time' and spell the words. He was patient. He's my friend. He helped make this." Regardless of how silly I sound, the words ring true.

The front of the sign is a carved book. It's open down the middle with a castle etched on the top left hand side of the open page. My way of telling her she's my fairytale. The lines of the pages are there too, and in gold letters it reads, 'Once Upon A Comet', and then on the bottom right side of the page in burnt black letters says 'BOOKSTORE'. It took a long time to make, but if she doesn't want to hang it and use it as her sign, I'll understand. I'm sure she has her own vision.

TONGUE'S TARGET

She rubs a hand down the gold letters, then caresses the book, outlining every detail with her finger. Every inch of the sign has been sanded and smoothed, and then has a waterproof protectant on it, on top of the shiny finish. There's no way she can get a splinter.

The wood is as smooth as a baby's butt.

Not that I'd know. I've never seen a baby's butt, but Dawn says it all the time when she changes Joey's diaper.

"Tongue, this is… this is amazing. I love it so much. It's perfect. I love you!" She throws her arms around me and cries loud tears that shake her entire body.

"But you're crying. You're unhappy."

She pulls away and keeps her arms on my shoulders, tears freely running down her cheek but her mouth in a big smile. "These are good tears. Happy tears. I love you, Wayne Hendrix. You're so thoughtful. This sign is everything I wanted. It's a symbol of our story, where it all started and where it will go. Our fairytale. This is our book."

I did something good. I made her happy. A crooked grin tilts my lips. "Our own book? I hope it's a million pages long so I can hear you read it to me forever."

"And I'd read every word a million times if it means making you happy."

Happy.

Such a new concept. It makes me exposed.

But it isn't so bad. Not with Daphne.

She's the new chapter in my life after so many others came to a horrible end.

"Can we hang it now?" she asks eagerly.

"Sorry, we still have work to do outside. It will have to wait a few days," one of the contractors says.

"I'll make another, a smaller one, one that you can carry with you." I think about a necklace and a charm. I bet I could go to a local jeweler.

"You're too good to me, Tongue."

Is she kidding? I'll never be good enough. Not when it comes to Daphne.

CHAPTER NINE

Daphne

"Oh my god, that's so sweet," Juliette praises the sign as I show her a picture of it.

"Let me see. Let me see." Melissa snatches it from my hands and her lips part. "Aw, that's so cute."

"What are you guys looking at?" Mary asks as she and Joanna walk into the living room. We are all sprawled on the couch watching Dawson's Creek reruns. The men are in Church, and sometimes that lasts a while. While the boys are away, the girls will play, and right now, we want the seventy-inch flat screen to ourselves.

Melissa turns the phone to show Mary and Joanna as they plop down on the couch, groaning at the same time, but they peek at the phone and squeal when they see what Tongue did for me. Everyone in this house is pregnant it seems. Mary isn't too far along, but Joanna is around thirty weeks. Her belly is as round as a basketball, but from the back, you can't tell she is pregnant. Sarah is the same way.

Dawn didn't want another baby right away, but Skirt was chomping at the bit. He wanted an entire clubhouse full of kids. Sunnie and Patrick want to wait until they have a few more years of sobriety under their belts, which I respect them for. Completely.

"Oh my god, someone take this child," Dawn says, wobbling into the room with her daughter latched on her breast and Aidan gripped on to her leg. She's sliding him across the floor since he won't get off. The poor woman looks like she's about to pass out from exhaustion.

"Aidan, leave your mom alone!" Maizey shoves him and Aidan falls right on his ass. "You are such a brat."

"Am not!" Aidan tosses at her, then shoves her shoulder.

Their fight reminds me of the little spat Tongue and I had yesterday.

"Are too! You're a baby."

"You're a baby, Maizey!"

"I'm rubber and you're glue whatever you say, bounces off me, and sticks you!" Maizey sasses. I have to hold back a snort, because she flips her dark hair over her shoulder and lays her hands on her hips in triumph.

Sarah trudges into the main room next, her face pale. She's walking a bit slower and gripping her stomach.

She and I might be on different pages right now, but I don't want to see her in pain. Her hair is up in a messy bun and it looks like she hasn't slept in a week. "Maizey, Aidan, enough. I don't want to hear your bickering today. Go play in your room."

Even though they just got into a spat, the kids run down the hall laughing, screaming 'you're it!' as they disappear into Maizey's room.

"Sarah, are you okay?" I ask, pushing myself off the couch. Tyrant and Yeti lift their heads and watch me as I walk over to her. She leans against the bar that hasn't been used since Patrick and Sunnie came back from rehab. "Sarah?" I lay a hand on her arm and the girls crowd around me.

Sunnie comes into the room next, a bowl of popcorn attached to her hip so we can marathon our show. We are all in need of some serious girl time. When she sees us, she sets the bowl on the bar top, then presses her hand against Sarah's forehead. Sarah and Sunnie look similar in a lot of ways: blonde hair, small frame, but while Sarah has brown eyes, Sunnie's are blue. Her hair is a bit whiter while Sarah's is more of a dirty blonde. Sunnie has more color too, a natural golden hue to her skin.

"You're warm, Sarah. How long have you been feeling like this?" Sunnie asks, brows drawn in concern.

"It's nothing," she waves the issue away.

"Honey, you don't look so good. I think we need to interrupt Church," Dawn says, hissing as the baby latches onto her nipple harder. "I'm breastfeeding a vampire, I swear." Her face pinches in pain before Joey relaxes and stops sucking so hard.

"No, no. Reaper's been worried enough as is. I don't want him to worry. It's just a bad case of morning sickness. I've been really looking forward to this girl time."

I worry my bottom lip and Mary hands me my phone while we all think about what to do. I tuck it in my back pocket, then glance toward the closed Church doors. No one can hear a thing anymore, not since Reaper soundproofed it. The only way to get their attention is to ring the doorbell he installed. "I agree with Sunnie, Sarah. Are you in pain?" It's another big black cloud that hangs over our heads. She's a high-risk pregnancy, after Tongue stabbed her. It was an accident, but still, she wouldn't be at such high risk if Tongue didn't stab her.

My argument? Tongue wouldn't have stabbed her if he hadn't been in that position where the guys invaded his privacy, sending him into a whirlwind of bad memories and flashbacks.

She cups the bottom of her stomach and hunches over, a muted cry leaving her lips as another wave hits her.

"Oh my god, someone go get Reaper."

"No! Not again," she cries when she falls to her knees. Her hand won't leave the small swell. "No, please, no." Her broken sobs have tears pooling in my eyes. I fall to my knees, then rub small circles across her back to try and make her feel better. "I can't do this again. Oh my god," she screams, then flips to her back. She rests her head in my lap, and I swipe the hair off her damp face.

"Nothing is going to happen to you," I tell her, then I lay my hand on top of hers, protecting her unborn baby with her. "We won't allow it."

"It hurts so much," she wails, her big brown eyes bubbling with fat tears. "I'm losing her. I feel it. I'm losing her." She clenches her eyes shut. Another roar of pain escapes her. A deep, agonizing, guttural, shattering sound has a tear escaping me. I hate this for her. She can't lose this baby. Reaper and Sarah don't deserve that kind of pain, and I know Tongue will never forgive himself if she does. He already wakes up in cold sweats at night when he dreams of stabbing her.

"A girl?" I try to take her mind off the pain. "How do you know?"

"I just feel it. I can't have this happen, I can't."

Melissa and Sunnie bang on the Church doors, yelling for someone to answer.

"Ring the bell, remember? He soundproofed it last week," I remind them. I have no idea what to say to Sarah. Nothing can take this fear from her. All I can do is be here.

Sarah digs her cheek into my leg and her arm curls up against my thigh. Her nails dig in against my skin, right where the hem of my pajama shorts ends.

"It's okay. Reaper will be here soon. Doc will take care of you," I tell her, trying to soothe her the best I can. I pet her cheek to dry the tears, but they are coming too fast.

"What is it?" Badge snaps at the girls when he opens the door. He sure is an asshole on most days, but he's there when it matters. His eyes widen when he sees Sarah on the floor. "Reaper! Doc! It's Sarah."

Melissa and Sunnie move out of the way just in time before the heavy *boom, boom, boom*, of boots stampedes toward us.

"Sarah, Doll! Fuck, what happened? What is it?" Reaper slides his arm under her and moves her from my lap to his. He sets his sights on her belly and his left palm swims over his child, his fingers curling over the bump. Sarah takes his fingers in hers. "No," he chokes. "No, it isn't the baby? Please, tell me it isn't the baby."

"I'm sorry. I'm so sorry."

"Shh," he blinks back tears. The badass President embraces his emotions, not giving a damn if any of us witnesses him break. "It's okay, we will get through it. We always do."

"Hey, Sarah," Doc kneels beside her, just as Tongue watches from the Church doorway. His eyes are wide, and he is frozen in fear seeing Sarah on the ground like this. "What's going on? Talk to me." He rolls her to her side and checks out her rear, but not sexually. With a slow, timid motion, he places her on her back again.

"It hurts," she whimpers. "So bad. I almost can't breathe."

"Well, you aren't bleeding. I didn't see any blood, which is a good thing, but I need to get you downstairs so I can do a full evaluation. I think it's what we talked about before, remember? Your muscle in your abdomen didn't get a chance to properly heal. It's scarred and stretched thin. It's weak. You're growing, which is stretching that muscle. That's the cause of the pain."

"I'm not having a miscarriage?" she asks, hopefully.

"Really?" Reaper smiles and starts to laugh, but the laugh falls short when it morphs into a choked sob. "You're sure?"

"I won't be positive until we get her down there. Pick her up and follow me?"

Reaper's hope flees. He gives a solemn nod as he carefully holds Sarah to his chest, one arm wrapped around her shoulders while the other is tucked under her legs. When he stands, Sarah moans in pain and he kisses her forehead. "I'm sorry, Doll. I'm so sorry."

Reaper and Doc leave the room, their boots echoing loudly.

And then everyone around us is silent.

"Tongue don't blame yourself," Poodle starts, noticing how Tongue is frozen in one spot. "Tongue." Poodle reaches out to comfort him, but Tongue shrugs it away.

"You can't blame yourself anymore," Slingshot adds. "It was a horrible accident. You didn't do it on purpose. Give yourself a break. She's going to be okay."

"You don't know that," Tongue replies, swallowing so hard I can hear the gulp from across the room.

"It's scary, and I know you feel guilty, but you gotta learn to let go." Tool glides over to Juliette and wraps an arm around her shoulder. We all quietly gather in the main room, not knowing what we can do. We want to help, but how can we make a difference?

"Learn to let go?" Tongue growls. "Learn to let go?" he repeats, slamming his fist against the wall.

Poodle leans against the couch and opens his arms for Melissa, who eagerly runs into them.

All the men pair up with their ladies, but Sunnie walks to Patrick so he doesn't have to go near the bar and sits on the couch next to him.

"It's easy for you to say. You won't have to live with the guilt of knowing she lost her second child, and the reason is because of you. Don't sit there and tell me everything is going to be okay. Nothing is going to be okay. This isn't fucking okay. I need… I need…" Tongue starts rambling. His nerves are getting the best of him. "I need to go." Tongue fishes out his keys from his pocket. They jingle, a sound I don't want to hear, especially when it's punctuated by a heavy crack of thunder rolling in the sky, shaking the foundation of the clubhouse. "I'm going to go."

I get up from the floor and brush my butt in habit. I walk toward him and for the first time in our relationship, he holds up a hand to stop me from coming closer.

"I need some time, Comet. I need to be alone. I love you, but I can't be here right now," he says, his voice breaking. The haunted expression in his chocolate brown eyes will be an image I'll never be able to forget. He brushes by me. The electricity crackles across our skin like it always down when we are near one another.

Everyone watches him leave. He opens the door and even from where I'm standing, I can see the grey skies looming in the distance. The kiss of rain pecks against the room, dripping off the edge onto the porch steps. Tongue doesn't care. He takes his leather jacket off the knob against the wall that's dedicated for him. All members have one. He doesn't put it on. He hangs it over his shoulder as he slams the door behind him.

He must jump down the steps because I can't hear him pound down the wood like usual. A grumble cuts through the white noise of rain and pulls away, idling when he gets to the gate where Braveheart is along with Tank.

My eyelids ease shut when I try to understand what just happened, but my heart is crushed. Tongue never denies me, and today his denial hit me right smack in the chest.

"Don't take it too hard, Daphne. Tongue gets that way sometimes," Poodle says, and I know he meant to calm me, but it doesn't work. If anything, I feel a giant need to stand up for Tongue.

"Don't tell me how he gets. Don't tell me how all of you know him and know what he is like. You don't know. You don't know anything about him. And that's your fault. All of you!" I whip around and point a finger at each of them. Tool's brows rise in shock, Juliette can't bear to look at me, and Melissa is rubbing Poodle's chest. "You paint him as the bad guy every day because he is so different. He's Tongue, right? He can't feel anything? He's just the guy you call to do the dirty work that you can't do. He's different. But he isn't a damn leper. He deserves more than what all of you give him. None of you have faith in him. Can't you see him?" I yell, pointing toward the door, then hit the side of my head as if they are too dumb to realize the damage they are doing. "Can't you see he needs more? He's different in the sense that he's learning life all over again. And no matter what I do, I can only put him together so many times before all of you break him again. He's more. He's fucking *more!*"

When the door opens again, I hold my breath, hoping Tongue has changed his mind, but it's the silver-haired man again.

My hope deflates, shoulders sagging, and of course, Mercy's eyes are on me.

And of course, Tongue isn't here when I need him most.

"Reaper around?" Whistler asks, coming around Mercy. "We need to talk to him."

"Sorry, he's busy right now with Sarah and Doc."

"Everything okay?" Mercy's brows bend in concern as he shakes off his jacket. Water droplets fling and scatter along the floor. "Does it have to do with Tongue barreling out of here like a bat out of hell?" Mercy's eyes are making me uncomfortable, and I am too heated to deal with stares that are full of questions.

The more he looks at me, the more familiar he becomes, and I don't like it.

I need to get out of here too.

I just wish Tongue would have taken me with him. We could have ridden to the center of the storm together.

CHAPTER TEN

Tongue

THE RAIN STINGING ME IN THE FACE IS WELCOME AFTER WHAT I JUST WITNESSED. My cheeks are getting the brunt of the pain, and my hands aren't gloved, so my knuckles are white, and my fingers are cold. I deserve the pain. I need the rain to soak me to my bones to the point that I can't be wrung dry. To the point that my insides drown. I deserve that and so much more after seeing Sarah lying on the floor, cupping her stomach as she cried.

Fear.

Pain.

Devastation.

And it's all my fault.

My bike fishtails along the road and water flings up from the back tire, spraying against my jacket and the back of my neck. The roads are foggy and the clouds are low. The blacktop is shining from blankets of rain and oil from the traffic. One wrong move and I could end up as buzzard food.

I bet that would be a welcome relief to some. No one would have to worry about me anymore. Daphne would be okay. She'd move on. She'd find someone better, someone who can love her without the harmful tendencies my love brings.

A car horn honks and headlights shine in my face. I've swerved to the other lane and the massive semi-truck barrels forward since he can't exactly slam on the brakes. The grill is silver and the logo in the middle starts with a P. If I can see that, then shit is about to get messy. I jerk my handlebars to the right, the blowhorn of the truck ringing in my ear. I get in my own lane, and out of the corner of my eye I see the driver lift his hand out the window in a 'what the fuck' gesture.

My heart sledgehammers against my chest and my breath leaves my lips in an icy cloud. Holy shit, I nearly died. I could have not moved. I could have let the truck hit me and leave me in unrecognizable pieces along the highway.

But Daphne's face, Daphne's love... she's what had me jerk the handlebars at the last minute. I'd regret dying because I'd miss her. She's the only thing keeping me alive. If it weren't for her, I think I might have become a nomad eventually.

And that life is a rough one. Eventually something would kill me, but at least it would be on my own terms and away from judgement. Hell, my own club members don't even like me. There's Slingshot, but I don't know if he likes me or just deals with me.

Cue the smallest violin and let the devil play it on my shoulder, then let me dance in the flames of my 'woe is me' self-pity party.

I pass a yellow road sign and exhale my stress as I get further away from the club. The darkness hides the mountains in the distance, but they surround me. A perfect place for a man to escape and live off the land for a few days. But I can't leave Daphne alone. I'll bring her with me. Maybe we will get a cabin away from everyone and everything. We only need each other. As long as we have us, we will be okay.

Eventually, I turn around on the road and start to head back to the clubhouse. I've been gone for a few hours and I don't want Daphne to worry.

The road back to the clubhouse is straight, long, and goes on for miles. It looks the same going back as it did when I left. The asphalt is so dark it's nearly black, soaked through with rain. A white line on the right and a yellow in the middle to signal people can pass one another.

My headlight shines against the road. Every now then I see roadkill picked apart, probably by coyotes or buzzards.

Another sign comes to view, only this time, it's one made of wood, and just as old as the building Zain lives in.

Las Vegas Asylum, est. 1907.

Well damn, look at that. I read it.

I grin to myself and wish Daphne was next to me for us to celebrate. She always celebrates me. Every new word I can pronounce and sound out, every time she thinks I'm ready to upgrade to a more difficult book, she never fails to say how proud she is of me.

Taking the next right following the sign, my bike bounces from the uneven terrain. I slow down to give my suspension a rest and coast over a few potholes. I don't know what the fuck I'm doing here. Something is pulling me into this direction, it's only fair if I give it a chance to see why.

The bike comes to a rolling stop near a few cars. There's an old Lincoln Continental that has seen better days. The front end is still dented from when Porter smashed into Patrick and Sarah.

I hate that motherfucker.

I park my bike and take off my helmet, cross my arms, and just stare at the Asylum front door. What am I doing here?

Zain has done a good job of renovating the building while keeping its creep-tastic nature. Some bricks are crumbled in certain places. He told me he found a cemetery not too far in the backyard, from the Prohibition era. If that doesn't scream haunted, I don't know what does.

Even over the hiss of rain peppering the ground, the squeak of the front door sounds over the droplets, and Zain is poking his head outside. His shiny bald head reflects the porch light and his narrow eyes narrow even further to try to figure out who I am.

I can tell the moment he figures it out. He steps outside and the screen door slams. He takes three steps to the new rail on the porch, folding his arms as he stares off into the desert. I push off the ground and make my way toward him, my boots sludging through the mud with a squelching sound.

"I can't say I'm surprised to see you here," he starts, turning his head to pin me with black eyes.

"That goes for one of us. I'm surprised. I don't know what the fuck I'm doing." I take another look around the porch, impressed with how nice it looks compared to the slumping shit-fest it was before. There's a swing on the far right side of the porch. I can image sitting there and watching the sunset. Not with a beer in hand, but a cold sweet tea that really quenches the thirst. There are a few potted plants, and there is a small sign next to the door with 'Las Vegas Asylum' engraved on it. As if this place is a bed and breakfast.

Whatever tickles their crazy, I guess.

"I think you're here to talk to your brother."

I grab him by the back of the shirt collar and throw him against the side of the house. "Don't ever fucking call him that again or I'll kill you."

"You won't fucking touch him," Zain's ol' lady comes up to the other side of the screen door, a knife in hand. "Or I'll kill you."

"I don't take kindly to threats," I warn her, my voice bordering on a threat.

"I'm not asking you to," she sneers.

Zain lifts his hand up telling us to stop. "Jessica, it's okay."

"How do you know it's Jessica?" I ask, sizing her up as she does the same to me.

"Jessica is a bit more... protective."

"Chloe is a coward."

"Be nice," Zain orders.

"I will when he doesn't threaten you."

"I'll stop threatening his life when he doesn't refer to Porter as my brother."

"He is your brother." Jessica tears her eyes away from me and stares at her nails. Her tone is as if she's bored out of her mind, just repeating the obvious.

"He isn't!" I growl, slamming my fist against the side of the house. A piece of brick crumbles to the ground and lands on my boot. "He is nothing to me."

"Get over yourself." She drags her eyes from inspecting her fingernails and lands those empty and emotionless abysses on mine.

I don't like her.

"He's your blood. And if he wasn't your brother, what are you doing here? Dropping by to say hi?" She snorts in disbelief. "Please. I bet there is a small part of you that wonders what he is like."

"I know what he is like."

"Hmmm," she hums, unimpressed with my argument. "Then you know he's a lot like you, right?" She taps the door and with a confident smirk she turns around and walks away, heading toward the couch. She sits down next to a woman with blonde hair and a guy in a toga. That must be Apollo.

"She's a pain," I state honestly.

Zain toss his head back and laughs. "Isn't she great? I fucking love that woman." He slaps his hand on my shoulder as he comes down from his joy. "Tongue, can I talk to you about Porter? Maybe in some way you'll be able to see he isn't all bad. He didn't used to be. He's sick. Here." He taps the side of his head with his index finger. "I mean, we all are, but Porter is different. His identity crisis is similar to Apollo's, but Apollo literally doesn't have another personality. Apollo is... Apollo. I don't even know his real name. Porter? He thinks he does the world a favor getting rid of people like you, or people involved with you, because of his dad and mom."

"His mom was mine, remember? And what I remember of her, she wasn't bad. My parents were good to me." I think they were. I remember a few things, but I can't remember what they looked like. It's been too long, and I don't have any pictures of them. Life's unfair like that. I remember Mom making mac and cheese for me because I didn't like anything else as a kid. I remember her putting a band-aid on my knee and then kissing it better.

I don't believe kisses make wounds better anymore, but I did as a kid.

"I just think you should talk to him. Maybe you could find some common ground."

"The only thing I could tell him is that if I ever saw him again outside of this Asylum, if he ever roamed free, I'd kill him. I'd take my time. Not just for what he did to Sarah and Daphne, but Knives too. I'll kill him. He's lucky Reaper hasn't asked for his death. I don't understand why."

"You don't know why?" he asks in disbelief. "Reaper hasn't killed Porter because Porter is your family. Whether you want to admit it or not. You're more alike than you think. How many people have you killed?"

"That's different. I did it for the club."

"Any kills that weren't club business?" he asks.

I freeze like a deer in headlights. I want to say there haven't been any, but that isn't true. I've lost count of how many people I've killed just because they have pissed me off.

"You're more alike than you think. Maybe talk to him and see what he is like. He's been on his medication and he's improved."

"I'm nothing like him," I say, trying to convince Zain, but it's a sad attempt to try to convince myself.

"Then leave," he says. "If you aren't here for him, leave."

"I'm not here for him. I left the clubhouse to get some air and I wanted to come say hi."

"I don't see you leaving." He sits down on the swing and pushes off the ground with his feet to start to sway back and forth.

Leave.

Leaving is easy. I can leave.

But my boots are stuck to the porch. I stare through the screen door. The black sheer material fuzzes the inside of the Asylum. From here it looks like a real home on the inside. Wooden floors, coffee tables, a sectional couch facing the tv, décor up on the walls. It even smells like cinnamon candles are burning, giving a comforting aroma.

All the scent does is coverup the crazy inside.

"I'm waiting," he says, stretching out his arm to show me the way out.

It's pouring rain now, reminding me of static blaring from a TV that's turned up too loud. "I'm going," I say, but I still don't move.

I want to fucking move, but my brain and legs are not communicating. I don't want to be here. I want to go home to Daphne. I want to curl around her and lay the sharp edge of my knife against her skin, carve my name into the flawless flesh like I've always wanted.

But all I can think about is Porter. Why does he do what he does? Why does he insist on hurting the ones I care about? Why does he hate me? He has no right to, especially when I have every reason to hate him after everything he has done.

I'm not trying to form a brotherly bond, but I do want answers. I grab the silver lip of the handle and open the screen door.

All I need to do is turn around and leave. All I need to do is stop giving a damn, but lately, it seems I do give a damn, and I'm not liking it. I don't know how to process it. Just go inside and kill him. That's all it takes, and then I can never worry about him again.

But he's my brother...

Blood or not, my only family is Daphne. I don't need him.

But I still find myself walking inside, stepping into the air conditioning. My skin goosebumps from the cold since I'm wet, and I shake my hair out, flinging water on the mirror to my right.

"Take off your boots. They have mud all over them and I just mopped the floor. If you ruin it, I'll make you clean it again."

I roll my eyes and tug on my wet laces, then kick my boots off.

"Chloe likes the house a certain way."

I turn around to see Zain closing the door behind us, and I want to ask how he really knows that's Chloe, but when you love someone, I guess you just know.

"Come on, follow me. I'll take you upstairs." Zain locks the door and then turns off the porch light. "We're going to go see Porter."

"He is well today," Apollo says, flipping a page of a thick book that seems to be a thousand pages.

I'd die trying to read that.

"If he's related to me, he isn't well." I shrug off my jacket and hang it on the coat stand next to the shoe rack.

Zain bends down and kisses the top of Chloe's head. "I'll be back in a minute. Don't go anywhere."

"I'm going to make popcorn. You want some?" the blonde rises from the couch and sniffles. Her eyes are red and puffy, and her hair is a tad bit greasy.

"Make loads," Zain says, licking his lips. "I love popcorn."

"I'll help you, Goldie." A guy with stich crossings across his lips lays a hand on her hip.

"Thanks, Zipper," she whispers.

He stares at her adoringly. They don't kiss, but I can tell they want to. Why doesn't he just claim her? Own her. Show her who she belongs to.

Instead, he guides her toward the kitchen, and she wraps the baggy brown cardigan tight around her waist.

"Ready?" Zain asks.

I whip out my knife. It glitters in the light of the living room. "As I'll ever be."

Apollo sighs on the couch, then licks his finger before flipping a page. "Violence fixes nothing but love changes everything. Remember that, Tongue." His voice is calm and calculated, with a tinge of boredom and annoyance that he had to give advice to me.

"Well, maybe violence should be my answer when love fails me," I snap.

He closes his book and turns around, placing an arm on the back of the couch, then bends his knee as he lifts his leg from the floor. "Do you choose to be oblivious, or has oblivion chosen you?" he asks.

What the fuck?

"Maybe tell Daphne you said love fails. See what happens when her heart breaks. Love has not failed you. It has found you, but you choose violence instead. You will be the ruin of your own future. The destruction of love by using your violence will be your deepest regret."

"Come on or Apollo will keep giving you words of wisdom to live by. See you in a minute, Apollo," Zain says, waving his hand as he walks away.

"I'll be here, and when I'm right, you'll thank me." Apollo spins around and opens his book again, places a finger on the page, then drags it just below the sentence as he reads.

Interesting man.

His words find a way to the inside of my head, and I think about them as I follow Zain down the hall. We take a right down a dark hallway. Apollo is right. Love hasn't failed me. It did a long time ago, but it hasn't now in the present. I might get what I want from others, but I get what I want and need from Daphne.

Love failed me once, but damn it, it's brought me back to life.

And the more time I spend with Daphne, the less bloodthirsty I become. It's hard to change the core of who I am, when my core is damned and shredded. With one look, just by existing, Daphne is healing me from the inside out.

Let's face it, the inside of me is way more fucked up than the outside of me will ever be.

I keep my knife out and at the ready. I don't want Porter to try and get the best of me.

"Sorry it smells like paint. We just painted the hallway a few days ago, and the fumes will not leave, even with the window open."

"These rooms are nice," I notice to my left.

The metal doors to each room are open and they don't look anything like the crazy room I imagined in my mind. They have big beds, hardwood floors, and fashionable rugs.

"They used to be the rooms the doctors kept patients in back in the 1900s. I figured I wanted every room as nice as it can be, just in case we get more people who need a place. I wanted it to feel like a home as much as possible. There are some areas that aren't cleaned up yet but were used for the same purposes. Downstairs are the padded rooms, and the rooms upstairs are like the rooms here, but sparser. I don't trust Porter not to hurt himself."

"I don't know why you have faith in him."

Zain stops climbing up the steps and looks over the meat of his shoulder. "The same reason people have faith in you."

"People don't have faith in me. Faith isn't a real thing. They either trust or they don't. One person trusts me."

"Sometimes, one person is all it takes, isn't it? One person to make you look at the world differently?"

Damn, this fucking crazy house. Everyone is twisting my words and throwing them back at me. I rub my hand through my wet hair, stopping on the steps just below the one Zain is on. "Let's just go." I'm more confused than I have been in a long time. Do I give Porter a chance? Do I forgive him for everything he has done? I don't think I can. Burying me, coming after me and attacking Daphne, I'll never forgive him.

"I'm going to go. This was a mistake." I pound down the steps and Porter's voice echoes down the hall, making me pause mid-step.

TONGUE'S TARGET

"Come on, Wayne. You've come all this way." He sounds so much like me, it unhinges me a little.

I twist my body to the left and peer into the darkness above the staircase. There's a faint glow to the left down the hall, but it isn't enough to illuminate the staircase. I want to know how he knows about me and I never knew about him.

Despite my better judgement, I haul up the steps and grab the rail, swinging myself around to the left. Zain softly pads up the staircase behind me. The light flips on to my right, and Porter is there sitting on his bed, reading a book.

Reading a fucking book. Casually.

The bastard. He learned to read and here I am struggling.

"Hey, baby brother," he greets me, shutting the book and placing it on the nightstand next to his bed. He stands, placing his hands on his thighs as he pushes off the bed. He strolls toward me, wearing a white t-shirt and black sweatpants that do not have strings to tighten around his hips. He'd probably strangle himself or find a way to strangle someone. He lays his hands on the glass. We stare at one another. We're about the same size, but I'm a little taller.

His eyes are brown and as I tilt my head, he tilts his in the same direction.

We're too much alike.

"Oh, little brother, my, oh my, how I feel like I'm looking in the mirror. How are you doing?"

I slam my fist against the glass and curl my lip.

"You're doing good? That's great. Me too. How's Daphne doing? She's a strong little thing. I'm happy for you to have found such a strong woman."

"Don't you dare say her name after what you've done."

He lifts his hands off the glass, the heat from his palms leaving oily prints against the window. "No harm. I am sorry for what I did, for what I've done. I hated you. I still kind of do, but I think it's because you got the life I never had."

"Got the life..." I repeat back to him, stunned by what he thinks. "You know nothing about my life!" I roar, hitting the glass as hard as I can. Cracks like spiderwebs run along the surface. "You have no idea what I went through."

"I did you a favor!" he roars, banging his own head against the glass. He's rabid, untamed, and a primitive killer.

Just. Like. Me.

Fuck.

We are alike.

I stumble back and Zain catches me before I lose my footing. "You did me a favor? What did you do? How did you know about me? I knew nothing about you." I go to charge again, but Zain holds me back. It's a failed attempt. I swing him off me without breaking a sweat. He hits the end of the hall, smacking his back against the wall.

Porter pouts. "Aw, Tongue so mean hurting the nice man. Careful, he's my friend." He sighs, lifting one leg and balancing on the other. He stuffs his hands in his pockets and whistles. "I guess we deserve to know each other, don't we? Since we will be seeing so much of each other soon." He drops his leg to the floor, then sits down, cross-legged, right in front of the window. I could punch it one time and tackle him. Kill him like he deserves to be killed.

But then I think of Reaper and why he has been keeping Porter alive. It isn't because he doesn't want to kill him. He chooses not to.

For me.

Maybe he cares about me after all.

"Sorry, Zain," I whisper, throwing the man a bone.

"I'm staying here to make sure you guys don't kill each other. Porter is my friend."

"Hear that?" Porter puffs out his chest, then jabs his finger in the middle of it. "I am someone's friend."

"You'll never be mine," I sneer.

"Oh," He scoffs. "You wound me." But there.

I see it.

The flash of vulnerability that he and I both seem to hide so well.

What's beneath the violence, Porter?

And why do I fucking care all of a sudden?

CHAPTER ELEVEN

Tongue

I sit down on the floor, wishing I had something to drink in my hand. I want hard whiskey, the cheap kind; the kind that burns and unsettles my stomach. The kind that rips apart the back of my throat. Sipping something smooth and expensive is enjoyable.

And this moment is not.

I mirror his position, right on the other side of the barrier. What would life have been like if we hadn't been brought into the life we were dealt. What if I could have had a brother, and he could have been there for me? What if he existed and my uncle never touched me? Would I be the same man I am today? What if we had grown up together and were close?

All the what ifs, all the what ifs that don't matter because now we are on opposites sides of the glass.

"Porter? Stop with the taunting and just talk," Zain warns as he walks behind me. "I'm going downstairs. Hopefully if you guys fight, you kill each other, so I don't have to worry about killing the one that lives." His footsteps are quiet since he is barefoot, and the stairs creak as he walks down the steps.

I lay the knife next to my leg. Porter follows the movement, then grins when he sees it. "Well, I'm proud. Little brother comes prepared."

"Stop calling me that. We both know you hate me just like I hate you."

The mockery on his face is gone, and I'm not sure if I believe his sincerity. "I did hate you, for a really long time. I wanted to take from you, Wayne. I wanted to take, take, take, until nothing was left for you to live for. I was jealous. So damn jealous, and mad at you. Mad at you for existing, mad at you for not knowing you, and mad at her." He doesn't look away from me as he starts to speak.

"Her?" I ask, watching an orange tabby cat jump from the top of the dresser in his room and onto the floor. The fur ball struts toward Porter and purrs, rubbing his body against his side.

He scratches under the cat's chin. "Our mother."

"I don't remember much of her."

"Good. She was a lying whore. There isn't much to know."

I bang my fist against the glass again, causing another crack. "You don't know what you're talking about. She was a good mom. She—"

"She was with my old man for a long time, you know. The president of an MC. She was one of his whores at first."

"You don't know what you're talking about."

"Like I'd ever tell you a lie. The truth always hurts more than a lie ever does, baby brother."

I grit my teeth and any good memories of her I had start to tarnish. "I don't remember her much. She died when I was young."

"I know. I killed her and your dad," he says nonchalantly, leaning back on his hands.

The blood drains from my face and my hand curls around the knife. "What did you just say?"

"That little accident you were in. All of you were supposed to die, but only she did, and that man—"

"My father!" I slam my shoulder against the glass. The damn thing holds more than I expect it to. I try again and again.

Thud.

Thud.

Thud.

But it won't give.

"He was a good man!"

"Wayne, do you know nothing of them?" He scoots closer to the glass. My mind is whirling from the shock of his words. He has to be wrong. I know my parents. I know… I know…

Fucking damn it, I don't know anything.

"Your mom married my dad and got pregnant with me. They lived happily ever after for a while. Dad was a real asshole and hit me every chance he got. She fucked around a bit. Dad didn't care if she slept with other members. She got passed around. Then Dad died on a club run and she finally took that as the escape she needed, so she left. She left me behind. Me. Her own son, to start another family. And then you came along." He curls his lip in disgust. "I followed up with her the best I could, watching this family build themselves in suburbia."

I don't remember living in the suburbs. I don't remember much before my uncle.

It doesn't sound like the kind of life I'd live. Look at me. I don't look like I mow the lawn every Sunday and play golf with the guys every Wednesday.

"Come to find out, your dad wasn't so straight and narrow. He loved drugs. He worked for a cartel, smuggling all sorts of good stuff over the borders, which the MC loved by the way. Our mom knew." He continues to pet the cat with gentle stokes. I expect him to stop and to wrap his arm around the cat's throat and choke it to death, but he doesn't. He seems as though he loves the cat.

I didn't think such evil was capable of such a thing, but I suppose the same could be said of me.

"I came to visit once."

I jerk my head up from where I was staring at the cat, fighting... tears.

Of anger.

Nothing else. If this fucking glass wasn't in my way, I'd kill him.

"What?"

"Yeah, it's what kind of made me spiral out of control."

"You're lying. Mom would have never let you leave. She would have welcomed you—"

"Tell me, Wayne. What do you remember of Mom?" he folds his hands in his lap. "I want to know. You were a kid. I'm a little older than you, remember? I think I know more."

As much as I want to argue with him, he is right. Gritting my teeth until they might crack, I study the groove in the wood framing the window. Rings upon rings, which tell me the wood they used is older. It's a beautiful piece of wood.

"You don't remember much, do you? And what you do remember, I bet if you're wondering if you've made it all up in your head. Listen, baby brother—"

"Don't call me that. You don't give a fuck about me being your brother."

"I didn't use to. I had a vendetta to grind, that's for sure. I've had a lot of time to think in here. Zain makes me take my medication and I've leveled out. I'm not perfect, but I'd like to try..."

"You said you visited?" I force him change the subject. I'm not trying to get emotional with him when he is nothing but a liar.

He seems hurt that I don't want him to continue his confession, but it would fall on deaf ears. He nods and clears his throat. "I did. I had been watching you guys for some time, and I decided I wanted answers, the same way you want answers now. I wanted to meet my baby brother." He gives a low chuckle as he stretches his neck to the side. "Don't look so surprised. I wasn't always like this. I knocked on the door and no one answered, but I heard you crying. You were fucking wailing, so I checked the knob and it was unlocked. Man, you lived in this typical fancy rich house. Two stories, white picket fence, the works."

I still find that hard to believe.

"Anyway, I turned the knob and I let myself in. It was unlocked because every person leaves their house unlocked when you're in a safe neighborhood. You were in the middle of the floor. Dirty like you hadn't bathed in days. You had a diaper on, even though you were too old for one. The house reeked of meth, and you were probably crying because of the drug you were inhaling. I saw that and realized I had all the answers I needed, especially when I saw them passed out on the couch, naked. They couldn't even hear you. I went to take you, you know. I was going to get you out of there. I had no idea what kind of life I could give you, but it had to be better than the one you were living. A neighbor came over and caught me and threatened to call the cops. I had to get out of there. I regretted it for a long time, but then the regret turned to hate. This deep hatred. I blamed you for ruining her."

I probably did. I ruin everything I touch.

"I had to kill them for so many reasons. Her for turning her back on me, him for corrupting her, you for being involved, and because it was the only way to save you. I found you there and thought, 'I can still save him. I can still figure out how to bring him peace.'"

"Peace?" I choke out. "You have no idea what your actions did to me and what kind of life I lived after that. Maybe they were everything you said they were, but at least they weren't my uncle. Who I had to go live with, by the way," I shout at him, slamming my hand against the glass again. Even though it is cracked, it still won't budge. "Do you know what he did to me?"

I hit the glass again, wishing it was the memories I could shatter, then rip my shirt off and spread out my arms. "He burned me with cigarettes. He scarred my tongue. He raped me," I roar in a broken guttural shout. I ball up my fist and punch again, causing a crack in the glass to spread further. "Over and over and over and then again." With every word I slam my fist into the glass, throwing my whole weight into it.

Images of everything Justine did to me send fear clawing through my gut. I get up off my knees and slam my entire body against the glass wall. It shakes in an empty vibration from the weight of me but doesn't allow me inside to strangle Porter. "I wish you would have killed me in that accident. I wish you would have."

"Wayne," he gets up off the floor and shakes his head. "I'm not perfect. I never claimed to be. I've done fucked up, unforgivable things. I never expect you to trust me. I never expect you to be my baby brother, but I want you to know I'm trying here. I didn't know about your uncle. I'm sorry."

"Sorry doesn't fix the years of damage he did to me. You will never know the extent of it."

My phone dings, and I dig it out of my pocket, blinking back the damn tears from everything he just told me. I don't know how to handle it.

It's Daphne. She's sent me an audio message.

"Wayne, please." Both hands are against the glass and his brows are pinched as a sorrowful expression takes over his face. "I am sorry. I am."

"I don't believe anything you say. Daphne sent me a message. One minute." I press play and the tone hidden in her voice has my hackles raised. I bend over and pick up my knife and sheathe it in the holster on my pants.

"Tongue, please come home. Mercy is here talking to Reaper, but I don't like how he is looking at me. He's doing it again. Please. I love you, and next time you run off, take me with you. You know I don't like to be away from you."

The message ends. I want to replay it again and again to hear her voice. All of the discomfort, all of the pain I've felt, wishing I died when my parents did, all goes away. Nothing Porter says matters to me. His truth hurts, but what's done is done. I can't change anything. And while he says it's the truth, he could be playing me like a fucking violin for all I know.

I press reply and hold down the button. "I'll be there soon, Comet. I'm sorry. I love you too."

"Aw, baby brother in love is sweet. Daphne is a real peach. Strong and resilient. You got lucky."

The way he says her name pisses me off and that fuel I needed to break the glass ignites in my veins. I slam my body against the glass one more time and it shatters, finally. Heavy broken pieces fall across us as I tackle him to the floor. I can feel the pieces digging into my arms and hands. I wrap my hands around Porter's throat and squeeze.

"Don't you fucking dare speak her name again." I lift one hand, clench my fist, and punch him in the face. "I fucking hate you. You think this changes anything? Do you?" I pick him up by the material of his shirt and slam him against the floor, his head hitting with a hard crack. "You find ways to ruin my life. I'm fucking done with you. You hear me? No more curiosity, no more nothing. We are done here. You hear me? Fucking done?" I wrap the hand I just used to punch him around his throat again and squeeze.

And he just lies there. He isn't fighting back. He's taking it.

"Fight me!"

"No."

"I said fight me." I slam him on the floor again and a few broken pieces of glass skid against the floor.

"No. I've been fighting you too long. I'm done."

"You aren't allowed to be done." I shake him so hard his teeth clank together.

"Fuck! Tongue. Get off him. Get off!" Zain yells, grabbing one of my arms while Zipper grabs the other. The only reason they can get me off Porter is because I'm too fucking high-strung right now. I'm shaking all over.

"What the hell, Tongue?"

"Keep him away from me." I rip my arms from their hold, and without giving anyone a second look, I fly down the steps, not caring about the glass in my arms. So many things are running through my mind. The first thing is, why didn't I kill him? I've killed for so much less; and yet, I can't find it in me to kill him.

I slip my boots on at the door and leave them unlaced.

"Bye," Chloe or Jessica or whatever the fuck her name is says.

I don't bother saying goodbye in return. I take my jacket off the hook, shrug it on, and head out the door, slamming it shut. It's still fucking raining, but I don't care.

I want the storm to wash away whatever the hell is wrong with me, because I feel like I'm drowning. Either wash me away or set me free. I can't swim like this anymore.

Tossing one leg over my bike, I crank it, then slide my helmet on. I don't bother buckling it under my chin. I fly out of the lot, slinging mud all over their car as I leave. I probably did the damn thing a favor. The bike slips across the wet sand; it takes some direction to make sure she doesn't topple over. When I get to the end of the dirt road, I don't even stop. I crank the throttle and speed down the road. I'm about ten minutes from the clubhouse.

The only thing I have to do is make it back in one piece.

For Daphne.

The rain screams, echoing the sounds of a banshee in agony. The wind cuts across to the left and my bike dances with it for a second before I right it.

The driveway to the clubhouse is hard to see this late, but muscle memory takes over as I flip on my blinker and head down the road. Reaper finally fixed all the damn potholes. Not that the fix will matter after this storm. The damn potholes will be back.

When I get to the gate, Braveheart sees who it is and lets me in immediately. Poor kid. He needs to be inside where it is warm, but he refuses to leave his post.

He gives me a wave and I head under the awning where all the bikes are parked to get them out of the rain. I cut the engine off, already missing the vibration between my legs as they tingle. I take my helmet off and place it on the seat as I dismount.

I pass Mercy's bike and glare at it, wishing I was disrespectful enough to kick it over so it hits the ground, maybe breaking his mirror. Maybe I'll put sugar or sand in his gas tank one day. I'll just have to wait and see how I feel after I figure out what he wants with my Comet. I dig my boots into the steps, pounding up them until I get to the front door. I shake my hair out and wipe my boots on the 'welcome' mat and then pull my jacket off. I shake the leather out too, so I don't drip water all over the floor, then bang on the door so someone lets me in.

The small window opens in the middle of the door, and Slingshot's eyes widen when he sees me. When he opens the door, he throws himself at me, wrapping me in a hug. "Man, where the hell have you been? Do you know how worried we were?" He pulls back and analyzes my face. "Why are you bleeding? What happened? Why didn't you text me? Who are we killing? Did you kill them already? Do you need help burying the body?"

He throws question after question at me, but there is only one person I'm interested in talking to tonight, and she's on the couch, reading a book with her legs tucked under her. I scan the couch to see what the problem is and there is Mercy.

Sitting there. Ankle crossed over the other the knee, and his sights are set on her.

Again.

I push Slingshot to the side and take a step forward, bringing in mud and rain. Daphne unsticks her nose from the book when she hears the pound of boots against the floor. Her eyes light up and her shoulders deflate like, the weight of the world is lifted off her shoulders.

Mercy doesn't even notice me. I don't like that he is studying her. He scoots across the sofa to get closer and leans into Daphne. I can't hear what he says, but it has her sliding her legs out from under herself and trying to scoot over. And then his hand lands on her bicep. Her blue eyes land on mine and are as big as the moon.

She has no idea what to do.

But I do.

I push by Skirt next, careful not to hit him too hard since Dawn is in front of him holding Joey. I shove Patrick aside and his glass of water drops from his hands. It clatters to the ground, spilling water all over his shoes.

"What the fuck, Tongue?" Patrick asks with a hint of annoyance as he wipes his hands on his jeans.

I march toward the sofa and snag Mercy's wrist from her arm, then bend it back to the edge of a break.

"Ah, fuck!" he screams.

He stands as I yank him to his feet, and when he tries to use his other hand to hit me, I'm too quick with my knife. I slide it out of my sheath and plunge it through the second and third knuckle. I pick him up by his cut and drag him toward the nearest wall. I slide the blade out, uncurl his fingers, then shove the knife in his palm until the tip lodges in the wall. I apply more pressure to sink the knife into the drywall. Blood drips from his hand and down his forearms. That familiar bliss takes over, causing my cock to become half hard.

"Fucking hell, Tongue," he blows out a painful breath that's mixed with spit. "Shit, that hurts."

"Tongue, what are you doing?" Tool wraps his fingers around handle of the knife. I stop him by elbowing him in the gut, then whack him across the cheek when I drive my elbows upward.

"Get the fuck back or I swear to God, I'll become the monster you all think I am." Everyone forms a circle around me, but it's Daphne whose hand sears the middle of my back.

"It's okay, Tongue. I'm okay," she reassures me.

My arm starts to shake from stretching his hand too far back. I won't let go. I don't care how much pain he's in. "What the fuck do you want with Daphne?" I ask Mercy, curling my lip as the words leave me on a deep gravel.

"I swear, she's safe. I am not trying to hurt her."

"Then why are you looking at her? You stared at her in the bookstore. You stared at her here. She sent me a message. You're making her uncomfortable. I don't like it when she is uncomfortable."

"You've been looking at her? In front of Tongue? You're an idiot," Slingshot chuckles, and then pulls out said slingshot and launches a Skittle at him. The red round candy smacks Mercy in the middle of the forehead. "You deserved that," he says, pocketing his weapon. He sends me a wink. "I got your back, buddy."

"You are dumb," Tool says, rubbing his jaw.

"I'm staying out of this." Poodle continues to pet Lady. He is sitting on the ground, leaning against the side of the couch with his beloved dog on his lap.

"She looks familiar, okay? That's all. That's why," Mercy says quickly, grunting through the pain.

I grab the handle of the knife and twist. His screams send a pleasurable stroke down my spine, and I shiver. "Why?"

"I don't know you," Daphne says so softly, I can hardly hear her. "I swear, Tongue. I don't know him. I've only seen him around here."

"I know, Comet. I don't doubt that." I twist the handle again. His knees buckle, but the knife keeps him nailed to the wall, and the gravity tugging against his flesh is used against him. More skin tears and more blood pours. "So why?"

"She looks like someone I used to know, okay? She looks like Michelle Douglas, okay? She looks just like Michelle Douglas!" he roars when I twist the knife again.

Daphne inhales, then steps in front of me, her back against my front. No doubt she can feel my hard cock between the crease of her ass. "How do you know my mother?" she asks in a shocked whisper.

"Holy shit," Poodle repeats the stunned word in my head.

"Damn."

"Ye knew her mother? Shite, it's a small world."

"You knew her mom?" I ask again.

A bead of sweat drips down his temple. He closes his eyes just as I yank the knife from his palm. His arm falls limp to his side and a thick river of blood drips onto my boots. "I didn't know you were her daughter; I swear. You look so much like her I thought I was looking at her twin. You look so much alike. I'm sorry. I should have been more upfront, but I couldn't believe it. So many memories of her came rushing back."

"You knew her," Daphne sighs in disbelief and awe. "I've never met anyone else that has known her. Do you know a lot about her? How did you know her?" I can hear the pain in her voice.

"Did? What do you mean?"

"You don't know?"

Mercy glances at everyone in confusion before landing on Daphne. "No, what do you mean?"

"She died when I was eight," she admits, sadly.

Mercy's face falls. Any hope of seeing his old friend again fades; the color in his cheeks changes to a pale white. "She died? How? What? No." Mercy shakes his head. "No, that's not how it was supposed to be," he mumbles, eyes glossing over.

"She killed herself."

Mercy's head snaps up to stare at her and shakes his head, tears forming but not falling. His eyes are stern, and his lips are pressed in a thin line. "That woman was a lot of things, but she would never kill herself. Ever!" he yells at Daphne. She jumps back, slamming against my front. I place the knife against his throat in warning and he gives me a small nod. "I knew her back when we were just teens, Daphne. The woman was life. No way in hell would she kill herself, and I'm going to find out the truth to make sure you know."

I don't think she killed herself either, but Daphne is certain her dreams aren't real.

Mercy squints his eyes and bobs his head as he checks Daphne up and down. "How old are you?"

"Twenty-five," Daphne answers.

Mercy seems horrified. "I need to go."

"Wait, no! You knew her. I have questions. I hardly remember her. Please."

"I can't," he says, his tone full of regret. "I'm sorry. I need to go. I have... I have questions you can't answer."

"I might," she pleads. "I'm begging you, Mercy. Please."

"I'm sorry," he says.

I press my knife against his throat, warning him he better tell Daphne everything she wants to know.

"You want to kill me? Go ahead. I don't have answers. Not yet. I need to figure it out and when I do, I'll come back, and I swear I'll answer all your questions. Daphne, I swear." His aching hand, the one that's not bleeding, touches her cheek. "God, you look so much like her."

I see now he isn't looking at her like a lover would, but like a father would a daughter.

That's impossible, considering we know who Daphne's father is. Mercy has answers, though.

"Yeah?" Daphne's on the verge of breaking with how her voice trembles.

"Yeah, kiddo. It's uncanny." Mercy drops his hand, breaking the intimate contact, and starts to walk away. Whistler, who was standing near the pool table quietly, follows him. "I'll be back, okay? I'm sorry. For her death. She was too young."

"I'm sorry too." Daphne closes the space between them and hugs him, wrapping her small arms around Mercy's neck. "You obviously cared for her."

"Cared?" Mercy's eyes shut as he pats Daphne's back. "I loved that woman," he admits. "I loved her more than the—"

"Bees love honey?" Daphne finishes for him, pulling away and staring at him with curiosity.

He mirrors the same expression. "How'd you know that?"

"It's something she always used to say to me when she tucked me in at night."

Mercy's brows rise and his eyes turn red. He stares at his boots and coughs, clearing his throat. "I used to tell her that all the time. I'm sorry, I need to go." Without another word, he holds his arm to his chest and hurries out the door.

"No! Wait. Who are you?" Daphne screams in desperation for answers, for anything, but Mercy heads out the door.

Whistler gives a sad half smile. "It will all be okay. Mercy is the best at finding the right answers. He doesn't want to answer any questions without doing significant research. He'll be back."

Everything Daphne needs to know is gone when the door closes. Everyone is silent, everyone is staring at us in shock.

"I... I'm going to clean the blood off the floor," Daphne says in a daze. "Don't want it to stain."

"Daphne, I'll clean the blood, go take a bath," I tell her, not asking if she wants to, but telling her she has to.

"I'm fine." A tear rolls down her cheek, and I wipe it away, then bring it to my lips like I always do and kiss it clean.

"You aren't. You just met someone who knew your mom. Go, Comet. I made this mess, I'll clean it up."

"Thank you." She stands on her tip toes and kisses my left cheek. When her lips are gone, the skin burns, as if she's poured kerosene on me and lit a match.

A door bangs open in the kitchen and Reaper appears, dragging a hand down his face. He sees us and ignores the mess on the floor and the bloody knife in my hand. "How is she?" I ask, waiting for him to finally kill me.

"She's on bedrest for the remainder of her pregnancy, but she's okay. The baby is healthy."

"Oh, that's great, Reaper," Skirt exhales.

"I'm so glad she's alright." Juliette peeps from Tool's lap as she holds a pack of ice against his cheek.

Pussy. I barely hit him.

"Tongue, it's time we talk about your punishment," Reaper states.

"What? No! It was an accident, you can't," Daphne begins to cry again as she comes to my defense. "That's not fair, when you wouldn't listen! You drove him to break!" She shoves Reaper's chest.

I tug Daphne away from Reaper and pass her off to Patrick, who holds her still when he understands what I'm about to do.

"No, you can't. Please," she begs.

"I'll be alright, Comet. I got you now, remember? Pain is a momentary, necessary evil to move on in life." I kiss her forehead just as Reaper opens the Church doors to allow me in.

"Tool, start the fire and heat the poker."

My skin tingles with awareness, a blanket of fear cloaking my skin as the memories of being burnt hundreds of times washes over me. I hold my breath as I step inside the room.

He can't cut me because I'll like it.

Burning me is the only thing he can do, because it's one of the only things I fear.

CHAPTER TWELVE

Daphne

"YOU'D DO THAT TO HIM? YOU'D BURN HIM, KNOWING THAT'S WHAT HIS UNCLE did? Do you hate him that much?" I lift my body, kicking my legs up to try and get away from Patrick, but his hold on my arms is too strong. "Let go of me!" I scream through a closed jaw.

I thrash and pull against Patrick with all my might until I'm as far as I can go and just a hair away from Reaper's face. "This cannot be undone. You will not be able to fix this. Whatever shred of hope there is between the club and Tongue will be gone, and you will lose him."

Reaper's dark eyes dance between mine. I can tell he is contemplating what I'm saying. A variety of emotions flicker across his face. His shaggy, dirty blonde hair hangs in his face, and when he makes his decision, he thrusts his shoulders back, lifts his chin, and holds out his hand. "Tool, is the poker ready?" he asks, sending me into a blind rage.

"No!" The word is a broken scream leaving the depths of my chest. "I won't let you." I yank against Patrick, who is holding on tighter than I expected him to be.

"I'm sorry," he whispers in my ear, only causing more anger to boil away what's left of my soft, understanding nature.

"He will never forgive you," I whisper, my chin wobbling as I try to hold back my emotions. I look from Tool to Tongue, who has already whipped his shirt off and tossed it on the ground. He's kneeling on the floor, hands clasped behind his back and his head bowed.

He's defeated. He has already given up. Why isn't he fighting? Why won't he stand up for himself?

Tool takes the poker out of the fire, the wood crackling as if it is spitting hot hatred and sparking across the floor from the hearth.

There it is.

The hesitation.

He doesn't want to do it.

Tool spins the iron poker, watching the bright orange glow bright with heat. "Reaper... I don't know."

"Give me the goddamn poker! You think I'm happy about this? You think I want to do this? You think I don't care? I have to uphold our law. We will get through it. We always do," Reaper snaps.

Tool grudgingly holds out the poker and Reaper takes it from him. I can feel the heat of it caressing my skin like a hot summer's breeze as he walks by.

I give one last effort to rip myself from Patrick. I stomp on his foot and slam my elbow into his ribs. He grunts and his breath leaves his lips in a hard whoosh puffing against the back of my neck. I run into the room and block Tongue with my body.

"Comet, it's okay. Stand down. I'll be fine."

"I won't let them hurt you." My legs are spread, rocking right to left to be ready to attack Reaper. "I won't let you hurt him."

Reaper drags the hot poker behind him as he walks into the room, burning a line in the wooden planks. He reminds me of the Grim Reaper right now, but instead of dragging a scythe, he's dragging a flaming sword.

"Daphne, this will be quick, and Tongue will be fine. He always is."

"Yeah?" I shove at his chest. "Maybe it's time he isn't always fine. Maybe it's time to see him for a person. A real person. Isn't what happened to him punishment enough? Isn't the guilt he carries for what he did to Sarah enough?"

"No, because I have to make an example."

"I do too. I will die before I let you come near him."

"You're challenging me?"

"I'm daring you." I might be saying words that will lead to my untimely death, but I can't stop the tears. I'm afraid, but I will not let him hurt Tongue.

I don't care what I have to do to make sure that iron poker doesn't go near his skin.

"Daphne, please. I'll be fine. It's nothing I haven't felt before," Tongue says in a small voice behind me.

I spin around and drop to my knees. He is statuesque, a sculpted moment representing defeat. He's strong, made of stone, but is choosing to crumble instead of stand. My hand shakes as I lift it to his cheek. He tilts his head and leans it into my cheek, the killer stripped bare. Now the vulnerable boy who hides under the man who thirsts for blood, yearns for a simple touch.

For a simple love.

"You don't have to feel it. It's me and you, Tongue. You don't have to fight alone anymore. You have me now. Remember when you said my silence would be my tragedy? Because I do."

He nods.

"Your pain would be mine." My breath hitches as I comb my fingers through his hair and then lift his chin with my other hand. His eyes hold the weight of the world. The weight of life. Why can't anyone see just how pure Tongue is in the way that matters?

His heart is so big, and his love is one of kind.

"It's why I'm not going to let it happen." I turn counterclockwise, peering over the curve of my shoulder to fixate on the sizzling hot poker searing the wood. I stand and glance at Tool, who is blocking the doorway so no one can get in.

I remember vaguely someone telling me about the rules. I just hope I get it right.

"I want to be his champion."

Everyone gasps when they hear me, and the room immediately explodes into a conversation I can't understand due to how many people are talking at the same time.

"No!" Tongue staggers to his feet, and with a vehement shake of his head he pushes me behind him, nearly touching the poker with his chest as Reaper lifts it off the ground. "Don't listen to her. Her mind is obviously fucking warped right now. Prez, I'm here. I'm taking my punishment. I'm here. Just do it."

"My mind isn't warped! I know what I want. I want to do this."

"Not if you have a champion," Reaper states, glaring over Tongue's shoulder to look at me. "I'm not big on women getting punishment."

"Well, I hear declaring a champion doesn't have a gender specification." I step out from behind Tongue. "Don't you touch him with that or I will kill you," I threaten the Prez, keeping my tone soft but venomous at the same time.

"I don't like to be threatened," he sneers.

"What are you going to do about it?"

"Don't fucking tempt him, Daphne." Tongue pushes me away and Tool catches me before I can fall. I expect him to hold me, but he throws me back in the middle of the arena.

I know it's just a room, but right now I'm fighting for what I believe in.

And I believe in Tongue. I believe in his innocence and his good heart. People might laugh and wonder how I see all that. How can a ruthless killer be innocent?

But he is. He is naïve and innocent, in the ways that boys are when they don't experience life the way they should have. I won't have him punished for that.

"Go get 'em, tiger," Tool says to me, and Tongue whips his head at his friend.

"What the fuck, Tool? Grab her!"

"No. She's doing what Sarah got to do for Boomer. It's only fair. I think it's brave, what she's doing. If this is what she wants, then I think this is what should happen. Champion call always rules. Hands are tied. Sorry, Tongue."

I give Tool a thankful grin for being on my side. I didn't expect that. Out of all people, I thought he would hold me down while Reaper burned Tongue.

"Get Tank. I'll need him, you, Bullseye, and Skirt to hold Tongue down."

"No! Please. I said champion. I said champion! Why doesn't it count?" I ask, desperately pulling at my hair. I'm willing to do anything.

Tool exits, and a few minutes later returns with everyone. "Lock him down," Tool orders. All of the men move at once. Their footsteps march, the beating of their boots in sync with one another, and Tongue doesn't fight them when they get to his side.

Tank and Tool hold down his arms. Skirt and Bullseye hold down his legs.

"Please," I give one last attempt to offer myself instead. "I'll do anything. Please, don't burn him. You don't know the damage," I repeat, hoping Reaper will listen. "You have no idea what you'll do."

"Stand or kneel," he says, which I find an odd request, but I do it anyway.

"It's going to be okay, Comet. It will be over soon," Tongue says without a single hesitation in his eyes. It reminds me of a scene from a movie where a man is about to get executed. Instead of straps holding him down, it's people. "It'll all be over," he repeats, resigned.

Where will we go after this? I'm not going to have us stay here knowing they would use Tongue's fear as a punishment tactic. There are only so many times broken pieces can be put back together again until eventually, some broken pieces are lost forever. Let's face it, when things are broken one time, the integrity is never the same.

Reaper unbuckles his belt and whips the black leather out from the loops in his jeans, then folds it until it can't bend any further. "Open your mouth," he tells me.

Confused, I do as he says.

"Now, bite down."

I clench my teeth together and the burst of worn leather dissolves across my taste buds.

"Good. Now, keep doing that because this going to fucking hurt." He tugs the strap of my tank top down my left arm.

"What?" Tongue suddenly shouts, on the edge of delusion. "No! Let me the fuck go. Tank, let me go!" He manages to get an arm free and punches Tank across the cheek. Tank takes the punch in stride and catches Tongue's hand mid-air, then digs his knee into Tongue's shoulder until Tongue's warrior cry pierces the air.

My body quakes in fear from anticipating pain.

Tongue's back arches off the floor and he lifts the men with him, but he still doesn't break free.

"Christ, ye a stronger mother fucker, ain't ye, Tongue?" Skirt grunts, fighting Tongue as if he were wrestling an alligator.

"Big bastard." Bullseye lays his body across Tongue's legs to keep him still.

TONGUE'S TARGET

"I'll fucking kill all of you. You hear me? Don't you touch her! Don't touch her!" Tongue screams, his lungs exerting every ounce of air he possesses. His inability to save me echoes in the frequencies of his pleas.

"This is going to hurt," Reaper warns me again.

My eyes roam to the door. Everyone is watching me, but I'm not going to back down. If they want a show, they got one.

I nod, letting him know I understand.

"You're crazy," he mutters, not intending for me to hear as he exhales and inches the hot poker closer to my chest. My heart is trampling, bruising my breastbone the closer the flaming iron gets. The hot poker has my skin reacting, the scalding heat still inches away yet already stinging my skin.

Crazy people will do insane things for the people they love.

And I'm one of those people.

"Daphne! Comet! No, please, don't do this."

Sweat drips into my eyes, but it doesn't stop me from stealing one last look at Tongue. He is begging me, brows pinched and lifted.

No way in hell will I ever run from this. I bite down on the leather, keep my eyes on Tongue, and thrust my chest forward onto the flaming orange tip.

The first millisecond of sizzling has the smell of burnt flesh drifting in my nostrils. The belt in my mouth muffles my screams, and my teeth dig into the leather until I feel it give. I cry, tears as hot as the poker against my skin. Tongue's livid, panicked shout numbs my ears. My throat is raw from screaming, and the air from my lungs is being stolen from me, a sick game of tug-of-war. I only inhale because I have no choice, but a second later it's tugged out from me like a rope is tied to my lungs.

He's worth it. He's worth everything.

"There's one half," Reaper says, lifting the poker from my skin.

Dizziness takes over my head and I sway. My stomach churns and bubbles. Nausea clings to my insides and works its way up my throat from the pain. I swallow it down, not wanting to appear weak by puking or passing out.

I make a mistake of looking down. The tip of the poker is covered in my skin and dried blood, and the smell...

Oh god, the smell.

I gag again, the acid from my stomach burning a pathway up my esophagus, searing me from the inside while the iron poker ruins me from the out.

"Daphne," Tongue's voice breaks. "Daphne!" I hear Tongue's voice in the distance as my head swims. My vision doubles. I see two of everything.

Two Reapers.

Two iron rods.

Two Tongues.

If I was feeling better, I'd try to make a dirty joke about that.

But Holy Moly.

I'm about to pass out.

"There." Reaper tosses the poker on the ground and the metal hitting wood sings. High-pitched white noise blares in my head. "You did it. Fucking hell, Daphne." Reaper kneels in front of me and takes the belt from my mouth. "You have a heart on your chest. It's a warning. Second will be an arrow. You know the rest," he informs.

"Let me go! Let me the fuck go. I can't believe you'd touch her. Comet!" Tongue's pointless broken cries for me fall on deaf ears as he struggles against his friends.

I try to smile, but the pain and smell is too much to deal with. Another wave of dizziness hits and I sway like a flower in the meadow in the middle of summer, only less graceful. I'm floating away.

"Let's get you to, Doc," Reaper says, holding his arms out to me. I can't focus long enough on him to decide where his arms are, since there are two of him.

I sway to the left.

Then the right.

And this time, gravity wins, and I fall to my side. The burned flesh is still cooking and the agony spreading throughout my body is more than I could have ever imagined it could be. Even knowing the pain, I don't regret doing this. If I had to get my entire body covered in burns to save him from, not only the agony of what the burn brings, but of the everlasting torture his memories would cause, I'd do it every single day.

I hear my name being shouted somewhere. I'm sleeping and someone is trying to wake me up, but it isn't working. My eyes roll to the back of my head and darkness takes over.

I don't mind darkness.

It's safe here, peaceful, and quiet.

I fell in love in the dark.

And if I'm lucky, I'll die in it one day too.

CHAPTER THIRTEEN

Tongue

THEY FINALLY LET ME GO AND I'M TO MY FEET IN LESS THAN A SECOND. SHE'S LYING unconscious on the floor, her skin charred, bleeding, and bubbling. Reaper kneels next to her and goes to slide his arms under her body to take her downstairs. I cross the room with long strides and shove him away from her. He stumbles back and hits the wall with a hard thump. He is sweating. Sweating from the concentration and precision it took to burn her beautiful skin.

I want to kill him.

"Don't you fucking touch her." I slide my arms underneath her limp body and pick her up, holding her to my chest. Her skin looks fucking terrible. "I bet you liked that, didn't you?" I say to him, stopping in the middle of the doorway. Everyone parts ways, but I'm not done talking to Reaper yet. "This wasn't you following the rules for a champion, this was you getting your revenge. How do you feel, Reaper?"

"What? Tongue, it's nothing like that. I'd never hurt her intentionally."

"But you did. And the difference between me and you? When I hurt Sarah, I had no idea what I was doing." Talking to him is pointless, so I decide not to waste my breath with another word. He can tell me until he is blue in the face that he did this because she asked.

But I know better.

He's been dying to get back at me, because if I were him, I'd feel the exact same way.

I pass Poodle, Patrick, Badge, and a few ol' ladies. The girls are crying and Melissa steps forward from Poodle's arms. "Is she okay?" she sniffles, wiping her cheeks with a tissue she has in her hand. "I didn't know… I swear, I would have tried to stop her and convince her not to—"

"I know," I say as gently as I can, but it still sounds like there's a monster clawing up my throat. "She'll be fine. Especially when I get her out of here."

"When you get out of here? What the hell is that supposed to mean?" Reaper follows me along with everyone else.

While I was held there on the floor fighting the strength of four of my brothers and witnessing Daphne taking my punishment, I realized I didn't want this life for her. She's had enough pain to last a lifetime, and I won't subject her to any more. I thought the MC was my family, but the past few months have left me questioning otherwise.

Daphne is my family.

Ever since they found my journals, ever since I stabbed Sarah, nothing has been the same. I want things to go back to the way they were, but that's impossible. The best thing for us to do is leave. I don't want to go. This MC has been a part of my life for a long fucking time, but they have only ever needed me as a monster.

Underneath the rough exterior, I'm a human being, and it seems the club has no idea what to do with that bit of information. If they want a killer, they can do it themselves.

I'm done.

Daphne is my priority. We have enough to deal with together, like figuring out how Mercy knew her mom and if her dreams are real.

I need to convince Daphne about her dreams. She's the only one that doesn't believe them.

"Tongue, wait a minute. Just wait!" Reaper grabs my arm to stop me from opening the door and heading down to the basement. "You don't mean to leave? We need you here."

The basement door opens on a groan, the hinges creaking from years of use. "Please, the last thing you need is someone like me here." I give him my back, step onto the first stair, and hold her tighter as I use one hand to reach behind me to shut the door.

Exhale.

Inhale.

Everything will be okay.

I head down the steps. The lights are turned down low and the beep of machines tell me Sarah is okay. My boot hits the last step with a solid *thud* and Doc peers up at me as he places a gray monitor around Sarah's stomach. He dips his sights to Daphne and the burn she has on her chest and hangs his head. With a tired sigh, he pulls a knitted blue blanket over her body, then another tan throw before flipping a switch on it.

Must be a heated blanket.

"Come here. Bring Daphne to this bed," Doc waves me over to follow him and skips the bed next to Sarah. "Lay her down here."

I cup the back of her head and lie her down gently. Her body is on the mattress first, then her cheek is against the pillow, comfortable and unmoving. I expect her eyes to flutter, to show she's okay and to come back to me, but she doesn't.

"She pulled champion on me." I push the chocolate strands off her sweaty forehead and take her hand in mine as I sit down in the chair beside the bed. "Crazy Comet. What was she thinking? I could have taken it."

Doc busies himself with preparing the IV and pain medication. The wound on her chest is going to take forever to heal. I bring her knuckles to my lips and kiss them. "What were you thinking?" I ask her again.

"I think it's brave what she did. She did it because she loves you, just like you'd do the same for her."

"She's crazy to do something like this for me. I'm not worth it."

Doc pierces her inner elbow with the IV and taps it in place, so it doesn't move before hooking fluids up. "She thinks you're worth it. Isn't that what matters?" He grabs a syringe and then opens a medicine cabinet, taking out a clear bottle with a name I can't pronounce.

Small words are the only thing I can read at this point.

Doc inserts the needle in the tube, and I stop him by grabbing his hand. "What is that?"

"A sedative, and then I'm going to give her a pain killer. She'll be okay, but burns are painful, especially ones of this severity. It's third degree. I need to clean it and bandage it. Even then, she's going to be in a lot of pain."

"So give her more pain killers," I say, letting go of his hand so he can do his job.

His thumb presses against the syringe and the clear liquid enters the tube slowly. "It isn't that simple, Tongue. Remember Moretti? I kept him in a coma for a long time, because even when burn patients are asleep, they are still in pain. Medicine can only do so much. Imagine your nerves being split open and exposed to the world, hot and on fire, and over sensitive. Luckily, the burn is contained to one part of her body, so the process of recovery will be quick, but it doesn't mean it's less painful."

"She's in pain because of me?" I never want her to hurt. All I've ever wanted from the moment I laid eyes on her was to protect her and hold her. I didn't want the world to put a hand on her, including my world, and look at what I've done.

"I guess you can look at it like that," Doc says, tossing the syringe in the trash. "It's definitely half-empty glass."

"How else would I look at it?"

"Well, she's in pain *for* you. She decided this, not you. This is what she wanted. Who else have you known to want to do that for you? Besides us, of course."

I keep my mouth shut and decide not to breach that topic. The only people I know I can trust are Daphne and Slingshot.

"You're not going to want to watch this. I have to peel away the dead skin," Doc informs me as he snaps on gloves. He sits down on the stool that's on the other side of the bed and gathers his medical equipment. I don't know what they all are, but they look sharp, silver, and deadly.

"I'm not going anywhere." The only way I get up and walk out of here is if someone forcibly removes me. The heartrate monitor beeps the tune of her life and I hang my head, relieved. I know she is nowhere near dying, but still. Her heartbeat is soothing to hear.

The machines sound from behind me too, which reminds me of Sarah. I feel awful for not asking about her sooner, but my mind has been focused on Daphne. "How is Sarah?"

"She's fine. Tired. She admitted she hadn't been sleeping well because of the pain. Apparently it started in the middle of night, but she ignored it because she didn't want it to be a miscarriage."

"Is it?"

"No," Doc says, cleaning the burned heart on Daphne's chest. "It's the muscle, and it isn't your fault. I know a hundred people can tell you that right now, but only you can believe it."

"I don't believe in belief. Everything is black and white. It's either yes or no, you did or didn't. There's nothing in between."

"Oh, you can't really believe that? There are so many things in between. That's why the color gray matters. It's in the gray, Tongue. Look for belief there."

That makes no sense, and it sounds like a fucking palm reader, which reminds me of Seer. Why hasn't he called? Why didn't he see this coming? He always says he has to take a step away, but he never does. Maybe he listened to his own advice?

Damn it, Seer.

A pair of long tweezers in hand, he starts peeling the black flesh off her chest. My grip tightens around her hand as he tugs. "Is this necessary? It looks so painful."

"Unfortunately," he answers, dropping the dead skin in the silver basin. "I need fresh, uninjured skin to make sure this heals correctly, but I can't avoid scarring. That's impossible."

The sound of the basement door slamming open stops me from getting up and doing something I'd regret later.

"Man, you can't mean that! I'm not going to let you go. You can't leave me." Slingshot jumps midway on the steps and crashes against the floor, loses his footing, then hits the wall face first. "We just became friends, and you're just going to go?

What about everything we shared? Happy's swamp? Was it just me, or did we share something out there, huh? I thought we had something special, Tongue." Slingshot's hands fly to his waist, staring me down like some housewife who got cheated on.

"What?"

"Oh, what? Like you don't understand. We are friends. Best buds, bro-lios, bro-manos, brosephs, brochachos—no, we are better than that, we are bro-tacos. And you... you would just leave me."

"I have no idea what is happening right now," Doc singsongs under his breath. "But I never want it to stop." He releases another charcoaled piece of skin. Slowly, the patch of pink skin he wants is being revealed, but he still has a long way to go.

I squint my eyes at Doc, wondering if it would be bad for me to kill the doctor of our fine establishment.

Probably.

"Slingshot, I don't know what... a bro-rrito is, but I don't think I like the sound of it."

"Bro-rrito, that's good. I like that." Slingshot finger guns me and winks.

"No, you said Bro—no, you know what? It doesn't matter. I have to protect Daphne. It isn't safe for her here. We are friends, Slingshot, but you belong here."

"You're saying you don't?" he asks, dragging an extra chair from the wall to the front of the hospital bed.

"I know I belong with Daphne. Things haven't been the same here."

"Things have been rocky, but things will go back to normal—"

"—They don't trust me," I cut him off and give him my back. "I don't want to talk about this anymore. Daphne is my priority."

"Just promise you'll think about it. Promise you won't go without trying to mend what you think is broken here."

"I don't think, Slingshot. I know. There's a difference."

"Then make it different. Fix whatever is fucked up between you and Reaper. This is your home. I hate that we have been brothers for all these years and I'm just now getting to know you. You're my friend, Tongue. You can't go."

"You were thinking of leaving?"

"Come on, Doc," I groan and stare up at the ceiling to gain some composure when I hear the disappointment in his voice. "You know it was bound to happen."

"I didn't know, and it's a shame to hear. We wouldn't be where we are today without you."

"You only need me because I do what you all can't," I sneer.

Holding Daphne's hand, I press my forehead against the side of the bedrail. It's cool against my skin and exhaustion taps against the front of my skull. I'm tired of fighting. I want peace. I want a life with Daphne, and I want to be able to be good enough to be a father to our kids.

I'll teach them how to kill, of course. Every kid should know how to protect themselves, so what happened to me, doesn't happen to them.

"Tongue—" Doc drags another crispy chunk of skin off Daphne's chest. "If you really believe that, then it isn't you who has failed us, it is us who've failed you. Regardless of your decision, I will always be your friend. Selfishly, I want you to stay. Selflessly, I want you to do what you think is best for you and your family."

"No, fuck that. I'm selfish." Slingshot hits his chest with his hand. "I'm selfish as fuck. I don't want you to go. You've turned into my best friend. What's best is if you stay here. Things can be fixed. You have to give it a chance. I'm going to go check on Happy. He's been iffy the last few hours. since you haven't been here." Slingshot storms away and in a typical dramatic fashion, he stomps up the stairs as hard as he can. He never takes his eyes off me. With every thud of his boot, I bet he is picturing my head as he steps on it.

"You know he means well," Doc says, continuing to work on the burned heart above Daphne's breast.

"I know."

We fall into a comfortable silence after that, and I'm left thinking what kind of man I would have become or where I would have been if my life had been normal. Would I have met Daphne? Would I have a psychopath of a brother? Would I crave blood? An alternate life for an alternate man, a dream that will never come to formation in my mind, no matter how much I think on it.

"Have you thought about what she would say about leaving?"

"What?"

"Daphne." He squeezes a clear bottle, and some form of solution comes out of the nozzle, cleaning the wound of debris before he starts prying the skin off again. "What if she doesn't want to go? What if she wants to stay?"

"I…" I hadn't thought of that. I assumed she'd want to leave. "I don't know."

"Well, take it from experience, include her in on this decision. Because if you make it without her, there might be hell to pay. And there is no hell like a woman pissed off." Doc grins, patting the wound gently.

Damn, he's right. I have to give her a choice unless I want to sleep outside with Happy.

"So where did you go? You're all busted up," Doc notices the cuts on my arms and the one on my face. "Do you have any glass I need to get out of there?"

"Probably, but I don't care about me. Take care of her." I bite my thumb nail and shake my leg. The chair I'm in starts to squeak from the vibrations my leg is causing. I've always had issues voicing what I want to talk about. Sometimes, it takes me a minute to gather my thoughts and what I want to say, and other times, it's because I don't want to say anything at all.

"I'm going to guess you went and saw your brother. You had questions, he had answers. And you didn't like them."

"What are you, Seer?" I snort, ripping a hangnail from my thumb.

"No, but he did call me and tell me." Doc has a knowing expression on his face, one that is smug. He's enjoying this. "Told me to be prepared for a busy night. Damn, he wasn't wrong."

"He could have called me."

"You fuckers never answer him." Doc cracks his neck and rolls his shoulders before hunching over and starting on the other half of the heart.

I open my mouth to defend myself, but nothing comes out.

He's right.

"Maybe if everyone got their head out of their ass, a lot less discourse and more understanding would happen, but no. We have to be prideful and beat our chests. It's shit like that pushing people away," Doc confides. "So prove me wrong. Tell me about your brother."

"I can't, Doc. Not right now, please. And he isn't my brother. I need everyone to stop calling him that. Remember everything he did on Halloween? He's still that man."

"Mmhmm," Doc hums, clearly wanting to say something, but doesn't, which means he has a different thought process.

My mind is too fog-dense to care more than I'm capable of in this moment.

I'm lost.

Until Daphne wakes up, I'll linger in the dark, tucked away in the corners of my mind, and hope she's able to find me.

CHAPTER FOURTEEN

Daphne

Two days later

H̲oly Moly.
 If someone told me I got hit by a sledgehammer or by a truck, or a horse kicked me in the chest, I'd believe them. The sheets under me are slick, different from what I'm used to on Tongue's bed. I rub my hands over them, pinching the material in my fingers, then pop my eyes open when I know undoubtedly that these are not Tongue's sheets.

These are silk.

My tongue sticks to the roof of my mouth. My throat is raw and sore, as if I swallowed a thousand razorblades. My eyes are glued shut from the crust of sleep, and I squint them together, bring my fist up, and rub. I squint as my vision adjusts. I blink a few times to clear the blur and when my eyes finally focus, I notice I'm in a room that looks a lot like the master suite that is being built in our house.

I tug my arm and cringe when something jerks above my elbow.

An IV?

Since when?

I take a good look around the room. It smells of sawdust and paint. The bed is huge, and I'm nestled on the right side of it. There is a walk-in closet and an oversized black claw-foot bathtub near the window so we can look out toward the mountains.

Wondering if I'm in our room, I lift my lashes and blush, a fever drifting through the marrow of my bones when I see the mirror above us.

Oh yeah, this is our room.

I hold my breath and push myself into a seated position, grunting as the skin on the left side of my chest pulls. I cry out from the pain and slump against the bed.

I want to get up, use the restroom, and brush these fuzzy teeth. I feel disgusting.

The door is kicked open and the gold knob hits the wall, denting the new paint. Tongue is there. Shirtless. Chest heaving. His chest hair is covered in saw dust.

Someone send help. I can't breathe.

"Comet, you're awake." He runs over to my side of the bed, tracking in wood chips. When he kneels, I get hit with a fresh wave of sweat and pine with a hint of leather.

"I—" but I can't get the words out. My throat is as dry as cotton. I begin to uncontrollably cough, and my chest is screaming with a lash of fire.

"Sip." He brings a plastic cup in front of my mouth with a silver-reusable straw. "It's water."

I wrap my lips around the straw and the taste of metal reminds me of blood. I suck down the icy cold liquid and I groan in relief as it coats the back of my throat. I can't get enough. I drink quicker, as if I've been stranded in the desert for days on end.

"Shhh, slower, Comet. Don't get yourself sick," he croons, brushing a hand down my arm.

I don't listen. I keep drinking until there is nothing left.

"Do you remember what happened?"

Now that I've been awake for more than five minutes, I remember everything. I nod. "Reaper listened to me," I grin. "I was your champion."

His thick fingers land on the side of my jaw, adding pressure to turn my head. "Don't ever do that again. I can't stand to see you get hurt." His eyes lock with mine, turmoil swirling the depth of the earthy tones.

His eyes hold earthquakes that shake my core.

My eyes hold tsunamis to drown his enemies.

And one is always a possibility after the other.

Together, we destroy and give reason to rebuild.

"You scared me," he admits. "It's going to scar, Daphne. Doc did the best he could, but it's so deep. It's going to take a long time to heal."

"I don't care. I'd do it a hundred times for you."

"You're crazy."

"Crazy for you," I croak.

"Which I'll never understand as long as I live, but I'll never stop being thankful." His eyes drift over my face, then stop when he sees my hair. His eyes widen and his lips roll together to keep from laughing.

"I know, I look like I had a few too many."

"You look beautiful. I don't care when you think you don't, you always do."

"The charmer," I say with a roll of my eyes. "Can you help me to the bathroom? And is this our house?"

"The only room that's done is this room, the bathroom, and the kitchen."

"Why aren't we in the clubhouse?"

He picks me up, keeping my injured side on the outside and my good side tucked near his chest. "I didn't want us to be there. I needed space. It was too hard seeing Reaper do that to you. I swear, he liked it. I bet he thought he was getting me back."

"You can't really think that?" I utter in disbelief.

He sets me on the vanity and grabs my toothbrush.

Wets it.

Toothpastes it.

Wets it again.

Anyone who doesn't apply toothpaste like this is not human and needs lessons in brushing their teeth. He grunts and grumbles, muttering but not directly speaking to me. He shoves the toothbrush between my lips, and I nearly gag.

I take the handle and do my business, then scrub days' worth of bad breath off my tongue. I spit in the sink and he has a cup of water ready for me to gargle with.

"Are you in pain? I had to unhook your IV to come in here."

"Yeah, can we talk after I pee? Have I peed in the last two days? Oh my god, is my bladder going to explode?"

Tongue chuckles, lifting me again, tugs my pants down, and sits me on the toilet.

And doesn't leave.

He crosses his arms and waits. "Doc took your catheter out earlier this morning because he knew you'd wake up. He sedated you for a few days to give your body much needed rest."

"It's a small burn, Tongue. I would have been fine being awake. And I can't pee with you watching."

"You can do other things when I'm watching," he lowers his voice to a deep baritone, reminding me of a musician plucking a string of a bass.

"Go and close the door!" I giggle, then hiss as the pain ignites under the bandage.

"Fine." He closes the door, but I can see the outline of his body through the frosted glass.

I shake my head but smile, loving how protective and worried he is about me. I do my business and get up, open the door, and find him standing there.

Wayne Hendrix.

My once upon a comet.

And damn, I never thought the wish would come true.

"I love you too," he says, noticing the loving expression I have plastered across my face. "Let's get you cleaned up. I bet you'll feel better. Doc will be by again soon to check on you and later, after dinner, I want to talk to you about moving."

"Moving? Why would we move? Where?"

"Away from here. If you want. Since we aren't treated like we should be." He unbuttons the green plaid shirt I'm wearing and slides it off my shoulders. His fingers brush along my collarbone, staring at the wound. "This never should have happened."

"We aren't leaving. This is our family. Families fight sometimes, things get messy and out of control, but family always finds a way back. Plus, this is our home. The one you're building. Do you have any idea how beautiful this room is? We are staying."

He doesn't say anything. If anything, a cloud of disappointment hangs over his head, but he will thank me for it later. He scoops me up in his arms and takes me back into the bathroom where the bathtub is so I can look out the window. The faucet is gold and the handles glimmer in what's left of the sun dropping behind the mountains. The cactuses are a black outline in the distance, and the stars are poking through the last muted orange in the sky as nightfall takes over.

"We can't get your bandage wet, so no washing your hair yet," he informs me.

"I like it when you play doctor." I step into the tub, and the hot water has me sighing as the heat tingles the bottoms of my feet.

"I'm not good at it. I'm trying to listen to Doc," he says, grabbing a rag from the oak shelf he made himself. He dips the sage colored rag into the water, then squirts honey scented body wash on it and rubs the material together to create suds.

I don't want to let on how much pain I'm in. The burn on my chest is doing exactly that—burning. I want to be hooked up to that IV sooner rather than later to get the pain medicine. He drifts the rag down my leg, the white foam of the soap bubbling along my shin. He takes his time like he always does with me. He never hurries when my body is literally in his hands.

His callouses scratch the back of my knee as the rag drifts up to my inner thigh, then back down. Sex is intimate of course, but have you ever had someone choose to bathe you? To care for you? I never knew how connected it would make me feel. Having hands that have known no mercy on me, treating me like spun strands of gold, is like experiencing a miracle.

Naturally, my body responds to him. The space between my legs grows hot and my nipples tighten, but I don't have the energy to do anything about it. I want to enjoy his hands on me. I moan when he dips his hand between my legs and washes my most vulnerable place. He doesn't hover or linger like a part of me wants him to.

The warm water cascading down my right breast, careful to avoid the bandage, has my eyes hooding with lust and relaxation. *Who needs R&R when I have L&R? Lust and relaxation.*

Holy moly, his hands feel good.

"I can't get over the fact that I get to be the man that touches your body."

"I can't get over the fact that I'm the woman on the receiving end of your touch," I return his compliment and watch as he looks away from me.

So shy when it comes to compliments because he doesn't think he is worthy.

"Thank you," he whispers.

"For what?" I close my eyes when he starts to massage my calves. He digs into the muscle with his thumbs and I tilt my head back, resting it against the small pillow attached to the tub.

"For saving me."

I open my eyes and get a view of the high cathedral ceiling before tilting my chin to look at him. His beard has grown out a bit, and his hair is a bit shaggy and dark, matching the color of his eyes. The sage green of the bathroom wall brings out the golden hues in his eyes, but I can see a hint of garnet. The color really shines when he sees blood.

"I'll always save you, Comet. You never have to ask. It will always be something I do, like you do for me," I state the truest fact I know deep in my soul.

He washes me off and grabs a soft, green towel that matches the rag he used. Tongue helps me stand by wrapping an arm around my waist, so he doesn't have to tug on my arms. He pats me dry and his fingers brush down the side of my neck. I'm blushing fiercely.

"I like this," he says, talking about the pink tint spreading down to my chest. "I like that I get a reaction like this out of you." He places a soft kiss against the feverish skin, then wraps me in the towel. "Let me get you some fresh clothes and then we will settle you in bed again."

Even though he just bathed me, every time he picks me up, I can smell the sweat and wood all over his skin, getting me dirty all over again. He sets me on the bed and walks to the closest, grabs another button-up shirt so it's easy to remove for my bandage, and then a pair of panties.

In his large hand they look like pieces of scrap material.

I'm in the same spot he left me in. When he is in front of me, I lift my chin so I can see his handsome face. I have the luxury of seeing his body at this angle. It's sculpted out of the hardest rock known to man. It has to be. The swell of his pecs show the strength in his chest, and his abs are hard ridges and valleys.

All eight of them.

I outline the 'Unscarred' tattoo again, loving how his stomach trembles from my touch. "Comet," the name is shaking on a staggering breath. That beastly rumble in his chest has me looking down to see his cock hard beneath the prison of his jeans.

How does it fit inside me?

His hand tugs the towel free, his fingers teasing the curve of my breast. I gasp as the towel falls onto the bed and the air wraps around my nipples.

Instead of laying me down, he slides one arm through one sleeve and does the same with the other. "Tongue—"

"I won't fuck you when you're clearly in pain. I see it written all over your face." He begins to button the shirt from the bottom to the top. He leaves two unbuttoned at the top, so the shirt doesn't rub against my wound. He kneels, coasting his palms up the sides of my leg. Goosebumps arise all over my body, and my nipples tighten even further, something I didn't know was possible.

When he gets to my thighs, his fingers dig into my skin and yanks them open. He lifts one leg, loops the panties around my ankle, and proceeds to repeat the motion for the other. He tugs them up and I lift myself off the bed so he can pull them up my butt.

Puffs of hot air coast over my pussy with how close his lips are to me. "I can smell how sweet you are for me," he moans, burying his face between my legs and inhaling the scent he loves. The blunt edges of his nails pierce my skin and a sharp breath chokes me.

Holy Moly.

I want him.

"You test me, and in these moments, I do not want to be a good man." He lays his head on my thighs and my hands drift over his inky strands, then down his back. He is warm and tense, hanging on by a thread, and I want to cut that thread in half.

It's so tempting.

He stands slowly, dragging his nose up my body until he kisses the middle of my chest, works his way to my neck, and then his wide palm cups my cheek. I'm dizzy again, but not from pain, from him taking over my senses.

His lips slant over mine, and a slow dance of a kiss serenades my heat. I love his hand against my jaw, a gesture of how strong he is, how big his palm is compared to me, and how he controls the way our heads move for the kiss.

Control is Tongue's anchor. If he doesn't have that, he feels like he doesn't have anything to bind him to the world without him becoming a bloodthirsty killer.

"Come on, let's get you back to bed." Tongue pulls away, the magnetism between us pulling tight as he breaks our kiss.

I'm high on our kiss, dazed, and I can hardly feel the pain in my chest. It's a low throb compared the aching between my legs.

He tugs me around the bed, and I follow like a helpless puppy. I lay down and he hooks my IV up again.

"Doc filled these for me, so all I had to do was insert it."

It isn't long before my body feels numb. I hadn't realized how much pain I was in until now. I can't imagine how people with burns all over their body feel. It makes my heart go out to Moretti, even if he did turn his back on us and kidnap his brother.

"Can you hold me?" I ask him, not wanting him to go too far. I know I sound needy, but I just need to feel him surround me right now.

He strokes my cheek with his knuckles. "Like I could ever say no. I'm going to shower. I'll be right back."

"Okay," I slur a bit from the pain meds kicking in.

The mattress dips from the loss of his weight. He takes off his pants on his way to the bathroom and saliva pools in my mouth with I see that bubbled butt.

I want to bite it.

Grrr.

I giggle to myself.

"What's so funny?" he asks.

"Thinking 'bout that booty." I hold out my hands and pretend to grab.

He chuckles, but somehow doesn't manage to smile. "You're cute when you're high."

"You're cute," I retort. "Take that." I lift my nose in the air, proud of my witty comeback.

There it is.

That once-in-a-lifetime smile.

I could die happily right now knowing it's the last thing I ever see.

The hiss of the shower lulls me into a light sleep. I'm in the veil between awake and asleep, and it is the kind of fog that's wildly addicting. There are no thoughts, no fears, no panic, there's nothing because the only thing that matters is sleep. Nothing. Else.

I don't know how long I lie in the in-between, but the bed dips again and Tongue is there. His scent has my eyes opening, and his arm across my waist has me falling into a fog of safety instead. His skin is pink from the hot water and his wet hair tickles my shoulder as he puts his chin in the crook.

"Knock, knock."

Tongue is up and out of bed with a knife in his hand in a matter of two seconds. The door opens and Tongue throws the blade through the air, barely missing the man's head. It lands with a hard thump in the wall and Mercy ducks out of the way.

"Oh, it's you." Tongue sounds less than thrilled.

He snags the knife from the wall and when he turns around, I focus on the sweatpants he is wearing. They are gray, hanging low on his hips, and leave nothing to the imagination.

"It's just me," Mercy says. "I heard what happened, Daphne. Are you okay?"

"I'm great," I say, scratching the tip of my nose. "How are *you*?"

"Um, well, I have a lot to tell you."

"I want to know what you're doing here," Tongue interrupts him. He grabs the whetstone for his blade and wastes no time grinding the metal against stone.

"Reaper said I could find you here when I knocked on the clubhouse door. I came with those answers after doing some research. I figured you'd want to know, Daphne." Mercy takes a step forward, then stops. His hand is bandaged from the other day, but he seems to be doing fine.

"Well, you could have knocked on our door."

"I did, you didn't answer, and I got worried," Mercy says.

"Why? You don't even know me," I say, lifting my good arm in the air to make a point. "I just remind you of my mom. How did you know her?"

"May I?" Mercy asks Tongue as he eyes the spot at the edge of mattress to take a seat.

Tongue nods. "Any fasts movements and I'll kill you."

"No doubt about that," Mercy says.

The bed dips again, but Mercy weighs less so the motion isn't so significant. "What do you want to know first?" he asks me.

Even through my high goggles, I can tell he hasn't slept. His beard isn't combed, and his hair isn't styled. His eyes are tinged red, like he has been crying. "Did you love my mom?" I ask.

He smiles as if he is remembering her fondly. "She was my first love. Look." He digs into his back pocket, pulls out a black wallet, unfolds it, and slides out a square picture. "That's us. She was eighteen and I was twenty. I was about to go join the Navy, an idea she loved and hated. We had been friends for years, but it was only that summer we realized our friendship was more than that. It was love."

I'm careful with the photograph as I hold it. The edges are worn, the color is faded, but I can still recognize my mom. She has a beaming smile on her face that I had never seen before while growing up. I rub a finger over her face and inhale. She's sitting on a motorcycle, arms wrapped around a much younger Mercy, who has dark hair in this picture. He is wearing a leather jacket, and her cheek is pressed against his back, like she's holding onto him tight. She has on jeans and a t-shirt. Nothing fancy.

"I never saw her smile like this. I actually never saw her smile," I say with realization. "What happened? Why weren't you two together anymore?"

"I left for the Navy. I was in special ops, so the mission I was on was so secret she didn't know about it. It was only supposed to be a few weeks. But I got captured. I was a Prisoner of War for a few years. I never got to send her a letter explaining it. I bet she thought I died."

"But when you came back, why didn't you search for her?"

"She was with another man. She had a family. I didn't want to ruin that."

"You should have!" I throw the picture at him. "Maybe she'd still be alive if you would have done something."

"I didn't know," he chokes. His hand grips the middle of his shirt, right where his heart is. "God, I didn't know. It's all I have thought about. She was everything. She was… she was fucking everything, Daphne. I swear she's the reason I lived when I was captured. I'd see her face every time they tortured me, and all I wanted to do was to get back home to her. I didn't know…" he swallows, staring down at the black of his boots.

"You didn't know what?" I hiss, angry at him, happy that my mom knew some form of happiness, and sad she didn't get more of it like she deserved.

"I didn't know when I left for the Navy that she was pregnant." His eyes meet mine, then land on Tongue. "When I saw her with a little girl, my heart broke because we talked about having kids, and the man she was with didn't love her. Not the way I did, not in the amount I did. He couldn't." He slaps his chest again. "I didn't want to come between a family, but damn it, I regret it now. I regret it so fucking much."

"Why?" I yell at him through tears, the high gone, but my heart pumping adrenaline.

"The other night, when I got home, I did some research. You looked too familiar to me. I brought up your mom's name and your birth certificate, then checked the date you were born." He blows out a breath and rubs his uninjured palm on his knees. "Eight months after the day I left."

Holy Moly.

I suck in a deep breath. My mouth falls open in shock. I try to say something, anything, but the words don't come out. Mercy continues.

"And there, on the original birth certificate, the father's name was blank. She didn't put down your father. She didn't put down anyone, but you don't know how badly I wanted to fill in that blank with Andrey Machado." He reaches for my hand and rubs his thumb across it. "I also go by Mercy."

My mind tunnels, racing at a thousand miles an hour. The only thing I can focus on is the lie surrounding my life. "So my dad… my dad isn't even mine?"

"He raised you, so he is your father, but god, if I could turn back time, Daphne, I would have given anything to watch you grow up. I'm so envious."

I pull my hand away, unable to stop the flow of tears when I think about what could have been different. "You saw us, and you turned your back."

"Because I didn't want to ruin whatever life your mother built for you. I didn't know you were mine. I swear, Daphne. I had no idea or I would have."

"Please, leave," I point toward the door. My mind is swirling, and I hate it when it does this because usually it means I'm about to break. I don't want to break. Not here. Not now.

"Daphne, I want to get to know you. I want to make up for lost time. I want to be the father I never got to be for you. I'll do anything for a chance," he begs.

"I need time to think. Please, go." My voice hitches and I can't stop the tears. He reaches for my hand again, and I pull it away with a small shake of my head. "Don't."

He picks up the photo, takes a picture of it with his phone, then hands it to me, sliding it into the palm of my hand. "This should have always been yours." He bends down and presses a dry kiss to my forehead. "I didn't know I could love someone I didn't know so quickly," Mercy whispers. "But finding out I have a beautiful, strong daughter makes me realize the love a parent has for a child is instantaneous. I am so sorry."

The leather of his cut rubs together as he straightens. His lashes stick together, wet with the tears he is keeping at bay. "Take care of her," he tells Tongue, before doing what I want him to do.

He turns and leaves.

The door shuts softly and Tongue climbs onto the bed. We don't speak, he doesn't tell me everything is going to be okay, and he doesn't lie to me. He holds me while I cry. He knows that's all he can do because words cannot make me better.

I cry thinking about the life I could have had. I sob thinking about how happy my mother could have been. And I wail at the loss of it all.

I cry until I fall asleep while Tongue rubs his hands up and down my back to comfort me. I don't know how long I sleep for, but I wake up to my cellphone vibrating on the nightstand. Tongue is sound asleep.

I answer it quickly, keeping my voice soft. "Hello?" I eye Tongue to make sure I'm not waking him.

"Daphne," comes the voice of my father—well, the man I have always known as my father—stunning me silent. "You need to come home. Your Aunt Tina is in the hospital and it isn't looking good."

"Dad?" I ask, to make sure it's who I think it is. "Why are you calling me in the middle of the night? I haven't heard from you in months." This can't be him. He doesn't call. Ever.

"Get here. Now." Typical. He hangs up before I can ask if she is okay. He's always hated talking on the phone. I just thought he'd want to talk for a minute if he missed me.

But regardless, I have to go.

My mind numbs and something flips in my brain.

I have to go home.

I have to go to Nola.

CHAPTER FIFTEEN

Tongue

SOMETHING ISN'T RIGHT.

The room is different.

I sit up with a gasp and let my eyes adjust to the dark room.

It's colder, like something sucked the warmth out of it and left me for dead. I reach for my knife and the moonlight glitters across the blade. I listen, focusing on anything that doesn't belong, but I don't hear a thing.

And that's the problem.

The only breaths I hear are my own. My arm swings out to feel Daphne's side of the bed, but it's cold. I reach for the lamp, knocking over a glass of water onto the floor before I can pull the string connected to the bulb.

Click.

The light illuminates the room.

"Daphne?" I still sound sleepy but alarmed at the same time.

The silk sheets on her side of the bed are almost unbothered. I bought silk sheets because I wanted her to be comfortable, but maybe she doesn't like them and wanted to sleep somewhere else. I throw my legs over the edge of the mattress and my bare feet hit the hardwood floor. I try not to think of the worst. I try not to think like that, but negative notions are my specialty.

Negativity makes the world go round.

I flip on the bathroom light and peek my head in the bathroom. "Daphne? Comet? You here?" I ask into the acoustics of the restroom, but the only reply is the echo of my own voice. My heart is a wrecking ball threatening to crack my sternum

The floor creaks with every step I take toward the bedroom door. My breaths are erratic as I think of the worst.

It's fine.

She's here. Or she's in the clubhouse. She has to be. She said she didn't want to leave, so she's probably scared, wanting to be with the girls again since they have become good friends. Maybe I should have left her with Sarah to heal in the medical room. I just wanted her to wake up in our new bed, so she was comfortable. I remember hearing that silk sheets keep you cool when you're warm and warm when it's cold. I wanted what was best for her. That's all.

When I get to the bedroom door, I examine her side of the bed. She's unhooked her IV and fluid is dripping onto the floor from the bag hanging on the hook. Her phone is gone from the edge of the nightstand and her shoes, the blue Converse she loves so much, are missing. They were at the foot of the bed, the tips tucked between the space of the floor and the bedframe.

They were right there.

I open the door. The hinges don't squeak like a lot of others at the clubhouse because they are new. I flip the hallway light on. The floors aren't completed yet, and only a part of the wall is up. Everything else is just bare bones of the house's structure. I stand there and listen for her, her sighs, her yawns, her heartbeat, the way she moves, I know it all. I know what every sound she makes sounds like, but I don't hear anything.

This house is empty.

I sprint down the hall, my feet scratching against the unfinished floorboards—no doubt I'll have splinters to pull out, but I don't care—and throw the front door open. I don't bother closing it either. I jump down the eight steps, landing directly on my feet before taking off across the desert to the clubhouse. Behind me, I hear a scurry of claws scratching the sand, and I don't need to turn around to see who it is.

It's Happy.

I leap over the bushes I can see and step on painful sharp twigs and rocks along the way. The sting in the back of my eyes is there. I don't have a good feeling. My stomach hurts. My heart hurts. Something is wrong.

"No, please, no. I'll do anything," I beg to someone, to anyone, to fucking everyone. "She has to be there. She wouldn't leave."

She wouldn't leave me.

I pass the black metal building of King's Garage and head toward side door that takes me to Reaper's office. I try to open the door, but it's fucking locked! I bang my fists on the door rapidly, one after the other. It isn't a knock.

It's a plea to be let in.

Happy hits the side of my leg and I bend over to pick up him. He nuzzles his snout against my neck and the hug he is giving me means the world.

The hallway light comes on through the colorful stain glass window and the skull staring back at me appears to be on fire. I can't see who is walking toward me, but I don't stop hitting the door, even if it means I have to break it down.

The lock clicks, the knob turns, and a very tired, very sleepy Juliette answers. "Tongue? What's wrong? I was just making tea. My throat is killing me from singing three nights in a row. I have to tell Tool I need a break," she rambles tiredly, not giving me a chance to answer. She opens the door wider. "Gosh, come in. You must be so cold. Where is your key? You know you don't have to knock."

"Have you seen Daphne? Is Daphne here?" The words are rushed and hurried. I stumble against the wall and one of the pictures fall and breaks, which has a door opening beside us.

"Tongue?" Badge scratches the side of his head, then rubs his eyes, and scratches his chest. "It's so early or late… or both." He yawns. "What's the deal?"

I run to my room, which is opposite of the kitchen, and place Happy in his tank so he can be warm. "Daphne? Is she here? She isn't in bed. She isn't in bed! I need to know she's okay. She wasn't beside me when I woke up. She's gone." When I get to the kitchen, the only light on is above the sink and Juliette's mug is alone on the tabletop. A black mug with a teabag dipped inside has steam billowing out of it.

"No, Tongue. She isn't here," Juliette regretfully informs me, and worry frowns her lips. "How long has she been gone?"

"Are you sure she's gone?" Badge asks, checking to see if there is any water left in the kettle sitting on the stove. When he nods to himself, he opens the cabinet next to him and grabs a plain white mug, like the kind they have at diners. He pulls out a chair at the table and steals one of Juliette's bags of tea from the box. "Maybe she couldn't sleep. Happens to me all the time."

I run my hands through my hair and shake my head. "Sh—she wouldn't," I try to say. My thoughts are moving too fast. I turn around instead, ignoring them since they are no help, and try the basement. Maybe she was in pain and wanted Doc to give her more medicine.

Not caring about how quiet I am, I thud down the steps and flip on the light, but the beds are empty. "No." I hold a hand over my heart. Denial sinks its fangs into me, snaking venom through my veins. That sensation in my stomach, the one that's knotted and makes me feel sick, gets worse.

She's gone.

When I get to the top step, I trip, but Slingshot is there at the door to catch me by the arm, so I don't fall backward. He looks exhausted too. It seems the entire clubhouse is awake now, no thanks to me. Slingshot tugs me forward and shuts the door. His hair is wild. The man always has crazy bedhead. He grips my shoulders and tilts his chin down, lifting his eyes through his lashes. "Buddy, I need you to start taking some deep breaths. You're freaking out. We can't get anything done if you're panicking. Deep breaths," he reminds me. He inhales through his nose, lungs expanding, then exhales.

I follow his lead. I didn't realize how much I needed to calm down and focus. The short breaths were making me lightheaded.

The kitchen chairs grind against the floor as he pulls two out. One for me and one for him. I sit down and tug at stands of my hair. I can't do this. I can't focus. What if she's hurt? I grab the sides of my head and rock back and forth.

No one will ever be able to love you. You're a fucking idiot. You're nothing but a tight ass for my cock, Wayne. Nothing more, nothing less, and everyone will know that when they look at you.

My uncle's words run through my head. Is that what happened? Did she finally see who I am?

A backhand to my face has my cheek flaming and my anger snapping to Slingshot. His steely gaze is on mine and he points at a finger at me. "Get it the fuck together right now. You're fucking Wayne goddamn Hendrix. You cut people's tongue's out of their mouths and feed them to your swamp kitty."

"What's going on?" Reaper questions and everyone in the room sits up a little bit straighter.

Not me, though.

He doesn't give a fuck about Daphne.

"Nothing. I'll handle this on my own," I say as I get up from the chair. No one is taking me seriously, and I'm too tired to fight with them. I'll get more done on my own.

"Tongue, sit down, and tell us what is on your mind." Reaper turns on the faucet and fills the coffee pot. "Please."

"Hey, Tongue. How's Daphne doing?" Mercy comes through the hallway next, wearing sweatpants and a T-shirt. "I know. You're shocked I'm here, but I couldn't leave." He falls silent, having me connect the dots, which means he hasn't told Reaper the truth. "Reaper let me stay."

I fling the chair across the room and haul ass toward him, throwing my arm against his neck. "This is your fault. She left because of you! I should kill you. Right here. I'll fucking gut you, right where you stand. Where is she? Where is my Comet?" I roar, smashing my forearm against his windpipe. "She left me in the middle of the night, and I have a feeling it has to do with you paying a little visit and saying you were her fucking father!"

"What the fuck?"

"Shit."

"Holy fucking hell. The world cannot be that small…" Reaper grumbles under his breath just as he turns the coffee pot on.

"You want to know what's wrong with me?" I turn to them. "She's gone! You know better than to think she'd take a midnight stroll alone. She wouldn't leave me. She wouldn't." I know I sound like I'm convincing myself and maybe I am, but I'm desperate. "She was fine until Mercy came in to talk to her about how he knew her mother. We all know how fragile of a mind Daphne has. God." I let go of his throat and lace my hands behind my head. "What if she's in the middle of an episode and she needs me?"

"Episode? What are you talking about? And she had the right to know who her father was! I deserve to know my daughter. She was kept from me for twenty-five years. I'm allowed to talk to her!" Mercy defends himself, looking just as scared as I feel. "What's wrong with her?"

"Nothing is wrong with her. She's fucking perfect how she is." The blade in my pocket is burning a hole right through, begging me to grab hold and cut Mercy's tongue out.

"She has psychosis," Reaper tells him. "Her version of reality isn't always real."

Badge gives me a glass of water. The condensation on the glass is cold and slick against my fingertips. I take a greedy gulp, but it does nothing to put out the new hellfire in my veins. "She saw her mom die and her psychosis formed. I think she saw her mom get murdered. I don't think she killed herself. The dreams Daphne has been having lately are too damn real, and she wakes up gasping for air like she's run a mile."

"Dreams? Why didn't you tell me this?" Reaper asks.

"I didn't think you'd care," I state, adding a bite to every word.

He's hurt.

Good.

"Oh my god. I could have saved them so long ago," Mercy says to himself. He props himself against the counter and sags. "It's all my fault."

I want to blame him and right now, I will, even if logic tells me it isn't his fault. He didn't know about her past.

"Well, looks like we are having Church. We have a ton to discuss." Reaper checks the time on the clock hanging above the sink. "Five a.m. Hope you boys are rested."

The front door slams open and my hopes are lifted when I think it's Daphne, but it's Braveheart.

Wait a minute.

"Hey, guys," he greets, rubbing his hands together to get them warm again. "What's with the gloomy faces?" His eyes land on me and something resembling confusion crosses his face. "You just missed Daphne. She left a few hours ago."

Before I can blink, before I can breathe again, I have him face down against the table with a knife against the base of his skull. "You let her leave? Why? Why would you let her leave alone!" I apply more pressure to the end of the knife, a drop of blood pebbling on his skin.

"I didn't think anything of it. She's one of our own. I figure she can come and go as she pleases!" The last word is a loud shout as I apply even more force against his head.

"Fuck, I'll go check the cameras. I'll see if I can track the traffic cameras to see where she is going." Badge drains the rest of his tea, then pours a cup of coffee. "We will find her, Tongue. We care. She is one of ours."

I don't say thank you as he leaves the room to go to his office. I'm too fucking busy debating if I want to kill Braveheart.

"Tongue, I'm sorry. I didn't know. Okay? I didn't know. I thought maybe she was picking something up for you and wanted to keep it a surprise for your birthday or something—"

I stop him from saying anything else and pick his head up, then smack it down on the table again. "I don't even know my own birthday!" I roar into his ear and lift the knife in the air. My uncle never celebrated my birthday. I can't remember any birthdays before he had custody of me, either. I simply don't know.

Reaper grabs my arm as I slice it through the air, just before it hits Braveheart in the middle of the head, which would have decapitated him senseless. I fight Reaper, but it's my bad arm and the muscles start to shake. Braveheart takes the split second of my weakness for his advantage and rolls away.

"You need to calm down," Reaper orders, snagging my other arm and yanking it behind my back.

I cry out as the scarred gunshot wound tugs. Painful tingles cascade through my tendons, numbing the tips of my fingers.

"Let me go," I seethe, using my bodyweight to launch him to my left. He doesn't expect it and Reaper's grip loosens enough for me to shrug out of his hold. I reach across the table and snag the knife right before Slingshot tries to beat me to it.

I hold my trusty blade out in front of me, slashing it through the air. Sweat over my brows and down my eyes, stinging and burning from the salt. I'm frantic. I can't decide who to look at. Everyone is crowding me.

Just like my Uncle did.

Bend over, Wayne.

My uncle's cruel laughter echoes in my head.

No. No, I won't bend over. "I won't bend over!" I scream at them.

"Tongue, you're safe here," Reaper says with trepidation, slowly inching his way toward me. "You killed your uncle. Use that anger for Daphne."

Daphne.

"Where is she? Where's my Comet?" I swing the knife in front of Mercy's face. "It's your fault! It's your fault she left me. She's mine. She isn't yours. She was never yours. You waited to take action. I didn't."

"We don't know yet, but I swear on my life, we will bring your ol' lady home." Slingshot's words hitch as he speaks, the whites of his eyes turning red.

No one will love you like I love you, Wayne. No one will take care of you like I do. Don't you like this? Don't you like when I touch you?

Something drips onto my cheek.

Tears.

A concept I'm still learning. Something I've never done before I met Daphne. She isn't even here and she makes me exposed.

"I need her, Reaper." I hit the side of my head with my fist. "Like you need Sarah. I need Daphne. She makes me better. I'm better."

"You don't think I don't notice that? I do. I notice, and I'm sorry I haven't said it before, but I'm proud of you, Tongue. I'm so proud of you. You're a good friend. A good man. And you're smart. You've excelled so much, and I can't wait to see where this new you leads. But also, I'm going to need you to put down the knife."

She won't come back. She realized how stupid I am. My uncle was right. "He was right." My head sways back and forth. "He was right." I place the sharp tip into the middle of my elbow.

"Tongue, no, he wasn't. He wasn't right. You have proved him wrong, time and time again."

No. I was weak. I am weak. Daphne saw it just like my uncle did. I dig the knife into my skin and drag it down to my wrist. Blood spreads down my arm and spills onto the floor.

I go to cut the other, to release the pain, but there is a sharp pin prick against my neck. "I can't let you do that, Tongue. Not on my watch," Doc says, keeping an arm around my neck.

I tap his forearm with bloody fingers, but whatever he gave me begins to take over my body. The knife slips from my hand and clatters to the floor. I'm falling limp. The fight leaves my body and all I can see is Daphne's face.

"There you go," Doc croons, squatting to the floor as gravity takes hold of me so I don't hit the ground face first. "It's okay. We got you. Everything is going to be okay."

"We need to call Seer," someone says.

My vision darkens. Daphne's smile is the light at the end of the dark tunnel I find myself walking down more times than not. I close my eyes as her light fades and time is no longer a bitch I'm subjected to.

And then everything is black.

I don't know how long I'm out. Honestly, I don't care either.

My head swims as I open my eyes.

I blink. The room doesn't look familiar. I'm not in my room, or the house, or in the basement. But I shake that thought aside. I need to get up and find Daphne.

"Damn, looks like we're more alike than you think, baby brother."

My eyes finally come to focus, and I lift my head to look at the room across from mine. Porter is there, looking down at me from his standing position, smirking. He gives me a finger wave. "Good morning, Sunshine."

"Shove your morning up your ass."

"Oh, someone is cranky."

I'm going to kill him.

And then I'm going to find Daphne and fucking kill whoever the fuck put me in the Asylum.

CHAPTER SIXTEEN

Daphne

I FORGOT HOW HOT IT CAN GET IN NEW ORLEANS. MY HAIR IS STICKING TO THE BACK OF my neck from the humidity. The sun is hot and there isn't a breeze to be felt. I wait outside the airport for my dad to pick me up, but I don't see him yet. That's okay. He is always fashionably late.

A grumble of bikes passes by slowly, and one of the bikers stares directly into my soul. He has bright blue eyes. For some reason, their leather cuts look familiar. On them is emblazoned the words 'Ruthless Kings, NOLA Chapter'. I try to think of where I recognize it from but can't quite put my finger on it.

I don't know where I could have seen a Ruthless King before. I'm not exactly the biker type, but something about them feels familiar. The burn on my chest sends a stab of pain, like it's trying to remind me of something.

I think it was some freak accident. Daddy said when I was on the phone with him that I was on vacation. The trip must not have been very good because I don't remember a thing.

Daddy's rusted green Chevy comes to view through the pick-up lane. The muffler is off, and the engine is loud, followed by the smell of gas fumes. The grill is hanging on by a piece of wire and the passenger side door doesn't open from the outside. Daddy leans over from the driver's side and opens it for me. He has a cigarette hanging in his mouth and a flash of anger in his eyes, but it's gone the moment I notice it.

Probably my mind playing tricks on me. Daddy says that happens a lot, which is why he sent me on vacation, to clear my head.

"We need to go see your aunt. Get your ass in the truck and stop wasting my damn day." He smells of booze again.

"I thought you quit drinking." I yank the seatbelt across my chest and buckle up.

"Well, I fucking felt like starting again. That a problem?"

"No, Daddy," I whisper, a whirlwind of uneasiness settling in my stomach. My head hurts so bad and when I close my eyes, I see a face that eases the queasiness. He's handsome. Chocolate hair and brown eyes, tattoos, but I don't know how I know him.

But I think I do?

No. Maybe I've just seen him somewhere and latched on because I thought he was cute.

"What happened to your knuckles?" I question, staring at the broken red skin that looks a few days old.

"None of your business." He flicks the cigarette ash into the small tray that came with the truck, where a dozen other orange butts are buried. The car is just like I remember it, with burn holes all over the leather seat. An open Big Gulp cup is in one of the cup holders that has chewing tobacco stuck to the sides. A tangle of bat bones is hanging from the rearview mirror. Daddy says it keeps the ghosts away.

He grabs the black angled gear shift and pulls it down into drive and presses the gas. He turns the volume up on the radio, some classic rock station screaming about "Girls, Girls, Girls." I know it's code for not wanting to talk.

As we pass the bikers who are pulled over on the side of the pick-up lane, my eyes lock with the one I saw a few minutes ago. His eyes are the clearest blue I've ever seen. He stares at me until I'm too far away to look at him.

Daddy doesn't stop like he should when he turns onto the road to see if traffic is clear. Car horns blare and the tires screech along the road as he straightens the wheel.

The Mississippi River is to the right, and today it is murky and the water is high. The heat waves are ripping through the air, and I roll down the window to get some sort of breeze, since the air conditioning doesn't work.

"So, you go away for a few months and come back fat? What the fuck happened to you?"

I glance down at my body and frown. I don't think I look that different.

"This is why you need to always be with me. Plus, your aunt came to see me and started bitching at me about your mother's will. I need you here to help fight her with me. Me and you, the widow and the daughter, she won't stand a chance."

I don't like how that sounds.

The familiar rumble is distant and when I glance in the side mirror, I see the motorcycles a few cars behind us. I wait for the fear, but there isn't any there. I'm... relieved.

Why?

The side of my head is hurting again and the trees warp as the river's waves get abnormally large. I shut my eyes and take a deep breath. I'm fine. There's nothing wrong with me.

Comet.

A deep voice penetrates my inner thoughts, and I smile when I hear his voice. Who is it?

"I swear to god, if you aren't worth it," Daddy mumbles under his breath as he tightens his hand on the wheel.

I lean my forehead against the frame of the truck, letting hot air rush across my face. I'm trying to piece together where I've been or what I've done, but there's a wall in my head that I can't break down. Something is stopping me from thinking clearly.

What does Daddy do to make me like this?

"Get the fuck out. I'm going to go find a parking spot."

I open my eyes to see that we are in front of the hospital already. The bushes on either side of the automatic doors are bright green, and an alligator sticker on the side of the bench has my heart kicking up a notch.

But why?

"Hurry the fuck up, you idiot. Christ. No good, just like your—"

I don't hear what he has to say because I slam the door, not wanting to hear the hatred he spews. I don't know how I've managed to live with him all these years.

Something tells me I haven't, but I don't understand. I'm more confused than ever.

I head inside the hospital and the burst of air conditioning drapes over my sweaty skin. I sigh in relief. Damn, that feels good.

I pass a few people holding their stomach. One is puking in a barf bag and the other looks like he is thinking about puking. It's a cruel, sick cycle. Literally.

The nurse at the front desk is older, with dyed brown hair to cover the grays, and her lips are thin and wrinkled. She purses them as she talks on the phone. When she notices me through spider leg lashes, she holds the phone to her shoulder. "Sorry, sweetie. The man is just going on and on about how someone messed up his stitches. How can I help you?" Her southern accent takes away the edge gnawing at my stomach.

"I'm looking for my aunt. Her name is Tina Douglas. She's a patient here."

She types away on the keyboard and the jolly expression she had on her face is gone. "She's in intensive care," she says sadly. "It's the East wing. Just follow this hallway and look for one of the doctors there to update you on her condition."

"Intensive… oh my god, what happened?" Aunt Tina is the closest person I have to a mother. She has to be okay.

"We don't know. She was found beaten up pretty good. Sorry, sweetie. I'll keep her in my prayers." She touches the golden cross she has around her neck, as if what she says is supposed to bring me comfort.

I give her the best smile I can manage, which is barely there, with a tiny lift of my lips. I head down the hall like she says and follow the signs that lead me to intensive care. The floors wobble and I pause, holding out my hands to steady myself. It looks like lava.

No one else seems to be concerned. I get a few odd looks from doctors passing me by.

It's fine. I'm fine. Everything is fine.

Act natural. Your mind is playing tricks on you.

I step through the lava and wait for the undeniable pain, but nothing happens. When I don't feel the expected agony, the floor turns to normal again and I let out a deep breath.

See? I'm fine.

I get to the double doors with the words Intensive Care painted in red across them and step through. Now I have no idea where to go. Everyone is so busy. The doctors are rushing back and forth, and the nurses are helping the patients. I stand there, not knowing what to do, when an arm grabs mine and pulls me back out the doors.

I'm shoved in a closet and a hand is over my mouth.

Blue eyes.

"Do not scream," he whispers. His Cajun accent is slight, making him easy to understand. "My name is Seer. That name mean anything to you?"

I shake my head.

"I'm going to lift my hand from your mouth, and you need to promise me you aren't going to scream. I'm not here to hurt you, *cher*. I'm here to help."

As fast as I can, I nod.

"Okay, that's real good, *cher*. Real good." He eases his hand off me and keeps it hovered, just in case he has to silence me again.

"You're from the airport."

"I am. A friend of mine asked if I could find you. Luckily, they have a guy that's good at locating people. You, *mon amie*, were a good girl using a credit card."

"What are you talking about?"

"Daphne, you don't belong here. Don't you feel that? You are meant to be somewhere else. Men from the Ruthless Kings Las Vegas chapter are coming for you. Do you know them?"

I shake my head, but it does sound familiar.

And... "It feels like I do."

"Oh, *cherie*. You bet you do," he replies with a smile. His hand is back over my mouth when a doctor stops outside of the door to talk to a coworker.

"I don't know how she's going to make it."

"Me either. She received one hell of a beating. Whoever did this is a monster."

I wonder if they are talking about my Aunt Tina.

"You cannot trust your dad," Seer tells me, his blue eyes oddly bright as he stares at me. "I think you know that. Here." He points a finger to my heart. "And here." He taps my head. "The human instinct is some of the most powerful forces out there, *mon amie*. You just need to listen to you."

"What's happening to me?"

"Your mind is lost, Daphne, but don't worry. It's going to be found. Keep an open mind. And your aunt's abuser is closer to you than you think."

Riddles. I'm not good at riddles.

"I'll be keeping an eye on you while you're here."

"Why?"

"Mostly to keep my head on my body," he chuckles. "That Tongue is no man to mess with, especially when it comes to you."

"How do you know this?"

"Oh, *cher*. That's a story for another time, I'm afraid. Just keep yourself alive. Okay? I know you think you don't remember right now, but that is not true. You remember everything."

"I remember nothing," I hiss, unable to stop the pool of tears blurring my vision. "I know nothing."

His hand lands on my shoulder and he brings his lips to my ear, whispering, "Your dreams remember everything."

I close my eyes when his warm breath becomes too close. "But my dreams—" I snap my eyes open to find myself alone in the closest.

"He was here," I say to myself. "I'm not crazy. He was right here." I find myself staring at the corner, the darkest part of the room, and wait.

Wait for what, I don't know.

Something about the shadows calls me home.

I just wish I knew where home was.

CHAPTER SEVENTEEN

Tongue

I'M FUCKING FURIOUS.

"You think you're going to do what?" I snarl at Reaper as he speaks to me from the other side of the glass. I bang my fist against it. "You aren't going anywhere without me."

"Tongue, you're injured, and I think a few days here might help. We know where she is. Badge saw she bought a plane ticket to New Orleans. I've already called Pocus. They found her. Seer has already talked to her."

Bullseye and Reaper share a look. I hate that look. It tells me they know something else and they don't want me to know. "What else?"

Reaper rubs a hand over his day-old scruff and fogs up the glass as he sighs. I pound my fist against the glass again, right where Bullseye's face is. I want to punch it. "Tell me!"

"She doesn't remember anything, Tongue. She's in one of her episodes."

"Remember? Remember what?" I ask stupidly. By the expressions on their faces, it hits me like an anvil. I stumble backward from the hard hit of the weight.

"Wayne? Hey! Wayne!" Porter calls out to me somewhere in the distance.

"She can't remember me? She doesn't remember us?"

"No, she doesn't," Reaper says sadly.

She said she'd never forget.

And now… what am I going to do? My chest heaves as sorrow fuels me.

"We are going to go down to meet the NOLA chapter. We will be back, and she will come with us."

"You are going to let me go," I say to him. "I need to see her. I need to remind her of us. She remembers. Maybe not right now, but she will." She'll see me in her dreams. She has to. I have to hold onto that. I have to… I gulp.

I have to believe in that. I have to believe that our love is stronger than a memory. It's a comet that stands the test of time and burns forever.

"Tongue—"

I charge to the glass window and slam my head against it. Blood drips from the crack spidering outward. I don't even bother to wipe my face. "If you don't, I swear, I will break this wall down and find her my fucking self."

"Mercy, Bullseye—"

"She needs me!" a howl rips from the top of my lungs. "She doesn't have a damn thing to do with Mercy. Her memories run deep with me. Me! She's mine, Reaper. If this were Sarah, you would stop at nothing to save her. This is my ol' lady. Don't take this from me."

The last words make his face soften. "Okay," he says.

"Can I come, or is that asking too much?" Porter asks as he taps the glass.

"It's too much to ask. I don't trust you."

"I don't trust you either."

"You're staying. You're lucky I don't kill you where you stand. You are only alive for Tongue. That's it. Zain!" he calls for his uncle.

"Don't yell, I'm right here. Damn," Zain huffs as he comes out of the room diagonal from me. "I heard everything." He takes out the set of keys and slides one into the lock. "They only put you in here because they were afraid you'd hurt yourself."

"I already hurt myself," I say, slipping out the door when he opens it and grab the bag of my stuff they packed and left by the door days ago.

"Let's go. I don't want to waste any more time. Who knows what her father is doing to her? Who is coming?" I ask.

"No one besides us. Poodle has Ellie's ballet recital to go to, Joey is sick, so Skirt is staying, Doc doesn't want to leave Joanna, Tool has his first college night at King's Club, Patrick—"

"I get it. It's fine. Let's go," I say. "She isn't going to remember on her own." I'm so impatient. I want to get there already. Is she okay? Is she hurt? Is she happier without me?

Reaper, Zain, and Bullseye walk away and head down the steps.

"Hey, baby brother."

I look at Porter over my shoulder, wishing things could be different between us. I wish there was a possibility we could be brothers, but there isn't and there never will be. "What?"

"Be careful."

"Why do you care?"

He lifts a shoulder and strokes the spine of the book he is reading. "I don't know. I just know I do. Just don't go getting yourself killed."

I give him a slight chin tilt. "You too," I say languidly. I'm unsure about this new development, but it's hard to ignore that we share the same mom. It's hard to ignore he killed her too, but also, the hardest to ignore is the fact my mom didn't love me at all.

Porter is sick, thinking trying to kill me was in some way saving me.

Sickness must run in the family because I know I'm not right in the head either. How we get past this, I don't know. It's too much to think about right now. I run down the steps, needing to get away from him and remind myself he is the Groundskeeper.

A man that wanted to kill me and the only family I've known.

I can't forgive that.

I'm not that good of a man. Hell, I'm not a good man at all.

I stop in the bathroom to change and pull on my cut before I fly out the front door and see Reaper and Bullseye waiting near the truck.

"Do not make me regret this," Reaper warns. "Keep your head when we are down there."

"I don't make promises I can't keep," I tell him in earnest and hop in the backseat, then shut the door.

"I was afraid you'd say that." Reaper and Bullseye buckle their seatbelts at the same time. "Let's get this trip over with and bring home Daphne."

"Can we bring Tool? Please?" Bullseye starts to laugh. "It's been too long since I've seen him freak out over Seer."

"No. I need him here. Too many of our women are pregnant and need protection. I'm not leaving them alone when I have two of my best killers in the truck right now." Reaper turns the engine of the Ford Raptor and its horses shake the truck. He stretches his arm across the back of the passenger seat and turns around. "Tongue, we need to have a serious talk before we go."

"Can it wait? I want... I need to get to Daphne."

"I know, but this needs to be said." He turns his body, and the movement has his jeans rubbing against the leather. "I know things have been tense between us. I've been tiptoeing around you, and I'm sorry."

I stare out the window and stare at the cactus growing from the ground. I'm uncomfortable. The only heart to heart I want to have is with Daphne.

"What happened to you, I should have talked to you about it instead of walking on eggshells. It was wrong of me to invade your privacy. I exposed you. That was wrong of me, and it was my failure as President. I apologize."

I feel exposed now.

I rub my chest. The anxiety is almost physical, in the way it applies pressure.

"I didn't enjoy burning Daphne, but I was fucking proud of her for doing that for you. I want her for you, Tongue. She's strong. And I am proud of you."

I've never heard someone besides Daphne tell me they are proud of me. It's a strange feeling. I almost... like it?

"I know you've been having a hard time lately trusting us. And I get it. I would too, in your position. But I want you to know you always have a place here with us. No matter what, you're family, Tongue."

He stares at me, and I can tell he really means it.

"Can we go now?" This is too... uncomfortable. I want to cut the tongue out of her father's throat. She's mine.

"Yeah, Tongue. We can go." The truck reverses out of the dirty driveway. "We're flying there."

Great.

I hate flying, but it makes sense. The quicker the better.

Country music blares on the radio, but I don't know the song. We stay quiet and my mind drifts to Daphne. It hurts so fucking bad to know she can't remember me, but I'll fix this. She needs me. She has a lot to process right now. She just found out her dad isn't her dad. It makes sense that her psychosis would break free.

I want her to be okay. That's all. If she's safe and sound, I can take care of the rest.

I'll always take care of her.

After I carve my name in her skin, so she fucking knows she belongs to me. She can't forget me when she has to look at my name every day. Just the thought has my cock growing hard. Damn it, I miss her.

I take out my journal from my back pocket and open it, seeing the drawing of her naked I did the other night. Perfect fucking tits. When I get back, I'm going to have her push them together so I can fuck them, then I'm going to come all over her mouth and watch her lick her lips clean.

"Stop growling back there." Bullseye polishes his silver dart.

"Have you checked your sugar levels today?" I rub my finger over the soft curve of her face against the paper.

"Touché," he replies.

I hold a smile inside and flip the page of the journal. I reach into my cut pocket and pull out a pencil, sketching her face from memory. Her small, button nose, plump lips, and big eyes. I love that her bottom lip is a little bit bigger than the other. I growl again when I think about them wrapped around me and sucking me dry.

Reaper chuckles from the front seat. I don't care who knows how much I want Daphne. If it were up to me, I'd let the entire world know.

I concentrate on the wispy strands of her hair, making sure they are just right. They have to be perfect. Every single strand on her head is perfection. The way they curl around her chin as they hang loose from the messy bun she has on top of her head, or the way they blow in the wind as she's holding on to me tight as we ride the bike.

Or how she swings it through the air with a flip while she fucks me.

I growl again.

Bullseye and Reaper laugh.

It isn't funny.

"Alright. Empty your pockets. No weapons and shit on the plane."

"I need my knife, Reaper. You know I need it. I can't be anywhere without it. I need it to protect Daphne."

"They will have knives there, Tongue," he pinches the bridge of his nose, exasperated.

"Fine. I won't be happy about it."

"You never are, Tongue."

I mock him while I slide my knife into the pocket of the front seat, then open the back door, and hop out. The three of us head toward the departing flights in the same stride and I tuck my sketchbook safely in my pocket.

When we get to the front counter, the woman eyes us warily.

"Three one-way tickets to New Orleans, please," Reaper leans against the counter and gives his charming smile to the lady. She's older. Blonde hair turning white, but her blue eyes are clear as she was when she was younger, as light as the sky.

Not as pretty as Daphne. No one ever is or ever will be.

"My pastor on Sunday said I was going to be faced with darkness and evil this week. And look what the devil dragged in," she says, pretending to be unimpressed, but her wrinkled cheeks turn a brighter shade of red than the blush she's wearing today.

"I think you're getting us confused with our buddy Knives," Bullseye chimes in, taking a jab at his 666 tattoo above his dick.

"There are more of you?" she gasps.

"Oh, we are everywhere, ma'am," Reaper says, his eyes dropping to her nametag. "Gretchen. Whenever you need help, you find us, okay?" he grabs her hand and kisses her wrinkled, age-spotted knuckles.

"Oh, Pastor Dan was right. I'd be blinded by Satan in a Sunday hat. And you three are all wearing hats," she giggles.

"I'm not wearing a hat," I say, impatient. "Can we fucking go now?"

"It's a saying—you know what? Never mind," Bullseye says.

I don't get it. We aren't wearing hats.

Gretchen, the poor wench, hands over the tickets with shaky hands. "Satan," she points to Reaper, then to his head. "Hat. A big one."

"Oh, it's big, alright," Reaper winks.

"I'm telling Sarah," Bullseye snorts, holding in a laugh.

I snatch the tickets from her frail hands, annoyed with this fucking bullshit. I want to get on that plane, and I'm going to go with or without them.

"Sarah would understand. I saved us two hundred bucks and we have a kid on the way," Reaper defends himself as we slither through the busy crowd. Slot machines go off in the distance. Even people at the airport are drunk and wasting all their money. I see an Elvis in the corner, and I want her home so bad so he can marry us.

I'm determined.

"Shoes off. Phones in the bin. Empty out your pockets, please!" the agent shouts over the roar of people.

I don't want anyone to see my sketchbook. What if they look through it? Daphne is mine. No one else can see.

Bullseye places his boots in the gray plastic bin and empties his pockets. He heads into the scanner and lifts his arms.

I don't like this machine. It's small.

"Sir, please step over here." She ushers him to the side of the machine, and she takes a wand and roams it over his body until she reaches his zipper. "Sir, do you have anything in your pockets?"

"No, ma'am," he smirks.

She waves the wand again and it beeps three times. "What's in your pants, sir?"

"A Prince Albert, a guiche, and Jacob's Ladder. You want to climb it and see how high you get, gorgeous?" Bullseye offers with a salacious baritone.

"Next," she shouts, lifting a brow and unimpressed with Bullseye. "I have a taser, sweetie. Get to moving."

"Wound my heart, lady."

"Get a band-aid," she sasses, and Bullseye grabs his boots from the belt.

Finally, all of us are through the security and get to the gate. Bullseye is pouting, Reaper is getting grouchy, and I'm getting angrier.

This is taking too long. The longer it takes, the longer Daphne goes without remembering us.

The lady behind the desk smiles, her brunette hair pulled back into a perfect bun, and she grabs the microphone and announces. "Now boarding flight 1289 to New Orleans, Louisiana."

"First thing we do when we get there is go see Pocus."

"Not a chance in hell. I'm going to go see Daphne," I say to Reaper.

"Not without us."

"Yes, I am. I am not going to do anything. I just want to see her, that's it. Like I used to." I've missed watching her. It's how we started.

And maybe that's what she needs a reminder of.

This jet is going to fall to the damn ground when we get on it. It's so damn small. I really hate flying.

But I'll do anything for Daphne, even if my feet are thirty thousand feet up in the air.

And when my feet are on the ground, I'll show them what *anything* consists of.

I'll need to find this Satan hat that woman spoke of.

I'll need the extra edge.

CHAPTER EIGHTEEN

Daphne

I sit up in bed, my skin prickling with awareness. It's dark. The only sound is the *whoosh* of the ceiling fan.

But I feel someone in here. A presence. I'm not scared.

Ever since I came back home, there has been this cloud of danger hovering over my head. I'm in the same house my mother died in, and the way my dad looks at me… it's like he wants me dead too. The energy in the room is so powerful it dissipates the creeping chill over my skin.

The door my dad busted down all those years ago is still wonky. The trim is nailed in place. He hasn't even bothered to replace it.

I wait for my eyes to adjust to the night, and for some reason, I try to see if anyone is in the corner. It's reflex, like I'm expecting someone to be there.

"I feel you," I whisper into the room.

I wait for him to say something, to say anything, but he doesn't. Headlights peek through the window for a second as a car drives by, giving me a glimpse of the room.

I stop breathing when I see a flash of a tall, broad man in the far corner of my room, where my dresser is. It still has a butterfly sticker on the middle drawer. I turn on the lamp to get a better look at the man, but he isn't there. I check all of the corners of the room, but he isn't there. I know I didn't make him up.

He was there.

"Please, tell me if you're there. Mentally, I can't take anymore unknowns," I beg, my heart nearly bursting from my chest with hope.

I know him.

I feel him.

But how?

I expect him to say something, anything, but the ceiling fan is all I hear as it spins in circles.

Maybe he was in my head.

I don't even know who I am anymore. I don't want to be in this house. I don't want to be under the same roof as my father. I'm scared.

I miss… someone.

The cotton pillowcase rubs against my cheek as I bury my face into it and sob. I clutch my hand over my heart, hating how much it hurts and hating even more that I don't understand why. "What's happening to me?" I wail, stifling my cries in the pillow so Daddy doesn't hear me.

He'll get mad.

I rub my nose against my shirt and sniffle, then tuck my hands under my damp cheek. There are too many unknowns in my life.

And all of my questions revolve around Daddy.

What's that say about what I know?

I thought I remembered a time when Daddy got sober and our life together was good, but now that I'm here, I'm wondering if that's just what I made myself believe so I felt better.

If I felt what I feel now, then it isn't surprising I left. But why did Aunt Tina come back if Daddy is a bad man? Why am I here? What power does he have over me?

Did I make up the birthday parties? My friends?

If all of it is fake, then what happened to my mom?

The burn on my chest stings, and I hiss as I readjust myself in bed.

"Holy Moly. Just forget it," I gripe and sit up, then turn on the lamp again. I'm never going to be able to sleep in this hell hole.

A man laying across my tattered pink chaise lounge appears. I open my mouth on a scream, but when I see his face, no sound comes out. I crawl to the side of the bed to get a better look at him. The light moves across half of his face, and when his eyes land on mine, my worries halt. He has shaggy dark hair and a short beard. His gaze is penetrating, reaping my soul inside out and right side up. He is wearing a black leather cut that says 'Ruthless Kings', similar to the one Seer wore. His legs are long and encased in worn denim jeans with scuffed black boots.

The scent of pine and leather tickles my senses and the oddest sensation comes over me.

I *know* him.

I don't know how I know, but I do.

He's so familiar.

"Are you afraid of me?" he asks, his voice swinging low and deep as the lowest note of a trombone.

"Should I be?" It's the wrong question to ask. The man can obviously kill me with a snap of his finger.

"No, Comet. I'd never hurt you."

"Comet." My brows push together when I hear the word. "Comet," I repeat, a throbbing I my head pressing against my skull. There's a memory there.

"Yes." He rushes to the ground, falling to his knees. "You're my Comet. My name is Tongue, but my given name is Wayne Hendrix. Seer says you don't remember us."

I shake my head and my lips wobble. This unbearable feeling weighs down on me. "Not yet, but I think I remember how I feel, and I've felt…"

"What?"

"I've been feeling like I miss someone deeply. Like when I see shadows and an alligator sticker. It makes me feel… happy. Why is that?"

"We have a pet alligator. His name is Happy. And we met in the shadows, Comet. You made me feel what love was the moment I met you."

"Why can't I remember?" I begin to cry.

"You do," he whispers, knee-walking until he is at the edge of the bed. "Can I touch you? Would that bother you?"

I shake my head and lean to his hand when he lifts in the air to touch my cheek. One touch. Why do I have a feeling all it would take, is one touch?

"Who the fuck are you talking to?" Daddy yells. His drunken steps tumble down the hall to my room.

Glancing at my door, then back to Tongue, I'm surprised to see he isn't there. But he was. I know it.

Daddy opens the door and fumbles over his own two feet, then hits the side of my dresser. The light from the hallway trickles into my room, and that's when I see him standing in the far left corner. He's staring Daddy down, a furious expression on his face. A knife glints in the cheap yellow glow.

And that turns me on.

"You're lyin'!" he spits, turning up the bottle of Jack Daniels in his hand. "I heard you. Walls are paper thin, Daphne. It's how I caught your whore of a mother cheatin' on me! Fuckin' him in my own goddamn house." He points the liquor bottle at me and chuckles in his dirty tighty-whities. He isn't wearing a shirt, and his pot belly from drinking so much is pronounced. His boobs are nearly as big as mine, and he has sweat dripping down his chest. There are cigarette burns on his underwear, small black rings in the material from where he fell asleep with one in his hand in his recliner. "Keep it down in here. I won't say it again," he warns before storming out of the room the best he can, but not before his shoulder and the edge of the door meet. "Ah! Stupid fuckin' bitch." He pushes the door with his hand as if it's the one in the way. The knob digs into the cheap drywall causing it to crumble.

His ambling footsteps and incoherent mumbling gets further down the hall and Tongue's boot lifts from the shadow and slowly shuts it. "I can kill him."

"He's my dad." I say it in way that has an 'explanation to itself' tone.

"Family doesn't always mean blood, Comet."

I twist the yellow blanket between my fingers. It's something I've had since I was a little girl. It used to bring me comfort, but not anymore. Nothing does.

Except Tongue.

My mind might not recall my memories, but my heart remembers how I feel.

"We're more than friends, aren't we?"

He walks so quietly for a man that's as big as he is. He stops at the foot of my bed, and I'm drawn to the tattoos on his arms. "You're my best friend and the love of my life, Comet."

"Why can't I remember you, then?" I sob. "Why am I here?"

"You do remember." He makes his way to my side of the mattress, sits down beside me, and takes my hand. I inhale as his fingers brush over mine. Sparks—no, something more than sparks—dance over the nerve-endings on my skin. It's so much more.

It's fire and ice, a million needles dancing and whirling in a tango over my skin.

I imagine this is what the heat of the sun feels like.

"Yeah, Comet," his voice deepens. "You remember." The rough pad of his finger strokes the top of my hand.

I gasp, my eyes fluttering like the butterflies in my stomach as he travels up, caressing my bicep next. My entire body trembles, reacting to the simplest touch, but I have a feeling nothing is simple with this man.

"Every time I touch you feels like the first time. The way you feel right now—" his fingers drag up my shoulder and to my neck, grabbing hold of it like he has done it a hundred times.

My body tells me he has, because I arch my back, tilting my head to give him access to do with me whatever he wants. This is crazy. I've never met this man in my life. But then there is that push in the back of my mind, the one that bends reality, and most of the time in my life nothing makes sense.

When I look at Tongue, I know everything is going to be okay. A shift happens inside my soul and life makes sense. Then when he touches me, I'm yearning for the memories we have already made. I want to know what we have together.

"What if I never remember again?" The thought of that scares me to death. I hold a hand over my mouth and muffle a sob. "What if this is all I have? What if this life is all I know?"

"It isn't," he says, as if it is so simple. "What you feel right now says you know a lot more than you think." He rests his forehead against the side of my head. "And if I have to, I'll remember for the both of us. I'll tell you every moment we have ever had together."

"Yeah?" I ask him with a watery smile.

"Yeah, Comet. I'd do anything for you." He turns around and stares at the door when the sound of the TV gets louder. "You have no idea how hard it is not to kill him right now after....." He swallows and his Adam's apple bobs. "It isn't my place to say. You need to remember on your own, so you can make the right decision."

"He's mean and a drunk, a mean drunk, but he doesn't deserve to die."

"He does for what he did to you, your mom, and your aunt."

"My mom killed herself." My eyes widen when he grabs the sides of my face. His brown eyes dart between mine.

His thumbs trace the edges of my mouth. "I know you don't believe that."

I pull away from his touch and scurry out of the bed. My T-shirt falls to my knees. "No, I don't know you! You... You're here in my room. I don't even know how you got in my house—"

"—I broke the back window and climbed through," he says unapologetically, shrugging his shoulder. "And don't say you don't know me." He pushes off the bed and towers to his full height. I have to crane my neck to see his face. "You know me," he growls, my heart reacting to the gravelly timbers. He takes a step forward. "You know what you feel for me."

"You.... you...." I poke a finger against his very muscular chest and the air from my lungs escapes me. "Holy Moly." I don't mean to say that out loud, but *wow*, that's an impressive chest.

His lips tilt in an awkward smirk.

"I still don't know you." My vibrato is weak as he takes a step closer.

His lips curls in rage. "Yes, you do. You are mine, Daphne. I am yours. You know that."

"I know you are in my house. In the corners, hiding in the dark. Normal people don't do that. I'm going to have to ask you to leave." *Before I spontaneously combust with arousal.*

He buries his fingers in my hair, then yanks my head back as he fists the stands. "We are far from normal, Comet." He brushes his lips against my chest. "One thing you should know about us—" he skims his mouth to my ear and nibbles the lobe before he whispers, "—We fell in love in the dark. And make no mistake, you will fall in love with me again in the dark."

My eyes shut on their own accord, my body pressing against his.

He lets me go and his warmth leaves me as I open my eyes again to stare at a ghost. He's no longer there, but my door is open. I know my mind isn't playing tricks on me, not with how my body is yearning for his touch again.

I understand why my eyes have been drifting to the corners, examining the shadows, and why my heart has been waiting for a reason why.

I trust the dark.

The shadows are my home.

The corners are my comfort.

And the darkness is a place for me to be loved.

CHAPTER NINETEEN

Tongue

"**A**ND WHERE HAVE YOU BEEN?"

I pause as I'm entering through the window of the bedroom I'm staying in at the NOLA clubhouse. It's an old plantation-style home that's a little run down from how old it is. It has charm, though. Pocus said when he became Prez, the first thing he did was rip down the slave quarters. Then he brought in a witch to cast the ghosts to their resting place so they can finally be at peace.

He didn't want to be the reason why they continued to suffer, when they had suffered long enough.

I feel like I'm a teenager getting caught sneaking inside after my curfew. Reaper flips on the light and reveals himself. He is sitting in the corner, left ankle over his right knee, and his fingers are pressed together in a steeple position.

"I was with Daphne." Part of me hates that she can't remember, but it's kind of fucking hot too. My cock is still hard from how she reacted to me. Getting her to want me again won't be a problem. She feels we are meant to be. I have no doubt we will be together again.

"Did you kill him?"

I jump down from the window and close it, locking it in place. "No. I didn't."

He blows out a breath and snags the bottle of beer off the coffee table to take a swig. "Good. We need more information about him."

"I wanted to."

"I know."

"No, Reaper, I don't think you do know." I sit on the bed and lift my hands in the air to show him how bad they are shaking. "I'm so fucking mad. The restraint. I held myself back, but it was the most difficult thing I've ever had to do. He was there, drunk, wearing only underwear, and how he talked to her... it's no wonder she's so damn confused. His abuse is powerful, Reaper."

He squeezes my shoulder. "I know, Tongue. I'm sorry. Come on, let's go get you a beer and talk to their doctor and tech guy. We are going to see what we can find, okay?"

"What's there to find out? Her dad is a terrible man, and he needs to die."

"Terrible people always have a reason to do terrible things. What's his?"

"People don't need a reason to do bad things, Reaper. It's as simple as them liking the pain they inflict." I put myself in that category. I don't consider myself a good person, not with what I do and why I do it. Simple fact of the matter is, I love the pain I inflict. I love the suffering I bring to others. I know my soul is damned to the wicked. I'm going to go down in smoke and flames, and the ride to hell will be one I will enjoy.

We walk down the hallway, the brownish-red hardwood floors creaking under us. I take the time to look around and inspect the house. The ceiling is high, and there are chandeliers hanging low. They seem like they were installed with the place. They aren't illuminated, but there are lamps attached to the wall every few feet that are turned on to show us the way.

A cold chill rips through me, and I have to stop walking to catch my breath. I shiver. A cold cloud leaves from between my lips as if the temperature just dropped to thirty degrees.

Reaper is a few steps ahead me and he pauses, looks over his shoulder, and bobs his head as he waves his hand. "Well, come on what are you waiting for?"

"Sorry, cold chill."

"It's hot in there. What are you talking about?" Reaper takes out a black handkerchief and pats the back of his neck.

"Sorry, *mon amie*," Pocus apologizes as we come into the impressive main room. They have a large bar that takes up one entire wall with shelves of booze. We don't have that in our clubhouse anymore because of Patrick. I'm fine with it. It isn't a big deal.

But right now, selfishly, I'm glad to kick back and pop a top without feeling bad about it.

What can I say? I guess I'm an asshole.

"The air conditioning broke yesterday. We're waiting on the guy to come and fix it. Every now and then, you'll feel a cold chill. It happens in a house with old bones like this." When we get the bar, the guy behind it has a 'prospect' cut and Pocus slaps his hand on the black cement bar top. "Two beers, Buffy."

"You got it, Prez." The kid can't be a day over twenty-one, but he double fists the bottles and pops the tops off them at the same time. He places them in front of us and I can see the sweat dripping down the outside of the bottle. A beautiful fat droplet that I can't help but bring to mouth and sigh from how refreshing it is.

"Cold chill? That shouldn't happen when the air conditioning is out," I mention, following Pocus to the couch where a few of the guys are talking amongst themselves.

"*Mon amie*, haven't you ever heard of ghosts?" Seer reveals himself in the front entryway, leaning against the wall with his arms and legs crossed. He has a big smile on his face.

"Don't believe in ghosts," I say, lifting the bottle to my lips.

Seer's laugh booms, which somehow even has a slight Cajun twist to it. "Oh, I know that ain't right. You do, you just don't want to admit it. There are a few in this house. They're harmless."

"Yeah, they ain't no problem," Hex chimes in from the middle of the couch. His arms are spread wide across the back. "I've talked to them a few times to make sure. They like it here. They feel safe."

Reaper spews his beers out, then coughs, which makes me wonder how Tool would act. Damn it, I wish he were here.

"I'm fine," Reaper chokes again, his eyes turning red from the force of the cough. "Went down the wrong way."

Hex smirks knowingly, "Sure, *mon amie*. That's it."

New Orleans is a whole other animal. There is shit here I do not and will not understand, but that's the beauty about cultural differences. I can appreciate them even if I don't completely understand them.

"Go on, sit down. Don't let these fools scare you off." Pocus sits down and Seer takes the seat beside him. The couch is big enough for ten people to fuck and sleep on.

The leather gives and molds to my body. I groan and drop my head against the cushion. This is a comfortable couch. I turn my head right to left. "Where is Bullseye?" I notice he isn't around. I only see a huge flat screen TV hanging on the wall and a few portraits.

I swear, they are looking right at me.

"He's in bed. He isn't feeling too hot, but doesn't want to admit it because of his pride," Seer says.

"Dumbass," Reaper hisses and goes to push himself up when Seer lifts his palm to stop him.

"Leave him be. He will learn the hard way. Don't we have work to do for Daphne?" he asks, bringing us to the task at hand.

"Yeah." Fast typing from my right has me staring at a slim guy. "I'm Snake, we have met before. Briefly," he clarifies.

"Snake? What earned you that name?"

"I slither through all necessary evils to gain information." The reflection of the computer shines in the guy's eyes.

"I need to go check on Bullseye," Reaper says. "I don't feel comfortable not checking in."

"Graveyard is with him. He's fine. Getting the insulin he needs," Pocus states, placing his elbows on his knees. "He's our doctor."

"And his name is Graveyard? That's not too reassuring."

"Should be, considering his graveyard doesn't have anyone in it—"

The front door opening has everyone turning to see who it is. Lightning strikes across the sky and thunder rolls right after. The man shakes his jacket and pulls down his hood.

Oh, fuck no.

"What the fuck is he doing here?"

"He deserved to come, Tongue. Sit down and don't cause any problems."

"She's my daughter and you won't stop me from protecting her."

Mercy has the audacity to imply I can't protect her.

"Sit. Down," Reaper's tone leaves no room for argument as he grips my hand. "Now."

I crack my neck and do as I'm told. I never take my eyes off Mercy as he drags a plastic chair from the corner, spins it backwards, and sits down. Water drips everywhere around him, and he slicks his silver hair back over his head to keep the wet strands out of his face.

I hate him.

"You could have told me."

"And deal with your grouchy ass from Vegas to here? No, thanks," Reaper answers me and then chugs down his beer.

Snake claps his hands together. "Okay, before this bickering gives me a headache. Her father—uh—sorry, Mercy. Her other father? I don't know how to phrase it."

"It's okay. I haven't exactly earned the title," he says.

"Damn right," I grumble and it earns me a hard slap in the chest.

"He has a record a mile long," Snake ignores us and continues typing. "He has a crap ton of arrests from twenty years ago. All assault and battery charges, but they were always dropped."

Mercy inhales a sharp breath and rubs his eyes. I feel bad for him. I'm being a bastard to him, but he just found out the woman he loved was abused and he had a daughter. I need to learn to be nice.

"A few drunk and disorderlies from a few different bars. DUI. His license is revoked. He shouldn't be driving," Snake clacks away at the keyboard. I've never seen fingers move so fast.

I'm jealous. I want to type like that, but I need to learn how to read and write better first.

"It isn't too far-fetched he'd go too far. I'd say what happened to Michelle most definitely had something to do with him."

"Oh, it did," A guy coming from the hallway carrying a small black pack in one hand states. In the other, he has a file. "Here. This is for Bullseye. I know he already has one, but this is for you to keep if you feel necessary to check his sugar like he is a damn teenager."

"All of my members are fucking teenagers," Reaper snaps, side-eying me as if I'm a culprit.

Only right now... the rest of the time I'm not even noticeable.

"We haven't met. I'm Graveyard. You don't see me around because I work a few nights over at the local hospital. It's the only reason I was able to get this file. It was sealed."

Now that gets my attention. "Sneaky," I say, impressed.

"You have your ways, I have mine." He opens the file, and one flap hits the table with a small slap. "The autopsy report says she was shot in the head, but she was also shot in the shoulder."

"That isn't too common with suicides, is it?" Reaper asks.

"No. And statistically, it's more likely for woman to pick a less violent method, like overdosing on drugs or the car fumes in the garage. A gun to the head is a man's top choice." He pulls out a few pictures and lays them on the table. "These are pictures of the crime scene—"

"Oh, Michelle," Mercy's voice breaks as he reaches for a picture. He rubs his fingers in his eyes to stop the tears, but it's no use. The longer he stares at the image of his dead lover, the more emotional he gets.

"You know her?" Graveyard asks. "I'm sorry, I didn't know."

"We should have told you. He is the biological father of Daphne, and this is her mother," Pocus advises with a regretful tone.

"Fuck, man. I'm sorry." Graveyard tries to pick up the pictures, but Mercy stops him by grabbing his wrist.

"Don't. I need to see what I could have prevented." He analyzes the photographs and closes his eyes. "She died wearing the locket I gave her."

I take a peek at a picture and see a silver locket covered in blood around her neck, hanging down to where it nearly touches the carpet in the picture. Mercy traces it with his finger, staring at her as if she had just died yesterday.

I guess she did. To him, at least.

No one knows what to say. There's nothing to say. Nothing can make him feel better.

The thick expanse of Graveyard's throat moves as he swallows. "So, it's impossible for these wounds to have been made by her. Her father's statement says he was trying to wrestle the gun away from her, but it backfired."

"That isn't possible?"

"No, the size of the wound, the gunpowder residue, the angle, she was most definitely shot at. And when he had her weak, he shot her between the eyes."

"Why wouldn't they catch that?"

"Twenty years ago. They probably saw a mess they didn't want to clean up, and suicide was the easiest way," Graveyard explains. "No real proof it was him either."

"That's not true," I realize. "Daphne witnessed it."

"She's an unreliable witness, because of the psychosis."

I slam my fist on the table and sneer my teeth at Graveyard. "Because she saw him kill her mother."

"Doesn't matter. Besides, there's no way for us to prove it in court. It's been too long."

"So I can kill him?" I say happily.

"Like we were going to do any different." Reaper rolls his eyes.

"Y'all, I just found a pretty good reason why her father attacked her aunt," Snake pipes up.

Mercy stands and drops the picture in his hand. "Tina was attacked? What the fuck? Is there anything else you're leaving out?"

Reaper rubs his temples. "No, that's it. I'm sorry for not telling you."

"Is she okay?" he asks, black brows so tight together they look like one.

"She's hanging in there," Seer says with a positive nod and gives Mercy a warm grin.

"Okay," Mercy nods. "Daphne can't lose her too."

"Snake, what were you saying?"

"There was a will that Michelle left. She left all of her money to Daphne, but she could only get it when she turned twenty-six. Until then she had a guardian. Her aunt."

"Her birthday is in June. He wanted her aunt to sign everything over, and she said no. That's the only thing that makes sense. And he called Daphne because he knew he could get into her mind and fucking manipulate her to sign over the money. It can't be much, right? The trailer is falling apart. She struggled growing up."

"Because her mom was paying into an account for Daphne. She only kept what she needed to get by. It's grown—" Snake whistles. "Two million dollars. No wonder her dad wants the will. He didn't get life insurance since it was suicide and not an accident. Fuck, that's why he wants Tina dead. If she dies, he is going to get that money."

"No fucking way am I going to let my little girl suffer more than she already has. I'm going to kill that sonofabitch!"

"We can kill him together." Lightning cracks outside, matching the fury in my heart. Mercy and I have a long stare off before he concedes.

Seer's eyes are bright as he looks off into the distance. "He's going to the hospital tomorrow." He blinks and then sags against the couch, then examines my arm. "He's going to rip a few of those stitches open."

"I don't care," I say, finishing off my beer. "It won't be the only scar I have."

"I can staple it tonight to give it a better chance at not opening up," Graveyard offers, picking up the pictures and putting them in the file.

"Can y'all bring the guy here? I want to see the Vegas boys in action, and see what the fuss is about," Graveyard says.

Well, the NOLA chapter is about to get one hell of a show, because I'm not going to stop until this man is disemboweled.

And if Hex can see ghosts, I hope he witnesses Daphne's father's soul being dragged to hell or I'll become the hellhound that rips him to pieces.

CHAPTER TWENTY

Daphne

A SLAP OF A HAND ACROSS MY CHEEK HAS MY HEAD JERKING TO THE RIGHT AND THE handle of the coffee cup slipping out of my hand. It shatters on the floor with the coffee, which earns me another hit on my other cheek. My eyes water and my jaw drops open from the sting. Something flashes in my mind, a vision of him hitting my mom in the same fashion.

"Since you can't make a decent drink, I'm going to the fuckin' bar," Daddy slurs, already drunk.

"How am I going to get to the hospital to see Aunt Tina?" I ask, holding in the tears as my cheek throbs.

"I don't give a shit. Figure it out, Michelle," he calls me by my mother's name and as he stares at me, I don't see love but pure hate.

He snatches the keys from the fruit bowl and leaves me holding my cheek. He kicks the coffee table as he passes by it, then kicks the screen door open with his foot. The door comes off its hinges, which doesn't seem too difficult since it's so cheap.

Crying, I kneel on the floor and pick up the pieces of the mug, careful to place them in my palm so I don't cut myself. I wipe my cheek on my shirt and think about Tongue, wishing he was here so I felt safe. Something about this house makes my nerves shake. My instincts roar at me to get out.

I toss the broken ceramic chunks in the trash, then grab a towel and clean up. The floor molts and moves, sways and dips, and I gasp. Someone is standing in front of me.

"No!" I scream and scurry away until my back hits the cabinet. The handle digs into the space of my shoulder and spine, a bruise I'll feel tomorrow.

It's my mother. She's in the dress we buried her in, drenched in dirt. Her skin is pale, and the gunshot wound in her head bleeds.

"You aren't real. You aren't real," I repeat, unable to take my eyes off her. Another form appears behind her.

Her mouth opens, her jaw continuing to the floor as she screams 'run' at me. My father is behind her, gun drawn. My heart is hammering as I stagger to my feet watching the horror unfold. The gunshot rings out. I hold my hands over my ears and close my eyes with a scream.

The ringing stops.

I can smell the gunpowder, like a bonfire's smoke clinging to someone's clothes. I peek one eye open to see if they are there, but the space is empty.

What if my mom didn't kill herself? What if I've been suppressing the truth?

I glance at the clock and see it's past ten a.m. and decide to get the hell out of here. I'm going to the hospital, and when I'm done, I'm going to find Tongue. I'm safer with him than I am here. I know that. I feel that. He would never lay a hand on me.

I run to my room and grab my purse, then sprint toward the front door. I step outside, one arm on the door handle as I turn around to take one last look at the place that's haunted my mind for far too long. Daddy's fear is no longer going to control me. I'm not going to fall into his ways again. Something about seeing my mother scream at me felt familiar, all too familiar. Like how it is with Tongue.

Which means I've experienced it before.

Damn this house.

Damn my mind.

But I won't damn what I feel.

My gut feeling is all I have to go on right now, and my gut is telling me to get the fuck out of here. My blue Converse sink into the mud as I cut through the pathetic front lawn and jump over a broken lawn gnome.

When I get to the road, I take a right and start the long journey to the hospital. It isn't too hot today since there is cloud coverage, but the air is still sticky. I swear, I can smell the rotten core of Bourbon Street too.

Like trash and booze.

And after a few days out in the New Orleans weather, that smell can even make a raccoon turn its nose up.

The sound of a motorcycle has me looking up from my feet to see down the dusty street. As it gets closer, a few bees fly around me, since I'm passing wildflowers. They don't bother me. A slap to the face doesn't hurt worse than a bee sting.

The bike rolls to a slow stop and Tongue places his feet on the ground. "What's my Comet doing out here all alone?" he takes off his sunglasses and grabs my chin. "Did he do that to your face?"

I lower my lashes, staring at the mud on my shoes.

"I'm going to fucking kill him." The gravel lodged in his throat makes me want to jump inside him so he can lull me to a deep sleep. His fingers play with a strand of my hair and he tucks it behind my ear. His lips are on my cheek next, warm and soft, a complete contradiction to the tough armor he wears. "No one hurts my Comet without paying a price."

My clit throbs. I don't understand why I'm turned on by him threatening to kill my father, but I am. Something about being overly protected has me wanting to mount him right on his bike. Maybe it's because the man who I was supposed to count on in life didn't do a bang-up job at protecting me, and now that I have it in spades, I want every ounce of protective instinct he can give me.

"You have no idea how much I've missed you, Comet. I'm not going to push you, but I want you to know how much I want to kiss you. I've missed your lips." His hot breath tickles the space under my ear and goosebumps travel all over my body, tightening my nipples from the chill.

And it is far from cold outside.

"Everywhere. I've missed your lips everywhere. My mouth, my neck, my chest—"

I whimper.

"My cock," his voice turns dark and sinful, twisting its way into my soul like a cruel addiction.

My mouth waters, and I ache to taste him in the back of my throat.

"I miss worshipping your body."

I turn toward him, our lips inches apart, and that familiar feeling returns.

I think I miss all those things too.

No.

I *know* I do.

"Kiss me," I say breathlessly, staring at the full red lips. My fingers hover over his cheeks because I'm afraid to touch him.

Afraid because he's the most magnificent man I've ever seen. His stubble scratches my palm and his head tilts back, so I roam down his neck, then over his shoulders and he grabs my hips. He groans when I skim along his pecs, feeling the muscle tense.

From me.

"Kiss—"

My words are silenced as he pushes our bodies together and slams his lips onto mine.

A flash of us tangled in the sheets slams against my mind. don't know if it's me thinking about what I want or what I've already had with him.

But I want it again.

And again.

Our tongues tangle, and he rocks my hips over the intimidatingly long erection tenting his jeans. I have to break away from him for a minute to catch my breath and a slight whine escapes me when he hits the bundle of electrified nerves.

He shoves me away, and for a moment I think it's because of something I did when he unzips his pants, fishes out his cock, grips the thick meat, and pumps twice.

"Comet," he shouts my name into the sky for any and all to hear, points his cock to the dirt, and comes.

My eyes widen as I watch the thick streams paint the ground. "Holy Moly," I rasp in awe.

"Ah, fuck yes. I told you," he gasps. "I've missed you so fucking much. Look what you do to me." He squeezes the last droplet out of the slit, and I don't know what comes over me, but the pearly drop is too pretty to deny. I bend down and lick it off the hot, red crown. His salty taste slides down my throat, and now I wish it hadn't all gone to waste on the ground.

He wraps his hands around my hair and pulls me back. "I might have come quick because I've missed you so goddamn bad, but my cock is always ready for round two. You suck me, I'm going to bend you over this bike and fuck you, Comet. My recovery time is impeccable. Don't you fucking forget that, and it always will be when it comes to you."

I moan against his neck and rock my hips onto his knee as I straddle him. I ache to be filled by him. I claw at his back and create as much friction as I can.

"That's it, Comet. Use me. "

"I want you." I have an eagle's eye view of his cock.

"Not until you remember."

"Why?" I cry out in frustration, dry humping his thigh harder.

He wraps a hand around my throat and forces me to meet his flushed face. "Because I need you to remember how much you love me."

My orgasm crashes over me and Tongue's arm wraps around my waist as I fall against him. I'm gasping the humid air and my entire body is shaking with aftershocks. I grin as he pushes the hair from my forehead. "I want to do that again."

"That's my Comet," he laughs, searching my eyes for… memories.

"I'm sorry, I don't…"

"It's okay. I mean it." He gives me a kiss on top of my head, then sighs as he pulls away. He tucks himself in. Even semi-hard, he is big. "Stop looking at me like that. I'm only so strong, Comet. Hop on and hold on tight." He pats the seat behind him, then hands me his helmet. "Are you going to see your Aunt Tina?"

"How did you know?"

"I know everything about you."

If any other man said that to me, I'd be scared, but knowing he cares so much to find out everything about me has that silly organ in my chest tripping over itself.

I throw my leg over the bike and settle in behind him. I wrap my arms around his waist and his rough hands that promise a hard day's work caress me for moment. My skin is alive, I'm alive, and I smile for the first time since…

Probably since I saw him last.

"Feels so good to have your hands on me," he admits. "You scared me when I woke up alone in bed and you were nowhere to be found."

"You were scared? You don't look like a man that scares easy," I reply, resting my cheek against his back. The leather of his cut is warm from the day, but comfortable against the bruise on my cheek.

"I do when it comes to you. Always when it comes to you." He cranks the bike again, and the vibrations tickle between my legs, igniting another round of sensations.

Why can't the veil in my mind go away? Why can I remember how he makes me feel but I can't remember what we have built together?

He does a U-turn in the middle of the empty road and applies pressure on the throttle. We speed down the narrow street, passing a blur of trees on either side of us. My hair whips behind me and the ends sting my shoulders as they lash around me, snapping like serpents.

It feels right. Being here, with him. Even if I never remember, I know where I'm meant to be and that is where he is.

We pass the loud jazz of the French Quarter, and I wish he and I could spend the night experiencing the wild haunts of New Orleans.

All too soon he is pulling up to the hospital. I undo the strap under my chin and take off the helmet, then hop off the bike. My legs are tingling and wobbly. I giggle when I stumble, and he catches me.

"You okay, Comet?" he asks with a crooked grin, one that doesn't show teeth.

"Yeah, I think I'll be alright. I'll see you later, right?"

"In every dark corner you can find," he states.

As I stare at his face, I have one thing repeating in my head.

How can I love a man when the only memory I have is the one my heart tells me?

CHAPTER TWENTY-ONE

Tongue

My Comet is crazy if she thinks I'm going to let her go in there alone. I park my bike in the nearest spot, place my helmet on the seat, and follow in after her. I don't want her to feel smothered, especially after what happened between us. I didn't expect that. I was on my way over to check on her when she was walking down the road.

And one thing led to another…

It always does with us.

Memory be damned.

I dig my phone out of my pocket and send a voice message to Reaper. "I'm at the hospital now. I'll update you if I see her father and I'll act accordingly." I press the send button, then press the audio message again. "I won't kill him here," I clarify. "No matter how much I want to." I press send again and tuck the phone in my back pocket.

I pass the lady at the front desk. She's too busy taking on the phone to notice me slip by. Only family members can get into intensive care right now, and that's where Daphne is headed. I keep my eye on her back and make sure she gets to her aunt's room safely. I hide behind the closest wall and peek my head around the corner to see her talking to the doctor. A smile ghosts over her face and then tears drip down her cheek.

I'd kill him for making her cry if they didn't look like happy tears.

She turns around, after giving the male doctor a hug, and heads toward a door on the far left. When she opens it, I rush after her and stop the door from shutting with my boot, then dip inside, then dart into the bathroom. I crack the door so I can listen.

Why am I doing this again? Her Aunt knows me. If anything, she can verify who I am... which might not be a good thing.

I'll stay right here for now.

"Aunt Tina," Daphne's cries. "You're awake. Oh my god, I came as soon as Daddy called."

"No," her Aunt cries. "No, you... you... need... to leave. Your dad... Your dad is not who he says. He.... he... did..." she struggles to say as her heart rate monitor starts to race.

"Aunt Tina? Aunt Tina! Someone help her!" Daphne's pain screams throughout the halls, and I want to go out there and pull her to safety, but I know I can't. Not yet.

A stampede of doctors and nurses fly into the room. "Wait outside," they say to Daphne.

"No! She's my aunt. I can't leave her."

"Ma'am, we will get you when everything is settled. Wait outside, please," the nurse says with a stern, no argument tone.

I watch through the crack as Daphne gets pushed out the door. I hate to see her cry. I hate to see her hurt. I wish I could take all of her pain away and protect her from all the horrible things this world has to offer. That isn't realistic.

But I can try.

I'm not sure how long I hide in the bathroom, but I hear the doctors speak a flurry of medical words I don't understand and then declare her stable.

Thank fuck.

One by one, two white coats and a nurse in blue scrubs leave the room.

It's a long shot that her dad will come here today, but we can't be too safe. We have to protect her aunt at all costs and it's better if Daphne doesn't know the plan, so she doesn't feel like she has to lie to her dad.

Even if the man is a piece of shit, she will love him for the simple fact that he is her father. A privilege he will never deserve.

"I... know... you're... there...."

Aunt Tina's struggling words have me stepping out from the bathroom and into the shadow the room keeps, which is usually close to the wall or in a corner. Her blue eyes follow mine as I stand against the wall.

"How did you know?"

"She said... your... energy... buzzed the room every time...you entered it," she coughs, then licks her dry lips.

I come around the edge of the bed and grab the water pitcher off the stand and pour her a paper cup full. I bring it to her mouth and she greedily chugs it down. "Thank you," she croaks.

If the desert had a voice, it would be Tina's right now.

"Do you know what's going on with Daphne?"

She shakes her head and swallows.

"She doesn't remember anything about me, us, or Vegas. She found out her dad wasn't her dad. Come to find out, her mom had a thing with Mercy, a close friend of the club. Then her piece of shit father calls and tells her to come home because you're in the hospital. Why can't she remember?"

"She shuts down… when… she thinks… she's protecting herself, when the truth is… too close to the… surface."

That has me straightening my spine. "You knew how her mom died?"

She nods and a tear runs down her cheek. "I… tried… to get her away… but… I had no proof. Her dad… brainwashes her somehow and she… believes everything he says."

"She's a daughter looking for her father's love," I say in sadness.

Tina agrees and I pluck a tissue from the Kleenex holder and dab her cheeks dry. She hisses when I apply too much pressure. "Sorry." It sounds like a weak apology, which means it probably is. "Did you know about Mercy?"

Her lip trembles and she stares at the ceiling, her eyes filling to the brim. "Yes."

"Why didn't you tell Daphne!" I hiss, and I mean to sound as deadly as I can, because I'm close to taking a pillow and killing her for what she did. How long did she let Daphne suffer needlessly?

"Michelle… made me… promise not to say a word… I didn't… know… he… was alive."

"Very much so, and he has an axe to fucking grind. You people have got to start telling the truth." I lace my fingers behind my head and wonder what position this puts me in now. If she feels like everyone has lied to her, she'll close herself off from everyone, and who knows what her mind will conjure up to scare her. "Why didn't you tell her about the money?"

"She was determined… to work hard… for herself. Money wouldn't have mattered."

I worry my bottom lip as I stare out the window into the parking lot. My mind whirls with how to protect Daphne, but I don't know how anymore. Everyone around her has lied. I don't want to be lumped in with those people. If there is one thing our relationship has been built on, it's honesty.

"I'm giving her time to remember me on her own without trying to push her, but you and her dad and her mom… you guys are making that really fucking hard."

"I'm sorry…"

"Sorry doesn't fucking cut it. Sorry doesn't make her worries go away, does it? Lying to her all her life, what the fuck is wrong with you?"

"I was… protecting… her too. In… my own way."

I get in her face, my arms gripping the sides of the hospital bed to cage her head with my arms. The whites of her eyes are red from busted blood vessels and she has a busted top lip. "You chose wrong."

"I... know."

I straighten, not expecting her to admit her wrongs, but she does.

"You'll take... care of her? She's... never had that."

"She will always have that with me," I say honestly, just as a doctor hurries into our room, slams the door and leans against it. He's sweaty and pale.

And reeks of fear.

When he sees me, his eyes widen, and he stays low to the ground, then dives to the right to get hidden by a wall. "Don't panic," he stammers.

While panicking.

I'm impressed with no one here. Everyone is a goddamn pussy.

I stomp over and pick the twig up by the collar of his white jacket and slam him against the wall. His toes drag along the ground. "How about you don't panic and tell me what has your panties in a twist, doc."

"The hospital is on lockdown. No one in. No one out."

"Why?" I growl.

"There's a man with a gun and he has a hostage. He's on this floor," the doctor squirms.

A gunshot echoes outside and the hallways act as tunnels to make everyone's screams travel.

"Daphne," I gasp with horror, wearing the same fear as the man in front of me. "What does the man look like? The hostage?" I slam him against the wall again.

"I don't know," he begins to cry.

I slap him across the face and push my own fear aside. "Fucking get it together and be a man. What does he look like? And If don't tell me, I'll gut you right here, right now. I'm just as dangerous as the man outside, only I'm giving you a chance to live, so fucking tell me!" I roar as quickly as I can so no one can hear us.

"He—he—is older. White tank top, greasy hair—"

"And the hostage?"

"I don't know. I swear, I don't know. They didn't say. They paged Code Black, which means active shooter."

I drop him to the floor, and he cries out when he lands on his foot wrong. "Ah!" he grabs his ankle. "You broke my foot."

"Better than being dead." I step on his leg as I walk toward the door, which has him whimpering.

I grin.

Yeah, I can be a sadistic sonofabitch.

I peek out the narrow rectangular window in the door and see papers scattered along the floor. I grip the handle and turn it, but it's locked. "What?" I hiss and try again. I jiggle the handle and tug, but it won't budge. "Why won't the door open?"

"All doors are locked for safety. Only doctors can get in and out."

I get my knife out and the doctor pushes himself across the floor as far away as he can get from me. "Tina, I'm busting out of this room. I have a feeling the hostage is Daphne. You'll be vulnerable since the doctor is useless."

"I'll... be fine."

"I'm not useless," the doctor tries to justify.

I dig my phone out of my pocket and see fifteen messages from Reaper. I press play and hold the speaker to my ear. "Tongue, we can't get in the hospital and no one can get out. It's all over the news. We are in the parking lot, brother. We're here, but they won't allow us in. Be careful," the last message says.

I press the record button and lower my voice, "He is on our floor. I'm busting out of the room and going to find him on my own. I think he has Daphne. I told you I should have killed him the other night and none of this would be happening." I press send, then give my phone to Tina by tossing it to her. "Use that if you need to. The guys know I'm here."

"Be... careful. If it's her... save her."

"Always." I focus on the task at hand, push the panic and terror aside, bad thoughts, and breathe. I take the handle of my knife smash it against the glass.

Thud. Thud. Thud.

It takes a few times before it cracks, it won't budge. "Shit, I'm an idiot," I say to myself, then rush to Doctor Pansyass and grab his keycard. "Thanks for doing your part."

"No problem," he says with chattering teeth. He's in shock.

I slide the keycard over the black square and the door clicks when the light turns green. When I step into the main area of the intensive care unit, I'm shocked by how abandoned it is. Paper is everywhere, IV bags are busted on the floor, and that scent of fear is there again, making it hard to breathe. I take a right, down the hallway, listening.

"Oh, fuck," I whisper when I see a man lying face down in a puddle of his own blood. Gunshot to the abdomen. It was not a quick death. Looks like he traveled pretty far, according to the blood path. It leads all the way down another hall.

It's so quiet.

Too quiet.

The kind where something could happen at any moment.

Silence is loud if one listens carefully enough, and right now, it's telling me to be prepared for death.

I loop around by going down a back hallway. The lights flicker from being shot. There are a few more dead bodies. A nurse with a gunshot wound to the head and her elderly patient.

Another gunshot wound to the head.

He knows what he likes, doesn't he?

Blood is everywhere.

And for the first time in my life, I dread seeing it.

I do another loop and find the rest of the halls empty and find myself back at Tina's room.

I hear a click and the warm barrel of a gun pointed against the back of my head.

Execution style.

His favorite.

The End… for now.

TONGUE'S TARGET PLAYLIST

GOOEY BY GLASS ANIMALS

DEVIL LIKE ME BY RAINBOW KITTEN SURPRISE

GLASS HEART BY CAPTIVES

NO MATTER WHAT BY CALUM SCOTT

SOMETHING WONDERFUL BY SEAWAY

SEE YOU IN HELL BY WSTR

DROWN IN MY MIND BY STORY UNTOLD

I'M SORRY BY MOKITA

WORKDS OF PROGRESS BY ACROSS THE ATLANTIC

HOME BY SECRET EYES

ACKNOWLEDGMENTS

To our Ruthless Readers we just couldn't let go of Tongue. Thank you for sticking with us!

Give Me Books here's to another great release.

To all the bloggers and reviewed and shared Tongue's Target thanks y'all are the best.

To Wander and Andrey you truly are the best! Thank you for being my rocks.

Donna we love you! #BOOMERISDONNAS

Stacey at Champagne Book Design thanks for all your amazing work.

To my Instigator you are stronger than you think.

Lynn you're the best friend a girl could ask for.

Silla thanks for everything you do!

Carolina the torture continues, but I know you like it.

Harloe you are amazing

Mom love you

Jeff 5 LITTLE WORDS

Austin as always y'all are such a blessing

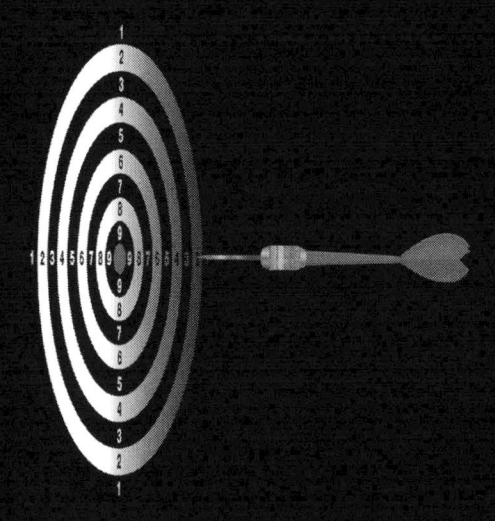

BULLSEYE
RUTHLESS KINGS MC
BOOK TWELVE

COPYRIGHT © 2021 BULLSEYE BY KL SAVAGE

All rights reserved. Except as permitted by U.S. Copyright Act of 1976, no part of this publication may be reproduced, distributed, or transmitted in any form or by any means, or stored in a database or retrieval system, without prior permission of the author. The scanning, uploading, and distribution of this book via the Internet or via other means without the permission of the publisher is illegal and punishable by law. Please purchase only authorized electronic editions and do not participate in or encourage electronic piracy of copyrighted materials. This book is a work of fiction. Names, characters, establishments, or organizations, and incidents are either products of the author's imagination or are used fictitiously to give a sense of authenticity. Any resemblance to actual persons, living or dead, events, or locales is entirely coincidental. BULLSEYE is intended for 18+ older, and for mature audiences only.

COVER DESIGN: LORI JACKSON DESIGN
EDITING BY: INFINITE WELL
FORMATTING: CHAMPAGNE BOOK DESIGN

FIRST EDITION PRINT 2021

To all the children who are lost. We think of you, we hope for you, and we pray for you. Every 40 seconds, a child is missing or abducted. According to Bureau's National Crime Information center in 2017, there were 32,000 missing persons under the age 18.
We love you and we hope you come home.

"He who passively accepts evil is as much involved in it as he who helps to perpetrate it."
—Dr. Martin Luther King Jr.

PART ONE

Note: If you do not care for the backstory, flip to Part Two.

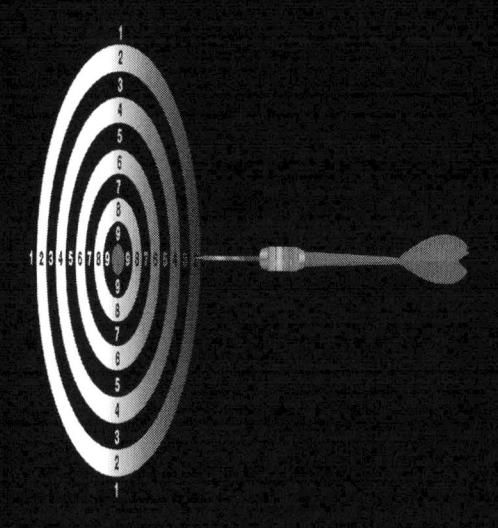

CHAPTER ONE
Bullseye

Eight years old

There is one thing I love more than pizza, and that is having pizza at the fair. Mom and Dad promised they would take me when it came to town and today is opening day. I can't wait. I've been dreaming about pizza for weeks now, but I haven't eaten any because I want it to taste like I've never had it before. It's going to be cheesy and greasy and delicious, and I need it now!

I throw my Batman blanket off me and climb out of bed, then do what I always do first thing in the morning—brush my teeth.

It's the first thing they always ask me in the morning. I want to make sure I do everything right today, so nothing messes us up going to the carnival.

I flip on the bathroom light and giggle when I see my hair. It's crazy, standing up in all directions. Dad says it's nearly impossible to tame my hair. I like it. Makes me feel like it's my superpower or something. Every strand holds something I know.

Smiling at myself, I stand on my tiptoes and reach for my Superman toothbrush. I think he's the best superhero, and he has all the powers. I'd love to fly one day.

I squeeze the toothpaste container a little too hard, and the toothpaste shoots out all over my toothbrush. Some of it falls down into the sink, and I make a face at it as if it committed the ultimate crime. Mom will not be happy if there's toothpaste in the sink. I shove my toothbrush in my mouth and turn on the sink, scrubbing the pink paste so it can go down the drain.

Spit leaves my mouth and drips down my chin. It's gross but so cool at the same time. I wonder how far I can spit.

I brush my teeth fast and grin at myself in the mirror to see the foam all across my mouth. I stick out my tongue and scrub just like Dad taught me. That's where all the stinky breath lives. Once that's done, I spit in the sink and wash my mouth out with water, then I dry my face with the towel hanging on the silver rod beside the shower.

With too much excitement and energy, I bolt out of the bathroom and use the wall to swing through the doorway and run down the hallway. There's a bunch of pictures lining the wall of all of us, but it's the last one on the right that I love the most.

It's of the three of us at Disneyworld, taking a picture in front of the castle. I loved it there. I hope next year we can go to Universal when I grow a little more, so I can fit on the rollercoaster. I can't wait to grow up. Being small sucks.

Oops.

I'm not allowed to use that word.

Their bedroom door is cracked, and I slam into it so hard, the door slams into the wall. The metal of the doorknob crashing into the wall sends my Dad jackknifing forward with sleepy eyes. He's lost and has no idea what's going on right now.

I jump in bed between them, and it bounces, which disrupts Mom's sleep.

"What is it? What's wrong?" Dad grumbles, rubbing his left eye with his fist.

"It's so early." Mom's voice is muffled by the pillow.

"It isn't! It isn't! It's seven. I waited a whole hour to get you. Please, please, please. We have to get up and get ready. The fair is here. The fair!" I squeal and begin to bounce again.

"Sweetie, the fair doesn't start until the afternoon," Mom chuckles, wrapping her arm around me to pull me down on the bed. She gives me a kiss on the side of my cheek.

"Afternoon? I've waited forever," I groan, displeased to learn this new information.

"Tell you what," Dad offers, swinging his legs over the bed. "I'll fix us breakfast. Bacon, eggs, pancakes, orange juice, maybe a mimosa for your Mom...?" Dad questions slowly and sends me a wink.

I look over to see Mom peek an eye open at us, which makes me giggle.

"With some mango juice?" she asks.

Dad rolls his eyes. "Obviously. What else is there?"

"What's a mimosa?" I've heard Dad say it a few times, but I've never asked.

"It's a drink that will get Mommy out of bed."

"Like a superhero drink? I want one!" I say excitedly.

"Oh no, buddy. This drink is for adults only. Your little body can't handle it. It's made for grownups."

I fall back dramatically and sigh. "Everything good is."

Mom's lighthearted laugh sounds like music when she finally sits up. I love Mom's laugh. It's my favorite. "You know what isn't just for grownups?"

I drop my arm from my eyes and sit up on my forearms. "What?"

She wiggles her fingers. "Tickles," she playfully growls before launching herself at me and digging her fingers into my ribs.

I scream and try to roll away, but I'm trapped with Dad's legs on one side and Mom's on the other. "Okay, okay, stop it," I beg, laughing as I hold my tummy.

"Okay, I'll put my fingers away." She brings her fingers to her lips and blows on them as if they're hot, then puts them in a pretend holder on her sides like I see my favorite cartoons do.

"Alright, my little bullseye, let's go to the kitchen." Dad ruffles my hair as he gets up.

"Daaaad," I pout. "You know I don't like that nickname." They've always called me that ever since I can remember. Apparently, I never missed the toilet when I learned how to pee standing up. It's embarrassing. I'll never tell that secret.

"But it's funny, and it's a good thing," he says. "You're a quick learner, and I bet you'll get a bullseye every time you try something new. You'll get it right the first time. You always do, kiddo."

"That sounds better than being a champion pisser," I mutter under my breath as I follow him down the hall.

He spins around on his heel, a finger in my face, and he's hiding a smile as he tries to be stern with me. "You can't say pisser or piss or anything like that, Waylon Justin Presley. Do you understand me?"

"You say it all the time," I point out.

"I'm an adult. That's different."

"It shouldn't be."

He opens his mouth and closes it again when he can't come up with an answer.

"And I'd rather you call me Bullseye. You and Mom are such hippies for naming me, Waylon Presley."

"Are we going to get into this again, Waylon? Waylon Jennings and Elvis Presley are—"

"—Two of the greatest musicians to have ever lived. I know, Dad." He makes me listen to them, and I can't stand them.

"Your Mom and I—"

"—Danced to Waylon and Elvis the night you fell in love. I know. It's sickening."

"Brat."

"Old man."

"Champion pisser," Dad throws back at me.

"You said—You said it. That's not fair."

"Life's not fair, kiddo." Dad shrugs and opens the fridge to get out the bacon, eggs, and milk.

"Okay, be nice. I heard that, by the way," Mom scolds Dad.

I stick my tongue out at Dad, and he makes a face at me. Mom takes a seat next to me, and like every morning, she places her word search book on the counter between us. Word searches are something we do every day.

Clicking the pen, I run a line through a word that goes from one corner of the word search to other. "Haberdashery," I announce proudly.

"Oh, good one, Waylon. That was a big word." She nudges my arm with hers, and I feel stupid for being proud of myself. It's just a word, but when Mom can't find it and I can, it makes me feel really smart.

While we search for words, the smell of pancakes fills the kitchen and my tummy grumbles. "Dad, do it. Do the thing," I tell him, hoping he puts on a show.

He grips the handle of the pan. "You mean this?" He flicks the pan up with his wrist. The pancake flips through the air, and Dad spins around, catching the pancake just in time.

"Aye-oh!" he cheers.

I clap as he does it again.

Mornings are the best. Why do they think I always want to wake up early?

"Oh, hey. Check it out, the fair is opening earlier because they have a petting zoo from ten to noon. Do you want to go, Waylon?" Mom shows me the picture in the newspaper. There's an entire page dedicated to the goats, alpacas, and pigs.

"Oh my gosh, can we please? Please, please, please, Dad?" I fold my hands together and give him the big eyes he can't stand.

The pan sizzles when he adds the bacon. There's nothing like the smell of bacon.

"Of course we can. I wonder if we can feed the animals too."

"Oh, I'm sure. I'll buy the tickets now just in case they sell out before we get there. I wonder if they take payment over the phone." Mom reaches for her billfold that's on the edge of the counter and gets up, walks over to the pink corded phone, and dials the number on the newspaper. "Hi, is it possible to buy tickets in advance?" she grins. "Excellent. No, I understand it might take a minute. The internet is so slow. With all the advances in the world, you'd think they would come up with something better besides dial-up. Oh, yes, of course, the card number is..." she rattles off the card number, and I'm about to burst with excitement.

"Today is going to be the best day ever." I click the pen again and find another word.

"Okay, eat your breakfast, then everyone will shower, get ready, and we'll have an amazing day at the fair." Dad carefully sets the plate down in front of me, and I narrow my eyes at the pancake.

He made a bullseye on it. There's whipped cream in circles with blueberries in between and a raspberry in the middle.

He laughs, and I grab a blueberry and throw it at him. "I'm so funny," he tells himself. Mom snorts as she sips her mimosa.

She smacks her lips together. "Oh yeah, babe. Hilarious."

Dad leans over the counter and kisses her.

"Ew," I say, wrinkling my nose in disgust.

"One day you'll want to 'ew' with someone, Waylon," Mom says, giving Dad another kiss.

"Will not. Girls are gross." I shove a forkful of pancake in my mouth and lick the whipped cream from the side of my lip.

"So icky." Dad shivers in disgust, and Mom pushes him gently on the shoulder. "I'll show you icky."

"Promise?" Dad wiggles his brows.

I don't know what that means, but it sounds disgusting. "Stop. I'm trying to eat here."

We eat quickly after that, and I practically lick my plate to get the last of the syrup. I jump off the stool and run down the hall, but Mom's snapping fingers stop me in my tracks.

"And what are you forgetting, young man?"

I roll my head on my shoulders, run to the kitchen, grab my plate off the counter, run around the island, and then wash my dish off in the sink. I reach down to open the dishwasher and then set the plate inside.

"Thank you," she sings.

I run up down the hall to hear my parents laughing behind me, probably flirting, which is gross, and I head up the steps to go to my room so I can get ready. I take the quickest shower of my life and grab a pair of jeans and my Ghostbusters shirt. The ghost glows in the dark.

So cool.

I slip on my sneakers and run down the steps again. Mom and Dad are still being disgusting in the kitchen, swapping cooties, and I stomp my foot. It echoes down the hall, and Dad turns around, not pleased with my slight tantrum.

"You guys aren't ready yet!"

"Waylon, we have time. Don't stomp your feet in this house, we've talked about it. Do it again, and we won't go to the fair," he warns.

"I'm sorry," I say automatically. It's the one thing I do that really upsets Dad.

"It's okay. We live, and we learn. We'll leave in about an hour, okay?"

"Longest hour of my life!" I hang my head and drag my feet toward the steps.

"How about you hop on the Sega to kill time?"

I snap my head up. "Really?"

"Really." He sips his coffee while grinning.

"Sweet. Thanks, Dad." I run to the living room and jump on the couch, then wince. I know what's coming.

"No jumping on the couch, Waylon!" Mom yells after me.

I always realize what I did a second too late.

"Sorry!" I call back. I turn on the TV and the Sega, then blow in the Sonic the Hedgehog cartridge that goes into the slot of the Sega.

I'm going to catch all the rings.

I get lost in the game. I die a few times, but I get back up and try again, jumping and rolling, running really fast through the loops.

"Alright, kiddo. You ready?" Dad asks as he steps into the living room.

I groan again when I see the tacky shirts they're wearing. They match.

His says, "If found, bring me to my wife."

Hers says, "I'm the wife."

"Out of all the clothes you have, you pick those?"

"What? We like them," Mom shrugs.

"You guys are trying to embarrass me."

"Us?" Dad gasps. "Never."

They're so corny, but I love them anyway.

"Come on, we don't want to be late." Mom ushers us out the door while putting an earring in her ear. "And remember, Waylon. Always stay close to where we can see you, okay? You know I don't like when—"

"—When I get out of eyesight. I know, Mom." I try not to groan again. I tend to do that when I'm fed up.

She grabs my chin and kisses me on the cheek.

"Mooom."

"So stinkin' cute."

"Mom! I'm not cute. I'm ruggedly handsome. I'm even growing a mustache. See." I tilt my chin up and rub my finger through the blonde hair above my upper lip.

"Goodness, look at you. On your way to being a man."

"I know," I say, a little impressed with myself.

"Come on there, Mr. Man. Get in the car and put on your seatbelt." Dad points to the backseat, and I climb in, using the handle above to help me.

I lick my lips and taste the syrup from the pancakes.

I'm hungry.

"When can we get food?" I ask. I'm starving.

"You just ate four pancakes, eggs, and bacon. You aren't hungry." Dad turns on the truck, and the engine rumbles as we pull out of the driveway.

"That was an hour ago! I'm starving."

Mom chuckles and flips down the visor to apply lipstick. "When we get to the petting zoo, we can get something, okay? Chunky Monkey," she says.

Dad flips on the radio station, and I can't help but roll my eyes at the oldies song starting to play. He and Mom sing together to a song that shouldn't even be allowed on the radio, and I stare out the window, watching the trees pass.

My favorite thing to do on car rides is to pretend I'm racing the car. I imagine I'm on a horse, on the side of the road where it's grassy. We're running full speed, trying to beat Dad's huge truck. I have no idea how to ride a horse, but I bet it's so cool.

A log is in the way; we jump over it, landing perfectly as we pull ahead of Dad. My imaginary horse is pitch black with curly hair. His name would be Midnight.

Riding Midnight, even if it's just in my daydream, makes the ride to the fairground go by quick.

"Okay, we're here," Dad announces, pulling into a parking spot.

"Finally, I'm starved." I unclick my seatbelt and jump out of the truck, landing like Spider-Man would. I hold out my hand and pretend to shoot spiderwebs from my wrist.

Thwip, thwip.

My fake webs land on a nearby car, and I jump in the air, launching myself as far as I can.

"Okay, Spidey, let's go." Mom waves me over, and I jump to my feet to stand and rush over to take her hand.

It's the one rule we have when it comes to walking in parking lots. I always have to hold Mom's hand so she can make sure I'm safe.

I'm a big kid now. I don't need to hold her hand. It's embarrassing, but I won't argue about it. I always lose.

Dad takes my other hand, and we walk connected to the entrance of the fairgrounds. Dad's hand is calloused from his construction job. Mom's is soft from the lotions she uses while giving massages since she owns her own spa.

I look up at Mom, who is smiling, staring up at the Ferris wheel. She points. "Look, Waylon. Look how high. You want to go on it with me?"

"Yes! I know you don't like heights, but I'll protect you."

"Oh, sweetie. I know you will. You're the best." She bends down and kisses the top of my head. I won't ever tell anyone because it's embarrassing, but I'm a mommy's boy. She's pretty much my best friend.

"You look pretty, Mom," I say to her. I always tell her that 'cause Dad does, so I think that means she likes to hear it.

She brings her blue eyes to mine as she stares down at me, and her brown hair whips over her shoulders like octopus tentacles from the wind. "I think you might be the best son in the world."

"Duh." Obviously.

"She is the prettiest woman alive," Dad says after me, leaning across my head to give Mom another kiss.

Blah. Gross. Cooties.

I'm happy my parents are together. A lot of kids at school have divorced parents and go from house to house. That sucks.

Oh, I'm not allowed to say that.

But it does suck.

My parents are always going to be together.

We come to a red ticket booth with a teenage girl inside blowing bubbles with the gum she has in her mouth. "Hi, we bought three tickets in advance," Mom says into the hole cut through the plastic barrier.

"Cool." She rips three tickets off and hands them over to us without asking for proof. "Would you like to buy food for the animals?" Her voice is flat as if she's bored.

I guess I would be too if I had to sit here all day.

"Yeah, that would be great."

"Cool," she says again, plopping down a plastic bag that looks like dog food. "Have fun and enjoy your day."

'Montana Fairgrounds' is spelled across the big arched sign as we walk underneath it. The dirt is red; on either side are wooden fences to block the animals from coming onto the pathway. There's a big red barn up ahead, the doors wide open.

I wonder what's in there.

An alpaca stretches its neck from the other side of the fence and bumps its nose against my head. I giggle.

"I think he wants you to feed him, Waylon," Dad grins, opening the plastic bag.

I dig inside the bag and grab a handful of the brown pebbles that looks disgusting. There's a nasty grime to them that leaves crumbs in the palm of my hand.

"Hold your hand flat," he tells me, grabbing my hand and having me curl my fingers from the middle of my palm. "There you go."

The alpaca's nose tickles my skin, and his tongue flicks out to gather the food.

"Gross," I chuckle but dive my hand in the bag again to give him more food.

I reach for his long nose and pet him from the middle of his forehead down to his nose. He's soft and fluffy and has brown eyes with really long lashes. He's cute.

A pig oinks from a little further down. I skip down the fence and squat so I can be on his level. He' fat, pink, and has dirt on his nose.

"The sign says we can't feed him this kibble, but we can pet him," Dad says, pointing to a small sign nailed on a wooden post.

With a shaky hand, I reach through the boards and pet the back of the pig. "He's softer than I thought he would be. Can we get one?"

"No," Dad and Mom say in unison.

"A dog? A cat?"

"Oh, boy. I should have known this was coming." Mom throws her hands on her hips. "I don't know. I don't think we are ready for a puppy, Waylon. It's a lot of responsibility."

"Please," I beg, giving my best puppy dog eyes. "I swear, I'll take care of him."

"You'll make sure to potty train him? Every fifteen minutes, you have to take him outside to use the bathroom."

"Okay. Please? Please?" I beg again, folding my hands together.

Mom sighs, and I know that sigh; it means she's giving in.

"How about we go to the shelter after the fair and look? We're only looking. If we're getting a dog, we're going to rescue it."

"Ah! Really? Thank you, Mom. Thank you, thank you, thank you." I throw my arms around her and give her a big hug.

"Don't get too excited yet. It takes time to find the right dog. Come on, let's feed that food monster inside you."

"Kendra? Kyle?"

I look up to see our neighbors from across the street come up to my parents.

"Katie. Brett. It's good to see you guys," Mom greets them, leaning over to give Ms. Katie a hug. She's been my babysitter a time or two.

I don't need a babysitter. I'd be just fine on my own. I'm practically a grownup now.

"And how are you, Mr. Waylon?" Katie ruffles my hair.

"Great! Mom and Dad are going to let me have a dog."

Ms. Katie's smile has wrinkles forming on the sides of her eyes. "Is that so? Well, every kid needs a dog, in my opinion."

"We're just going to look," Mom reminds me, giving me 'the look' by raising one of her eyebrows.

"Yeah, that's what we said, and now we have three dogs, a bird, an iguana, a cat with one eye, and a hamster," Mr. Brett mumbles under his breath.

"Oh, you love that cat. She only cuddles you, honey."

I tug on Mom's hand. "Can I go to the cart over there and get fries, please?"

Mom scans her surroundings to see how far the food cart is and when her eyes land on it, she nods. "Yes, you can go. Come right back, okay?"

"Promise."

"I loves you big, baby," she says.

"I loves you too."

She hands me a twenty-dollar bill. Just like in my video game, I run toward the cart with my supersonic speed, barely missing people as they pass me.

My stomach grumbles as the scent of French fries wafts over me. I read the menu, and my eyes widen when I see all the French fry choices. I'm not like most kids who only like their food plain. Mom and Dad, from the time I could eat real food, always had me eat what they ate.

So I want barbeque fries with pulled pork and sauce on them, maybe with some pickles and onions.

"Oh my gosh, Waylon? Is that you?"

I turn my head to see a woman standing there. I don't think I've ever seen her before. She's around my mom's age with blonde hair. I notice her eyes are red, puffy, maybe from crying. She's skinny, too, like maybe she doesn't eat enough.

Maybe I can share my fries with her, but Mom said to never talk to strangers.

"I don't know you."

"Oh, yes, you do. It's just been a while. My name is Patricia. It's been a few years. You probably wouldn't remember me."

"Mom said for me not to talk to strangers."

"Your Mom is very smart." Her eyes get glassy like she's about to cry. "You want to go see these horses in the barn? They're huge, and they have apples to feed them."

My eyes widen. "Whole apples?"

"Yep. How cool is that? Their teeth crunch the entire apple easily. It's pretty neat to see."

I look toward my Mom, and she waves at me before turning her attention back to the neighbors. "I don't know. I don't remember you, so I shouldn't go."

"Kendra won't mind, I promise. Just five minutes. I want to catch up and see how you're doing in school."

I don't know what to do, but I feel obligated to go. "Okay, but it has to be fast. Mom doesn't like for me to be out of sight."

"What a good Mom." Her voice sounds funny like she suddenly has a sore throat. He holds out her hand. "Come on, I won't let anything happen to you."

I slip my hand in hers, and we walk inside the barn. A few horses are poking their heads out of the stall, and I reach for an apple and feed one. He's not like what I imagine when we drive, but he's a pretty tan color with a white strip down his nose.

"Wow." I've never seen a horse up close before. They're so big. I look around, and the woman is standing off to the side, watching me. "I better get back. Thanks," I tell her. Something is telling me to get away, but I'm too scared to make quick movements.

"I'm sorry," she begins to cry. "But you can't." She wraps her arms around me and shoves a stinky cloth over my mouth and nose, then drags me out the back doors of the barn. I try to kick and scream, but my head starts to feel loopy, and my body becomes heavy.

I don't understand what's happening. "Mommy…" I try and scream, but I can't. The word is slurred, and I don't know if Mom would know it's me calling for her. I haven't called her Mommy since I was six. I wanted to grow up.

But I want my Mommy now. I'm scared.

"You did good, Patricia," a deep voice growls like a villain in the movies I watch.

I wish I had powers. I could break free.

"I did what you asked. Let her go."

"No," he says, and a loud slap sounds.

I try to open my eyes, but I keep getting sleepier.

"Let's go. We need to leave before someone notices," the man says.

My back hits something hard, and I manage to blink my eyes open enough to see Patricia and this man staring down at me. I'm in the trunk of a car.

"He'll be perfect for her when the time is right."

I don't know what that means, but the guy slams the trunk closed. I don't have the strength to fight, but maybe when I wake up, it'll all be a really bad dream.

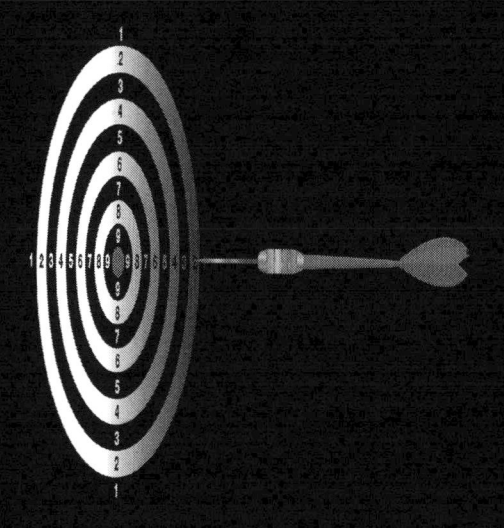

CHAPTER TWO
Bullseye

Ten years later

"**H**APPY BIRTHDAY TO YOU. HAPPY BIRTHDAY TO YOU. HAPPY BIRTHDAY TO ME, Happy Birthday to me," I sing the song to myself pathetically and pick up the piece of metal I got from the broken spring from the mattress. I carve a line on the wall to keep count of how many days I've been here.

It's my eighteenth birthday, so I've been here for ten years. That's 3,652 days, 87,658 hours, 5,259,492 minutes, and 315,569,520 seconds.

I can't remember what happened to me ten years ago. All I know is that this family is the only one I can remember, and I hate them.

Something tells me I'm not supposed to be here. Something tells me this isn't how a man is supposed to be raised. I would have killed these people already and left them bathing in their own blood if it weren't for Georgia.

Their daughter.

At least, I think she is, just like I'm their son.

I'm missing something important—some vital piece of information that would make sense to me. There's just this massive dark hole in my mind that I can't seem to shine any light in. I can't remember anything that hasn't been here in this cold, cement room.

I think I've lived another life, though.

Or maybe that's just wishful thinking.

Georgia is my best friend. We've grown up together here. She's made this place and these people tolerable.

Patricia and Ronald Jennings.

Ronald wants us to call him Dad, but I'd rather get whipped a million times than to ever call him that. I hate him too much. Patricia is the reasonable one, a bit kinder, but she does the devil's bidding, so I know she can't be trusted.

I hit the back of my head softly against the wall, sitting on the lumpy and uncomfortable mattress as I stare up the wooden staircase.

And I wait for them to come down and get me.

They are sick, twisted people who deserve to rot in hell for what they make me and Georgia do together.

Ever since we were sixteen, Ronald has made Georgia and me have sex. He records it, jacks off to it, and tells us what to do. If we don't listen, we're beaten until we can't move. He keeps us weak by not giving us proper food and water so we can't fight back, but if we perform well, he gives us a good meal. We all sit down at the table like a real family.

A real fake fucking family because Ronald keeps Georgia and I chained together by binding her left wrist and my right together while keeping our ankles trapped in chains too.

I know this isn't normal. None of it is.

And I want out. I want more, but I won't leave Georgia behind. They might make us do things we wouldn't ever do, but I love her deeply, as much as someone can without being in love with someone. I know she feels the same. We've talked about it before. Maybe if our situations were different. Maybe if we lived another life, we could be in love, but this isn't a fairytale.

We're going to die here.

Even with all the horrors, these people put us through, I don't regret Georgia. I regret how things have happened between us. I regret our situation. I regret that I am not strong enough to protect her. I regret that I can't be who she needs me to be.

But I don't regret her.

She's the only good thing in this fucked up life.

I pick up the chain attached to my ankle and wonder what my life was like before all this. The life I can't remember.

Maybe that's just wishful thinking. Maybe I've never had another life, and I've always been here. No, that's not right. I'm not supposed to be here. I feel it.

I just don't know where else I'm supposed to be.

I look around my room as my stomach growls. There are a ton of books. At least I have that. I've taught myself everything since I've never been to school, but why bother continuing? Why did I bother at all? It's how I've been able to keep up with my birthdays, and I don't know how I know it, but I do. It's like it was ingrained in me.

What else is ingrained in me?

I know when I fall asleep at night on this twin-sized bed, I dream about a woman with brown hair and blue eyes, but I can't see her face. It's like everything is blurred. And then there are pancakes and Superman? It makes no sense, but dreams never do.

I think it's my soul telling me what it wished it could have.

Wishing is a bitch.

I exhale and give my sorry excuse for a room the finger. I fucking hate it here. I want to burn this place to the ground with Patricia and Ronald inside. I'll take Georgia with me, and we can start life over together. We've only ever known each other, so it would make sense to stay together. Not as a couple, because I don't know if either of us want to be with someone who's experienced something so terrible. It would be a constant cloud over our heads. She deserves more than that.

She deserves to be happy.

Drip. Drip. Drip.

The drops of water pooling on the floor from the pipe in the corner bring me out of my depressing thoughts.

I'd kill myself right here and now if it weren't for Georgia. Fuck living the rest of my life like this.

Okay, now my depressing thoughts are done.

The door opens, sending light from the hallway spilling down the stairs. I wince from how bright it is and lift my hand to cover my eyes. It's dark in my room with one small, rectangular window that's frosted over so I can't see outside. It doesn't bring in enough light at all.

"Lunch," Patricia raises her voice from the top of the steps and slowly comes down the steps carrying a tray of food.

It isn't every day we get lunch. I can smell the food. It's warm and hearty. I try not to get too excited, but like a desperate, weak man, I get on my knees and get as close to her as I can because I want the food so bad. The chain around my ankle tugs once I run out of slack.

What am I doing? I'm not going to fucking beg for food.

I sit down and lean again the wall, my back sore from how long I've been in this position. Fuck her, fuck him, and fuck their food.

Patricia sets it down next to me. The beef stew has my mouth-watering. There's even toast and mashed potatoes with a Coke for a drink. "Please. Eat," she says softly. She's always been nicer, but I don't understand why she listens to Ronald.

Does she not care how miserable Georgia and I are? Does she not care about the child pornography Ronald made from the time Georgia and I were sixteen? Does she not care just how sick the man is?

"Has Georgia gotten food?" I ask, only wanting to eat if she has been taken care of.

Patricia nods. "I just gave her some. She got the same thing with a salad on the side. I know how much she loves her veggies."

Veggies.

It's as if Georgia and I are still kids when Patricia speaks.

I pick up the tray and set it on my lap. This is a huge serving for lunch. This is actually the biggest serving of food I've ever received. What's going on? I don't ask because it doesn't matter, does it? No matter what, I have to do what they say.

Or they'll kill Georgia, something they've warned me about a hundred times. Or Ronald will rape her after beating her first.

That's not something I can risk.

Even knowing all that, even knowing the monsters they are, part of me loves them. I think. I don't know where else I'd go, and I don't know what other kind of life there is out there. Maybe this is as good as it gets. Not being here scares me. Not having them feed me terrifies me.

And not having their fucked-up version of love? It fucking somehow hurts me.

What kind of person does that make me? Does it mean I like what they make Georgia and I do together? Sex is supposed to feel good, but this kind doesn't.

Do I like that?

No, I can't be that ridiculous. Of course, I don't. I can't stand for her to cry because I know there's nothing I can do to make this situation better.

What can I do when I have a gun to my head or a whip to my back?

I'm a weak, pathetic man. I can't walk up the stairs without getting winded. I'm just not strong enough to be who I need to be.

And that is something I'll never be able to forgive myself for.

"Can I eat with Georgia?" I dare to ask, swirling my spoon in the mashed potatoes.

Her eyes take on this typical sad look to them, and they create their own frown. Bitch.

"I don't think I can do that, Waylon. You know how Ronald is."

"He isn't even here, Patricia." I know that because I don't hear drunk yelling in the middle of the day and the breaking of glass. "Please? I want to see her. I need to know she's okay. I won't eat unless she eats with me." I have never given an ultimatum before, but I know if I don't eat, they can't use me later since I'm so weak.

I would skip this meal, but I've already skipped the last few days to buy as much time as I can.

"If I do this, you better put on a good show for him because if he finds out, I did this—"

"—He won't. I won't say a word."

She stands, wiping the palms of her hands on her jeans. "Okay, I'll bring her down. You're too weak to move."

It isn't often I feel excitement or happiness, but my heart kicks up a notch when I know I'm about to see Georgia. "Thank you," I say softly, wrapping my hand around the cold Coke bottle. Seeing Georgia earlier than I'm supposed to is my birthday present.

Not that they know it's my birthday, but Georgia does. It's our little secret.

I run my hands through my hair, even though I know I can't look good. I still want to try. She deserves that.

I watch as Patricia runs up the steps and slams the door, leaving me in darkness again. Picking up the tray, I set it aside and decide to wait for her.

I've had all my firsts with Georgia.

First kiss.

First touch.

First blow job.

First everything.

And it all started at sixteen.

I hate Patricia and Ronald for ruining our first experiences, but the bright lining to this fucked-up situation is Georgia. Deep down, past the fear and the pain, I wouldn't want to experience this with anyone else. And maybe that's selfish to admit, but Georgia makes me feel safe.

It's an impossible feat, considering more than half the time, I have a gun pointed at me.

The creak of the door opens again, and the chains thud on the staircase as Georgia takes the steps casually. Patricia flips on the light, and a wide smile takes over Georgia's face. There aren't often times where happiness exists here, but right now is one of those times.

"You have thirty minutes. And Waylon, since you haven't been taking your pill, I crushed it up and put it in one of the items on your tray."

My guts turn with hatred. I clench my jaw, wishing I could kill this woman. I'm eighteen. A young, virile man who should get an erection by watching paint fucking dry, but no. The situation is too damn stressful. I'm constantly afraid, and it is affecting my ability to get it up. Poor Georgia, she asked me one time if it was her fault. If it was because I didn't find her attractive.

I told her it was the furthest from the truth, that in this bad fucking dream of the reality we live in, she was the only beauty in it.

My shortcomings are all me. I hate what they make me do to her, I hate that she cries every time, I hate how dirty and useless I feel. I hate I can hear Patricia and Ronald in the corner, moaning as they watch us.

So yeah, I can't get it up because I'm filled with so much hatred and disgust. I'm okay with that. I think that says something about me.

So they make me take Viagra so they can get the footage they want. I last for hours until Georgia physically can't take anymore.

It breaks me as a man.

Or whatever the fuck I am.

Georgia's smile slips off her face, and she tripsfalling against the floor. I reach for her, but she's too far away for me to check on. Patricia is holding a tray with one hand and the chain leash with the other.

They treat us like fucking animals.

"Georgia, are you okay? Talk to me," I say, my voice cracking from worry.

"I'm fine." She places her palms on the floor and pushes herself up.

Her dirty blonde hair is a curtain around her face, and the ends drag along the grime on the floor.

"Get up." Patricia yanks on the chain, which pulls Georgia's head back.

"Hey! She's trying. Give her a minute," I shout.

"I'm sorry, I just... Ronald needs to know I'm not nice to you," Patricia says as if she's ashamed of herself.

She should be.

"You aren't fucking nice. I hope you burn in hell in one day," I spit.

"Stop, Waylon. It's okay, I'm fine." Georgia stands on wobbly legs. Her gown is stuck to her knees. Blood stains the material, along with dirt and whatever other filth finds us. We are only allowed to bathe once every two weeks, and that's when we change clothes too.

No matter how much I hate Patricia and Ronald, they love Georgia and me. They have to. I mean, if they didn't, we wouldn't be here, right?

I just want to know what it's like to be loved, no matter how fucked up it is.

And if this is it, love is very disappointing because it's painful.

"You're bleeding," I gasp, lifting her gown above her knees when she sits down next to me.

She has a few scratches on her right knee. I wipe the blood away with my thumb. She leans her head on my shoulder and lifts her golden-brown eyes at me. "It's okay. It's just blood, Waylon."

Just blood.

Just pain.

Just torture.

How bad do things have to be when 'just' means we have grown too accustomed to abuse?

"Blood that shouldn't be there," I tell her, taking my napkin and pressing it against her wound.

My eyes lift to meet Patricia's, and she sets the tray down on top of Georgia's lap. "I'll be back in thirty minutes to take the trays. There's a little something in your food, too, Georgia. Ronald wants more from you."

I wrap my arm around Georgia's shoulder as she turns her face against my chest to cry. She shakes; her cries are silent.

Mine are too when I'm alone at night. Learning how to be quiet is a way of life; if not, you get punished.

Patricia leaves the light on, and the stairs groan under her plump weight. She's put on few pounds over the years. The door shuts, and a lock clicks, finally leaving us alone.

"I fucking hate her. One day, I'm going to get us out of here. I don't know how, but Georgia, I swear I will."

"We can't be without them. We need them."

"No!" I yell a little louder than needed, and she flinches away. I cup her face with my palm and look into her teary gaze. I take a deep breath to calm myself. "No, we don't. I know we only know them and our life with them, but it isn't right. We deserve more."

"But... they need us. We pay their bills."

She's right. I feel a little guilty since they're the only parents we know. "They don't feel guilty for what they do to us; we shouldn't feel guilty for dreaming of more. Come on, babe. Let's eat. We've put them off too long, and I can tell you need food."

"But it's spiked, Waylon."

"I know," I say sadly. "We do this. We don't have to do it again for few days, but you've lost so much weight, and I don't know if we should keep putting it off. You're skin and bone. I can't do that to you. You have to eat."

"Will you?" she asks, lifting her head off my shoulder to stare at me.

"Yeah, babe. I'll eat with you. You never have to do anything alone." I pick up the plastic spoon in her stew and bring it to her mouth. She hums contentedly.

While she chews, I take a bite, and while it tastes delicious, I know there is poison in this food, but at this point, it's the lesser of two evils.

We eat in silence, and when we're done with the stew, she has enough energy to feed herself. She digs into the mashed potatoes, then eats the salad, slurping down the Coke before I'm halfway done with my food.

I chuckle. It's good to see her eat.

"Waylon? Can you promise me something?"

"Anything," I say, taking her hand in mine.

"If anything happens to me, promise me you'll leave this place."

"I'm not going anywhere without you. Fuck that. You're my world, Georgia." I know it's odd to say because we aren't in love, but she's all I've known. I don't know how to be without her. She's my soulmate, in a way—my best friend. I get anxious when I think of life without her. "You can't think like that. Nothing is going to happen to you. It's you and me to the end. If something happens to you, I'd rather die than live."

She grips my face, and her eyes dart back and forth between mine. "No. Promise me you'll live your best life. Promise you'll love and make love or fuck or whatever you're supposed to do and feel good doing it. You deserve to feel good, Waylon. Live your life."

"I won't do it without you." I won't make promises I can't keep.

"Where the fuck is she?" Ronald shouts from upstairs.

The trays on our laps crash to the floor when Georgia crawls into my lap.

"She's downstairs. It was the only way Waylon would eat," Patricia explains, a lilt of desperation to her voice.

A loud slap follows a second later, and Georgia wraps her arms around my neck, placing her face against the side.

She hates it when Patricia and Ronald fight. It scares her.

"Stupid bitch. They aren't allowed to be together until I say!"

"You needed them tonight. I only thought I was doing what was needed," Patricia cries. A large thump vibrates the floor.

He's beating her.

I close my eyes and rub my hand up and down Georgia's back.

And it isn't long before I feel a tingling in my cock, since she's on my lap, wiggling around to get comfortable. On a normal day, I wouldn't be bothered, but since I'm drugged with Viagra, the lust factor is too hard to control.

"You have to stop moving around," I whisper, trying to force the unwanted desire down my throat as I swallow.

"I can't." Her words are breathless, and she willingly kisses my neck.

"Georgia, we can't," I hate to say. We've never had sex outside of when we've had to in front of Ronald. This isn't how things are supposed to happen.

"I know, it's just… we never do anything without them in the corner. They aren't here. We have fifteen minutes. Can you have sex with me the way you want? Not what he tells you to do?"

"We don't have a condom." It's the one thing that Ronald makes sure I wear.

"Pull out?" She removes the soft silk of her lips from my neck to look at me.

Her face is flushed, and her eyes are glazed over. I can't be with her like this. I know it wouldn't be what she really wanted.

"Waylon, please. I know what we are to each other. We might not ever get out of this place. I want to experience something that's just you and me. We won't ever get this chance again. They won't allow us to eat together again after this, and you know it."

Every word is true. It's becoming harder and harder to deny her. How much Viagra did Patricia slip me? My cock feels like it's about to explode.

Georgia trembles in my arms as she slips the strap of her nightgown off her shoulder. "I know I'm not what you want all the time, but maybe once you can really want me? I want to know what real bliss is like, Waylon. Please," she begs, inching forward and presses a tentative kiss to my lips.

"Look what you fucking did," Ronald shouts at Patricia.

God, the walls are thin.

"I have to clean your blood up now. It's going to be an hour before I can go downstairs to get them. I swear, you dumb cunt, if you stain this rug, you're going to be scrubbing it until your fingers bleed. Get in the room and don't come out!" he ends his statement with a final slap to her face, silencing her.

"We have more time," Georgia whispers. "Want me, even if it's only for a minute."

"Babe, it isn't about not wanting you. It's about not wanting you in the situation we're in, but you're beautiful."

She grinds against me helplessly, and I tilt my head back, squeezing her small waist as my control gets thinner. It's about to break.

Her nightgown slips lower, revealing her tits. They're just the right size with hard, rosy nipples. I hate that I want her right now, but she wants me to, so it's okay.

No, it isn't.

"Stop thinking so much. I want you. I want us to experience another first together." She tugs her nightgown over her head and tosses it on the floor. "Let's just have one time where they aren't in the same room." Her hands clutch the stained tank top I'm wearing, and I lift my arms over my head so she can yank it off.

My hands roam down her skinny frame—too skinny—and my brows pinch together, wishing I could take better care of her. I can count her ribs. My fingers trace the ridges, and her skin fills with goosebumps. I palm her tits, rubbing my thumb over her nipples.

Ronald always wants hard, fast, dirty, and degrading, and I'm good at it, but I don't always want that. I want what my partner wants.

I bend down and suck her tight bead into my mouth, flattening my arms around her back as I pull her close. She whimpers for me.

She has never made that sound before.

This feels different.

She's right. We need this. We need to know what it's like to be together without force.

I know there's some force at play with the medication, but at least they aren't here. I can show her how good it can be, and she can show me.

Her breasts are soft. Her skin is surprisingly smooth since we don't have access to lotion or anything. I let go of her nipple with a soft plop, then give it a goodbye kiss. I drag my tongue up the middle of her chest until I'm at her lips and kiss her, like really kiss her.

It's slow and timid on her end. Delicate, yet perfect. The tip of her tongue flicks against mine, and I groan down her throat, so she does it again, which makes me lose control.

I flip her onto the cot and spread her legs apart. She's beautiful, laid out under me like this, more than any other time she's been in this position. Because I know she really wants to be here.

Slipping my thumb to her clit, I begin to circle it, something Ronald doesn't allow me to do.

"Oh, Waylon," she moans, and I shove my hand over her mouth.

I grin, feeling good about my ability for the first time. "Shh, babe. Walls are thin, remember?"

She nods and grips the sheets as I move my thumb quicker. Her whimpers and moans come out faster, and her back arches.

I think she's having an orgasm. I know she fakes it most of the time while Ronald is watching us. I don't have that option. It's why it takes so long sometimes. Ronald always inspects the condom to make sure I wasn't faking it. I did one time, and he beat me so bad I couldn't see for a week because my eyes were swollen shut.

I dip my fingers through her folds, and she's nice and wet. I drop my hand from her mouth, and she giggles, hiding her face in her palms. "That felt so good," she says.

"Let me see you because watching you fall apart has been the best part of today."

She drops her hands, and she has a bright blush on her cheeks. Our eyes meet when I slide a finger inside her, and her mouth drops open. "So tight," I growl, my cock pressing against the thin material of my sweatpants.

"I want you, Waylon." She sits up and tugs my pants down, wrapping her hand around my cock to give it a quick stroke.

I toss my head back and bite my lip until I draw blood to keep quiet.

"Come here," she purrs, lying down on the bed again.

I curl over her and reach down to press myself against her entrance. She gasps when I slip inside; her eyes roll to the back of her head while I push myself to the hilt.

She's never been so wet before. It's so hot. My god, I don't think I'm going to last. I have to. I have to make this good for her. Instead of fast thrusts, my strokes are long and slow.

"I love you the only way I know how," she whispers in my ear.

I don't break the pace, but I do lift up on my forearms and nod. "Me too, babe. The only way I know how." I kiss her again, slow and steady. I intertwine our hands and keep them gently pinned next to her head.

"Oh god," I groan, then bite into the mattress when she starts to feel so damn good.

We've never done this before.

Christ, I think I do love her.

Actually, really love her.

The realization is heavy, slamming against me to the point where I can't breathe.

I blink away the tears because loving someone in a place like this is hell. Loving her only makes me realize how little of a man I really am. I need to fight, but every time Ronald is in front of me, I shrink to an eight-year-old boy again, dying for his love.

"Stay with me. It's just us, Waylon. It's just you and me." Georgia kisses the side of my neck, then sucks my earlobe into her mouth.

Another thing she's never done.

Her nails dig into my scalp—another new thing to add to the list—and she lightly trickles them down my back, careful to not leave a mark. If Ronald were to find out about this, it would mean trouble. Georgia grips my ass, pulling me deeper inside her. I curl over her, wrapping an arm around the top of her head as I drive in.

"It's never been—this so good, babe. I've never felt this good."

"I know," she mewls. "I'm so close."

I jerk back in surprise and smile. "Really? Again?"

She nods, sucking in her bottom lip, still not letting go of my ass. Her eyes drop to my abs as they flex. I glance between us, watching as I slide in and out of her.

It's beautiful.

I change positions, wanting to see her riding me. I flip us over until I'm staring up at her. What a sight. She's never been on top before. Ronald doesn't allow it.

"You're so beautiful, Georgia," I praise her, rubbing my hands up and down her sides. I can't help but rub my palms over the slight undercurves of her breasts.

"Waylon, I don't know what to do. We've never…"

"I know. Just do what feels natural. It's going to feel good."

She situates herself on top of me, and my cock slides in another inch. We groan at the same time, and my hands grip her hips, rubbing my thumb over the ridges of bone protruding from her skin.

"So full," she moans, her hands slapping against my chest for leverage.

Georgia begins to rock. Uncertain at first, but her clit rubs against my pelvis, and she slaps a hand over her mouth to swallow a loud sound.

I take her hand away and replace it with mine instead, so she can do what she wants. She moves faster, back and forth, rocking against me like a boat at sea caught in raging waves. My eyes roll to the back of my head, and the tingle at the base of my spine tells me this is about to be over.

"Oh god, Waylon. I'm so close. Don't stop, don't stop—"

But it isn't me that's moving. It's her. She rocks me faster, harder, chasing her orgasm.

"I can't hold back," I grit, my teeth tight together. I flex my hips, thrusting deep inside her and trying to hold back my orgasm. She has to come first. It's the only way I can pull out.

"Yes, yes!" she flips her hair over her head. Her hips stutter as her pussy pulsates around my cock.

I tap her hip, warning her to get off. "I'm too close, babe. Oh, fuck. Get off, Georgia. I can't." My toes curl, and I squeeze my eyes shut.

"No, it's okay. Do it, fill me up, Waylon."

I snap my eyes open and shake my head. "You could—"

"I don't care. I want this with you. I need it." A tear drips down her cheek, and I sit up, wiping it off her face.

Happy tears.

Needy tears.

Once-in-a-lifetime tears.

I pull her off me and flip her back over so I can look into her eyes while I do this. I feel like it's beyond basic sex, beyond personal. I steal her lips with my own, kissing her until I know my lips will be bruised tomorrow. I grip the top of her neck with one hand, controlling the kiss, slipping my tongue between her lips with a moan.

"Georgia," I whisper between us, burying myself as deep as I can as I come. I punctuate my hips with every spasm that leaves me.

I kiss her again. Lazy and messy, but I don't care.

This is perfect, and I never knew perfection could exist in my life.

"I do love you, Georgia." My fingers slide down her arm and back up, all while I press a kiss on her dainty collarbone.

"I know. I love you. A different life—"

"—another world—" I interrupt.

"—in a different place—" she says.

"—then maybe we'd have a chance." I close my eyes as my heart fucking aches.

This is real misery.

Because this love will kill us.

The door slams open, and I jerk away from her, my semi-hard cock slipping out of her. I scramble for her nightie, pluck it off the ground, hurriedly pulling it over her head. "I'll take care of this, babe. I'll take care of you this time."

And I don't care if it kills me.

I barely have time to put on my sweatpants when Ronald is at the bottom of the steps. I just pull them above my hips, and I forget about the damn chain around my ankle. I can't go more than three steps outside the bed. My leg tugs when I try to attack him, but I'm stopped short. I growl, stepping in front of Georgia so he can't see her.

"And what do we have here?" he sucks his tongue across his teeth. "You being a little whore, Georgia? You don't get enough of him, so you gotta sneak down here and get it, huh? Is he not enough? Do I need to bring you another man to add to the mix?"

His hand grips her ankle and yanks her down on the bed. The collar around her neck digs deeper from the awkward placement of the chain being hooked on the other end of the wall.

I lurch forward again, trying to wrap my hands around his throat. "Don't fucking touch her!"

"Why not? You can. Been thinking about this pussy for a while now. She's legal now. Or maybe I'll beat the shit out of her for spreading her legs before I could tell her to." He pinches the side of her leg until a spot is left, and she cries out.

She scrambles away from him, but he yanks on her chain, sending her flying backward on the bed. Georgia is on her back, staring up at him with fear in her eyes. He wraps his hands around her throat and unhooks the chain, lifting her by her neck.

She chokes, gags, and claws at his arms.

I step forward, the chain tightening when I try to get closer. "Let her go. Whatever you want to do, do it to me. Leave her alone, please," I beg him.

The worst part of all this is how I still have lust coursing through my body and an erection that won't go down because of this goddamn Viagra they gave me.

He tsks when he sees my come dripping down her thigh.

Fuck.

He wanted to be the first to...

The thought makes me want to puke.

"I'll literally do anything," I manage to choke out the words.

Anything.

"Patricia!" Ronald yells, and a few seconds later feet, hit the floor upstairs.

Patricia runs down the steps and stops short when she sees the sight before her. "Oh no," she whispers.

"Take Georgia to her room." Ronald tosses her over to Patricia, and she has a gentler touch, taking Georgia's hand instead.

"Waylon," Georgia calls out for me, scared and white as a ghost.

I don't have time to answer her. Patricia drags Georgia up the steps and slams the door. It only takes Ronald a split second to throw his fist and land it against my face. Blood fills my mouth. I try to fight back, but these chains are making it hard for me to stand my ground. I throw my fist next, clocking him right in the chin, but I don't have the same stamina.

I'm weak.

He throws a fist against my side, and I double over. He grunts as he lifts his knee and rams it against my face. My head snaps back, and blood gushes from my nose.

"You'll do anything, huh?" he backhands me across the face. My vision hazes from the force. "Would you suck my cock to save her?"

Would I want to? No.

Would I do it to save her?

Yes.

"My cock is worthy of so much more than your useless mouth." He slaps me again, and this time I fall to the ground. He kicks my back, and something cracks inside me. I howl in pain. "I'm not fucking gay. You're sick." He squats down and grips my face with his hands.

I wheeze, struggling to breathe from the pain.

"Dad—" I let slip because he has to be.

"I'm not your father. I'd never love you. You're nothing but a way for me to live, boy."

Boy.

"Love deserves more than a boy like you."

I curl in on myself as he starts beating me again, feeling like a little boy all over again.

I can't protect anyone. I can't save her.

All I want is to be loved.

But love is hard to come by when you've never experienced it.

You get the love you think you deserve, so I obviously hate myself.

Love is learned, and it doesn't live here.

The only thing I'll ever learn to do is hate.

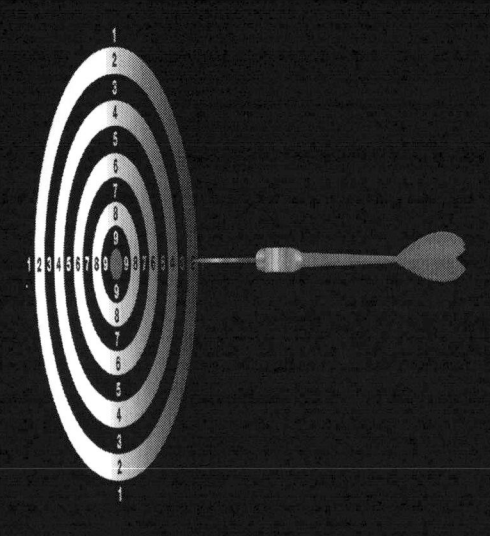

CHAPTER THREE
Bullseye

Seven months later

I FOUND OUT FOUR MONTHS AGO THAT GEORGIA IS PREGNANT. I HAVEN'T SEEN HER. THAT'S been our punishment for what we've done. I want to say it was worth it, I do, because it was fucking beautiful. I've never felt anything like it before and will never feel anything like it again.

Not seeing her has been torture. I know what they made us do together is terrible, but not being able to touch her and make sure she's okay is unbearable. I don't know if that hour was worth seven months of pain. I miss her. What's happened to her during this time? Is the baby okay? How have Ronald and Patricia made money if they haven't been recording us?

A bunch of fucking perverts all around the world has seen me and Georgia. It makes me sick to think those same people have gotten to see her pregnant belly, and I haven't. It's my fucking kid. I deserve to see her. God, I want to kill all the sick assholes that have seen her, which have gotten off on her not because of her beauty but because of our child growing inside her.

I might be too young to be a father, but I'd be a good one if ever given a chance. My soul and mind are older than the years I've been alive.

The door cracks open, and I wince from the light. It's Patricia. I can tell by the silhouette at the top of the stairs. I lift my hand to block the light. I don't have the energy to argue, to fight, to do anything.

They win.

I haven't eaten in days. I haven't had water in days. I haven't slept in months. It feels that way, at least. I'm too worried about Georgia.

"Oh, Waylon. You need to eat and drink water," she whispers, kneeling at my feet.

She places her hand on my forehead, and I jerk away from her. "Don't fucking touch me, you sick fuck. I saw you," I rasp in disgust. "I saw you in the corner touching yourself, fucking Ronald, moaning at our expense." I gather spit in my mouth and spew it against her face. It lands on her cheek, but she doesn't look angry. She looks... regretful.

Which only pisses me off more.

"You don't understand," she starts, wiping her cheek on her shoulder.

"I'll never understand perverts like you. You are our parents. You're supposed to love us." It sounds automatic as I say it because I've said it so many times in my head.

I didn't know it was possible for her to look guiltier. "I love you in the best way I'm allowed, Waylon."

"Whatever the fuck that means."

"I slipped Ronald a sleeping pill in his beer. He will be out for a while."

I wait for her to continue, but she doesn't say a word to explain herself. "Well? What the hell does that mean?"

She hands me a bottle of water. I don't even care if it is laced with Viagra; I'm too fucking weak to fuck. I twist the cap off and guzzle it down. It spills over my lips and refreshes my dry, cracked lips. It tastes so fucking good.

"How is Georgia? Please, tell me. You haven't given me an update. Is the baby okay? Is she okay?" I gasp for air, tired from drinking the water so fast.

"You want to go see her?"

"Seriously?" I don't know if I can believe her.

"It isn't right that you haven't. I've been doing the best I can," she whispers, turning her head against the light to show a black eye. She unlocks the chain from the wall, and the shackle falls off my ankle. "Don't try to run," she says, pulling a gun from her red hoodie pocket.

"I barely have the strength to drink water. I won't run. As fucked up as it sounds, you're my family. I don't run away from family." Because I'm somehow sickly attached to these people.

"You first," she says, waving the gun in the air.

She's a frigid, fucked up cunt, but you know what? She knows how to shoot a gun. When I was fifteen, she aimed it at me and fired, but it hit the wall behind me. She said, "Next time he asks me to shoot you, I won't miss."

A bullet rarely misses twice.

I'll never forget that as she walked away, leaving me holding my breath, shaking, and on the brink of pissing myself.

The barrel of the gun presses against my back. It never fails to make my bones tremble. The tips of my toes graze along the edge of the steps. The muscles in my legs shake from being so stagnant. I try to do a few exercises when I'm locked downstairs to try and keep my muscles from becoming atrophied.

I read about atrophy in a book, and now I'm paranoid about it.

Sure, I've been locked up in this room for years and treated like shit, but I don't want my muscles to atrophy. Sue me, I guess. I do what I can to stay sane.

"Be quiet. You know he's a light sleeper," she whispers, shoving the gun against the knobs of my spine. "First door on the right."

I try to be as stealthy as I can, sliding my feet across the hardwood floors. When I see the door, I'm relieved to know she isn't in the room where we would put on a show. "Has she still been recording for you?" I turn around, my eyes burning with tears at the terrible thought.

Patricia shakes her head. "No, just pictures, but not her face. Pregnant belly photos go for a good price. We've been doing well."

I clench my jaw shut, hating that my daughter or son is being exploited. I reach my hand for the doorknob, and she stops me, sliding her body between me and the door. I want to kill her, but how do I kill the only Mom I've ever known?

"You need to know something," her voice drops to a worried tone. "Georgia isn't well. She's had complications."

I shove her out of the way and open the door, my heart slamming against my chest when I see Georgia lying in bed, still as a corpse. Her eyes fling to the door. Fear flashes over her eyes for a split second as she cups her belly, but then she sees it's me.

Choking back a sob, I run to my best friend's side and clutch her hand.

"Waylon," she says weakly, but a smile as wide as the ocean graces her beautiful face. "You're here." Her voice cracks, and her terrifyingly skinny hand places mine on her belly.

I can't help it.

The tears fall. "I'm so sorry, babe." I clutch her stomach fiercely, protectively, and lovingly. Georgia's health isn't worth risking for this. She's skin and bone. Her cheeks are gaunt, her eyes are dark, and she's just so damn small.

I'm afraid if I kiss her, I'll break her.

She looks like she's dying.

All of her weight is in her stomach. It's like the baby is a vampire, sucking the life out of her. She's all belly, round and tight.

My baby kicks my hand, and I smile, leaning down to press a kiss to him or her. Lifting her shirt, I see a few stretch marks, and I kiss every one of them. "I love you both so much."

"I tried to see you, they wouldn't allow it," she explains.

"Shh, I know. I tried too, babe. Patricia drugged him. We have a little time." I sprawl next to her and wrap my arm around her belly. "I was worried this would happen. Of course, pregnant on the first try, and it's killing you."

"I'll be okay. We'll get out of this," she says lowly, so Patricia can't hear her. "We'll be a family."

I rub her stomach, loving every second of this. I can't imagine not being by her side now that I've seen her like this. She's had to go through this all alone. "Babe, why are you so sick?" I ask, rubbing my finger along her jaw. It's sharp with an edge, not plump or filled out like it used to be.

"My body is rejecting the baby, but I want to have it. It's us, Waylon. They will be the only thing good about this."

"It's killing you."

"This place is going to kill me anyway. Death is relative. It's about how, not when, and I choose this path."

I lean my head against her stomach and shake it in disagreement. I hold her tight, too tight, too afraid to let go. "I love you in the way I know how," I whisper.

"Me too, Waylon. So much." She runs her fingers through my hair, and a hiss leaves her mouth. "Oh god." She clutches her stomach. "No, it's too soon." She cries out and arches her back.

"What? What is it?" I yell, but she can't hear me through the pain. She's sweating, large drops flowing down her temples.

"Baby. Coming."

No. She's way too early. "She needs a hospital."

"That's not going to happen," Patricia says, cocking the gun. "Stand back and get out while I take care of this."

"I'm not fucking going anywhere. Kill me if you have to," I reply, thrusting my shoulders back. I look down to see blood coming from between Georgia's legs. "No, no, no, babe, you stay with me, okay? You're going to do this."

Her eyes are fluttering, and more blood is coming from between her legs.

"Let me do this. I used to be a nurse. Wait outside," Patricia says, pointing me to the door.

"I'm not leaving her."

"You will, or you won't be alive to see this baby's breath, I can promise."

Fucking bitch. This isn't how life is supposed to be.

I bend down and kiss Georgia's forehead, then her lips. "I love you. I'll be outside. I'll be right outside, babe." Patricia pushes me out the door and locks it. The click is loud and deafening. I press my hand against the door and roll my forehead against the cheap wood. "I love you in the only way I know how," I whisper, hoping she can hear me.

I don't know what happened. There was no blood, and then… she screamed, and there was so much of it. I lace my fingers behind my head and fall back, hitting the wall across from the door. I sweat. I ache. I hope.

And all I can do is watch the handle turn. All I can do is wait.

I don't hear anything. I don't hear screaming, or her pushing or Patricia talking to her. Silence can't be good.

I rub my hands down my face. The thought of living life without Georgia or our baby kills me. I have to start thinking of a plan to get us out of here.

A loud snore comes from the living room, and an idea starts to form. I could kill Ronald in his sleep, and when Patricia is done, I'll kill her too. Georgia and I can run away together. Yes, that's it. We'll run far away from here. I don't know where we'll go, I don't know what I'll do, but that doesn't matter. I'll do whatever I need to do to provide for them, to care for them, to make sure they never have to want for anything.

I don't know how. I don't have a high school degree. I've never had a job. I don't have any skills. Well, not true. I've had a lot of sex. I could be a prostitute. Is there another word for a guy selling his body for cash?

No, I can't think like that. I can do better than that. I'm smart. I can provide for my family while not having to sleep with other people.

The only thing I need to focus on right now is killing Ronald and Patricia.

The click of the lock has my eyes zeroing in on the doorknob as it turns. I kick off the wall and bounce on my feet. I can't wait to see my son or daughter. I hope being born so early is okay? I know nothing about babies or children.

Patricia slides through the crack of the door. She didn't open it all the way, so I can't see inside. From her neck down, she's drenched in blood, her hands are shaking, and there's a smear of red across her cheek.

"I… I tried, Waylon, but there was so much blood."

I scoff. Her words don't make any sense. "How are they? Boy? Girl? How is Georgia? Can I see her?" I step forward and reach for the handle, but she sidesteps me to block my way.

She places a bloody hand on my shirt, and I look down to see that the red has pooled under her nails. "They didn't make it, Waylon. The baby was too premature, and the cord was wrapped around her neck—"

My knees buckle, and I hit the floor. The hardwood digs into my bone, bruising my flesh, and I let out a piercing, murderous roar.

A girl.

My daughter.

"Can I see them?" I croak, the tears streaming down my face until all I taste is blood.

"She wouldn't want you to see them like that, Waylon. There's so much blood."

"I don't care."

"She asked me not to," Patricia says, placing her hand on my shoulder. "She asked me to tell you to remember her before, not like this. The baby… it would hurt you worse to see her."

I fall onto my ass and punch the floor, screaming at the top of my lungs as I clutch my chest from the pain ripping it apart. Georgia has been my solace, my safe place, my best friend since I can remember. She is my life. She is the reason I stayed alive and didn't kill myself.

She was the reason.

And she taught me how to love.

She was the only salvation in this hell.

She died because of them, but also because of me. I should never have given in when she said for me to come inside her. I should have been stronger, but for once, we wanted something beautiful to happen between us, something that wasn't spoiled by Patricia and Ronald.

She's dead because of me.

I slowly stand, the guilt eating away at me for not being the man she needed me to be. I don't deserve to walk through that door and hold Georgia in my arms to say goodbye.

Not after I've failed her.

I wrap my hand around Patricia's throat and slam her against the wall. "You have ruined my life," I sneer at her. "I hate you."

"Waylon," she struggles to say, gripping my wrists with her hands. "It wasn't me. I—I—"

I slam her against the wall, and her head snaps back with a sickening crunch. Her eyes roll, her body going limp. I drop her, hoping I didn't kill her, but at the same time, I hope she's dead. The silver of the gun shines from its spot tucked in her waistband.

My hand trembles causing the reflection of the gun to glide across the polished metal. I wipe my arms under my nose and sniffle, then glare at the door that Georgia is behind. Dead. Bleeding. With my baby.

Our baby.

I sob and sag against it, punching the wood with frustration. I want to go in there. "I'm so sorry, babe."

"What the fuck is going on? Patricia?"

I whip my head to peer over my shoulder and look down the hall when I hear Ronald coming out of his drugged state. His words are slurred, so he's still weak.

"I'm going to fix this for you, babe," I say to the one and only friend I ever had. "Goodbye, Georgia. I'll see you and our daughter again." I'll be counting down the days.

I take a deep breath and cock the gun, then stare down the hall.

"Get me a goddamn beer. Oh, and I want to video Waylon and Georgia together. I bet it will make us a ton of money."

The sound of her name coming out of his disgusting, perverted mouth fills me with a new rage. My heart is crying for who it's lost.

My time here with these fucking assholes is over.

My footsteps are soft as I tiptoe down the hallway, the gun heavy in my hand.

"Actually—" he laughs, which sounds forced and drunk, "—Don't get Waylon. I want to fuck her tonight. Been waiting too long to feel that pussy. You can have Waylon. We can watch one another. I know you'll like that. Come help me, Patricia. I can't get up."

I lift the gun and step out of the shadows, aiming it directly at his greasy fucking head. His hair is dirty, his skin shines with sweat and oil, his shirt is stained, and he's wearing tighty-whities that have turned a light yellow color from sweat.

Filth.

Pure fucking trash is what he is.

"Patricia can't come to the phone right now," I say, my voice shaking from fear.

Yeah, I'm scared. I've been scared of this man for years. I've never stood up to him because he was the person who took care of me. He was all I had, but now I know I never had him.

I only had Georgia.

Patricia and Ronald are monsters. We weren't their kids. I don't know how we got stuck with them, but they're the kind of people who need to die. The world would be better off without them.

Waylon's eyes finally leave the TV; the bright light from the screen flashes across his face as he stares at me. A crooked, villainous smile takes over his face. "Well, look who found their balls," Ronald sneers, scratching the front of his crotch.

That's when I hear whimpers coming from the TV, not the good kind, the sad kind. I know those sounds. I've had to hear them enough over the years to learn them.

I take a step deeper into the living room and turn my head to see me and Georgia on the screen. She's crying, and I'm whispering in her ear, trying to tell her how sorry I am.

At sixteen.

We were sixteen in this fucking video.

I bring the gun up and shoot the TV. It sparks and smokes, cutting off the horrific moments of me and Georgia. Scared kids who thought we were being good kids, but we were manipulated and taken advantage of. I often tried to hold back my own fears and emotions for Georgia when we were younger. I had to be the strong one. I had to take care of her.

And I failed.

"What the hell do you think—"

I swing the gun toward him and cock it again. I take a step closer to him, my heart raging inside me. "I think I'm finally doing what I was supposed to do a long time ago." I place the hot barrel against his chest.

"You think you have the balls to kill me? You think you're man enough?" he laughs, which sends his disgusting cigarette-ridden breath wafting in my face.

"Georgia's dead. My kid is dead. I have nothing to lose here."

His eyes widen, and his frail chest starts to pump faster. "Dead? Fuck, that's a problem."

I push the gun against his chest. "It's my fucking problem because she was my family!"

"Boy, I'm your goddamn family. I feed you. Clothe you—"

"Barely. I'm done with you." The curtains behind the TV catch fire from the sparks coming from the exposed wires. "I'm taking everything bad you've ever done to us, and I'm burning it to the ground." I meet his beady eyes, and a flash of me looking up at him in a dark, tight space fills my mind. A memory, maybe. I don't know.

I don't blink.

I don't look away.

But I do pull the trigger.

Bullseye.

The gunshot is loud, and the spray of blood against me is warm as it rips a hole in his chest where a heart used to be. I wait for panic, but it never comes.

He's dead. There's no lingering torture of waiting for him to die. His eyes are open, staring right at me, but he doesn't blink. Wrinkles form around his open mouth, making that stupid shocked expression he died with even more satisfying. Blood soaks through his shirt, dripping down to his underwear.

I'm calm. I wipe the gun down to get rid of my prints and throw it on his body.

I just hate that I'm leaving Georgia behind, but I have to know she's in a better place and at peace. No more struggles, no more pain, no more videotaping or threats, just… solace.

And I miss her so fucking bad.

Smoke is starting to fill up the living room now. I cough heavily into my elbow, but I'm not leaving until those videos are destroyed. I hold my arm over my nose and open the huge filing cabinet next to the TV. All of them are filled with videos of us, neatly organized by the month and year they were filmed. With a roar, I empty out every drawer. They clatter to the ground in a large heap. I want to throw up.

Every encounter, every forced kiss, every tear, every painful memory lies in that pile, but there is one that these films will never have.

And it's the night Georgia, and I risked everything together.

I run to the kitchen and look for some type of accelerant. I find a bottle of lighter fluid under the sink. I grab it, along with the laptop and video camera on the kitchen table.

It's where they uploaded all their work.

I open the laptop and snap it over my leg until it's in two pieces. I add it to the mound of abuse with the video camera and douse everything in lighter fluid. I back away as the flames whoosh up above my head, engulfing my past with all the heat and fury I've felt all these years.

People have seen enough of Georgia. Once the police find this place, I didn't want them to find tapes of us and end up seeing her. I don't care about myself, but she deserves peace.

I squirt the last bit of accelerant on Ronald and throw the empty bottle at him. The tendrils of the fire inch their way closer, burning the recliner. I make my way to the back door and look back to see him in a red-hot blaze.

I'm free, but why do I still feel chained?

I stand in the middle of the yard, the desert beneath my toes cold compared to the heat blaring from the house. I watch as the only life I've known goes up in flames.

I thought I'd feel liberated, but it's the last thing I feel. My freedom, my dreams were supposed to happen with Georgia.

The window in the kitchen shatters, and black smoke billows to the sky.

Slow tears drip down my face as I walk, dazed and nearly catatonic, out of the backyard, turning my back on what was. I climb the fence, not feeling the pain of a splinter digging into my toes as I use the beams to push myself up and over.

I'm numb.

I don't feel anything.

I don't think anything.

I walk. I don't know where I'm going. I don't even know what state or city I'm in. I follow the narrow road. I think it's a road. It's smashed red clay, a dirt road. There's a lot of that around here.

Exhausted, I drag my feet. The grains of sand lodge in my toenails, and I become dizzy. It's been a few days since I've had an actual meal and a good amount of water—more than a damn bottle.

I look around, passing large patches of empty land. I didn't know I lived in the middle of nowhere, but wow.

I stumble, and the jerk of my body has me dry heaving. Nothing comes up.

I spit, but it's just dry. I debate on sitting down to die so the crows can have me, but think better of it. I don't know what keeps me going. Georgia, maybe. She wanted me to live and get out, but I feel selfish for even considering it.

I'm not sure how long I walk, but I come upon a big building with a row of huge motorcycles outside. Loud rock music is coming from the inside, and I can hear laughter and talking.

I've never heard real laughter before; Only Patricia and Ronald's sick, mocking laughter.

"Shit, Hawk. Incoming."

I lift my hand to wave, but it's all too much. I fall to the ground, and their boots scuff against the ground.

"Hell's bells. He looks rough. He's skin and bone." Someone lifts my head up, and I groan. "Kid, what's your name? What happened to you? You're safe here."

"Hawk, he looks in bad shape."

"Go get the doc. Now!" Hawk yells.

"What happened, kid? It's you and me now."

"Bullseye," I rasp. "Bullseye. Always a bullseye." I never miss.

"Stay with me, Bullseye. You're going to be alright. You're with the Ruthless Kings now." The man's brown eyes are concerned as he stares at me, shaking my head to keep me awake.

I have no idea what a Ruthless King is, but this place has to be better than where I've come from.

PART TWO

Present Day

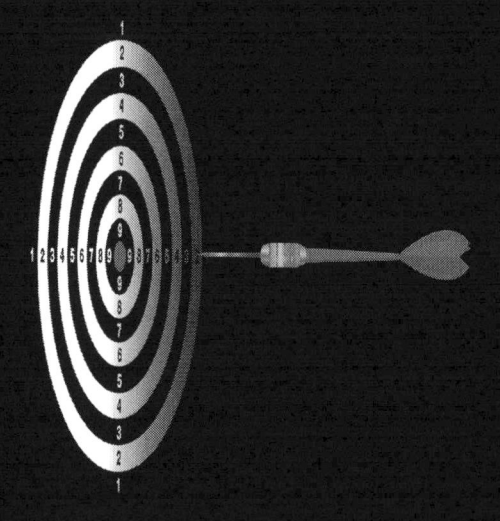

CHAPTER FOUR
Bullseye

THIS IS FUCKING BULLSHIT.

I can't believe Reaper is sending me to involuntary therapy in order for me to remain in the club. Apparently, I've been difficult to get along with. Whatever the fuck that means. I'm sitting in a swanky office with light blue painted walls and 'calming' pictures of landscapes and oceans.

I'm not crazy. Therapy is for people losing their minds, and that isn't me. I'm fine. I don't need anything or anyone. I understand myself just fine.

"You can go. I don't need a fucking babysitter," I grump, crossing my arms over my chest as I stare at Skirt.

"Aye, ye do. Yer being a wee little dick about this entire thing. Reaper wants me—" he points to himself, "—on you—" he points to me, "—like glue. Yer stuck with me." He leans back and spreads his arms wide, showing me he's getting comfortable and not going anywhere.

I hate this.

Not once have I ever been to therapy. I'll go. I won't say a word-no need to because nothing is wrong with me.

"Great," I mutter, less than enthusiastic about him being here.

Reaper doesn't even trust me enough to go to therapy alone. He thinks I'll ditch.

I would, but I won't admit that out loud. That would mean Reaper is right. I'm stubborn and hardheaded. The last thing I ever want to do is admit when someone's right.

Skirt leans forward and places his elbows on his thighs, folding his hands together. "What's yer deal, Bullseye? Why ye so angry?"

"I'm not fucking angry. I just don't want to be here," I snap.

Fuck. He just proved his point.

"Therapy is for weak people. I'm not weak."

"Yer wrong. It takes a lot of guts to admit what's going on inside ye to someone ye don't know. People find it easier, ye know, than talking to someone they know, like a friend. Something about less judgment."

"I don't give a damn who judges me."

"Ye know what I think?"

I let out a long exhale and play with the threads sticking out of the hole in my jeans. "I don't care what you think, Skirt."

"I think ye do. Ye know, we've been brothers for a long time, Bullseye. I don't really know a thing about ye. What's that say?"

"There's nothing to know." The words come out sadder than I mean to when a flash of Georgia's eyes plays in my mind. I might have a club to back me, I know I'd die for any of them, but none of them could be as close as me and Georgia were. None of them can be my best friend. Half of my soul died when she did.

Another pair of eyes flashed in my mind, green instead of blue. She has a pixie haircut and the personality of a firecracker, Ruby, the girl from the boutique over by Daphne's shop. Seeing her has me… feeling things.

I don't want to feel anything, and it's better off that way since she wants nothing to do with me. I wasn't sure if I wanted anything to do with her anyway.

And the last thing I want is to feel. Best bet is to stay away from her. No one can replace Georgia and what we could've had.

"I don't believe that."

"And that sounds like your problem, not mine."

His eyes soften around the edges. "Ye didn't use to be so angry, Bullseye."

"I've always been angry."

"At what? At who?"

I clench my fists at my sides and grind my teeth together. "That's none of your business." I run my hands through my hair and begin shaking my right leg. "When the fuck can we get out of here?"

"Ye have to meet with the therapist first," Skirt says, right as the door to the right opens, revealing an older woman.

Great.

Now I have to worry about grandma's feelings when I tell her I don't want to talk to her.

She isn't too old, I guess. She has gray hair in her fading auburn hair and laugh lines around her mouth, telling me she's had a good life.

"Waylon Jennings?" she holds the side of her glasses as she reads the name on my file.

"Yer name is Waylon Jennings, like the singer? How did I not know that?" Skirt asks, a note of pain in his voice. "That's what I mean, Bullseye. We don't even know the most basic things about ye."

"And I want to keep it that way." I push myself up by using the arms of the leather chair and tower over the tiny woman. "I don't go by Waylon. I don't even know how you got that name. I go by Bullseye, and only Bullseye," I tell her, staring at her in the eye.

"Waylon makes you uncomfortable?"

Oh, she's already doing her psycho-babble bullshit on me.

"Why is that?" she asks, swinging her door open to allow me inside, wanting to find out.

I begin to sweat. I rub my palms on my jeans as I stare inside her office. I can see a long desk with a small waterfall fountain plugged in on the side of her desk to probably give a calming effect.

Well, I'm not fucking calm.

I don't think I've ever felt what calm is.

"I'll be out here waiting, *Waylon*," Skirt bites, narrowing his eyes at me.

I roll my eyes and step forward, turning my body, so I don't run into the therapist. She shuts the door quickly and walks confidently behind her desk. She's pretty for an older woman. She's kept her figure, and the suits she wears emphasize it. Right now, the skirt is professional to her knee, and her blouse is tucked in, paired with a black blazer to match.

She's fashionable. I guess she can be when she's charging people an arm and a leg to sit in uncomfortable chairs to talk about 'feelings.'

It's bullshit if you ask me.

"Please, take a seat," she gestures to the chair in front of her desk.

It's a large leather chair, like the one she's sitting in.

Interesting. I wonder why we have the same chairs.

I take a seat and look around her swanky office. It's painted a calming color too, a soft gray, or maybe it's blue. I can't tell. To the left are built-in bookshelves, filled with books I know I'd never read. I hate reading. I read enough growing up to teach myself about the world.

I don't give a fuck about the world now.

The world can keep spinning, but I'm stuck in place.

"I'm Doctor Sylvia Gerard. You can call me Sylvia if you like."

"Aren't doctors snobby about their titles?" I ask, not caring if I sound rude.

She chuckles and takes off her glasses, folding them gently and setting them in the middle of the desk. "I don't care about that. It tends to make my clients feel intimidated, and I want them as calm and comfortable as possible."

"How did you get my real name?" I ask, wanting to cut to the chase.

I never use my name. I put Bullseye on everything. All my paperwork, all my information. I don't even have a bank account. Everything I have is cash.

"Hmm," she opens her folder to find the answer. I bet she doesn't give it to me. Therapists like to leave people guessing. "Someone by the name of Badge?"

My cheeks heat. Badge looked me up. What else did he find? It's none of his business. I can't believe he'd do that to me.

"I only have your name and birthday. It seems he didn't find anything else."

Load of fucking crap. Badge turns over every rock and looks into every nook and cranny in existence. Whatever he found, he didn't tell this therapist. Or maybe he did, and she's being cool about it.

"Well, I don't go by that name anymore."

"I understand, Bullseye. Your friend, Reaper," her brows pinch while she says the name. She's clearly not used to road names. "He says he is making you come here. Why do you think that is?"

I spread my legs to get into a more comfortable stance and cross my arms. I don't say a word. I'm not doing this.

"Mmmm, I see," she chuckles. "You want to do this the hard way. Is that what you like, Bullseye? Do you only do things the hard way? What do you get out of that besides self-loathing?"

I grind my jaw back and forth to stop myself from speaking. What sucks is there's a part of me that wants to say, "Because it's what I deserve."

But I stop myself.

"Reaper paid for the entire day, Waylon. So we can sit in silence for eight hours if you wish."

I slam my fist on her desk and drop my tone to a threatening level, one that scares most people. "That's not my name!" The agony is loud in my yell.

She doesn't flinch.

She's a tough old broad. I'll give her that.

"You can't scare me, Bullseye. I deal with worse men than you over at the maximum-security prison. Tell me, why does your name bother you?"

I tilt my head back and stare at the ceiling, trying to figure out what is going on inside me right now. All I know is it's usually worse around this time of year because it's when I lost Georgia.

"Why do you go by Bullseye?"

I inhale a sharp breath and look away. The truth is, I don't know. Everyone thinks it's because I never miss with darts, but that isn't the truth.

I actually can't remember the 'why', but I know how it feels. It feels right.

She sighs, and her chair squeaks as she leans back.

My eyes catch a photo on her desk of her and her family. The older man has his arm wrapped around her, and her two kids are sitting down in front of them, smiling at the camera. They seem happy.

"Nice picture," I grumble, ignoring all of her other questions.

Her brow raises, and her mind is spinning as she picks apart my curiosity. "Thank you. My family means the world to me. My sons' names are Jake and Liam."

"Good names. Strong. I like that," I say, a bit softer. If my daughter was still alive, she looks like she'd be around the same age as Sylvia's sons.

"You like family, Bullseye?"

I nod. "Family is important."

"Want to tell me about yours?"

"My MC is my family," I say automatically. I don't want to get into what I don't remember. It's too soon.

"You like them?"

"I'd die for them."

"But do you like them?" she repeats.

"Of course," I nod. "I wouldn't die for someone I didn't like."

She scribbles something down, and I roll my eyes. What could she possibly be getting from this conversation?

"And your biological family? Do you still keep in touch with them?"

The rage I always feel when I think of my past builds up inside me. It's getting hot. I rub my chest.

"You're angry with them?" she questions. "Why? What do you remember about your childhood?"

That's it.

I get up, take her picture, and throw it against the wall. The glass shatters, and she still doesn't flinch. I'm huffing, staring daggers at her. "Your family is nothing. That's all family is. It's nothing."

"But you just said family is important. Which one is it? Is family nothing, or is it everything?"

"You're so fucking annoying." I begin to walk around the room. I feel restless.

"Yes, so are you."

I stop walking, surprised to hear her say that. It makes me smile.

On the inside.

"I don't want to talk about them," I say.

"Well then, what do you want to talk about? Pick something, and that's what we'll discuss today."

"Anything?" I ask.

"Anything."

I head back to my chair and sit down. "I'm sorry about your picture."

"It's fine. Happens more than you think. I keep extra frames nearby."

I chuckle. I hate that I kinda like her.

"If we talk about the weather, that stays between us?" I pick at the threads in my jeans again.

"Always, Bullseye. If there's one person in this world you can trust, it's me. Think of this room as a safe haven, a place where you can come and unload everything off your shoulders and hand it over to me."

I shake my head. Years and years of my past are slamming against me. My eyes burn; the build-up of keeping everything inside threatens to come out. I can't. I need to bottle it up.

"There's no rush. Take your time."

"I don't believe in trust. I think you're lying. I think you're untrustworthy. I don't think you care as much as you think you do."

"Why?" She doesn't sound surprised or hurt, just curious.

"No one does. Trust is an act meant to lure people in, and once they're there, trust turns to betrayal."

"That's a very cynical way of thinking."

"If there's one thing that's never let me down, it's cynicism."

Being cynical is what kept me alive. I won't change that in exchange for trust when trust has never done a damn thing for me.

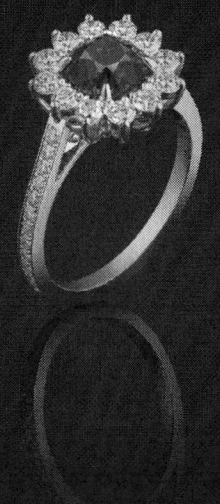

CHAPTER FIVE

Ruby

"NO, I KNOW. I JUST NEED A LITTLE MORE TIME." I PRESS MY FINGERS AGAINST MY forehead as I talk to my bank. I'm three months behind on my rent at Ruby's Rarities. "I almost have the payment in full. I need a week, tops. Please." This store is my life. I only just recently opened, and I poured every drop of savings I had into it and took out a business loan. I make decent money at the store; it just isn't enough yet.

"Ms. Raine," the man types something vigorously on his keyboard since it's clacking in the background. "I'll give you one more week, but after that, there's nothing I can do. I'm sorry."

I let out a breath and smile. "Thank you. Thank you so much. I'll have the payment to you in a week. I'm close, I swear."

"I hope so, Ms. Raine. Have a good day."

"You—" He hangs up before I can finish. "Too."

I hang up the phone and tuck my cell in my pocket. Having my own vintage-style store was something I always wanted. I don't remember a time when I didn't. This store is my dream. But I just don't know how to make it successful.

I fall against the counter and rub my temples as my frustration turns into a throbbing headache. I need another job. I wait tables at Kings' Club once a week and I like it there, but it isn't enough. I want more hours, but I don't know how when I have the store to run.

I'm screwed.

Flat out, ass up, tits down, screwed.

No lube.

Up the ass.

Yep. That's my life. Painful with no pleasure.

I slam my head against the counter and groan.

"Shall I come back another time?"

I pause in my self-destruction and turn my head to see a man dressed in an expensive suit. It's black, and the shirt underneath is dark blue. His hair is styled back, and he grabs the hem of a lace dress as he walks by it.

"Sorry. Rough morning." I straighten and plaster on my best fake smile. "Welcome to Ruby's Rarities. How can I help you today?" This guy seems familiar. A wicked storm is hanging around him, screaming danger.

"You are Ruby?" he asks, an Italian accent bending his words.

"That's me," I say happily.

"Mateo Moretti," he greets, holding out his large hand for me to shake.

Oh, shit.

Moretti.

I know that name. He's a very dangerous man. Holy hell, what is he doing in my store? I flush and take a step back. "You're welcome to anything in the store. Free of charge, Mr. Moretti. Um, yeah. Just don't kill me."

A young woman bounces in behind him with long brown hair and a big smile on her face. "Mateo, you better not be scaring her."

"Stellina, I would never do such a thing. She drew conclusions about me," Mateo explains, wrapping his arm around the woman. He kisses the top of her head, and his dark eyes find me again.

I swallow.

"He's a teddy bear, I promise," the girl tells me.

Right.

Maybe a wild, feral teddy bear that cuddles with dead bodies.

"Go pick out whatever you want, Stellina. I'll wait."

The girl grins and walks away, but he doesn't let go of her hand. He brings it to his lips for a quick kiss before letting her go.

Okay. That was cute. I want a man that kisses my hand. Talk about panty-melting. One guy comes to mind that melts my panties into a giant puddle.

But I can't give in. I have to get my life together first.

Bullseye is a flirt, a charmer, and I don't want to like a player. He only wants me for one thing, and I'm not going to give it up to him. Most girls would throw themselves at a guy like Bullseye, but I know myself. I'm sensitive, and I get attached. My heart desperately wants love and is tired of being alone, so I'm not going to settle for someone who just wants to fuck me and leave me.

I'd end up with a broken heart and eat five pints of Ben and Jerry's ice cream.

And while Chunky Monkey is my favorite, it's not good for my hips.

Broken hearts lead to pants that don't fit.

I watch the scary Moretti man watch his woman, his eyes never leaving her as she flutters around the store, picking up anything and everything she likes. His gaze is intense. It even has me feeling flustered, and I'm not even the one on the receiving end of it.

I stroll around the counter and sit on the high barstool I have behind it. I'm super short, so I want to make sure I can see every corner of my store, and I can't do that without the stool. While she's looking around, hopefully buying everything in the store because it's the only way I'm going to be able to make the payment the bank wants from me, I pick up the account book.

It's time I mess with the numbers.

For the thousandth time.

"My Stellina likes your store," he says, leaning his elbow against the counter. "It's hard for her to find something she likes. I get her expensive things, but she doesn't like them as much as something with a history attached to it."

"I'm glad she found my store. I'm grateful for your business." I tap the pencil against the book, take a quick peek at Mateo then avert my gaze. He's a very handsome man with a dark, calculating gaze and a sharp jawline. Someone that good-looking can only be dangerous.

And it's the kind of danger that reels you in. It's no wonder that girl's so happy. I bet he treats her like a queen while everyone else gets the deadly side of him.

"You're behind," he states.

I jerk my head up and find his eyes on my accounting book. I cover them up with my arms. "I'm sorry, I'm not trying to be rude, so don't put a bullet in my head, but this isn't any of your business."

He holds up his hands in surrender, a wicked smile on his devilish face. *"Mi perdoni.* My apologies. I do not mean to offend you. I'm good with numbers."

The Armani suit says he's great with numbers.

I'm not looking to get rich, but is it too much to ask to live comfortably?

Why be embarrassed about it now? It's not like he can't leave here and use the money he has to find out what he wants to know. "I'm failing," I state bitterly.

"Babe! I'm going to try all this on. Look at this stuff? I love it, and I'm nowhere near done." The woman is holding a mountain of clothes she can barely see over. She's cute.

Moretti chuckles. There's a dark rich hue to his laugh that makes me uneasy. "Stellina, no rush. It's our day, remember? I want you to have whatever you want."

She giggles and throws open the curtain, tosses the clothes inside, and slides the drape closed.

"She's adorable," I tell him, hoping the word isn't offensive.

"She's everything." He folds his hands in front of him on the counter. "So," he switches gears to change the subject. "You're failing."

"It's not something I like to admit, especially to a stranger."

"Sometimes talking to a stranger is the perspective you need. I'm a successful businessman. Tell me, what's failing?"

"Me," I toss the pencil on the counter and exhale. "The business does okay. I haven't been open that long, so I know it takes time to see profit, but I have other bills—medical bills. I can't pay them and my rent here at the same time. It's drowning me. I just... I can't do both, not for much longer. I have a week to come up with five thousand dollars, which I guess isn't a lot in the scheme of things, but to me, it's a fortune."

I can't believe I'm blabbering my business to this man. Rumors have been flying around Vegas because of him. He's killed and conquered. I even heard he tortures his own brother.

But that's all hearsay.

I think it's the truth.

"How much are your medical bills?" he asks, grabbing the pencil off the counter and ripping a sheet of paper out of the accounting book.

"Fifty thousand."

"Not too bad for medical debt."

Says the guy wearing the damn Armani suit.

"I have a deal for you."

A deal.

Why does it sound like he's about to ask for my soul in exchange for ten years of service?

"A proposition, if you will," he rephrases. "My Stellina loves your store. I will pay off your debt, medical, and business."

That sounds too good to be true.

He pulls out a black card with gold lettering, laying it on the counter.

Club Lussuria.

I've never heard of this place.

"You work for me until your debt is paid off."

"What kind of work is it?"

"Come tonight. Around ten. I'll show you."

I slide the card closer and pick it up. The gold lettering looks like real gold, and the cardstock is heavy, solid. I tuck it in my back pocket and nod. "I'll be there."

"Good. No need to live stressfully. There are always options. Plus, I hear you're a friend of the Ruthless Kings. Any friend of theirs is a friend of mine," Moretti says, the smile on his face a little deceiving.

"Babe, I don't know what to pick. I love all of them," the woman says from behind the curtain.

"Stellina. Get it all. No need to wish for some of it when you can have all of it."

Good lord, how does the woman not drop her panties every time he opens his sexy mouth with his sexy Italian accent?

I wonder if he has any brothers...

His... Stellina comes out of the fitting room, carrying every single item she took in with her, places it on the counter in front of me, and then starts to wander around the store again. I start ringing up the items and begin to feel bad. He offered to pay all my debt. Do I give him this purchase for free? The scanner dings every time it passes over the barcode, and the weighted sense of guilt irks me.

I don't even know if I'm going to accept the guy's offer. I should. It's not like I have anything else to fall back on. It's him, or I lose the store.

"You'll be paying me back in less than a month's time if you work for me," he says.

My mouth drops open, and he reaches a hand to my face and closes it.

"Listen, I'm not fucking anyone," I blurt out.

He turns his head and scoffs. "There is no fucking unless you want there to be."

Before I can respond, his girlfriend—sorry, fiancée, by the size of the rock on her finger—takes the spot next to him. She places a few items of expensive jewelry—my most expensive—and sets them down.

"You have everything you want, Stellina?"

She nods. "Thank you. After this, can we go to the bookstore next door?"

"Once Upon a Comet?" What I'm about to say next is going to disappoint her. "Sorry, it isn't open yet. The owners are out of town. They're going through something personal."

"Ah, Tongue," Moretti snaps his finger as he remembers the creepy man. "That's right."

"Darn. I really wanted some new books," Stellina sighs.

I don't know what else to call her. I don't know her real name.

"There is a nice place about two towns over. I know it's a drive, but there's a delicious Greek restaurant out there that's to die for that you might enjoy."

"Mmm, that sounds good," Moretti growls, wrapping his arms around her. "What's the total?"

"One—" I swallow my tongue when I see the number. "Fifteen hundred dollars."

Without blinking, he takes out his debit card and hands it over.

The charge goes through without question, and with shaky hands, I hand him the receipt. It's the biggest purchase ever made in the store.

"Come see me. Flash the card at the entrance, and you'll be treated like a VIP. Dress to impress." His hand falls to the curve of his fiancée's lower back and carries her bags in the other, guiding her out the door.

"Why are you helping me? It can't just be because Stellina likes the store," I shout after him.

The woman giggles. "My name is Nora. I'm so sorry for not introducing myself. I got lost in your store."

"Sorry," I flush, embarrassed.

"Giovanni, take Stellina to the car. Wait there."

An older man waiting by the door nods, his silver hair parted perfectly to the side. He takes the bags from Mateo and holds the door open for Nora, who waves goodbye to me.

She seems nice. Someone I could be friends with, maybe?

"As I said, my Stellina likes your store. To see it go under would make her sad. I have the funds to change that."

"You're helping me to keep her happy?"

"Is that such a horrible thing?" he shrugs, taking a step forward to go out the door. "I plan to see you at ten tonight. Do not be late. I'm not the kind of man who takes kindly to people taking advantage of his time."

"Late isn't even in my nature. I'll be there early." An entire hour early. I'm not about to give the man a reason to kill me.

"*Magnifico*," he smiles, reminding me of a cat who just ate the canary.

I shiver.

"See you tonight, Ms. Raine." With that, he heads out the door, leaving me alone in my tiny shop with my heart racing.

Wait a minute… I didn't tell him my name.

Which meant he knew everything he needed to before he walked inside the store. Great. Well, at least he can't call me a liar. If anything, I was way too honest with someone I've never met before.

"Crap." I sink onto my chair and take out his mysterious card again, shining it against the light. It sure is pretty. The black is rich, and the gold shines brighter than a freshly polished diamond. If this is my way out, just what exactly is he going to have me do?

I turn on my computer and bring up the browser, then type in *Club Lussuria*.

No hits.

His hotel comes up—*The Lussuria*—a five-star hotel on the Vegas strip. Why didn't the club come up on his site? I think that's odd. Is it illegal?

Would I do illegal things to get rid of debt?

Yes.

I stopped caring about morals when I started drowning. If someone would tell me to spend a month in prison for my debt to be gone, I would without question.

I won't kill.

I ponder that thought for a minute.

I don't *think* I would kill.

Well, okay.

It depends on who it is. I wouldn't kill an innocent grandma, but I would kill a rapist. That's good to know. I'll need to remember that.

The bell above the door rings, and I snap my head up to look who's coming in. My heart stops when I see Bullseye standing there. I hurriedly tuck the card in my back pocket and stare at him.

He makes my heart do funny things, things I don't want it to do. He's changed since I first met him. Angrier, paler, and a bit skinnier. He's diabetic, but it's not just his condition. Especially today. He seems tired. Dark circles are under his eyes, and he has a resignation about him that stabs me in the chest.

Bullseye has been asking me out for ages, and I've constantly been saying no. Not because I don't want to. He's a beautiful man. Tall, muscular but not overly so, a face that belongs in a magazine, and those eyes.

A bright, crisp green, but right now, they are murky.

"I just came in to say I won't be bothering you anymore."

What? No, that's not what I want.

"I realized a lot today, and the truth is, going after you was something I should never have done." He scratches the underside of his chin but never takes his eyes off me.

Christ, that hurts way more than it should.

Skirt is outside, idling on his bike as he waits for Bullseye. His words are almost drowned out by the exhaust grumbling.

"I'm not good for you, and you obviously see that. Have a good life, Ruby." He turns around, and the bell dings again. The door slowly shuts behind him as he mounts his bike, and I finally get out of my stupor and run after him.

I push against the door with my shoulder and yell, "Bullseye!"

He pretends not to hear me and guns it out of the parking spot.

Why does it feel like everything just changed for the worst?

"It's for the best, Ruby. He isn't in a good place," Skirt explains. "Have a good one." He follows Bullseye a second later, and I'm left dumbfounded wondering how the hell so much could happen in one hour.

Bullseye is a rarity. There aren't many like him. Coming across someone like him is like looking for a gem that's never been discovered before.

I just missed out on a chance of a lifetime because of my own insecurities.

It's always me.

I'm always a failure, and I have no one to disappoint but myself.

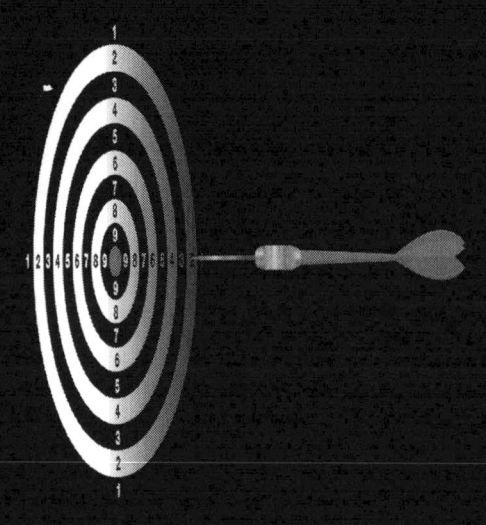

CHAPTER SIX
Bullseye

I'M GLAD I DON'T HAVE TO GO TO THERAPY FOR ANOTHER WEEK. TODAY WAS EXHAUSTING. I didn't even say that much to Sylvia, but being there with her had me thinking about a lot of things. I've fallen off the wagon. I've enjoyed a little too much of my life, fucking cut-sluts and doing whatever the hell I wanted. I have briefly forgotten that I don't deserve anything good in my life.

Georgia and our daughter deserve more respect than what I've shown them.

I hate myself so much. Can no one see it? Can no one see how much I regret my life?

I should have laid next to Georgia and killed myself, then let the flames take me. I'd be with her and my little girl right now.

Instead of this.

But again, I don't deserve the peace that comes with death, which is why I ended things between Ruby and me. I don't know what it was between us, but it was me chasing her, and she was obviously not interested. I don't need to be chasing tail anyway.

No more whores.

No more sex.

I've lost myself in sex for most of my life. It's ruled me for too long. I thought it would feel different after what happened when I was a teenager.

It doesn't.

I still feel like I'm performing, and I'm tired of it.

I'm tired of everything.

I walk into Kings' Club, a local bar a club brother of mine started from the ground up. Tool and his ol' lady own the place. Everyone in the MC has a few shares in the club, so we get revenue. I like the place. It's got a sultry vibe to it, especially when Juliette is singing on the stage. The girl has a set of pipes on her that has this place packed on Thursday and Friday nights.

Tool is behind the bar and placing fresh bottles of booze on the liquor shelf. "Tool," I call out as I head his way.

He looks up from the box and smiles when he sees me. "Well, look what the cat dragged in! How you doing, Bullseye?" he asks as I take a seat on a plush, purple velvet barstool. "You look like shit."

"Thanks. You don't look so good either."

"I always look good," he says.

"Yeah, he does. Ow! Oww!" He seizes up and whips his head around to see Juliette running away, giggling after slapping his ass.

"I'll get you for that, little sparrow!" he shouts.

"I hope so!" she replies, her voice a soft echo in the club.

"Damn, woman." He doesn't say it with malice but with a huge lovestruck grin on his face. He reaches behind the counter and pulls out two glasses, then pours about two fingers' worth of scotch in each. "What can I help you with, Bullseye?"

I pick up the glass and take a sip. I close my eyes and hum as the smokey flavor warms my stomach. "You are helping me."

"Drink to feel better, not worse," he says.

"What do you think I'm doing?"

"I think you're one glass away from falling apart. Tell me, what's going on?"

I've known Tool a long time. I even knew Hawk, Boomer's dad, back in the day. If I could tell anyone what was eating me, it would be him.

No one knows my story. They all know I wandered in from nowhere and that I'm somehow connected to the fire I set on that horrible day, but I never told my story, and no one ever pushed me to tell it.

"How's your diabetes?"

I clutch the glass so tight I'm afraid it will break. "Fine," I seethe, downing the rest of the whiskey.

"I shouldn't be letting you drink if you haven't been responsible about your sugar levels."

"I said I was fine." I reach around the bar and pluck a bottle from somewhere. Vodka. I can get down with that. I pour myself enough to make me sick later and take a huge swallow. I'm not much of a drinker, not like Patrick used to be or anything, but today I really need it.

"You don't look fine. Why are you torturing yourself? Why won't you let us help you?"

"I don't need help, and last time I checked, Reaper is making me go to therapy. There. See? I'm getting help." Stupid goddamn diabetes. That's what everything is about these days.

"Bet you didn't talk about anything with her either. She's the best damn therapist on the West Coast, and you won't let her help."

I snort and take another gulp of vodka. "Like you would? Don't act like you'd gush your feelings to a stranger."

"I don't know, but if whatever is eating you ate me, I probably would. You're killing yourself, Bullseye. Slowly. Can't you see that?"

I down the rest of the vodka and slam the glass on the counter. "I do," I say, standing up from the barstool. I bring out four twenties, hoping that's enough to cover what I drank—and toss it on the table.

"You're a stupid man, Bullseye. We care about you too much to let you destroy yourself."

It isn't up to them.

If I want to self-destruct, if I want to explode, then I'm allowed to set the timer. But I know I can't pull the trigger myself. Someone will have to do it for me.

"See you around, Tool."

"You can't fucking drive right now." Tool runs after me and grabs my arm to take the keys out of my hand.

"I'm fine, Tool." My head is buzzing, but it isn't enough for me to not drive.

He plucks the keys from my hand and tucks them in his pocket. "I don't give a damn. I'll call someone to come get you. I'm not letting someone I care about drive drunk. Go sit down. I'll bring you some food and water. Christ, Bullseye. What the fuck is wrong with you?" Tool storms off, huffing and puffing like the big bad wolf.

I take two steps forward and plop down in one of the booths. I fold my arms on the table and place my head on top of them.

I don't know what's wrong with me. Anything. Everything. I don't know who I am or why I exist anymore. I want to turn back time and be with Georgia. I want to fight differently. I want to risk my life for her. I would rather her and our baby be alive than me.

It isn't about me trying to be a hero. It's about what's right.

She deserved more than she got, and here I am bitching and moaning about the life I have. Well, life ain't worth shit without her and my baby. My daughter didn't even get a chance at life.

Tool is right about one thing: my past is eating away at me. It's slowly consuming me, making it hard to breathe. There's so much I owe to the Ruthless Kings for teaching me about life. When I first came to them, the only thing I had ever seen was my room. Now that I know, I don't care.

I don't care that I have a bike out there worth more than what some people make in a year. I don't care that I have a job at a garage, where I can build cars from the ground up. I don't care that the family I have is amazing. I know I'm lucky to have them, but I don't care right now.

They can't ever replace what I lost.

And what I lost, I want to find again.

Which is impossible.

It's not in the cards for me to have what I've lost twice.

I'm breaking apart, and I don't know how to put myself back together. I'm a sad, pathetic case of a man, just like I was all those years ago.

"Bullseye!" Reaper's voice cuts through the air like a knife, angry and ready to jab me through the chest.

I don't bother to lift my head. I don't want anyone to see me like this. I was okay living my life by fucking my way through it since that was really the only thing I was taught. Then I got diabetes, and I had to actually fight to survive. I had to watch my sugar, or else.

I never wanted to fight that hard to live. I just wanted to coast until I died.

Boots kick mine under the table as Reaper takes a seat in front of me.

"Look at me," he says softly.

I shake my head, rolling my forehead over my forearms. I know I don't have a say in the matter. When Prez says 'jump', you reply with 'how high'. I know what he sees when I lift my head up. A weak man unable to care for himself. I know.

I'm not asking for pity.

I just want to be left alone.

Tears fill my eyes, and I close them, the pain becoming so unbearable inside me that I don't know if I can let it out. It's too much.

It's a bomb.

"Bullseye."

I open my eyes to see him sitting in front of me, a concerned look on his face. "I want to fix this for you. Tell me what I need to do, and I'll do it."

I look away. "There's nothing to be done."

"What happened? Tell me. What has you like this?" Reaper has grown up with me, and all he knows is I came to them in a bad way. He saw the shape I was in. "Is it that day you found the club?"

"Reaper, come on, man. You don't get it. No one will get it."

He gets up and grabs me by the shirt, then drags me to the back. My hip runs into a table, and I hiss. He yanks the curtain back but doesn't let go of me. When we get to Tool's office, he opens the door and throws me inside.

He steps in and shuts the door. "Rage," he says simply.

"What?" I look around the room to see stacks of paper, a couch, a desk, and few other knickknacks.

"Rage. You want to destroy something, fine, but it won't be yourself. Tear the room apart. I'll pay to get it fixed."

"It won't be enough."

"You want me to punish you?"

"That won't be enough," I state, debating if raging is exactly what I need.

Because I am so fucking angry.

"What will be?" Reaper asks.

I take a minute to think about it. Nothing is coming to mind. "Tool won't care I trash his office?" I'm starting to breathe heavier, the need to destroy searing my veins like a hot flame to wood.

"He needs an excuse to remodel it. He's been putting it off." Reaper leans against the door and crosses his ankles over one another. "What will be enough? What do you want?"

I don't answer. I clench my fists and grind my jaw together.

"I asked you what the fuck you wanted, Bullseye. What the hell do you want?"

"I don't know!" I roar at him, then swipe my arm over the desk. Papers fly into the air, and the keyboard to Tool's computer hits the opposing wall, clattering to the ground.

"I don't fucking know!"

My eyes blur when I think about Georgia, Ronald, Patricia, and my daughter. The pain that I've kept inside for too long is boiling over. How much longer can I pretend to be someone I'm not?

I slam my arms on the desk. It's old, cheap, and the wood cracks to the four corners.

It feels good.

Real fucking good.

I let out another painful scream. Sounds that have been building up for years, pain that I've never been able to let go of, are exploding out of me. I slam my arms on the desk again, my bones aching from the force. I don't stop. I keep pounding it, and the wood splinters, digging into my arms as I smash it with every ounce of anger I have.

I'm sweating. The salt is stinging my eyes, but the exertion feels liberating. I imagine Ronald and his face. His confident, evil, vile fucking face. I pretend it's him I'm breaking. I wish that's what I did. I wish I broke every bone in his body before I killed him. I was too quick to pull the trigger. I should have made him suffer for what he did to Georgia.

To me.

To us.

To my fucking life.

"He ruined me!" I scream.

I take a sidestep from the desk and stare at the wall.

And all I see is his face.

I lift my fist and punch the wall.

No.

I don't punch.

I plummet.

My muscles ache as I rotate my hands, taking turns to smash against the wall. The hole gets bigger. Dust from the drywall flies, and my knuckles split open, a small amount of blood staining the white plaster.

I don't punch it anymore.

I grip the jagged edges and rip the drywall apart. I grunt, growl, sneer, and hate.

Oh my god, the hate that is consuming me feels so good. I need this. Reaper was right.

I ram my shoulder next to the hole, and the wall gives again, crumbling to pieces onto the floor. I breathe in fiberglass and dust and whatever else is floating in the air right now. It burns my eyes and my lungs, but my heart is still numb.

A thousand shards of fiberglass could puncture my heart, and I doubt I'd feel a thing.

Or maybe that's the problem.

I'm feeling everything. It's hitting me all at once. I can't tell what I am feeling because there's too much. It's making me confused.

There's no room inside me for puncture wounds.

Because that is all I am.

My arms slow as the exhaustion hits me. My muscles ache and tremble. It's getting harder to breathe.

"I want it to be over," I choke, holding back a sob as I break in front of one of the most powerful men I've ever known. I stumble back and swing my head toward him, my knees buckling when I suddenly become dizzy.

"Whoa, I got you, Bullseye. I got you." Reaper catches me and helps me to the floor.

I try to regulate my breathing by inhaling and exhaling deeply.

All this is this stupid therapist's fault. I was fine. I was fucking handling my shit, and she had to go prying me open, thinking I was this unsolved mystery. That bitch. Oh, when I see her again, I'm going to break her picture frame again.

I was fine.

I am fine.

"I want to go back in time, Reaper," I say solemnly, half-dazed as my vision blurs.

"And do what?" he sits back on his knees and cocks his head, waiting for me to answer.

I remember falling on the Ruthless Kings doorstep and how they took me in. A stray, a worthless, forgotten person. I could have fallen off the face of the earth, and no one would know.

But they took me in.

"I want to die."

He pinches his lips together, not liking my answer. "I'm sorry, but I can't let that happen."

It isn't up to him.

All I know is I can't live like this anymore.

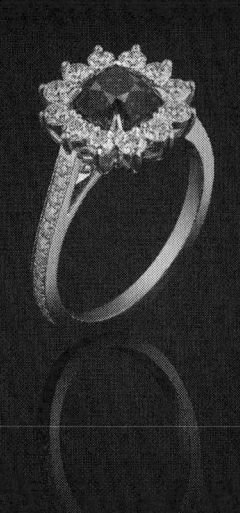

Chapter Seven

Ruby

I look up at the expensive, massive, luxurious building. Lussuria Resort and Casino. I'm standing there in a simple black dress, nothing too expensive, but it will get the job done. It hugs my body in all the right places, and it's strapless, which shows off the small tattoo of a heart I have on my left collarbone.

"You can do this. If you say no, he'll kill you. Probably fast, like a gun to the head or something." I blow out a breath and fiddle with the ruby ring I have on my right ring finger. It's a family heirloom; the ruby itself is huge—six carats of pure ruby-ness. I don't know if that's a thing, but it is right now. Actually, this is the ring that I'm named after, along with the four Rubys before me in my family. The ring itself is old. Just this year, I had to get it reset since the prongs in the old one wore out. I'm careful to get it inspected at a local jeweler every three months.

It's the only thing I have that links me to my family. It's been just me for as long as I can remember. I've survived this long without help. I think I deserve a break.

"You know, it just gets bigger as you look at it."

I stumble in my red high heels at the sound of a familiar voice. I hold onto my ring as if that can ground me and look up to see a few of the Ruthless Kings there, including Reaper.

My shoulders deflate with disappointment when I don't see Bullseye. Where is he? Is he actively avoiding me?

"What are you doing here?"

"Guy's night," Reaper says, tossing a cigarette onto the ground and stomping on it with his boot.

"Liar. Sarah kicked you out because you're annoying the hell out of her," Poodle cracks, wiping his long, wavy hair over his shoulder.

I've met all of the Kings over the last few months. They're a good group of guys, loyal to a fault. And their edges? Rough as hell. There's no smoothing them out. If a girl is lucky enough to be an ol' lady, they just have to deal with the pain of getting pricked every now and then.

By their edges... not their...

"She isn't annoyed with me. She wants me to get out and have a good time," Reaper clears his throat, then tugs on the hem of his shirt.

"Right, right. So when I heard her yell, and I quote, 'Reaper, I swear to god if you don't go out tonight, I'll murder you in your sleep then feed you to Happy!' That was just all in my head?" Poodle teases, and Skirt gives him a fist bump.

"Yep," Reaper pops the p. "My doll can't get enough of me."

"You're so full of shit," Tool chuckles.

"God, I know." He drops his head in his hands. The move makes him less intimidating and frightening. "I'm just worried about her. Doc said that trip to Portland wasn't the best idea. Now she's completely on bed rest for the remainder of her pregnancy. She's cranky."

"No shit," Badge grumbles.

If I thought Bullseye was an asshole, Badge beats him by a million yards. He isn't very likable, and he doesn't seem to care.

Well, I don't want to be late meeting Mateo. Or is it Mr. Moretti? Shit. What do I call him?

I take a small step forward, careful to keep balanced on my high heels. What was I thinking wearing this? I can't walk in them. I wear flats all the time. I wanted to look taller, more intimidating, and maybe I'd be taken more seriously if I didn't look like a runt.

Not that it matters. Even with four extra inches, I'm still a pipsqueak.

"May I walk you inside?" Tank asks, holding out his arm on my right side. He's so cute with his kindness; I hardly know what to do with it.

"Me too," Braveheart says, coming up on my left.

I look around again for Bullseye one last time. Not that I'm disappointed these men want to walk me inside, but my eyes still search for him.

They always will.

He's a beacon in a long dark night, and I can see that he's lost. He thinks he's alone in the night, but I still see him because I'm there too.

"He's not here, Ruby," Tank leans in and whispers. "He's having a tough time."

"I don't know what you're talking about," I reply, swallowing thickly, then straight ahead toward the entrance of Lussuria. "Is..." I gulp again when my voice cracks. "Is he okay?"

"No," Braveheart states.

"Braveheart!"

"What, Tank? You want me to lie to her? He isn't okay."

The wind breezes between us, and I'm able to smell both of their colognes, which are a bit heavy. Not that they're wearing too much, it's just that I have a sensitive sense of smell. It's one of the things I like about Bullseye. He always smells like leather and pine. I can never get enough of it. It's a hint barely there, like his scent is wind-blown, leaving just enough behind to leave me wanting.

And that's the root of all the problems between him and me. In one little word, the man threatens my independence.

Wanting.

I've never wanted anyone like I want Bullseye. It's why I pushed him away all those times he attempted to ask me out. I'm good at being alone. I know at the end of the day, the only person I can depend on is myself.

Bullseye's presence is suffocating, leaving me gasping for breath every time he is near. Part of me wants to drown in him, but the other side of me always wins.

I don't drown in him.

I swim away.

And now, he is going through something alone. Maybe I should forget the offer Moretti offered me. I'm a big girl with big girl problems. I know I'll be alright one day, even if it won't be today. Bullseye is more important than some missed opportunity.

He is the missed opportunity.

Ah, I hate that little voice in the back of my head.

"Tell you what, let's take a picture and send it to him. I'll make sure to tell him you hope he feels better," Braveheart offers kindly, but there's a tone to his words that tells me he is up to something else.

Well, that sounds nice. It would be good to let Bullseye know I care. "Alright, but if I don't like it, we take another. It needs to be my good side." Good thing I put extra product in my hair today to slick my pixie cut down and added an extra coat of mascara.

Tank scoffs. "Please, like you have a bad side." He freezes as he leans in closer to me, realizing what he just said.

"Aw, thank you, Tank." I give him a quick kiss on his cheek, and he blushes-what a damn cutie.

"Okay, cuddle close, everyone." Braveheart tilts his head to mine, and I do the same, wrapping my arms around both of the guys. He holds out his phone in front of us, and our three faces fill the screen. "One, two, three..." he says.

I plaster the biggest smile on my face, a genuine one, hoping it makes Bullseye happy.

"Aw, look at Ruby being a King sandwich," Poodle teases with a wink.

"It isn't such a bad place to be," I whip in return, and the guys laugh as we walk together toward the big golden doors.

Two doormen open them by the handles, and the same older man with silver hair greets me at the entryway. "Ms. Raine. Mr. Moretti is expecting you."

I unhook my arms from Tank and Braveheart and open my red clutch to dig out the business card Mateo left me. "It's here somewhere, sorry." The tube of my lipstick rolls under my fingers. A foil of a condom wrapper sounds, which has me blushing as I dig.

"How have you been, Giovanni?" Reaper asks the scary bodyguard guy in front of me.

I forgot to take that out. Better to be safe than sorry, right?

"What ya got in there, Ruby Red?" Poodle peers over my shoulder to try to get a peek.

"Like I'd tell you," I snip, finally feeling the heavy edges of the card. I hand over the card, but as I remove my hand from the bag, the condom wrapper slips out of my purse and lands right in front of the silver fox's Italian black shoes.

Oh my god, this isn't happening.

A few of the guys snicker behind me. My face goes up in flames. Kill me. Weld my coffin shut and let me sink to the bottom of the ocean.

Giovanni bends down and clears his throat, gripping the condom between his fingers and holding it into the air. "I believe you've dropped this, Ms. Raine."

I close my eyes and take a deep breath. "Seems that way, doesn't it?"

"Oh, this is gold." Braveheart takes a few more pictures. "Bullseye is going to throw a fit."

I open my mouth to stop him from sending anything to Bullseye, but I stop myself. Maybe him being a little jealous is a good thing. He can come back, and I can somehow convince him to give me another chance. Maybe I can ask him out instead of waiting for him to come around again.

Lifting my head high and thrusting my shoulders back, I pluck the condom from Giovanni's fingers and tuck it back in my clutch. "If a woman wants to have sex and be prepared, I think she's allowed to be, don't you all? Or are you sexist and think only men can be prepared?" I level my eyes with all of the Kings. "I'm ready to see Mr. Moretti now, Giovanni."

He has a proud glimmer in his eyes and offers his arm to me again. What is it with men and offering their arms? Bad, murderous men aren't supposed to be gentlemen. They are supposed to hold a knife to my neck or rip my panties off.

Heat pools in my panties when I think of Bullseye doing both.

What the hell is wrong with me?

I bet he would, too. I bet Bullseye has an animal inside him waiting to be unleashed, and I want nothing more than to unlock the cage he keeps it in.

"Right this way, Ms. Raine," Giovanni's baritone voice has a sliver of what danger sounds like running down my spine.

The Ruthless Kings follow, and Giovanni holds up his hand to stop him. "Mr. Moretti only wants to meet with Ms. Raine. If you don't have a card, you are not welcome."

"We have an open invitation, Giovanni. Don't forget that." That sounds a hell of a lot like a threat from Reaper.

"I haven't, but he has business to discuss, and his business is always private," Giovanni says with a bite. "Come, Ms. Raine. We can't keep him waiting." Giovanni tugs on my arm gently, and I wave goodbye to the Kings.

I feel guilty leaving them behind. They have all tried to support my store, but sometimes, desperate times call for desperate measures.

We pass a few drunk people. Women are laughing, stumbling in their high heels, and whatever man they are with tries to hold them upright, probably praying they get lucky tonight. A drink clatters to the floor, and a splash of a cold beverage lands across my foot.

I yelp, running right into Giovanni's side. "Sorry, I wasn't expecting that."

"It's okay. I understand." He snaps his fingers, and two men run down the hall until they are at our sides. "Clean up that mess. There better not be a wet spot on that rug when I walk out of Club Lussuria, do you understand?" he darts his eyes from one man to the other.

"Yes, Mr. Moretti," they say in unison.

"You're a Moretti too?" Duh, that makes sense.

He chuckles. "I'm his uncle."

"Oh, that explains a lot," I let slip. "In a good way," I rush out, hoping I didn't offend him. Sleeping with one eye open for the rest of my life is something I do not want to do.

He tosses his head back and laughs, patting my hand that's hooked on his arm gently. "Oh, Ms. Raine. You're a flatterer."

Uh… yeah, totally.

When we get to the entrance of Club Lussuria, I expect there to be a line, but there isn't. The doors are black, and I can't see inside, but a man is standing to the side. He's wearing a crisp black on black suit, standing there with his hands crossed in front of him. He's also tall and broad, with olive skin and ink-colored hair. He isn't older like Giovanni, but young, maybe in his twenties.

The outside of the club is surrounded by black and red sculptures swirling toward the ceiling. I narrow my eyes as I try to figure out what I see about them but can't see at the same time. My brain is trying to figure out the trick. I tilt my head, and that's when I see it.

They are bodies pressed against each other, a clear message of what hides behind the doors.

Lust.

Which makes sense, given the name.

"Piero, if you'd open the door for the lady," Giovanni hisses when Piero takes a minute too long. He's staring at me.

"Apologies, Mr. Moretti. My focus was captured by a stunning sight."

Oh, wow. He's good.

Too young for me. I like my men a little more… damaged.

I dip my head as we walk through the doors, the base of the music vibrating deep within the walls. It's dark in here but not packed.

"It's membersonly," Giovanni yells into my ear, so I can hear him over the music.

That makes sense. Everything screams sex and wealth.

Neither of those things comes cheap.

"Come. He is this way, in the VIP area." He leads me through the dark, passing people who are dancing with one another.

On every table, there is a black rose, a color I've never seen before on a flower. It's decadent, sexy, and while it screams beauty, it also promises danger.

I carefully walk up the black velvet steps, the plush cushion giving under my spiked heels. The cool air wraps around me, causing goosebumps to rise on my skin and make me shiver. I'm surprised, given the humidity sticking to the air. It's a dense fog curling to the ceiling as the bodies gyrate. Giovanni spreads out his arm to allow me to sit down in the booth. The seats are lush, an intoxicating plum color that tricks the eye into thinking it might be black. The back of the booth reminds me of an old Victorian couch. It swoops around in a half-circle to give everyone enough space.

The table is a bright cherry red with a flaming spade in the middle. A single black rose sits in the middle in a crystal vase, and across the other side is Mateo Moretti.

He has his arms stretched out over the back of the booth, dark eyes watching me as I get settled. He looks… casual.

As if I'm not about to sell my soul. No biggie. It's fine.

I rub my hands down my thighs and clear my throat. I'm always fine.

I wish someone was by my side right now, someone that I knew, maybe Braveheart or Tongue.

Bullseye.

No, not him. He's done with me. I should have said yes to him the hundred times he asked me out before. I don't know what's changed with him. I don't know if he met someone else, or maybe whatever illness he has requires him to be in quarantine. Maybe has the flu.

Moretti holds up his finger and closes his eyes, his body giving a half jerk before a euphoric grin takes over his face. Nora pops her head out from under the table and crawls up his body, not seeing us yet.

Oh.

Yum.

I take a sip of the water in front of me and watch as they devour each other. His hands are on her ass, squeezing the globes with his large hands. My breasts are heavy and aching, my nipples turn tight, and my clit begins to pulse as they give in to their carnal desires.

His eyes meet mine as he whispers something to Nora. She turns her head and holds a hand over her mouth, giggling. She slides off his lap and plops down in the spot next to him.

"You came," he says to me, reaching for the scotch glass.

"So did you." I slap a hand over my mouth and feel the tips of my ears heat.

They're going to shoot me dead. I'm not going to make it through the night.

Mateo grins, taking a sip of his amber beverage. "I come every day and night, Ms. Raine, and so does my sweet Stellina."

"I really do," Nora seconds, sounding a bit drunk off lust.

Maybe they pump pheromones into this club.

"Would you like a drink before we get started?" he asks.

I turn to see Giovanni sitting next to me, casually staring at his phone as if his nephew wasn't just getting a blow job right in front of him.

What kind of world have I stepped in?

The desperate kind.

"I would, please. Spiced rum with a splash of pineapple juice, please."

"Anything for you, Mrs. Moretti?"

"Another daiquiri. They're yummy."

"Stellina, you know what happens when you get drunk."

I watch their exchange, and her eyes go round and innocent as she sips her straw. Clearly, they have played this game before.

"No," she says, slurping away.

He bends down, and whispers in her ear and her eyes roll to the back of her head.

Oh my god.

What if they're asking me to be their third or something? Could I do it? I mean, he is handsome, and she's pretty, but that's pretty far out of my comfort zone. I guess I could for him to pay off my debt. Money talks and sex feels good, so fuck it. Why not?

"You're probably wondering why I asked you here, Ms. Raine," Mateo turns to me, kissing the skin of Nora's shoulder.

I fold my hands on the table just as Giovanni comes back with drinks. Thank god. I take it from him and chug half of it down. "Listen, I'm not into it, but if you're looking for a temporary third, I'll do it. But I don't do anal with strangers. Sorry." I lay it all out there so no questions can be asked about my limits. "Other than that, I'm pretty open." It's obvious that's what they want, with how they can't seem to keep their hands off one another. They are kinky.

I can respect that.

I take another big swig of my drink and stare at Giovanni, Moretti, and Nora. I meet their gazes individually, and they're staring at me like I've lost my mind. "Ooo-kay," I drawl. "Is it about the butt stuff? Because—"

All three of them burst out laughing, and Nora reaches for my hand, grabbing it as she shakes her head. "Oh my gosh, no. I'm so sorry that's the impression you got. Mateo didn't think you'd actually be early, so I slipped under the table to kill time, but no, sorry, you aren't who we're looking for when it comes to a temporary third."

Ouch. Okay. I mean, I'm relieved, but rejection still sucks. "Oh. Okay, that's good. What a relief. Wow. I apologize for jumping to conclusions. This place tends to make the mind be on one track, and that track is sex." I drink to shut myself up.

"I like you, Ms. Raine." Moretti shakes a finger at me and smiles.

That's good. At least he isn't offended. I can sleep well tonight, knowing I'm not dead.

"Please, call me Ruby."

"Ruby," he says with a lick of his lips. "I asked you here because there's a certain aspect of my venue that I am hiring for. You'll make good money if you agree, but there are stipulations. Considering you were willing to be our third, it gives me hope you'll consider my offer."

I sip my drink again, only to realize I'm out. I'm going to need more.

As if Giovanni is reading my mind, he places a taller glass in front of me. The same drink with a slice of pineapple.

"My hero," I say to him before greedily sliding the liquid courage over to the edge of the table. I wrap my lips around the straw and take three huge gulps. "Okay," I blow a raspberry with my lips and shake my arms to get the nervousness out of me. "Hit me with it. What's your offer?"

"If you turn around, you'll see a sign that says, 'Hall of Lust.'"

I keep my drink close as if it's my body armor as I spin around. Just as he said, a neon sign is flashing those words, illuminating bright light everywhere. Another set of black doors hide what's behind them. A man sits there, collecting the black roses as a few people go inside.

"Do you know what it is?"

I shake my head as I turn around to stare at him. "No."

"It's for voyeurism. In that hall are separate rooms. In those rooms, there is a one-way mirror, so the customer can see what they've purchased. You would be their purchase."

I choke on the rum, and it burns my nose, throat, and eyes. I cough and hold up my finger as I take a swig of water. "I'm sorry, what?"

"You can request a partner, or you can perform by yourself. When the customer orders, they're specific with what they want because of the choices on the list. For one month, you work for me, and your debt will be clear."

"Are you—are you trying to pimp me out?"

"Nothing like that, I assure you," he says. "You'll merely perform-dance for their amusement. Put on a show. There is no touching. There is no sex—unless, of course, you have chosen to do so."

"Why this? Why not make me a waitress?"

"It will take you twice as long to pay me back that way. You'll be safe here. Every single one of my Lusters, that's what I call my employees who work the Hall, have a bodyguard. No one has to know your identity either. I need a body. The last woman quit due to becoming pregnant. You're in a pinch, and this is me willing to help."

"Here?" I squeak.

"No, with her husband. This life isn't for everyone."

I take another drink and consider his proposal. Could I do it? It would be nice not to wake up with looming debt. "Before I agree, can I get a tour?"

"Thought you'd never ask." Moretti slides out of the booth and holds out his hand for Nora to take. She lifts her eyes through her lashes, staring up at him as if he hung the moon. Maybe for her, he did. It's sickly romantic.

And I want it.

Yes, I'm whining because I fucked up my chance all on my own.

Giovanni slides out of the booth and holds out his hand too. I don't feel a spark with the handsome silver fox like I do with Bullseye.

I miss his annoying visits. I need to check on him. The more I think about it, the more I want to flee from Moretti's offer, but I know this is a one-time opportunity. If I don't take it now, I might not ever get a chance like this again.

Bullseye doesn't want me anyway, right?

What's it matter now?

My breath stutters as I inhale, the sharpness in my chest making it difficult to breathe.

"You okay?" Nora leans in and questions, placing her hand on my arm.

I nod. "Yeah, just nervous."

"Don't be. It's amazing if you're into this kind of thing," she says.

I am into it. I've never had the opportunity to truly experience it.

The guard opens the onyx door, bringing to view a long, wide hallway. It seems never-ending. The doors are made of steel, and Mateo opens the first one on the right.

"Ladies first," he purrs, watching Nora with eyes that promise wicked, terrible, amazing things.

I enter the room and gasp at the extravagant curtains and bedding. Everything is silk. There's a chandelier above the bed and a small fridge to the left. It imitates a bedroom.

"You could turn on a black light and find this place clean as a whistle. Everything is replaced after every visit," Moretti explains.

I take a seat on the bed and reach for the list that's lying next to a touch screen panel. The black silk sheets slide against my legs, and I have to hold in a moan. Wow, they feel good.

Everything in this room is meant to make someone's body feel good.

"I used to have a colored-light system, but I upgraded. I found the lights tacky." He tugs on the sleeves of his suit.

"Right, of course." I try to sound agreeable, but I'm in shock while I stare at the menu. He has everything. I shouldn't say menu. It's not like I'm ordering dinner, but reading the options makes me feel like I'm at least ordering dessert.

Male on male: full sex scene with toys.

Male on male: Without toys.

Male on male: Without protection.
Male: Solo act.
Male on Female.
Male on Male on Female.

The list goes on and on. After I pick who I want, it asks what I want. If there's a certain scene, I'm craving.

"Have a good time. Let me know your decision when you're done."

"Wait! What—" But I'm not quick enough. Moretti locks me in the room, and I spin around, gasping for breath as I stare at the floor-to-ceiling mirrors taking up the entire wall.

Fuck.

What the hell have I gotten myself into? Do I succumb to pleasure to erase debt? *To hell with it all.*
What do I want to choose?

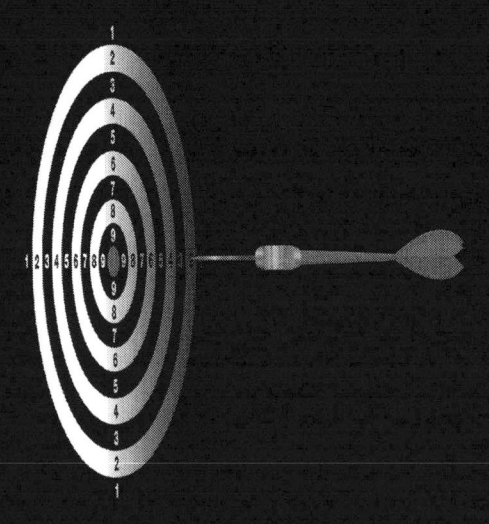

CHAPTER EIGHT
Bullseye

Everyone knows I like to do the watching.

No one knows *I* crave to be watched.

It's in my DNA. It's what I was shaped to want, and no matter how much I fight it, I can't anymore. Watching Skirt and Dawn, no matter how fucking hot it is, it isn't enough for me.

Everyone thinks I'm at home wallowing in my discomfort, but I'm not. I'm at Club Lussuria, and the only person who knows I'm here is Moretti.

After the last few days of diving darker into my mind, I need this. Fighting who I am and what I need is exhausting. I know I'm fucked up.

No, not fucked up.

Broken.

I should hate being watched after everything, but now it's like I don't know who I am without it. I've been lost for eighteen years, stuffing this need down in my soul until I couldn't taste it anymore. I was lying to myself.

I always tasted it. The forbidden nature, the darkness of it, the way my skin crawled from eyes wandering over my body… I miss it.

I miss being wanted.

Christ, I really am fucked up in the head.

The worst part?

I'm wondering if I miss *them* wanting to watch me. They created this monster inside me, and now I need to figure out how to tame it before it kills me.

In the confusion, I know there's a part of me that wants to heal. I want to get better. Everything I've stuffed inside me over the years to try to live a normal life is cracking me from the inside out.

If I have to heal, I have to break.

Maybe breaking won't hurt as bad as suffering.

A knock at the door sounds, and Moretti enters. He doesn't know why I'm here, and he hasn't asked. What I like about him is that he's discreet, secretive, and only thinks business. That's what I am right now.

"You sure you want to do this?" he asks.

"I'm sure." He has no idea how much I need it.

"Sign here." He places a piece of paper down on the table along with a sleek gold fountain pen. No doubt it cost a fortune.

I pick up the pen and scribble 'Bullseye.' I never write my real name. Anywhere.

"Cash only?" he double checks.

"Cash only."

"How many times a week do you want?" He folds the contract and tucks it in his pocket.

Patricia and Ronald had me performing twice a week until the end. Would twice be enough? "Twice, if that's alright."

"Of course it is. This will be your own room. No one will be allowed in or out. You will not share it. You can keep all of your personal work items here, and before you go out, you will check your blood sugar. You even signed the contract stating as such." He pats his jacket pocket.

How the fuck does he know about my diabetes? You've got to be fucking kidding me.

"I know everything there is to know about my investments, Bullseye. In that refrigerator, you'll find everything you need, including your testing kit. Another one of my men and I will be in here to check on you to make sure you do it."

"I'm not a child," I say through tight teeth.

"That's not what I hear." Mateo strolls to the fridge and pulls out a black bag.

I hate that thing. It only makes me feel weaker. How the hell can I be a man again and claim who I am when I can't get over the fact I have a disease that makes me weak? Type 2 Diabetes can reverse itself, but it hasn't with me yet.

Patiently fucking waiting for it to get on with it.

He tosses it to me and crosses his arms. "I'm waiting, Bullseye. I don't have all night."

I jerk the bag open, clenching my jaw. I insert the test strip in the handheld vampire, as I like to call it and prick my finger. I plop a drop of blood on it and watch as the machine thinks. "There." It beeps. "120. Happy?"

"As a fucking clam," he says with zero enthusiasm.

My tablet dings, and I hold my breath as I stare at it on the coffee table next to the chair I'm in. It's the tablet for Club Lussuria. Someone has already requested me. How the hell am I already in the system?

"Fresh masks are in the closet since you care about your identity. Welcome to Club Lussuria, Bullseye. I can't wait to buy you for an hour and see just what you can do," Moretti darkly states. I'll be putting on a performance for him sometime in my future. Great.

I wait for the disgust to hit, the sickness of wanting this, but it never comes. I'm nervous, but I'm more excited. It's liberating, giving in to this need I've suppressed for so long. I know for a lot of people like Skirt and Dawn, it isn't a big deal for someone to watch them.

For me, it's carved into my skin like some of the other scars I have on my body.

I've been shot.

I've been hanged.

I've had my own darts used on me.

But the pain doesn't compare to the pain of not being watched.

Knowing someone is getting turned on because of me is invigorating.

I blame *them*.

I get up and walk to the large modern armoire. There's a full-length mirror on the wall next to it, and I look at myself for the first time in a while. I've lost weight. I have dark circles. I don't look the same. I'm shriveling to the man I used to be when I was eighteen. Slowly but surely, if I don't get my head out of my ass, I will become that useless boy again.

I avert my eyes and open the closet, noticing new costumes with tags and masks. Let's not talk about the toys sitting on the bottom of the closest still in the packaging. How did he know I'd officially say yes? All of the costumes are my size.

My tablet dings again, and I'm reminded that I need to make sure my customer doesn't want anything special; otherwise, I can do what I want. I reach for it and slide the notification to the side.

Solo play. Wants to see muscles flex, but not in a regular bodybuilder way-a natural way, like working out.

That's it.

I can do that.

I drop the tablet onto the chair and rummage through the closet. Options aren't something I'm used to. My service was just demanded from me when I was younger. It's nice to be in a safe environment. I forgo the costumes and reach for a leather mask that covers my entire head and face, minus my eyes. There are nose holes so I can breathe, but other than that, my mouth will be covered.

It's perfect.

I don't want anyone to see my face.

Plenty of the sick world has already seen it.

I glance down at the toys again, and one grabs my attention.

A cock cage.

Before I feel pleasure, I deserve to feel pain.

I bend down and push the ends of the costumes out of the way. There are a number of cages here, in various sizes.

Christ, there is a mini one.

Well, I sure as hell don't need that one.

I grab the second largest and close the armoire door and begin to undress. The air is cool, wrapping around me like an ice sheet. My nipples bead; even the tight contraction has me gasping for breath since my nipples are pierced. I slide off my pants next, and my cock comes into view. It's pierced from top to bottom with a Jacob's ladder, a Prince Albert, and behind my sack, I have a guiche piercing.

Like I said, pain before pleasure.

It's going to hurt when I get hard. My piercings are going to press against the cock cage, and the anticipation sends a shiver running through me. I unwrap the cage from the packing and inspect it. It's round, with metal spirals around it to encase my cock. It snaps at the top where the lock goes. The key is in my hand, but I need to figure out how I want to unlock it.

The customer will have to tell me when they want me to unlock it, or maybe they can. I wonder how that would work.

I slip my flaccid cock into the cage and hiss. The metal is cold. I slide the lock into place and groan. Fuck, this is going to hurt. I have no room to grow.

Perfect.

I slip my mask on, right as a knock on the door sounds. "Come in," I answer.

The door swings open, and Moretti runs his eyes up and down my body. Everyone knows he is bisexual; he doesn't care to hide it. I'm straight, but it doesn't bother me. I'm used to men looking at me.

"Aren't you a vision?" His nostrils flare.

I clear my throat and hold out the key to him. "Is there a way for the customer to unlock it when they want, or is it no touch?"

"I apologize, Bullseye. There is a no-touch rule. I can tell her to tell you when she wants you to come? She will bang on the glass?"

"Yeah, that works." My words are muffled by the mask. I slip the key through the mask, and it holds tightly against my cheek.

"I'm not going to ask why you're doing this. It isn't any of my business."

"It isn't."

He charges at me and wraps his hand around my throat. "You'll watch how you talk to me," he sneers.

"Fuck you." I shove him away. "I'm not someone you can boss around. If you can't handle that, let me know, and I'll walk out of here."

"You've been bought and paid for. You'll bring in great money. Keep your temper and attitude in check, Bullseye. Just because you're a King doesn't mean you can't be punished."

Punished.

He knows nothing of punishment.

"Your punishment would be a fucking playground," I growl, taking a step forward, squaring off to one of the most powerful men in the city.

Do I have a death wish?

Yes.

But wishes don't come true if they're spoken out loud.

I'm fearless and afraid.

Anyone who says they aren't scared of anything is a liar.

Life is too fucked up to not be terrified.

"I can't tell if you're brave or stupid, but I respect you either way. Come on, your customer is waiting."

"Who is it?"

Moretti shakes his head and levels his eyes with mine. "The reason this business does so well is because of anonymity."

"Of course." I can't believe I even asked.

We walk out the door, and my sack rubs against the metal of the cage. It's a delicious tease, creating a different kind of hunger.

One that I've let starve for far too long.

"Have fun," he smirks, opening the door for me to enter the room, where only the customer can see me through the glass.

I step into the room. The floor is lukewarm under my feet. It's smooth, shiny, like polished cement. There's a red glow encompassing the space, making it difficult to see at first. There are two silver bars attached from one side of the room to the other, a few seats if I choose to sit, and a bed.

I don't care about any of that.

If she wants to see muscle, then she wants an up-close show.

My feet patter against the floor, and I cock my head to the side as I stare into the glass, hoping I'm capturing her gaze, whoever it is.

When I get there, I lift my arms above my head and drag my fingers down the mirror, flexing my biceps as if I'm dying to get inside. I angle my body and place my hands parallel to my shoulder and push up, staring into the glass.

Are they already touching themselves?

Do they want more?

Are they fantasizing about me?

The thoughts have blood flowing to my cock, plumping against the cage, negating any possibility of becoming fully erect.

I groan and take a step back, running my hand down my chest and playing with my nipples. I flick them, tug on the bars until it hurts, and a bead of pre-come leaks from my begging dick.

I fucking love this. How have I been denying myself all these years?

I drop down to my forearms and imagine a beautiful woman under me, Georgia, but her face doesn't last long. She morphs into a short little spitfire with a pixie cut and burgundy colored hair. Her green eyes are wide as I drive into her, fucking her raw.

She'd scream my name, shout it the heavens—or maybe hell, depending on how good I make her feel. Ruby would cream all over my pierced cock, milking me for every drop.

I rut against the floor, waving my hips back and forth. The cage clinks onto the floor with every stroke. My arms shake as I hold myself up. My cock wants to burst free from its cage. It's painful. I can feel the agony deep in my sack.

I shake my head of the thoughts of Ruby. My desire for her grows, as does the need to move on from Georgia. I would be cheating if I loved again.

I jump my feet between my hands and stand, strut close to the mirror again, and grip my caged cock.

Right above me is a rod. I jump up to grab onto it, giving her a full view of what she's paid for. I lift myself slowly above the rod, keeping my abdominals flexed, and rub my cock against the mirror, hoping she sees how many piercings I have.

Clink.

Clink.

Clink.

The cage scratches against the glass.

My cock becomes harder, and the flesh starts to swell outside of the metal springs. Fuck! It hurts. It hurts so fucking good.

The sweat behind my leather masks begins to build as I pull myself up faster, showing this stranger my endurance.

I concentrate on keeping every muscle in my body strained so she gets what she wants. I can feel her eyes on me, and it has my heart pumping, my cock leaking, and my mouth watering for release.

Bang. Bang. Bang.

The vibrations shake the mirror. I release the tight grip I have on the rod, drop to my feet, and slip my fingers in the space of the mask between my cheek and eye. The key is slippery from perspiration, and I slide it out.

My fingers shake as I insert it into the lock. The slide of the lock is music to my ears. I toss the lock through the air, and it smashes against the glass. I yank the cage apart and groan with relief as my cock finally becomes fully engorged. The imprints from the cage remain along the silky length, and my piercings seem irritated from the pressure. The head is an angry blood red, and precome is spilling from the tip, glossing my shaft.

I wrap my hand around myself, and my body bucks. I'm tender and sensitive, but it isn't enough. I pinch the Prince Albert at the same time I stroke the Jacob's Ladder creating a unique massage along the hard muscle.

"Fuck," I growl to myself. My spine tingles and, my balls pull tight against my body as my orgasm threatens me. I reach a hand between my legs and press against my guiche. My moan is a strangled sound as my entire body tenses. The tendons in my neck strain, and I can't breathe as my orgasm wrecks me.

White come shoots through the air and lands on the glass, similar to paint strokes. The next three spurts don't have as much momentum. They drip over my hand, puddling onto the floor. From head to toe, I'm shaking. I don't move to clean up. I'm staring right into the glass, knowing her eyes are on me too.

My shoulders rise and fall as I take in harsh breaths, my heart stutters an even, strong beat, and a euphoria takes over my head. I'm dizzy. I'm high.

I surrendered to my need.

And it feels so fucking good.

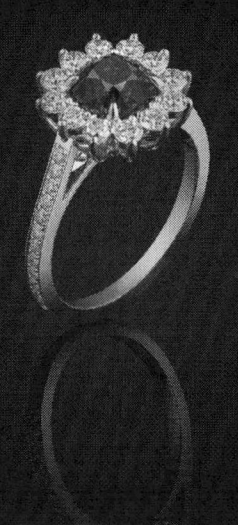

CHAPTER NINE

Ruby

O^{H.}
My.
God.

What the hell did I just watch? And can I please watch it again?

This man is pure, explicit, panty-melting sex. I can't rip my eyes away from him. His body is glistening under the red light, and with every ragged breath he takes, the sheen of sweat reflects against his broad chest. Come drips from the tip of his cock; for some reason, I find myself licking my lips, wanting a taste. The piercings call to me. My tongue twitches to slide over the metal studs and suck them into my mouth one by one.

I don't even know if he could fit in my mouth. The man is big, long, and thick. Even semi-hard, he is impressive. The beast lies against his thigh, smearing his come against his leg. He's so close, I can see the dark hairs becoming wet.

God, he is beautiful.

A man like this deserves to be worshipped and praised. By the brutality of scars on his body, I'd say being praised is the last thing that has happened to him.

I pull my fingers from between my legs and whimper. I'm still sensitive from one of the most explosive orgasms of my life. If this is what Moretti wants me to do, I'm fucking for it.

Who needs morals? They never got anyone anywhere, anyway.

I swallow as my gaze runs up his body, pausing at the bead of sweat curling around his nipple before sliding my eyes to the masked face. There's no mouth. I can't see his lips, but I can see his eyes. So familiar, yet distant at the same time. I feel like I know him.

He turns around and bends over, giving me a gorgeous view of his ass. It's round and firm, an athletic butt I want to grab and bury my face in. I love rimming if the guy is into it. Most straight guys aren't because it's such a forbidden place.

Pleasure is pleasure; who cares what kind of form it comes in?

He grabs the cock cage and then takes two steps to the right to grab the lock. He gives me one last look by peering over the swell of his shoulder before walking away.

"My god," I whimper, clawing at the damn glass to grab that ass as it jiggles with every step away from me. "Come to Mama."

Okay, I'll pretend I didn't just say that out loud. I'd never have a lover call me Mama. It's weird.

The stranger walks out the door and leaves the viewing room empty, leaving me wanting more than the show he gave me.

Love isn't born out of lust. Love only grows if the environment is right, but lust? It's an emotion anyone can give into at any time; the environment be damned.

I let out a breath I had no idea I was holding and walk over to the sink and wash my hands. Club Lussuria is unlike anything I've ever experienced. I never thought voyeurism would be a job opportunity for me. While I'm still nervous at the prospect of performing in front of someone, I'm also kind of... excited? It's new and different—a change of pace that I need in my life. Something other than working myself to the bone.

I wipe my hands off on a disposal towel and toss it in the hamper. My legs wobble as I try to remember how to walk. I tug the hem of my dress down to where it belongs as I unlock the door.

Damn it! I could have fled this entire time.

No regrets.

I thrust my shoulders back and open the door, then strut down the hall with a flushed face, wet panties, and a deal to make.

I have never felt more like a boss in my entire life.

I open the door to leave, and Giovanni is there waiting for me. "Did you have a good time, Ms. Raine?"

"The best," I scoff on a laugh. I school my features when I remember this is a business meeting. "I mean, it was good. Very classy rooms." The blush creeps up my neck, and I'm thankful it's dark in here.

"I'm glad you find it to your liking. Come this way, please. Mr. Moretti is waiting at the booth for you." Giovanni turns on his heel, and I follow him blindly, catching glimpses of people making out and moaning on the dance floor.

When we arrive at the booth, Giovanni has to clear his throat because Moretti has Nora spread out on the table.

Moretti lifts his head from the side of her neck, and he growls in displeasure, removing his hand from the apex of her thighs. I turn my head away to give them privacy, and when I look back after a few minutes, he is licking his fingers clean.

Good lord, the man gives no fucks about where he takes Nora.

This is the perfect example. Lust has no environment. It lives everywhere in every situation.

"Ruby, did you enjoy your show?" he asks, wiping his hand on a black cloth napkin.

"I did. Very much." My voice cracks, and I stuff my mouth with a straw from my new drink. I gulf eagerly, quenching the dryness in my throat.

"Would you like to work for me?"

"Am I allowed to work for you after the month is up?"

His mouth tilts devilishly to the left. "You think you'd want to be here longer? I'm not so sure. Let's start with a month, and we'll see where we're at."

"Thank you." The straw makes that terrible slurping suction sound when I'm done.

Mateo slides a piece of paper across the table and clicks a pen. "Just sign on the dotted line, and I'll see you first thing tomorrow night."

I pick up the pen and read the contract he made for us. It's short, simple, and I have no doubt he'd aim to kill me if I broke this contract.

This is a contract between Ms. Ruby Raine and Mr. Mateo Moretti. Ms. Raine has agreed to Mr. Moretti's terms. Mr. Moretti will pay all of her debt, and in return, she is to work for him for one month. At the end of that month, whatever money Ms. Raine makes that surpasses the amount owed will be paid to her in full.

Below the simple statement is his elegant signature, and just below that is a space for mine. When the pen hits the paper, he stops me. "Let me make myself perfectly clear on something, Ruby. No one fucks with me. No one fucks me over. If you plan on doing that, I'll pry that family heirloom off your finger."

My eyes round in shock when he says that. How did he know? I drop the pen and swirl my ring passed down from generation to generation back and forth.

"I'm a businessman, and I pride myself on being smart. You are in debt, Ruby, yet you refuse to sell the one item you have that will not only pay everything off, but you'll have some cash left over too. I know a gem like that has to be worth a pretty penny."

I protect my ring by holding my left hand over it. He's right. I won't have to struggle anymore if I sell this ring, but I can't. It's all I have left of my family. I'd rather die than give it up.

"Do I make myself clear?"

"Crystal," I say on a slight growl. "I won't disappoint you. I'll be here. I'll show up."

"Excellent. Also." He reaches into his pocket of fucking wonders and slips out another tightly folded piece of paper. "I want to buy 49% of Ruby's Rarities. In one month. We can discuss business later."

"What? No, that wasn't part of the deal—"

"It's a business opportunity. Do you really want to say no? You'd never have to worry again."

"Why are you doing this? Why are you so interested in me?"

"Mmm," he hums, lifting the scotch glass to his lips. His dark eyes sparkle in the light, revealing a devious nature lurking beneath.

The abyss.

"Because I know someone who has an interest in you. Besides, Ruby's Rarities has potential. I am part of said potential," he says. "Plus, my Stellina loves that store. Whatever she loves, I buy, but I know you love it too. I don't want to take away your dreams. I know how important those are."

"Can I think about that, please?" I ask in a small voice.

"Don't take too long to think. Opportunities like this only come around once," he tells me.

Yeah, the implication is clear.

He won't be offering this again.

I pick up the pen and sign our original contract. I'll work for a month, pay off my debt, and I'll see where we are.

"I paid your debts earlier today. You're free and clear when it comes to collections."

When it comes to collections...

Man, Moretti really doesn't beat around the bush, does he?

"You can stay and enjoy yourself, or you can leave. You're free. For now."

"I'll go. I'm starving," I say, suddenly feeling uncomfortable and second-guessing everything.

"We have a wonderful restaurant here," he offers.

"Good to know." I hold my clutch to my chest and get the hell out of this club.

I make a beeline for the door, trying to duck through all the people dancing. It's no use. I'm getting bumped around by all the people writhing around. A waiter nearly runs into me with a plate of drinks. The music is loud, but even still, with all the distractions, I can feel the threatening gaze of Mateo Moretti searing my back. I don't need to turn around to see. I grab the silver, gothic handle of the door and push it open with my hip. A burst of cold air hits my heated face, and I sigh in relief.

I fan my face with my clutch and head to the right, where the doorway is. I need to get the hell out of here. Too much has happened.

"Hey! Ruby!" I hear my name called, and I look around to see Slingshot at the blackjack table with Poodle. "Want in?"

I give him a wave and shake my head, then mouth 'hungry' knowing he, of all people, would understand.

"Okay, have a good night!" he shouts over the loud shouts and cheers of the crowd as they win.

I wrap my arms around myself and head out the doors. Once I'm outside, I walk to the nearest wall and slump against it. I feel dizzy, out of my element, and in way over my head. There's one person I want to call. One person I want to talk to about this.

But I know Bullseye won't answer.

"Everything will be okay," I mutter to myself as I put my hands on my hips and bend over to take a deep breath. "Everything will be fine. You're doing the right thing." I'm sure I sound like a crazy person talking to myself. It happens a lot.

I finally catch my breath and straighten back up, looking out to the Vegas nightlife. It truly is a beautiful place. Bright lights. Busy people. Shotgun weddings. Gambling. This city has anything and everything. I don't often get a chance to come all the way to the Strip from my little town a ways over, but when I do, I love it.

My thoughts are interrupted when my stomach grumbles, reminding me that I haven't eaten since breakfast. I know of a great sushi place that's nearby. It would be good to walk under the stars. That'll clear my mind and calm my racing heart. I keep my arms tight against my body as I put some distance between myself and The Lussuria. My stilettos kiss the pavement, clicking rhythmically down the sidewalk.

Being alone on the Vegas strip has my thoughts whirling. I can finally think without the chaos in the background and temptation all around me. I stare down at my ring. The big, beautiful ruby ring that everyone would want and no one can have. I've got plenty of offers on it. Mateo is right. I could sell it and would never have to worry about anything ever again.

Selling it would be turning my back on my family. I've been alone for a while, but that wasn't by choice. The only family I had died when I was younger. Everything we owned got turned over to the state, but not this. I stole it from the estate sale. I knew it was the most important thing to protect. This ring was promised to me by generations of my family before. And that's a promise I intend to keep.

I'd rather be homeless and live on the streets than give this up. I remember my mom wearing it, whether dressed to impress or in pajamas. She never took it off.

"A lady can always look nice no matter what clothes she wears, as long as her jewelry is beautiful," she used to say.

I wonder what she'd say now? What would she think of me performing for money? What would she think of me failing? The medical bills I can't pay for were from when I lived on the streets for a year after my family died. I got stabbed, and someone found me, rushed me to the hospital, then I got an infection, and the rest was history.

I was left with fifty thousand dollars to pay.

Life hasn't been easy. I've clawed my way to get to where I am. I never need anyone. I'm the strength I'll always need.

But sometimes, I get tired of carrying the weight around. Fighting all the time just to survive is almost suicide. I can feel the urge to give up in the marrow of my bones. I can sell the store to Mr. Moretti, and with the cash, start over somewhere else.

No, I can't give up.

It isn't in my nature.

"Mother fucker," I curse when my heel gets stuck in a grate.

That's what I get for not paying attention to where I'm going. I twist and dance, giving people a small smile as they walk past me and not help.

"Tonight! Come tonight and get the show of your life! We have strippers for everyone and back rooms for your pleasure!" a man announces as he hands out flyers with naked women on them to the people around me. "You want one?" he asks.

"Does it look like I give a damn about your flyer right now, buddy?" I finally rip my shoe out of the grate and stumble over to the sidewalk. I snatch the flier from his hand and wave it in the air. "It's been delivered."

"Bitch," he grumbles before shouting his little mantra again.

Ugh! I could just cunt punt that bastard to the next city. I swear. Who waves a flyer in someone's face when they are obviously stuck in a grate? "I hate people," I sigh.

Maybe I should just go home and warm up some noodles instead of spending money I don't have. I decide to take a shortcut home. I live in an apartment above the store, and if I take a cab, it's only a few minutes away. I can make it. But I'll never be able to hail a cab with all these bustling crowds and traffic. I cut through a back alley away from the bursting sidewalks filled with drunk people. I inhale deeply when I smell Chinese food, and my stomach roars at me, pissed off that I haven't eaten.

The one streetlight in the alley flickers; I'm reminded of what happens to women in movies when they're alone.

Now I'm just paranoid.

I gasp when I hear a trashcan lid hit the ground. I spin around to see who's there, but I don't ask. I might be dumb enough to walk alone at night, but I'm not dumb enough to ask a cliché question. A raccoon scurries across the alley and lifts a piece of garbage to its mouth with its tiny paws.

I press my hand to my chest and laugh. "You cute little asshole. You scared the hell out of me." It stands on its hind legs and nibbles the apple core, staring at me with its big black eyes. I turn back around and run smack into a chest. The first thing I notice is the pungent stench of alcohol and cigarette smoke. I slowly tilt my head up, and fear pools in my stomach when I see the arousal on the man's face.

He's older, maybe in his fifties, with gray hairs in his beard. He has a shaved head that shows his tattoos. His eyes are void of kindness. All that's in them is hunger.

Damn it.

"I'm just trying to go home," I start slowly, backing away step by step. "I don't want any trouble. Please, just let me go home." I've never been in a situation like this. I've been one of the lucky women who has never experienced sexual assault. When I got stabbed, it was over where I was sleeping. Apparently, I took a guy's spot without knowing.

"You don't want trouble?" he mocks me, his voice like a rockslide crashing against the ground.

My spine tingles from the sinister gravel in his tone.

"If you didn't want trouble, a pretty thing like you wouldn't be out here all alone dressed like a whore." He sucks his tongue over his teeth.

As I back away, his face fades into the shadows as he follows me, and when he steps into the light again, the hatred in his eyes confuses me: hatred and arousal. Men like him hate women but want to use them anyway.

As punishment for who they are: women.

"Is that what you are? Do I need to pay you to suck my cock, whore?"

"Fucking pay me, and I'll drop to my knees and bite it off," I sneer, letting my six-foot-five temper out of my four-foot-eleven body.

He backhands me so hard. My vision blurs for a split second. Blood lingers on my tongue, and tears sting my eyes. I get my footing under me and try to run away, but my heels are too high, and I trip on that goddamn apple core.

He grabs my wrist and jerks me back. I slam into his chest, and he wraps his other hand around my neck.

I'm frozen.

I know what I need to do. I need to fight. I'm not a weak person, but as I stare into his cold eyes and taste the iron on my lips, I can't seem to figure out how to come out of the scared trance I'm in. I'm pathetic.

He slams me against the wall and shoves his body against mine. He growls, then takes his other hand to grab my breast.

Cunt punt.

I grab his wrist with both of my hands and use it as leverage to lift my body. Then I shoot out my leg, putting all of my force behind the knee to the balls this disgusting man deserves.

I make contact, and I swear I hear a nasty squelch—or maybe that's wishful thinking—but he lets go of me to double over. I do not take the opportunity for granted. I kick off my shoes and make a dash for the exit.

Only to slam into another chest.

"Oh, little one. We never hunt alone." The new stranger is skinnier than the other.

I look back to see the first guy still cupping his balls. I doubt he could even get it up right now.

I lift my fist in the air and swing, but he dodges it, grabs my arm, and wraps it around my back, shoving me face-first into the brick. He grinds his erection against my ass, and I whimper, tears brimming my eyes when I realize I'm not going to get out of this.

He reaches under my dress and rips my panties off. The air tickling my bare skin makes me remember my voice. It's the reminder I need that I still have one last weapon.

I scream.

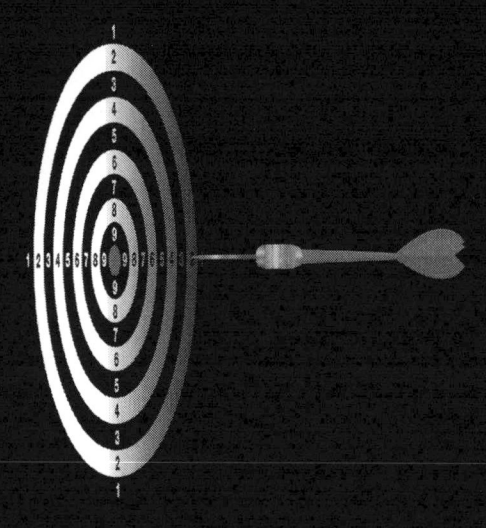

CHAPTER TEN
Bullseye

I FEEL BETTER THAN I HAVE IN A LONG TIME. I KNOW I HAVE A LONG WAY TO GO TO FIGURE myself out, but I think accepting who I am is a good place to start. I was conditioned for this lifestyle, and not having it has left an uneasy, unfulfilled emptiness in me.

Sure, I watch Dawn and Skirt, but that's not what I was conditioned *for*.

I need to be watched.

And tonight, I didn't feel shame. I felt empowered because I had control. Things are different now. I'm different. I'm not a weak fucking kid who can't do anything. I'm a grown man. I can conquer my demons; it just may take longer than others for me to do it.

Moretti said I was done after one performance tonight. I don't know if it's because he reads people really fucking well or if I didn't do a great job, but I'm glad not to be pushed to do more. I need to take this at my speed because it's my pace that matters.

Not anyone else's.

So I'm walking the strip to try and clear my head when I realize I feel lighter than I have in ages. I'm actually enjoying the nightlife of Vegas. I was getting so rundown. The burden of everything weighed on me so much it was pushing me to the ground.

I still have a lot I need to accept that makes me realize I'm not a weak man.

I'm just a man who *needs* differently than others.

All of a sudden, a scream rips through the air—at least, I think it does. I'm not sure. Vegas is filled with so many sounds. I freeze mid-step and listen, then dig my hand into the inner pocket of my cut to grab my darts. If there is one thing I've never failed at, it's always hitting my target.

I tilt my head and roll the steel dart between my fingertips. It's smooth, sharp, and ready to kill. If I'm not aiming to kill, then I'm not doing it right, am I?

I'm about to chalk up the scream to just being in my head when I hear it again coming from my left. How can everyone else go about their business and not run toward where the murderous wail is coming from? People are so selfish.

I run to the left and jump over a line of trimmed bushes. My boots hit the sidewalk with a thud, and I hear the commotion coming from the alleyway squeezed between two buildings.

"No! Fuck you," the woman hisses. I hear the guy groan, but painfully, not in a good way.

She's a fighter. That's a relief.

I sprint to the entrance of the alley and see one man on the ground cupping his balls and the other shoving a tiny woman against the wall. I can't see her face, but her dress is hiked up, so it isn't a mystery as to what the guy has planned for her.

Not tonight.

With all my might, I sling the dart through the air, and it lands right where I want it to, right against the side of his neck, where his jugular is. He releases her and stumbles back, his hand touching the side of his neck as he tries to take a deep breath.

I debate if I want to attempt throwing a dart at the guy holding his hand between his legs as he rolls on the ground in pain. He's a little far, but these babies are made to fly true, with way more yardage than a regular dart.

Fuck it.

I take a few steps and throw my body into the shot. The dart slices through the air, and by the sound of his scream, it's a bullseye.

I just don't know where it landed on him. I'll deal with him when I'm done with the guy who has one of my darts in the side of his neck.

"Who the hell do you think you are, taking advantage of a woman?" I roar. There is nothing I hate more because I felt like the scum of the earth when Ronald made me and Georgia have sex. How can a man justify himself for doing this?

"She's just another whore," he gasps as blood tints his lips.

"Yeah, I wouldn't try to speak." I squat down and flick the dart. "Those aren't regular darts. See, the metal has latched onto your muscle, and if you pull it out, you'll probably bleed to death since it will take the jugular out too. So sad," I pat his face and pretend to pout.

"W-wait, man," he stammers. "You can't do this to me. My life—"

"I don't give a fuck about your life."

I rip the dart from his neck. Blood gushes out in a heavy spray, just like I thought it would. The attempted rapist tries to suck in air like a fish out of water as his blood bubbles onto the filthy alleyway floor.

No doubt the rats will come out to play soon.

I stride over to the other man who was writhing in pain not moments ago and realize he killed himself. Well, I killed him, but he pulled the dart out from the side of his head, which made his brain swell.

Oops.

I grab my dart from his hand and whip my wrist to get the gunk off the dart before tucking the two back into my pocket.

A whimper from behind me reminds me of the girl. I was so caught up in these two assholes, I completely forgot about her. I sprint back to where she's huddled against the wall, head hung between her arms as she sobs.

"Hey, it's okay. They're dead. They aren't going to hurt you anymore," I say soothingly, but she doesn't answer. I check her out to make sure she isn't injured. She has a bite mark on her shoulder and a few scratches and bruises that no doubt hurt like hell, but she looks like she'll be okay-no major damage, from what I can see.

And then I notice the ring on her finger. My heart begins to thump, and fear, real fucking fear, seeps into me. "Ruby?" I whisper, hoping like hell it's someone else with the same ring and pint-size height.

She jerks her head up and spins around. Those light neon green eyes are full of fear, but the panic fades to relief when she sees me. "Bullseye? Bullseye!" she throws her arms around my neck and holds on so tight I think she might choke me.

I don't care.

I wrap my arms around her and try to comfort Ruby. "Shh, it's alright. I got you now. You're safe." I close my eyes and think about what could have happened to her, the first woman I've given a damn about romantically since Georgia. I tighten my arms again and hold her close as she sobs, her body trembling with fear.

I'm proud of her for fighting. She took one guy down, and I know she gave the other a run for his money.

She pulls away, staring up at me with those fucking eyes that soften the hard shell encasing my heart. Her mascara is running down her face in thick black lines. She has scratches on the side of her cheek from the brick wall, and a bruise is forming on the other side of her face, along with a split lip. "Thank you," she trembles.

"You never have to thank me for something like this," I tell her.

She nods and wipes under her eyes, but it's no use. The tears keep coming, and the shock is causing her to shake. Her gaze turns hard as she looks down at the guy who almost had his pants down around his ankles.

"You fucking bastard! I wish I could've cunt punt you to hell!" she shouts, slamming her foot between the man's legs.

I have to roll my lips together to keep from smiling because now is not the time.

Cunt punt. Only she'd say something like that. Only she'd want to give her attacker a final blow to the crotch after nearly being attacked.

She's so tiny but so far from helpless, and that's one of the many things that drew me to her. From the moment I saw her, my soul felt this connection, this peace. I got addicted to it, so I kept coming around. She has this energy about her that's infectious. It makes me feel alive. It's her spunky nature. I've never met anyone like her before. It's hard not to be drawn to her when she makes me feel… better.

It doesn't hurt that she's incredibly beautiful. Her short pixie hair cut matches her personality: sassy and strong. It takes a lot of guts for a woman to cut off all her hair. Not many can do it—something about long hair and femininity or some bullshit like that.

I like that she has no give-a-damns.

Like mine, hers are all busted and fucked up.

She's still kicking the guy until she hiccups and covers her mouth with her hands. "Oh my god. I can't believe this happened. I was fine. I was on my way home, and I tried to fight them, Bullseye. I swear, but he was so strong—" she begins shivering again.

"—I know you did. You're nothing but a fighter. I'd never expected you to give up and take it, spitfire. Not in a million years." I slip my finger under her chin and lift her eyes to mine. Her face is delicate, the bones fragile and angular like an elf. Her eyes are big and watery, while the tip of her nose is red. "Did I make it in time? Did he…"

She shakes her head. "No. He didn't. I don't have any underwear… I don't want it after he touched it." She tugs her dress down, and that's when I see a bruise on the upper part of her chest, where the middle of her dress is torn.

I shrug off my jacket and lay it over her shoulders. "I'm glad I got here in time." I refrain from saying, "I don't know what I would have done if anything happened to you if I got here too late."

For months, Ruby and I have been dancing around each other. I figure she was telling me no because she could see just how fucked up I was.

But I'm working on it.

I'm a work in progress with a lot of failures in my wake.

"I'm… I'm…" her eyes roll to the back of her head, and I catch her before she hits the ground.

I press two fingers against her neck and blow out a relieved breath. Her pulse is steady. She's in shock, and the adrenaline is crashing her system. This would be a lot for anyone to go through. "Ruby?" I try shaking her awake, but she's out cold.

"I got you, spitfire. You did so good," I whisper into her ear, hoping she can hear me in her subconscious. I lift her into my arms, careful to keep her dress tugged down, but my jacket is so big, it covers her completely, so I don't have to worry about anyone seeing her.

I'm going to take her back to the clubhouse, where Doc can look at her to make sure she's okay. She can't fit on the back of my bike like this, but I know it will be safe at Lussuria, so I hold her tight against my chest and get my phone from my back pocket.

Damn, she needs to gain some weight. She isn't taking care of herself. I don't like that. I want to take care of her, but I don't know if I'm ready to take care of someone else when I can barely take care of myself.

Ruby is a sick game of tug-of-war on my soul. Do I give in? Do I let go?

Either way, I fall.

And I'm either going to hit the ground so hard the earth shakes, or she'll manage to catch me. She deserves more than a freak like me.

She's dangerous. She has me wanting and hoping to change.

My phone vibrates, and when I look down, the Uber is right around the corner. I tuck my phone in my pocket and hurry to the end of the alley, then take a right to get on the main sidewalk. I keep her head hidden so no one can see the bruises and blood. It's best if we get away from the crime scene I left behind before the cops show up.

The further away we are, the better.

The Uber comes to a stop, and I open the back door, cup my hand over her head, and duck into the backseat. I fasten the seatbelt over us, which is difficult, but I manage. I find myself kissing the top of her head and pressing my cheek against her, inhaling the faint scent of her perfume and sweat.

"Too much to drink, huh?" the driver tries to make small talk as he puts the car in drive.

I grind my teeth together, the muscle in my jaw clenching. I wish this were from too much drinking. Maybe then, Ruby wouldn't be so damn traumatized. "Yeah, you know how Vegas gets."

"Sure do. You should see the sloppy drunks that I get in the car. If they puke, I charge them extra."

"I don't blame you." I run my fingers through her short hair, and my brows crease when I feel a lump. When did she hit her head? I look down and part the short strands to see a deep cut. It isn't long, maybe two inches, but it will need stitches. I didn't even notice the blood on the back of her neck. I lift her hand next and study the scratches on her knuckles.

She fought like hell.

I don't know what comes over me, but I bring them to my mouth and kiss them. Part of me hopes it soothes the wounds and makes them better. It's a childlike thought process, but I never had it done to me. I would think being taken care of makes everything a bit better.

"Whoa, check out this place. Ruthless—" the driver's eyes widen, and he gulps. "—You're part of the Ruthless Kings?"

I don't answer him—there's no need. I toss a twenty-dollar bill at him and get out of the car, then kick the door shut with my boot-the driver slams on the gas, and the tires spin, burning rubber into the air. I curl my lip.

I hate that smell.

Adjusting her weight in my arms, I run as quickly as I can down the driveway. I miss the potholes and kick-up dust from the desert. The iron gates are open, which is unusual. Braveheart never leaves it like that. I use the open gate to my advantage and bolt to the front door, passing a long line of motorcycles. There is a faint fire crackling in the firepit right below the steps, which tells me someone was just out here.

I love the smell of a bonfire.

I clunk up the steps; my boots are heavy. I relax my arms and look down to see if Ruby is awake yet, but she's still out cold. I hold her with one arm and open the door, noticing the main room isn't full of bikers, but just their ol' ladies.

And they are all crying over The Notebook.

Crap, it's the scene where they're dancing in the hospital. I can't watch. I'll get teary-eyed too.

"Doc!" I bellow, slamming the door shut. "Doc, I need you!"

"Oh my god, is that Ruby?" Sarah asks from the loveseat. She's supposed to be in bed, but she said she wanted to be included with everyone, so she and Reaper live out in the living room now.

"What happened?" Jo asks, rocking back and forth to get to her feet. She's as big as a house and about to pop any day now.

Makes me think of the daughter I lost. She'd be… eighteen, I think? A pang hits my heart when I realize how much I miss what I never had.

"She was attacked. I need Reaper too. Where is he?" I ask, pounding down the hallway as Mary and Dawn run after me.

I've seen Dawn naked. Hell, I've seen Dawn on her knees sucking Skirt's cock. I've seen her moan and come and shake. I've seen what every inch of her looks like. Usually, when I see her, I imagine the three of us in the back room Sarah and Reaper built as a Christmas present.

But I'm not.

I only care about the woman in my arms.

"Most of the guys are out. Sarah wanted some alone time, so they went to Lussuria."

I freeze. Fuck. Did they see me there? I hope not.

"But Doc's here?"

"Doc wasn't going to leave all the pregnant women alone," Dawn says.

"Is she okay?" Sarah yells from the main room as Mary opens the basement door to Doc's makeshift hospital.

"I think so. I'll keep you guys updated, okay?"

"Thanks, Bullseye," Dawn says, placing her hand on my arm.

I guess you could say me, Dawn, and Skirt have a pretty odd relationship compared to the others. More intimate. I mean, I don't kiss or touch her. It's a rule. But I find her leaning on me sometimes, and Skirt doesn't care. Skirt says she feels safe around me, and with our arrangement, Skirt is okay with the friendly touches.

But that might all have to come to an end. I'd give that up to make something with Ruby if I ever get the chance. If I think I'm deserving enough. I've got a lot more healing to do before I'm even close to being worthy of someone as strong as she is.

Hell, I'm a brute of man, and she's stronger than I'll ever be.

"Doc! Doc!" I call out for him, but all I hear is silence. "What the fuck?" I growl, placing Ruby gently on the bed. I straighten to try to find him when I'm tugged down. Her eyes are still shut, but her fingers are curled in my shirt.

She doesn't want to let go.

Damn, it shouldn't melt me because of why she's holding on, but it does.

"I'll be back, spitfire," I whisper into her ear and kiss the top of her head. She must hear me because she lets go and flips to her side. When she's settled, I march into Doc's office and see him doing paperwork with headphones on.

What if one of the girls went into labor? He wouldn't be able to hear them.

I march up to him and yank the headphones off his head. "I've only been calling for you for the last two minutes."

He groans, stretching as he leans back in the chair and reaching his arms above him. "I'm listening to a new podcast on surgical scars. I shouldn't have put them on, but I get too distracted when it's on the wireless speaker."

"Well, I need you to look at Ruby. She was attacked, and she's unconscious."

Doc is out of his chair in less than a second and runs to the treatment room. I'm right on his heels. Ruby is asleep or unconscious; I can't tell anymore. Doc pulls out one of those tiny flashlights and opens her eyes, shining the light at her pupils.

She's unconscious because a sleeping person would've woken up from that.

"Tell me what happened," Doc says, flipping her onto her back.

"I heard a scream, and I ran to an alley. She was being attacked by two men. She took care of one, but not the other. He was pretty close to… getting his way, but I stopped him."

"These scratches look like she fought."

I puff my chest out with pride and nod. "She did." My little spitfire.

"I'm going to have to place her in a gown and check her for other injuries."

"You aren't going to fucking touch her," I sneer, this overwhelming need to protect her and her body from anyone else needing to see it.

"Not me. Juliette will do it."

I let out a breath and nod, then rub my hand on the back of my neck. "Sorry, I didn't mean to snap."

Doc's fingers fly over his phone as he texts, and a second later, the basement door opens. Juliette is light on her feet as she comes down the steps. "Oh my god, what happened? Sorry, I was taking care of Lady. She's on her last few days, Doc."

Damn. Poodle is going to be a wreck when that happens. Lady has held on longer than any of us could have hoped. Poodle will be lost without her.

"We're ready. I have the medication to make her go easily. And Ruby here was attacked. I need you to change her into a gown so I can examine her, please," Doc says.

"Of course." Juliette walks to the closet and grabs one of the gowns, then comes to Ruby's side again.

Doc guides me to his office to give them privacy. "Her pupils are responsive. That's a good sign."

"She has a gash on her head that needs stitches," I rub a hand over my mouth, suddenly feeling sick. "Is she going to be okay? Does she need surgery?"

"I won't know until I examine her, but I don't think she will."

I close my eyes and lean against the wall, suddenly spent. "That's good."

"How are you doing?"

Oh, I know that tone of voice. "I'm fine, Doc."

"What's your sugar?"

"It was 120 a few hours ago." I leave out the fact that it was Mateo that made me check it.

"Good. Keep checking it. Don't forget. You can contract type one diabetes if you don't regulate your type two."

I get it. It's just another thing to add to the list of things for me to conquer. One more thing that makes me weak. "I know."

"Okay, Doc. She's ready," Juliette announces.

I push off the wall and run to Ruby's side. She looks sick in the damn gown. I don't like it. Doc checks her over for other injuries, probes the bite mark on her shoulder, and then finds the cut on her head. "Juliette, I need you to check between her legs."

"What? No. you aren't going to violate her—"

"—It's procedure. We want to make sure there wasn't any sort of penetration. She might not know. Things like this happen so fast," Juliette says, taking a seat on the stool and scooting forward.

Doc is cleaning out the cut on her head wound while Juliette is spreading Ruby's legs. I take her hand and rub my fingers over her knuckles. She's a warrior.

"There's some bruising along her thighs, nail marks, but no damage from force. She was very lucky."

"She wasn't lucky. This isn't fucking lucky, Juliette. She fought like hell. That's what saved her, not something as superstitious as luck," I snarl. My hands begin to shake, and I have to let go of Ruby's hand.

"I think we need to check your sugar—"

"—I'm fine. Take care of Ruby. I can take care of myself."

"Yeah, you're doing a really great job of that," Doc mutters as he begins stitching the wound closed on Ruby's head.

I don't have the energy to bite his head off, so instead, I take a seat in the recliner. My head begins to pulse. I rub my temples to ease the ache.

"The bite mark didn't puncture the skin, so that's good. Won't have to worry about any diseases or infections. I've cleaned up the scratches on her body, but other than that, she'll be sore for the next few days. She'll be fine. She'll wake up soon." Doc covers Ruby up with one of the blue blankets at the foot of the bed. "She just needs rest, and depending on how she bounces back, she might need some therapy."

Fucking therapy.

"You can go, Bullseye. She's fine here."

"I'm not leaving her." I'm never leaving someone I care about alone again. I don't care if it kills me.

"Then let me check your sugar. I think it's low from all the activity in the last few hours." Doc opens the medical cabinet to grab a kit.

I take Ruby's hand with my left hand and hold out my right for Doc. I feel steady, no longer afraid of the outcome anymore.

"It's a bit low like I thought. Nothing some juice can't fix." Doc walks over to the fridge and grabs me an orange juice.

My reactions take me by surprise as I take it from him instead of throwing it against the wall. My reactions are changing, and Ruby is the catalyst.

Maybe I don't hate myself anymore.

Just a strong dislike.

And I have her to blame—or thank—for that.

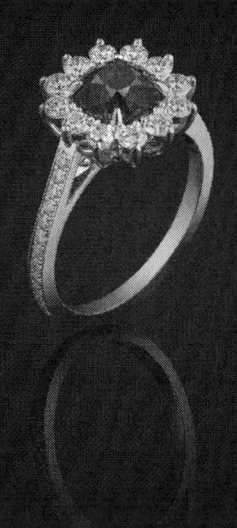

CHAPTER ELEVEN

Ruby

Ow.

My head hurts.

My entire body hurts.

I blink my eyes open, and every time my lids close, the throb in my head beats harder.

"Hey, you're awake," comes a familiar, deep voice. The soft, rich tones flood my chest with warmth and bring me out of my sleepy stupor.

I open my eyes and blink a few times to clear the fuzziness. Bullseye's handsome face is the first thing I see. I have to admit; it isn't the worst thing to wake up to. His dark lashes are stark against the green iris of his eyes. His thick, unruly brows squeeze together as he looks at me with concern. My heart flutters when he cups the underside of my jaw. I lean into his touch, loving how his hand swallows me. I feel so secure with him. I regret all the months wasted saying no to him when I could have felt like this.

"You with me, Spitfire?" he asks.

"I need to pee." Why is that the first thing I say? No wonder he ended things with me before they even had a chance to begin.

Bullseye chuckles, then hangs his head. "Of course, you do. You've been out for hours. I'll get Juliette to help you—"

"—No!" I shout at him wrap my fingers tightly around his wrist, holding on for dear life. I lick my lips and take a minute to compose myself. Wow, I panicked. "I mean, no. It's okay. I can go on my own. I don't want to bother her." And I don't want to be around anyone else right now.

"Ruby, do you remember what happened last night?" he asks.

I nod, and instead of becoming a crying mess, I get angry. "I cunt punted those assholes, and I'd do it again." I lift my chin defiantly, and there's a sharp pain on top of my head. "Ow," I mumble, reaching for the top of my head.

"Ah." Bullseye stops me, snagging my hand just in time before I touch it. "You have stitches, little miss. It's best not to get yourself hurt unintentionally." He helps me off the bed and to stand up. Every muscle in my body hurts. My knees give, but Bullseye is there to wrap his arm around me. "I got you," he says, taking most—if not all—my weight.

I scoot my feet along the floor and hiss with every muscle I use to move my legs. We pause at what I assume is the bathroom door, and I tilt my head to look up at him. "You were there. You saved me."

"I think you would have saved yourself. With your cunt punts and all," he smirks.

"Maybe," I say with doubt. "I think you're just saying that to make me feel better, but we both know what would have happened if you didn't show up. Thank you, Bullseye. I don't know why you were there, but I'm so thankful."

"I'm glad I was, too," he says, rubbing his calloused index finger over my jaw. "Now, go pee before you piss on my boots." He opens the bathroom door and flips on the light.

"I wouldn't piss on your boots. *In* your boots, maybe, if you *pissed* me off enough." I shuffle inside the bathroom and giggle when I see his face before I shut the door. Oh, those cute lips parted in shock have me wishing I could stand on my tiptoes and kiss the bottom one. They are full, plump, and impossible to deny.

So why have I denied it?

"Cause you're stupid, that's why," I mutter to myself as I lift the hospital gown and pop a squat.

I squeeze my eyes shut as my muscles protest. I'm surprised at how sore I am. I remember everything from last night, so I'm scratching my head, wondering why my muscles hurt so bad. The fight didn't last long.

The struggle.

Whatever it could be labeled as the five minutes of fighting off two grown men really left me hurting. I remember feeling tense and scared. When they hit me, they really didn't hold anything back. I'm trying to process how I feel about it, how to react and cope. I know other people would be crying and freaking out, screaming, or maybe in a catatonic state. I don't judge anyone for that. I was assaulted, but I wasn't raped, and I'm sure that has a lot to do with how mentally stable I am right now.

I am good at processing when bad things happen; I seem to recover quickly. Maybe it's the way I categorize things or because I've been through bad shit before. I'm shaken, that's for sure, but I'll be okay. I know I'm not ready to curl up in a ball and die. That's for sure. I've worked too hard to get to where I am to give up now because two assholes thought they could have their way with me.

"Damn it," I groan in frustration. I can't seem to get up. My thighs are killing me. I wipe and flush, then close my eyes from the embarrassment I feel, knowing what I have to do. "Bullseye?"

"Yeah, Ruby?" he answers through the door.

"I can't get up. My body really hurts." This. This is what I hate most—feeling like a victim, not being able to rely on myself. I almost hate that more than the actual act of what those men did to me last night. If there is one thing I pride myself on, it's my goddamn independence.

Asking for help tastes just as bad as regret, in my opinion.

My pride might be a little over six feet as well.

The door cracks open, and Bullseye keeps his eyes on the ceiling, which causes him to slam his shoulder into the wall. "Ow, damn," he curses.

"Yeah, there's a wall there," I point out and grin, then wince from my jaw hurting. "Damn, I forgot the guy slapped the daylights out of me."

"He didn't. You're still here. He isn't. You punted him straight to hell, remember?"

"Mmm, I did, didn't I?" That makes me feel great about myself.

"Sure did. Alright, can you wrap your arms around my neck?" he asks.

I lift them, and while it hurts, they don't hurt as bad as my legs. That's probably because I have deep bruises and scratches up and down my thighs from where that man tried to take what wasn't his. He didn't get it because I slammed my head into his face.

And Bullseye came to the rescue, just like he is now. He scoops me up effortlessly and brings me to the sink. I unwrap my arms and wash my hands, then dry them off by plucking a towel that's folded next to the sink. I discard it in the laundry bin in the corner and wrap my arms around Bullseye's neck again.

I inhale deeply, leather and pine soaking into my lungs to remind me I'm safe. Bullseye sets me on the bed, but I don't unwrap my arms. I don't want to stay down here. This hospital-like room only makes me feel worse than I really am. "Can't you take me to your room? Or take me home? What time is it? I need to open the shop. I have an appointment tonight—" Damn it. I'm not going to be able to perform. Moretti is going to think I'm standing him up. He's going to find me, gut me, and pry my ruby ring off my cold dead finger.

"Listen, you're in no shape to run a store or whatever else you have planned. I'm sure as fuck not leaving you alone. Okay?"

"I can't afford to stay closed." I pinch the bridge of my nose, and the sting of tears hits my eyes. Ha. Of course, I'm crying over finances instead of what happened last night. What the hell is wrong with me?

"You'll be okay—"

"—No, you don't understand. I have to be there. I have to." I know how desperate it sounds, but I have no choice. I made a deal with Moretti, and if I don't follow through, then I don't know what I'll do. Would Bullseye understand? Would he judge me? If I stay here, I'm going to have to tell him everything. "You have to let me go."

"I don't have to do anything," he corrects me. "But we'll talk about it more after you eat, maybe shower? You'll feel better after. And if it is so important to you to open the store, we can send Tank and Braveheart down to run it, and Mary. They will need a woman's touch, and Mary knows that vintage stuff, right?" he offers, brushing his thumb over my cheek. "I shouldn't be touching you after what you've been through. I'm sorry." He pulls his hand away, and I snatch for it again, grabbing it just before he drops it to his side.

The skin across my knuckles is broken and red. I remember my fists scraping against the brick as I tried to get away from the hold the man had on me last night. "I'm not afraid of you, Bullseye." I rub my thumb over his knuckles. The skin is softer than what I thought a dart-slinging, grumpy-going, car-fixing man ought to be. His fingers are calloused, his skin has an olive hue, and he has scars randomly all over his body. But I think he's beautiful.

He's a story. A long series I could get lost in, and I want to know every detail. I bet the details would be like pulling teeth.

"You should be," he rumbles. "I'm no good, Ruby. I did us both a favor the other day. Besides, I know you aren't interested. It's alright. We're friends. I'm going to be here for you."

But I don't want to be his friend.

I scoot closer to him and lean in, watching his tongue flicking out over his lips.

"What are you doing?" he asks, a curiosity to his tone. He doesn't move away. His eyes land on my mouth, and his breath is minty from brushing his teeth.

"Doing what I should have done a long time ago, and I'm sorry I waited so long to do it." I close the distance between us, going all the way—the full one hundred percent—and gently take his lips in mine. I don't deepen it; I don't try to slip him my tongue. I don't try anything fancy because I'm not sure if I'm welcome after ruining my chances.

Oh, his lips are softer than I thought they'd be, just like his skin. He's a pleasant surprise. The kiss isn't heated as much as it is an experiment. After a few long seconds, I pull away and close my eyes, feeling like I've been swept away into a dream. Kisses, simple or intense, are supposed to feel just like that—all-consuming and daydream-inducing.

I lift my fingers to my bottom lip as we stare at one another. He's surprised by my move. My heart is pounding, wondering what he'll decide. "You aren't in some fragile state, are you? You aren't seeking comfort after what happened?"

"I can't lie and say I don't feel comfortable with you. I do. It was one of the most unsettling things I felt about you when I met you. You were so cocky all those months ago, yet you still made me feel comfortable. Then I don't know what happened. You changed. You still brought comfort, but you were so mad."

"I'm still mad, but I'm not mad at you."

"Oh. Okay. That's good," I nod, biting my bottom lip. Where does that leave us? "Well," I clear my throat. "Can we go to your—" I'm silenced when his lips find mine this time, but this kiss isn't timid or experimental.

There's more pressure, and the cut in my lip stings, but it isn't enough to stop this. His hand grips the back of my neck, deepening it, sliding his mouth against mine as if it was always meant to kiss me. God, he feels good. He's gentle, opening his mouth on a shaky breath before slanting his lips on mine again. I open up on a whimper, and his tongue is a tease of silk against mine before he pulls back.

Yes, just what I like. I don't like too much tongue.

Since I'm on my knees on the bed, he wraps his arms around me and lifts me, plopping me right on his lap. I keep my legs closed because I don't want the marred skin to pull. I won't lie; I'm not ready for him to take this further than kissing, but I will be.

"God," he groans, pulling away from me as if it's taking him all his will. "You taste like fire." He leans his forehead against mine, a slight growl to his heavy breaths as he exhales. "I don't know what you do to me." He sounds vulnerable and nervous. "I'm not ready for someone like you," he admits after a few beats.

I nod slowly, trying to understand his words. We've been tiptoeing around this thing between us for a while now. I want to know if we're going to give in or if I need to seal myself off again from him. I can, too. I'm the kind of person that, once I decide someone is out of my life, or I'm done with them, that's it. I put whatever I felt for that person and throw it away, never thinking about them again. I don't believe in wallowing over something or someone I can't have. I won't cry over a broken heart for months, and I won't cry or feel sorry for myself after the attack from last night.

The only thing I can do is move on with my life and once again try to claw my way through this life like I always have. "What's that mean? You aren't ready for someone like me?"

He sighs, and it's full of burdens he's been holding in. "It means I've got a long road before accepting myself, but I want to." He looks down and draws circles on my knee with his fingers. "I want to be ready for someone like you."

I cup his face and press another kiss to his sweet mouth. "Then I'll make sure to accept you enough for the both of us, okay?"

He gives me a sight tilt of his lips before he rubs the kiss away with his hand. There's a smile there, but it's distant like there's a secret behind it he's not ready to tell me.

"Come on, Spitfire. Let's go get you some food and figure out what to do about your appointment."

Crap.

Since we're talking about acceptance, is he going to accept me and my issues too?

Maybe neither of us is ready for one another. That thought has a deep sadness pooling inside me. It's like getting ready for a wonderful and exciting trip to the beach, only to find out it's going to rain.

I hate to admit this, but maybe Bullseye is right.

Maybe we aren't ready for each other.

But shouldn't we at least try?

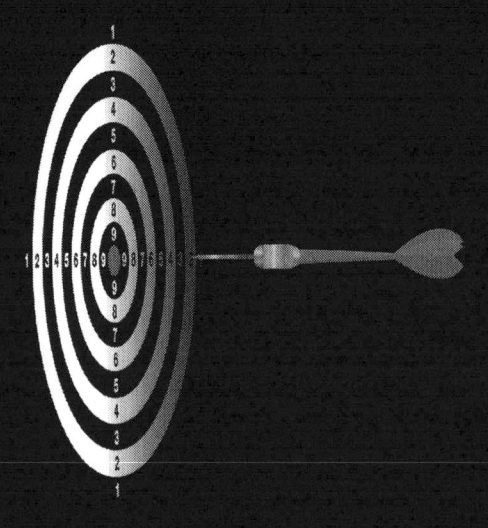

CHAPTER TWELVE
Bullseye

If her lips are sinful, then call me a sinner. I know there's no way she's holy because that would mean I'm a saint. And my demons are far from the praying type.

Holy hell, that kiss.

That kiss was… transformative.

She's transformative, and it scares the hell out of me.

When I see her, when I really look at her, I feel something I haven't been allowed to feel for myself in a long time.

Hope.

I haven't dared to feel that damned emotion. I don't think I ever have. There hasn't ever been a time in my life where I remember thinking, "Hey, there's hope. Everything will be okay." I don't think I like how it makes me feel either. Hope makes me believe I'm allowed to have something as good as a life without suffering.

And I don't deserve that.

"Come on, let's get you upstairs and get you some clothes, maybe some food?" I ask her, staring at her lips that are still swollen from our kiss.

She lifts her arms in reply, and I lean in, allowing her to wrap her hands around my neck as I swing her into my arms.

Goddamn, she feels so good here against my chest. Her lips are so close to my neck. I can feel her breaths. I close my eyes and take a minute when my chest swells with relief.

Relief because a small part of me, the tiniest part of me, has let go of the past. It feels so damn good, like a million pounds lifted off my shoulder.

But then guilt slithers in like the serpent it is, and I'm weighted down again.

I hold her close as I walk up the steps. My fingers curl into her torso before I open the basement door. I know when I walk into the kitchen, and everyone is around the table enjoying their breakfast and drinking their coffee, they're going to have questions.

Because I never, ever, hold a woman close like this. I've never given a damn about anyone else since Georgia, but it's fucking hard to say no to Ruby when she's so damn strong. God, I just want to soak up her courage and her will, then maybe I'd be able to get over myself.

Even with the cut-sluts, who haven't been around in a while since the compound got attacked, I never held them.

I'd fuck them and leave them with their panties around their ankles while I tucked my cock back in my jeans. Hell, I'd be zipping up as I walked out the door, still hearing them panting for breath.

I was an ass, but sex was all I knew, and hanging around with a woman intimately who wasn't Georgia was something I wanted nothing of.

Until now.

I swing the door open and pause in the entryway. Just like I thought, most everyone is around the table—every single head swings in my direction. Reaper pauses as he drinks from his 'President of the United States of Ruthless America' mug Slingshot got him. Joanna has her hand on her stomach, rubbing her large pregnant belly while her brows raise in question. Skirt is eating pie, but he doesn't stop eating his pie—he never does. Badge doesn't give a fuck. He's on his laptop while Maizey puts his hair in small ponytails all over with pink bows.

He acts like he doesn't like kids, but he lets Maizey do whatever she wants.

Doc gets up from the table and rushes over, wiping his hands on his shirt since he was eating toast. "Is she okay?"

"She's right here," Ruby mumbles against my chest before turning to look at Doc. "And I'm fine, just sore."

I smirk at her attitude. "You heard the lady," I say.

"Lady," Poodle repeats sadly. Melissa begins to rub his back to calm him down as he turns in his chair and hides his face against her shoulder.

That's right. Lady is on her last few days, and Poodle is taking it very hard.

"Good. Get Ruby settled. I expect everyone in Church in twenty," Reaper announces from the head of the table. His coffee mug hits the table with a louder thud than necessary. Now that I'm really looking at him, he has dark circles under his eyes and worry lines etched in nearly every crevice of his face.

I don't ask questions; I just nod and begin my way to my room, which used to be Tongue's.

He and Daphne now have a home outside of the clubhouse waiting for them as soon they get back from New Orleans. If they come back. The issues with Daphne are... delicate. Reaper went ahead and hired a few contractors to build other houses, too, so the other couples don't have to wait if they don't want to. Skirt and Dawn have a place now for themselves, baby Joey and Aidan.

Everyone's finding their home except me.

"What do you mean you can't do my tea party?" Maizey screeches at Badge.

I'm taking that as my cue to leave.

"I have Church in twenty minutes. I can do it after."

"The tea will be cold," Maizey argues with Badge.

"Yes, the pretend tea will be cold. Tragic," he replies in a flat tone.

"Badge," Reaper warns him.

It's all I hear as I close the door to my bedroom and place Ruby on the bed. I'm sure she's less than impressed with my room. There isn't much here. A bed, a dresser, a closet, and that's about it. I don't have any pictures hanging on the walls or shit I'm proud to show off.

I open the closet and grab one of the King's Garage shirts. "It will be big, but it's all I have. I can ask one of the girls if—"

"—No." Ruby stands up and takes the shirt out of my hand. Our fingers brush. I'll never admit this to her out loud, but I hold my breath. Every touch with her feels intimate. "I want your shirt." She brings it to her nose and inhales. "You know when you'd come to visit me at the store—"

"—And you'd kick me out? Yeah, how could I forget?" I say dryly.

She chuckles and nudges my arm. "I kicked you out because I didn't take you seriously, and I'd know what you'd do to me if I allowed you to," she sighs, inhaling my shirt again. Maybe it might be weird to some, but I find it flattering that she loves how I smell. "You'd leave, but the scent you left behind always lingered. Leather and pine. If I could bottle it up and spray it around the store, I would."

"Well, I'll gladly walk around your store every half hour as your air freshener."

"Aw, isn't that romantic," she smiles wistfully. "Nothing like my own badass biker air freshener."

The way she says badass takes the wind from my sails. I've been weak for months. She could do better.

"Hey, where'd you go?" she asks, taking another step forward until there's no space left between us. She has to tilt her head to look at me, and she barely reaches my chest. *Barely.*

But I see her rebellious nature in her eyes, readying herself for a fight.

"What? Nowhere. It's fine. I'll give you some privacy while you change." I turn around to leave, and Ruby's hand shoots out, grabbing my wrist. Her fingers are so slender; she can't even wrap them all the way around and touch them.

Which only makes me wonder how'd they look wrapped around my cock.

God, I can imagine her jerking me off in that tight fist, brutally, maybe hatefully. She'd tug and pull, yank, and maybe bite.

I like it a bit rough.

"No, you don't get to run away from me." She moves to stand in front of me and grips my chin, forcing me to look down to meet her eyes. They're like a storm, firm and ready for any amount of destruction that's about to come her way. "You've been doing that lately. Running. Why?"

God, what is she? My therapist?

Christ, if I want to run, I'll run as far as I want.

"That's none of your concern," I reply through gritted teeth. "I have Church."

She blocks me from leaving and shoves me against the chest. "It's my concern when I have a feeling this dance between us has finally come to an end, and we're going to do something about it. I want to know you. Let me."

"There's nothing to know." The sadness in those words reminds me of how hollow I am on the inside. I'm nothing special. I'm just like everyone else with their fucked-up pasts, and it's all hitting me at once. It's like I never grieved all those years ago when I escaped Patricia and Ronald. When I got diagnosed with diabetes, it was the cherry on top. Everything inside me collapsed. I don't know how to put myself back together.

Her hand lands softly on my chest, right above my heart, and she stares up at me with tender eyes. Why do I feel smaller than she is? How does she hold so much power in a simple stare? The longer I'm with her, the more I crumble.

"I don't believe that for a second, Bullseye. Tell me one thing while you help me get dressed. One thing about you that you haven't let anyone else know." She spins around to show me the ties that hold her gown together. "Undo my gown, Bullseye. Help me get dressed." Her tone is firm and bossy; my cock plumps from how demanding she is.

I lift my hand without question and do as she says, which makes me pause. Why am I listening to her like some obedient dog? That's not who I am.

Yet, it feels good not to make any decisions. Not to have to think. I don't know what's wrong with me. I like to be in control. That's been my problem for the last few months. I haven't been in control, and I hate the spiral.

I blow out a breath, and her skin pebbles with goosebumps. I swallow, pinching the ties between my fingers, and pull slowly—the shoulders of the gown part, showing more of her alabaster skin. Unable to stop myself, I run my index finger down her spine before getting to the next tie. Her skin is soft, beyond silk or velvet. If I imagine what clouds could feel like, weightless and airy, they wouldn't be as soft as Ruby's skin.

I tug the next tie free, closing my eyes and inhaling a sharp breath as the dip of her waist comes into view and the material slips off her shoulders.

She's nearly bare.

If she were to turn around right now, I'd get a full view of her breasts. I bet they'd fit in my hand perfectly.

The gown barely manages to hang on her hips from the last tie, and I pull the knot free, allowing the gown to slip onto the ground around her feet.

I growl with lust and appreciation when I see the swell of her ass and the flare of her hips. "You trust me not to touch you after what happened last night?" I ask, my voice deeper, becoming hoarse from the desire simmering in my blood.

"I'm not too hung up on what happened last night like you are," she says, turning her head to her shoulder. Her chin lies artfully on the slim curve. I never had an appreciation for photography, but her standing like that, bare, vulnerable, and seductive, is the perfect kind of image I could lose myself in. "I like to move on with my life when a curveball gets thrown."

I keep my hands to my sides and bury my nose in the short strands of her hair. A rumble builds in my chest when I smell cinnamon. Figures she'd smell spicey with an attitude like she has. "I envy your ability to do that," I tell her.

She leans back, her shoulders against my chest. "Everyone can do it, Bullseye. It's all about being honest with yourself and what you want. If you want to be happy, be happy. If you want to be miserable, be miserable."

"You make it sound so easy."

She spins around, naked and completely fucking beautiful. My eyes roam her short stature. I close my eyes again as she leans forward. Her hard nipples rub against my shirt, tickling my skin. "It's easy, Bullseye. It's the overthinking that makes it so hard."

The way she says the word hard makes me fucking *hard*.

I need to get out of this room.

I take the shirt from her hand and tug it over her head before I place her on the bed and fuck the hell out of her. My shirt drops to her knees, which makes me want her even more. Fuck, she looks good in my clothes.

"I'll be back after Church to check on you. The kitchen is right outside the door, so" I clear my throat. "Yeah, if you need anything—"

"I need you to tell me one thing about yourself," she reminds me. Fuck. I haven't held up my end of the agreement.

I place my hand on the door, readying myself to leave. I want nothing more than to walk out the door, but I can't. I have to be honest with her. She deserves that much. "I hate having diabetes. It makes me feel weak." Amongst other things. "Makes me feel like I don't have control of my own body."

"It doesn't look like you've lost control." The warmth of her hand lands in the middle of my back.

I shake my head. She doesn't get it. No one gets it. The diabetes is only the tip of the unstable mountain I have become. If she knew everything about me, she wouldn't even like me.

"What is it, Bullseye?"

"Honestly?" I stare at the door, numb, my boots bolted to the floor.

"Only honesty."

"I haven't had control of my bod—" I catch myself when I realize what I'm about to say. I can't tell her the darkest part of me.

"Talk to me. Choose to let go," she urges me. "I'm listening to you."

"I can't. I don't trust myself enough to confide in you, and that isn't on you. That's on me." I open the door and take a step into the kitchen, where only Skirt remains eating his pie.

"Hey, Bullseye."

I turn around to give her a departing glance. Goddamn, she's a sight for sore eyes like mine. I lift a brow, silently asking what she wants.

She begins to shut the door, staring at her feet, when those dark lashes lift and those emerald gems land on me. "I can trust enough for the both of us." And with that, she closes the door, leaving me wishing I was half as strong as she is.

"She's got a pair of big balls on her, that one, aye," Skirt grumbles around a mouthful of food. "She'll whip ye into shape in no time."

I flinch at the word 'whip', and my skin begins to tingle. A memory surfaces of Ronald whipping me over and over again because I didn't hurt Georgia the way he wanted me to.

"Aye, ye okay there, lad?" Skirt's hand lands on my shoulder, and I blink back to the present day. Ronald is gone. All I see is Skirt in front of me chewing. He has crumbs all in his beard and concern written in his eyes.

I shrug out of his hold and curl my lip. "I'm fucking fine."

"Liar," he says. "Always lying."

I give him a brisk, narrowed expression and shoulder bump him as I head toward Church. There are a few minutes left before the meeting officially starts, but there are a few guys seated in the room already. Slingshot is there and somehow got his hands on tacos. Reaper's going to kill him.

"Oh my god, Bullseye. I had some tacos delivered—"

That explains it.

"—And they had fried tacos on the menu. It's a taco, but fried."

"I gathered that when you said, 'fried tacos.'"

"But it's so good. You want one? I ordered fifteen of them."

My stomach grumbles, and I lift a shoulder and shrug. "Sure. I'll take one."

He slides over a white-wrapped taco with grease spots on it, and I snag it. I don't expect to be impressed, but when I unwrap it and pick it up, the shell is warm and inviting. I bite down.

Wow.

Slingshot must see how much I like it because he laughs. "Right? So fucking good."

"It is. I'll give you that," I acknowledge, taking another bite, a string of melted cheese hitting my chin.

The door slams shut, and Reaper stomps his way to the head of the table. "Slide me a fucking taco, damn it," he grumbles.

Oh, he's in a mood.

He unwraps the taco, and right as he's about to put it in his mouth, Sarah yells,

"Does someone have fucking tacos and not bring me any?" she practically roars like a savage beast.

Reaper hangs his head and groans. "She's been so crabby and hungry all the time. It's like a never-ending craving. She asked to spank me last night. *Me.*" He points to himself.

The guys snicker around the table, then fall silent when Reaper narrows his eyes at everyone. I don't say a word. I stuff my mouth with a fried taco.

"But the question is... did you let her?" Poodle asks, still hiding a laugh.

"Would you tell an angry, very pregnant, always hungry woman no? Who, may I add, is also on bed rest?"

"You would be cranky too if you had a bowling ball inside you, sucking the life out of you," Slingshot points out. "Open the door," he says. "I'm not going to let a pregnant lady go hungry."

I roll the chair back and twist the handle, and open the door.

Sarah looks up from the loveseat. Poor thing, she does look miserable.

"Heads up, Sarah." Slingshot takes his slingshot out, puts a taco in the strap, pulls it back, then launches it across the room.

He just slingshotted a taco.

I've seen everything now.

Sarah catches it mid-air, and she unwraps it like a Christmas present, growls, and stuffs half of it in her mouth.

"Jesus," I mutter under my breath, closing the door slowly as not to disrupt the animal outside.

"Scary shit, right?" Reaper asks, wincing when he adjusts himself in the chair.

Damn, she must have really spanked his ass. It's so hard to hold in my laugh, but I keep a straight face, which should earn me another taco.

"Okay, down to business. Fuck, these are good," Reaper says, staring at the taco. "A deep-fried taco, who would have thought?" he speaks to himself more than he does to us. "Okay." He shakes himself, clear of his thoughts. "Okay, first thing on the list. Bullseye," he spins his chair a little to the left to look at me. "How's therapy?"

I growl in response and rip another bite off the taco.

"It's going well, then? Good. You have another appointment in two hours."

I slam my fist on the table and sneer. "I'm not going. Ruby needs me here."

"She has us. She'll be fine."

"Well, someone needs to open her store, and she has an appointment she needs to cancel tonight."

"Wow, another appointment with Moretti? Wonder what that's about," Slingshot says as he unwraps another taco.

"What the hell did you just say?" I better not have heard what I think I just heard.

Slingshot licks his fingers. "Last night, when we were out at Lussuria, Ruby was there. She had a meeting with him, and by the look on your face, you didn't know. Awkward," he says in a higher-pitched voice. "Could have been innocent," he shrugs.

Nothing with Moretti is innocent.

I dig my nails into the table and try to take deep breaths. If Ruby was there last night, she might have seen me, but I'm not even upset about that. I don't like that she's meeting with a man like Moretti alone.

Well, that won't be happening again. After this meeting, I'll talk to her, and whatever is going on, it stops right fucking now.

"Well, this makes the next part of the meeting even more awkward. Moretti believes some of the men he fired, those who worked for Maximo, are plotting something. He killed one lurking around his home, and since he still has Maximo locked away, he thinks their unwavering loyalty to his brother means they're going to try and set him free. So he's hiring a few of us as security. And he has requested you personally, Bullseye."

It means I have to leave Ruby.

I growl in dissatisfaction.

"Maybe you'll change your attitude after your therapy meeting. I can already see a few of those dark clouds over your head changing to sunshine," Reaper jokes.

I sit back and cross my arms. I am not a fucking ray of sunshine.

I'm not. I don't even like sunshine. I don't.

Fuck.

I do feel... something.

And damn it, it is kind of warm.

It feels... nice, but it has nothing to do with therapy and everything to do with Ruby.

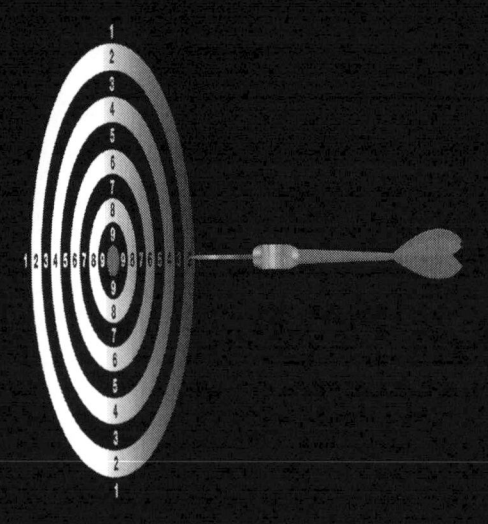

CHAPTER THIRTEEN
Bullseye

AAAAND I'M BACK HERE STARING AT SYLVIA'S DOOR. I DIDN'T GET A CHANCE TO TALK to Ruby before I left, so now I'm stewing in questions wondering why she met with Moretti.

"You act like it's the end of the world. How do you think we babysitters feel being here with you? If we could trust you not to ditch on your appointments, you could do it alone." Badge is such an ass. He leans his head back against the wall and shuts his eyes. "Don't know what's crawled up your ass, but you need to get it out. I miss the old Bullseye."

Yeah, well, I'm starting to realize that Bullseye never existed. He was a fraud.

Sylvia opens the door and takes off her glasses when she sees me. "Bullseye, it's good to see you again." She smiles.

She looks like she's actually happy to see me too.

And when I find myself getting up, I don't feel as angry as before. I want to walk inside. I want to get better. I think it has something to do with Ruby's words.

If you want to be happy, be happy. If you want to be miserable, be miserable.

I don't want to be miserable anymore.

"Have fun talking about your feelings," Badge says, his eyes still closed.

Sylvia doesn't seem amused. "And I'm sure you're a big strong man without issues. I'm sure I'll be seeing you sooner than you'd like." She tilts her nose in the air and walks into her office, leaving Badge with one eye open.

Dare I say, he looks nervous.

I huff a chuckle and slip inside the office. Sylvia closes the door, her heels softly clicking against the carpeted floor. Her posture is straight, and her stride is so smooth. It's as if she is floating as she walks around her desk and sits down in the chair.

I sit down too, and the comfortable feeling I felt begins to flee. She looks at me with a relaxed expression, but the walls are already closing in. I crack my neck. I've never been good at talking about myself because I've never understood myself. I don't know where I come from. I don't know who I am.

I know my name and my birthday. Everything else has been a 'learn as I go' in life. And really, who wants to know I grew up as some sick man's sex slave, forced to fuck the only friend I ever had? That was my existence.

"You don't seem too excited to be here now, Bullseye. What happened? It' as if a switch flipped," she notices, gently placing her glasses to the side.

"I don't know," I tell her honestly. "I was hopeful walking in, but now that I'm here, I don't know." I look around the room again. There isn't anything threatening about it besides the woman behind the desk holding all the fancy degrees to map out what the fuck is wrong with me.

I know what's wrong with me. I'm just fucking broken, and I should have killed myself a long time ago.

No, I can't think like that. I don't want to be miserable anymore. I want...I want to change. I just need to learn how to let go of regret and guilt.

"I understand. Maybe it's easier if we aren't in the office? Would you prefer to take a walk outside? We have beautiful gardens here," she offers.

"You can grow flowers in this heat?"

"No, we have a greenhouse. It's huge. Enough for us to walk around uninterrupted."

"Yeah, I think a change of scenery would be good." I get up from the chair and rush to the door to open it first, for Sylvia.

"Oh. Why, thank you, Bullseye. Aren't you a gentleman?"

Huh. Never been called that before. Small changes, I suppose.

When we walk out of the room, Badge stands and clenches his fists. "Where the hell do you think you're going? I know you aren't done."

"You can sit there. We're going on a nice walk, and then you can sit here and think about how you speak to people," Sylvia huffs, then begins to saunter down the hall.

And I'll be damn if Badge doesn't listen to her.

I give him a middle finger wave before following behind my therapist. She makes it difficult not to like her. If I'm honest, it isn't about not liking her. It's about not liking the fact that Reaper finds me so unbearable that he wants to fix me, so he sends me here with Sylvia.

We walk in silence, not saying a word. I pull out my phone and send a text to Juliette to see how Ruby is doing.

My phone dings a second later.

Juliette: Oh my god, she's the same as she was five minutes ago—the last time you asked.

I growl at the screen, wishing she could hear me.

Juliette: She's fine. She's asking about you and wonders when you'll be back from therapy.

My heart hits against my chest like a wrecking ball swinging to break concrete. She knows? I didn't want her to know I'm in therapy. Fuck, she probably thinks I'm so weak now.

I need a scene.

Only this time, I want to do the watching.

I tuck my phone in my pocket and let out a breath. I want things to be simple. Why can't I choose it? Why can't I choose simplicity?

The only thing I know about simple things is that they are really not that simple.

Complicated is in my nature.

"You're stressed all of a sudden," Sylvia states, opening the door to the greenhouse.

The air in here is cool and damp. I'm able to breathe easier in here. These plants are no joke. Some trees touch the top of the greenhouse, and bright flowers are blooming in every corner. I even hear a waterfall trickling in the distance, and I smell the fresh air of all the plants. I'm immediately more relaxed.

Ah, that's why she brought me here. "You knew this would calm me," I say, taking a right to start the trail. My steps are languid; I want to take my time to stare at all the greenery. Hell, I don't think I've ever seen a place so green in my entire life.

Concrete walls and dirt. That sums up what I've seen of life.

"Guilty as charged," she says without regret. She laces her hands behind her back. "It's relaxing here. It's good for the mind. So tell me, what has you so stressed on the phone?"

I pinch a large leaf in my fingers as I walk by. "A woman. She knows I'm here, but I didn't tell her. I don't want her to think I'm weak. She's far from it. She's one of those people who's able to let go of things. She got attacked last night, and it's like it didn't even happen. She wants to move on."

"Everyone is different. That doesn't mean you're weak for being here. Your friend Reaper must care for you very much. He told me he was so worried about you, and he signed you up for this against your will. I imagine that wasn't a strong point in his mind either, but something that needed to happen. Tell me, why do your closest friends not know you?"

"I haven't shared," I say simply. "I consider it a way to protect myself."

"From what?"

I open my mouth to tell her, but I don't have an answer. "Getting close to people is something I stopped doing a long time ago, that's all." There. That should be a good answer.

"Why don't you like your name? I think Waylon is unique and different," she asks, changing the subject as we pass a koi fish pond. There are rails for people to lean on to look at the water. To the left of me is a fish food dispenser. I crank it and catch the pellets in my palm, then toss a few into the pond.

The black water ripples as the fish swim close to the surface. There's a white one that's bigger than the rest, and it has a red spot on top of its head. Another one swims next to it, this one smaller but searingly bright orange. I toss a few pellets its way, too.

"I wish I could tell you. I really don't know. I just know I have to rebel against it for no reason," I say, then frown when I realize that doesn't make sense.

"What can you tell me about your childhood, Bullseye?" she asks.

"Ah," I click my tongue and toss a few more pellets in the water. "You probably know more than me," I say sadly. The koi fishes' mouths are huge as they gulp in the food, creating bubbles in the water. "I can't remember anything about my childhood."

"Well, that isn't unheard of. It's so long ago," she tries to explain.

"No, I really don't remember anything. People have memories of when they were kids, their parents, their best friends, pets… anything. I don't remember a thing." It feels so good to say that out loud. I'm a grown-ass man nearing 40, but it bothers me that I don't remember anything. "It's like my slate was wiped clean."

She purses her lips and takes a few pellets from my palm, throwing them in the water. "What's the last thing you remember?"

Georgia's sweet, innocent face comes to mind, and I sprinkle the rest of the food onto the water. "It doesn't matter. What I do remember is gone too." I lean my elbows on the rail and hang my head, then fold my hands behind my neck as I try to take a deep breath. "I don't know how to do this, Sylvia."

"Okay, let's not talk about that. Come on, let's sit." She guides me to a nearby bench. A light mist from the sprinklers fills the air. It feels good.

I close my eyes and tilt my head back and breathe in the fresh scents of flowers.

"What's the one thing that bothers you today? In the present?" she asks, her voice calm and soothing. I could listen to her talk all day.

"My diabetes," I admit for the second time today. "I'm not handling it well. It's what kind of made me spiral. When I found out, it was like everything I was trying to be just came crashing down. I don't take care of myself like I should."

"Why not?"

"I don't deserve to," I say automatically. I've said it so often that it's all I think now.

"Why is that?"

"I can't tell you that, Sylvia. You won't look at me the same again."

"I'm not here to judge you, Bullseye. I'm here to help you. But I can't do that if you don't allow me."

If you want to be happy, be happy.

If you want to be miserable, be miserable.

I chant Ruby's words over and over again. Being miserable all the time is exhausting, and I apparently don't want to die because I haven't offed myself yet. Speaking what's wrong with me out loud is different. Talking about what happened all those years ago with someone I don't know... I'm not sure.

"What I say stays between us? You aren't going to tell Reaper?"

"I'd never do such a thing. Patient confidentiality, Bullseye. I'll swear my life on it. And for that matter, my job. I could get arrested if I tell anyone. What you say to me stays with me."

Maybe talking to someone, I don't know will be easier. I won't be so afraid to see the disgust in their eyes. "You can help me?" My throat deepens with emotion.

"I can try, but I can't if you don't talk to me."

I want to. The words are right there. They're clawing at my throat, dying to get out. They're choking me.

Come on. Just speak. Just say the words. Tell her how much of a freak you are. I groan and slam my fist on the bench. "I can't," I grunt, fucking pissed that I can't manage to say what's eating away at my soul.

"Alright," she smiles with all the patience in the world. "Tell me something else about yourself, then."

What's another fucked-up twist I can share about myself that won't rip me from the inside out? "I like watching people have sex, but what a lot of people don't know is that I also like to be watched."

"Nothing wrong with a healthy sexual appetite, Bullseye. I think it's good to try new things. It's important to know what you like."

"But what if the reason why I'm like this is because of a habit that I was forced to create?" Fuck, I've said too much. "I need to go." I stand, feeling lost and cornered. "I need to get out of here." I begin to sweat. It's becoming hard to breathe and even harder to focus.

"Bullseye, what do you mean? No, we're getting somewhere. Sit down and talk to me. Don't run from this. Don't run from the truth. Stop lying to yourself," her voice is harsh yet caring. I can hear the *want* in her voice to help me. "We both know you would have found a way out of coming to therapy if you didn't want to be here."

I look for the exit. It's right there, just past a massive bush with white blossoms. I could make a run for it.

"I'm too weak," I repeat.

"His fears define a weak man," she says, punching right in the gut. I'm sick of being weak. "But a strong man is defined by what he does even when he is afraid."

I slowly sit back down and slump. I think of Ruby, and if I want a future, I've got to let this go. I have to let Georgia go. I spin the silver ring on my index finger and swallow the lump in my throat. "I was conditioned to be the man I am. I was conditioned to be watched, but it's the watching that makes me feel in control because that's what he did. *He* watched us."

Her hand lands on me. It's a gentle touch. The kind I've never really had in my life. "Who watched you? Give me details, Bullseye."

I give up the fight. I'm tired. I'm so tired of not understanding. My eyes burn as

I take a trip down memory lane. "I remember growing up in this house. And when I say grow up, I mean from the time I was eight or so, I was with these people... two people. A man and a woman. Ronald and Patricia. I loved them, and I hated them. I thought they were my parents, but they always denied it. God, I fucking hate them so much. They ruined my life. They made me into this... person I don't even recognize. I hate myself because of them." I take a deep breath as my eyes water and remember that I don't want to be miserable anymore. I need to be honest. If there is one person I can tell my truth to, it is Sylvia.

I bend down and unlace my boot. "They kept me downstairs in the basement. I wasn't allowed to eat most days. Wasn't allowed to bathe. Wasn't allowed to do anything but sit there in the dark.." I take off my sock and show her the faded scar around my ankle. I feel like it all happened yesterday, but I know it didn't.

Losing Georgia feels the same now as it did when she died. The only difference is I have something to look forward to for the first time in my life.

I want to get better.

I want to be better for Ruby.

She deserves a man to be every bit as strong as she is.

A strong man is defined by what he does, even when he's afraid.

I'm going to be strong.

Let's do this.

"They chained me against the wall so that I couldn't escape. What they didn't know was that I wouldn't have tried. As fucked up as it sounds, I loved them. They were all I knew." I inhale a sharp breath and continue, "They did have another girl there. I don't think she was related to them either. She was my only friend. We didn't go to school like other kids. It was just us. And then we turned sixteen."

I put my sock back on and then shove my foot in my boot, lacing it back up. "Everything changed at sixteen. Bodies changed. Ronald and Patricia noticed. They made me and Georgia have sex together, filming it every time, to sell it off to I don't even know who. They watched from the corner, directed us, beat us, yelled, cursed, and touched themselves to us. And I knew it was wrong, but over the years, I just kind of thought, 'This is how life is for everyone.' And Georgia and I expected it. God, she cried every time, and I felt so bad. I should have let him shoot me, but I didn't want to die and leave her there alone with them."

"That was the best choice," Sylvia whispers, still listening to my flow of words that are bursting out of me. "Go on. I'm listening." I can hear the horror in her tone, the tremble of shock shaking her core as she listens to me.

"He'd even put a gun to my head." A tear drops down my cheek and I make a hand gesture, pointing my index finger and thumb in the shape of a gun. I sneer the exact words Ronald used to say to me all time, "You better take that Viagra, boy." I mock the words with hate, spit flying from my mouth. "You better fuck her harder, boy. I got a lot riding on this show." I shove the gun in the air, remembering how it felt when he hit the barrel against my head. "Fuck her face harder, boy. I want my audience to see the spit dripping from her chin."

My lips turn downward as I hold in my emotions, but the tears are dripping onto my arms. I shove the fake gun again. "Spank her to where it hurts, boy. Make her cry. Tell her how worthless she is." I growl, and I begin to raise my voice, the agony ripping me apart when I hear his words. "Turn her around, boy. Let the camera see those young tits bounce. Don't be worthless, boy. I want to hear noises, boy. Our people pay a lot of money for this." I hit the side of my head and then grip the bench with my hands, staring at the ground in a daze.

I remember him talking to Georgia, gentler but still disturbing. "Ride him faster, Georgia, you sweet thing. Ride him harder. Slap his face, sweet thing. Ride him reverse, let the audience see that mouth making those sexy sounds, girl. Stare up at him while your mouth is full of his cock, Georgia. You know you want it."

I can almost hear Ronald's voice in my ear again, barking his orders, the smell of beer and cigarettes always wafting from his mouth. "That's it, sweet thing. That's it. One day, all of us will get together and perform a show. Bet that slutty cunt would like that."

"Oh my god," Sylvia whispers.

"She tried not to cry, and I always told her how sorry I was. Patricia seemed to care more than Ronald. When they would keep me and Georgia apart, sometimes weeks at a time, Patricia would let us sneak a visit to be together. She was my best friend. My soul mate, I think. I mean, what do I know? She was all I had for so long; of course, I loved her. But then, one time, we were eighteen, and she wanted something neither of us had before. She just wanted regular sex. Without them watching. Without them controlling us. Something we deserved for each other. Patricia left us alone while Ronald was out doing whatever the fuck he did, and it was as perfect as it could have been given the situation."

Sylvia sniffles, and when I look over, she's patting underneath her eyes.

"But she got pregnant, and then they wouldn't allow me to see her. For seven months, I was in the basement, wondering how she was. She was already so skinny, so malnourished. I was worried. I stopped eating, and Patricia finally let me see her." I hold my face in my hands and weep. "She looked terrible. I had done that." I hit my chest violently with my fist. "I was killing her because I should have said no. I shouldn't have let us have something beautiful because beautiful things didn't happen for people like us, not without consequence. She died twenty minutes later. Bled out. Miscarried. I don't know. I lost her and my daughter."

I wipe my cheeks, promising myself that this is the last time I'll shed tears for a past I can't change. I already feel lighter after spewing all that built-up hate. "And that's why I like to watch," I finally answer her question.

"Because you feel in control, but why do you like to be watched?" Her voice is heavy with emotion, but she maintains her professionalism.

"Because it's what I'm used to. I need it now because it's been carved into me." I dig my nails into the bench—the grains of wood scratch the calloused skin on my fingertips.

"I am so sorry you had to go through that, Bullseye. No child should be subjected to such abuse. What they did was child pornography, physical abuse, child trafficking, and the list goes on. I don't know how you ended up with those people, but aren't you curious?"

"No. I never questioned it because, through it all, I had Georgia. She was the biggest part of my life since I was eight. She was my lover at sixteen. She was my everything at eighteen. I'd do it all again if it meant having her."

"And now you don't think you deserve happiness because of what happened to her."

I nod.

"Oh, Bullseye. You're still abusing yourself after so many years. Would she want that? Georgia?"

I shake my head. "She made me promise that I wouldn't."

"Why are you breaking it?"

"Because I feel like I'm betraying her."

"You're betraying her by not living the life you fought so hard for. If she were here, I bet she'd be so disappointed. She loved you. Don't you think she'd want to see you loved and to have the happiness you were denied for so long?"

"I don't know how to be happy, Sylvia," I admit. "I don't know how to love the right way."

Her hand grips mine a little tighter, and it has me turning my head to see the sincerity in her eyes. "I'll tell you this, love isn't supposed to hurt, and if it does, it's the wrong kind of love. The right way—" she sighs happily and stares off into the plants that surround us "—The right way leaves us feeling whole, centered, and wanted. The wrong way only has us questioning everything."

"But what if all I know is the wrong way? What if the only love I have to give is the wrong kind?" I press my palms against my eyes and take a deep breath. I feel so much fucking better admitting all this. I know I have a long way to go, but I already feel better.

She purses her lips as she thinks. "Until I see you again, I want you to do something with this new woman, something you wouldn't usually do, and I want you to write down how many times you smiled. That's it."

"I don't smile."

"I know. I'm going to change that, Bullseye. I promise," she replies.

I grip Sylvia's hand in return and meet her gaze. "I'm sorry. I'm so sorry. I wasn't who I needed to be for her."

She gathers me in her arms and holds me tight. I feel like I'm eighteen again, finally dealing with the demons that have been haunting me. "It's okay, Bullseye. Oh, you were just a boy. You were only a boy. You did everything right. It was them.

Don't for a second blame yourself for the misguided actions of sick people. You'll see, Bullseye. You'll see."

Hearing her tell me it's okay lifts a massive weight off my chest. It's what I needed to hear. I don't know why, but coming from Sylvia, I know it means something. I know I have a long way to go until I can accept myself fully, but I think I'm on the right track.

God, I hope so.

Because I honestly do want to know what the right way is and how it feels.

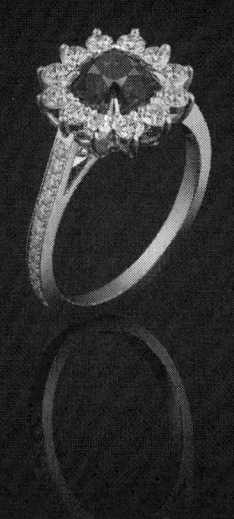

CHAPTER FOURTEEN

Ruby

It's been a few hours since I've seen Bullseye. Juliette said he went to therapy, which only made me more curious about the man who likes to hide away. I know everyone has their problems. I know it isn't every day someone can try and talk about what's eating away at their soul, but I find a huge amount of respect for them when they do.

Solving problems isn't easy, especially when they are your own.

While I'm waiting, I'm getting a little bored sitting in his room. I want to snoop, but he doesn't have much to go through by the looks of things.

Fuck it. I'm going to do it anyway. I roll off the king-sized bed and open the nightstand. There's your typical stuff: lube and condoms.

Magnum.

My cheeks heat when I think of why he must have that size. I clear my throat and slam the drawer closed, then fan my face when an image of us rolling around in his bed comes to mind. "Get a grip, Ruby. He might not even want you after you admit the Moretti thing," I say to myself, opening the closet next.

Just shirts, and at the bottom, there are a few different pairs of boots. One pair is filthy. Another the leather is cracked, and the last pair is shining as if they are brand new. Those must be his 'going out' boots.

A wave of jealously slams into me when I think about him going out and meeting other women. Of course, he does. It's Bullseye. He's fucking gorgeous. He probably has three women at a time.

And I want to kill all those bitches.

I don't care how long it takes or what I have to do to secure Bullseye, but he's mine.

Only mine.

I slam the closet door closed a little too hard, upset that Bullseye seems to have just been dropped here from out of nowhere. How does he not have pictures? Albums? A history? Everyone's room has a little history.

Where is his?

I tiptoe to the dresser. Pause. I cut a glance back to the door as if I'm about to get caught, but nothing's there. After a minute, I continue. I open one drawer and roll my eyes.

Socks.

All mismatched.

"Of course," I mumble.

I close that drawer and open the next.

Oh. Underwear.

Sexy underwear. None of that saggy Fruit of the Loom shit, but Grade-A nut hugging undies. I hold one up, and it feels like spandex. It has to be some type of stretchy material. Damn, I bet he looks so good in these as they cling to every curve.

Imagining them stretched over his tree trunk thighs, suctioning over his cock, and pulled taut over his plump ass like a second skin.

"God bless the woman who made this man," I say silently to God, or whoever's idea it was to make such a fine specimen.

I keep the drawer open because I'm nowhere near done with it. I want to see what else he has in the goody forbidden drawer. "I'll be back," I whisper to the sexy spandex briefs. "I'll miss you."

My knees pop as I squat to open the last drawer, and what I find surprises me.

It's empty.

I tap my hand around the drawer, and the back end pops. I freeze. Oh, shit. I'm about to find something I'm not supposed to see. That was the point. This was what I wanted. I take a deep breath. Here it is. Here is Bullseye's history that he keeps hidden away. Part of me feels terrible for just snooping around like this, but he left me in here, so...

With a slow, careful hand, I take out the board, ready for whatever surprises might be waiting for me. My imagination runs wild—maybe it's photos of him and his lovers. Maybe it's a secret stash of mementos. Maybe it's... oh.

It's nothing.

Just a bunch of cash and darts. That's disappointing. I frown and dig around, even more, trying to find a dirty secret, but that's all I see. Just stacks of cash and some of his darts. Nothing that tells me about Bullseye's history. I'm coming up empty-handed.

"What are you doing?"

I scream, then hold my hand to my chest when I hear Bullseye's voice. I look up to see him standing in the doorway, arms crossed and staring at me. "Uh, I'm snooping," I answer honestly.

His eyes drop to my chest, and that's when I remember I'm still holding a pair of sexy undies. I'm holding them close since he scared me.

"Need some underwear, Spitfire?" he tsks, walking into the room and shutting the door. "Cash? Both?"

"No." I toss the underwear in the drawer they belong in and close it, then close the secret cash drawer. "I wanted to find something personal, I guess."

"Disappointed that you didn't?" He takes a seat on the bed, and the springs groan from his weight.

"A little bit." I take the spot next to him and evaluate his face. His eyes are red, as if he's been crying. A few things start to click together. He doesn't have anything personal in his room because everything he deems personal, he keeps close to his heart.

So if I want him, if I want to get to know him, I have to earn him.

"I'm not a sharing kind of guy," he grunts. "Most of the guys here don't even know my name. Badge probably does cause he's a nosey fuck, and Skirt on accident when he had to come with me to therapy." His throat bobs as he swallows.

"Can I ask what you're going for?"

He blows out a breath and nods. "You can, but I can't get into it again today. It's exhausting. I did something I thought I'd never do. I told my truth. That's because of you, you know." He reaches up and rubs his knuckles across my cheek.

"Me?"

His touch makes me breathless. I press my thighs together as a buzz hums through my veins.

"You said, 'If you want to be happy, be happy. If you want to be miserable, be miserable'. And I want to be happy. I have to learn how to be. I have a lot let go of, but I want to."

"I'm glad I could help."

"You've helped more in the last twenty-four hours than anyone else has in the last eighteen years." He drops his hand from my face, and he sighs. "I'll tell you soon, I promise, but what you need to tell me is what kind of business you have with Moretti and why."

The threatening tone in the timbre of his voice has my body awakening, wanting to reach out and cut this sexual tension with some actual sex.

"I'll give a secret for a secret." I quirk a brow at him, challenging him to defy me.

He picks me up around my waist and plops me on his lap. "You drive a hard bargain, Spitfire." He slides his hands up my back and growls as he slides them back down. There's an ache in my shoulder where that attacker bit me, but other than that, I feel fine. His hands feel good. "You don't play fair. I'm a man full of secrets."

"I know." I wrap my arms around his neck. "And if driving a hard bargain is how I get to know the man, then that's what I'll have to do."

"Tell me why you met with Moretti last night, and you can ask me anything," he offers.

I tap my fingers along his neck, and he closes his eyes, soaking up the touch. It's simple, not a huge gesture, but it's like he can't get enough of it. Why is that?

I play with the ends of his hair on the nape of his neck, and he hums, a hint of a smile ghosting on his lips. "One," he mumbles.

"One?"

He shakes his head. "Just something my therapist told me to do. Tell me why you're meeting Moretti," he says, switching the subject instead of allowing our conversation to flow.

I decide to let it go.

For now.

"I'm in financial trouble. I have medical debt, and I'm behind on rent for the store because everything I have is going to medical bills. I went to him because he came to me with an offer. He paid off my debt, and I work for him for a month."

His hands tighten around my hips, and the muscle jumps in the carved edge of his jaw. "You got into bed with a snake. No way in fucking hell will I allow that."

I'm going to ignore the 'allow' part of that statement. He doesn't control me. I make my own decisions, and whatever we're doing, whatever this is between us, it hasn't been signed and stamped or written in blood. Until then, I'm my own damn person, and I make the decisions about my life.

"That actually wasn't an option. I thought it was. I thought he and Nora wanted a third to add to their relationship. Talk about awkward," I blow out a breath. "I was sweating as they laughed."

"No," he states on a cruel bite. His fingers add delicious pressure to my hips as he grabs onto them with fury.

I lean back and lift my brows. "Excuse me? It isn't up to you. Moretti offered me a way out of the damn struggle I've been dealt. I'm an independent woman who doesn't need a sexy biker." *Lies. Save me. All-day.*

I want to punch my inner voice in the face.

"Are you a performer?"

My cheeks heat under his calculating gaze. "Yes. He gave me a tour. I saw a show."

"I won't allow you to perform alone," he says. "Take the offer, or I'll take all that cash in the drawer and pay the man myself. You won't be going to Hall of Lust alone."

I bite my lip as a thought occurs to me. "And how do you know about the Hall of Lust?"

"Let's just say, I have a few kinks I need to settle inside me," he says.

A breath hitches in my chest when I think of us performing together. My breasts become heavy, and my nipples are tight, scratching against the material of his shirt.

"In fact, while you were there, I performed a show too." He flips me over, and I wrap my legs around his waist, staring up at the intimidating man as he zeroes in on me, as if I'm one of his targets. "Maybe you saw me there," he whispers, tickling his nose across my cheek. "I was in a red room, a leather mask covered my face—" he moves to the other side of my neck and presses a kiss under my ear.

My heart thumps wildly against my chest when I remember the long, thick cock hidden beneath the cock cage.

No.

It couldn't have been him. He could not be that beautiful, sexy, breathtaking man who danced in front of me and gave me everything I ever wanted when I couldn't touch.

"—I wore a cock cage."

I gasp when he confirms it. All the blood in my body boils under my cheeks as he stares down at me, smirking.

"So it was you I performed in front of," he grins when he sees my face. "Two," he whispers to himself, then returns his focus to me.

He spreads my legs, and his jean-covered cock rubs against the flimsy material of my panties. "Did you like watching me, Ruby? Did you like seeing what you couldn't touch?" He rolls his hips, and a whimper escapes me when the fat head of his cock presses against my center.

I can feel his piercings rolling over the bundle of nerves.

"Did you fuck yourself as you watched me, baby?" he practically purrs against my ear. My eyes roll to the back of my head. "Did you put those sweet fingers into that tight cunt for me while I put on a show for you?"

"You better fucking believe I did." I grab his shirt and pull him closer to me, smashing my mouth against his and taking it into a brutal kiss. His tongue slides against mine; the strokes are rough and demanding. We don't tease or lick or enjoy.

We try to take from one another.

We fight for dominance.

Backing down isn't something I do. I like a good power struggle before I give in.

If I give in.

"Seeing that big cock constrained in that cage had me wanting to hold the key." I break the kiss and bite his bottom lip. "And I don't know if I would have unlocked it if I wouldn't have been able to touch you." I claw at his chest; his leather cut digging into my nails.

He growls and flips us over until he's on his back and I'm on top, his hands on my thighs. I hiss as his thumb digs into a sore spot on my inner thigh, and I know right then the mood is going to be killed. I yelp when he flips me onto my back again and lifts my legs into the air, each foot on his shoulder.

His brows pinch as he lifts the shirt covering my legs. I don't look away from him because I'm not ashamed. I fought like fucking hell for those bruises not to turn into more. I'm proud of myself.

His fingers trace the scratches, one by one, he follows them down my thigh.

"I'm fine. They're just bruises. I'll heal."

A growl leaves his throat, and the heat in his green eyes has me holding my breath as his rough hands skim lower, below the bruises, below the edge of pain. "I love a woman who can take care of herself." He hooks his fingers in the waistband of my panties and pulls them down my legs, then stuffs them in his pocket. "I'll be saving these for later."

I inhale a sharp breath when his finger rubs against my slit. It's a lazy motion as if he isn't in a hurry. He isn't trying to pleasure me. He's just... feeling.

And that makes me so much wetter.

His eyes fall between my legs, and he groans, licking his lips. "What a pretty pink pussy." He lowers himself to his elbows and lies down on the bed. "I've been dreaming about this cunt for fucking months. You've denied me." He gives a long lick to my center, and my thighs tremble.

A knock sounds at the door, interrupting us, and I slam my fists on the bed.

Bullseye sucks my clit into his mouth, which has my back bowing off the mattress. He lets go with a soft plop and kisses it. He slides the shirt down over my legs, and he smirks, "But I think it's my turn to deny you, don't you think?"

He rolls off the bed and readjusts the massive cock that's tenting his jeans.

"Bullseye, we have to roll out in ten," Skirt yells from the other side of the door.

"You've got to be kidding me. You're going to leave me like this?" I sputter. Legs spread, wet, aching, and throbbing for an orgasm.

"Spitfire, you've left me in a whole lot worse."

"I doubt that. I never had your juices shining on my lips," I spit.

He grins and rubs his lips together. "Fuck, you do taste good. It's a good thing it's there too because when I'm talking to Moretti about you not working there alone."

"I'll work there if I want to work there."

He's at my side in less than a second, and his hand is between my legs again, his thumb pressing against my clit and his index finger at my entrance. "No one—" he growls, pressing into me.

My mouth drops open on a moan.

"—Fucking no one is seeing your pussy without me there. They can watch us, they can wish they were me tasting this sweet fucking cake, but leaving you alone with eyes that want to eat you up is out of the question. You fuck me and only me, or you don't fuck at all, Spitfire."

He slides his finger in and out, slow and steady. "So fucking tight. I can't wait to feel you wrapped around me one day." He pulls out and brings his finger to his mouth, and sucks it in. "By the way," he closes his eyes as if he just tasted the sweetest thing on Earth. "I have an arrangement with Skirt and Dawn. If you're interested, maybe we can do something about that later."

The thought of watching another couple has me sliding my hands down my body to take care of the ache he has created.

"Fucking hell, you're perfect. You aren't allowed to touch yourself until I come back, do you understand me?"

"And what are you going to do to me if I do?" I smirk, kneading my breasts and pinching my nipples, giving them a good hard tug.

"It's what I'm not going to do to you if you do. If I don't come, you don't come." He snags the back of my head and pulls me in for another kiss. It's heated, quick, and our tongues duel for a sweet, too-short second before he breaks away. "If I come home and bury my face between those legs and smell the sweet scent of your come, your pussy will not be my target tonight." He begins to walk away, but his parting words leave a bad taste in my mouth.

I slide out of bed and grab the back of his shirt before he opens the door. "No other pussy will be your target either," I clarify.

I'm not stupid. I know bikers. They fuck anyone they can, and I know Bullseye's reputation. The girls told me. He loved the cut-sluts when they were around. "I don't share, Bullseye. Not physically."

"Waylon," he says out of nowhere.

"What?" I blink up at him, confused as to where that name came from.

"You wanted to know something about me that not everyone knows. My name. It's Waylon Jennings." He kisses my forehead and a sigh escapes him. "And I don't share that information."

I smile up at him, realizing what he means.

He doesn't want to share me either.

Because he plans on sharing *who* he is with me.

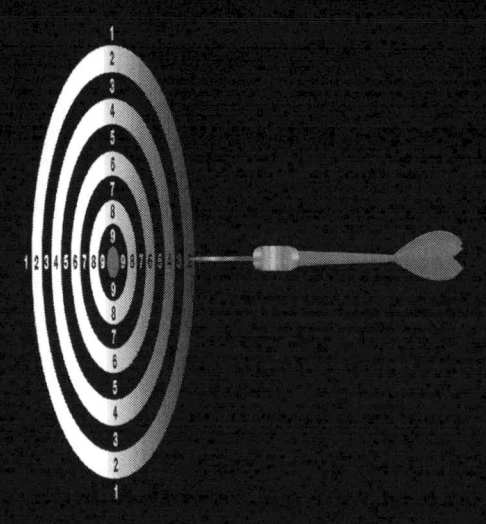

CHAPTER FIFTEEN
Bullseye

MY GOD, MY FUCKING COCK HURTS. I WANTED NOTHING MORE THAN TO FUCK RUBY right then and there on the bed. My old self would have unzipped my pants, slid on a condom, and fucked her without consequence.

I don't want that with her.

It's why I didn't give in for a quick fuck before I walked out the door. I wanted more than that for our first time.

Skirt smirks at me as I walk by him. "Did I interrupt?" he asks, following behind me as we head to the front door.

"Yes, but it was for the better," I reply, fidgeting with the darts in my pocket. They always make me feel better. They remind me of part of the man I am on the inside, the Sergeant-at-Arms, who Prez always wants at his side when torturing people.

I love playing human darts, and he always lets me practice.

"So I was wondering, later, if ye wanted to come into the room? Dawn's been asking."

I almost trip over myself as I walk, but it's subtle. I want nothing more than to have a scene with Skirt and Dawn. I remember when he first asked me, he was so nervous, but Skirt had no idea how the person he picked was indeed the man for the job.

Like it's a hardship to watch a beautiful woman moan and asked to be fucked harder? Watching them gave me power again, but it also made me realize how badly I needed to be watched.

How likely is it that Ruby will want to watch with me?

I know I'd give up the dynamic with Dawn and Skirt for Ruby, but I wouldn't be happy about it. We've become close. We aren't a throuple or anything, but there is a deep level of trust there I don't have with anyone else in the club. The relationship is hard to explain, but it makes me happy, and thinking about not having the one thing that kept me somewhat grounded over the last few months hurts more than I care to admit.

"Absolutely. Like I'd ever say no."

Skirt's shoulders sag, and he blows out a breath. "Good. I'm always nervous about asking. I don't know why."

"I know, but you and Dawn are important to me. I like doing those things with you." I have never admitted that before, and I start to get nervous that Skirt thinks I'm going to move in on his woman. "Listen, I care about you both, but I'm not after Dawn or anything."

Skirt tosses his head back and laughs. "I know that, Bullseye. I know. Don't worry. We feel the same way." He pats my shoulder. "Is yer lady going to join us?"

I scratch the back of my head and think about how to answer. "I think so. She's into watching, so maybe?"

"I'll talk to Dawn and make sure it's okay. I don't think she'll mind. Never thought our little party would grow," he snorts, making his way around me. His brass knuckles drop on the ground. "Damn it." He bends down, and his kilt lifts.

I've seen Skirt's ass plenty of times, but out of the room, I don't want to see it. The son of a bitch is hairy.

"Aw, don't act like ye don't like it," Skirt says playfully.

"Get the hell out the door, Skirt, before I need someone to bleach my eyes." I shove his shoulder, and he stumbles out the door, cackling like the crazy Scot that he is.

I look over my shoulder and down the hall as I grab the door handle. My bedroom door's shut, but I know Ruby is there, safe and sound. I don't want to leave her, but I need to deal with fucking Moretti.

Just the thought of her performing in front of him or some strangers has me slamming the door shut behind me harder than necessary.

"Ye okay?" Skirt asks, stopping on the third step of the porch.

"I'm fine. We aren't killing Moretti, right?"

Reaper's lighter strikes, a flame is swaying as he cups his hand over it so it doesn't go out as he inhales on the cigarette. The end turns orange, and ash trickles off the end. "We can't kill a man who gives us a fat paycheck," he shrugs, tucking his Zippo lighter in the inside pocket of his cut.

I sneer, wishing money didn't talk so damn much. "Fine." As much as I'm disappointed, I understand. A job is a job, no matter how much we don't like it.

Reaper flicks his half-smoked cigarette onto the ground and blows out the cloud, polluting the air. "Let's ride," he announces over the grumble of his bike as he starts his engine.

My bike is next to his, and as I mount it, he's strapping his helmet on.

"Tank and Braveheart are on their way to Ruby's store. It'll be covered for a few days until she's back on her feet," he says to me, flipping the kickstand up with his boot.

Honestly, the way Ruby bounces back from the cruelty of life hitting her out of nowhere, I bet she's already ready to go back to work. She'd push through the pain and soreness in her bones because she always had to work through the pain.

I'm just an over-protective ass. I know there aren't many things about Ruby I can control, but I know I have control over this. I'm not ready for her to go back to work so fast. I think she needs time to relax. A part of me also believes she isn't as good as she says she is. I'm waiting for the other shoe to drop, so to speak. I'm so used to things falling apart. I might be wrong. Maybe she is as strong as she says, and I'm being a skeptic.

I nod to Reaper. The rumble of bikes is music to my ears as we head out of the front gate. Even over the loud engines, I hear men cursing because of the potholes in the driveway. Reaper refuses to get them fixed again after the storm washed the dirt he filled them with away. He always says, 'it's a way of slowing down the enemy', which I think is a crock of bullshit. But what he isn't thinking about is what it's doing to our bikes.

One by one, we turn right onto Loneliest Road. I follow behind Reaper and place a hand on my thigh, casually sinking into a relaxed ride. Damn, it feels good to ride. I'm thankful Skirt picked up my bike for me from Lussuria without asking questions. He probably knew what it was doing there and put two and two together.

The hot sun on my arms and the breeze across my face feels so good. I look around and find myself surrounded by my real family. Life isn't bad at all. Now that I've slowly started healing, my eyes are more open, and I can see everything I have around me.

Plus, who can deny this gorgeous view of the rocky desert with the mountains in the background? For the longest time, all I saw were four walls, and now I have the opportunity to see everything. Sylvia is right. Georgia would be fucking pissed knowing I haven't been taking advantage of life the way she would have loved to.

The ride is quick and easy. Too quick. I want to go on a longer ride, one where Ruby is riding bitch with her arms wrapped around me.

And then, when we're secluded, I'll pull over on the side of the road and fuck that tight cunt until she's screaming my name across the highway.

Skirt's whistle of appreciation brings me out of my thoughts, and I look up to see a huge gate blocking our entry into Moretti's Italian-style mansion.

"Damn, this is fancy," Skirt comments.

"Just remember, everything is dipped in blood."

I snort. "So are we."

Reaper presses a button on the intercom. "Mateo, let us in. I gotta piss."

The intercom clicks, and Moretti's dark chuckle emits from the speaker. I tighten my hands on the handlebars and keep my lips pressed together. I didn't mind the man but knowing Ruby signed a contract with him has all my protective instincts flaring up.

"It's always a pleasure to see you, Reaper," Moretti says. "Please, come in," he adds just as the massive gate begins to swing open.

The feeling is not mutual. It is not going to be a pleasure to see him.

The gates take forever to open, and I huff in annoyance. I look at the two gargoyles perched on the concrete posts, staring at me with big stone eyes. They creep me out. What's the point of damn ugly gargoyles? It's not like they can come to life and protect the place from an intruder.

The gate finally opens enough for Reaper to nose his way through. He fires up his engine, leading the way for us to follow, the sun glistening off the chrome of his bike.

The driveway is long, made of gorgeous red cobblestone that circles a giant fountain. Full green bushes with pink blossoms surround the extravagant structure. We park our bikes and turn them off. I take off my helmet and lay it on the seat.

Skirt whistles again as she stares up at the mansion. "Good lord, can ye imagine the size of the fridge in this house? It bet it could hold so many pies."

That gets us all laughing, and I slap my hand on his shoulder. Skirt always says the right thing to make things better.

Reaper walks up the bifurcated staircase. I've never seen one outside before, but as we climb up the stairs and stop at the front door, on either side of us, the stairs continue to a balcony, maybe? I'm not sure since I've never been here before.

The intricately carved arch-topped wooden doors swing open, and a younger version of Moretti greets us. Unlike the serious expression Mateo keeps, this Moretti is all smiles. "Hi, I don't think we've met. I'm Salvatore. Mateo's brother." He holds out his hand, and Reaper goes to shake it, but Mateo steps beside his brother, and like the dark cloud that he is, he slaps his brother's hand away.

"Don't let his friendly demeanor fool you. He isn't to be trusted." Mateo narrows his eyes at his brother, and the fun light that was shining in Salvatore's eyes dims.

"He's fine," Reaper says, entering the house without permission. His wide shoulder bumps into Moretti's, and Moretti's lip tugs in the corner in a sneer. "He's nicer than you," Reaper informs him. "Matter of fact, I think I like him more."

Salvatore grins. "See? I knew I was the brother everyone preferred."

"Well, the rest of you come in. You're letting all the hot air in." Moretti walks away, his expensive leather shoes clicking against the floor. There's a chandelier above us shining and sparkling like a million diamonds. It's pretty, expensive, reeking of wealth, but I think rubies are prettier. "Follow me to the living room," he orders, lifting his hand in the air and crooking two fingers over him. His suit sleeve drops down to show his Rolex, and it only makes me hate him more.

I have money, and I have no reason to be flashy with it. I don't understand it. He has a Rolls Royce, a Range Rover, a Mercedes, and a Tesla sitting in his driveway. I bet he has countless more cars he doesn't drive in his garage. What's the point of all that?

I'm not rich, but I do pretty fucking well. All I need is my bike and Ruby by my side. That's it. We could travel the world.

That would be so nice.

The realization almost knocks the breath out of me. Is that really what I want? Is that the thing I crave? The life that will make me truly happy? Love, companionship, and adventure? Just the thought has one of those fluttering things flapping in my stomach. I've never had that before.

I can't do that if Moretti keeps his fucking claws in Ruby. I can't have what I want if his shadow always lingers. I'm done with people trying to control what's mine and what's supposed to be my fucking life. I dig my hand into my pocket and roll the sleek edge of my dart against my fingertips.

Moretti turns around to speak, and before he can get a word out, before I can stop myself, I throw the dart in the air so quickly that no one has any idea of what is going on. I intentionally only nick his neck. He hisses, slapping his hand over the left side of his throat.

The dart lands with a hard thud against the wall, and I'm in front of Moretti in three angry strides, my arm against his throat. I slam him against the wall, a trickle of blood dripping from where my dart hit him. I'm tempted to lick his skin clean, so he knows how serious I am about wanting his blood anyway I can fucking get it.

"Bullseye! Stand down!" Reaper yells the order, but I'm too fucking pissed off to listen to anybody.

Several guns cock around me, and the slightest tremble of unease settles in my spine. I hate guns. I can't break the eye contact I have with Moretti, though. He needs to see how serious I am. I won't let my fear of what might happen to me ruin that.

A strong man is defined by what he does, even when he is afraid.

Besides, anything that would happen to me will be a walk in the park.

"Bullseye, I won't ask again. You have no idea what you've just done."

"Oh, I have an idea," I hiss, shoving Moretti again.

He lifts his hands to his men to tell them to hold off on shooting me.

"Now, Bullseye. Is that how you treat your employer?" he asks smugly, and the back of my neck begins to burn when my brothers murmur behind me.

I won't be ashamed.

"I don't give a flying fuck who you tell anymore. I'm not here for me." I press him harder against the wall.

"Well, we both know you never miss when it comes to your darts. So why don't you indulge me and tell me?"

"Ruby. I want her out of the contract you have."

Reaper and Skirt take a step forward. "You went into business with her?" The gravel of anger charring Prez's words have me grinning like a smug bastard.

"She's a grown woman. I gave her an opportunity, and she took it."

"Well, she can't perform for you. She was attacked last night, so I'm telling you the contract is void."

The dark coals of his eyes spark like fire when he hears she's been attacked.

"I am not an unreasonable man no matter what you think, but a contract is a contract. We agreed."

"She isn't performing without me, or I give you the cash, and we can be through with it."

He eyes me, contemplating my offer. I reach next to his head and yank my dart from the wall, leaving a small circular hole in its wake. "You're going to want to fix that," I say, blowing the dust off the sharp metal tip of my weapon.

Mateo tugs his suit straight to get the wrinkles out and then brushes the dust off his shoulder.

"I want to own forty-nine percent of her business, and for one month, you perform together. That's my new offer. Take it or leave it."

I stand toe-to-toe with him. "I don't know if Ruby will sign over her business. I'll pay you in cash for the debt you paid."

"You have nearly $100,000 in cash?"

"Yes," I say without flinching or blinking. Everything I've ever earned is in my room. It's not the safest place for it, but I don't like the thought of using a card. If Ruby and I go further, I'll need to get over that.

"Hmmm," he thinks about it, dabbing his bleeding neck with a silk handkerchief. "Consider my payoff for Ruby's debt my buy-in into her business. If she says no, you'll give me $150,000."

Before he can blink, I have the sharp tip of my dart under his chin. "Why the fuck are you increasing the amount owed?"

"For pissing me off and making me bleed in my own home," he sneers. "Now, can we get to the matter at hand, or are you still going to be selfish?"

I flip the dart in my hand, then tuck it in my pocket. "Nope, I'm done."

Skirt slaps the back of my head, and I do not doubt with how Reaper is looking at me that I might get a heart carved into my chest. I could have started a war, I incited violence in an ally's stronghold, and I ignored his order.

But it was all worth it.

"Oh my god!" Nora, his fiancée, places the tray filled with coffee cups on the counter, pulls her robe tight around her waist, and ties the belt. She runs to Moretti's side and fusses over him, which has me rolling my eyes.

The bastard has been through much worse, like an explosion, for starters. He's lucky he came out looking as good as he does. His burns healed nicely, nearly unseen, but she's bitching about a small cut on his neck.

"What happened? Do I need to go get a band-aid?" she asks, her eyes big through the glasses she wore.

"No, Stellina. I'm fine. Bullseye here lost his temper, that's all."

Nora whips her head to me, her brown hair swinging over her shoulder as she marches up to me. She lifts her hand in the air and slaps me across the face.

"Oh, shite," Skirt gasps.

"He deserved it," Badge grumbles.

"He might make deals, but I will make death threats if you ever touch him again. I don't care who you are. I will go after the one you love if you ever go after who I love again."

"Stellina, shhh, all is well." Mateo grabs her hand and brings it to his mouth to kiss. He speaks to her in Italian. She giggles then bounces away happily on her heels.

I rub my cheek from the slight sting. "She hits like she loves you, that's for sure."

"Mmm," he agrees. "My Stellina is protective. She's perfect. I won't apologize for her actions. She did nothing wrong." He takes a seat in the chair next to the fireplace and places his hands in a steepled position as he stares me down.

"It's not the first time I've been hit. It won't be the last," I say.

"Okay, enough of the bullshit." Reaper takes the lead and rubs his hand over his mouth. "Bullseye, sit the fuck down and don't say another word until I say otherwise."

I do as he says and take a seat on the couch, but a gun hits the back of my head. "Get that fucking gun off me before I ram a dart in your eye," I threaten the person behind me.

"Piero." Mateo motions for the guy to drop the gun, and the steel barrel finally leaves the back of my head.

I crack my neck. "Sorry, Prez."

"It's fine," he sighs, exasperated. He knows how much guns make me uncomfortable, especially after being shot in Atlantic City. He pinches the bridge of his nose. "Why are we here, Mateo? Why do we care what happens to your brother? And you have men here. You don't need us," he points out.

"My men are young and inexperienced. You're not. You should care because I need to make sure my brother doesn't escape or get freed. What I have planned for him is much crueler than any quick death. Plus, my Stellina is here. I need to make sure she's safe. If my brother's loyalists get their hands on her, it would be like someone taking Sarah, Reaper."

Prez's nostrils flare at the thought, and the tendons in his neck tighten. "Okay, well, I don't think so many of us need to be here. Bullseye, Poodle, Patrick, you three head back."

"Sounds good to me," Patrick says. "I'd rather be with Sunnie. Moretti, I'm sure I'll be seeing you soon."

Moretti nods in agreement as Patrick and Poodle leave, but I'm confused. "I thought I was requested here. Why am I leaving?"

"Because you've pissed me off," Reaper snarls. "Go back to the fucking clubhouse and get your head on straight. I'll deal with you later."

Moretti smirks, but the last thing I do is break eye contact with him. "I look forward to it, Prez." I get up slowly and spin around, passing the guy still holding the gun in his hand. I might hate guns, but I know how to use them. I steal it from him in a quick move, empty the chamber along with the ammunition, then proceed to take the gun apart. "You need to hold your gun tighter, dumbass." I drop the gun on the floor, where it makes a hard thud, the clinking of bullets still sounding as they dance along the floor.

I open the door and slam it shut behind me.

"Man, you just love making friends, don't you?" Poodle jokes as he puts on his helmet.

"I don't need any more friends anyway." I hurry down the steps and mount my bike.

My bike. Ruby.

I have everything I need.

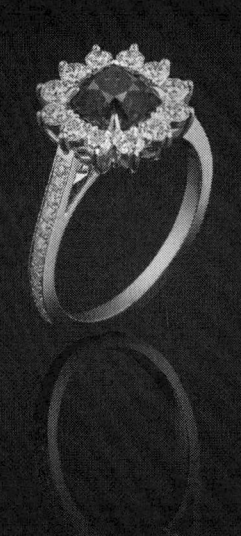

CHAPTER SIXTEEN

Ruby

I CAN FEEL HIS HANDS ON ME, HIS BREATH TICKLING MY NECK, HIS TEETH SCRAPING AGAINST MY shoulder. I kick and scream, but the darkness mutes my screams.

No one can hear me. No one is coming. No one is going to save me.

My panties are ripped from my body, and my dress is hiked up as my attacker smashes my face against the wall. The brick scratches it. It hurts, but the pain doesn't register as much as the panic and fear do. My nails claw at the wall, threatening to break.

I rear my head back, and it hits against his nose, but it doesn't stop him from gripping my thighs to spread my legs. He sinks his teeth into me, and another scream leaves me. I can feel myself wanting to increase the volume, but it's as if I'm underwater, trying to yell for help.

Why can't anyone hear me?

His fingers pinch my ass, and right as I hear the zipper of his pants—

"Whoa, hey, Ruby. I got you. It's okay." Bullseye's voice is calming as I gasp awake. He wraps his arms around my waist and pulls me close. I turn to my side and bury my face in his chest. I don't know when he came back home, and I don't know what time it is, but I'm thankful. He is warm, strong, and his presence is soothing. The fear I felt from my dream fades the longer I inhale his scent.

Safety.

He's safety.

"Waylon," I whimper his name as I rub my cheek across his chest. Saying his name, his real name, makes me feel closer to him. It's like I have a part of him that no one else has.

He inhales a sharp breath and cups the back of my head while his other arm wraps around my stomach. "I'm not going anywhere. It was just a bad dream," he croons. "You're safe. You're safe with me."

I wrap my arms around his broad back, squeezing him tight as I fight the tears from the overwhelming emotion of terror coursing through me. I don't want to cry. In a few days, I know this will all be behind me because of how I am as a person.

But right now, I'm so glad I'm with Bullseye. There's nowhere else I'd rather be. His arms feel good. He's like a sturdy, well-built house, and the foundation that makes him the man he is made of concrete and steel. Nothing can bring him down, no winds can make him waver, and no sea can rage against him.

I'm secure in the walls he's built for himself.

He's the home I've been looking for. I've never felt so good.

A hurricane could blow through, and he'd stand firm, bracing effortlessly against the havoc the storm brings.

His hand lazily rubs up and down my back. It's surprising, in a way, the gentle touch from a man who's accomplished so much violence in his life. The same hands that have killed, tortured, and who knows what else are caressing me as if I'm the most fragile thing he's ever known.

I let out a shaky breath and close the last inch of space between us. I'm practically wrapped around him now. It's like I can't get close enough. I rub my nose up his chest, inhaling again, and stop at the crook of his shoulder. His skin is hot, and he has scruff on his face from the day, softly bristling against my neck.

He's all hard muscle, and power. He's too impossible not to become addicted to. How did I deny this for so long?

"Are you okay?" his sleepy voice is deep and rough, which has my body waking up as if it's morning. I'm putting the night behind me, even if it's still dark outside.

"I'm getting there," I tell him breathlessly.

A low rumble shakes his chest. "Are you not as okay as you say? It's okay to be scared and need time to heal."

"I'll be okay. Like I said, in a few days, I'll be good as new. I'm glad you woke me up. I feel better here with you," I exhale, finally relaxing against him as the nightmare fades. The only thing on my mind now is Bullseye.

My mind wanders elsewhere as my body grows heavy with need. I run my hand down his chest and press a kiss to the side of his throat.

"What are you doing?" he asks, his words strangled with lust.

I grin against his throat before pressing another kiss to the large knot of his Adam's apple as it bobs. "Isn't it obvious?"

His chest is bare; all that muscle is on display. I can't see since the lights are off, which is a shame. A man that looks as good as he does deserves to be appreciated more.

"I don't think it's a good idea with everything you've been through."

I sigh and roll over, flipping on the lamp so I can see him. The light isn't bright, so it isn't enough to hurt my eyes. I settle on my side again and keep myself propped up with my elbow on the bed and face in hand.

The impressive width of his chest is illuminated by the faint light, which casts a yellow glow onto the olive hues of his flesh. I'm sure beautiful is not the word women use to describe him, but he is. From the curls at the ends of his hair to the tips of his toes, the man is the definition of beauty.

His eyes dart back and forth between mine. "What are you looking at?"

I press my palm against his chest, the primitive beat of his heart runs rampant under my palm. "I'm looking at you, Waylon," I make sure to repeat his name. "You're gorgeous." I bend down and press a kiss to the top of his chest, then trace the defined pectoral with my finger. "I just appreciate the sight." I lift my eyes and notice a faint blush on his cheeks as he looks away from me, a smile stretching his lips.

"Three," he says.

"Three?" I'm confused. What is he counting exactly?

"Nothing, don't worry about it," he says, turning onto his back. "I don't know why you'd want to look at me. I'm..."

"—Fucking sexy? Yes, yes you are." I drift to the wound on his shoulder. It's a puckered scar that's not faded but not a fresh, bright pink either. "What happened?"

"Gunshot."

"Hmm. Hot," I joke, watching another smile grace him.

"Four," he says to himself again.

I have no idea what he is doing, but I'm not going to ask. My fingers drift to another scar, smaller, perfectly round. "What about this one?"

"One of my darts," he says unhappily.

"Oh, kinky." I decide not to ask for the stories because I don't want this moment to turn heavy. I want Bullseye. Now. But I think I have some buttering up to do with him. He can act big and bad to the world, but I think he's never had someone take the time to touch him, to relish in everything he is. I'm going to show him it's okay to let go of that bit of control and hand it over to someone else.

He grins again. "Five," he whispers.

"And this?" I ask, tracing a line on one side of his throat. It's faint. Maybe the wound hadn't been that bad.

"I was hanged. The rope burn was nasty, but it healed. I can barely see it now," he explains.

"So you liked to be tied up? That's good to know," I say, watching him try to hide another smile.

"Six," he mouths.

I swing my leg over his legs and bend down, kissing each scar that I've touched. I continue my way down, kissing the abs that glisten in the pale light until I get to the sheet covering his hips. "And here?" I ask, rubbing my bottom lip against the thin, faded line. It looks like nothing, but any mark on him is anything but nothing.

"Whip," he says but doesn't elaborate.

A whip.

That left a scar.

When I think about it, my brows furrow, and I have nothing clever to say because being whipped so hard it leaves a scar isn't for pleasure. It's for pain.

He has a novel written on his skin, and I want to know his story so badly. I tug the sheet down and fling it off the bed. He's in his sexy underwear, tight and stretchy, forming over his thighs and cock like a second skin. The waistband is black, a thick cotton material that feels soft under my fingers. I run my nails down his sides, and his stomach hollows as he inhales a shaky breath.

"What are you doing?" he asks again through tight jaws.

"Appreciating," I answer honestly as I scrape my nails down his legs.

I lower my body and come face to face with his covered cock. I can see the outline of the piercings; the very tip of his crown is peeking out from the bottom of his underwear against his thigh.

He is big.

Hard.

Straining.

And that glistening silver Prince Albert piercing is begging to be played with.

"I think you're still… in shock from your dream."

What happened to the confident guy that left me wanting while he went to see Moretti? This Bullseye is almost… shy. I like it. Makes me feel powerful.

"I think I'm a grown-ass woman who knows what she's doing and what she wants." I mouth a wet spot over his cock, soaking the material from my spit. "And I want you. I don't know how many ways I have to spell it out, hint at it, or tell you I'm fine, but I guess I'm going to have to prove it to you." I tug down his underwear, keeping my eyes up at his face, so I don't look at the glorious weapon hanging between his legs. If I remember correctly, he is just the right size.

And I don't care what women say; it's the size of the dart that matters, not the toss. Because no matter the aim, sometimes the target is missed.

When I tug off the underwear from his ankles, another scar catches my eye. It's nasty looking. There isn't any hair that grows there. It looks like it's from something round, maybe like a cuff or something? But that doesn't seem right. His entire body tenses as I run my fingers over the flesh, and I know this is one that I'll be most curious about.

I ignore it, filing it away in my mind for later as I kiss up his right leg. He squirms and groans, his hands fisting the sheets tighter the closer I get to his cock.

Now that I'm face to face with it, it's even bigger than I remember it being. I blow a cold breath on the throbbing flesh, and a bead of pre-come trickles out of the slit. I don't take him in my mouth just yet. I want to play and explore.

I want to show him what it feels like to be the one not having to worry about a thing. As alpha as he is, he's just as submissive.

On the inside.

I doubt the cut-sluts got him in this position.

I think he's going to be sharing a lot more of himself with me than he initially thought.

"I love your piercings," I purr, scratching my nails down his chest. "Metal looks good on you." I pinch his nipples between my fingers and twist, tugging on the bars unforgivingly.

He growls, arching his back, which causes his cock to hit me on the chin. "Are you going to get on with it and suck my cock?" he growls, staring at me through impatient eyes.

"No," I chirp with a devious grin, twisting the barbells in his nipples again.

His mouth drops open on a silent moan, and his brows dip in the middle, creating a crease in his forehead. "No one has ever played with my piercings before."

"That's a shame. It's obvious you like pain. You haven't had the right kind of lovers, then."

"I haven't been looking for love."

There is an underlying statement there, one that has my heart fluttering with hope. I sit up and grab the hem of my shirt, then pull it over my head. I'm still not wearing panties from when he took them off earlier.

His hands are quick as they rub up my stomach and knead my breasts. I gasp at how rough his hands are. He pinches my nipples next, and I toss my head back as the sparks tingle my entire body. He wraps his arms around my body and flips me onto my back.

My legs are parted.

His cock is at my entrance.

And we stare at one another.

I'm not ready to move on so quickly. I reach between us and squeeze him until I know it hurts.

"Fuck," he grunts, squeezing his eyes shut.

"I want you to straddle my head and fuck my face. Do you think you can do that?"

He snaps his eyes open, and before I can say another word, he is straddling my face, and the Prince Albert piercing is nudging my lips. I twirl my tongue around it, sucking the jewelry into my mouth stretching the spongy flesh of his crown.

"Fuck yes. God, you could keep doing that, and I'll come down your throat."

I hum in approval. I want his come down my throat.

He wraps a hand around my neck and squeezes. "You like that, don't you? Your belly full of my come and my taste lingering on your tongue?"

My eyes hood from the filthy words. A gush of wetness starts to spill between my legs. I press my thighs together to help with the throbbing, then flatten my tongue along his heavy cock, tracing the outline of the Jacob's Ladder.

"I've been waiting for fucking ever to feel your lips around me." His fingers tighten against my scalp, and he manages to pull on my hair.

I kiss each silver stud along his cock and give it a good lick. "I thought you were going to fuck my face?"

"I'll fuck it when I'm damn good and ready." His eyes are laser-focused on my mouth, watching as my tongue slips from between my lips. I'm taking my sweet time, adoring the long thick inches, brushing my lips up and down him.

Finally, after he seems like he's about to burst, I suck the flared tip into my mouth, my lips stretching to accommodate the girth. His hand moves to the back of my head as he groans.

And that's when he snaps his hips.

His cock hits the back of my throat, and I gag, which has him shudder above me. He holds my head in place as he rams himself into my mouth. I choke and cough around him, the piercings rubbing against my cheeks as I try to suck, but it's pointless when he's moving so fast.

His heavy sack hits under my chin with every thrust. My eyes are watering from the lack of air. Tears begin to stream down my face, and when he notices, he swipes a finger through them, sucking his index finger into his mouth.

"Taste so good when you're crying from my cock," he rumbles, popping his finger out of his mouth.

I narrow my eyes the best I can and bite down on his cock—gently, not too hard, but he stiffens inside my mouth and shouts. He slams his hand against the headboard, and a devilish sound escapes his throat as he picks up the pace, his hips bucking against me over and over again.

My hands grip his ass, squeezing the firm globes as I hold on to the ride of my life.

"Fuck, you're going to make me come taking my cock like this, baby."

I rip my mouth from him, spit dripping down my bottom lip and push him away. "The hell you are. We're nowhere near done." I place my hand on his shoulders and push him down between my legs, telling him what I want.

He spreads my legs as wide as they can go, which leaves my clit vulnerable. He licks his lips before he dives his tongue inside me, then laps his way up my center. He circles his tongue around the sensitive bead, and I whimper as he sucks my clit into his mouth.

I run my fingers through his hair, holding onto the strands like reins as I ride his face. I rock my pussy against his mouth, needing every sensation I can get from him. His finger circles my aching entrance.

I want him so much it hurts.

He slips a finger inside and kisses the inside of my thigh as he watches me. "This cunt is so tight. I can't wait to feel you around my cock." He inserts another finger and picks up the pace. "So wet, Ruby. This is the prettiest fucking pussy I've ever seen." He buries his face between my legs and sucks onto my clit again, then licks between my folds. "The tastiest, too," he adds.

He reaches out a hand and begins to fuck me with his fingers. It's as if he is mimicking the way he wants to fuck me. It's hard; he is burying himself to the knuckle. I tug on my nipples, becoming even wetter. The sticky sound of his palm slapping against me only fuels the fire between us.

"Oh, god. Yes, Waylon—"

He freezes for a moment, and I thought I said something wrong, but his eyes are blazing with need before he begins thrusting his fingers inside me again.

"That's it, baby. That's it. Call out my name." His other hand presses against the lower half of my stomach, and his fingers hit the spot inside me that has me grabbing the pillow and shoving it over my face to scream.

He hits the spot with every thrust, and my legs begin to tremble. My eyelids are fluttering. My jaw is falling open. My orgasm is building, and my body tingles in awareness, warning me of how high I'm about to fly.

"I'm so close. I'm close," I whimper.

His bicep is flexed as he fucks me harder, and right as I'm about to fall over the edge, he pulls his fingers out of me. I cry out in frustration.

"You deny me. I deny you," he growls, licking each finger clean of my juice with a cocky smirk.

Oh, he wants to play.

I tackle him backward and kiss him relentlessly. I can taste myself on his tongue, sweet yet subtle at the same time. I suck his tongue into my mouth. His fingers dig into my ass, and then his hands are gone. I miss them on my body, but I know he is enjoying himself.

Until his palms land hard on each cheek, a loud clapping fills the room, and my flesh stings. I let go of his tongue, and he brings his hands down again, his eyes never leaving my face.

I gasp, my mouth falling open from the delicious sting. "If you keep doing that, I'll come."

"Christ," he glowers. "You're fucking perfect." He spanks me again, and my nails dig into his chest. I can hardly focus. The only thing keeping me, in reality, is the delicious burn on my backside and the thick cock pressing against me.

I begin to rock against him, my folds embracing his girth. His piercings rub against the right places, the Prince Albert hitting against my clit with every upstroke. "I need you," I beg him as I reach for the nightstand with one hand and hold onto his shoulder with the other.

I grab a gold foil packet and rip it open with my teeth.

His nostrils flare. I don't break eye contact as I take the large condom in hand and roll it down his impressive cock. I lift myself to sink onto him when he suddenly spins me around and slams me face-first into the headboard. His hand is between my shoulder blades, the pressure hard and uncomfortable. I can't move.

It hurts.

It hurts so fucking good.

He yanks my head back and brings his mouth to my ear. "You've got to be out of your fucking mind if you think I'm taking this perfect pussy with a condom." The snap of latex tells me he has taken it off, and he confirms it when he dangles it in front of my face. "I'm clean. Are you?"

I can't speak, so I nod.

"Good," he says again, dropping the condom in the waste bin beside his bed. "It was sexy watching you put it on me, but this cunt is mine, Spitfire." The wide tip of his cock presses against me, and I shiver with anticipation. His hand strokes down my back, and he holds onto my ass again. "I'm going to fill you up with my come, and then maybe you'll get the fucking message of my obsession with you." He lines himself up and thrusts inside me in one hard stroke.

We moan in unison at our connection, like it's the thing we have been for waiting all this time. Bullseye rests his forehead on my back. He's pushed to the hilt, and I'm stretched to the brink. I'm at my limit. His piercings rub me perfectly, creating a ripple effect in my most delicate and intimate area.

"Don't move. God, don't move." He squeezes my hip to keep me in place.

But me being me, I lean back and use the space to flip around so I can look at him. I wrap my legs around his hips while keeping a good grip on the headboard.

It's his turn to quake.

His big, powerful body seems like it's about to come undone. The veins in his arms are protruding, he has sweat dripping from his temples, and every muscle in his body is tense.

He looks down where we're connected and slowly pulls out. I can't help it. I have to look too. I've never had sex without a condom before, and it feels so damn good. I can't catch my breath. Every motion of his hips makes his piercings massage my insides, sending roiling shockwaves of pleasure through me. He slowly pulls out, the metal rubbing against me until all that's left is the tip.

There's still this sense of urgency to fuck, but there's a want to slow down too.

Both of us want submission.

Both of us want domination.

Both of us want to take charge.

The power struggle is one of the things turning me on the most.

Fight me.

Tease me.

Submit to me.

Then turn the tables around and make me.

Make me fuck.

Make me fight.

Make me submit.

It's the best of both worlds.

And I can't wait to experience it.

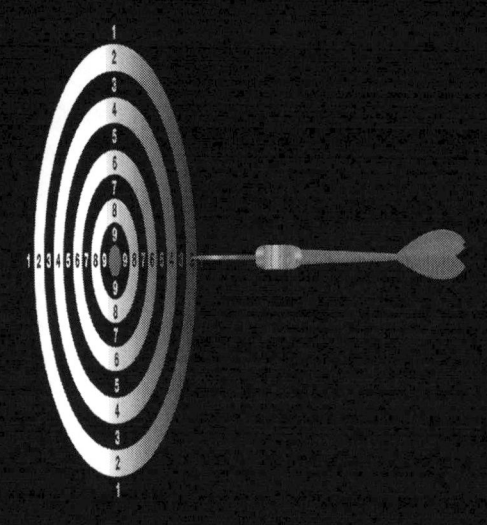

CHAPTER SEVENTEEN
Bullseye

I CAN COUNT ON TWO FINGERS HOW MANY WOMEN I'VE FUCKED WITHOUT A CONDOM.

Georgia.

And now, Ruby.

It's been eighteen years since I've felt the bare, hot, wet flesh of a woman around my cock. And fucking hell, it feels good.

No, not good.

Phenomenal.

I can't even remember what it felt like before because it had been so long, but damn it, I'm never fucking with a condom again.

There will be no need.

Ruby is mine. This solidifies it.

I don't go barebacking every woman I want to fuck. It's too personal. At least it is to me.

And I'll never go a day without being ten inches deep inside her tight heat as long as we live.

I don't move. Not yet. I want her to beg me for my cock. I want her near tears. Hell, maybe I do want her to cry. I want to see how fucking bad she wants me.

Her hair is short, but it's long enough for me to slide my hands through and grip the strands. I yank, and her head tilts back. She whimpers, tightening her muscles around my cock, fucking me from the inside.

I growl, deep and threatening—a warning to tell her to stop. I nip at her chin, my breaths leaving me in desperate trembles. "You know what I want to do to you?" I flatten my tongue across her neck, and her hands fall from the headboard. She wraps them around me and grinds her nails into the skin of my back.

"Bull—"

I smother her mouth with a kiss. I've always hated my name, but the way she says it has me wanting to hear it more.

She's somehow managed to make me love myself. I don't know how or why or when it even happened. "I want to hear you say my name," I say, still not moving like I want to.

Her eyes are glazed over, shining like polished gems. "Waylon, please," she begs.

It isn't enough.

I want to hear her whine.

I want to feel her take.

I want her to lose control with so much desire, so much fucking need that it causes pain.

And I want her to relieve herself by letting that animal go inside her.

My fingers pinch her left nipple. The dusty red bead is tight and stiff, beckoning for my mouth. I lean down and nibble it, kissing it the way I'd kiss her. I suck the flesh into my mouth, moaning from how perfect her breasts are. Round, perky, and bigger than I thought they'd be.

"You haven't answered me," I mutter, my words muffled against her chest. "Do you know what I want to do to you?" I lift my head so she can see the seriousness of my gaze.

She licks her lips; her cheeks flushed with arousal. "What do you want to do to me?" Her voice is soft and compliant as if I'm bending her to my will.

She's bending me. That's for sure.

That's when I take a moment to sink back in her warmth, slow and steady, to drive us both mad. I haven't given enough to make her come, but I've given her enough to make her beg. "I'm going to buy us toys, and one of those will be a plug. Do you know what I'll use it for?" I slide out, and the feel of her has me digging my fingers into the soft flesh of her ass, so I don't break control.

She shakes her head, her eyes wide with curiosity and lust.

"The plug will be to keep my come in this addictive cunt. And then when I want you, whenever the time of day, you'll be wet and ready for me." Fuck, just the thought has me close to losing it.

"Please, Waylon. I can't wait anymore. Fuck me."

"Not yet." I pull out, loving the look on her face as I stretch her when I thrust in. Her eyes close, and her swollen lips part.

"I can't wait." She tries to start fucking me herself, but I grip her hips with my hands and push her against the headboard.

Readjusting my stance, I close a few inches of space between us, which has me sliding in deeper. She can't move now.

I'm in control.

"I'll fuck you when I'm damn good and ready. I'm enjoying having you around me too much to rush this."

She shoves her shoulder between my chest, which knocks the breath out of me. My back hits the mattress, and she's on top of me, smirking. Her hands are in the middle of my chest as she hovers over my cock.

"Well, that's a problem," she says. "Because I'm ready now." She slams herself down on me, taking every inch to the hilt, and begins to ride.

She doesn't start easy.

She doesn't take time to adjust.

Ruby moves back and forth, fucking me as hard as her body will allow. "Oh, fuck. Waylon," she gasps. "You feel so fucking good." She cups her breasts, her hips gyrating front to back. "So big. I love the piercings. I can feel them." Her mouth opens, and a whimper slips out. It's high-pitched and broken like she can't breathe.

Hell, I can't either.

I've always been the one to do the fucking. I've never had a woman take me like this.

God damn.

I love it.

"You like that cock filling you up?" I grab onto her ass and move her body with her, quicker and harder.

"Yes," she nods quickly.

"You've always wanted me, haven't you?"

"Yes."

"You want me to claim this cunt, don't you?"

"Mm-hmm."

Goddamn, she's so wet. Her sweet honey is drenching the inside of my thighs.

"Over and over again. You can't wait to feel my come dripping from you." I push against her hips faster as her breathing picks up. She's already close.

I debate on denying her, edging her to orgasm only to back off again.

I decide against it.

We've both been denied too long.

She falls against my chest, grabbing onto my pecs as she continues to fuck me. "Yes, yes, yes," she chants.

"Are you going to come for me? Are you going to squeeze my cock with this cunt?"

She nods before taking my lips for a kiss, but the momentum prevents us from staying lip-locked. She rears up, and her hips stutter, her tongue paints her lips, and her eyes widen as the pleasure washes over her.

"Waylon, oh god, Waylon! Yes! Oh, fuck!" She grinds herself against me as she falls apart.

Seeing her face pinched with pleasure has my lips parting. I'm close, but I'm holding back. I don't want to come yet. I want to see her fall apart again.

And again.

She tosses her head back as she begins to slow down, her body spasming again and again as the space between us becomes slicker with her come.

She is a fucking sight. The way she bends. The way she gasps and kneads her breasts while she comes down from her high, I'm hypnotized.

I flip us over until she's on her back, trying to catch her breath. Her body is slick with sweat, and her face is flushed as red as that ring on her finger. I can't help myself. I bury my face between her tits, lick the beads gathered there, and thrust into her at the same time. Her leg wraps around my hip, and somehow I'm on my back again.

"I'm not done, and I come quickest on top."

I bite my lip and rub my hands up her back. "You're going to come anyway I make you, Spitfire." I maneuver us again by sitting up and shove her over onto her stomach. I groan when I see her pink star winking at me. There will be a day where I own that too.

The round globes jiggle as I part her cheeks. I spit onto her hole and rub my finger around the forbidden place.

She twists her head and narrows her eyes at me, pressing her cheek against the mattress. "I don't do butt stuff, Bullseye."

I answer in a dark chuckle, then press my finger into her at the same time I plunge my cock into her pussy again.

"Oh, god," she moans, hanging her head in defeat.

"Not only are we going to do 'butt stuff,' Ruby, but you're also going to beg me for it. I'm going to own, claim, and ruin every hole, so you know that your body is no longer yours. It's mine."

"Mmm, it's mine, good-looking. Sorry to break it to you."

I slap a hand down on her reddened cheek. "It isn't, and you know it." So stubborn. So independent. So bound and determined to convince herself she doesn't depend on me.

Tsk. Tsk.

I grab her hip with one hand and start a hard, punishing rhythm. Her ass sucks in my finger, and her cunt massages my cock, rubbing against the piercings in a way I've never felt before. "Fuck, look at you taking my cock and finger. You feel so good."

"God, it feels so good. I'm so full. More," she pleads, yet at the same time, she tries to get away from me by clawing at the bed.

I shove her head down against the bed so she can't move and slide in a second finger into her star, which has her screaming, no doubt waking up different parts of the house. My fingers are engulfed in a vise. I can feel the ridges of my piercings as I take her pussy too.

I don't give her time to answer me.

I fuck her senselessly.

Her ass shakes with every punishing thrust. I don't take it easy on her. I give her everything I've got, needing to prove to her that I can make her come in any position.

I refuse to be like any of the men she's been with before. If she could only come while she was on top, they weren't doing it right.

My fingers are knuckle-deep, and my sack is swinging, slapping against her clit. Our skin slaps together, and sweat drips into my eyes. Heat and exertion cloak my skin. I plant my foot against the bed and keep one knee on the mattress to get a better angle and leverage.

And I pound her. Again and again and again.

Her body is a damn temptress, wringing out the best I have to give.

"Fuck, Waylon. Oh!" she tightens her hands on the edge of the mattress, clasping it for dear life as she muffles her cries into the bed.

I can't wait to hear her when we don't have to worry about waking anyone up. The Hall of Lust will be perfect for that. Or the soundproof room Reaper and Sarah built me, Skirt, and Dawn for Christmas.

A gush of fluid hits my leg, and I smile wickedly, licking the sweat off the top of my lip. Seven. I love knowing that she's coming again.

No, she's doing more than that.

She's orgasming so hard that she's squirting all over me.

My mouth waters, needing a taste, so I pull out of her but keep the same rhythm with my fingers in her puckered hole. I bury my face in her cunt and lick her clean, growling like a beast. I swear I taste strawberries and cream. I slide my tongue in her swollen, used hole, and another small tremble shakes her as she comes yet again.

I hear my name on the sheets as she cries for me. Nothing has ever sounded better. Her gasps, moans, and whimpers are a symphony being played just for me.

My fingers slip free of her, and I spin her around. I sit back on my feet, and she straddles my lap, wrapping her legs around my waist as she engulfs me again, taking me straight to the hilt. Our mouths collide, our teeth clink together; she whips her tongue against mine, bringing a moan from the depths of me.

As I thrust up into her, she meets my move with a roll of her hips: something changes, the pace, the mood, the emotion.

It's desperate.

And I have no idea what to do.

I circle my arms around her, hold her close, and our foreheads fall against each other. Both of us are slick with a sheen of sweat. Our fingers slide against our flesh, unable to gain any traction. I breathe in every breath she exhales.

She circles her arms around my neck and pulls herself closer, holding on tight.

God, I never want to let go.

I haven't felt a connection like this... ever.

Not even with Georgia.

I groan her name, "Ruby." My hips stutter when my orgasm causes my cock to become harder. Tingles drift from my spine to my sack as it pulls tight against my body. "Damn it, baby. Damn it. You feel too good." I grab at her back desperately to bring our bodies closer, but it's impossible.

She steals my lips again, but this time, she isn't fighting for dominance. The kiss is sweet and slow, the soft skin around her mouth brushing against the course shadow of my stubble. Our tongues dance, but mine overpowers hers as she lets me take the lead.

I cup her throat, deepening the kiss, wanting to get lost in her. I can't hold back anymore. I rip my mouth away. My breaths come out choppy, along with deep moans that rattle my chest.

"Ruby," I warn her, but she only picks up the pace by moving her hips faster. "Ruby," I sneer her name, trying to hold back my orgasm to make her get off because that's the only way I'm not coming inside her. I thrust one more time and bury myself as far as I can go. "Fuck! Fucking hell. God," I groan as I come, bathing her depths.

I punch my hips three more times, then finally come to a stop.

We collapse against each other, dying for our next breath.

I hold onto her tight and kiss the slender collarbones.

I don't want to let go.

And if history has proven anything, I'm bad at letting go.

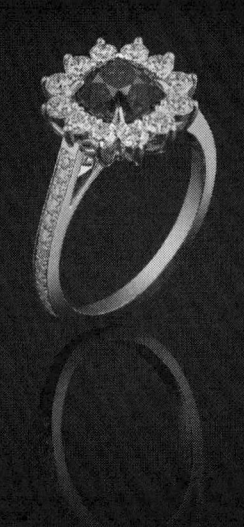

CHAPTER EIGHTEEN

Ruby

I somehow, vaguely, sort of remember him carrying us to the en-suite bathroom and filling the tub with water. It was hard to focus since he was still inside me, and I was too tired to open my eyes to double-check to see where we were going.

I just had the best sex of my life, and I feel drunk.

And I haven't had a drop of alcohol unless Waylon Jennings is considered a drink.

Then call me an alcoholic and pour me another glass.

I lean my head against his chest as I sit between his legs, watching as the water cascades from the faucet to fill the soaking tub. Waylon even put bubbles in it. They smell good too, like lilacs in summer.

I'm getting drowsy in my bliss, especially since he's rubbing the loofah down my arm. He dips it into the hot water, then brings it to my neck, squeezing it, so the veil of bubbly liquid falls down my chest. The steam billows upward from the water, causing my hot skin to become even warmer, but I don't want to move from this spot.

I know I've always been eager in bed. I can be mouthy and selfish. Guys are usually turned off by that, but not Waylon. I like when I push for the man to push back, and that's exactly what Bullseye did.

He seems perfect.

And perfect always comes with a catch.

That's fine by me. I just want to know what exactly I'm catching.

"Tell me about yourself." My voice is hoarse and groggy, probably from screaming his name over and over again as he railed me into next week.

"What do you mean?" he asks, squeezing the loofah over my shoulders again.

"Like, tell me things about you. What's your favorite movie? Do you have a favorite color? What do you like to drink?"

He chuckles, then sighs. "You want to play twenty questions, huh?"

"I feel like it's the only way I can get to know you. You aren't exactly forthcoming," I tease.

He grunts but doesn't say anything. I get the impression I said the wrong thing. I'm afraid I hit a nerve. "You don't have to—"

"—Promise not to laugh when I tell you my favorite movie? You can't judge me."

I sit up and look over my shoulder. "Oh, I'm interested. I can't promise I won't laugh. I'm only human."

"Brat," he says, pinching my still sensitive buttcheek.

"An honest brat." I flutter my lashes at him.

"My favorite movie is A Walk to Remember," he mumbles under his breath, hoping I don't hear him.

My mouth falls open, and I spin around, nearly splashing the water over the edge of the tub. "You're kidding?" I ask, shocked, then throw my hand over my mouth as I laugh. I can't help it.

"You're laughing! This is why I keep all of my personal things to myself." He splashes me playfully with water.

"I expected… I don't know, a guy movie. Die Hard or Ocean's Eleven. One of those Fast Furious whatever's."

"Well… while I have an appreciation for those movies, I'm a sucker for chick flicks. Mandy Moore is amazing in A Walk to Remember. And it's so sad." He gets a forlorn expression on his face, and his hazy green eyes take on a sad hue.

"It's a really good movie. I'll give you that. Maybe we can watch it some time?"

"I'd like that, but you can't laugh at me when I get teary-eyed. It happens every time, and I've seen the movie a hundred times."

"Again, I promise I can't make any promises."

He tickles my sides, and a burst of loud laughter escapes me. "I can live with that." He leans in and kisses me on the cheek. "What about you?" I don't miss how he mouths the number 'eight' on his lips.

I still want to know what he is doing when he counts.

"Hmmm," I think about it and snuggle against his chest again. "Rose Red by Stephen King. It's a mini-series, not technically a movie. It's long. But it's so, so good."

"What do you like about it?"

I sigh when I think about the last time I watched it. "We watched it all the time. It used to be something my Dad, and I did together before he and my Mom died. I think that's why it's my favorite. One of the last memories I have of him is watching it. We'd get popcorn, different sorts of candy, drinks, and pig out on the living room floor for like four hours."

"That sounds like a great memory. I'm sorry you lost them," he says, wrapping his arms around me.

"It's alright. I mean, I learned how to live on my own. It took a while, but I did it. It's how I got this." I move his hand to my stomach to feel the scar from the stabbing.

"What happened?"

"After my parents died, I lived on the streets for a year, and a guy stabbed me. It's why I was in so much medical debt. I don't blame him or anything. I was in his spot when I shouldn't have been, and I didn't know."

"My god, I'm so glad you're okay. You must be the toughest woman I've ever met." He tightens his arms around me again.

"I have my moments. Anyway, favorite color, go." I don't want to get stuck on depressing things.

"Black."

I groan at how stereotypical that is. "Seriously? Black? Why am I not surprised?"

"It goes with everything, and it looks sharp. What about you? Is it pink?" he sasses.

I feign a gasp, placing my hand against my chest. "How dare you insult me like that. I'll have you know my favorite color is green."

"That's up there in the top three for me."

"Good. Then we won't have problems," I tease him, lacing my fingers through his to hold his hand. "I have a question, and if you don't want to answer it, I understand."

"Shoot."

"Why don't you like your name? Why doesn't anyone know it? And why tell me?"

He turns me around and settles me on his lap. "It's hard to explain, but bear with me."

I lift my arms to his shoulders. Goosebumps are rising on my skin from the cold air. "Take your time."

"I don't know," he says with a shrug of his shoulder. He runs his free hand through his hair and slicks the thick locks back over his head. "I don't remember anything from my childhood. When I hear my name, I get a feeling, and I just shut down. When I came to the Kings, I was in a really bad way. I never opened up to anyone." He swallows thickly. "Getting close to someone isn't what I do. I don't typically like how it feels."

I cock my head and rub my hands down his chest, knowing he is keeping something big from me. "Why me?"

His eyes finally meet mine, and that cute wrinkle between his brows forms. "Because for the first time in a long time, you make me want to try and be happy. I think I knew that from the moment I saw you. I was just drawn to you. I loved your energy. I loved how it made me feel. That's why I kept asking you out. But then I started to think getting away from you was best. I had just started therapy, and I had a fucked up day. I was pissed at Reaper for making me go in the first place. I was living my life fine—or so I thought—but it hit me all at once that I wasn't really living at all. You were the catalyst. You stopped me from offing myself."

I throw a hand over my mouth. "What? You can't be serious."

"I told you, I was in a bad way." He leans his head back against the edge of the tub and stares at the ceiling. "I can't remember when it was, but it was recent. I was in my room, and I took one of the guns Reaper keeps in his office, and I sat on my bed just staring at it, just daring myself to do it. I was so tired of living, Ruby. You have no idea how dark it is inside me. How fucked up and ruined I am. You have no idea of the things I've done or the things I've should have done, and I just... gave up for a minute. I hate guns." He squeezes his eyes shut and rocks his head back and forth. "They aren't my choice of weapon. I hate them so fucking much, but it was the easiest way out of the hell I created for myself. I put the gun in my mouth, cocked it—"

"No." I throw my arms around him and squeeze him.

"And I pulled the trigger."

I lean back, unable to hide the tears in my eyes. "How?"

"The gun jammed," he begins laughing. "I dropped the gun so fast. I immediately regretted trying and was thankful that it didn't happen. I don't know how it jammed because the next time Reaper fired it, it was fine. Some divine intervention, maybe? I knew then I had a long way to go to recovery, to stop hating myself, but I wanted to try. Trying for me wasn't enough. It isn't enough." He tilts his head up, and his palm gently holds my cheek. "So I'm trying for you."

I choke out a sob and take his hands and press them against my chest. "God, please don't ever do that again. Please. Even if you ever decide not to be with me, I can't live without knowing you're in this world, Waylon. Don't ever leave me. I'd miss you so much."

"I won't."

"You promise?" I ask him through watery words.

He gives me a sad smile and brushes his nose against mine. "I promise."

"Why?"

"Why what?" he cups his hands in the water and splashes water on his face.

"Why did you try? What happened that was so bad?"

He dips his head underwater for a second and bobs up, pushing his hair back. "I was a sex slave from sixteen to eighteen. I lived with these terrible people who locked me up ever since I was eight or so. Not my parents, but they made me believe they were. I was kept in a basement, chained to the wall so I could never escape. I never saw the outside of that room until they made me... perform."

I don't know what I was expecting, but it wasn't this. I clap my hand over my mouth. I might be sick.

No. I have to hold it together for him. He's sharing his truth with me. This is the dark secret he's been keeping.

He continues: "They videotaped me and Georgia, the other kid my age there. They forced us to have sex. Threatened us when we didn't. Guns, whips, beatings, whatever. They denied us food and water. I was so unhealthy and thin. I couldn't protect us. So many times, I debated on having him shoot me, but I couldn't leave Georgia alone."

"Oh my god, Waylon." I lay my hand against his heart as mine breaks.

"It doesn't hurt to talk about as much now. It's easier since I talked to my therapist, but yeah. It stayed with me. It *stays* with me. Georgia was all I knew from the time I was eight to eighteen. I loved her. She was my first everything. One time, we found ourselves together without the camera, and she wanted to have sex without the pressure. Without them hurting us or watching us in the background. Just us. It was the one, and only other time I had sex without a condom, but she got pregnant. And then I was forced to stay away from her. I only saw her when she was seven months along. She was weak, skin and bone. She died twenty minutes later, she and my daughter. They both died. I couldn't tell Georgia no, and maybe she wouldn't have died because she wouldn't have been pregnant."

I'm covering my mouth with both hands now, crying for him, crying for the boy that lost the most precious years of his life, crying for the man that's trying so hard to claw his way out of the blanket of depression his past has put him in. "You lost them. Both of them."

He nods, the muscle in his jaw twitching. "I never got to say goodbye. I didn't deserve to. I killed them, the people that did that to us. I finally had my chance, and I killed them, then burned every tape they ever made. I burned down that house with their bodies in it. I wandered to the Kings; they took me in, didn't ask questions. That's it." I know he is trying to sum up everything that happened by leaving out horrible details.

"My little girl would have been eighteen last month," he whispers, a tear leaking out of the corner of his eye. "Eighteen."

I sob as I hold him. "I'm so sorry."

His arms slowly find my backside, and he squeezes me.

I can't believe what I just heard. No wonder he keeps everything to himself. He hates talking about himself because he thinks there's nothing but bad memories. He doesn't have much to relive, only pain and sorrow.

"It will always hurt like hell, but I'm getting better. I'm putting it behind me. Besides my therapist, you're the only one I've ever told."

He's sharing another part of himself with me.

"You'll always be safe with me, Waylon. Any part of you, anything you share, I'll take care of it. I'll take care of you."

"I know, and I'm learning how to take care of you by figuring out how to take care of me. I want to. Don't give up on me, okay? I can do this. I'm stronger than the pain. Just don't give up on me."

"I promise." The mood is solemn as we sit in the tub. I'm horrified and heartbroken with what he just admitted to me.

It's fucked up. What happened to him as a boy should never have happened. As we sit there in silence, my mind is racing. Why can't he remember anything from his childhood? I think it has something to do with the people that made him perform.

Internally, I gasp.

No wonder he likes to watch and be watched. It makes sense now, but damn it if the knowledge doesn't hurt me too. He only likes it because it's what he knows.

It's literally all he knows.

I squeeze his hand in mine and do my best not to lose control of my emotions. I do my best not to cry. I hate weakness, but Waylon is slicing away at my soul bit by bit.

I want to help him remember where he came from because maybe, there is happiness there. Maybe there's something that can make him see through this dense fog that's congested his big, beautiful mind. There has to be something good to remember to outweigh the bad. And maybe we can hold a funeral for Georgia and his baby daughter that he never got to hold.

My heart squeezes painfully at what that must feel like. The self-wrecking emotions he must feel all the time because of that must be drowning him.

He's strong, muscular, a man's man, but even then, sometimes men need help from a little pixie like me. I can help. I know I can.

If we can say goodbye to his family properly, it might help him let go.

Not let them go, but let the pain, self-sabotage, guilt, and blame go. It wasn't his fault.

Wanting to make him laugh again, I try to change the mood. "If you had to choose between A Walk to Remember and The Notebook, what would you pick and why?"

"Aw man, those are two of my favorites. Not fair."

Unbelievable that a man who can kill other men with a dart loves Nicholas Sparks movies. "Pick one," I say. "Hurry. They are both going to fade away into Neverland if you don't."

"A Walk to Remember."

"Why?"

"Cause it's always been the two of them. She changed him for the better, and he didn't want to let that go until he had to let her go. The Notebook, I don't like that she fought her feelings for him. I don't like love triangles. They piss me off, but yeah, A Walk to Remember. It's a story about a love that lives on forever, a love that was never lost. I like that."

What a romantic.

"The love you and Georgia shared will never be lost, Waylon." I brush my thumb against his cheek,` and the stubble scratches the pad of my finger. "It will live on forever." I think that's why he likes that movie so much. He can relate to it in a way.

He inhales a shaky breath and gathers me close. "Thank you for not taking her away from me."

"If there is one thing no one can take away from you, Waylon, it's her memory and her love. That will always be yours."

He smiles a real genuine smile that shows his teeth.

"Nine," he mouths.

Whatever that means.

"And what about you?" he questions.

"What about me?" I rub his shoulders, digging my fingers into the unforgiving, knotted muscle.

"Can I have your love too?"

I smile to myself, knowing he is going to have my love. I tsk, "Jeez, greedy much? My love, her love, you just want all the love." I joke with a roll of my eyes.

I yelp when he playfully throws me under the water and immediately pulls me back up. I sputter, tasting bubbles, and that's when I'm thankful I have short hair, so I don't have to rub it out of my face.

"I guess that just means I'm a lucky guy," he says. "Ten."

And I'm a lucky girl.

Men can fight. Men can kill. Men can threaten or be possessive.

But a man who battles his demons and tries to overcome them?

Now that is what I call fucking hot.

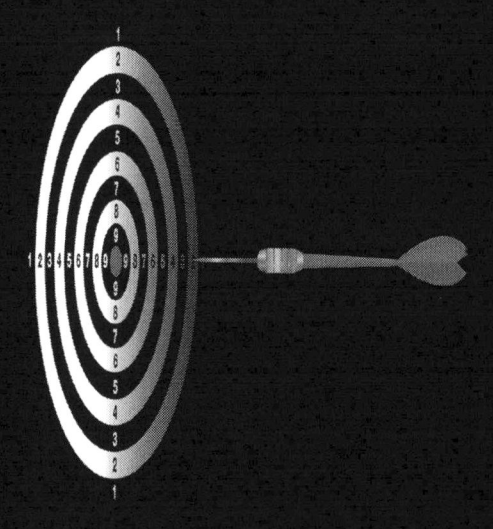

CHAPTER NINETEEN
Bullseye

I can't remember the last time I felt so good. I think my steps are bouncier too. I think... I'm happy. I feel lighter. Talking about it instead of keeping my pain bottled up really made the difference. I whistle as I flip the thousandth pancake.

I feel like a new man.

I am a new man. I'm well on my way to becoming someone my old self won't even recognize. Someone better.

"What the hell is this? Is this a feast?" Badge tiredly walks into the kitchen and stumbles into a chair.

"You look like shit," I observe, pouring him a cup of coffee and sliding it over to him.

He lifts his head from his hands and grunts. "And you're unexpectedly cheery. It's too early for that bullshit," he gripes.

"I had a great night," I tell him, my stomach fluttering as if I'm young again.

"Yeah, we all heard. Why do you think I'm so goddamn tired?" he sips his coffee and crosses his arms.

I smirk. "Can't help how good I make my girl feel, Badge. Don't be jealous."

He snorts. "I wasn't talking about *her* noises."

There have been a few times in my life that I have blushed. Very few. So few, I can't remember them much, but this moment I want to shove my head in the sand. Better yet, dig a grave and cover myself up. I didn't realize I was loud.

Ruby comes out from the bedroom in my dark green King's Club t-shirt with a pair of my sweatpants that she's had to tie in a knot at her hip. Like a cat, she sneaks behind Badge and takes the coffee right out of his hand. "Now, now, Badge.

No need to be bitter. I like it when Bullseye's loud. Let's me know I'm doing my job right." She shoots me a wink, and I don't know why it makes me so flustered. I'm a fucking wreck. I spin around and grab the spatula, shove it under the pancake, and flop it onto the plate.

I'm shaking. Why am I shaking?

I grab the plate of bacon and set it on the table, too, then the syrup.

"Bullseye!" Reaper shouts from his office, and my eyes fall to Ruby.

She looks worried from the sound of his voice, but everything will be fine. I know what this is about.

I walk around the table and kiss the top of her head. "It'll be fine."

"Oh, pancakes." Maizey runs into the kitchen wearing a pink princess dress and a tiara. "Badge, I brought you a crown because you're a king." It takes her a second to crawl up onto the chair, and when she does, she plops the plastic crown with fake red and blue gems on top of his head.

The hard edges around Badge's eyes soften. He'll never admit it, but he loves that girl more than anything in the world.

"Well, Princess, it's time to eat. You have to eat all your breakfast if you want to go to the royal tea party." Badge places five pancakes on her plate, and Ruby giggles.

Maizey can't eat all that.

"What are ye doin' Badge?"

"What? Fuck off. This is royal business, Skirt," he growls, his sour mood returning. He plops a handful of bacon on her plate.

Maizey's eyes are wide and intimidated by all the food on her plate.

"Eat up," he grunts, scooting closer to the table. He folds a pancake in half, sets his elbows on the table, and digs in.

"Hey, Skirt? Can you grab Delaney and Micah from downstairs?" I ask, wanting to make sure they eat. They are trying to come around more, but they feel safer together still.

"Aye, I'll try."

"Thanks," I tell him as soon as he opens the door to the basement.

Giving Ruby's shoulder one last squeeze, I head down the hallway, and the morning sun shines through the stained glass on the door that leads outside. Greens and reds reflect against the floor like diamonds. It's a pretty sight before experiencing an ugly one.

My punishment.

"Come on in, Bullseye." Reaper doesn't look up from the paperwork he is scribbling on to greet me. How he knows I'm here is beyond me.

I count my blessings and take a step into the wolf's den. There is one chair in front of his desk, and I take a seat, crossing my legs. Throwing the dart at Moretti wasn't a good idea, but at the moment, it seemed like the best idea.

Reaper finally sets down his pen and sits back in his chair, lacing his fingers together across his stomach. His 'Long Live the King' tattoo shows along his chest since his shirt is unbuttoned. "You've been my Sergeant-At-Arms for a while, and for that time, I trusted you to take care of business."

Trusted.

Which means he no longer does.

"The shit you pulled with Moretti, knowing the history we have with him, was uncalled for. I don't give a fuck about your reasons or excuses." He leans forward, and the leather of his chair squeaks. "I don't know what's going on with you because you've been sealed tight from the moment you stumbled onto us, but that shit ends now. Anything you tell your therapist, she's going to tell me. If she tells me anything that requires me to yank your patches, I will, Bullseye."

"What? Prez, that's a little extreme. I might be fucked up and working shit out, but it isn't enough to throw me overboard. You didn't with everyone else." Sylvia can't tell him. She said she wouldn't tell because of doctor/patient confidentiality. Do I care if he finds out?

I'm not sure.

"And I know you the least out of everyone. Even though we've been brothers for longer than almost anyone else. Why? I'm waiting for you to get your head back in the game. I need you by my side, and you can't be there if your head ain't right. Mateo, for some reason, has asked me to spare you punishment. He seems to really like you. So to keep the peace between us, I won't carve a heart in your chest like you deserve."

I bow my head. "Thank you," I nearly croak, wondering why Moretti is being my advocate.

"Don't thank me yet. You'll be switching out with Tool at Moretti's in two hours. And Bullseye, I expect you on your best fucking behavior. I better not hear about you throwing a dart at him because if I do, not only will you get a heart carved in your chest, but an arrow too."

I stand and bite the inside of my cheek to help keep my temper at bay. "Yes, Prez." I walk away. The urge to throw a dart at some useless fuck is making my fingers twitch.

"And don't think I don't know *anything* about you."

I stop mid-stride out the door, keeping my back turned toward him.

"I know all those years ago you had something to do with a large house fire. I don't know how or why, but I hope one day you tell me, so I don't have to force my hand to find out."

I turn around and stomp toward his desk and press my palms flat against his desk. "I'm not hiding anything anymore. You want to know so much about me? Fine. Ask my therapist because I don't feel like repeating myself." I turn around and grab the handle of the door behind me and slam it shut, just asking for punishment now.

Fucking carve me up. I don't care.

Anything anyone does to me now can't compare to what I've already lived through.

I march down the hallway, and Ruby is standing against the wall by my room, watching everyone in the kitchen. She must hear me because she unfolds her arms and pushes off the wall. I'm so fucking pissed off. Reaper really pushes the power boundary sometimes. I understand he's President, but I think it's okay for people to have secrets.

Well, until they affect the club. While I have been moody, throwing a dart at Moretti wasn't exactly best for the club.

And him being right only pisses me off more.

I grab Ruby's hand drag her into the bedroom. I'm all worked up, and I need some relief. I lock the door behind us and stretch my neck left and right, popping it in all the right places.

"Are you okay? What happened in Reaper's office—"

I don't give her time to speak. I grip her shoulders and shove her to her knees. "—Put that mouth to fucking work, suck me, and shut up." I grab her chin, sounding more hateful than I intend to, but she likes it.

She sags, and her eyes dilate.

Ruby doesn't know that before I made breakfast, I took a trip to the adult store, purchasing nearly everything I want to use with her.

"I'm waiting," I growl viciously, a primal animal wanting release.

She fumbles with the button on my pants and drags the zipper down. Ruby reaches her hand inside, and her slender fingers wrap around my aching shaft to pull me out. I'm so fucking hard. I need release. I need to calm down before I go out, and what better way than for Ruby to swallow me?

Her pretty pink lips wrap around the tip, and her tongue flicks along the head. I reach down and wrap a hand around her throat. "Don't tease me, Spitfire. Make me come."

Her hand wraps around my base, her thumb and index finger rub against the piercings on either side, which sends a delicious zing to my balls. While she fits me into her mouth, sucking the tip in and playing with my Prince Albert, I grab her other hand put it under my sack, where my guiche piercing is. I take her index finger and have her press against the stud. I hold in a groan and pinch my lips together. Her eyes widen in surprise when she feels the piercing. She applies pressure and tugs, humming around the length of my cock as she sucks me down her throat.

Fuck yes, I love that she wants to play me.

"Just like that," I praise her, my hand on the back of her head as she bobs up and down. The slurping and sucking noises have me losing control and thrusting my hips to quicken the pace. I can't decide if I want to come down her throat, her face, or lift that shirt up, pull those sweatpants down, and finish inside her tight body.

And then I'll pull out that plug I talked about last night and keep her full of me. Mmm, yes. That. I choose that.

And then, when I come home later, I can slide back inside and have my way with her.

She quickens her strokes, twisting the base of my shaft with her fist and sucking on half my cock with the hot abyss of her mouth. I'm touching the roof of her mouth, the sides of her cheeks, the back of her throat; with every second that passes; she sucks me down in the hungriest of ways. She moans, and her spit makes squelching noises while she jacks me.

Her finger twists the guiche piercing, and I snarl, take her head in my hands, and begin to fuck her face like I did last night. "You like that? Do you like being my little slut for me, baby? You look so good on your knees, sucking my cock. Is this the only way I can shut all that sass up?"

I expect her to mouth off at me, but she just nods and rakes her nails down my legs, humming, so the vibrations wrap around my girth, splitting her lips wide. She knows I need this, and she's backing down so I can have what I need.

And right now, I need more than Ruby on her knees.

I pull my cock out, and a string of spit stretches from her mouth to the Prince Albert. She looks debauched with those swollen red lips. Her short hair is messy, sticking up on its ends from my fingers. I don't say a word. I pick her up and roughly push her down on the bed, yanking the sweatpants down below her ass. I just need rough enough to slide into her pussy.

I don't take off her shirt. There's no time. My need is too much. I grab her hips and slam into her in one long stroke.

And I don't stop.

I pound into her, shoving my cock as deep as I can go with every stroke.

"Waylon," she whimpers my name in a lust-induced frenzy.

My hand lands on the back of her head. "Be quiet. Do I need to gag you to get you to shut up?" she becomes wetter and groans, trying to be quiet like how I want. "I think someone likes that idea." I dig my fingers into her hips, plummeting my cock as hard as I can. She's going to be sore later. I'm probably taking her too hard, but she'll be fine.

I wrap my hands around her shoulders and swing her around, slamming her against my closet door, continuing the harsh rhythm. Our skin slaps together, and she begins to make those fucking sounds again. I want to record the sounds for myself and listen on repeat like a favorite song. I shove three fingers in her mouth to keep her occupied; she sucks on the digits greedily. She loves having her holes filled. I'll have to keep that in mind for next time.

She bites down on my fingers and shatters, another wave of her nectar slicking my cock, causing the wet sounds of our skin making contact to become louder.

"I don't remember saying you could come." I bite the shell of her ear and press her flat against the door to bury myself. "Take every fucking drop. Take it!" I grip the back of her neck and hold her down, punctuating my hips as another spasm leaves me. My eyes roll to the back of my head as wave after wave of pleasure melts my bones.

"God," I exhale, stumbling us back until we hit the bed. I slip out of her and roll her to her back, then lift her legs. "Like I said, I don't want a drop to leave this cunt." I wrap a hand around her ankle and lean down to open the drawer of the nightstand. I pull out the plug I bought, and her eyes round. "This better be inside you when I come home. I won't be happy if it's not." I wet the plug with the mess of our come and slide it inside. "Look at that. Your greedy walls sucked it right in. Your hungry pussy doesn't want to miss a drop either, does it?" I lift my eyes to meet hers, and her cheeks are flushed. "Does it?" I repeat myself.

She shakes her head, and I drop her legs to tuck my semi-hard cock back in my jeans. I bend down and kiss her, slipping my tongue inside her tired mouth. "Fucking perfect for me, Spitfire. I'll be back later. Rest up, okay?" I'm starting to calm down now that she's taken such good care of me. I trace her jaw with my finger. "You're beautiful."

Her eyes soften around the edges. "So are you. Hurry. The quicker you go, the quicker you can come back to me."

"Alright." I bend down to kiss the tip of her nose. "Braveheart is at your store today. So just rest, okay? I'm afraid I took you too hard—"

"—Whatever that just was, feel free to do it again. I'm boneless, and I'm going to nap." She moves up the bed and gasps when she looks between her legs.

I straighten and take a few steps toward the door. "Oh, yeah. Did I forget to mention that the plug is pushed against your G-spot with every move you make?" I tip her a wink and head out the door, double-checking to make sure I shut the door all the way.

"Whew. You smell like sex," Knives comments, throwing the ninja star in the air and catching it without cutting himself.

"Shut up, let's go to Moretti's and get this over with."

"Aye, Bullseye? Let's plan the room, ya?" Skirt asks, catching me before I can get down the hall.

Fuck. I haven't talked to Ruby about it yet. I don't want to agree if she isn't ready for that. "Yeah, sure. I'll make sure Ruby is with me."

Skirt smiles, his rosy cheeks becoming full. "Sounds good."

"Knives, ready?"

"Yeah, let's roll out. Bye, Hellraiser. I'll see you later." He leans in and kisses Mary within an inch of her life.

I don't blame him. Every time we walk out the door could be the last time. We never know what we're getting into when we leave the gates, especially since we're getting into bed with Moretti, so to speak.

I have a feeling our hands are going to get dirtier.

I pass Maizey sitting on the couch with Slingshot and jut my chin toward the door, telling him it's time to go. Sunnie is next to Maizey, painting her nails so she won't be too bored without Slingshot. Patrick must have already headed out for the day. He'll probably already be there waiting for us.

"Time to go, Slingshot," I say, opening the front door.

Maizey jumps off the couch and begins to cry. "No, Uncle Slingshot, you can't go."

Oh, man. The waterworks.

"It'll be alright, Maze. I'll be back. I always come back." Slingshot picks her up, and her princess dress flutters around her as he plops her on his hip.

She buries her face in his shoulder. Her dark hair fans around her face as her little shoulders shake with tiny sobs.

"Aw, Maze, baby. It's okay. He'll come back. Come here." Sarah holds out her arms as she sits on the loveseat.

"No! No! I want Uncle Slingshot." Maizey kicks her legs and wails into his shoulder.

"Hey, hey, hey, look at me," Slingshot says softly, leaning away, so Maizey has no choice but to look at him.

Her big brown eyes are filling with tears, and her bottom lip is pouted as it wobbles.

"I'm going to be just fine, sweetheart. I always come home, okay? No more tears. I think someone needs a nap." He kisses the top of her head, and I swear the women around him melt and sigh dreamily as they look at him.

I bet their ovaries are exploding right now.

"You taco swear?" Maizey hiccups as she blinks up at him with wet lashes, rubbing her left eye with her tiny fist.

Now it's his turn to melt. "I taco swear, Maze." He folds his hand like a taco. "Come on, do it."

She grins and copies him.

"Now, wrap your arm around mine, and let's take a bite out of our taco. It's the only way the swear will be promised."

They bite down on the pretend taco and pretend to chew. "There," he grins, setting her next to Sarah.

"I love you, Uncle Slingshot," Maizey says.

"I love you too, Maze." Slingshot slides on his sunglasses and clears his throat as his boots pound out the door.

Knives and I share a grin as we follow, the metal door clanking and locking automatically behind us. "That little girl has you wrapped around her finger, Slingshot."

"No shit," he huffs, mounting his bike. "It kills me when she cries, man. And then she had to taco swear? Taco. Swear. That's huge. I have to come home. I can't break our taco swear."

"Right? It would be so messy. All that cheese and lettuce everywhere." Knives laughs and knocks Slingshot's shoulder as he gets on his bike.

Slingshot isn't laughing.

"Ah, man. Lighten up. We always come home. It will be alright." Knives starts his bike, and Slingshot and I follow suit.

God, I love the vibrations between my legs. The power gets me semi-hard every time. It never fails. "Let's go see if we can't save a man who already has a death sentence, boys." I shake my head at the time wasted trying to make sure Maximo doesn't get taken. I'd rather kill the bastard myself, and then we wouldn't have to worry about this shit anymore.

We can get Moretti's drugs, drop them off, get paid, and go about our fucking lives, but no, now we have to be the security detail too because his men are too fresh in the gills. Well, the only way to learn is to be thrown into the life. Either sink or swim, die or live.

That's how this life is.

And I'm man enough to admit it's nearly defeated me a few times.

Tank waves at us from the front gate to allow us through, and we begin our journey to Moretti's. I can smell the heat in the air, and it's nearly suffocating as the bikes roar down Loneliest Road. As we ride, we pass a rotting coyote on the side of the road. The buzzards are picking at it, then attacking each other when one gets a bigger bite.

Circle of life.

The grumble of my Harley eases my thoughts. While I'm on the open road, my brothers flanking me, it gives me time to think about everything that's been going on and how much I've improved over such a short period of time. I know it's only a matter of time before the guys find out about my past. It used to bother me, but now I feel bad for keeping such a big part of myself hidden away.

There is a lot to know about me. It just isn't going to paint a pretty picture.

But the rest of my life is a blank canvas. I plan on using the brightest colors to fill in my life.

We ride under the burning sun and blue sky. A few white thunderheads are building in the heavens to the left; when they block the sun's rays, the shade is a welcome relief.

It's a beautiful day to ride.

Look at me, appreciating nature and shit. That wouldn't have happened a week ago.

I check my rearview mirror when a car pulls up behind us, riding our asses a little too close for comfort. Knives sees them too, along with Slingshot, and the hair on the back of my neck stands up.

Something ain't right.

Slingshot reaches into his cut pocket and slows down to hang back.

The glint of a gun shines right under the tint across the top of the windshield. The Dodge Charger inches closer, revving its engine.

"Fuck," I curse, knowing this is about to end badly.

I don't know how many men are in that car, but encounters like this rarely end well. It's harder to communicate with each other when we don't want the bastards in the car to see us. Me, Slingshot, and Knives have to read one another's body language to see what our move is.

The black Charger's tires squeal across the pavement, wafting burnt rubber in the air as they speed into the other lane. The window rolls down just enough for the gun to poke through.

Double fuck.

The three of us slam on our brakes at the same time, and as we skid to a stop, Knives flicks a ninja star through the air, which lands in the back right tire of the car. Our options are few and far between right now when it comes to weapons.

I hate guns, but I can admit there are certain circumstances they come in handy. This is one of those times. Luckily, Slingshot carries one in a holster under his cut.

The car sways right and left as the driver tries to keep control. The gunman rolls down the window all the way and leans out, pointing the gun directly at us. At the same time, we hit the throttle and drive straight toward the danger. Knives dives left and slings another star through the air, just missing the back left tire.

I reach into my pocket for one of my darts. They are sharp enough to penetrate rubber, but the car is fishtailing, making it almost impossible to get a decent aim. I try anyway, throwing the dart through the air, but it lands just above the left-back bumper.

Damn it. I fucking hate it when I miss. It isn't often, but those few times really piss me off. Moving targets are the hardest to try and get a good bead on.

The car finally slides sideways, and Slingshot fires round after round into the car. Knives flings another star, which hits the front right tire while bullet holes pepper the glass. The passenger leans out the window, and time slows down.

Being on a two-lane road gives us few options to escape, especially when the car is sideways, blocking our way out, and right now, we're moving too fast to turn around. Plus, never give a man who has a gun your back.

That's how you die.

The screeching tires and glass shattering onto the pavement mute the chaos of my pounding heart. All I can think about is Ruby, my brothers, and my family. Now that I'm finally overcoming my bullshit, I'm ready to live.

But sometimes, living isn't always in the cards.

The car spins until it's head-to-head with us. The bumper's chrome gives one last glint against the sun before the driver slams on the gas. The passenger leans out the window, holding the gun in the air, and fires. Knives throws one last ninja star while I toss a dart, and Slingshot fires his weapon. My dart lands right between the passenger's eyes, and the gun drops to the pavement, igniting the trigger once more.

Momentum and speed are lost against gravity, and the Charger loses its composure, spinning into the air and heading right toward us.

There isn't anything we can do but brace ourselves.

Metal crunches against the road, launching forward again in another turn.

We punch the throttle and hang right, damning the road and taking our chances with the desert instead. Knives makes it onto the sand first, but the back end of the car clips Slingshot and me. The hit is hard enough to send me flying off my bike.

I soar through the air watching cactuses and the red, cracked dirt under me pass by. My shoulder hits the ground first, and the breath leaves my lungs. Something cracks—I don't know what yet—and I'm suddenly in searing agony.

Instinctually, I cover my face with my arms as the car spins over me, landing in a useless heap a few yards behind my head.

"Knives? Slingshot?" I grunt as loud as I can. When I don't hear them, I yell and hold my hand to my shoulder. "Guys!"

Silence.

People think screams are scary, but that's not true.

Silence is the scariest sound to hear.

It's where the unknown lives.

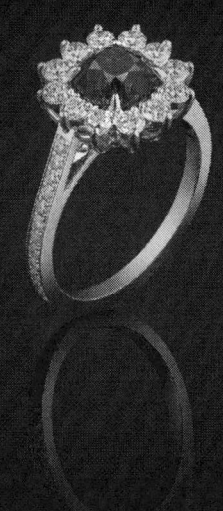

CHAPTER TWENTY

Ruby

I DON'T THINK I CAN MOVE MY LEGS.

Actually, I don't think I can move.

Why would I want to move?

Oh, yeah.

I sit up, giggling to myself as the plug rubs me in all sorts of delicious ways, sending that promise that Bullseye made to take me again later rushing toward my throbbing clit. I can't believe I can't touch myself, but I'm going to listen to him. I trust him to make me feel good later.

I gasp as I stand and head to the bathroom. "Oh god," I groan with every step. How am I going to get through the day?

Maybe I should take it out? I'll put it back in later, and he won't even know…

But I don't know if disobeying him is a good idea. That's asking for punishment. It's something to keep in mind.

I flip the silver knob of the shower and step into the hot spray. I tilt my head back and wince, forgetting about the small cut on my head. I let the water flow over it, warming the stitches until the pain fades and the ache is gone. I stretch my neck and let the water hit my face. All the bruises and scratches from the attack the other night no longer hurt.

There's a sliver of me that's still uneasy about the attack like any person would be, but the majority of me is moving on. I don't like lingering in the past. It doesn't get anyone anywhere but pain and suffering.

Why would anyone choose to suffer when they could live?

A contented exhale escapes me as I scrub my body with the honey-scented soap. There are a few things I need to be worried about since I've been holed up here for the last few days—like my shop and Moretti—but I trust Bullseye to tell me the truth. When he says he has it taken care of, I believe him.

Turning off the shower, I reach for the fluffy gray towel hanging on the silver rod and dry off. There's still a wanton heat building between my legs, but my body is becoming accustomed to it.

The mirror is foggy from the steam, and I swipe it with the palm of my hand, staring at my reflection. My hair needs a trim, and my cheeks are flushed from the shower. There's a small red mark on the side of my neck, where Bullseye latched his lips and sucked when he pressed me against the closet door.

I like it when he gets carried away.

I spin around and turn my head to look over my shoulder and notice the attacker's bite mark is still there. It looks worse than it feels. Black and blue with teeth indentations. Damn him. I could cunt punt him all over again.

Sighing, I open the cabinets looking for a toothbrush, something other than his, but when I come up empty, I'm satisfied.

If I can suck his cock and he can eat me out, why is sharing a toothbrush so forbidden? I snatch the electric brush from the holder and squirt a line of minty paste across the bristles. While I'm unfortunately scrubbing the taste of Bullseye off my tongue, I think about everything he has shared with me. The faith, love, and hope he has put in me. I never want to give him a reason to doubt me.

Doubt brings hate, and hate brings war.

The last thing I ever want to do with Bullseye is fight.

Because losing him would kill me.

I stop brushing my teeth when the realization slams into me.

I'm in love with him.

Was my heart his target, or was he hoping for a shot?

And do I dare ask him if he loves me, or have I missed my mark?

I spit into the sink and rinse my mouth out, then run the toothbrush under the water, staring at the green, deceiving eyes glaring back at me in the mirror. I never want to hurt Bullseye, but what I'm about to do will hurt him.

He will think I'm going behind his back. I'm not. I want to help him remember who he is. I think there's a reason he doesn't remember his childhood. I think it's blocked out from the pain and horrible experiences he had with those people who took advantage of him and Georgia.

I think Georgia would want him to remember if he had loving parents, a dog, a favorite food if he liked school, something. Anything good. If I can help add anything memorable to his experiences, I want to do it. He deserves to have them.

He needs to know if he was loved before he experienced so much hate. If I lose him for this, if he hates me for this, I'll have to live with that.

Risking my love for him so he can regain the love he used to have as a child is a chance I'm willing to take.

I hope he can forgive me.

I head to the bedroom, running my hand over the top of the dresser. It's sleek, old, and worn. It's chipped and dented in various places. It's obviously used, something maybe everyone in this house has used at one point or another. It has a history.

I like things with history.

Throwing the towel on the bed, I open the drawer and snag a t-shirt, pull it over my head, and tie the loose material to my hip. I really need my clothes from my apartment. His are way too big. Next, I steal a pair of gym shorts and roll the waistband to get a better fit.

Blowing out a nervous breath, I keep the reasons for doing this running through my mind and open the door. There's no one in the kitchen, but the smell of coffee lingers. I get the idea that maybe if I pour this grumpy bastard a cup, he'll be more likely to help me.

The kitchen is huge but has an old feel like a grandma's house. The cabinets are oak to match the table, and the wallpaper behind the oven has apples on it. Every other part of the house has been updated except this one, and I wonder why.

The restaurant-style coffee maker is to the left of the sink, and I open the cabinets above it, thinking that's where the mugs would be. I'm right. I grab two diner-style mugs and pour two black coffees. I like a ton of sugar in mine, so I reach for the sugar shaker and pour.

And pour.

And that's good.

They even have little compostable stirrers.

Aw, they give a shit about the environment. Who would have thought?

I mix the sugar in with the coffee, toss the stirrer in the trash, huff a nervous breath, wrap my fingers tight around the handles of the mugs, and begin my journey down the hall. My heart is hammering in my chest.

Badge isn't nice, but he's the only person I can think of who can find the answers I'm looking for. I tiptoe as quickly as I can so I don't make any noise, passing dozens of photos hanging on the wall. I take my time looking at them. Some are in black and white with past MC members, and some are new, with Reaper leading them.

I pause at one picture. Everyone seems younger, but adults all the same, and there is a teenage boy with a mop of brown hair standing next to a very young Reaper. My heart melts a bit when I realize it's Bullseye. He isn't smiling, and in this photo, it's obvious he's a few years younger than Reaper. He's so skinny. A tiny gasp escapes me when I realize this must have been soon after he found the Kings.

My sweet man. All he ever wanted was a family. All he ever wanted was to be loved.

He has it now. He has a big family, and if love could sink the earth, the love me and the club has for him would.

I touch the frame gently before moving on, letting the smell of the coffee remind me of the task at hand. When I get to the end of the hall, I peek around the corner to see Badge typing furiously on his computer. If he weren't so burly, I'd find him handsome, but then he opens his mouth, and I want to slap him across the face.

"Don't just stand there and look at me. If you have a question, ask it." He spins around in his leather chair and crosses his arms.

His very large arms are attached to very massive hands that probably choke cute kittens in his spare time.

Oh god, those poor kittens.

Does Badge even care about the kittens?

I'm getting way off track here. I don't know if Badge ever harms innocent kittens.

"That for me, or are you just going to continue to stare? Want a picture? Not sure how much Bullseye would like that, but whatever."

Bullseye might like it, and I might too. But that's a conversation for another time and most definitely a different person. I step into his office and hold out the coffee. "I'm here to talk about Bullseye, actually."

He lifts a brow and brings the coffee to his lips, sipping it. He chokes and hands the mug out to me. "You're trying to kill me before we can talk? Christ, that's sweet."

My eyes round, and I steal the cup from him and exchange it with the one in my hand. "Shit, I'm sorry. That one is mine."

"You'll be on your way to getting diabetes, too, if you aren't careful. That is pure sugar."

Well, if I did get diabetes, at least I'd know Bullseye's would be controlled. He isn't fooling anyone. He thinks it won't affect him. One day it's going to catch up to him. I just hope I'm here to help because he won't be able to help himself.

"I'm more responsible than he is. That's not why I'm here. I want to ask you what you know about Bullseye?" I lean against his computer desk and try not to stare at all the monitors above one another lining the wall. These are security feeds from different establishments the Kings own, I think. I hope. If not, it's just creepy.

"I know his name and his birthday," he grunts, taking a big swig of his coffee. "That's better." He smacks his lips together.

"No, what do you really know?" I prod. "What do you know about him? As a person."

He sighs, and it sounds weighted with guilt and regret. "I can tell you everything about every member, down to their first sneeze, but not Bullseye. He's my brother. I'd die for him, but knowing him isn't something he has ever allowed. Not with anyone."

Except me.

"Bullseye came to us in a rough kind of way. I never asked questions. He was loyal, is loyal," he corrects himself. "I figured he'd tell us when the time was right, but he never did, so I respected his privacy."

"Why? Did you ask questions with anyone else?"

"Yes, Poodle," Badge grinds his jaws together. "I'm older than I look."

Okay, I don't know what that has to do with anything.

"Listen, we saw Bullseye in the worst way when he came to us. I've never seen anything like it before. He obviously had been abused. I wasn't going to prod. And then the time had passed, then more time, and then it didn't matter. He was a King. A brother. I'm not going to question it now or ever."

"I'm not asking you to, but I think you need to do some digging," I tell him, hating that I'm going against him like this. "The things I know, there is a part of himself he can't remember, and I think remembering that will make him realize who he is."

He leans forward, his dark brows pinching together to give his stern face a soft edge. "He might not forgive you for this if you tell me."

"I'm doing what is best for him, whether he realizes it or not. This is what is best. He needs to know. He has accepted this because of his fucked up past. I know all of you have stories, but Badge, his is unlike anything you've heard. He can't remember the first eight years of his life. I know, kids don't remember, but I mean nothing. Not a damn thing."

His eyebrows move toward his hairline as he sits back in his chair. Badge laces his hands behind his head and clicks his tongue. "That's unusual. I'll give you that."

"You've never looked into him?" Call me a skeptic.

"I never went back more than ten years, and that was only recently."

"Why?"

His eyes narrow. "Because I didn't want to go behind his back." Badge is accusing me. That's fine. I'm a big girl. I can handle whatever life decides to throw at me. "I did what was necessary for his therapist. If she wanted to know anything, she was going to have to get from him."

"Very noble of you," I mutter.

He grabs a notebook, opens it to a blank page, and clicks his pen. "Tell me what I need to know."

"I, unfortunately, don't know much. I know he grew up with a man named Ronald and a woman named Patricia for most of his life. They weren't his parents. There was another girl there, Georgia. They... umm..." I debate if I want to give any more information and decide against it. "Anyway, that's the most important information. It happened here in Vegas. So maybe... maybe try missing persons or something?" I wrap my hand around my coffee mug and try not to stare at Badge. I know what I just insinuated was huge. It could all be in my mind, but something doesn't feel right.

"You don't think he is from Vegas? You think he's a product of child trafficking?"

"I think—" tears sting my eyes, and I hold my mug to my chest "—it's more than that. I won't give you the details. I'm sure if you find anything, you'll figure it out on your own."

"You really think that this was his life? You think he has parents out there, and the people that raised him... what are they?" he asks.

"Monsters." A tear drops from my lashes to the spot between my thumb and index finger on my hand. "They are fucking monsters for what they made him and Georgia do." I shut my mouth before I say anything else. It isn't my story to tell, but someone needs to look into this. It can't be swept under the rug anymore.

"Just please look into it, and if I'm crazy, tell me. I'll let it go, but something is going on Badge. I feel it." I press my hand against my stomach and gasp, forgetting that damn plug is there. And the pressure I just gave it, even the smallest amount, has made my clit throb.

Now is not the time.

"Hey," Badge's hand rests on my knee, and even the pressure from that has me holding back a whimper. When I'm aware of the plug, I feel it everywhere. When I forget about it, it's like it isn't there. Bullseye knew exactly what he was doing, leaving me like this. "If your instincts are telling you to look into this, screaming at you that something is wrong, then you're most likely right. Our guts are never wrong. I'll look into this, I swear."

"Thank you, Badge."

"Don't thank me yet. Whatever we find, it's going to hurt him, and in turn, that's going to make us feel like real fucking assholes."

"So you'll feel about the same?" I tease.

His lips tilt to the left in, dare I say, a smile. "You're funny. I like you."

I push myself up and plop myself on the desk with a grin. "I'll remind you of that later."

He grunts and turns to begin typing when a loud crash comes from the front of the clubhouse. I jump, and coffee swishes out of the rim of the mug, the warm liquid wetting my lap. I hiss at the same time Badge stands up. He draws a gun from his back and cocks it.

"Stay behind me," he orders.

"Are you kidding? Give me a gun! I'll point and shoot."

"Slingshot! Knives! Oh my god," Mary screams.

By the fear trembling her voice, whatever is happening doesn't sound good. Badge keeps his gun drawn as we run as fast as we can to the main room. The photos along the wall are a blur, and my heart is in my throat.

She said Slingshot and Knives.

Where is Bullseye?

The house is in utter chaos. Everyone meets in the main room at the same time. "Oh my god," I somehow manage to say as I see Knives gently place Slingshot on the ground.

Is he dead? He looks dead.

"Knives, what the fuck happened?" Reaper pushes between Badge and me. I happily get out of the way and press my back against the wall.

Doc is kneeling on the ground and rips Slingshot's shirt down the middle to show two gunshot wounds. One to the chest. One to the shoulder.

"Where is Bullseye?" My words tumble out of me, emotion thick as my lip wobbles and tears threaten. Knives just stares at me. "Where the fuck is he! What happened!" I shout, needing someone to answer me.

"We... we were—"

"Uncle Slingshot! No, Uncle Slingshot," Maizey cries and tries to crawl to him.

"Aye, get her out of here. Put her in Aidan's room with Joey, Dawn," Skirt says, grabbing Maizey by her stomach and handing her to Dawn, his ol' lady.

"He promised! You taco swore, Uncle Slingshot, you taco swore," she screeches and wails at the same time as Dawn carries her through the hall, to the kitchen, then down the steps to the basement. That isn't where Aidan's room is. That must be where Aidan is, though.

"Okay, Knives, what happened?" Reaper asks him again.

Doc snaps his fingers at Juliette. "There's no time to move him. I need you to go get blood. I have his already. It's A positive, and it's labeled Slingshot. Get three O negatives, too. Okay? Bring me all of my supplies."

"Okay, yeah, alright," she nods, and Tool follows behind her, right at her heels.

"Where is Bullseye? Why doesn't anyone care about him? Where is he?"

"Knives, we need to know where Bullseye is. Can you do that? Don't focus on Slingshot. Focus on me." Reaper shakes Knives by the shoulder, but he is pale, and his eyes are glazed over as he watches Doc try to stop the bleeding from the hole in Slingshot's chest.

"Knives!" Mary, his ol' lady, slaps him across the face. He blinks, finally coming back to reality. "Where is Bullseye?"

"We were riding to Moretti's when this black Dodge Charger came out of nowhere and tailed us," Knives explains, wiping the back of his arm on the cut on his forehead. It seems to be the only injury he has. "They attacked us. I threw my star and busted a tire. They had a gun, Slingshot drew his, and it was fucking crazy. Bullseye threw his darts, and I don't even know what happened. The car lost control after another tire blew, and it flipped in the air. I made it to the desert first, but the car clipped Slingshot and Bullseye. I didn't know Slingshot got hit until I woke up, and when I woke up, Bullseye was gone. The bodies in the car were gone. I drove Slingshot and me here since my bike was the only one not fucking ruined. I swear that's all I know."

Bullseye is gone.

The breath leaves my lungs, and Badge catches me as my knees lose control.

Reaper is stomping his feet furiously.

"Goddamn it! Badge! Figure it out. Find him. I'm going to Mateo, and when I get there, I swear to god if he has anything to do with this, I'll kill him. Doc, how is Slingshot?"

Juliette sits down next to him with a bag of supplies and blood and gets the transfusion going right here in the living room. There's a puddle of red on the floor, staining the edge of the carpet, and Slingshot's eyes are closed.

Doc rolls him over to check the wound. "Both gunshots are through and through. That's good, but I have to stop this bleeding. He's lost too much. Way too much. I don't know, Reaper. I'll get him stable and move him downstairs but he cannot fucking move from this spot."

"What are his chances?" Skirt asks.

"I don't know," Doc whispers.

"He'll make it, right? He has to. It's Slingshot," Tank says, standing in the middle of the entryway.

"I don't fucking know!" Doc shouts as he meticulously cleans out the wound.

If there is one thing I know about Doc, it's that he's level-headed and calm all the time. He doesn't yell.

Everyone in the room is quiet, and Sarah is on the couch with Jo, cradling their stomachs as they cry.

"We can't lose him," Knives whispers.

"You think I don't fucking know that?" Doc snaps then wipes the sweat off his forehead. "I know," he says brokenly, and that's when it hits me.

He doesn't know if Slingshot will make it. He isn't confident.

He's scared.

"I need Bullseye." I lift my eyes to Badge, tears breaking free of my lower lash line. "I need to find him. His diabetes, you know he doesn't take care of it. I have to get him. We have to find him." I'm a blubbering mess, just like everyone else in the room.

"We will. None of us ever lets one of us be lost. I swear, we'll bring him home." Badge does the one thing I don't expect him to do. He wraps his arms around me and holds me as I cry.

These arms don't wrap me in the same safety as Bullseye's do. But I'm appreciative anyway.

Bullseye isn't gone. He'll come home.

He has to come home.

Because *he* is my home.

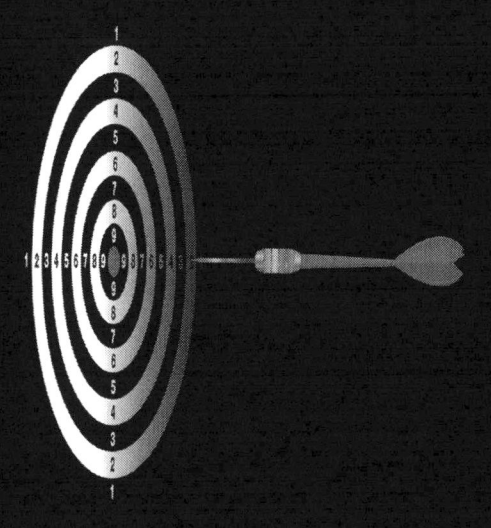

CHAPTER TWENTY-ONE
Bullseye

THE LINGERING SMELL OF SMOKE WAKES ME UP, NOT CIGARETTE SMOKE, BUT OLD SMOKE. Like this place has smoke in its bones. It has my head throbbing. I've been in and out of consciousness for a few days now. I haven't been able to pinpoint where I am exactly. I'm not awake long enough to try and figure it out. I think I have a concussion from the accident.

Now that I'm blinking my eyes open, I don't feel a sickness swirling around in my stomach. My eyes adjust to the darkness for the first time since arriving at my cage.

I shake my head free from the dizziness, still trying to tickle the back of my brain.

"Well, well, well, look who has finally joined the party," someone says from the shadows.

I look around the room, and at the same time, something tugs on my ankle. The sun is pouring down the staircase into the basement.

No.

Impossible.

I cannot be back here.

I turn around and check the cement wall behind me. Frantically, with my heart in my throat and fear in my mind as the worst memories play on repeat, my fingers trace the marks I made all those years ago. I scramble to the corner, and my leg tugs on the chain just like it did in the past.

My boots scuff against the floor, sliding through the buildup of black soot from the fire I caused eighteen years ago.

Bursts of sunlight peek through the broken floor above, which tells me the entire house burnt down like I wanted, but this fucking hell hole remained.

I should have known. It's a cellar.

Mother fucker. How did I end up back here? No one knows about this. I'm the only one.

"You look like you've seen a ghost," the man says, creeping out from across the room.

A ghost? No.

Am I freaking out about going back in time? Fuck yes. How is it possible that I can still smell the fire burning?

"Why the fuck am I here?" I demand. The soot is affecting my voice, grabbing it by the vocal cords and poisoning it. Every time I inhale, I inhale the rotten memories that have turned to dust in the ash settled in this place. "And who the fuck are you?" My head hits the wall behind me, sending a fresh wave of pain through my already aching head.

The crunch of debris tells me he's walking closer, and I force myself to stand, swaying on my feet. Fuck, I really don't feel well. How long has it been since I've eaten? Since I drank anything?

"You killed a few of my friends in that car," he says, leaning against the old wooden rail of the staircase.

"They tried to kill me first, so better them than me." I spread my arms to the side. "Now, are you going to keep the suspense high and drag this out for a few more days? Or are you going to tell me what you want? Who are you? And why the hell am I in this shit cellar?" I want to make sure I come across as clueless. The last thing I need for this guy to do is to find out that I grew up in this room, in this very fucking spot I'm standing in.

That the degraded cot frame a few inches in front of me is where I made love for the first time.

No one needs to know that.

This has to be a coincidence. He's a bad guy. They all have a space they like to take their victims. Like the Kings, we have the playroom.

This cellar has been here for years, so who knows what other horrible things have happened in this room?

"I'm one of Maximo Moretti's men. It didn't take too many brain cells to figure out Mateo would call you. He's always been a fucking pussy. He can never do the job himself."

"Well, I hope you didn't fry the brain cells you have left. That would be tragic." I place my hand to my chest, faking that I give a fuck.

I'll never give a fuck.

Ever.

He tucks his hands in his trouser pockets and confidently struts around the room. He's older, maybe in his fifties, and has silver throughout his hair.

"You have a mouth on you, *Waylon*."

The shock must be evident on my face because he laughs, the sardonic echo bouncing off the prison-like walls. "Mmm yes, how do I know all about Waylon Jennings? I bet you're wondering. I can tell by the stupid look on your face."

If my closest brothers don't know my name, how in the hell would one of Maximo's men?

"I've been a big fan of yours, Waylon." He stops right in front of me and hums as he looks me up and down. He reaches for my face, and I block his touch, slapping his hand away.

I inch forward and tighten my jaws together. "Don't fucking touch me."

"I'll do whatever the fuck I want to you." He punches me across the face and takes advantage of my moment of weakness by handcuffing my wrists together.

Damn it, I want to fight back, but my body feels sluggish. Tired even. Maybe it's the concussion.

He yanks my head back with a thick grip of my hair and sneers, "I've poured so much money into you—so much time. I had no idea it was you while I was working for Maximo until recently. You looked so familiar." His finger outlines the edge of my jaw, and I launch myself at him.

He steps away, and I land right on my stomach, unable to go anywhere.

"How could I ever forget this handsome face, the sharp edge of your jaw? Your green eyes?"

I snatch my head away again, but his fingers trail over my lips next, which makes me gag. I try to bite his index finger, but he yanks his hand back just in time.

"Oh, I fucking loved watching you and Georgia. I must have been your number one fan." He falls to his knees in front of me and grins. "To get my revenge for you killing my friends is one thing. To say I killed a King to complete our mission to free Maximo another—but to enjoy the last fleeting moments of the boy I enjoyed watching so many times..." his eyes close, and his nostrils flare. His hands press against his thigh.

"...That's a fucking gift."

All the fury and hatred I had for Ronald and Patricia hits me like a freight train. My eyes begin to water as I think about the agony they put me through for him.

Their customer.

The torture this man put me through by sitting back and watching me, watching Georgia, has been permanently carved into my bones.

"You were so beautiful. You are now, but nothing compared to the delicate lines and youth you had as a boy."

Fucking pervert.

"Ronald really groomed you and Georgia to be the perfect couple for us. You were starting to get too old for my liking around the time everything went silent. No more videos, no nothing, and do you know what that did to me?" he yells, spit flying in my face.

A curl of his hair falls across his forehead as he shoves me against the wall.

Another level of weakness hits me. Did he drug me?

"It left me dying for another glimpse of you. Just one more. That's all I wanted. And someone listened to my prayers because here you are. You've been in Vegas this entire time," he says, rubbing his fucking hand down my chest.

I swing the leg out that isn't chained, but he grabs it since I'm so slow.

What the fuck is wrong with me?

This isn't normal.

"Did you know Ronald had set up a live show? Invited his best customers to come to see and sample the two of you?" he grabs my cock, and I freeze, too nervous to move. It's a delicate fucking position I'm in, and I can't fight him off. I happen to like where my dick is, and the last thing I want is for him to rip it off. Not like I could fight anyway with how my body is shutting down.

I think I'm dying.

"I paid top dollar for you, boy. The highest fucking bid. I couldn't wait to get my hands on you. I couldn't wait to see this pretty mouth wrapped around my cock. God, I dreamed of those pouty lips. Mmhmm," he hums as if he just tasted the best treat of his life. "I dreamed of sinking into that young ass and claiming it. I bet no one has claimed it, have they?"

"You're fucking disgusting." I gather a wad of spit and launch it in his face. It lands on his cheek in a thick glob. "People like you make the world worse. People like you ruin lives. You ruined my life. You enabled that bastard."

He wraps his hand around my throat. "People like me are what make this precious world go-'round, Waylon." He runs his hand up my chest and I'm relieved that he has let go of my cock, because his hand down there was making me want to throw up. He swipes his finger through the spit and wraps his lips around the digits, sucking them dry.

I curl my lip in disgust.

How the fuck did I get here for the second time in my life? The universe must really hate me. Even in the back of the room, there are books sitting on the shelves covered in remaining soot that haven't been moved in eighteen years. This place is a time capsule.

And I want out.

I refuse to die here. Not when I lost everything just to get out.

"It was so easy finding this place. All I had to do was remember where I had kept my invitation he sent me in the mail and the picture of the beautiful boy he sent." He pulls out a faded envelope and pulls out a picture of me.

I turn away, disgusted with myself, when I see the kid in the photo. It's me. I couldn't have been more than seventeen. I'm naked. Skin and bone, but my cock is hard from all the Viagra they pumped in me. This was just before a show.

And there is no life in my eyes—just a dark, useless void.

I wished for death.

"Does your cock still look like that?"

I pull against the cuffs, knowing I can't get out of them, but it's worth a try. They break my skin and turn my fingers purple from the pressure.

"I bet it is. All long, thick and glorious. I couldn't wait to get my hands on you, and then you had to go and ruin everything." He stands up, drops the picture, and kicks me in the stomach. "I waited my entire life for a boy like you, and you fucking ruined it!" He slams his shoe into my ribs again, and I cough, gagging from the pain.

"Sweet fucking karma is what this is. I would never have thought I would see you again, and then we cross paths, just by chance. You see, fucked worlds always find a way to collide, Waylon. We were bound to meet again. How perfect is this? I kill you, prove to the Kings how serious we are, they back off, we get Maximo. Piece of fucking cake."

I snort. "Your brain cells must really be gone if you think for one minute Reaper will ever back down because one of his men is dead."

"I know he will. He barely tolerates Mateo."

No. Reaper can't. He can't fucking do that. If these men get Maximo, who knows what they'll do. What if this sick fuck puts children at risk? How many lives has he ruined? How many would he continue to ruin?

I had to survive this. I had to dig down deep for more energy. Where is my will to survive?

It's fucking lost because my head won't stop spinning. I can hear my heartbeat in my ears.

He tucks a piece of my hair behind my ear, then runs his fingers through my hair. "So soft. It's softer than what I imagined. God, I bet you were so perfect when you were younger. Soft skin, no hair, sweet and naïve. You aren't now. The world has hardened you, and your skin isn't soft, but I'll take you anyway. I can have you, Waylon. I bought you for a night. Don't you think it's about time I get what I paid for?" He begins to undo his pants. I try to tell myself to fight, to pull on these chains, that no one can fucking beat me. I am a killer.

And the more I try to strengthen myself, the more exhausted I get.

Something is wrong.

My eyes hood, and the guy in front of me doubles. My body sways back and forth.

Stay awake. Stay conscious.

But I can't.

"Actually—" he zips his pants up, "—Better yet. How about we put on a show? I know a few people who would love to see you again," he chuckles with his brilliance.

I groan when my face hits the floor. Dust and soot gather in my mouth, the fire trying to come back to life across my tongue.

The world always makes sure it comes around again, doesn't it?

Of course, how I was brought into this world is how I'd be taken out of it.

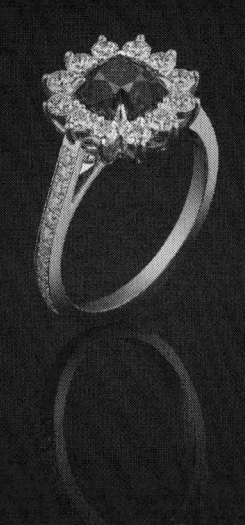

CHAPTER TWENTY-TWO

Ruby

I'VE BEEN BESIDE MYSELF FOR DAYS.

We could have had this amazing relationship between us for months, and I didn't take a chance because I'm an idiot. Now what? All that lost time, and I might not be able to get it back. What if Bullseye is dead in a ditch somewhere? What if he's in another state by now? Another country?

I wipe my cheeks with the sleeve of his shirt that I'm wearing. I need to feel close to him. I press my hand against my heart and take in a shaky breath, playing with the ruby ring on my finger to try and calm my nerves. I'm a nervous wreck.

"Here, I brought you coffee." Badge sets down a white diner-style mug and takes his usual seat in front of his wall of monitors.

I've been working with Badge side by side. He finally got tired of me breathing over his shoulder, so he got me a chair. I've gotten no sleep. When I try, I fail. My mind is racing a hundred miles an hour. I can't stop thinking about Waylon. He doesn't deserve this. He deserves peace.

Because of all the time spent working with Badge, the shop has been neglected by me. I've been tempted to place my shop up for sale and maybe just hand it over to Moretti, but Reaper won't let me. He said Braveheart and Tank have the shop under control, and whenever I'm ready to return to work, I can.

Bullseye is the priority, and everyone has been looking for him nonstop. God, Reaper, and Knives went to the accident site yesterday and brought Slingshot's and Bullseye's bikes back.

The two bikes had fused into a tangled heap of metal that looked like they came from the junkyard behind King's Garage. The sight only replaced the small amount of hope I had with the rotten sludge of dread.

"Thank you," I whisper, taking the cup in my hands. The heat feels good against my palms. I bring it to my lips, blow on the java, and take a sip. The warmth is comforting against my raw throat since I've been crying so much. The taste of a ton of sugar tingles my taste buds, and it's the first time a smile wants to form on my lips in days.

"What?" he grunts. Typical Badge. I've gotten to know him a little better in the last few days. He puts on such an act of being a tough guy, but he's a total softie. He types away on his keyboard, diving deep into the dark web where horrible things lurk.

"You remembered how I like my coffee. Thank you."

He shrugs. "It's not a big deal."

"Badge!" Maizey cries out for him as her little feet patter down the hall. "Uncle Badge!" she screams again.

He spins around in his chair just in time to catch her as she launches herself at him. He looks annoyed, but I'm starting to think that's just how he looks.

"What is it, Maze? I'm working, trying to find Uncle Bullseye," he says gently, barely hiding the hint of annoyance in his voice. He wants to get back to work.

I take another sip of my coffee just to hide my mouth behind the mug.

"I'm scared. I don't want Uncle Slingshot to die. He won't wake up." Her nostrils shrink as she breathes in rapidly to catch her breath and her bottom lip is a quivering mess. "I even held tacos under his nose, and he won't wake up," she wails. "He taco swore."

"Aw, Maze."

I think I hear a slight crack in his voice.

"He's going to be okay. He hasn't broken your swear yet. He's alive. He's just resting, healing. You have to give him time, okay?" I've never heard him sound so gentle before.

She sniffles, and her big, brown watery eyes are staring at Badge as if he holds all the answers to the universe. "You swear?" she questions, rubbing her runny nose on the back of her hand.

I don't miss his cringe of disgust.

"I taco swear, kid. Go hang out with your Mom, okay? I need to find Bullseye." He lifts her off his lap and sets her on the ground.

"Okay. I love you, Uncle Badge."

His shoulders tense, but the wrinkles around his eyes disappear. "I love you too, Maze."

"I hope we find Bullseye. He promised to teach me how to throw darts!" she spins around, her blue princess dress of the day fanning around her as she sprints down the hall.

"You're good with her."

"Only cause I have to be," he says.

Yeah, I don't believe that for a minute.

"Fuck, I found something. Many, many somethings, and I hate to say this, but you're right, Ruby." Badge punches a few more items on the keyboard and brings up another tab on the screen. He doesn't dive into the dark web just pulls up a missing person's report. "Missing Child. 1992. Waylon Justin Presley. Eight years old. Last seen wearing a Ghostbusters shirt. He has brown hair and green eyes—"

"—That's not his name, though. His name is Waylon Jennings."

Badge presses his lips together.

"I know. But I got to thinking—his kidnappers wouldn't have kept his name the same, would they? It would be too easy for him to look himself up. If he didn't remember his real birth name, he couldn't find his past. Look," he clicks on another screen, and a video feed pops up. It's old, grainy, but in color. "I cross-referenced Waylon Presley's face on the missing person report. There are hundreds of videos." He clicks on the very first one uploaded.

Oh my god.

It's him.

It's Waylon.

It isn't sexual, which doesn't make sense because Bullseye said they started filming him at sixteen. Badge points to the kid wearing a Ghostbusters shirt. "They had a live video feed on him since he was eight," he sneers. "People were just paying to watch."

My stomach rolls with nausea.

He clicks to another video, then another, and another. They are all the same. It's just him sitting there, crying for his mom, which has me silently crying for him as well.

But in the following video, things change.

He isn't crying anymore. He's not wearing a shirt. And he seems... different.

"That's the moment where his brain shut out his past. It was too much trauma for him to handle, so the mind did what it does best. It tried to protect him." Badge clenches his fist together and slams it down on the table. "I've seen this before when I was a cop. It never gets easier, especially when this is hitting us so close to home." Badge clicks through other videos and then clicks on one where Bullseye was made to perform but quickly exits out. "I feel like the scum of the earth for seeing that."

"Why are these videos up? Why haven't the cops or the FBI taken them down and arrested the bastards that watch this shit?"

"Because this is one out of hundreds of thousands."

"That's terrible." My Bullseye slipped through the cracks because there were too many like him. How unfair is that?

"Wait a minute." Badge stares at the screen and tilts his head. "There's a live feed, but Bullseye's face just dinged it. Not when he was younger. I can trace it," he says, elated with a big grin on his face. "We can find him. I just need some time to pinpoint this asshole. Hopefully, he is sloppy." Badge clicks on the video, and this time, the feed is crystal clear and in color.

I gasp, and Badge and I lean forward at the same time. Bullseye is lying on the ground, eyes closed, but I see his chest rising and falling.

"Oh my god, he's in the same house." I point to the chain on the wall attached to his ankle and then point to an older video with the same chain in the same spot. "They took him back." I can't hold it back anymore. I lean over the chair and grab the wastebasket and throw up. It's just coffee and water. I haven't been able to eat much since he's been gone. I've been too worried.

"It's a live feed, taking bids. High bids. It's for a front-row seat."

"To what?"

"To whatever this guy has planned with Bullseye."

"We have to win those seats, Badge."

"What would you have me do? The bid goes up every second. It's already at a million dollars."

"What? That makes no sense. He's a grown man. He isn't a boy anymore. Don't people pay that kind of money for their... perversions?"

"Bullseye himself is a perversion to this man. He never got to have Bullseye before, but he gets him now. I bet the audience he is gaining is the same audience Bullseye has had before. We don't fucking have a cool million just lying around."

I stare down at my finger and lift my hand up. "We have a cool two million."

Badge's eyes lock on the ring, and he whistles. "That ring has been in your family for generations. Are you sure?"

I don't know how he knows that, but I'm not going to ask.

"I'd give up all the rubies I had for him if I had more. This is worth two million, or it was two years ago." I could have lived a really great life if I sold this ring when I lived on the streets, but now I know why I didn't. It was for this moment.

Badge brings up a chat window and types. *"Ruby ring worth 2 million in exchange?"* he asks. "Now, we wait."

Three dots pop up, and both of us scoot closer to the desk.

"That was fast," I note.

"They are all about making money and getting their dicks wet."

I cringe at how crude that sounds.

"Sorry," he states unapologetically.

The computer dings in a reply, which steals our attention again. *"Seat is yours. Bidding's over. Be here in one hour. If you don't have the ring, I'll kill you."*

The chatbox closes, and while the live stream is still up, the countdown clock begins, and the bidding numbers switch to a four-letter word.

SOLD.

My throat tightens. I never thought I'd be right here bidding to get my boyfriend back to me.

"I'm tracing it," he informs me.

It would be easier if we had Ronald and Patricia's address, but Badge came up empty. He thinks those were aliases, not real names for us to go by. We will never know their true identity, but I'm fine with that. I just want Bullseye back.

"I hate that you were right."

I give Badge a curious look when I see guilt written all over his face.

"I might have been able to prevent this if I dug deeper. Maybe I could have found this guy."

"Don't put this on yourself. There's no way you could have known this. No one did. I wanted to think his past was behind him. I only wanted to help him. I had no idea it would be tied into the present."

Badge hits one of the keys harder than necessary and gives me a toothy, villainous smile. "Well, let's go end it for him because I just got a hit. It's only a twenty-minute drive." Badge stands and, without another word to me, walks away.

Um, I... okay.

I hurry behind him and follow him to the main room. Slingshot's blood has stained the floor, and everyone is solemn, sad, and quiet. Practically every single member of the Ruthless Kings, and all the ol' ladies, are in the living room. It's as if we all need to be close to one another.

"We found him, and he's close," Badge announces, pinching the bridge of his nose. "It's pretty fucking terrible. I won't give details. It isn't my place. Ruby and I are going. Who else wants to go?"

"Why is Ruby going? She should stay here safe with the women and children," Skirt says.

I know he doesn't mean it in a bad way, but it ticks me off. "I'm going to kill the son of a bitch that has done this to Bullseye, again. It will be the last time anyone ever retakes advantage of him. If you have a problem with it, maybe you should stay and sit this one out," I sneer, readying myself for a fight.

I'll throw hands right fucking now.

"Crivvens, a little pitbull lives in that chihuahua body," Skirt chuckles and holds up his hands. "Ye won't hear me say another word, Ruby. Apologies."

"We're all on the same team here, tiger. Retract the claws." Badge jerks me backward by my left shoulder, muttering curses out of his mouth that only I can hear. "Anyway, anyone want to come?"

I'm not surprised in the least when everyone raises their hand, even the pregnant women.

Doc snorts. "Nice try. This pregnant group is staying home. Right here where I can keep an eye on everyone." He bends down and kisses Joanna on top of her head. "I know you might need me, but I'm needed here. I have to keep an eye on the ladies and Slingshot."

"I'll go," Juliette pipes up. "You've been teaching me. I can go out into the field without you."

"If you're sure..." Doc sounds hesitant, but I would be too. Juliette is going to school to be a nurse, not a doctor.

"I'll go too." Reaper places his glass of water on the table. "It's the least I can do. Tool will stay here, and so will you, Skirt. Where the hell is Patrick?"

"I haven't seen him," Poodle says, petting Lady's head. Doc told Poodle it would be time to let Lady go once everyone is home. "He's been M.I.A. a lot lately."

Reaper tilts his head back and stares at the ceiling. "Don't let it be his sobriety. I can't handle this shit right now. Okay, we're taking the truck. I don't know what we'll find, but we need to be prepared. Where's Sunnie? Melissa? I want to make sure the girls stick together while we're gone."

"Downstairs visiting Slingshot," Doc answers, keeping his arms folded across his chest.

"Okay, let's go. I don't want to waste another minute." Reaper reaches for the hook on the wall and snags the keys to the black Ford Raptor outside. "If anything happens to Bullseye, I'll never forgive myself."

Touching the ruby on my finger one last time, we head out the door to reclaim the most important person that's ever been lost.

The weather fits the mood. The skies are gray, and the color against the desert has the red sand bright and popping as if a camera filter has been placed over it. A tumbleweed blows by just as thunder rolls above. An eerie feeling hovers over me as if a shoot-out is about to go down.

Badge opens the back door for me, and I roll my eyes when I see how high up the truck is. How the hell am I going to get up there? I yelp when Badge picks me up by the back of the shirt and tosses me in the back seat without a bit of finesse, then slams the door.

I'm fine.

No big deal.

Poodle's hand wraps around my elbow and helps me sit up even though I don't need it. "Thanks," I tell him, the polite mannerism haunted as it leaves my lips.

He must feel it, too, because he only gives a grim expression in return. The truck roars to life, loud and boisterous. On any other day, I'd be glad to ride in a truck this big. The leather seats are pristine, and the hint of the new car smell still hangs in the air, but I'm too worried to enjoy such a luxury. I'm afraid.

I plop my chin in my hand and prop my elbow on the door. The bikes get further away as we reverse, and Reaper presses a button that reminds me of a garage door opener, which has the iron gate swinging wide to allow us out.

As we drive, I fall into a trance. My mind is blank as I watch the cactuses and scrub grass pass us in a blur. I don't hear the conversation in the truck's cab, and I don't answer questions asked of me. I don't do anything.

I'm too focused emotionally. I know the guys think I'm coming along because I want to make sure Bullseye is safe, but that's not the only reason. I'm coming because, like Bullseye, I have a target in mind.

I'm going to kill the son of a bitch doing this to him. And when I hit my mark, that's when I'm going to breathe again. That will be the only time I'm truly invested in what is happening around me. Badge didn't have time to get me a gun, but I did snag a handful of Bullseye's darts from the secret drawer in the dresser.

They are pressing against my leg from the inside of my pocket. I'm borrowing a tight pair of jeans that no longer fit Sarah, and they barely fit me. They are snug, and the sharp points of the darts are poking through the blue denim.

I know nothing about darts. Bullseye has only shown me once—I nearly took Skirt's eye out. But this time, I think I have the right motivation to get the job done.

"We're here." Badge announces, turning off the GPS and pointing to a half-burned-down house.

"How is it still there after all these years?" I ask in a hushed whisper, afraid that whoever has Bullseye will hear me.

It's completely irrational.

"I bought it."

A stunned silence fills the truck as everyone stares at Reaper.

"I didn't ask questions. When the bank put the house up for sale, I knew Bullseye was attached to it. He came to us with soot all over him, and then the next day, we find out a house burned down? If I was wrong, so be it, but I wasn't. I didn't even think of this address, or I would have given it to you. I thought a rival took him—"

"—This is a rival. It just isn't the kind you're used to," I cut him off before he can say anything else. This is the enemy.

Reaper nods in agreement. "You're right."

"I think it's best if I go in alone. He won't expect me, and I'm the one with the ring."

"No," Badge replies immediately, shaking his head. "Out of the question."

"Why? Give me ten minutes and the call the cops," I protest

"We don't do cops. We'll do this the Ruthless way." The way Reaper's voice deepens has me afraid for my own life.

"I think that's a good idea. We'll surround the place. We'll make sure you're okay and covered, but if we come in with you, it could cause alarms to go off," says Badge.

"If anything happens to her, it's on you, and you get to explain to Bullseye how you let her walk into a dangerous situation," chimes in Poodle.

"I'll be fine. I don't think this guy is too smart. He didn't think this through."

"Don't underestimate him, okay? Guys like him are sick and twisted. Don't take his sickness for weakness. He's gotten away with this for a long time." Reaper levels me with a firm stare. In his eyes are something I never thought I'd see from him:

Trust.

The Ruthless Kings are trusting me to get their brother back for them. And in return, I have to trust that they will protect me.

I open the door, jump to the ground, and carefully close the door with a soft click. "He won't be getting away with it anymore."

I thrust my shoulders back and strut to the half-burnt down house. The only thing left of the ranch-style home is the half of the frame that seems untouched by the fire but is darkened with smoke damage.

The other half of the house is burnt to a crisp. The windows are gone, but the frame managed to survive even if the wood is black. I pause in front of the house, staring at the place Bullseye once called home.

It's not a home.

It's a house of horrors.

I don't give a damn what I have to do. I will free him from this place.

The mailbox on the left looks untouched. The post is rotted, and the plastic bin is covered in dust. I open it to see if there is any mail, but there isn't. I don't know why I checked—part of wants to know their names.

There's a walkway that leads from the mailbox to where the front door used to be, and I take the first step toward Bullseye's salvation. I don't know how he'll feel about a woman coming to his rescue. He's definitely the kind of man who does the rescuing and killing, but this time, he has me.

He isn't alone anymore.

And that's all that's needed truly to save someone.

A slight breeze pitches through the air, bringing the faint scent of soot. Makes sense, since half the house is covered in it.

Out of the corner of my eye, I see movement. It's Poodle and Juliette hiding behind a neighboring tree. I can feel the rest of their eyes on me, and I know I'm safe.

I'm not scared.

I'm restless now.

And I'm ready to get even.

I might be small, but I'm goddamn mighty. I'll go down kicking and screaming before I ever give in. I step through what used to be the threshold. My borrowed sneakers are immediately ruined with black. I'll have to make an apology to Mary.

"Hello?" I call out. "I won the bid. I'm here for front row seats to the show?"

The crunch of rotted, burned-out wood under me snaps in half, and I lose my footing, tripping over a piece of... something. I can't tell what it is.

Arms wrap around me and the hairs on the back of my neck stand up. The way the man's skin glides against mine makes me shiver. He feels like a snake, a smooth caress, but I know he has venom in his bite.

"I believe you're looking for me."

I shudder on the inside when I hear his voice. Some people just sound creepy, and he is definitely one of them. He speaks slowly, precisely, and there is a slight break in his words—a natural crack.

I spin around, and I'm not surprised at all by what I see. A middle-aged man with gray hair, a nice suit, money to burn, and no fucks to give. "I'm..." I catch myself before I say my real name, "...Rebecca."

"Rebecca. It's nice to meet you. I'll show you the merchandise, and then I'll expect your payment."

"In full. And this viewing is private? I want to make sure I'm getting my money's worth before people start seeing what is mine." Something about the way I say it has a power rushing through me. He is mine.

Only mine.

"Of course. You have thirty minutes before the show begins. There is plenty of time."

"I didn't catch your name?" I remind him.

"Diego," he says with a flashy smile.

"Diego. Why here, out of all places? It's a bit... run down. It isn't what I expected. I've been to so many of these. The venues were much nicer. For instance, actual auctions. They are marvelous." Thank god I read that romance book about a virgin auctioning up her virginity, or I'd have no idea how to make this guy believe I'm the real deal.

"This place," he sighs fondly. "This place holds so many memories of this boy and me"

"—man," I correct him.

His eyes flash for a second. He doesn't like to be corrected, but I couldn't help myself. I know in his eyes, Bullseye might always be a boy.

"I've known him for a long time," he confirms my thoughts immediately. "I'll always see him differently, I suppose."

"Where is he?"

"Down this way." He gestures to the stairs that lead to the cellar. He pauses. "Actually," he turns around and plasters a sleazy, up-to-no-good smile on his face. "I want my payment now."

"And if I don't like the goods?"

"No refunds. Sorry."

I'm going to enjoy killing this asshole. Without thinking twice, I grab the ring off my finger and shove it in the middle of his palm. "Paid in full."

He whistles low when he holds it up to the natural light. "It's a beauty."

I'll miss it, but I won't miss it as much as I do Bullseye at this moment.

He smirks and places the ring in a small lockbox, which snaps closed with a complex series of gears and clicks.

"Follow me," he says.

He gives me his back. I could throw a dart at him right now, but what if Bullseye isn't down there? I need to see with my own eyes that he's alive. If he isn't down there, we'll need leverage. I can't kill him yet.

So disappointing.

When did I become so bloodthirsty?

When I fell in love with Waylon.

The wood creaks under my first step onto the staircase. The sun peeks through the floor like the heavens do through the trees. Dust particles float in the air, and the light shines upon a still body in the corner. I almost scream in relief and yell his name when I see him, but I keep myself under control. He's in the same position I saw him in on the video feed.

Something's wrong. I feel it.

"What's the matter with him?"

"Nothing. He hit his head. He's fine. He'll be *up* just in time." The man shakes a bottle, and that's when it hits me he's planning on drugging him with Viagra.

You've got to be kidding.

"Oh, nice," I try to sound convincing, but I know I don't. I'm heartbroken. My mask falls, and that split second is all it takes for Diego to see through my bullshit.

He pulls out a gun, and I take a step back. "Who the fuck are you?"

Yeah, I'm fucked. There's no getting out of this with words. I dodge to the left, and he pulls the trigger. The gunshot has me cupping my hand over my ears. It's so loud.

The bullet pierces the concrete wall, mere inches away from me. Diego must not have expected it to be so loud because he groans, holding his hand over his ears.

I take his moment of weakness as my moment of strength and dig in my pocket for the darts. I grab three of them. I stagger on my feet, the high-pitched ringing causing me to be off-balance. I launch the first one unsuccessfully.

The glint of the gun blinds me as the sun sears it. He fires again.

And misses, thank god.

I crossed my fingers on that one.

I shake my head, take a deep breath, and focus on Diego.

Oh, fuck this.

Instead of throwing a dart, I throw myself at him, tackling him to the ground. It knocks the breath out of my lungs. I know I don't have long before he gets the upper hand.

"Stupid fucking bitch." He lifts his hand and backhands me.

Blood slides down my cheek, and I laugh. "You're going to have to do better than that. I've been hit a lot harder." I lift my arm in the air and bring it down, stabbing the dart in his eye.

He screams at the top of his lungs, hands shaking as he touches what's protruding out of his eye. I grab the gun from his hand and place it on the barrel on the side of his head. He's trembling, and blood is pouring from his eye. "Please," he begs. "I'll give you the ring back."

"I don't give a fuck about the ring. I want him." I yank the dart from his eye. The teeth that spear out of the tip when they land against their target take a chunk of meat out.

The whole. Damn. Eyeball.

He has a hole where his eye used to be.

He cries, begging for his life.

"This is for Waylon!" I shove the gun in his mouth and don't hesitate.

I don't think. I don't second guess.

I pull the trigger.

I'm gasping for breath from the exertion it took to take that man down. My entire body hurts. I drop the gun as if it's burned me, and I scurry off the dead body and scurry to Bullseye, who still lies unconscious on the ground.

Chained.

Cuffed.

"Baby?" my throat clogs with emotions as I lift his head onto my lap. "I'm here. You're okay. You're safe. I have you. That man can never bother you again." But he doesn't wake up. "Bullseye." I shake him, but he doesn't respond. I gently trace his jaw with my hand, stroke his cheek, then bend down and kiss him. "I love you. You have to wake up. You're my future."

The hard pound of boots comes down the steps, and Reaper stops at the bottom, staring at the dead body. "Damn, you really fucking killed him."

"Of course, I did," I hiss. "Sarah would do the same for you."

"Damn, remind me not to get on your bad side," Poodle comments, stepping out of the way to let Juliette through.

Juliette checks his pulse, and the first thing she does after that is check his blood sugar. "I wouldn't be surprised if he's in a diabetic coma, and that's what made him pass out. It's common with type 2 diabetes when they don't take care of it."

"I'm going to kill him when he wakes up for not being better about it." I'm going to check his damn sugar every day if I have to.

"Yeah, it's 30. We need to get him fluids and another cocktail mixture, but first," she says, stabbing a needle in a small glass bottle. "Insulin."

"Poodle, help me with these chains and cuffs. We'll carry him to the truck and take him home."

Poodle taps Diego's dead body and pulls out the keys, along with the small lockbox that holds my ring. "I think I know how he got in touch with Bullseye." He lifts an employee badge of the old casino before it was Lussuria.

"One of Maximo's men," Reaper kicks Diego's body. "Mateo will answer for this."

Poodle unlocks the chain around Bullseye's ankle, then the cuffs, and Bullseye groans but doesn't wake.

"Come on. Let's go home."

"And then burn the rest of this fucking place to the ground," I add, remembering Bullseye had told me he set the fire to begin with. "And then maybe Badge can look for the people who were interested in this?"

"He's already on it. A lot of people are going to jail. And as for Bullseye, he can finally know his past can't come back and haunt him," Reaper states, picking Bullseye up from the shoulders, which takes his beautiful freaking head off my lap. Poodle takes his feet, and they climb up the steps.

"I'll be up in a minute." I throw my hands on my hips and hold back the emotions. No tears. No tears.

It's hard not to cry when his pain surrounds me. I run my fingers over the wall and the lines etched in stone. This place is so cold. Haunted by a little boy's fear. He made these lines. He kept a tally.

My heart fucking hurts for him.

I lay my hand across my chest and take a deep breath, stepping over the man I just killed. I don't feel bothered by it at all. My way of thinking is that this man deserved it. I hold no guilt for what I've done. Maybe it's my way of categorizing things. Maybe it's how I deal with pain in order to overcome it.

I run my fingers along the spines of the books that Waylon used to touch, aged soot falling off in chunks. There's one book that isn't pushed in all the way, and I open it to the bookmark.

It's an old polaroid of Waylon and Georgia. Young. Maybe ten? Before things went to hell. They are smiling.

One of the last times he was happy.

I tuck the picture in my back pocket, then do what needed to be done years ago. I pull all the books out of their spot. They crash to the ground; some open, some don't, but I don't care. Paper is paper, and when I set this place on fire, these books will help it burn.

The past deserves to remain in the past.

Burned.

Buried.

And behind us.

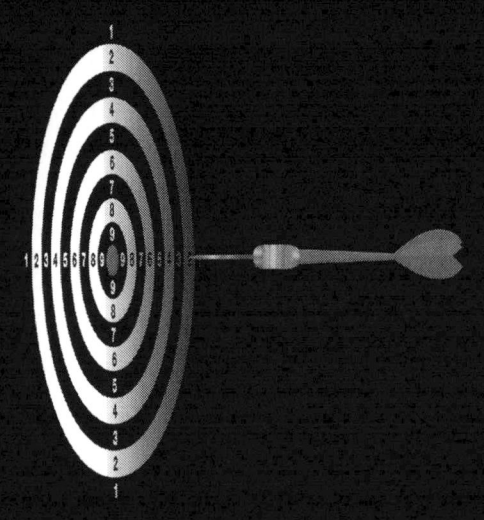

CHAPTER TWENTY-THREE

Bullseye

"STOP FUSSING OVER ME. I'M FINE," I COMPLAIN, YANKING MY BODY BACK TO PUT on my own shirt. "Spitfire, I love you, but if you don't let me put on my own damn shirt, I'm going to scream." I stomp my foot on the ground like a child.

I don't give a fuck.

It's been five days since I woke up back at the clubhouse, out of harm's way, because my Spitfire saved my ass. Other men might be bothered that their girl saved them, but not me. Ruby is a raging ball of badass waiting to be unleashed, and she fucking unleashed it.

For me.

And she gave up her family heirloom for me.

She risked it all for me.

All. For. Me.

Any man who would take an issue with that needs to get his head examined.

"I just want to make sure you're okay," she whines. "It's only been five days—"

"And I'm fine. I'm alive and well. My sugar is doing great because of you. You keep me in line. I'm healthy as a horse, Ruby."

"You're really okay? Not just physically, but mentally?"

She's talking about when she broke it to me that I was kidnapped when I was eight years old. I still don't remember that life. Sylvia thinks I might not ever get those memories back. Honestly, I don't know how I feel about the information. I'm not surprised, but I am at the same time. It makes everything make some sort of sense, but then it leaves me dumbfounded.

I still can't quite put together that my real name is Waylon Presley. Not Jennings. Saying it somehow feels right, but it also makes me sound like an oldies singer.

I hate oldies.

"Knock, knock," Badge announces before entering anyway. "I have something to show you. We're all in the living room. Whenever you're ready."

I groan. I want to be left alone. I want to be alone with Ruby, actually. I want sex. I want her on her knees sucking my cock, but since everyone thinks I need more time to heal, I've been abandoned. No one is listening to me. Ruby is slapping my hands away when I try to palm her tits when we go to sleep.

I just want to fucking come. Using my hand isn't the same. I know there are more important things in life, like my life. I'm thankful to have it, but I'm ready to live it now. I'm ready to start my life with Ruby officially.

I want to move on.

"Be there in a minute," I sigh, dropping to the edge of the mattress.

I want five minutes where people don't surround me. The only alone time I get these days is when I go visit Slingshot downstairs—poor bastard. If I'm grouchy, I know he is being stuck in that basement. Maizey hasn't left his side. He has makeup on, his nails painted, tiny pigtails, and whatever other girly shit exists he has on him.

She's happy he is alive. We all are.

"Are you—"

I hold up my hand to stop her from saying another word. "Please, for the love of god, don't ask if I'm okay. I've been saying I'm okay, but everyone keeps hovering over me. I get it, you're concerned, but hell, let a man breathe." I rub my temples, hating how I sound like such an asshole. "I'm sorry." I fall backward and bounce on the bed and throw my arm over my eyes. "I'm an asshole."

"No, you aren't." Ruby takes my hand and straddles my waist. "I'm sorry I've been handling you like glass, but you scared me so much. I never want to live through that again."

I intertwine our hands and immediately feel the space where her ring used to be. I feel so damn guilty. The lockbox is sitting on the kitchen table. We can't open it. We could never find the key, and even the combined lockpicking skills of the whole MC can't seem to get it open.

I've offered to break it open, but she doesn't want to damage the ring.

"I know." I sit up and seal our mouths together. "I'm sorry." I wrap my arms around her waist and groan when her tits press against my chest.

Fuck. I need her right now.

"How sorry are you?" I growl, lifting her shirt slowly.

"Super sorry," she bats her eyelashes, playing along. "I just don't think there is anything I can do to make it up to you."

I finally, fucking finally squeeze her tits, and my cock plumps as her hard nipples rub against my palms. "I can think of a few ways. I have two in my hands right now."

"Bullseye," she giggles, which turns into a moan when I twist the sensitive beads. "Bullseye." This time when she says my name, it's with want and need, not laughter and fun.

"Hey, you guys coming or what?" Badge shouts from the other side of the door.

"Will you fuck off? Christ, what's a guy got to do to get fucking laid around here?"

"Fuck off. We need ten minutes," Badge barks, stomping away in a fit.

Ruby snickers and crawls off my lap, which takes my hands out of her shirt. "No, no, no. Come back," I beg.

I'll plead. I'll buy her diamonds. I'll do anything. A man is fucking desperate.

"Come on. Let's go, and then after, I'll give you a treat." She fixes her bra and her shirt. Her cheeks are flushed, the tip of her pretty pink tongue is swiping against her bottom lip as her eyes lock onto my erection.

I can't hide how she makes me feel. I always want her. No matter the time or place, no matter my health.

I want her.

"Hey." I tug her to me, inhaling her honey scent, and relax. I need to just relax. Everyone has been supportive and what I need to do is appreciate more than I am right now. "I love you. You know that, right?" I stand up and cup her face with my hand. I don't miss the way her eyes flutter and the way she leans into my hand.

"I love you too," she says wistfully.

"Now that I've come to terms with so many things, I want you to know I'll be different. I'll be better—the man you deserve. I'll love you fiercely. Protectively. I won't be so afraid of the future. I want to give you everything, Ruby. Especially since you've given it to me." I slide my hand into her back pockets and steal a quick squeeze of her sexy ass.

Next time I get her naked, I'm going to bite it.

"Bullseye, you're everything I want. Always. You're the strongest man I know."

I scoff, remembering all the vulnerable moments I've had with her just within the last few weeks. I didn't realize how much I needed to heal until Ruby touched me for the first time. She broke the fragile shield I had around me and made me face the painful memories I've tried to bury deep.

I was weak.

"It takes a strong man to better himself. It takes an even stronger man to overcome himself." Her hand is cold as she presses it against my cheek, but I don't mind. Even though it is so much smaller than mine, her hand can still bring me to my knees.

The power she holds over me is more power than I've ever allowed anyone to have.

"And it takes the strongest man to realize he isn't perfect, but it takes a smart woman to know that man is perfect for me." She stands on her tiptoes, and I still have to bend down to meet her for a kiss, or she can't reach me.

I wrap my arm around her shoulder and steer her to the door. "I'm going to need those darts back, you thief."

"No way in hell," she huffs, placing her weight against me as we walk out of the bedroom.

The main room is packed. Everyone is here, including Slingshot in his glittery lipstick. The only ones not here are Tongue and Daphne. I miss the hell out of them, and I hope they come home soon. The kids aren't around either.

"They are in Maizey's room playing," Ruby leans over and whispers as if she can read my mind.

Patrick is sitting on the edge of the couch, and Sunnie is whispering something in his ear. By the look on his face, he isn't happy with what he's hearing.

I hope everything is okay in paradise.

"Alright, I know when we told you that you were kidnapped, it was a shock, and we didn't give you any information. I didn't have much at the time, but I do now, if you're willing to hear it," Badge starts, sitting on a barstool and pointing the remote at the TV.

Sarah and Joanna are crying already, and Slingshot is in the recliner, leaning back with an IV attached to him. I don't know how the hell he got up here with those injuries because Doc wouldn't move him unless Slingshot moved himself.

"Okay, sure," I shrug, uncertainty coming through my wavering words. I've come to a conclusion my life before the one at Ruthless doesn't matter. I don't need to know because it doesn't change anything. I hope this isn't some type of intervention about how I need more therapy.

Really, I haven't felt this good in a long time.

"Okay," Badge blows out a breath. His leg is shaking. He's nervous; it isn't like him to be nervous.

My fingers curl, and I make a fist. "Badge, if it's bad, just tell me."

"No, it isn't that. I found a few things I think you should see, and maybe you'll remember where you come from. Maybe you'll remember that you've always had people that have cared about you." That's oddly sweet of Badge to say—Badge is sour most of the time like bad milk.

I don't think I like where this is going.

"Okay, just... keep an open mind and don't hate me for showing everyone."

Why would he care if I hate him? Everyone knows my darkest secret now.

He turns on the TV and presses play. A news clip from South Montana's Local News comes up from 1992, with the headline, "FBI Now Searching For 8-Year-Old Boy."

"There's a tragedy hitting close to home today, just outside of Billings, where an 8-year-old boy has gone missing early yesterday morning," the news anchor announces. "His name is Waylon Presley." A picture comes up of me in a superhero t-shirt. My hair is too long, but I'm happy and smiling. The background is blue, and I'm posing, so maybe it's a school picture. I take a step closer to the TV and hold onto Ruby's hand as long as I can until I'm too far away.

"If you've seen him, please contact the authorities. We want Waylon home soon. Safe and sound."

Another date pops up at the bottom of the screen. It's about a week after the first announcement. Instead of a news anchor, two people are standing at a podium. A woman with brown hair piled up in a messy bun. The camera focuses on her, and her bright blue eyes suddenly unlock something inside of me.

I gasp. I can hardly breathe as memories assault me.

Pancakes for breakfast.

Taking me to the fair.

Petting the animals.

My Dad calling me Bullseye.

My chest tightens, and my eyes fill with tears as I listen to Mom—my real mom—beg someone to bring me home.

"Please, if you have him, if you have my baby, please bring him home. He can't sleep without the night light on. He's afraid of the dark. Please, don't keep him in the dark."

They did. I lived in the dark.

"I just want my Waylon home. Please. Waylon, if you can hear this, I love you so much. Mommy and Daddy love you so much, and we miss you. We will never stop looking for you. I swear to you. I swear it."

A tear breaks free and slides down my cheek when I see how heartbroken she is. Her eyes are red and puffy, and Dad has his arm around her, holding her tight.

"He's our only child. He's my baby. I just want him home," she sobs.

The video flips to another date.

Three months later.

"We haven't given up our search for him. I don't care what the authorities say. It isn't a rescue search. They aren't going to bring home a body. My boy is out there, and he's alive." She clutches her hand to her chest. "I feel it. He's alive, and I will search every inch of this world to find my son."

Another date appears one year later.

"Waylon is nine years old today," she begins to cry, then clears her throat. "It's hard to find the motivation to celebrate when he isn't with us, but we did. We made his favorite breakfast pancakes and bacon. We decorated his to look like a bullseye, a running joke between him and his Dad. He isn't forgotten. He will never be forgotten, and I'll celebrate every single one of his birthdays until I die."

Another year passes.

And another.

And another.

"There's a recent one," Badge says.

I hold my breath and watch the TV unblinking. I don't want to miss a thing. It's my Mom. She's older, tired, and her hair has a few streaks of silver in it. My Dad has started to lose his hair, and he has deep wrinkles around his eyes. It looks like this video was made and posted on YouTube instead of broadcast on TV, which makes sense. I'm sure the authorities closed the case.

"It's been twenty-eight years since our baby boy went missing. Everyone has told us to give up, to let him go, to be at peace—" my mom shakes her head and dabs her nose with a tissue "—but they aren't the ones with a gaping hole in their chest. Our son is out there. I believe that. And if he sees this, I know it means he is a grown man now, and god—" she chokes on a sob, "—I hope whatever happened to you wasn't as horrible as the things I imagined. I hope you have a good life, but please come home. Let me see you. Please," she begs. "We love you so much. Happy Birthday, baby." She blows me a kiss and waves goodbye.

The video ends, and I'm left staring at a paused, broken expression on her face. *I'm right here, Mom.*

I turn to Badge, whose eyes are glassy. There isn't a dry eye in the room.

"They made a video every year and posted it on your birthday."

"Are they still alive?" I choke, not knowing what to say. "Do I have parents?"

Badge nods. "They still live in Montana. In the same house. They never moved. They always wanted you to be able to find your home," he clears his throat and coughs. "Excuse me." He shakes his head, trying to rid himself of the damned emotions.

"I have parents." My eyes land on Ruby, and she smiles, her face a watery mess. "They looked for me. They're still looking for me. They didn't give up on me."

"They didn't give up on you. No one has ever given up on you," she says.

I hold out my arms, and Ruby crashes against me. Feeling her breaks something inside me. I bury my face in her shoulder and squeeze my eyes shut. God, I feel like that eight-year-old boy all over again. "I remember everything," I whisper to her. I remember my parents' love, how they looked at me, and how happy a family we were.

How much I loved playing Spider-Man. How much I loved joking with my Dad. How Mom would kiss my scraped knees when I fell off my bike.

Then life turned cruel, but knowing I had a good life before all the bad shit happened kind of makes the scars and wounds feel a little bit better.

"I need to go. I have to see them. Do they know?" I rush the questions out to Badge.

"No. I didn't say anything. I didn't want to jump the gun. I didn't know if you needed time."

I let Ruby go and stand in front of Badge and do the one thing I never thought I'd do with him.

I hug him. Tight. "Thank you for looking and not giving up."

That was the toughest thought growing up. I always thought I was forgotten, that no one wanted me, and I was left in a situation because I was hated.

That wasn't the case at all.

I just couldn't be found.

"Always, brother. Always." Badge pats my back, and I turn around and stare at Ruby.

"I already bought us plane tickets," she says. "We leave tomorrow morning."

"Do you want to contact them?" Badge asks.

I shake my head. "No, I... when I first talk to them, I want to see them."

He nods. "I understand that. Do you need any of us to go with you?"

"No, I think I have everything I need." My eyes lock on Ruby, and she blushes.

There is a knock on the door that interrupts the moment, and Reaper claps his hands. "Okay, everyone, let's get our emotions in check. I think we need to plan a big fucking party to celebrate. Maybe when Bullseye and Ruby get back. Bring the folks. I'll spread the word to the other clubs." Reaper opens the door, and the last person I want to see is standing there.

Mateo fucking Moretti.

"Reaper."

"What the fuck do you want, Moretti?"

"I come with apologies. My brother's men were horrible. It's why I fired them. And Bullseye," his attention swings to mine, "I truly had no idea about Diego and how he was connected with you. I want your club to know—anything you need, consider me in your debt. Ruby, your debt has no strings. I'm wiping it clean. Consider it the one thing I can do for my brother's mishaps about the company he kept. And I believe you were looking for this?"

Moretti reaches in his pocket and pulls out a small key, emblazoned with a letter M. It almost looks sticky, like there's dried blood on it. Ruby gasps, sprinting to stand directly in front of him, but I grab her shoulders not to take a step closer. Mateo seems hurt for a moment that I'd think he'd hurt her, but I don't trust him just as much as I don't trust his brother. "Badge told me what you sacrificed. He told me that none of you could open the box that *coglione* put your ring into."

He holds it out to Ruby, who takes it, staring closely at it.

"This key is special," he explains. "The lockboxes my brother's men used were designed to destroy whatever is inside, if not opened with a special key that only he made."

"Where did you get this?" she asks. "And why is it covered in—"

"Respectfully, *mia cara signora*, you don't want to know," Moretti interrupts.

That sends a shudder down everyone's spine.

"Thank you, Mateo."

Tool ducks into the kitchen and grabs the box then hands it to me.

"Are you ready?" I ask her, kneeling low so she can open it.

Ruby nods. She takes the key and gingerly twists it in the tiny lock. The box seems to rattle and shake and move as the gears inside finally give way.

And there it is.

A beautiful ruby ring for my Ruby.

Her eyes sparkling, she slips it on her ring finger and takes my hand.

"Excellent, I hope…" Mateo turns around and pauses before going down the steps. "I hope to see you both at Hall of Lust."

Reaper slams the door closed with a snarl. "How a man can be hated and liked at the same time is a fucking trickery he perfects."

"We love you, Bullseye," Sarah says from her spot on the couch. Her lip wobbling. "I'm so scared," she wails. "I don't want my baby to leave me. They are safe, you know?"

"They'd miss out on a lot of love, though, especially when it overcomes all the hate," I say to her, hoping she understands what I'm saying.

I have finally let go of all the hate.

And now I have space in my life for love.

"And I want to give you this," Ruby smiles, holding out a picture frame for me to take.

It's a simple frame. Silver edges. Lightweight.

But the picture inside is far from simple.

I rub a hand over my mouth when I see a Polaroid of me and Georgia.

"I found it in one of those books. I thought you'd like to have it."

This woman... how the fuck did I get so lucky? I knock the breath out of her when I pull her close. "I fucking love you. I have no idea where I'd be without you."

"You'd be a pain in the ass, just like you were before," Reaper says jokingly.

Everyone laughs, starting to clear the room and wipe the tears from their eyes.

The only people remaining are Skirt and Dawn.

"Thank you," I whisper against Ruby's cheek.

"Don't thank me yet." She takes the frame out of my hands and lays it on the side table. She tugs my hands to the back room where Skirt, Dawn, and I have our fun. "How about we try something new?" her eyes flicker behind me to Skirt. "If you're up for it."

Am I up for it?

I've been *up* for five days.

"Oh, Spitfire. You have no fucking idea how badly I need this."

"Us too," Dawn says a bit flirtatiously behind me, the caress of her hand against my arm.

I think that the party Reaper talked about has just started. I'm going to be the first one to arrive and the last one to leave.

"Oh, and Waylon?" Ruby beckons me to bring my ear to her mouth.

"What is it?"

She raises her head to me and whispers.

"I have the plug in."

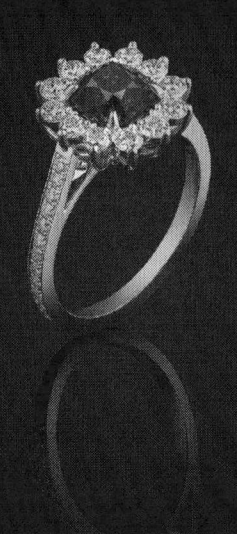

CHAPTER TWENTY-FOUR

Ruby

There are a lot of things I haven't done before, this being one of them. I don't know the rules. All I know is when I talked to Skirt and Dawn privately the other day about setting this up. I wanted to do it. Bullseye loves voyeurism, and I think I do too. I'm open to it, and that's what's most important right now.

On the door is a dartboard with a large peephole in the middle where the bullseye belongs, so anyone interested can peep in as well. Bullseye takes one of his silver darts and inserts the tip in the knob, twisting it until it clicks. My heart thumps as he pushes the door open, and a spacious room comes into view.

Red velvet walls.

A black ceiling with mirrors.

A gold chandelier is hanging in the middle.

The floor is so polished the stone almost looks wet.

I step inside, and the atmosphere around me changes. There are already sexual vibrations coursing through the air, and my nipples bead with anticipation while liquid heat pools between my legs.

I'm excited.

There are two king-sized beds put together. The black headboard seems to be custom-made, with the Ruthless Kings' skull in the middle. The sheets are silk, and on either side of the bed, on two perfectly placed nightstands, is an assortment of lubes.

But I want to know what's in the drawers.

I want to ask how this works and how we get this started because I have no idea. If I ask, does that ruin the mood?

"There is one rule." Bullseye lifts his index finger in the air. "We don't switch partners. We don't touch. We look, we can talk, and since there are four of us, I'm sure accidental touching will happen. It's just us in here. No judgments. You can stare, you can fantasize, you can do whatever you want." He crosses his arms as he shucks off his shirt and tosses it on the ground.

Dawn inhales a sharp breath as she stares at Bullseye. She bites her lip, and her cheeks begin to redden.

"Ye like that, baby? Ye like to see Bullseye's body?" Skirt rubs his hands up and down her arms as he stands behind her. "What else do ye want to see?" he whispers, never taking his eyes off me.

I swallow.

Right.

He's waiting for me.

"Nervous?" Bullseye nips at my earlobe, and I hiss, tilting my head back to give him access to my neck. His tongue slithers along my throat where my pulse is. Lust rears its head like a serpent, hissing inside me. "It's okay. You're safe here," he reassures me.

"I know." My eyes meet Skirt's over Bullseye's shoulder, and Skirt's nostrils flare. Dawn's shirt is off, and Skirt strokes her stomach, where a few stretch marks are from when she was pregnant. She's wearing a cute black lace bra; her skin is smooth and flawless. Skirt's eyes never leave mine as he nips at her shoulder and unhooks her bra.

I hold my breath when the straps slip off her shoulders, and Skirt tosses it onto the floor. His hands are all over her now, gripping and kneading the mounds and twisting her pale pink nipples.

Bullseye's fingers curl around the bottom of my shirt and lift it over my head. "I want you to watch Dawn get on her knees and take Skirt's skirt off." Bullseye swiftly unbuttons my pants and tugs them down my hips. He wastes no time roughly pulling my panties to the side, yanking out the plug, and shoving his fingers between my folds, delving in the slick heat that's ready and wanting.

"Mmmm," he rumbles, taking a deep scent of my juices from the plug. "You have no idea how much I've missed this."

I whimper when he rubs his thumb over my clit. "Are you watching?" he licks the shell of my ear. "I am. Dawn's tits are fucking gorgeous, aren't they?" he speaks a little louder so Skirt can hear, then lowers to a hushed tone for my ears only. "But yours are perfect, Spitfire. They were made for my hands." He uses his free hand to unclasp my bra.

"Aye, Dawn—" Skirt twists Dawn's chin to the side to stare at me. "Look at her. She's a sight, ain't she?" Skirt's brown eyes are a glowing copper as he stares at me.

Lust on fire.

Desire to see me naked and moaning, burning bright in his eyes.

And I ache for the same.

Dawn tugs Skirt's kilt off. He isn't wearing underwear. His long hard cock slaps against his belly, and I gulp.

He's just as big as Bullseye but without the metal.

I wrap an arm around Bullseye's neck. He bends down when I stand on my tiptoes, a gush of liquid slicking my lips as I watch Dawn suck Skirt into her mouth.

"Ah, fuck, that mouth," Skirt growls, his hand on the back of her head as she bobs, yet he still watches me.

"Oh, you like that, don't you?" Bullseye rasps when his finger easily glides back and forth over my hole. "Feels like you like it."

I nod. I do. I love it.

Skirt is gorgeous with all of his tattoos. He is completely different from Bullseye in the looks department. Where Bullseye is has a cleaner appearance, Skirt is grungy, with his lean body and tattoos. His red hair is different from Bullseye's brown. His cock, while veiny and no doubt pleasurable, has no piercings. The piercings along Bullseye's shaft make me come harder than I ever have.

Dawn turns her eyes the best she can as she busies her mouth on Skirt's cock to look at me.

To look at Bullseye.

Bullseye's fingers become drenched, and he growls low in his throat. He slips his hand out of my pants, leaving me aching and on the verge of tears because my orgasm is building. He walks over to Dawn and squats onto the floor, watching as she slurps and sucks Skirt's cock.

"You like sucking your man's dick?" he asks her.

She nods the best she can.

Bullseye slips his fingers that are drenched with my juices into his mouth. "I like sucking Ruby too. She tastes really fucking good. Like honey and strawberries."

"Fuck, that sounds good." Skirt fists Dawn's hair like reins and uses it as leverage to fuck her mouth. She chokes, spitting onto his cock when he pulls out only to shove back in, using her to his delight.

"It is good. It's fucking delicious." Bullseye turns around and unsnaps his jeans, then unzips them. "And I want more." He kicks off his jeans, and his cock is at the ready, solid and thick. The piercings shine in the light, and the studs along either side of his shaft make the ladder.

And I want to fucking climb it.

Bullseye picks me up by wrapping his arms around my ass and lifts me into the air. His face is between my legs, but he can't reach what he wants because my pants are still on. He tosses me onto the bed and, in one swoop, has my jeans on the other side of the room.

Along with my panties.

I'm naked.

In front of Skirt and Dawn.

And I feel empowered.

Skirt tosses Dawn on the bed next; both are naked.

Dawn stares at Bullseye. Skirt stares at me.

Something devious has me turning to him and parting my legs so he can get a good look at me. Bullseye groans and slips his fingers inside me. I clutch the bed, twisting the sheets with my fists, and arch my back.

"Such a pretty pussy," Bullseye praises, then takes his fingers out and slaps his hand against my clit.

"Bullseye," I whine, his name a high-pitched note leaving me.

"Again." He slaps me again, and the jolts shake my thighs. "Come on, Spitfire. Show Skirt how wet this pussy gets." He brings his hand down on me again, then again. It's too much. I'm so heightened from having everyone watch me.

I come.

My entire body spasms as fireworks go off all around me.

"She liked that, Bullseye," Skirt grins, stroking his cock with his hand as he watches me come down from my high.

Bullseye hums in agreement as he rubs his fingers through my sheath, getting them nice and wet with my come. He crawls onto the bed and lowers his head between my thighs. "Time for my strawberries and cream," Bullseye's voice drops an octave to sound seductive.

"Aye, me too." Skirt grabs Dawn's legs and spreads them apart. "Mmm, so beautiful. Can't wait to taste ye, love," he says to her, sending me a wink before disappearing between the apex of her thighs.

I can't take my eyes off Dawn as she whimpers, running her fingers through Skirt's hair as he licks her pussy.

My mouth falls open when Bullseye latches on my clit, sucking it between his teeth and gently rolling the sensitive bead.

"Oh god," I moan.

"Make me come, Skirt," Dawn begs, tugging his hair.

His fingers dig into her thighs, and he yanks her harder against his mouth, snarling like a beast as he laps at her center.

The wet sounds from both men feasting on us have another orgasming brewing.

"You like hearing her moan? You like knowing what Bullseye is doing to her?" Skirt flattens his tongue, circling it around her bundle of nerves. She cries out, wrapping her legs around his neck.

"Fuck, I can't get enough of this cunt, Ruby." Bullseye spreads my legs as wide as they can go and massages my clit until my throat hurts from screaming so loud.

"It's too much. I can't," I gasp, thrashing my head back and forth. I try to close my legs, so my clit isn't so sensitive, but he won't let me. He gives me a warning growl.

"Ye can and ye will. I want to hear ye come again, Ruby. It gets me so fucking hard."

Skirt's admission is enough to send me over the edge.

Bullseye moans as I flood his mouth, and the wet sounds become louder as he becomes greedier, licking and sucking me.

"Yes, oh god," Dawn whimpers, doubled over to hold Skirt's head against her. There's no way he can breathe. She comes too, her legs quaking around Skirt's neck.

Bullseye and Skirt lift their heads at the same time, their faces shining with our juices. Both of them lick their lips as if they have just tasted the best dessert ever made.

I'm on cloud nine with the orgasm high cloaking over my body as he lifts me. "Get on your knees," Bullseye orders.

I do as I'm told, and he spins me around until I'm facing Dawn and Skirt.

"Watch them." Bullseye settles behind me. His cock pressed against the crease of my ass, rutting it slowly as he plays with my nipples.

Dawn's hair fans over her face as Skirt bends her over, pressing his cock against her entrance. My throat goes dry as Dawn turns her head to stare at us. I get to watch the pleasurable expression take over her face as Skirt sinks to the hilt.

His low rumble fills the room when his pelvis hits against her ass. "So fucking tight," he praises. "So wet." Skirt holds onto the thickness of her ass and slams into her unforgivingly. He's rough and unapologetic as he plummets into her depths.

My eyes fall to where they are connected; I can see the pale flesh of his cock shining with her slick as he saws in and out. His balls slap against her with every stroke. "I love this cunt. I'm going to fill you up and get you pregnant again, Dawn."

She cries out as he speeds up his thrusts. He curls over her back and grips her hair, forcing her to turn her head to look at us. Bullseye is worshipping my body, rubbing every inch, kissing along my neck and shoulders, massaging my breasts, rubbing the space between my legs.

He doesn't once ignore me while we watch them.

"Look at him lovin' her," Skirt rumbles. "All gentle—" he punctuates his hips almost violently "—And sweet." He slams his hips against her again, moving her a few inches up the bed.

"Not for long," Bullseye says, suddenly flipping me to my back and ramming his cock into me one stroke.

"Bullseye! Fuck," I whine and sob at the same time with how good he feels.

He stretches me wide, and the pinch of pain from his piercings bites along my walls. It hurts so good.

"I know how much ye like looking at Bullseye's cock. It's filling her up and stretching her out."

"God." Dawn's eyes roll to the back of her head and Skirt smirks, loving how he drives her insane with the dirty talk.

Hell, it's driving me insane too.

I meet Bullseye's thrusts with my own while watching Skirt curl over Dawn, his lithe, muscular body flexing as he drives his hips forward.

He must feel my eyes on him because he looks up through his lashes while kissing along Dawn's spine. When he gets to the base of her neck, he bites down, slamming himself against her again.

My nipple is engulfed in a warm wet mouth, and teeth scrape along the sensitive buds. I break eye contact with Skirt to watch Bullseye switch back and forth between each tit.

He feels so good. Everything feels so damn good.

I rake my nails down his back just as the bed dips. I turn my head to the right and see they have switched positions. Dawn is on top of Skirt now, fucking him with every forceful thrust he gave her.

Skirt's hand touches my arm on accident, and I gasp from the quick, forbidden touch.

"Did you like that?" Bullseye whispers against my ear. "Maybe you want more one day. Maybe—" he next stroke is slow and hard. "—Maybe you want more than a quick touch." He kisses along my collarbone until his lips are tickling my other ear. "I can imagine fucking you while your mouth is full of cock. The image is gorgeous, but I don't know how I'd feel about another man touching you just yet."

The space between us becomes wetter than it has ever been, and he groans, grinning as if he is satisfied that I like that idea. "Maybe one day," he finalizes, then pushes me to the edge of the bed until my head hangs over the mattress, then flips me over. "I love this ass." A sharp pain has me yelping, then moaning when a hard slap follows it. It stings. It burns.

I want more.

He bites into the other cheek. It isn't soft and careful. I'll have a mark there tomorrow.

Dawn has a great view of Bulleye's ass right now.

"Fucking look at them, Dawn. Look at his cock sinking to her. Ye see it? I bet ye do, my filthy fucking girl."

A loud thud sounds, and I wish I could look over my shoulder. Bullseye must sense it because he flips me back over and drags me across the bed by my neck. "Is this what you want to see? Is this what you want to watch?"

Skirt has Dawn pinned against the wall, and every time he slams into her, she cries out. The tattoos on his muscles dance beautifully.

"Oh, god. I'm going to come." Dawn stretches her arms above her head, trying to find something to hold onto.

Bullseye throws me against the wall by my neck. I'm right next to Dawn. I can feel the heat of her body against my own heated skin.

"I think I'm going to take a page out of Skirt's book." Bullseye slides his fat cock in my pussy, continuing to choke me with his hand. "I'm going fill this cunt—my cunt—up with come until you're overflowing and pregnant. Fuck, just thinking about you carrying my kid has me close." He tosses his head back, his neck tendons protruding as he controls himself.

I gasp, wondering if he really knows what he is saying. If he really wants that with me, I'm elated. I didn't think he'd want kids again after...

I claw at him desperately, wanting him to fill me now. "Yes, I want that. I want—" I take a deep breath. "I want—" Then another. My toes curl, and that's the only warning I get before my orgasm hits me, breaking me from the inside out.

My nails dig into the wall, and I accidentally scratch Skirt. I'm too out of my mind with how high I keep climbing as I clench around Bullseye's cock.

"I love watching you fall apart," Bullseye croons, holding onto my ass with a firm grip. He backtracks and falls on the bed, feet on the floor, knees bent, and I ride.

I'm sweating, gasping, and I feel amazing. The air smells of sex and come; I never want to breathe anything else in. "You like that, baby? You like how I ride this cock?" I twist my nipples, wishing they were pierced like his. I bend down and bite one of his dusty brown discs into my mouth. The piercing clinks against my teeth as I roll it around.

"Fuck. Fuck!" Bullseye curses.

I sit back up and moan, sucking my bottom lip into my mouth while I fuck him. "This is my cock, isn't it?"

He nods and his hands are on my hips helping me ride him faster. "Only your cock, Spitfire. Forever."

"Forever," I repeat.

"Just like this is my pussy."

"Yours." The word is broken when the rush of another orgasm hits me. It's right there.

"Look at her tits, love. Look at them bounce. They are fucking gorgeous. Ye aren't even looking. Yer too busy staring at his cock disappearing inside her."

Dawn's eyes are glossed over and glassy when her eyes meet Skirt's. "I can't help it. He's thick like you. So hot. God, I'm burning up, Skirt."

"I got ye, sweetheart." Skirt falls down next to Bullseye.

Dawn's knee touches mine, but it doesn't bother me. It's like fuel, causing me to ride faster. I love watching Bullseye stare at Dawn. His eyes watch her tits bounce, and his tongue pokes out of his mouth. I glide my eyes over to Skirt. He's really great at sensing me because he locks his attention on me. His usual pale cheeks are flushed, and his biceps are flexed while he grabs onto Dawn's hips.

His eyes roll back, and he jackknifes up, holding Dawn close and kissing her chest. He turns his cheek against her, closes his eyes, and settles in the valley of her tits while holding her close. His lips part, and his brows furrow together as sweat gathers along his temples.

His breathing changes, and he snaps his eyes open, staring directly at me as he holds Dawn against him so she can't move. He thrusts his hips up and shouts, filling her like he promised.

Dawn follows next, scratching her nails down his shoulders and leaving bright red trails across his freckled skin.

Bullseye flips us over until I'm on my back again. "Seeing them come has me close," he admits, driving into me unrelentingly.

Skirt and Dawn collapse on the bed, still watching us. I look down to see Skirt's come trickling down her thighs. It's filthy. It's forbidden to see such personal things, but I love it.

My pussy spasms when my orgasm hits, milking Bullseye's cock as he comes at the same time as me.

"Drive in deep, Bullseye," Skirt says. "As hard as ye can. As far as ye can."

"Fuck yes," Bullseye says through a clenched jaw, punctuating his hips with every hot stream flooding my womb. His hand wraps around my throat again, and he jerks my head from looking at the mess between Dawn's legs to focus on him. He bites my bottom lip and tugs it, letting it go with a plop. "Take every goddamn drop, or I'll never give you my come again." He plants himself inside one last time before collapsing and giving me a bruising kiss.

We gasp for breath, and after a few quiet seconds, all of us chuckle at the same time.

"Fuck," Skirt announces, pleased with how that experience went. "Let's do that again."

"All night," I grin, hooking my leg over Bullseye's hip to turn him over. "I'm ready." I lay my chin on my shoulder as I turn my head to Skirt. I glance down at his impressive, semi-hard cock. "If you can handle it, that is," I challenge.

A bead of come drips from his slit as his cock grows to full mast again.

There's my answer.

And I couldn't be more excited to explore this kind of lifestyle with Bullseye.

Alongside people, I trust.

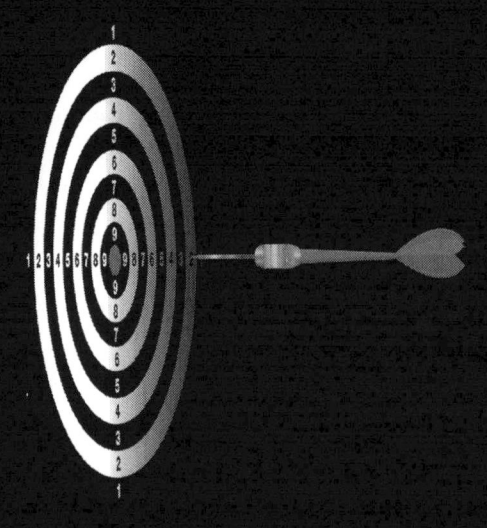

CHAPTER TWENTY-FIVE
Bullseye

"**N**ERVOUS?" RUBY ASKS AS WE PARK DOWN THE STREET FROM WHERE I GREW UP. It's surreal that I'm here again. I never thought I had any of this. I never thought I had a home or people who cared about me, but with one look at my Mom through the TV, everything rushed back. I remember it all.

I curl my hands over the steering wheel of the rented car, staring out the windshield at the house. It's a typical two-story home with a mowed front yard, an American flag waving high from the porch, and perfect flower beds. It looks like they put a lot into their yard. They didn't so much before. Maybe that's what they focused on when I never came home.

The house's siding is pale yellow, and the roof is a rich brown with white rain gutters flowing down the sides. Their mailbox is boxed in red brick, and on the side, it says 'Presley' in big block letters. Even the mailbox has perfect flowers around it.

If I meet them, won't I wreck their lives all over again? They've lived so many years without me. Won't my popping up out of nowhere ruin what they've tried to build? They've tried so many years to overcome their grief, and I'm going to drudge it all up again.

"I don't know if I can do it. They've worked so hard to get where they're at—"

"—Waylon, they miss you. They want you." She slides her hand over my sweaty one. I'm so fucking nervous. "Anyone who doesn't want you is a fool. And they do. They make a video every year, hoping you're out there to see it. You finally saw it. It's their message. It's time to come home, Bullseye. It's time to see them again. I'm here, and I'm not leaving your side."

I nod, blowing out a stressed breath as butterflies fly around in my stomach.

I want to throw up. "I look okay? I look okay, right?" I have my cut on over a gray button-up shirt and have on a new pair of dark denim jeans. I have on my good boots too, but I know that won't be what they're looking at.

They will look at my cut. It's who I am, and besides Ruby, it's the only thing bringing me comfort and settling me. I have the power of the Kings behind me, and it gives me more strength than they'll ever realize.

"You look handsome as ever, baby," she smiles, bringing my hands to her lips and kissing them. "You ready?"

No. God. I want a drink.

"Let's go." I open the door, and the Montana air hits me in the face. It feels and smells different. It's light and pure. It smells like grass. I haven't smelled grass for years.

We shut the doors, and Ruby is in front of the car waiting, holding out her hand for me to take. I do, greedily and needy. If she lets go, I might blow away.

I'm barely managing to keep my feet on the ground.

The house comes closer as we pass their neighbors' driveway. When we get to the yard, I pause. "Maybe we shouldn't walk on it. It's so green and perfect," I mumble, dragging her around to the driveway.

There are two cars that I don't recognize. One a family-size SUV, and the other is a new Toyota Camry. Both vehicles are white. I hang right to the walkway that leads to the porch. My legs are shaking as I climb the steps. The same steps I ran down as a kid to play in the sprinklers in the yard.

Ruby rubs my back. "You okay?"

"Just remembering," I reply.

I remember everything.

The wind blows, and the chimes ring.

The breath leaves my lungs when I see what they're made of. It's the window I broke when I was a kid. I accidentally threw a baseball too hard, shattering the kitchen window.

They kept it.

I look down to see a brown mat that says 'Welcome,' and I almost feel bad for stepping on it because it seems new and crisp without the grunge of dirt and a biker like me.

My finger shakes as I ring the doorbell.

"Kyle, I have the door! Don't let the burgers burn," Mom calls out to him.

"My mom's name is Kendra," I rush out to Ruby. I can't believe I didn't tell her on the flight. I was too caught up in my own shit.

The door opens, and the same blue eyes that haunted my dreams for so many years stare up at me with kindness. Her brown hair is in that messy bun again. There's a lot more gray than before, but it's still a beautiful color. She's wearing glasses, a plain t-shirt, and khaki capris with white sandals.

"Hi, how may I help you?" she says.

"Who is it, Kendra?"

"Don't know," she shouts back to my Dad.

I can't speak. The words aren't coming out of my mouth. They don't recognize me. So I think of the only thing that comes to mind. "You're still the prettiest woman in the world," I rasp through tears.

She inhales. "What did you just say to me? What did you say?" Immediately her eyes water.

"You're the prettiest woman in the world," I whisper.

Mom looks me up and down in disbelief, and in that moment when she realizes it isn't a stranger at her door but her son, she breaks. She sobs and launches herself at me.

"Waylon!" she screams, wrapping her slender arms around my waist, and she squeezes me tight to the point I can't breathe.

"Mom," I struggle to say as I hold her close to me.

The woman who never gave up on me.

"I'm home," I say, kissing the top of her head. I'm taller than her now. She's so small. I don't remember her being so tiny.

Ruby wipes her cheeks and gives me a blinding smile.

I bury my nose in my Mom's hair and inhale. She smells like maple syrup. It floods my mind with memories. "I'm so sorry. I'm sorry. I'm sorry," I repeat, knowing I could never apologize enough.

"No." She lays her palms on each side of my cheek, rubbing my tears away. "Don't you dare apologize. You're home. I knew it. I felt it. I knew my baby was alive." She pats her heart.

"Who is it, Kendra? Are you okay—" Dad stops short when he sees me, and he doesn't doubt for a second who it is because I know it has to be like looking in a mirror for him. "Waylon?" he takes a slow step forward, tentative.

"Dad."

He covers his mouth and catches himself against the wall as he collapses in on himself. I run forward and catch him, wrapping him tight like I did Mom. "I'm here. It's me. I'm right here." He grips the back of my cut so hard I'm afraid he might rip it as he lets out painful, agonizing sounds that tear me apart inside.

"I'm so sorry. I didn't know. I'm sorry." It's all I can say.

Twenty-eight years is a long time to be gone.

"You're real. You're home." He pulls back and touches my face. "Let me look at you. Let me see you." He grabs my neck, shoulders, arms, then back to my face. "I can't believe it. I can't." He holds his hand over his mouth again to try and compose himself. "You look good. You look good, son. You're all grown up. You're a man."

I'm still very much a boy on the inside, mentally. I need that love I never got to have, but now it's right here in front of me.

"Who's your friend?" Mom asks, staring at Ruby with a smile.

"This is Ruby Raine. She's the reason I'm here." It's true. I wouldn't be here if Ruby didn't push and figure out where my past came from. "She made me remember where I came from. I didn't know... when I was taken, my brain shut down. I didn't remember my childhood at all until a few days ago when Ruby talked to a mutual friend, and they looked into my past. They found your YouTube videos. We tracked you down, and I'm here..." I stretch my arm out to Ruby, and she nestles herself in the nook of my side. "She's going to be my wife one day."

"This is the best day of my life," my mom smiles, tears openly running down her cheeks. "Come in. Let's sit down. I'll make tea."

We follow her through the living room. On the walls are pictures of me as a baby all the way through the day, I was taken. Ruby stops at one and tilts her head, laughter in her eyes. I'm happy, smiling, and petting a pig.

"You really wanted a pet pig, and I said no, then your Mom said she'd get you a dog." Dad starts to get emotional again.

"Did you? Ever get a dog?" I ask.

"No. We couldn't. Even your room... it's still the same as you left it. We can't... we couldn't have..."

Damn it, is it normal to cry so much?

I bring him in for another hug and pat his back. "Thank you for never giving up."

"You're our boy. We'll never give up on you." He holds the back of my neck and presses his forehead to mine. "I can't wait to hear about your life. Let's go to the kitchen and talk. Catch up. God, I can't believe you're real. My life is complete."

Mine is too.

I smile and then remember the task Sylvia gave me before everything happened. I've smiled so much that I've lost count.

Happiness was always my goal, but Ruby was my target.

I can't have one without the other. She's bettered my life, made me a better man, and she's brought me home.

Even if my home is with her now.

That's a pretty good bullseye if you ask me.

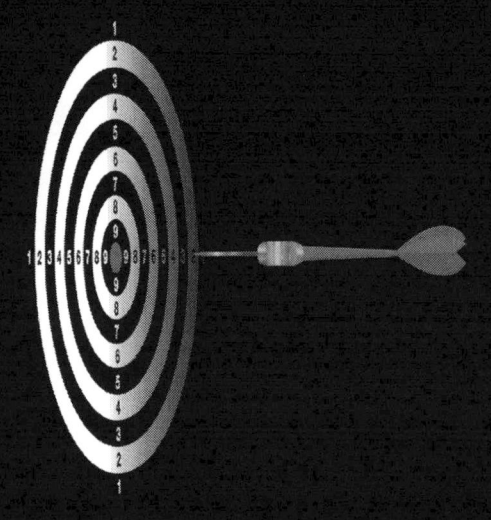

EPILOGUE
Bullseye

Two weeks later

While I was asleep, Ruby locked the cock cage on me. Fuck, I'm already fighting an erection. Thankfully, I'm in baggy sweatpants, and the bulge in the front just looks like my dick. Dawn must know because she's been staring at it all morning. The four of us have gotten a pretty good rhythm down in the last week. We really like same room sex. We have it nearly every night now.

"Like what you see, Dawn?" I tease her as I walk by, sitting next to my one and only.

Ruby Raine.

"Don't I always?" Dawn sasses back. "I can't wait to see Ruby unlock your cage."

"What cage?" Slingshot asks, shoving a scoop of eggs in his mouth, wincing when he bends over too far. He keeps pushing, and Doc keeps yelling at him. He isn't even supposed to be up and walking around. Doc has changed his stitches twice already because Doc had to tranquilize him mid-speed walk to get to his bike to get fucking tacos.

When he hit the ground, the stitches popped open.

He isn't allowed to have tacos, and he hasn't had them in weeks. He's driving us crazy. I didn't realize how many tacos he ate until now since he can't have any.

"Nothing. Inside joke," I say.

The backdoor opens, and my Dad and Reaper come in, laughing their asses off as my Mom follows behind them with Mary.

"Hey, son," Dad greets me, slapping my shoulders then rubbing them for a second. He's done that every morning. They are very touchy-feely parents, but I don't mind. They probably still don't think I'm real, plus I'm soaking up all the attention.

I'm an attention whore.

I love it.

It should have been obvious since I like to be watched.

My parents sold the house and one of the cars and moved right in when Reaper offered them a place at the compound. The premade homes are up and move-in ready, and they jumped at the opportunity. My parents went from being so far away that their existence was so far out of my mind to living just a few houses down.

My life is everything I have always wanted it to be.

"Hey, Bullseye! You got a girl here asking for you," Badge shouts from the main room.

Ruby gives me a sassy look, laying her arm down on the table. "What fucking girl?"

"I have no idea, Spitfire. You're my only pixie. You know that." I kiss her cheek and make my way down the hall, grinning when I hear the patter of Ruby's feet behind me.

Yeah, she's territorial.

I love it.

When I get to the door, a young girl is standing in the middle of the doorway. She's got a large pregnant belly that she is currently rubbing. She's got long blonde hair and dark circles under her eyes. Poor thing looks exhausted.

When she sees me, she straightens, fidgeting with nerves. She lifts a stack of letters in her hand. "Are you Waylon Presley?" she asks, her eyes shimmering.

"That's not my baby," I blurt. "Ruby, I swear—"

"—No, god... No. He isn't the father of the baby."

Phew. This girl can't be more than eighteen. That would have been rough. "Come in. Let's get you a chair. You look like you're close to your due date."

"Any day now," she says softly.

When she sits on the black leather couch, the girls eye her but don't say anything. I pull the ottoman toward her and sit down. As I look at her, some things are familiar. Her eyes. A deep, rich golden brown. Just like Georgia.

"Oh my god," I gasp in shock as I stare at her. The longer we look at each other, the more I know that this girl, this pregnant teenager, is my daughter. Her eyes well with water, and I fall to my knees, running my hands through her long hair.

This feeling. This has to be what my parents felt like when they finally saw me.

I wrap my arms around her and hold her close while her shoulders shake. I stare up at the ceiling and blink the tears away. "You survived."

She nods, and the letters crunch in her fist. "I've looked for you ever since I found the letters." She pushes away from me, but I'm not able to let go. I press my hand against her stomach, feeling the baby kick.

I have so many questions.

"These letters explained everything. Mom wrote them while she was pregnant with me, and she didn't leave out details. I know what happened to you and Patricia—"

"—That fucking bitch. What did she do to you? I'm going to kill her. I thought I did that already," I sneer.

"She's the one who raised me, but she raised me the same way she raised you..."

"No..." I gasp in horror. "No! No, I didn't... I didn't know. She said you died. You were so early... I didn't know."

"I know, Dad. I don't blame you. I'm not angry. Patricia told me everything before... she tried killing the guy I loved like you loved Mom."

God, no.

This is my wildest dream and my worst fucking nightmare.

I get to see the daughter I missed for all these years, only to find out she suffered just like I did.

"He killed her, but he died in the process. I found these letters in Patricia's nightstand when I was looking for cash to leave."

"I'm so sorry. It's..." I swallow. "It's hard to lose the person your world existed around in that environment."

She clears her throat, and I snap my fingers at one of the guys. "Water for my daughter, please."

"Your what?" Badge sounds like his balls haven't dropped yet.

"Daughter. Go get her water, please."

She and Badge stare at one another before he finally leaves to do what I asked.

"What's your name, sweetie?" I finally ask her.

"Hope. Hope Georgia Presley," she says.

I clutch her hand and smile, happier than I've ever been in my entire life. "Hope? Your Mom loved the idea of hope. I am so happy, that's your name. I don't know how that happened."

"Mom survived for a few minutes. Patricia had a birth certificate there. She signed your real name. Not Jennings. Rest is history."

"I didn't know that either." I wish I could have spent the last few minutes with her. "How did you find me?"

"You must have finally registered with the state or something because I searched your name every day, and this address came up."

"You found me," I say with pride. My daughter is strong and independent. "Thank you." I hold out my arms again, and she comes willingly, tired yet relieved. "You're home now. Dad's got you." I'm a fucking Dad. I finally get to be a father to the daughter I never thought I'd get to have. I want to know everything. I need to know everything she knows about the fire and how Patricia escaped with her. "I can't wait for you to meet everyone. The crying girls are Joanna and Sarah."

"Hi," they say in unison, watching us.

"This is my fiancée, Ruby."

"It's so nice to meet you, Hope," Ruby smiles through some tears of her own. "Your Dad has wanted this moment for a long time."

Hope smiles. "Really?"

"Losing you and your Mom… it nearly killed me." Multiple times throughout my life.

"I'm so glad I found you." She hisses. "Oh." Hope leans back and presses her hands against her stomach.

"What is it, Hope?"

"Nothing. I'm fine—" she screams, and then water wets her pants.

A lot of water.

"Holy shit, you're in labor."

"No. No. I can't be. Dad, no," she cries. "I can't do it without him. I can't."

"Someone get Doc!" I crawl in behind her and sit down, leaning her back against my chest. "You can do it. You're not alone, and you'll never be alone again." I take her hands in mine.

"Fuck!" Joanna doubles over next.

No.

Fucking.

Way.

Another splash hits the floor, and the room falls silent.

"Ow, ow, ow! No! Jesse," Sarah screams bloody murder. "Jesse!" She's clutching her stomach, too, tears in her eyes. "Too early. Way too early."

Reaper picks her up and heads out the door without a parting glance to anyone else to rush Sarah to the hospital. Doc finally enters the room, and he is shocked when he sees me since he doesn't know this is my daughter. "One woman is on her way to the hospital, and there are two here still needing to go too."

"No," Joanna reaches out and twists Doc's arm. "Now. The baby is coming now."

"Okay, babe. We got this. I love you," he says, pulling down her pants just in time as her water breaks. He points to me. "Someone take off…"

"Hope," I finish for him.

"Hope's pants."

Ruby gets to work and slings the wet material on the ground.

"Juliette?"

"On it," she answers Doc, snapping on a pair of gloves. She gets between Hope's legs just as Hope and Joanna let out matching screams. "Okay, this baby is coming now. I can see the head."

"Me too. Holy shit, I'm going to be a father. Jo-love, you're doing good, baby. So good." Doc praises her.

"Oh my god, I'm going to be a grandpa." I'm too young to be a grandpa. I literally just found out I'm a dad, and now I'm a grandpa too? My parents are great-grandparents. I look around for them and see Mom and Dad smiling, crying as always as Dad records. They know who Hope is.

I didn't leave out any details when I explained where I was. They deserved to know the truth.

It was a lot of tears and a lot of emotion, but that's okay.

I am not afraid of sharing myself anymore.

That's what makes me strong.

"I can't," Hope gives up, sagging against me.

"Yes, you can. You do not give up. I love you more than anything," I choke, clutching her hand. "I want to see my grandbaby. You better push, sweetheart. Squeeze my hand."

"Ahhh, god!" she yells while she pushes for ten seconds.

"I'm never having another baby!" Joanna shouts at Doc. "Never!"

"You're doing so good," Doc urges her. "So close."

And at the same time, the babies are born. Both are crying at the top of their lungs.

"You want to cut your granddaughter's cord?" Juliette plops a gross, wet, adorable, potato-looking newborn in Hope's arms. The baby is loud, showing off her new set of lungs.

My hand shakes as I grip the scissors and cut.

I wrap my arms around my family while Juliette delivers the afterbirth. "She's perfect." I rub my thumb over her plump cheek. "You did so good." It's easy to fall into the fatherly role since I've always wanted to be a father to Hope. It's like this void inside me is finally full.

Mom and Dad come closer to help Hope up. Ruby reaches from behind me and squeezes my hand. Finally, we're all together—a real family.

"What's her name?" I ask.

"Faith Georgia Presley. Without faith, I wouldn't be here."

"Perfect." I give Ruby a watery grin and mouth, "I love you."

Faith.

The one thing I never had, and now the one thing I'll always love.

My name is Waylon Presley, and I deserve hope. I deserve faith.

I deserve love.

I'm going to live the rest of my life surrounded by family who gives me all that and more.

ACKNOWLEDGMENTS

To our Ruthless Readers we couldn't have done this with out all your support, we love you.

Give Me Books thanks for making this release go smoothly.

To all the bloggers and reviewer, we know you have so many books to review and we're extremely grateful that you choose to read Bullseye thanks y'all are the best.

Wander and Andrey I am so thankful for you both, we could of never gotten this far without you. Bullseye is our 20th cover!! Here to our next 123 other images Andrey claims I have. lol

Donna have been my voice of reason, my biggest supporter, my eye opener when I need it, someone asked what's Donna's role?? Which goes to show how much you do for us lol they think we're paying you. There is no role for you though, even if Andrey would share, I could never give you a role because you don't confine greatness to 1 specific role! BOOM like how I did that? Are you crying? #BOOMERISDONNAS

Lori Jackson Designs thank you for everything, you are always there day or night, I really appreciate all you do.

Harloe thanks for always being there, I miss your face.

Jordan Marie I can't believe it took us this long to talk, my twin wanted to hog you, until the very last minute he could I guess. But's ok the world was not ready for our world to collide, oh the things we'll get into now.

Cassandra Robbins your friendship means the world to me, your positive spin on things always helps me see things differently.

Stacey at Champagne Book Design you never cease to amaze me with all of your designs.

To my Instigator as always you're the best impulsive decision I've ever made.

Lynn as always thanks for being my rock and my better half all these years

Becca, you have been such a huge help thanks for all you do.

Silla, even though we ended up on different paths I didn't forget #bullseyeissillas

Mom love you

Jeff 5 LITTLE WORDS

Austin as always y'all are such a blessing

ORBITING MARS

RUTHLESS KINGS MC™
BOOK THIRTEEN

COPYRIGHT © 2021 ORBITING MARS BY KL SAVAGE

All rights reserved. Except as permitted by U.S. Copyright Act of 1976, no part of this publication may be reproduced, distributed, or transmitted in any form or by any means, or stored in a database or retrieval system, without prior permission of the author. The scanning, uploading, and distribution of this book via the Internet or via other means without the permission of the publisher is illegal and punishable by law. Please purchase only authorized electronic editions and do not participate in or encourage electronic piracy of copyrighted materials. This book is a work of fiction. Names, characters, establishments, or organizations, and incidents are either products of the author's imagination or are used fictitiously to give a sense of authenticity. Any resemblance to actual persons, living or dead, events, or locales is entirely coincidental. ORBITING MARS is intended for 18+ older, and for mature audiences only.

COVER DESIGN: HANG LE
EDITING BY: INFINITE WELL
FORMATTING: CHAMPAGNE BOOK DESIGN

FIRST EDITION PRINT 2021

PLAYLIST

DON'T WORRY BABY BY: THE BEACH BOYS

YOU ARE MY SUNSHINE BY: JOHNNY CASH

SIMPLY THE BEST BY: STEPHANIE RAINEY

THE KILL BY: THIRTY SECONDS TO MARS

LOVE IS MADNESS BY: THIRTY SECONDS TO MARS

TENNESSEE WHISKEY BY: CHRIS STAPLETON

DRUNK ON YOUR LOVE BY: BRETT ELDREDGE

CIGARETTES & ALCOHOL BY: OASIS

HARD TO LOVE BY: LEE BRICE

HOW DO I LIVE BY: TRISHA YEARWOOD

WHISEKY LULLAY BY: BRAID PAISELY, ALISON KRAUSS

IT'S YOUR LOVE BY: TIM MCGRAW, FAITH HILL

BEAUTIFUL CRAZY BY: LUKE COMBS

MAKE YOU MISS ME BY: SAM HUNT

H.O.L.Y. BY: FLORIDA GEORIGA LINE

HOLDFAST BY: MONUMENT OF A MEMORY

PROLOGUE

Patrick

NO ONE KNOWS WHERE I AM. I HAVE MY PHONE OFF. I DIDN'T TELL ANYONE WHERE I was going, and I didn't speak a word to Sunnie about it. I'm too afraid to. After all the progress I've made and all the steps I've taken, I'm starting to relapse.

I want rum.

I want it so fucking desperately it keeps me up at night. I dream about it. When I drink coffee, I find myself wishing rum were in the cup instead. I'll settle for anything at this point. Vodka. Whiskey. Gin. I don't care. My mouth is watering for it.

My body aches for it. My muscles hurt and spasm, and there is this constant throb in the base of my skull.

Slamming.

Pounding.

Screaming at me to give in.

I rub my temples and exhale a shaky breath. My fingers tremble around my sobriety chip as I fumble with it, twisting and flipping it in my palm.

The room fills with people, and the cheap metal chairs scrape against the floor, echoing in the wide-open space. To the left is a table topped with coffee, tea, water, and soda. To the left of the coffee maker are packets of sugar in a container and a bottle of coffee creamer.

Maybe I just need to drink something, and the craving will stop. I stand, rubbing my sweaty palms against my jeans. There are a few new faces here tonight, and they're hovering around the beverage table, away from the regulars. Ah, I remember standing in the back, hoping to not be seen. It'll get easier. It helps being surrounded by people with the same struggle.

I grab a Styrofoam cup and fill it halfway, adding a dash of creamer. I don't bother stirring in it. It isn't to wake up. It's just to do something other than think about alcohol. I take a sip and let the hot java sear my throat, hoping like hell it burns the addiction right out of me.

A younger woman, possibly no more than eighteen, is stirring her tea next to the table. She looks like she's seen better days. She has bright blue hair, which I think is so cool. I've never seen anyone pull off a color like that. She seems sad and is a bit too thin. By the track marks on her arms, I'll say that has something to do with it.

Maybe I can introduce her to Sunnie.

"Hi, I'm Patrick." I introduce myself to try and break the ice, showing her that we aren't a scary bunch.

"Poppy." Her hand meets mine in a firm shake.

I thought it would be limper, considering how she looks.

"So, what's your vice, Poppy?" I lean against the pillar and sip the bitter coffee. It sure the fuck don't go down as smooth as rum.

"Heroin and Vodka. You?" She lifts her eyes to mine, and the dark circles take me back to the early days of recovery.

"Rum, but I drank just about anything."

She nods as if she understands. Her eyes dart around the room. I can tell she's feeling overwhelmed. "I don't know if I can do this," she admits.

"I get it, but don't put so much pressure on yourself. You don't have to speak, but it helps."

"Is this your first meeting?" she stares at me, hopeful.

I snort, bringing the cup to my lips. "Try my thousandth, maybe? I don't know. It's up there. I don't come much anymore because I've been doing better."

She cocks her head and analyzes me. "Why are you here today?"

"Because right now, I wish this coffee was rum, and I'm this close," I hold my finger and thumb barely apart, "*this* fucking close, to saying fuck everything just to get a drink." I toss the cup in the trash and feel a pinch better than I did a minute ago. "Anyway, I'm around if you need a friend. My ol' lady was hooked on heroin too." I pull out a business card with the Kings Garage's number and address on it, but Sunnie's and my cellphone numbers are written on the back. "If you ever need a place, some friends, we know what it's like."

Her small, slender fingers take the card, and she holds it to her chest as if I've just saved her life. "Thank you. That… that's exceedingly kind." Her eyes drop to my cut. "You're a biker."

"I am. We're a rough bunch, but we're good people. We'll help, alright?" I pat her shoulder before I turn around and head back to my seat. There are a few open on either side of me. Everyone tries to leave space between each seat. No one wants to crowd an addict, and everyone respects the other's boundaries.

I dig my hand into my pocket and pull out my chip again, flipping it across my fingers.

"Can I sit here?" Poppy whispers, wrapping her beige cardigan around her torso tighter as she hunches in on herself.

"Yeah, of course." I pat the seat, and her shoulders sag in relief.

The slightest smile tilts her lips to the left. "Thanks. You're the only one I kinda, sorta, know."

"I get it," I reply as Wendy, an older woman who's been coming to meetings for twenty years steps up to the podium.

She clears her throat in the microphone, and everyone quiets down. She has short gray hair, longer on one side than it is on the other. When she smiles, it's reassuring and hopeful, reminding me of a grandmother.

My grandparents died a long time ago, and I haven't talked to my parents in so many years that I've lost count. When Macy died, they pulled away from me with grief, and when I turned eighteen, I left and never looked back.

I don't know if they even noticed I was gone.

"Hi, thanks to everyone for coming tonight. I know it isn't easy to come to these, but AA is here to help you. We are a family in our own way. So I'll start every meeting like I always do, to set the stage for the next person who wants to come up and talk. I see a few new faces, so I hope we get to know each other by the end of the night. I'm Wendy. I've been sober going on twenty-five years. My addiction is going to come as a shock, but it's beer. I loved it—do love it. There isn't a day that goes by where I wish I could have a taste. I've lost plenty to this addiction."

Her voice reverberates off the walls. Her sighs are as heavy as the burdens I've been carrying for far too long. "I've lost my husband, my daughter, my house, my car, my job... I lost it all. When I was at my worst, even when I had nothing, I wanted a beer. I stopped at nothing to get it. I'd beg people on the street. Every penny someone gave me didn't go toward bettering myself. Finally, my son found me sleeping in an alleyway. No matter how much I used him for money, no matter how many times I told him I loved beer more than him—" she chokes on her words and tilts her head down. "—He never gave up on me. He should have. God knows I gave him every reason to. He dragged me to rehab. Now I'm remarried, and I'm an amazing grandma. I live next door to my son, and my daughter has come back around. It isn't easy getting your life together, but it's worth it."

She gives a final grin, and her eyes drift around the room. "Alright, who's up next?" she asks, pursing her lips when no hands are raised. "Oh, come on. Don't be shy. There are no judgments here."

The ache in the back of my throat hits me full force, and I glance toward the exit. My panic rises as my legs shake with the need to run out the doors and find the nearest bar. My nails dig into my palms as I curl my fingers, and I swear to all things, I can hear Macy's voice again.

Taunting me.

Begging me.

Crying for me.

I stand abruptly and lift my hand in the air.

"I'll go," I say.

Wendy gives me a wide smile that takes up her entire face. She scurries away from the podium and takes a seat on a chair against the wall so she can see everything going on.

"Catch ya later, Poppy." I try and squeeze through the aisle but accidentally graze her legs before I make my way out.

"Good luck," she whispers so softly. If I weren't standing next to her, I wouldn't have heard her.

I can feel everyone's eyes on me. It's never easy to speak in front of a large crowd, let alone talk to them about your darkest fucking secrets. I've gotten better at it. I talk about my pain and past, and when I do, the urge to get drunk lessens.

As I stride toward the front, the people sitting in the aisle chairs on either side turn around to stare at me. Their attention has my entire body heating, and my shirt begins to stick to my back from sweat. My boots scuff against the floor, which tells me I need to pick up my feet when I walk.

But I'm too fucking tired to care.

I climb up the steps to the stage, and Wendy stands to give me a hug. "We'll talk after," she whispers, giving me a comforting pat on the back. Not only is Wendy a friend, but she's my sponsor. She's kept me on the path of sobriety since I've gotten out of rehab.

I'm not so sure she's enough anymore.

My feet are planted behind the podium as I look out to the sea of fellow addicts. Some are crying, and others have dazed expressions in their eyes as they daydream or get lost in thought. Most, however, give me their full attention. People have all sorts of horrible stereotypes about what addicts are or what they do. But they're just regular people who are struggling and could use some help.

"Hi everyone. My name is Patrick, and I'm an alcoholic." I grip the sides of the podium, my nails digging in the wood.

"Hi, Patrick," they all reply in unison.

I blow out a breath, and the microphone enhances it. I wince from the sudden whooshing sound. "Sorry. I'm a bit nervous, even though I've done this a hundred times," I admit.

That breaks the ice, and a few people laugh and smile, making what I'm about to say easier. I lean down, bracing myself on my elbows against the wood of the podium. "Anyway, like I said, I'm Patrick. My vice, unlike Wendy's, is rum." I close my eyes as my taste buds come to life, my mouth pooling with saliva as I say the word. "Just saying the word makes me want it."

I hang my head. "It's been hard lately. So hard. I want to walk into a bar and order a drink so badly. I'm tired of not sleeping. I'm tired of dreaming about it. My sister's voice... I've been hearing it in my head the last few days. Her birthday is coming up, and I think maybe that's why I'm having such a hard time. She'd be grown now. Probably successful and caring, beautiful, but she died too young." My eyes begin to water. "I was kidnapped when I was a kid. My sister was too. She was so little. So it was up to me to protect her, and I failed. And now her birthday is around the corner, and I can hardly take it."

I blink up at the ceiling, rocking on my heels. "All I want to do is lose myself in booze, and the more I try not to lose myself, the more lost I become. I want to walk out of here and find the nearest bar, buy an entire bottle, and drown myself in it. Macy, my sister, when I think I hear her voice, she's telling me to drink. She's pushing me to. I know... I know it isn't her. Rationally, I know it's my guilt, but it doesn't ease the craving."

Nothing ever does.

No amount of meetings.

No amount of talking.

No amount of fighting the good fucking fight.

Nothing.

Maybe I should stop pretending to be something I'm not.

The truth is, I'm an alcoholic.

I'll die an alcoholic.

CHAPTER ONE

Sunnie

"**O**H MY GOD," I CROON, FEELING MY OVARIES EXPLODE WHEN I SEE JOANNA LYING in the hospital bed holding her newborn son. Doc is sitting right next to her, arm around her and one hand on the baby. They look like the perfect family.

I wonder if Patrick and I will ever be the picture-perfect couple with children. I didn't think I wanted kids for the longest time but seeing Doc and Joanna holding their son has something inside me stirring.

I want this.

I want this unconditional love.

"We followed behind the ambulance. They wouldn't allow us to see you until you they examined you," I explain, holding Patrick's hand in mine as every other club member and we enter the room.

"Oh, it's okay," she croons, rocking her son gently. "I'm so glad you guys are here. I'm sorry I ruined the couch with my water breaking." She chuckles. She finally looks up from her son. "Is Bullseye okay? How is Hope? That's her name, right? Wait, where is Sarah? Is she okay?"

"Bullseye and his daughter," Poodle emphasizes because we're all still shocked to find that out. "Are doing well. They are in the next room over. We just came from there. Sarah is down the hall; they are trying to stop the labor, but it doesn't look too promising." He pinches his lips together in distress.

Doc strokes his son's cheek and starts to speak cutesy to his newborn. "Well, what's so great is that she's far enough along that there shouldn't be any issues. Isn't that right, Dean? Isn't that right?" he smiles at the baby. "Cutest potato in the world."

"Eric! Stop calling our son a potato," Joanna scolds. I can't help but laugh.

"So you named him Dean?" Knives asks, pressing his hand against Mary's stomach. She'll be next to give birth.

Babies galore.

"Oh, guys. I'm sorry. Meet Dean Eric Forester," Joanna lifts him up so we can all see him.

His face is scrunched up, and his eyes are closed. Dean has pudgy cheeks and a cute dimple in the middle of his chin. What I know about Dean is that he was conceived in a terrible way. Joanna didn't know if she wanted to keep him since she was date raped. I understood where she was coming from since something similar happened to me, and like me, she chose to raise him.

She didn't miscarry like I did. The memory hurts like hell, but I'm so happy for her.

"He's beautiful," I smile, and Patrick takes the time to wrap his arms around me, holding me close.

Something in my chest tightens, and paranoia sets in. I want all this with Patrick, but I'm starting to wonder if he wants it with me. He's been acting strange lately. I think he's having a hard time because of Macy. Her birthday is coming up, but when I ask him about it, he gives me a smile and a kiss and says he's okay.

How can I help if he won't talk to me?

"Thank you," Joanna whispers.

Skirt stands next to Doc and stares down at baby Dean, then looks at Dawn. "This is going to be ye soon," he tells her.

Dawn snorts. "I swear all you want to do is keep me pregnant."

"That's such a bad thing? Ye look so sexy carrying me baby, Dawn."

"Okay, calm down. There are children in the room." Doc covers his son's ears, and everyone chuckles.

"He cannae understand me," Skirt defends himself.

"He's a boy. He'll always understand what S-E-X is." Doc spells out, and Joanna rolls her eyes.

"Eric, he can't spell either. I'm sure it's fine."

"You can never be too safe, Jo-love." Eric bends down and kisses her forehead. "You did so well. So strong. I'm so proud of you."

Joanna tilts her head back and stares at Eric as if he's the reason why the moon hangs high in the sky and the stars twinkle. "I couldn't have done it without you," she says, blinking up at him with all the love in the world.

Doc takes Dean from her hold, and his cheeks become red, and his eyes become glassy. "No, Jo-love, I couldn't be here without you. You have given me... everything. I didn't think it was possible to love someone so much, but I feel like I'm about to explode." He lifts baby Dean and kisses his cheek. Dean begins to fuss, and a loud wail leaves him. "I think my big man is hungry."

"That's our cue to leave," Tool says, placing his hand at the bottom of Juliette's back. "Congratulations, guys."

"I'll make sure tacos are waiting for you," Slingshot grins with a happy farewell wave.

"Yum," Joanna rubs her still-swollen belly.

"Thanks for stopping by. We should be home soon," Doc informs us, not even looking up. His eyes are focused on his son.

I really want to hold him. I know I have plenty of time, but I've never held a baby before. My maternal clock is ticking, and my ovaries are on fire. I want a freaking baby. Maybe I can talk to Patrick, and we can plan if that's what he wants.

If I'm still what he wants. I'm starting to have doubts, the way he's been going missing without saying a word. What if he's met someone else?

His lips find my temple at the ridiculous thought, and I sigh contentedly, remembering he'd never do that to me. Those are my insecurities. They have to be. He loves me. He's saved me. He's killed for me. Doubting him is something I can't do. With our personalities, doubt can lead us to a very dark path.

In the fear and torment of who I used to be, I met Patrick, whose fear and torment twisted with mine, and we somehow canceled each other out. Somehow, we are each other's puzzle pieces.

"Next stop, Reaper?" Patrick asks the crowd of bikers.

"Hell yeah."

"Let's go."

"I hope Sarah is okay. She deserves happiness," Mary adds after everyone has said their peace.

"Has anyone contacted Boomer to let him know she's in labor?" I asked, sweeping my eyes across the men.

"I called him. He's on his way with Scarlett. He'd never want to miss this." Tool wraps his arm around Juliette's shoulders.

I nod, relieved her brother was called. "And Tongue?"

A moment of silence passes between everyone. "No one has called him. Why? You know how close he and Sarah are."

"They're kind of on the outs. I didn't know if she'd want him to know, and I didn't know if he'd want to know." Tool scratches the back of his neck. "Which sounds way more dramatic than it is. I'll call him. I know he has a lot going on with Daphne still."

"I'm sure he'd still like to know. Maybe he'll surprise us all and finally come home," Knives comments, rubbing Mary's belly when she groans. "I miss that crazy, blade-licking bastard."

We all do. The clubhouse isn't the same without him.

Patrick's hand slides down my arm until he intertwines his fingers with mine. "I love you, Sunshine," he says.

Then why are you pulling away from me?

"I love you too." I squeeze his hand, doing my best to calm my whirling thoughts and stop overthinking everything.

Doctors and nurses part as the sea of bikers wearing cuts and heavy boots walk down the middle of the hall. It's an intimidating sight. In all honesty, everyone should be intimidated. All of these men can kill—and have.

But don't undermine the ol' ladies.

We can kill, too.

"I don't give a fuck what you have to do! You'll stop this fucking labor, or I'll cut your goddamn heart out. You got me, Doctor?" Reaper roars from inside the patient room.

"Oh boy," Tool mutters, hurrying between us from the back of the crowd. He swings the door open to find Reaper slamming the doctor against the wall.

Sarah is lying there calmly reading a magazine as Reaper puts the fear of God into the doctor.

"We can only stop it for so long. We're doing the best we can." The doctor squirms in Reaper's hold. He is smaller and skinnier than the Prez. Reaper looks like he could break him in half.

"Do fucking better!" Reaper roars, throwing his fist next to the doctor's head, which puts a hole in the wall.

The doctor's eyes follow his fist, and his prominent Adam's apple bobs when he sees the destruction Reaper can do.

"Reaper, let the poor doctor go. He can't help if our baby wants to come early. He's doing what he can," Sarah drawls out slowly as if she's bored. She licks her fingertip before flipping the page of the magazine.

"He needs to do more." Reaper cocks his head and inches his face closer to the doctor, engulfing him with his menacing presence. "And you're going to, aren't you?"

"I—um, I—there, well… maybe," he stutters over his words.

Tool grips Reaper's shoulders and drags him away from the poor man. "Okay, Reaper. You need to cool it. Calm down. Go take a walk. We'll stay here."

"I'm not fucking going anywhere," Reaper snarls, charging at the doctor again.

Tool snags him by the cut and tosses him backward. "Reaper, go take a fucking walk. Now. The stress your causing isn't good for the baby. You aren't helping the situation."

Reaper's face falls, and when he looks at Sarah, he's as white as a ghost. His hands tremble when he runs them through his hair. "I'm so sorry, Doll. I just want you safe. I need you to be safe."

She holds out her hand, and he rushes to the left side of the bed, taking the hand without the IV in it, then cupping her pregnant belly.

"I love you both so much. I'm so scared something will go wrong." Reaper glares at the doctor with watery eyes. "I guess I'm sorry. I'm worried."

Patrick snorts. "That's one hell of an apology."

"I'll take it," the doctor says. "I'll be back to check on you every fifteen minutes, okay? Your baby is healthy. Might spend some time in the NICU, but I don't see any detrimental problems. I'm more concerned with the tear in your abdominal muscle. The longer we wait, the bigger it can become. I know you wanted a vaginal birth, but I don't think that can happen. If we do a C-section, I can repair the tear too."

"You'll do whatever the fuck is necessary," Reaper sneers, and Sarah slaps him on the back of the head.

I giggle.

"Be nice."

Reaper grumbles. "Sorry."

"I understand, doctor. Thank you," she glares at Reaper. "For being so professional while my caveman guy here is an asshole."

"Doll, I'm only looking out for you two."

"You're being a dick," Sarah snips as she adjusts herself in the bed. "Listen to the doctor. If you snap at him again, I'll withhold the things you love most."

His mouth opens, then closes, then opens again, but Reaper gives up and sags in the chair. He crosses his arms and pouts but doesn't say another word. Sarah is the only one I know of to calm him down and shut him up without him getting violent.

The doctor leaves as fast as he can, his white coat floating behind him like a cape. Skirt grabs his arm on the way out the door and leans in to whisper in his ears.

"She might have him by the sack, but not me. If anything happens to that woman or her baby, each and every single one of us will come after ye. No one will be able to find yer body because yer limbs will be scattered along the desert. Do I make meself clear?"

"No pressure, right?" the doctor nervously asks, his voice cracking from fear.

"Nope. None." Skirt lets go of his arm, and the poor guy runs toward the nurses' station for sanctuary.

"That wasn't necessary. Come on. Give the guy a break," I pipe up, taking a seat against the wall by the window. "I'd like to see you bikers do better to deliver a baby."

"Thank you, Sunnie. That's what I've been trying to say to Reaper all morning, but he won't listen to me," Sarah replies.

"I'm listening now," he mutters unhappily, kicking the floor with the steel-toe part of his boot.

I open my purse and grab the book I always read to Patrick. Samuel and Elizabeth have an entire series of books, and I read it to him every night. I don't know how we bonded over a historical romance, but we have.

It's our thing.

"You reading without me, Sunshine?" Patrick takes a seat next to me, and I snuggle into the crook of his arm, inhaling the leather of his cut. "You know we save the dirty parts until later," he whispers into my ear so no one else can hear.

I look around to make sure no one is watching us before replying, "Maybe I want to read the dirty parts now. Have you aching for me all while I'm wet for you?"

"You better hush that mouth, or I'll take you to the nearest closet and fuck that mouth until you can't speak for a week," he warns.

I inhale a sharp breath, and my cheeks redden. I tuck a piece of my blonde hair behind my ear. "Well, maybe that's something I want. Ever think of that?"

He growls low in his chest, and I ignore him, humming happily as I open the book to where we left off.

"You're a tease."

"I know," I say, matter-of-factly. "Don't you love it?"

"Hey—" Sarah's voice cuts through our lustful daze. "How is everyone? Joanna? Bullseye? Is anyone going to talk about the biggest shock ever? Hello! He has a daughter. He isn't that old, and she's grown."

"I'm happy for him after everything that's happened," I say, turning the page mindlessly. "He thought she was dead for all these years. He's so happy. She's healthy, and her daughter is healthy too. He can't stop holding Faith. Hope is resting, and Ruby is so supportive. We walked in, and he didn't even notice us. His focus was on Faith. Ruby had to update us."

Sarah wistfully sighs. "So sweet. I'm so happy for him. I can't wait to meet the babies, which reminds me—" she glares at Reaper and narrows her eyes.

"—I'm being quiet. I haven't even done anything," he protests.

"Well, I remember a certain someone saying they're going to bring the cut-sluts back on Friday nights?"

"Doll, for the single members. Not for me." He strokes her cheek with his knuckles.

"Well, I think something else needs to happen. Maybe you need another business, so cut-sluts can go there. We have kids in the clubhouse now. I don't want them around a bunch of whores trying to get on their knees. And I know they'd try to suck everyone's cock. That's what they do. And that's drama—Ohhh," she winces and clutches her stomach.

"Doll?" Reaper stands and hovers over her. He turns his head to stare at the monitor that's beeping fast. "Doll, what's wrong?"

"Thinking of those fucking sluts has got me all pissed off, and I'm having contractions again." She cries out, doubling over in pain again like she did at the clubhouse. Tears drip down her face, and the baby's heart monitor is beeping fast.

Too fast.

The doctor quickly runs into the room at the sound of the monitor.

"Oh my god," I gasp in horror when I see blood pooling on the bedsheets.

"Why is there blood?" Reaper rasps. "What's happening?" he yells as the doctor lifts her gown to examine her.

Sarah's body begins to shake, and her eyes roll to the back of her head as she seizes.

"Doll? What the fuck is happening?"

"Everyone out!" the doctor yells over the havoc. "Out. We need to rush her to surgery now."

Nurses come into the room next, giving her some type of medication the doctor shouted to stop her seizing.

I'm being ushered out of the room, and I can't stop crying seeing her like that. Why can't Sarah have an easy birth? Why does her pregnancy have to be so complicated?

"I'm not leaving! You can't make me leave. That's my ol' lady. I'm not going anywhere."

"Sir, you have to leave. She's being rushed to surgery," one of the nurses explains.

"I don't give a fuck. I'm staying. Doll, I'm here. I'm right here."

Tool wraps his arms around Reaper to stop him from following them out of the room. Prez fights him, kicking and pulling, then smacks his head against Tool's. Tool tackles him to the ground, with Skirt and Patrick following, holding down his arms and legs.

The wheels of the bed track a thin line of blood across the floor.

The doctor runs next to her as they disappear into the elevator at the end of the hall. All that's left is a path of blood against the white floor.

It's haunting.

"My babies," Reaper gasps, sweating as he struggles.

Patrick's hair becomes damp with sweat as he fights to hold Reaper down. It takes three men to hold down one. Reaper is a madman when it comes to Sarah. He's unstable.

He turns his cheek against the floor, and his wet eyes land on the blood. "My babies," he chokes, sagging against the floor as fear takes hold.

We're all scared.

Fear has the ability to multiply and divide, hitting anyone and everyone if it wants.

It never just takes one victim.

It takes everyone it touches.

A nurse comes in with a syringe for Reaper. "It will calm him but won't knock him out."

"Do it," Tool orders.

"No! No, don't you fucking dare, Tool. I'll kill you. You'll get an arrow for this," Reaper thrashes against him, and the nurse stabs him in the neck without hesitation. "You'll... I'll never... forgive you." The words slur as he begins to calm, but it's followed by quiet sobs. "I can't lose them. I can't lose another child again," he admits on a strangled croak.

"Go. Everyone out. Leave us!" Tool raises his voice and points to the door.

Skirt and Patrick get off Reaper, and once they're out in the hall with the rest of us, Tool slams the door to the room.

An earth-shaking, groundbreaking, soul tearing roar thunders in the room behind the door.

The sound of pain reminds me of how I used to feel. I scratch the inside of my left arm where my track marks are.

My heart breaks at the sound of his agony, and the urge to shoot up again chips a small piece of my stitched soul.

Sarah has to be okay.

They have to be okay.

Or nothing will ever be the same.

CHAPTER TWO

Patrick

SHE CAN SENSE THAT I'M PULLING AWAY. I DON'T MEAN TO. I DON'T KNOW HOW I'M doing it; I don't know where to start to explain or how to tell her that she has fallen in love with a weak man. She stood by me at my worst, read to me, and nursed me back to health when alcohol had poisoned every inch of my body. I can't do that to her again.

I can't put my Sunshine through that again.

She lets out a big exhale and rests her head on my shoulder while reading her book. I slip my hand into hers. I need to feel her, need her to ground me before the craving becomes too much. Before I float away.

Sunshine is my anchor.

I'm her raging sea.

And yet she holds fast and stands firm, bracing herself against the heavy winds and rains from loving me.

She takes the black, cloudy skies of storm and turmoil always wrecking my insides and clears them up with her sunshine.

Rehab didn't save me.

Sunnie did.

And I'm afraid she's going to have to save me again. Will she still love me? Will she love me through it? Is saving me twice something she has the strength for? Or will I drown in the raging waters because I've sucked all the strength from her?

No. No, I can't think like that. I can't be selfish. Sunnie is my priority. I can't fall back into my old ways. I refuse.

We're in the waiting area right now, hoping for an update on Sarah. Reaper is sitting on the floor, leaning against one of the pillars. He might appear to be calm, but I know this Reaper. He's barely holding it together, and if he breathes, if he suddenly moves, he will kill someone. He's sluggish from the medication the nurse gave him to calm down.

He hasn't spoken to Tool, Skirt, or me since we held him down. He won't even look at us. I can't blame him for being mad, but he was losing it.

Understandably.

"Hey, Reaper—" Skirt tries to break the tension by talking to him.

Reaper lifts his hand. "—Don't fucking talk to me. No one fucking talks to me. The next person who tries, I'll cut your heart out right here in the goddamn hospital, and they can use it to save someone who's fucking useful." He keeps his eyes shut the entire time and speaks evenly, without yelling, at the same volume level.

It's scarier than the anger because he's letting the rage brew and simmer. All of us are in danger of his fury. Sitting here waiting for an update on Sarah, and the baby has my nerves shot. I'd give anything for a small sip of alcohol to calm my nerves. Reaper had a lot of patience with me over the years when I was a constant drunk, so his being furious with me makes me uncomfortable.

"Family of—" the doctor isn't able to finish his sentence before all of us stand.

The leather of our cuts creak, and the chairs groan from the sudden weight difference. Reaper pushes everyone aside, swaying from being drugged, but still manages to walk to the doctor.

He's currently shaking in his scrubs, staring at all of us.

"Is it Sarah? Is she okay? She's okay, right? The baby? Is the baby healthy?" Reaper slurs over a few words as he worries his fingers through his hair. He isn't shouting like I expect him to. He's quiet, and his voice is trembling.

"Yes, your daughter is okay," the doctor informs us with a smile.

A few of us gasp, and Sunnie grips my wrist with her hand from shock.

Reaper's breath whooshes out of his lungs. "A daughter? I have a little girl. Really?" As he talks, his voice becomes higher with emotion. "She's okay?"

The doctor places his hand on Reaper's shoulder, which is funny to see considering how much smaller and shorter he is. "Mister, um... Reaper, I promise your daughter is extremely healthy. She's on her way to the NICU, nothing serious, just a precaution, okay? I want to get her lungs a little stronger. Other than that, she'll be ready to take home in a few weeks."

"And Sarah? How is Sarah? What happened? Is she going to be okay?" Reaper sounds desperate. He's wringing his hands together, shuffling his weight on either foot. "Please," he begs, something that a man like him never does.

"Reaper—" the doctor begins to say.

"—No." He shakes his head. "No. No. No." Reaper's knees buckle, and Tool is the one closest to him, reaching out to catch Reaper as he crumbles. Reaper holds on to Tool for dear life, fisting the back of Tool's cut to hold himself up.

"Hey, no, I'm sorry. I didn't mean to scare you."

I let out a relieved breath like everyone else, but then I narrow my eyes at the doctor. Why the fuck would his tone sound so serious if she isn't dead?

Reaper's eyes are red, but his cheeks are dry. There are a few things I've seen that man cry about, and it's Sarah and Boomer. To him, the world stops and starts again with those two. Reaper licks his lips and swallows. "She's okay?" he asks, blinking at the doctor with hope.

The doctor winces and pinches his lips together. "She's alive. The pregnancy was overly complicated, but it wasn't the tear in the abdomen that caused it. Her placenta tore and
then she had a seizure."

"A seizure? What the fuck are you talking about? She's young. She's healthy." Reaper's shoulders rise and fall as his breathing picks up. Slingshot and I both take a step forward at the same time to try and calm our Prez down, but Tool shakes his head for us to stop.

"Things like this sometimes happen, for reasons we don't understand. I need you to understand something," the doctor gestures for Reaper to sit down, and Reaper runs his hands over his exhausted face before plopping in the seat across from him.

Everyone follows the Prez's lead after that, and we all take a seat.

"Just give it to me straight, Doc. Don't bullshit me. Don't give me false hope. Don't fucking do that." Reaper levels him with his menacing eyes. Braveheart and Tank shrink back from the icy daggers Reaper is throwing at the doctor.

"Okay," he sighs, ripping the scrub cap off his head, showing messy damp hair. "Sarah's condition is severe. I don't know when she'll wake up. We got her on medication as soon as possible, which helps if you catch it right away. The sooner, the better, and the side effects won't be so extreme. I don't know what her prognosis will be when she wakes up. She could be fine and normal, but she could have issues speaking or issues with certain cognitive functions."

"But she's alive?" Reaper asks again to double-check.

"She's alive, but she won't be able to have any more children after this. I tried to save her reproductive organs, but I couldn't get the bleeding to stop. There was so much damage. She kept hemorrhaging, and as much blood as we would put in, she'd lose minutes later. I'm sorry, but I had to perform a hysterectomy."

"A hyster…" Reaper drops his head in his hands. "She's so young. She wanted more kids."

"With her history, I doubt future pregnancies would have been easy on her."

"But she's okay? She'll wake up, right? She has to. We have a newborn who needs her mom. I can't… I can't do it without her. She has to wake up."

"She'll wake up," I say with conviction. "She's survived so much more than this. She's strong, Reaper."

"That she is," the doctor agrees.

"Can I see her? Can I see my daughter?" Reaper questions, pressing his palms against his eyes. "I need to see her."

"You can hold her too. We just ask you provide skin-to-skin contact because usually, that's the first thing they experience with their mothers."

"I'll do anything, but what about Sarah?"

"She's still in surgery. They're closing up as we speak. Why don't I take you to see your daughter?"

"We don't have a name." It dawns on him, and his eyes widen. "She doesn't have a name. What am I going to do if Sarah doesn't wake up? I don't know what to name her."

This time I close the distance between Reaper and me and squat down in front of him, squeezing the side of his arm as I look him in the eyes. Damn, he's hurting. "You don't have to ever worry about that. Okay? The name will come to you when the time is right, and Sarah will wake up. She would never leave you, or Maizey, or your newborn daughter. She'll come back to you. She always does."

He nods, standing, looking like he might either puke or pass out with how pale his face is. "Right. She always does." He rolls his shoulders and pops his neck. "Tool, from this moment on, you're acting President."

A dead silence washes over everyone, and Tool clears his throat. "You sure? Think about this, Prez."

"I don't think I need to. I can't focus on anything other than my girls right now. As for club business, I don't want any part of it. Don't come to me unless someone is dying. My focus is on my daughters and Sarah. Can someone please get Maizey from the babysitter and bring her here? I want her to meet her sister. I want her to see her Mom." He coughs to cover up his emotions. He claps his hands together and announces, "From this moment on, Tool is acting President until I say otherwise. Patrick? Come with me, please. Doctor, take me to my girls." Reaper doesn't give anyone a second glance as he turns around and follows the white coat.

"I'll be here waiting when you get back," Sunnie says, stepping on her tiptoes and giving me a kiss on the cheek.

"You better be." I cup the back of her head and smash my lips against hers, my soul feeling settled for the first time since this morning. I squeeze her hand as I walk away, and Tool is still standing there staring off into the distance. He looks odd without his screwdriver in his ear. Hospital policy won't allow him to have it, but I'll bet anything it's in his pocket. "You'll be great, Tool. Don't sweat it." It's the wrong choice of words, considering he's actually sweating. Several large drops slide down the side of his temple. His brown eyes are round, and the way his lips are moving tells me he's silently talking to himself.

I can't hear him.

"Tool?" I snap my fingers in front of him, and he blinks out of whatever trance he's in. "You're going to do great."

"Let's go, Patrick. I don't have all fucking day," Reaper yells from the double doors we have to enter through.

I give Tool a strained smile before jogging across the worn blue carpet to catch up with Reaper. I nearly run into a nurse wearing seafoam green scrubs carrying a container full of... yep... that's piss. "Oh shit," I curl my body away from her, but she's startled. It's too late.

She drops the container to the ground, causing the lid to pop off.

And now I have piss on my boots.

Slingshot snickers as he watches the ordeal from the waiting room. His fist is pressed against his chin, and his elbow is propped up on the armrest of the chair.

"I'm so sorry. Oh my god, I didn't even see you there." She spins around and runs down the hall, leaving me alone to deal with the piss.

Are you fucking serious?

"I want to see my daughter, Patrick. I'm leaving you here. Come back when you're done." Reaper slams the double doors open, making them swing so hard that the left side hits my shoulder when the momentum carries them backward.

Son of a bitch.

My eyes search for Sunnie, and she's with Juliette, Melissa, and Dawn, huddled up in a small circle as they point and laugh. What is this, high school? Sunnie blows me a kiss and winks at me. For some reason, that makes me feel better about the piss on my boots.

And I just cleaned them.

The nurse comes rushing back down the hall with her arms full of towels and cleaner. Oh good, I was nervous she left me for a second. "I am so sorry. I can't believe I did this. It's my first day on the job. All I had to do was take the urine cup to the lab, and I wasn't watching where I was going. I was too nervous that I'd drop the cup. So I didn't look away from it, you know?"

I open my mouth to answer and tell her it's okay, but without taking a breath, she continues, "And I stayed up so late last night because I couldn't sleep. I was so nervous about today. I showed up an hour early only to clock in five minutes late because on the way here, I got coffee, and I spilled it all over me when I tripped over the curb."

This girl is a walking, talking disaster.

She's on the floor cleaning up the pee, then spritzing the cleaner on my boots as she cleans them. I lift a brow and look at Slingshot, who is laughing so hard he has tears coming out of his eyes.

"So then I spilled the coffee on my scrubs, right? And luckily, there are always extras around here, but as I was walking to the locker room. I didn't see the wet floor sign, and I slipped and busted my butt on the floor."

Isn't a wet floor sign bright yellow? How does someone miss that?

"So then I finally get to the locker room and change, only for my hair to get caught in my locker as I closed it."

"Sounds like a rough morning." I clear my throat and bend down, gripping her by her shoulders to help her up. I glance at Sunnie so she can see me. She's covering her mouth with her hand chuckling up a storm. I'm glad everyone else can laugh about this. I bet all I'll be able to smell for the next week is piss.

"Listen...."

"Ari," she beams up at me with a bright smile.

Whew, she's happy, too. She kind of reminds me of Sunnie.

All the happiness all at once... I'm never ready for it. It's still kind of annoying, but I love Sunnie and all her quirks. This girl acts as if she had cocaine instead of creamer in her coffee. Christ.

"Ari, that's a nice name. I have to go follow my friend to go see his baby now. I'm sorry about your morning and thank you for cleaning my boots. But do you see that guy there?" I point to Slingshot, who immediately stops laughing. "He's too afraid to admit it, but he has this terrible rash... you know... down there," I point to my dick, and she gasps, her cheeks turning bright red. "And it's getting pretty bad. Someone needs to look at it. Do you think you can do that for me?"

"Of course. I'm a nurse. That's my job." She straightens her spine and flips her short hair over her shoulder.

"Thanks, Ari. You're a gem." I gently push her forward, meeting Slingshot's confused gaze. I flip him off and head through the double doors, hoping like hell Reaper isn't going to take me to an operating room and cut out my heart.

Only thing is...

I have no idea where to go.

And I don't ask where to go. I'm a man. I never need directions.

Ever.

It's simple. All I have to do is follow the signs. My freshly-cleaned boots scuff against the floor, and the bright lights have me squinting my eyes. My breath comes in short pants as an eerie feeling takes hold. The fluorescent lights strobe above me, and a dull ache begins to throb at the base of my skull.

This reminds me of rehab.

A tendril of sweat breaks from my hairline as I turn the corner and start to walk faster.

Bubba.

I skid to a stop. The rubber of my boots squeaks against the tile floor.

That's impossible. Her voice isn't inside my head anymore. I'm not drunk. I haven't touched a drink. It's my nerves or paranoia, maybe stress.

Bubba.

I close my eyes and count to ten. "One, two, three, four, five—"

Bubba.

"Six—"

"Sir? Do you need help?" a woman's concerned tone has me snapping my eyes open. Her head is tilted to the side. A piece of hair sticks out of her messy bun she has plopped on top of her head.

"Sorry. Yeah, I'm fine." I wait for a beat to make sure Macy is gone. "I'm so nervous about seeing my niece. She was just born. I needed a minute." Not a total lie. I'm good at tiptoeing the line of truth.

Her face softens. "Aw, that's so sweet. I understand. I just wanted to make sure you were alright."

"Actually, I'm a bit lost." Someone take my man card. I'm asking for directions. "Can you point me to the NICU?"

"Down the hall, take a left, down another hall, take a right, and you'll see it."

"Thank you." I quicken my footsteps to get out from under the haunted light that's taking me back to my worst moments. "It's all in your head, Patrick. She isn't real. She's been gone a long time. Cool it." But the self-pep talk doesn't really seem to work on me.

Something is *wrong* with me. I shouldn't be hearing her voice.

I rub the muscles in my neck as I turn the corner, and when the walls turn from a dull white color to a pale yellow with butterflies, I know I've made it to the NICU. On either side of me are huge glass windows full of incubators with babies struggling to live.

After today, I hope Sunnie doesn't want kids. I can't go through this with my own child. What kind of father would I make anyway? Sunnie is strong, kind, and caring. She's a fantastic nurturer. Me? I'm a fuck-up. I don't deserve to be a father. What son or daughter would want me as a dad?

I'd be an embarrassment.

How many games would I miss because I fell off the wagon and was drunk? How many dance recitals? Birthdays, anniversaries... the list goes on and on.

The steady beeping of the machines fires sorrow into my heart like a freshly shot bullet. Fuck. Why do these little ones have to struggle to live when a man like me deserves to fight for his life after everything I've done?

These babies are innocent.

I'm a guilty man using up oxygen and the space they need to thrive.

I keep checking each room I pass for Reaper. I pass decorations and drawings hanging from the ceiling from parents and siblings to wish their babies well. They've made the NICU as warm, comforting, and friendly as possible, given the circumstances.

Being here surrounded by all these people that give a damn has me feeling better. Wanting to be better.

But we all don't get what we want.

I get to the end of the hall and peer into the window on my right when I see Reaper. The pediatric nurses are helping him get settled, and they all have big smiles on their faces. I don't want to interrupt Reaper's moment with his little girl.

And it's a beautiful moment.

He isn't a badass biker right now. He isn't the President of the Ruthless Kings MC. He isn't the man who cuts out hearts just to watch them beat.

Instead, he's something better than all of that.

He's a father.

One nurse is an older woman with long dark hair that's streaked with gray. She's wearing pink baby scrubs, and the smile on her face is infectious. It is for me, but for Reaper, it doesn't work. He's red-faced as he stares down into the incubator, big fat tears rolling down his face. I have no doubt he wouldn't care who saw him like this right now.

It's an emotional time. Hope is high, but so is fear.

The nurse—let's call her Fiona because that's what she looks like to me—helps Reaper take off his leather cut. He barely puts in an effort to get undressed. He's focused on his daughter, smiling at her as if she made all of his demons disappear. I don't think I've ever seen him so happy before.

Happy and devastated.

The nurse whips off his shirt, folds it, places it on the nightstand, and then guides Reaper to the chair. Fiona, our nurse friend, opens the incubator and gathers a tiny baby wrapped in a pink blanket. She has tubes and hoses and stickers all over her body so the machines can do their job to keep her alive.

Reaper swallows and holds out his arms. He's shaking, and when Fiona places Baby Reaper—let's call his newborn that, since she doesn't have a name—in his arms, he breaks.

He holds her close and kisses the top of her head, and breathing her in. He says 'I love you' over and over again.

I knock on the outside wall and peek my head in. "Does someone have a baby for me to see, or what?" I ask, trying to lighten to mood.

It's intimidating to see such a small person hooked up to all these machines. I hope her condition isn't as bad as it looks because all this equipment is freaking me out.

"Yeah, Patrick, yeah, come here. Come look at the most beautiful girl in the whole world." Reaper holds her carefully, like a delicate family heirloom, holding her out for me to see. She's small, and I can tell she's premature, but she looks good. "Isn't she perfect?" his voice cracks. "I never thought in a million years I'd be here. Look at her little hands wrapped around my index finger. How can something so tiny hold so much power?"

"Baby Reaper is adorable, Prez. She looks good too. Strong."

"Oh, she is. Her oxygen levels are better than we hoped. I think she'll be out of here before you know it," Fiona pipes in. "I'm Nurse Felicia."

Damn it! I'm so close.

"I'll be taking care of Baby… Reaper? Tonight." She sounds unsure, and I can't help but snort.

"Let's not call my beautiful angel Reaper. What the… heck—" Reaper remembers he' in a room full of children "—Are you thinking?"

"Well, she's a fighter. A survivor. Just like her dad. I think Baby Reaper suits her," I offer. The annoyance drains from his face.

He nods, stroking his finger down her cheek. It's funny that her entire face is so tiny compared to his hand. I'm witnessing a beast becoming tamed. "Yeah, I can see that. Hey, video call Tongue for me. I know he'd want to see this since he can't be here right now."

"Sure." I'm still wondering why I'm back here with him, but instead of asking, I dig into my pocket, get my phone out, pull up his number, and hit video call. I scoot behind Reaper's chair as the phone rings.

Tongue answers the phone with a grunt. "Is Sarah okay?" are the first words out of his mouth.

Reaper sighs. "It's going to be a long road, Tongue. They just got done with her surgery, but I wanted to show you someone."

I angle the phone down to show him Baby Reaper.

"It's a baby," Tongue whispers with awe.

Reaper chuckles. "Yeah, Tongue. This is my daughter."

"She's tiny. Why the tubes?"

"She's premature, so she has a little more developing to do before she can be released. But she's okay. She's healthy."

"Did the doctors do everything right?" Tongue growls. "Do I need to kill them? I'll kill them."

"I know you would. I know with everything going on, you'd still want to see her."

"She's cute. I'll get her a stuffed animal swamp kitty."

"I wouldn't expect anything less," Reaper laughs.

"The baby is okay? What's her name?"

"Baby Reaper," I chime in before Reaper can answer.

"That is not her name," Reaper glowers at me.

"I like it. It's tough. No one will fuck with her. I'll have to get her a knife."

"Tongue, babies can't have knives. They're too little."

Tongue's dark brows furrow together as he stares at us like we are the dumb ones. "Well, she needs to learn how to protect herself."

"That's up to us right now. We have to protect her," Reaper informs him.

Tongue grunts again, clearly not agreeing with us. "So what's her name?"

Reaper stares long and hard at his daughter, then back to Tongue, and it dawns on him. "I think she takes after her Uncle Tongue. A total badass." Baby Reaper coos and stretches, which turns into a yawn, and all of us are hooked. We can't look away.

In unison, we say, "Aw."

Even Tongue.

We're goners.

"Hendrix," Reaper says with finality. "It's badass and unique. Sarah brought it up to me a long time ago. To name her after you."

"I..." Tongue's tongue-tied. "I... thank you," he whispers, his voice gravelly. "This means everything."

"You mean everything to Sarah. Stay safe and come home soon with Daphne. How's that going?"

Tongue growls and hangs up the phone, leaving us staring at a dark screen.

"It's going that well, got it," Reaper says sarcastically.

I snort a laugh and tuck my phone in my pocket.

"You like that name, little one? Hendrix?" He waits for her to respond, but all she does is yawn again. "Me too, Hen. Me too." He places her against his chest and leans the recliner back, holding her with both arms wrapped around her tiny body.

"Congrats, Reaper. I'm happy for you. I'll update everyone." I go to leave, and Felicia walks by with me with a blanket.

"Patrick?" Reaper calls out for me. "I wanted to talk to you."

I swallow and turn around, tucking my hands in my pockets.

"I don't know what's going on with you." He holds up his hand when I try to defend myself. "I don't want to hear it. Think about what you're doing, but if you become the man you were before, I'll have to ask you to leave the clubhouse. I don't want someone like that around my daughter, or children for that matter. So you have a decision to make. And I hope like hell you make the right one. You're family, but I won't hesitate to put you back into rehab. Understand?"

I nod. "Understood, Reaper." His words leave a bad taste in my mouth. I know I shouldn't be offended, but I am.

Yet, at the same time, he can see right through me.

What I hate most about being an alcoholic is no matter how hard I try, how hard I fight, how many steps I take, I'll always be an alcoholic. It isn't something that can ever go away.

My disease constantly lingers. It has made itself home in my blood. The marrow in my bone is tainted.

My parched soul is crying out to have a drink, and no matter what I do to ignore it, it's a thirst that will never be quenched.

CHAPTER THREE

Sunnie

It's been a few days since everyone in town has had their babies—okay, just three of my friends, but it feels like everyone. The feeling inside me telling me something is wrong between Patrick and me is growing stronger.

I scratch the inside of my arms, more out of habit than the actual need to scratch. He's growing distant. There's no denying it now. He isn't even home right now.

I don't even know where he is. I sniffle and do my best not to cry at the kitchen table.

Again.

I don't know what happened to us. For all, I know nothing has. It could all be in my mind, but my gut is hardly ever wrong, and it's telling me he's up to something. What if he is seeing another woman? Would Patrick do that to me after everything we've been through? My heart says no, but my mind is wondering what else it could be?

A woman always knows when a man is cheating. At first, they start acting different, and you blame yourself, which is the stage I'm at. Then you're in denial because they would never do that to you. And the constant swirling of a churning stomach makes you want to puke at the thought of their betrayal, so you stay sick for days, weeks, months—until the problem is discussed.

But that feeling? The one in your gut saying something is going on?

It is never wrong. If you feel that way, there's a reason.

And I have a reason, even if I don't know what it is just yet.

I know he loves me. I don't doubt that.

Does it make me a horrible person if I'm hoping the reason for his distance isn't because of cheating but because he relapsed? God, I know. It makes me a fucking terrible person. I can't believe I just admitted that to myself. I can forgive him for relapsing because, in my eyes, there's nothing to forgive. Both of us have to work hard every day not to give in to the urge to get high off our vices. I understand. I'd be by his side every moment if he gave in.

Honestly, I expected one of us to have relapsed by now. It happens in the beginning before you can really get your feet under you.

But cheating? Imagining him sleeping with another woman? I have to hold back a sob when I imagine him naked, thrusting into another woman.

No, I could never forgive him for that.

The sound of a baby crying tugs at my heartstrings, as a loud cry sounds from one of the bedrooms. I want that so badly. I want us to grow. I want Patrick to be the father of my children. I want a family of our own.

Doc stumbles down the hallway, still half-asleep, and slams his shoulder into the wall. I turn my head and wipe my eyes, stifling a laugh when I hear him grumble profanities.

"Everything okay?" I ask, wrapping my hands around the warm mug of tea I made.

He jumps from the sound of my voice and slaps his hand against his chest. "Shit, you scared me. I didn't even see you there, sorry." He yawns.

The baby is still crying, and when the wails become louder, Doc's eyes widen as he spins around. "Shit, I forgot the baby." He runs back to his room, and I'm in stitches, chuckling so hard. Ah, the exhaustion of being new parents.

I sip my tea, and his footsteps echo as he walks through the hall again. When he comes out, he has a tiny Dean cradled in his arms. Gosh, he's just adorable. He has a head full of hair that is bigger than the rest of his body. He's still crying and trying to latch onto Doc's nipple since he's shirtless.

"Hey, whoa, there. I'm not Momma. I don't have what you need. I'm going to warm up some milk for you, though."

"Oh my god, that's adorable."

Doc shakes his head as he grabs a bottle from the cabinet. "Yeah, you'd think so, except he won't latch onto Joanna's breasts. She's had to pump, and it makes me feel terrible because it hurts, but when this little guy gets in my arms, he gums me half to death. My nipples are sore. I can't imagine how Joanna feels." He tries to open the fridge with one hand, but he hasn't mastered holding the baby with one arm yet.

"I can hold him," I offer, swiftly pushing myself from the chair. I'm beside Doc in less than a second, eagerly holding out my arms.

"You sure? I don't want to make you feel like a babysitter."

"Oh my god, please let me be your babysitter anytime you and Jo need some alone time or a date night," I say as Doc slowly puts baby Dean in my arms. I bounce him gently, smiling down at his chubby face. "Look at you. Aren't you handsome?" I coo at him, wiping away the tears under his eyes from his crying. "I know. Daddy is getting you milk, handsome man. It's just you and me right now, though." I probably baby talk him too much, but I can't help it. I just want to curl up with him and never let him go. He's so stinking cute.

"You're a natural." The fridge closes, and Doc pours the breast milk into a bottle and sets it on the warmer.

"I love babies. Well, I didn't think I did, but I do now," I correct myself. "For a long time, I didn't think kids would be in the cards for me because of the drugs, but now, I don't know." I continue bouncing Dean as I walk, trying to calm him while the milk is getting warm. "I think I might be okay, you know? Thinking of someone else's well-being instead of my own might be good for me. I get stuck in my head sometimes about who I used to be and if I'm still that person, but I don't think I am, Doc."

"I don't think you are either." Doc flips off the warmer and brings the bottle to me. "You want to feed him?"

"Are you sure? You don't mind?"

"Are you kidding? I'm starving. You're going to give me a chance to eat. I missed dinner last night."

Deep down, I want to squeal with excitement. "I'd love to, Doc. Feed yourself. I'll take care of Dean." Dean is rubbing his lips across my right breast, trying to get my nipple through my shirt, and I can't help but giggle. "I don't have anything for you either, buddy."

"Sorry, I'm starting to think he just likes the feel of a chest."

"Oh, it's okay. It's natural. He just wants some food." I take the bottle from Doc and rub the plastic nipple against Dean's pouty pink lips coated in baby spit. It's so gross and cute at the same time. He greedily latches on and sucks ferociously, nearly taking the bottle out of my hand. "Goodness, you're a strong little thing."

"My boy has a strong appetite." Doc opens the refrigerator again, takes out a few containers of leftovers, and begins making a plate. There are leftover steak bites, mashed potatoes, green beans, and mac and cheese.

And he piles it all on his plate.

"Can you make me some too? I don't want all that, but maybe some mashed potatoes? Please?" I ask him while holding the bottle that feeds his hungry child.

He can't say no.

"Sure. No problem. It's the least I can do for you taking over for a bit."

The sound of the microwave hums and the smell of savory food hits my nose, making my stomach grumble. Multiple beeps chirping from the counter tell us that the food is done. Doc sets my bowl of potatoes in front of me as he takes a seat, scooping his food onto the fork as if it's a spoon and chowing down.

He groans, setting his fists on the table. "I don't know if it's the best thing I've ever tasted because I'm hungry or if it's really the best thing I've ever tasted," he says through a mouth full of everything.

"Both. It's delicious. Melissa really outdid herself to try to make up for the fact Sarah isn't here."

Doc stops eating for a second, and a wave of guilt washes over his face. "Yeah, I feel so fuckin' bad about that. I should have been there with her. I'm her doctor. I should have—"

"—Hey, it wasn't your fault. No one expected this to happen. It was unfortunate that it happened, but it isn't on you. You had your own baby to deliver. She'd understand that. She'll be okay, Doc. Nothing can kill her. She's too strong-willed to die on anyone else's terms besides her own, you know that."

"I know. I just hope she comes home soon."

I stare down at Dean and sigh, staring at his fluttering eyes as he fights sleep, sucking on the nipple. "I do too. It isn't the same without her. Hey, do you know if Reaper called Delilah? I'm sure she'd want to know."

"Yeah, I reached out the other day. She's on her way here too."

Sarah's brother Boomer got here the night Hendrix was born. He's stayed in the hospital with Reaper ever since. I know when Reaper's sister Delilah shows up, we'll probably not even see her since she'll most likely stay at the hospital too. I'll have to go to the hospital to see everyone soon. I want to check in on Sarah and baby Hendrix.

It's such a sweet name dedicated to Tongue since it's his last name.

Everyone has respected giving Reaper and Sarah space. We don't want to bombard them at such a critical time.

"So why are you awake at two in the morning? I know you didn't plan to sit out here and feed a baby," Doc wonders, shoving another scoop of green beans in his mouth.

"I couldn't sleep. I have a lot on my mind."

"Like? I'm all ears if you want to talk about it. You know it'll stay between us."

I do know that, but I'm not ready to talk about it yet, because what if I'm wrong? I don't want anyone to think badly of Patrick. "Macy's birthday is coming up, and Patrick's been distant."

"Ah, okay. I understand. You aren't blaming yourself, are you? It's normal for people to retreat into themselves when a day that holds meaning to them comes around, and with how she died... the day is no longer happy for Patrick. I'm sure if you ask him, he'll talk to you about it."

Patrick won't talk to me about it until he has no choice. He'll wait, wait, and wait until it's literally eating him alive or having him drink again.

"Yeah, I'm sure you're right," I say, taking the bottle away from Dean since it's empty. "I also want to get a job other than answering the phones for the garage. Don't get me wrong, I like it, but I want to feel more independent. Staying so close to home makes me feel like no one trusts me to do anything."

"Good for you, Sunnie. You deserve to do that and explore what makes you happy."

"Thank you," I reply, feeling humble.

I press Dean against my chest and start patting his back. "How's Joanna doing? She recovering okay?"

Doc takes a long swig of water before answering. "Oh yeah, she's great. She's resting, which is what I want her to do. It's why you always see me with Dean or doing the laundry. She birthed a bowling ball. The least I can do is be a good dad and man to her."

Melt my fucking heart and ignite my ovaries.

"I think that's amazing, Doc. You bikers surprise the hell out of me. You're so damn gritty, but you really know how to treat your women. It isn't expected by looking at you all. Looks really are deceiving when it comes to the Kings."

"Eh." He waves his hand in the air. "It's how it should be. Men need to fucking care more about their women. We wouldn't be here without them, so maybe they need to be more appreciative."

Dean burps loudly, and spit-up runs down my chest. It's warm and wet. "I don't think Dean agrees with you." I frown when I feel it trickling down between my breasts. I'll need to shower, or I won't be able to sleep.

Doc tosses his head back, a deep bellow that's loud throughout the entire house. "Give him a break. That's his way of saying he likes you." He pushes himself out of the chair and tosses his empty plate in the sink. "Here. Let me take him. Thanks for feeding him while I fed myself. I was so hungry."

"Hey, anytime. Really, I don't mind at all. He's precious." I reluctantly hand over the precious bundle, even if the spit-up is now drying onto my skin.

So gross.

So worth it.

"Goodnight, Doc." I grab onto Dean's little cute fucking foot and give it a little shake. *Gah!* I want to scream at him for being so adorable. "And goodnight to you, handsome boy." He isn't even my kid, and I hate that he's leaving me to go to his mom.

I grab my mug as I leave the kitchen, glancing down to see the milky puke on my chest. Yeah, that's real cute. I'm sure Patrick would be all over me right now.

Not.

Right before I get into the main room, I hang right down another hall, then turn left. I pass a few doors, including the bathroom, which always smells like lavender from Poodle's shampoo. We had a home on the property, but it got damaged, so now we're waiting for it to be fixed before we move back in. I actually prefer the clubhouse. I don't want us to go anywhere. I love seeing our family every day and hearing the kids and dogs play.

It's lively, and I've been in the quiet for far too long. I want to live in noise as a reminder that there's more than the silence being high can bring.

I push open the door to my bedroom and sigh when I see that it's empty. The bed is messy, just as I left it when I woke up about two hours ago. My pillowcase is wrinkled, while his is smooth and pristine, showing me he really hasn't been home.

Nothing good happens after midnight.

Only mistakes and heartbreaks.

I close the bedroom door and make my way to the en-suite bathroom we're lucky to have. My shoulder clips the edge of the dresser, and I hiss, spilling half of my lukewarm tea all over me, adding it to the baby spit.

Good thing I'm about to take a shower.

I set the mug down on top of the dresser. The bottom of it's wet, it's going to leave a ring, but I need to get this spit off me. It's starting to smell like funky milk. I tug my shirt over my head and use it as a napkin to clean up the milky spit from my chest. Balling up the shirt, I toss it in the laundry hamper, then slide out of my sweatpants.

The water hisses and plummets against the bottom of the bathtub when I flip the shower on. While it warms up, I take a minute to stare at my reflection in the mirror. My blonde hair is long and wavy, and my blue eyes are tinted red from being so tired. My under-eyes are puffy from crying so much in secret.

Patrick has no idea how much his distance has hurt me, and if I talk to him about it, I'm afraid I'll just make matters worse.

I'm not ugly. I know I'm not about to grace runways with my presence, but maybe Patrick found someone who isn't a junkie? I have needle marks in every spot on my body where there's a vein. I'm not scar-free.

The steam from the hot water blurs the glass, and I can't help but wonder if it's some sort of divine intervention, so I stop criticizing myself. I know that isn't likely. I know it's because of the shower. Steam is natural. Nevertheless, I'm thankful.

I start getting angry at Patrick for acting this way, which has me doubting myself. He isn't making me feel like anything. I want to clarify. No one can make anyone *feel* anything. I control my own feelings and actions, and right now, I'm pissed.

How can he treat me like this? How can he be gone in the middle of the night and not explain anything to me? I deserve that much. I deserve for him to treat me with respect.

Love doesn't come easy, but it sure as hell isn't supposed to be this complicated.

I thought we were partners in every sense, and yet he's feeling more like a stranger than ever. When I met him in rehab detoxing, I felt closer to him than I do right now.

Patrick was an honest man then, but now? He's lying.

Lying doesn't earn love; it's for dirty deeds and bad intentions.

Truth doesn't earn love either, but at least it gives freedom.

I jerk the curtain to the side and step into the water, blowing out a deep breath to try and relax. The hot water massages the tension in my neck, and I tilt my head back into the veil of the spray.

If Patrick breaks my heart, there's no amount of drugs that can put me back together.

CHAPTER FOUR

Patrick

I SHOULDN'T BE HERE.

But I can't help myself.

I can't fight it anymore. The need is too strong. I can walk in, stay for a minute, scratch my itch, and then walk right out. I'll be fine.

The temptation has my cock half hard.

I stop in the middle of the gravel parking lot, unsure if I really want to do this. Do I want to go inside? I rock back and forth on my heels. The gravel digs into the rubber of the sole of my boots. The rocks grind together, creating the same friction I'm feeling inside my chest.

The night is hot. There isn't a breeze to cool me as my heart races at a dangerous speed. What the fuck am I doing? Can I really do this to Sunnie?

Can I do this to myself?

I stare up at the neon sign glowing orange, yellow, and red. I can hear the faint buzzing coming from it as one of the letters flickers on and off.

Electric Paradise.

Name suits the sign, that's for sure. Looks more like a dive bar than paradise, but maybe that's the point.

I had to drive to the next town to come to a bar where I thought I wouldn't be recognized. If anyone I knew saw me here, I'd be in deep shit.

I didn't drive all this way for nothing.

I inhale deep. The smell of cigarette smoke and exhaust fumes wafts over me as I take a step forward to the front door. I know with every step I take, I'm risking everything.

Everything means nothing if I don't test myself.

I reach out a shaky hand and wrap my fingers around the rusted door handle. The hinges squeak, and when I take a deep breath, the fog of smoke infiltrates my lungs, and I relax. The bar itself is old school, with a retro '80s vibe. There's a jukebox in the back, shining with red and white neon lights. A Bon Jovi song is blaring through the speakers, and there are a few people gathered around the pool table. I don't recognize any of these guys, so things are already looking up.

A few girls catch my eye and look me up and down. I curl my lip at them to show them I'm not interested. I'll never be interested. I'm forever a taken man.

Maybe. Not if you become a drunk again.

I'm not going to drink. I just want to sit. I'm only here to socialize.

"What can I get ya, mate?" The guy behind the bar is older, with silver hair, but his face has no wrinkles, and his accent tells me he's from Australia. What the fuck brought him to America? He wipes down the counter in front of me, which doesn't help polish it since the wood is so old, then slings the dirty towel over his shoulder.

"Just a club soda with lime." See? I can be good. I can control myself.

"Comin' right up." He muddles a lime first, adds ice to the glass, then pours the lime juice before adding the club soda. He garnishes it with a wedge of lime. "Tell me not to give ya anything else, and I won't." He sets the tall, slender glass in front of me, then presses his palms against the counter.

I smirk. "Don't get many people that don't order alcohol?" The glass is already sweating under my fingers. The condensation is cold and slick against my skin.

"Everyone that comes in here wants a drink. Not all of 'em order it. You're in recovery?"

I sigh heavily and take a long gulp of my drink. "That obvious?" Damn, the carbonation feels so fucking good against my throat. I close my eyes and think of rum, wishing I had a mixed drink instead of this shit.

"Not obvious. I've just been doing this a long time. No judgments here, mate," he replies.

I dig out my sobriety chip from my pocket and smack it down on the counter. "Well, you're damn good at your job."

He whistles low. "Man, what are you doing here when you have a bloody gorgeous thing like that proving you don't need this place?"

"Eh, I'm sure you don't want my sob story. I'm just like every other guy, I guess."

"I'm a barkeep, mate. I can guarantee listening is part of the job. Plus, we aren't too busy. I'll make me a club soda too, and I'll be all ears."

I scratch under my beard that I've grown out a little too much, wondering if talking about this again is a good idea. "Alright. You asked for it."

He makes himself a club soda real quick just as one of the pool table guys comes up to the bar. "Hey, can I get a pitcher?" he asks, eying my cut. "You're in the Ruthless Kings? Man, that's fucking dope. I've wanted to prospect forever."

I look him up and down, lifting a very unimpressed brow at him. Who the hell has he been talking to prospect? We haven't been accepting anyone.

"Tim was a friend of mine back in the day before I got into law school. But you know, he's a fucking twerp. I figure if that little nerd can get in, so can I," he shrugs, slapping down a fifty. Probably Daddy's money. He's wearing fucking khakis and a polo shirt with boat shoes.

Fucking boat shoes.

What a dick.

"Braveheart is a good member of the club. Don't talk about him like that."

"Braveheart? Is that what he told you? He's a fucking coward—"

I'm out of my chair quicker than he can push the money to the edge of the counter. I wrap his arm behind his back and slam his chest on the bar top, pushing his wrist against the small of his back. His friends see the commotion and begin to walk over with pool sticks.

I chuckle and reach into my waistband with my free hand to draw the gun I've been carrying. I don't cock it, but I do aim it at them. "Don't fuck with me. I'm not in the fucking mood." I hold the other frat boy down that bad-mouthed Braveheart and push him harder into the counter. "I said not to talk about him like that. He's done more for this club than you've done in your pathetic fucking life spending Daddy's money."

"Please, man, I—I'm sorry—" Daddy's boy cries.

What a pussy.

"Don't kill me. I just got into law school. I have my whole life ahead of me," he blabbers.

I bend down, keeping my eyes on his friends and my gun trained on them while whispering in his ear. "I've killed men for much less, frat boy." I yank him back and toss him to his friends. He tumbles and his buddies catch him just in time before he hits the floor. "Pay your bartender and get the fuck out. If I hear you talking shit about Braveheart again, frat boy, I'll fucking kill you, you got it?"

All of them fumble for their wallets and they toss bills on the floor before dragging their piece-of-shit friend out the door.

"Fucking dicks," I mumble, plopping back in my seat and taking another gulp of my watered-down drink. The bartender is staring at the gun in my hand and I raise it slowly, barrel pointed away from him. "I'm sorry. Let me put it away. I'm not going to shoot you. I just don't do well with people talking shit about my brothers." I tuck it into my waistband and lift my hands in the air to show him I'm not armed.

"You're lucky I like ya. I don't do well with people coming into my bar with weapons."

"Sorry about that." It will probably happen again.

"No wucka's." He leans his forearms against the counter. "So spill." He flips my sobriety coin in the air. "Why are you thinking about giving it up?"

I swing back as if he has hit me. "I'm not," I say weakly. "I'm just testing myself." My eyes flicker to the bottle of rum sitting on the shelf.

He turns around and follows my line of sight before flipping the coin again. "You're full of shit, mate. You're close to breaking. I can tell. You want to take that next step and throw all this," he lifts the coin into the air, "All that work away. Tell me, what started this?"

"My sister died in front of me when we were kids, and her birthday is soon. It's never easy around this time. I couldn't save her." I decide to spare him all the gory fucked up details. They don't matter to him.

"Fuck, mate, I'm sorry to hear that." He slides the coin back to me. "What happened, if you don't mind me asking?"

Damn it.

"I don't really want to get into that. It was bad. Let's leave it at that." I finish off my drink, and he pushes himself up to stand straight to make me another club soda and lime.

"I hate to hear that, mate, but just think all that work you had to do to get to where you are now. Is your life better?"

"Yeah, I have everything I never had before."

"You're going to go through all that again to get this?" He picks up the sobriety chip at the same time he sets down the fresh drink. "All that shit you had to deal with, probably rehab, and god knows what else, and you're going to throw that all away for what? For this?"

He points to the shelves behind him. "Your sister wouldn't want that, and if you have someone now, they don't want this for you. You know the blokes that come here who give their lives up for the stuff and get pissed all hours of the day? They're fucking losers who don't have shit in their lives. They lost everything. Everyone they loved. All their families. All they have left is the drink. Are you ready for that, mate? You'll lose it all. If you're ready for that, tell me now, and I'll pour you a shot of your favorite. I'll take that sobriety chip as payment."

Am I ready to lose it all for a taste? I see Sunnie's face while I think about what he said. I couldn't breathe without Sunnie. Christ, if she ever left me, I'd die. I have no doubt about that.

The bottle is the devil, but Sunnie is the baptism.

With every touch, she cleanses the craving.

Until I have to be alone.

That's when the demon rears its ugly head, and right now, I'm dying to give into him.

"No. No, I don't think I am." I slap two twenties on the bar and get up, staring longingly at the rum on the shelf.

It's good.

But what I have now is better.

I pinch the sobriety chip between my fingers and tuck it in my pocket. "Thanks, man. For talking me off the ledge."

"Hey—" he holds out his hand for me to shake, "—Anytime you find yourself on that ledge, you come back to me, and I'll try every time. Bloody oath."

I give him a crooked, sad grin. I hope he doesn't ever have to see me again. "I'll keep that in mind…"

"Martin," he says.

"Patrick." I give his hand a firm squeeze before letting it go.

"More like Mars," he adds before wiping down the counter again.

"I don't get it." I'm confused. He doesn't explain himself as the rag swipes left and right, probably slinging dirty water everywhere.

"Look it up when you're ready and see what it represents. You'll get it then. Go on, I'm closin' up. I have me own Sheila to get to."

I give him a salute. "See ya, Marty." I head out the door, and the warm air bites my face, making me sweat again after leaving the air-conditioned bar.

The gravel crunches again while I head toward my bike parked at the edge of the parking lot. The stars are out, and the crickets are singing. I actually feel better than I did walking into the bar. I grin from the realization and swing my leg over the bike.

I think… I think I might be okay. I might make it through this.

With a new self-confidence, I crank my bike, throw on my helmet, and peel out of the parking lot to get home to my girl. I haven't been a good man to her recently, and if I don't get my shit together, she's going to get tired of me and leave.

That cannot happen.

No matter what, no matter the shit going on inside me, no matter how fucked up I am, Sunnie is my home.

She's mine.

Without her, there's no hope for me to get better.

I hit the throttle and speed down the road, wanting to get back to her as soon as I can. I miss her so much. I hate how I've pulled away, but I don't know how else to deal with my issues. I think being alone is better than putting my issues on someone else, so I try to figure it out.

And I fail.

It's something I need to get better at.

I'm anxious by the time I pull up the clubhouse. The gate is closed, and I reach into my saddlebag to grab the 'opener' Reaper gave us, so Braveheart didn't have to stand watch at the gate so much. Reaper had to threaten him to do something else with his life, and Braveheart didn't take it well at first. He feels guilty about a lot of things that happened because of the gate, but no one blames him.

I drive through the gate slowly, so the engine isn't so loud, and park. I slip off my helmet and run to the porch steps, slipping across the dirt and nearly hitting the back tire of Tank's bike.

Damn, that would have sucked. I wouldn't even be able to use the excuse I was drunk.

I climb the stairs, the thud of my boots echoing loudly across the porch and out into the desert night. I place the key inside the lock, open the door with a soft click, and hurry inside. The door locks automatically when it closes. When I look around, Tyrant and Chaos are on the couch sleeping and snoring out of sync with one another. Lady is probably in Poodle's room, and I'd bet anything he's cuddling her.

The house is quiet, which makes sense considering it's three in the morning. A stab of guilt pierces my chest when I realize I'm that guy that's walking through the door at ungodly hours. Sunnie deserves more than that.

Not wanting to waste another minute, I stride to our bedroom and carefully crack the door open, wiggle in the crack, and shut it behind me. She's sleeping. She must have showered because I can smell her coconut body wash lingering in the air.

She smells like vacation, and in a way, she is.

I get undressed and climb into bed with her, the mattress squeaking from my weight. I settle in beside her, wrap my arm around, and tug her close until her back touches my front. "I'm so sorry, Sunnie. I love you." I kiss the top of her head. She rouses but doesn't turn over.

I hope when she wakes, her love for me is enough to forgive me.

Even if I don't deserve it.

CHAPTER FIVE

Sunnie

I WAKE UP TO A WARM BODY PRESSED AGAINST MINE. I DON'T TURN OVER YET. I TENSE. I'M still mad. I have every right to be angry with Patrick. I don't think it's asking too much to know where he was last night.

Again.

I stare numbly at the wall. My eyes burn as I imagine him out all night with another woman, dancing, laughing, flirting. A tear drips from my left eye, and I wipe it on the pillow. When did we become so disconnected?

When we met in rehab, I thought, 'Hey, this is the guy I'm going to be with for the rest of my life.' But now I'm wondering if this has been one-sided.

Ugh, damn it. I fucking hate doubt. I go down the rabbit hole with it every time. The thoughts and paranoia turn worse, and every scenario in my head becomes more vivid.

He meets a girl.

They talk.

They flirt.

He pushes her hair behind her ear, and she blushes.

They kiss…

Okay, horrible—but not as bad as when my mind takes it a step further and pictures their tongues colliding.

I bury my face in the pillow, wishing I could scream. I'm holding back sobs that will no doubt wake up Patrick.

God, what if they go back to her place? He undresses her like he does me, appreciates her body like he does mine, and they get tangled in a mess of limbs as they have protected sex.

But then my mind races…

What if he fucks her without a condom like he does me?

And then she gets pregnant, and then he leaves me for her?

I'm dramatic and ridiculous. I'm better than this—so many what-ifs. My mind is playing tricks on me when I don't even know the story.

Just ask him.

A kiss on my shoulder halts all my worries. Like a typical woman in love, I make excuses for him when I feel his lips on my skin. He wouldn't pay me attention if he were cheating on me. I want to roll my eyes at myself, but feeling him against me, his warm body, his hard cock pressing against the back of my thigh, how can I ignore the sparks that always fly between us?

"Good morning, Sunshine," he says for the first time in days.

I want to cry right now. He hasn't called me Sunshine since he started acting weird. I know it's my name, but coming from him, it's like I'm *his* sunshine.

I open my mouth to say good morning in return, but that's not what I say. The words blurted out of me before I can stop them.

"Are you cheating on me?"

I slap a hand over my mouth.

Wait. No. I will not be ashamed of needing to know this. I'm standing my fucking ground.

"What?" He lifts up on his elbows and pushes my shoulder down, so I have to roll onto my back and face him. His eyes search mine, and the wrinkles between his brows tell me he's confused. "Sunnie—"

"Are you cheating on me?" I sit up so we're somewhat eye level and cross my arms, but I can't hide my emotions. I'm pissed, hurt, and I want to scream. My bottom lip starts to quiver, and my eyes begin to water as I stare at his stupidly handsome face I love so damn much. His hair has gotten longer, and his beard is scraggly. I love it. I love being able to run my fingers through it.

"What in the fucking world would make you think that?" he asks. His eyes dart between mine, but my line of sight is on the 'Macy' tattoo he has on his chest. Right below her name is mine, 'Sunnie Sunshine,' and there is a big sun shining over our names. It's gorgeous.

I lift my gaze from his stupid muscular chest to meet his stupid gorgeous honey brown eyes. He makes it so damn difficult to be mad at him when he looks like a model.

Asshole.

I choke on a breath when my mouth falls open. "What would make me think that? Are you kidding me right now?" I swing my legs over the bed, bend down and snag my fluffy robe off the floor, and cover my naked body. I feel exposed right now, and I don't want him seeing me. I have to protect myself somehow.

He doesn't bother covering himself up. The blanket is pooled across his lap, and I can see the base of his thick cock nestled in a brown bush.

So distracting.

He notices when I cover up and rolls his lips together, clearly stricken and disappointed. I never hide my body from him, but right now, the last thing I want is him looking at me or touching me, especially if he was with another woman last night.

I check his chest and arms for any claw marks from a night of wild passion and find none. There would be some. I've had sex with him a hundred times, and I always leave a mark.

He frowns. "Sunnie..." he starts, but it's too late. My emotions are getting the best of me.

I wave my hands in the air and lose it, crying as I shout at him. "You're pulling away from me. You haven't been the same for weeks now. You're distant. You don't talk to me. You barely call me Sunshine, and you've been staying out late. You think I don't notice? Is that it? You hope I stay silent and let you leave me feeling like this empty shell of a person because you ignore me?"

I let the tears fall so he can see how hurt I am. "I don't like feeling like this. I don't like feeling insecure, Patrick. Just tell me the truth. Be honest with me. Is it someone else? Are you seeing another woman?" God, the question burns my tongue as I ask it. It hurts.

He scoots to the edge of the bed, and the blanket moves another inch. His eyes cloud, and a piece of hair falls into his face as he reaches his hands out to me. I shake my head and take a step away. I can't be touched by him right now. I'll give in. I'll let everything go and sink into his embrace, and I want answers. I have to stand up for myself.

He stands, and the sheet falls away. His body is so impressive. I can't help but look at him. He's carved, lean, yet *big* in all the right areas.

"Sunnie." He grips my hands, and I try to pull them away. "Stop it. Damn it! Stop it, Sunnie," he yells at me, and I stop struggling, freezing in place. He never yells. "I would never cheat on you. There are no other women. There will never be another woman. You're it for me, Sunnie. God, I'm so sorry I made you feel like that, but I swear to you, I'm not cheating on you. You're... you're everything to me. I love you. You are the love of my life. I want no one else and will never want anyone else."

"Then where have you been?" My voice cracks with the words.

"Lost," he answers with a sigh, and the word is heavy with emotion. "I've been going to meetings and taking long rides to clear my head." He rips his gaze away from me and stares at the floor in shame.

I gasp. "Patrick, you haven't been to the meetings in months. I thought everything was okay?"

"I thought so, too. Macy's birthday is soon. It's getting hard for me to handle, and I can't promise I'll magically stop pulling away. I don't think I'll be better until that day has passed, Sunnie. Just... don't give up on me, okay? Please, don't give up on me."

I believe him, but I have an inkling he's hiding something else. I don't want to worry about that right now. He isn't cheating, and like the horrible person I am, I'm relieved. I don't want him to relapse, but we can work through that. We couldn't work through unfaithfulness. It's one thing I can never forgive.

"God, Patrick." I throw my arms around his neck, and he wraps his arms around me tight, his calloused palms scratching against the material of my robe. "Talk to me next time. You scared the hell out of me. I'm always here for you through this. If you were to pick up a bottle tomorrow, I'd help you get back on track. I'm always here for you, baby. Always."

He leans back and cups my face, those tough calloused rubbing over the fine edge of my jaw. "You'd be there for me? You wouldn't hate me?"

"Hate you? No, baby, no. Never. I love you. We're a team. Partners. You fall. I pick you up. I fall. You pick me up. This is how it works."

Patrick tightens his arms around me, sliding his hand up my back to hold the back of my head. He runs his fingers through my hair and kisses my forehead. "I'm sorry, Sunshine. I never ever wanted to have you think I'd ever do something as terrible as cheating. God, I'm so fucking sorry. I love you so fucking much. It's the only thing I think about when I want a drink. You're all I think about. You save me every day, Sunshine, and for you to think I'd ever even glance at another woman—" he swallows and shakes his head. "It tells me how terrible I've been to you. I'll never be able to apologize enough for that. I love you. I fucking love you, Sunnie."

His fingers tighten on the back of my head, and he smashes our lips together. The kiss is hard and desperate. Our tongues slip together in a wicked dance. His mouth is hot and needy, his lips soft and pliant against mine.

His kiss melts every worry away.

Every bad thought.

Every horrible dream.

Every what-if.

His kiss reminds me of the fireworks between us at all times.

I follow his lead and grip his long strands of silky hair. He growls down my throat.

Mmm, I love it when he gets like this.

"I fucking love that mouth," he rasps, mumbling over the swollen pillows of my lips.

"It loves you back," I purr, feeling lighter and better than I have in weeks. It's like a weight has been lifted off my shoulders, but I know this battle is far from over.

I can still feel him holding back, but I won't push for more. Not right now, not when it feels this good between us.

He tugs the belt of my robe and the fluffy material parts, revealing the valley of my breasts. "I hate when this body is hidden from me," he says, sliding his hand across my stomach and settling it on my hip.

"I'm sorry. I felt exposed when I was feeling so many things," I explain. I need him to understand I didn't feel comfortable showing my body if it meant he was sleeping with someone else.

"I know, and it's my own doing." His other hand lands on my right hip, and he slides both up my body, over my breasts, and slides my robe down my arms. "But I want to see what's mine, Sunshine. You going to show me?" his voice deepens when the robe stops at the crease of my elbows, my nipples beading as the cool air licks them to hard points.

I straighten my arms, and the robe slips off a useless heap on the floor around my feet. He flicks his thumbs over the sensitive peaks, causing me to arch my back. "Yes," I hiss. I never want him to stop touching me.

He takes my hand in his and wraps it around his cock. "You feel how much I want you?" he rumbles. I tighten my fingers around his thick shaft, and he groans from the feeling. My thumb and forefinger don't touch, and it always has me wondering how he fits inside me. "You're the only woman that has ever made me feel this good," he says as I stroke him, lifting my chin with his fingers. "This cock is yours, Sunshine."

My eyes are forced from his cock to stare at his face, which isn't a hardship, but I really love looking at the girth in my hands. It's so heavy and intimidating. The thought of him driving inside me has my pussy pulsating with need and my clit throbbing.

"I'm yours." He takes my other hand and places it on his chest. "Every part of me is yours. Nothing and no one else will ever be like you."

I stand on my tiptoes and kiss him again, stealing his lips in a gentle, timid way. His bottom lip slips between mine. When I move my head to the left, our lips glide over one another. We've done this thousands of times, but every time feels like the first.

One of the dogs barks somewhere in the house, but it isn't enough to break the sexual tension between us. Someone yells 'hush' next. It sounds like Ellie, Poodle's daughter.

Nope. Still not enough to stop us.

I push Patrick onto the bed and straddle his waist, rutting his cock between the folds of my pussy. We don't break the kiss, but I have to take a breather when the thick crown rubs over my clit. "Oh, god," I whimper down his throat. Another rumble vibrates his broad chest.

I rub my hands from shoulder to shoulder, unable to get enough of the impressive body. He's perfection.

He flips me onto my back, and I reach up, running my fingers down his pecs, onto his abs, and over the scar where he had his liver transplant. That was by far the scariest point of my life. I'm so glad he took that liver. I'd be living a life without him. Honestly, I'd probably be dead right now if he were gone.

"You're thinking so loud, Sunshine." He drops over me and rubs the crease between my brows. "What's on that beautiful fucking mind I want to devour?"

I grin, continuing to rub the puckered flesh. "Just thinking about how happy I am that you're alive. You have no idea what this process did to me."

He lowers his forehead against mine. He doesn't say a word; there's nothing he can say, nothing to say. It was an experience I hope to never repeat. His hair fans around us, and the faint smell of smoke tickles my nostrils. It has other questions popping up in my mind, but not enough for me to ask them. It doesn't matter. I don't want to pick.

Especially since this will be the first time in two weeks, we're going to have sex. When Patrick shuts down, he shuts down everywhere. He holds me close and shows attention, but when his mind is reeling with havoc, that's where it all stops.

He kisses my nose, my left cheek, then my right, until all that's left is my mouth, and he wraps his arms around my shoulders to deepen the kiss. "Fuck, I love how you feel against me, Sunnie." My tits are pressed against his chest, and my legs spread to welcome him. He settles his hips against mine and presses right against my clit.

He breaks our mouths apart and kisses along my jawline, then down the column of my throat. I expect Patrick to slide into me and begin fucking me. We don't have foreplay often. We like to fuck—hard. The buildup for both of us is torture.

It seems that isn't the case today.

He continues to pepper kisses down my body, then licks down the middle of my chest. His lips are feathers against my flesh, and he slides them to the right, wrapping them around my nipple. I groan and arch my back into him as he nips the tender point while massaging the other breast with his hand.

"Patrick," I pant his name, digging my nails into his scalp as his tongue assaults me. "Please, fuck me. I need it."

"I'll give you what you need when I get what I need," he mumbles around the mouthful of flesh before traveling to the other one, so it isn't ignored.

"And what—" I gasp when he licks and blows on the tight nipple, "—And what's that?"

"I want to kiss every inch of you," he says, humming in satisfaction when he looks at each breast. My nipples are red and swollen from him, and as he kneads me, I rut my hips up and down to give myself some type of friction. "Naughty girl," he grumbles, holding my hips down so I can't move.

"Patrick," I huff. I'm becoming impatient.

"I said I'll give you what you need when I'm ready." He slaps my clit with his hand, and I cry out from the sting. He slaps me again and again, and my legs shake. My mind is reeling from the sensation as I'm possessed with wanton, feverish lust.

I'm close.

"Mmm, someone likes that. Look how wet you are," he praises, sliding his finger through my drenched folds. He scoops the cream with his finger and sucks the digit into his mouth.

So fucking filthy. I love it when he does that.

"So tasty, Sunshine." He slides onto his stomach and spreads my legs wider. "Look at this pretty cunt. So wet, so pink, dripping for me."

"Just for you," I moan.

The puffs of hot breath leaving his mouth against my center have my skin pebbling in goosebumps. "So perfect," he whispers against me, his lips barely moving against the soft petals. He licks up the center, gathering my juices, and swirls his tongue around my clit.

"Yes!" I moan, fisting the sheets as pleasure unfolds inside me. "More. Finger fuck me, baby. God, I need it. Please," I beg on a pathetic whine. I've always been vocal in bed with him, and he seems to eat it up.

"So mouthy." He bites down on my clit as punishment, and I yelp, but then two thick fingers enter me, stretching me open. "But so tight. I love this cunt." He pulls them out and roughly shoves his fingers back in.

The bed starts to squeak from how hard he's finger fucking me now. The motion is fast and hard, and I reach above the bed to grip the iron bars of the headboard to hold on for dear life. "Yes, Patrick. Oh, god. Harder. Another finger."

Patrick doesn't argue. He adds a third finger and curls them up in a 'come hither' motion pressing against the spot that no other man has ever been able to find. Every time he rubs my G-spot, the pressure intensifies low in my belly. I can feel every thrust like a bolt of lightning coursing through my veins.

He's fucking me in earnest, mimicking how he would fuck me with his cock. He pushes up on his knees, supporting his weight on the bed with one fist while using it as leverage to move harder and faster.

"Fucking look at you. So gorgeous. Your pussy takes what I give so prettily," he croons at me. His appraisal has me bending back, thrusting against his fingers. His thumb rubs against my clit with every upstroke, and the dual sensations are too much.

"I'm close," I whine, tightening my fist around the rods of the bedframe. "Patrick! I'm going—I'm—"

"—Come all over me, Sunshine. Come on. Give me that sweet orgasm so I can claim what's mine."

My body must be conditioned to listen to him because I explode—Fireworks dance in my eyes, and my entire body tenses. My muscles clamp around his fingers, trying to suck him in deeper. My orgasm goes on and on, wringing my body of all its strength like a wet rag.

When I finally sag against the bed, there's a light sheen of sweat over my body. I'm gasping for air, swallowing to coat my dry throat as I watch him pull his fingers free. His hand is soaked. His palm is wet, and he licks his lips when he sees the mess I made.

"All this is for me? I feel so special." He licks his palm, closes his eyes, and hums in delight. "Fucking delicious," he purrs.

He wraps his wet hand around his cock and uses my nectar as lube. His cock shines from me, and he tugs on his sack before angling his cock into my entrance. He lifts my right leg, places it on his shoulder, and drives in one full stroke.

"Christ." He tilts his head back and groans. "You feel better than any shot of alcohol."

I know most people would think that admission is weird, but for me, it's the best compliment I could ever receive.

To Patrick, nothing feels better than alcohol burning his body alive.

Except me.

I drop my leg and wrap my thighs around his waist, maneuvering myself into his lap. He falls onto his calves, his hands gripping the globes of my ass.

"And you feel better than any high I could ever chase," I gasp, circling my arms around his neck as I lift myself up until all that's left is the tip of his cock. I slowly lower myself and watch as his face lights up with pleasure. The tendons in his neck stand strong, the pulse in the side of his neck jumps, and his cheeks turn red.

He lifts me up again by my ass, and both of us groan in unison. I dig my nails into his shoulders and bury my face into his neck, moaning when he thrusts up at the same time I stroke down. With every withdrawal, he brings a whimper out of me.

I nibble the sensitive skin below his ear and suck. I want to leave my mark. I want to show everyone he's claimed and taken.

Mine.

"Yes, Sunshine, fucking mark me," he groans, tilting his head to the side to give me more access. He loves to bite and be bitten.

Like a vampire, I widen my mouth and strike, biting the skin so hard I'm afraid I might break it.

"Harder," he begs through clenched teeth.

I do as he asks, biting until the faint metallic taste of blood hits my tongue and his cock jerks inside me. Warmth floods my insides, and his come bathes every depth. Patrick cries out and groans with every jerk of his cock.

Smirking, I let go of the tender skin and see my teeth indentations. The wound is red, purple from sucking, the divots from my teeth are deep.

His eyes are glazed over. I kiss the middle of his chin. His cock is still ready, pressing against my center, and when his brown honey irises lock on mine, his eyes dilate, and he comes back to reality. His lip curls in a snarl. He tackles me to the bed, roughly flips me over, and rams into me.

"Fuck, Patrick!" I reach my arms behind me and dig my nails into his thighs.

He uses my legs as reins, clutching them tight to yank me back on his cock with each thrust. God, I feel like I'm about to die in this position with how he hits that spot again. The wet slap of skin is loud from the mess of his come dripping out of me. It's so dirty. I can feel the wetness dripping down my thighs.

Patrick drops my legs and curls his body over, gripping the edge of the headboard.

"Fuck me, Patrick. Fuck me, harder. Use me." I turn my head to try to look at him, but he shoves my head into the pillow.

"Oh, I'm going to. This cunt is going to ache for fucking days. You're going to feel me sliding out of you, gliding between those pussy lips." He bites the nook between my neck and shoulder. The iron rods creak as he uses the board for leverage to fuck himself into me harder.

He pulls apart my ass cheeks while his cock fills me to the brink and circles my puckered star with a finger. Oh, it's been a while since he's played with me there. The tip of his finger breaches me, and I clamp down instinctively.

It takes me a second to relax as his finger slides to the knuckle. I groan.

"That's right, Sunshine. You love all your holes filled, don't you?"

I nod. My cheek rubs against the pillow, my nails digging into his skin so hard I know it has to be broken. I rake my nails down his thighs as hard as I can.

His finger rubs against the thin barrier where I can feel him rub his own cock that's sliding into me. My eyes roll to the back of my head from the intensity.

My orgasm is building.

And it's going to be earth-shattering.

My legs tingle, and my toes begin to curl. I muffle my noises against the mattress, remove my hands from his thighs, and slap them against the pillow. I fist the material so hard I hear a rip. I can't breathe. Oh god, I can't breathe. It feels too good.

"You're going to come, aren't you? I feel you squeezing my cock so tight. You're starting to come."

What does he expect when he's filling me to the brink?

The bed smashes against the wall with every thrust. Patrick's firm biceps flex above me as he uses his strength to hold on tight to give me what I crave.

I turn my head to the side to take a breath, and that's when it hits me. My entire body tenses, and good thing I took that gulp of air because now I can't breathe.

"Fuck, Sunshine. Oh damn it, you're milking me. I can't…" He fucks me straight through my orgasm, his rhythm becoming more ragged and unsteady. The bed finally stops smacking the wall when his warm come fills me for the second time tonight.

He collapses on top of me, the sticky ends of his sweaty hair brushing against my shoulder. He kisses down the back of my neck, and my eyes begin to droop again.

I feel fucking fantastic. I'm on cloud nine.

This high, right here—while my body is floating and we're trying to catch our breath—is better than any other I've ever chased.

"I love you so fucking much, Sunshine. My only Sunshine," he sings the last bit, which makes me laugh. It sounds tired, but it's real.

"I love you too."

He turns us to our sides, still connected to me, as he wraps me up tight in his arms, bringing me to his chest. As we fall back to sleep again, there's a hint of a smile on my face.

Why was I hurt earlier?

What was the doubt?

When I'm in his arms, doubt doesn't exist.

Only happiness and sunshine.

CHAPTER SIX

Patrick

I LIED AGAIN.
    I'm a fucking liar now.
    What kind of piece of shit lies to the woman he loves?
An alcoholic.
I didn't tell her about going inside the bar because I didn't want her to think I was on the verge of breaking. I didn't want her to worry more than she already is because it isn't going to happen again. I'm not going to walk into a bar.
I hope not.
There's a loud bang on the door that shakes the entire room. "Hey, get your asses out here," Tool bellows.
I was almost back to sleep, too.
"It's Lady," Tool adds.
Sunnie inhales. "Oh no. It's time."
I kiss the back of her neck and nod. "It's been a long time coming. Poor thing just doesn't want to leave."
"I know. This is going to be so sad," she whispers.
I slide out of her, and we groan in unison. I already miss her heat as the cool air wraps around me. "The last thing I want is to leave this bed."
"Me too, but Poodle needs everyone right now," she says. Always so damn kind. That's what I love about her.
"I know," I whisper in a reply. "We'll be out in a minute!" I shout to Tool.
"Make it quick," Tool grumbles from behind the door.

Sunnie rolls out of bed first, and my eyes lock on her perfect ass. Not too big, not too small. It's perfectly round, with the right amount of jiggle.

"Stop it," she giggles, a sound I'll never get sick of. "We need to get ready."

"I can't help it. You look like a snack, and I'm hungry."

"You're always hungry." She turns her head and places her chin on her shoulder, looking coy and beautiful.

"Well, when you're looking like that, what do you expect a man to do?"

She shakes her head and walks into the bathroom, flipping on the shower, which has me dragging my ass out of bed. "What do you think you're doing?"

Sunnie leans backward to peek out from the door, and the ends of her blonde hair tickle the top of her ass. "I'm taking a shower."

"The hell you are," I grumble and stalk toward her with heat in my eyes. "I'm telling you right now, you aren't allowed to shower today until I tell you too. You think I was kidding when I told you're to feel me slipping between those pink pussy lips all day?"

"Patrick." She blushes and leans back against my chest as I wrap my arms around her.

"Sunshine." I bend down and kiss down her neck, tasting the hint of salt on her skin from the sheen of sweat we worked up with hot sex. "Are you going to listen to me?"

She nods absent-mindedly, the back of her head resting on my shoulder as I skim my hands up her body.

I want to explore every inch of her, never taking my hands off her silky skin or my lips from hers. The only air I want between us is the air from our own lungs.

Breathe each other in.

Breathe each other out.

And become high from what we feel for one another.

"Come on. Let's get dressed. I don't want to keep Poodle waiting."

She nods, spins around in my arms, and presses a kiss against my right pec. "Maybe we should all pitch in and get another poodle for him? He seems like the kind of guy that would need another because he likes taking care of things. And when we get him, we can name him Mister, so it is still fancy like Lady's name."

"You're so fucking thoughtful. I think that's a great idea. We should talk to Melissa, but not today. It's going to be rough. He's had Lady since she was a puppy."

"I'm going to cry. I love Lady," she says.

I can't remember a time when the clubhouse existed without that dog. Poodle came to the Kings with Lady when she was just a little fluff ball. She isn't a dog. She's family. I think everyone is going to feel it for a few days.

While we brush our teeth, we hip bump each other while our mouths foam with toothpaste, still flirting after how long we've been together.

God, I don't think there will be a time when I'm not flirting with her.

She's too damn perfect and makes me feel like a teenager all over again.

We watch each other as we get dressed, and I make sure not to put on underwear. I tuck myself in as I zip up my pants. I don't miss the quick flick of her tongue across her bottom lip.

"You're fucking gorgeous," I growl, eating her up with my eyes as I check her out from head to toe.

"And you're fucking sexy. I want to spend all day in bed and have you fill me up over and over again until you don't have another drop to give."

I close my eyes and imagine that perfect day, groaning in frustration that that wonderful day can't be today. "You're killing me." I tug on a King's Garage shirt while she throws on a King's Club tee.

"Only killing you in the best way," she corrects with a wink.

I take her hand and kiss her knuckles while opening the door. "There's no other way to go, am I right?" I tug Sunnie through the door and place my hand on her lower back as she laughs, staring up at me with those big blue ocean eyes.

I want to dive in and never come up for air if it means I'm trapped in her endless seas.

I'm half Pirate, after all, right? Is it not my job to sail across her oceans to own every treasure she possesses?

When we take a right toward the main room, everyone is there besides Reaper. He's still in the hospital with Sarah and baby Hendrix. Bullseye is on the couch holding Faith while Joanna is sitting next to him holding Dean. Doc is on the floor next to Lady. Poodle is cradling his best friend in his lap, petting the top of her head. She's skin and bone, with labored breathing.

"Oh," Sunnie says sadly, pressing her hand against her chest when she sees the heartbreaking scene in the middle of the floor.

"Who has been the best girl?" Poodle croons at Lady while she stares up at him with big brown eyes, letting out a soft whine. "You have been my best friend, Lady. You're so fucking good. I'll never forget you." He kisses the tip of her nose and catches a sob in his throat. Ellie is sitting next to him, crying too, laying her head against his shoulder while Melissa is on his other side rubbing his back. "You're such a good girl, Lady. So good. I love you so much. We love you so much."

Poodle wipes his cheek on his shirt, continuing to pet the top of her head. "Such a Lady," he whispers. "It's okay. I'll be okay. You can go. I don't want you to go, but I don't want you to be in pain. You held on so long for me," he continues to talk gently to her, petting from the top of her head down her spine. I can see every vertebra, every rib, the sharp ridge of her hip bones. The poor thing just won't let go of Poodle.

She lifts her head, weak and slow, and gives Poodle a kiss on the chin, giving him one last lick before she puts her head in his lap for the final time.

"You always give the best kisses, Lady. Such a good girl. The best girl. Shhh, it's okay," he chokes. "It's okay. I love you so much, and I'm going to miss you so much. Thank you for so many years by my side. I'll never forget you and the memories you gave me."

Lady whines as if she can understand him.

"Are you ready, Poodle?" Doc asks, preparing the medication that will give Lady peace without suffering.

"No," he answers honestly. "I'll never be ready to let her go, but I know I have to."

Doc lifts up the needle and taps it. Lady looks at him, then Poodle, and with the remaining strength she has left, she climbs up his body until her chin rests on his shoulders, nestling her head in the crook of his neck.

He wraps his arms around her, squeezing his eyes shut as they give one another a farewell hug. Before Doc can put the needle into her leg, Lady closes her eyes for the final time, letting out the last of her remaining breath.

Poodle hears it, feels it, and cries silently as he holds his best friend that's been with him for so many years. Doc sniffles and shakes his head, trying to remain professional as he reaches for his stethoscope. He puts the ear tips in his ears and places the round metal circle against her chest, then her sides.

He frowns. "She's gone, Poodle. I'm so sorry."

Poodle tightens his arms around her and kisses the top of her head. "Oh, such a good girl, going out on her own instead of letting Doc stab her with a needle. You've always had your own terms. God, you were the best dog a man could ever have."

I don't know why I always find it a little harder when pets die than humans. Maybe I'm just a dick, but I'm finding it really hard to keep my composure. Sunnie's buried her face in my chest. I wrap my arms around her, rubbing my hand up and down her spine.

The entire room is heavy with sorrow and mourning; everyone loved Lady. Tyrant and Chaos are upset too. They're lying in front of her, chin on their paws, staring at her lifeless form.

"Christ, me eyes are lagoons. Someone make it stop." Skirt wipes his cheeks, and Dawn dabs a tissue under his eyes. "She was a good dog."

"She was," Bullseye agrees, rocking a fussy Faith to sleep.

"If I was able to, I'd take a shot in her name," I say, and everyone turns around and looks at me. Fuck. Maybe that wasn't the right thing to say.

"Thanks, man," Poodle states, his voice rough with tears. "That means a lot to me, but don't. I don't want you fucking up your sobriety. Lady wouldn't either."

"In spirit, then," I add.

Everyone nods around me. "In spirit."

"When do you want to bury her?" Doc asks.

"Well, I already have a spot dug. Her little casket is ready. If everyone doesn't mind, I'd like to do it today." He continues to pet her. "I don't want to wait too long. I don't want her to think I forgot about her."

"We get it. How about we head outside now? It's a beautiful day," Doc says, finally getting to his feet.

Slingshot clears his throat. "I have a taco for her. No one knew, but I fed her tacos in secret. So she had a really great breakfast this morning before... well... *before*," he says, pinching the bridge of his nose as he shuts his eyes.

"I'm sure she loved that. Thanks, Slingshot," Poodle says.

It takes a minute for everyone to get ready since most of the members have young children. Still, in ten minutes, everyone is following Poodle down the hallway. When we make our way into the kitchen, we hang left down another hallway that passes Reaper's office. The stained-glass door projects a rainbow of colors from the sun shining onto Lady's fur coat. Doc opens the door, and Poodle, Melissa, and Ellie are out first.

All the members follow in a single-file line. I'm holding Sunnie's hand while Bullseye is holding Faith. Hope is resting and can't join us, just like Joanna is resting with Dean, but other than that, it's most of us. The sun is hot while we walk, passing the garage since the small cemetery we have is in the back of the property. Small clouds of dust whirl around everyone's feet, creating a small sandstorm around us.

The cemetery comes into view, and a fresh grave is dug with a pink casket open next to it. The inside is white silk with a pillow, and Lady's name is in rhinestones on the side. Poodle really didn't spare a dime when it came to her comfort after death.

"Doc, can you double-check her again? Please? Just to make sure she isn't alive?" Poodle asks, and the question shoves a fucking knife right into my heart.

"Of course, Poodle. Anything." I don't miss the concerned expression he gives Tool as he whips out his stethoscope again. He cheeks for her heartbeat again, this time taking longer than he did before. Next, he grabs a small light from his pocket and checks her pupils for a reaction.

"I'm sorry, Poodle. She's gone. Her eyes aren't reacting to the light, and she has no heartbeat. She's gone."

Poodle nods. "I knew that. I just didn't want the truth to be real. Thanks for checking again."

"Anytime, Poodle." Doc squeezes his arm for reassurance, and Poodle takes a deep breath and kisses Lady on the snout before gently placing her in her small pink casket.

According to Poodle, Lady loved the color pink.

"Don't forget, you're my best girl. That's never going to change," he whispers into her ear. Giving Lady one last heartbreaking look with sad swollen eyes, he closes the casket. He rubs his nose on the end of his sleeve before biting the bullet and taking Lady's casket in hand. His hands shake while he lowers it six feet under.

He presses his hand over her name that's written across the front and bows his head.

The grief surrounding me makes me want to drink.

Fuck.

I can nearly taste the rum on my tongue if I think about it hard enough.

Especially in a time like this.

Seeing Poodle devastates me, and when I hurt, I crave rum—the entire goddamn bottle. And the struggle has been hard enough as it is. I've lied to Sunnie too much already. What else am I going to tell her? That I wake up in sweats, I dream about it, my tongue sticks to the roof of my mouth like a wad of cotton every day? Not very fucking likely.

And at this point, I'll take any kind of alcohol. Some are easier to ignore, like whiskey. At Christmas, I had temptation like no other while being captured by Tongue's brother, Porter, also known as The Groundskeeper. He set a big bottle right in the middle of the room, and I was able to toss it to the side like it meant nothing.

But if it were a bottle of rum?

Mmm, I don't think I could have denied it.

Like right now. I think I'd settle for any kind of alcohol.

Vodka.

Whiskey.

Gin.

I'd take anything I could get my hands on.

I run my fingers through my hair, shaking, barely able to hold myself together as we all crowd around the small grave for Lady.

"Are you okay?" Sunnie whispers as her arms hoop around my sides.

"I'm fine," I lie, wrapping an arm around her tight, needing to feel her, needing her to be closer than she's ever been.

I tug the collar of my shirt, trying to get fresh air against my sweaty skin. The sun is hot now that summer is inching around the corner. It's bearing down on my neck, the burn getting worse as the second's tick by. I glance up from the grave and look around, twisting my neck left and right to release some stress.

My vision blurs. Sweat drips down from my brows, turning the desert around me hazy. The heat waves through the dry air, and the crows spread their wings above us, slicing through the sky. Their shadows fall one by one as they circle us.

I bet they know about me. They can sense me dying on the inside, knowing that my greatest weakness will be my greatest downfall.

"We are gathered here today to say goodbye to one of our best friends and one of the greatest dogs—"

Poodle snaps, "—The greatest dog. Lady was the best." He traces her name with his finger along the casket.

Tool clears his throat and coughs. "You're right. My apologies. Lady lived a long, happy, ruthless life with us. She was Poodle's first queen. She fought cancer like hell and never left Poodle's side. She was more than a dog. She was family. I hate to see what the clubhouse will be like without her."

Poodle sniffles. Part of me feels for him—but the other part of me, the drunk, he doesn't give a fuck and wants to go drink.

"If anyone has any words or stories they would like to share about Lady, the floor is yours," Tool announces, as he tugs on the collar of his black button-up shirt.

Skirt is the first one to step forward. As usual, he's wearing a kilt. This one is green, and for a shirt, it's one with a fake tuxedo on the front.

"Lady was a good friend to me. When the compound got attacked when one of our own was missing, or whenever any of us needed comfort, she was there. She was trained to rescue, but she wasn't trained to love. That came naturally. I'll never forget the undeniable loyalty she had for us or the unwavering, unconditional love she had for Poodle. I'm so sorry for yer loss, lad. I know that can't bring her back, but know I'm feeling her loss just the same." Skirt reaches down and grabs a handful of dirt, and sprinkles it on top of her casket. "Rest in love and barks, Lady. I hope ye are chasing your favorite ball up in the high heavens."

"Thank you, Skirt," Poodle croaks.

"Aye, Poodle. I'm so sorry for ye." Skirt gives a friendly squeeze to Poodle's shoulder before taking his place next to Dawn. She's cradling baby Joey on her hip while Aidan runs around a few yards away with Micah and Delaney. A lot of the time, kids don't understand death, but these kids do. I just think they're trying to avoid it, which is understandable.

Next, Bullseye walks up, his tiny granddaughter nestled in his large bicep.

I still can't believe at thirty-six years old, the man is a grandpa, but he has a hell of a life, and I honestly have never seen him happier. Ruby is by his side. She's fussing over the baby hat Faith has on so the sun doesn't get to her.

She's adorable. Seeing them together has me wondering if I could be a father. How selfish of it would it be of me to reproduce, though? What if my kid grows up to be an addict because it runs in his blood? I won't do that to a child. I just won't.

"So a lot of people don't know this, or maybe you do because I was such an A-S-S-H-O-L-E for the longest time—"

"—Bullseye, the kid can't spell yet."

"You never know, Patrick," he hisses at me. "Don't be a... you know what, I'm not going to be lowered to your level," he says, making a much-needed chuckle trickle among us. Even Poodle manages a small smile. "Anyway," he clears his throat when the baby starts to fuss. He and rubs Faith's tiny back. It's completely engulfed with his hand. "I was in a bad way for a long time, and at night, when I'd be up playing darts when everyone else was asleep, Lady would accompany me. She'd stay up with me, and I'd be fuc—fudging angry."

Ruby snickers, which makes everyone else lose their composure.

"I had a lot going on inside, and when no one could see me, I'd make a shit ton of darts, I'd throw them as hard as I could against my dartboard, and I'd vent to Lady. Sometimes, I'd even cry. I knew she wouldn't ask me questions or judge me, so she made it simple." He bounces the baby against him to get her to go back to sleep when she starts to fuss again. "Any darts that fell on the ground, her pink painted nails would click along the floor, and she'd pick up the darts and bring them right back to me. We'd play for hours. She was just the company I needed when I felt like I didn't have anyone. She was a good companion, Poodle. A good friend. She showed me love when I didn't think I was worthy of any." Bullseye carefully squats and grabs another handful of dirt and sprinkles it over her casket, too, turning the baby pink to a light red.

I decide to tell a tale too. One that will seem unbelievable, but Lady was a brilliant dog, and everyone who knew her could see that. I take a spot next to Lady's grave next, and Sunnie refuses to let go of my hand, so she follows.

I let out a long sigh and run my fingers through my hair. "Everyone here knows how I used to be."

How I still am, because that man is now clawing at my chest to be let out.

"I was a drunk."

I am a drunk.

"And there wasn't a day where you wouldn't see me holding a bottle of rum, and when I was out, I'd look for anything else to replace it. You're probably wondering what this has to do with Lady." I cough when I remember the night. "I can't say for certain when it happened because I was wasted, but I remember being sick. I was throwing up, sweating, yet still drinking from the bottle in my hand. I passed out like I always did, forehead on the toilet, just low in my very existence as a man, and I felt something cold on me. It woke me up, and when I finally blinked my eyes open, I saw Lady there. She was jumping onto this water bottle and spraying me with it. Now that I say it out loud, I think I dreamed it—"

"—No, it happened," Poodle corrects me. "I was looking for that water bottle all morning, and when I heard you groan from the bathroom, I hurried in to make sure you were okay, and Lady was bouncing on the water bottle with her two front paws."

That makes my heart warm. "I drank that water bottle dry and thanked her, called her a good girl. She probably saved my life that morning. I was in a really bad way. I don't think I'd had water for days. I don't know how she knew to do that, but I'll forever be thankful. She really was the best and smartest Lady this world has ever seen." Sunnie and I squat down and pick up some dirt and let it rain over Lady's very ladylike casket. "She was probably the first one that ever tried to save me," I whisper. "Thank you, Lady."

I'm sad she's gone because I feel like I need her again. I bet she'd recognize the constant turmoil in me and try to give me water again.

Like Skirt said, Rest in Love and Barks—and maybe somehow, try to keep us all safe like you did before.

CHAPTER SEVEN

Sunnie

My phone vibrates in my hands. When I look down to see who's calling me, I don't recognize the number, so I decline it. I don't have time to answer it anyway. With the rest of the group, Patrick and I are walking into the hospital to see Reaper and Sarah.

I hate the circumstance, but I can't wait to see Delilah and Boomer. It's been too long since I've seen everyone.

I wish Sarah was awake. I have so many things I want to talk to her about, but maybe I can speak with Delilah instead.

Sighing, I tuck my arm through Patrick's as we bypass the front desk. We know where we're going, and it's visiting hours, so no need to check-in. It feels like it's been an eternity since we've been here, but really, it's only been a few days. The halls are plain, with medical carts lining the sides and generic paintings of the sea and meadows hanging on the walls.

There are lines of dust atop the frames, too, because who thinks of cleaning the edges in a hospital? It isn't the most crucial thing to get cleaned. I look behind me to see a crowd of black leather. Most of the members are here today, even all the kids. The only one who isn't is Poodle.

The man is devastated about Lady. It's warranted, given that we only buried her yesterday. Melissa hung back to stay with him.

Thinking about the quick dog funeral tugs at my heartstrings. I've never had to bury a pet before, but the clear destruction of Poodle's heart makes me wonder why people get them.

The boots of the bikers thud against the floor along with the beat of my heart. It's soothing, bringing me out of my depressing thoughts about a pet. Something about having a group of dangerous badass men at my back makes me stand taller. I feel stronger and more confident. It's hard not to when every guy is over six feet tall and has killed men with their bare hands.

"Do you remember where to go, Patrick?" Tool asks as we debate on taking a left or a right down the halls.

"Uh." Patrick looks left and right, then scratches the back of his head.

While he's thinking, I'm staring at his face, reading him, trying to decipher how he's doing. He has dark circles under his eyes from not sleeping well last night. I felt him toss and turn every few minutes and eventually give up and go to the chair in the corner to read a book after he flipped on the lamp.

I'm worried. He's getting antsy and reckless.

"I think it's this way..." he points to the left but then shakes his head. "No, it's definitely the right..." he stops walking when he looks around. "Wait. No, it's left then right."

Tool huffs and crosses his arms. "Patrick, are you sure? Are we lost?"

"No, we aren't lost." Patrick spins his body in a circle to see if he can notice anything, and I stifle a laugh.

We are lost.

We're blocking the hallway since there are so many of us. Eventually, a doctor is going to need to get through and be annoyed. "Maybe we should ask for—"

"—No!" all the men say at once, and I lift my hands in surrender.

"Jeez, alright. I just thought it would—"

"—No real man asks for directions. We're going this way." Skirt leads us to the right, and we meander down the hallway, passing rooms with open doors that have old people lying there, hooked up to machines. "I bet ye it's down this hall to the right." He taps the side of his head. "Men got senses for these kinds of things, ye know."

Me, Mary, Juliette, and Dawn do our best not to laugh. If a man's senses are so keen, then why did Patrick not know the way?

"Mmmhmm, babe. I know you know the way. You lead us here," Dawn talks to him as if he's a baby, which has all of us laughing again because he grins like a fool, and she's tugging his chain.

When we get to the end of the hall, I cover my mouth with my hand, then curl my hands into a fist, smiling at the men while they look so confused. I see movement out of the corner of my eye and see a nurse in one of the patient rooms, stretching an elderly person's limbs, so they don't become stiff. I bite my lip and tug on Mary's sleeve, sliding my eyes to the left.

She follows my gaze and nods, knowing precisely what I'm planning.

"I swear the hall was right here." Patrick throws his hands on his hips.

Skirt and Tool press their palms against the wall to see if it will move. Slingshot places his ear against it, knocking on it with his knuckles.

They're not doing what I think they're doing…

They're checking for false walls?

"My god, I'm worried about their mental state," Mary whispers while holding her belly. Her eyes widen when Knives throws his ninja star, and it lodges in the wall.

"Huh, they must have closed it in," Knives states with a click of his tongue.

Is it that difficult for men to admit they need directions?

I roll my eyes and duck into the room where the nurse is. She's pretty, young, with wide eager eyes, and she's talking the coma patient's ear off.

"And then this morning, I sprained my dang toe because I tripped on a sewer grate, can you believe that?" she laughs at herself while bending the man's arm gently a few times.

"Excuse me?" I make sure to keep my voice low, making sure it stays a whisper.

She squeals and drops the limb to the bed, startled. She lays her hand against her chest. "Goodness, you scared my lily pad straight off the pond," she gasps for air.

I don't know what that means.

"Where is the NICU? Our men are lost."

"Oh, straight down the other way to the right."

My eyes drop to her nametag. "Thank you, Ari."

She beams at me with a bright smile. "You're welcome."

I like her. She's a happy, positive person. "Have a good day, Ari."

"You too!" she chirps, swishing her ponytail left and right.

I turn around and head out the door, taking my spot next to Mary in a hurry, so hopefully, no one notices I was gone. "Hey, guys, maybe it's the other way. There's no harm in trying, right?" I offer, waiting to see what they decide.

Skirt and Patrick run their hands through their beards while they think, and Mary snorts, unable to hold in her amusement.

"Yeah, that's a good idea—no harm," Skirt shrugs.

Knives tugs his ninja star from the wall and tucks it back in his pocket. "Probably not there, anyway. I bet the babies are behind the walls." A look of horror washes over Knives' face, and his eyes drop to Mary's belly. "What if they keep the babies in the walls? We're having a home birth. No fucking way. We have a Doc," he points to Doc, who has been standing off to the side. He isn't paying attention. His focus is on his little boy Dean.

"Oh my god, Knives. It's a hospital, not a dungeon. They don't keep babies in the walls," retorts Mary. It's never good when they begin to argue. It always ends up with them fucking against the nearest wall.

"How do you know?" he sasses.

"Because we're at the wrong end of the damn hall. The lot of you are a bunch of doofuses. Tapping on walls, pushing against them to see if they're fake. All so you don't have to accept the fact that you're wrong." Mary spins on her heel and marches down the hall. "I'll freaking show you guys."

"Hellraiser," Knives chastises as he runs after her. His hand finds her ass and squeezes, and like I said, he shoves her against the wall and shoves his tongue down her throat.

No wonder they made a baby so fast.

No judgments.

I want a baby, but I'm on birth control until Patrick and I talk otherwise.

The group of us pass them as they dry hump against the wall—freaking animals. Knives is cupping her stomach, and something inside me aches for the same.

Would Patrick cradle my pregnant belly? Would he be happy?

I want to say yes, but there's a disturbing inkling in my gut telling me he wouldn't be. If I want kids and he doesn't, where does that leave us and our relationship?

It would mean it's over because it isn't fair to either one of us to give up or give into what we want. This is too big. This isn't about liking hamburgers or not liking them. This is a fundamental building block of a person.

We either build, or we leave what we have built behind.

And the thought is devastating because then it would mean I'd have to rebuild with someone else. I've never imagined my life with anyone besides Patrick.

"You're thinking awfully hard," Dawn whispers in my ear while we walk.

"Oh, yeah. Sorry."

"You know, you can talk to me about anything. I won't judge. If you need to vent or just have a girl's night, Skirt can watch Joey, he loves to, and Aidan can have a playdate with Maizey."

"I'll keep that in mind. Thanks, Dawn." I twist my body to the right to look over my shoulder to see Patrick talking with Tool. It seems like a serious conversation, so instead of going to him like I want, I stick with Dawn.

I smirk when we get to the end of the hall and take a right. Immediately there are yellow walls with butterflies.

"It's at the end to the right," Patrick grumbles when he realizes the men were wrong.

Men are always wrong.

Women aren't necessarily right all the time, but we know how to use our heads.

It's called thinking versus ego.

And men hate for their egos to be hurt.

When we get to the end of the hall, no one is there.

What. The. Fuck.

Where are Hendrix and Reaper?

"Fuck!" Tool runs back the way we came, and all of us follow as fast as we can. The stampede of boots echoes through the corridor.

"Hey, no runni—"

Knives punches the male nurse in the face to shut him up.

"We do what the fuck we want when one of our own is missing. Back the fuck off," he snarls.

"God, you're so hot," Mary purrs as she steps over the unconscious nurse.

"Later, Hellraiser." Knives winks at her, lifting her into his arms so they can run faster.

This isn't good. The Kings have made plenty of enemies. What if the President of the Ruthless Kings and his family have been taken?

I know what.

A blood-filled war.

Raise hell. Bring fury. Spill blood.

It's the Ruthless way.

CHAPTER EIGHT

Patrick

"Excuse me." Tool slides to a stop in front of the desk. "I'm looking for Reaper—"

The woman holds up her hand to stop him before he gets too far. "The biker guy, right?"

"Yes, the biker guy," Knives says with a bit of heat.

I don't like how she said that either.

"He's in Sarah's room. That's his girlfriend, right?" she begins typing on the keyboard, her nails clicking and clacking.

"His ol' lady," Tool corrects. "It's more than a girlfriend."

The nurse huffs and rolls her eyes. "Whatever. Same thing."

I clench my fists at my sides as I stare at Sunnie. She's more than a girlfriend. A girlfriend sounds temporary, replaceable, and immature. Sunnie's my ride or die. When a biker finds his ol' lady, that's fucking forever. No other bitch wears our property patch except the ones we want to spend the rest of our days with.

This dumb cunt. Someone ought to show her lesson, and if it weren't for the time and place, I'd love to.

"Anyway, he is in her room with baby Hendrix. Room 454," she says.

Tool grunts at her, and we all walk away again, relieved the Prez didn't get kidnapped but irritated with this woman's refusal to learn something new. We all mean mug her as we enter the hall, but Slingshot isn't done.

He pauses at the corner of the wall and eyes her, pulling out his slingshot from his cut pocket and then a skittle from the other. Slingshot is still moving slow considering he just got shot twice. I can tell he needs to rest with how pale he is, but no one can tell him otherwise. Doc stopped trying.

Slingshot winces as he pulls the strap of his slingshot back and launches the skittle, which smacks the bitch right in the head.

"Go, go, go," he ushers us down the hall before she can see us.

We're all quietly chuckling, and Sunnie says, "You'd think you all were a bunch of teenagers."

I wrap my arm around her shoulders and kiss the side of her head. "You love it."

"I do. Call me crazy." She wraps one arm around my hip as we stop in front of the elevator. Our reflection shines against the polished metal of the elevator doors. When they open, a few nurses in navy blue scrubs come out and then stop right in front of us with fear twinkling in their eyes.

A group of bikers is harmless.

We don't bite.

That's a lie.

We bite… until we kill.

The nurses scoot around us, and I don't miss Slingshot winking at one of them. She doesn't give him a second glance, and he pouts while sticking out his bottom lip.

We pile into the elevator, shoulder to shoulder, touching too close for my liking, and Doc's little Dean lets out a disgusting toot that stinks up the entire elevator.

De-Ja-fucking-Vu.

"Oh my god, I think he needs to be changed, Doc," I say, plugging my nose.

"No, sorry, that was me. I had carnitas for breakfast and—"

Everyone groans at Slingshot, and Tool points his finger at him. "What did we discuss? No fucking tacos before eleven. You know what it does to your stomach."

"But I wanted them."

"And now all of us are going to either pass out or die," Tool grumbles in displeasure.

When the doors open to the fourth floor, we stumble out at once and inhale fresh air. My eyes are watering, and I cut Slingshot a dirty look.

"You guys are so dramatic." Slingshot walks ahead of us and flips us off, looking left and right as he passes each room to look at the numbers on the sides of the door.

"Oh my god, what is that smell?"

We turn around to see a doctor gagging in the elevator as the doors slide shut, trapping him inside.

Yeah… we aren't dramatic. Slingshot didn't take his pill.

He passes a room and then backtracks, pointing at the door in excitement, then knocks. When the large wooden door opens, we expect Reaper, but what we get has me grinding my fucking teeth together.

Mateo Moretti.

"What the fuck are you doing here?"

He smirks, looking professional and wealthy in his expensive blue suit. "My daughter and I wanted to pay our respects."

"No one died." Tool pushes Moretti out of the way. When we enter the room, Reaper is talking with Natalia while holding Hendrix.

He's still shirtless. There is a NICU nurse in the room, just in case something happens to the baby. She's still hooked up to a ton of tubes and wires. I don't know how Reaper doesn't get tangled in it all.

"Hey, the calvary has arrived. Doll, everyone has come to see you and our beautiful daughter," Reaper whispers to Sarah while kissing her on the cheek. She hasn't woken up yet. I mask my worry because Reaper seems so hopeful carrying Hendrix and holding her against his chest.

"Oh my gosh, I can't believe they're allowing you up here with Hendrix," Juliette gushes, running over to Reaper's side first. She holds a hand to her heart as she stares at the baby with longing. "Isn't she just the best?"

"She's strong, so they allowed her to come see her Momma as long as a nurse was here, which I'll never be able to forgive them for. I'm thankful she's able to be up here. I mean, she has everything she needs, so it works out."

Juliette holds out her arms to take Hendrix, but Reaper pretends not to notice and bounces his baby girl in his arms against his chest.

She's already wrapped around his finger.

"Hey, maybe Dean and Hendrix will grow and marry one another," Doc stupidly suggests.

Reaper snaps his head up and narrows his eyes at Doc. "You're going to keep your son away from my little girl. She's never going to date or anything of the sort. Men aren't worthy of her precious time. Isn't that right, Hendrix?"

"Are you saying my son isn't good enough for your daughter?" Doc lifts a brow, challenging Reaper.

Reaper looks up from Hendrix and sidesteps Juliette, who is still holding out her arms to hold Hendrix. "You know what, Doc. That's exactly what I'm saying. No man is going to be good enough for my Hendrix. Ever."

"Yeah? Well, maybe your little girl isn't good enough for my son. Ever think of that?"

"What the hell did you just say about my daughter? Do you want to take this outside, *friend*?" Reaper hisses, taking a step forward to become nose to nose with Doc. The baby's butts are tapping against one another, and I roll my lips together to keep myself from breaking the serious expression on my face. Out of all the fights I ever imagined, I didn't expect this one.

"Okay, okay, the stress you two are inducing isn't good for the babies or for Sarah to hear," the nurse pipes in, scribbling something down on Hendrix's medical chart after studying the screens.

Doc and Reaper quiet down, but the looks they give one another are downright evil. Those poor kids. They have no idea what they're up against.

"So, how's Sarah doing, Prez?" It's a habit to call him by his title. "Sorry, Reaper," I correct myself. In my eyes, he will always be my President, no matter how great Tool is at the job. "Any improvements?" I ask, doing my best not to inhale too deeply because I can smell the hint of cleaner.

Cleaner that has rubbing alcohol in it or something that smells similar.

How sad is it that I find it to smell so fucking good?

Reaper comes around the hospital bed and takes a seat on the edge of the mattress next to Sarah. He stares at her longingly and places his nose against the side of her head, burying his face in hiding before he whispers something I can't hear.

"No," he says. "No, nothing yet. She's breathing on her own, which they say is a great sign, and no doubt it is, but I want more. I want her to come back to me and meet our amazing little girl."

"Why won't she wake up?" Slingshot asks, stepping next to Natalia. "Sorry if that's a dumb question."

"She's got some swelling in her brain, and for her to wake up, it needs to go down."

The nurse stands beside Reaper and reaches for Hendrix. "How about I take her so you can spend some time—"

"You need to back the fuck off!" he shouts, which causes the babies to cry. "Get away from me. Don't touch her. Don't you fucking dare take her from me." His voice is quiet, a dangerous hiss full of malice. He turns away from the nurse and presses a kiss against Hendrix's forehead. "I can't let her go," he admits, cradling Hendrix against his bare chest.

"I need to bathe her. It's almost time for the doctor to come in. Let me take her, Reaper." The nurse doesn't even flinch or tremble from his warning. "She's going to be okay."

"If not—"

"—You'll kill me. I know the drill, biker-man." She does something none of us would do and takes Hendrix out of Reaper's arms to place her back in the incubator. She immediately starts wailing, and Reaper seems torn.

"Let me have her back. She's upset. She needs me," Reaper says, pushing himself off the bed.

"It's normal for babies to cry, dear. It's okay," The nurse rolls the incubator to the back of the room, and Natalia stands right next to it as she watches the nurse perform her duties. Slingshot is next to Natalia, and Mateo is eyeing Slingshot as if he's gum on the bottom of his shoe.

The door opens again, and Zain walks in with Jessica.

No, Chloe.

Fuck, I can't tell who it is, considering she has a personality disorder.

"Uncle Zain." Reaper does something unexpected and rushes over to his uncle.

For the first time since being a King, I witness the power and strength drain from his body when his uncle hugs him. Reaper fists the back of Zain's shirt.

"It's okay, kiddo. It's all going to be okay," Zain tells him.

All of us look away from the two of them. It feels like we're intruding on a private moment. Reaper doesn't ever let us see him so stripped of what makes him... well... Reaper.

He's Jesse right now. He's just a man afraid he's about to lose everything.

"Where are Boomer and Delilah?" Tool asks to break the awkward silence.

Reaper pulls away from Zain, pats his back, and climbs onto the bed with Sarah again. He brings her head to his chest and runs his fingers through her dirty blonde hair. "You just missed them. They're at the clubhouse sleeping, grabbing a bite, and showering. I told them to go," he informs.

"You do have a beautiful daughter, Reaper," Natalia says from the back of the room.

"She gets it from her Momma." Reaper shuts his eyes and takes a deep breath. The room falls silent, and the only sound is the steady beat of the heart monitor.

"Thank god for that," Slingshot says. "Imagine if poor Hendrix got stuck with your ugly mug."

That loosens the mood, and Slingshot puffs out his chest, proud that he was able to help. "So do you want kids one day, or..." he asks Natalia, who turns a bright shade of red.

Mateo steps from the wall and slaps Slingshot on the back of his head. "If she does have kids, it won't be with the likes of you. Get away from my daughter."

"See, no man is good enough for another man's daughter," Reaper comments smugly to Doc.

Joanna giggles. "Okay, everyone play, nice. Everyone needs to remember they're just babies, and they're going to grow up together. They'll be like brother and sister rather than lovers."

"Oh, a forbidden love affair."

"Really, Ruby? You had to add that?" Bullseye teases his ol' lady.

"What? I wasn't the only one thinking it, so I said it."

"Let's just focus on the fact that they're newborns, okay? They don't even know their names yet." There's a hint of annoyance in Sunnie's tone.

I cock my head at her and notice her arms are crossed, and she's staring at the floor. "I'm going to go get something to drink," she says, excusing herself from the room.

"What did you do, Patrick?" Reaper jokes, but he has me wondering what I did too.

I'm rethinking the entire morning, backtracking everything that happened, but nothing comes to mind. Sunnie seemed fine until we went into the room.

"I'm going to go hunt her down and make sure everything is okay," I say. Before I go, I bend down and whisper into Sarah's ear, "You better come back to us. Your little girl needs her Momma." I give her cold, limp hand a squeeze before turning around. I head out the door in search of my Sunshine.

She's always so happy, though lately, Sunnie's sunny disposition is anything but. Maybe she isn't happy with me anymore.

Christ, that thought makes me want to go to the nearest bar and drown my sorrows.

If she isn't happy, what do I do?

Someone tell me what to do.

CHAPTER NINE

Sunnie

That was completely unnecessary, but I couldn't help but snap. I hated seeing Sarah like that. I hate being surrounded by children.

Children that aren't my own.

Everyone is moving on with their lives and growing their family, but what are Patrick and I doing? I feel like we're in a rut. We aren't moving, but I'm waiting for something more. I know we'll always have a lot of baggage and hardships to work through. I get it. I know we're addicts, and some believe we don't deserve to have kids or a future consisting of something other than fighting the urge to get high.

Do people think we addicts don't want more than our past?

I want to get married.

I want to have kids.

I don't give a damn about the order.

I want something good, something more than what already defines me as a person. I know I need to talk to Patrick about this because the more I bottle it up, the worse it gets.

Honestly, I'm afraid my truth is going to drive Patrick to drink. I haven't craved to get high in a long time, but I know Patrick is on the verge of breaking.

I insert two dollars into the soda machine and check out my choices while banging my fist against the image of a Pepsi bottle and a cherry dancing with one another. While I'm staring at the small boxes to click, a few have orange lights that signal they're out, so I decide on the boring bottle of water.

My fist connects with the button a little too hard.

"What did the machine do to you?"

Patrick's voice slides over me like a warm blanket fresh out of the dryer. There isn't a better feeling. He's home, and the thought of uprooting that scares the hell out of me.

I untwist the top and take a swig. The ice-cold water coats my throat, and I sigh. "They were out of all of my favorites." I really wanted a Dr. Pepper.

He grabs my arm and looks both ways before trying the handle of the janitorial closest.

The door opens, and he flings me inside, which has the water spilling out of the bottle onto my hand. Patrick shuts the door quietly, engulfing us in darkness.

The only amount of light we have is from the small crack between the floor and the door. He flips on the light, and the glow shines upon the seriousness masking his face. His deep-set brown eyes watch me like a hawk as he circles around me, then leans against the shelves. His hands fall to my hips, and as always, the touch soothes the anxiety building in my chest.

"Sunshine, talk to me. What was that about?" he asks in a whisper so no one can hear us from the hallway.

Do I tell the truth? He hasn't told me the entire truth. I don't want to lose him just yet, and I know I will. I feel it, and it's making me sick.

"I'm just sad seeing Reaper like that. I hate that Sarah is unconscious after everything she's been through. She deserves to hold her baby that they tried so hard for, and now… she might not wake up. What will Reaper do? What about Hendrix?"

I'm not lying.

Completely.

I am really upset about the situation. Sarah is my friend. She's like a sister to me, and I remember her crying in the bathroom with every negative test. I remember her coming back from the IVF appointments defeated. I was there for it all. They don't deserve this. They just deserve happiness already. How cruel can the universe be to people?

"I know, it's terrible. They deserve so much more than that." He skims his hands up my sides and cups either side of my neck. His thumbs brush against my jaw, and my eyes flutter in response.

Damn him and what he does to me. Maybe I'd give up my desire for children because I don't know if I could live without his touch.

I'm his.

Wants, dreams, and needs damned to hell, I'm his.

Is that so bad? Why can't that be enough?

"Is something else going on that you want to talk about, Sunshine? Talk to me." He brushes the back of his knuckles against my cheek. "Is there anything else going on in that beautiful mind of yours?"

I shake my head and decide to tiptoe around the conversation I really want to have with him. "I'm thinking of us, you know? What if that was you and me, and we just had a baby? It's terrible to think about." My fingers slide into his belt loops, and I use them to tug myself closer.

Being this close to him under a dim light has heat simmering low in my veins. He spreads his legs wider, which allows me to close another few inches between us. My heart pounds in my chest while we stare at one another. There's a tingle between my legs, and I rub my thighs together to ease the pressure.

I'm trying to read his reaction to what I said, but it's hard for me to focus while I'm so close to his wide shoulders and the warmth radiating from his sun-kissed skin.

I can't tell what he's thinking. I let out a shaky breath when he leans forward, the promise of a kiss tingling my lips.

"If it were us, I'd fall apart," he replies, brushing his bottom lip ever so slightly against mine without kissing me. "If it were us, I wouldn't be as put together as Reaper is. There's no way I can be without you, Sunshine."

That's a better answer than I expected. I thought he'd immediately say no about a baby, but he didn't say anything. Maybe he's more okay with it than I thought...

"If I weren't able to wake up to you—" His fingers pop the button of my jeans open. The loud clasp of the zipper lowering echoes off the cement walls "—Every day for the rest of my life. There wouldn't be a bottle that would be safe in this world that I wouldn't find." He tugs the jeans off my hips, then rubs his fingers against the lace of my panties.

"Don't say that. I never want you to relapse because of me."

"If anything happened to you, that's inevitable, Sunshine. You're the only one keeping my world from turning upside down." His fingers push the material of my panties to the side. He tugs on the tuft of blonde hair I keep trimmed down there.

I whimper, gripping the muscle of his shoulders with my hands.

"Patrick—"

"—It's okay, Sunshine. I know the only thing in existence keeping me strong is you. Night and day, I say no, for you." He dips his fingers through my wet folds, and I tilt my head back, doing my best not to moan. "But you aren't going to say no to me, are you?"

The heady scent of arousal soaking my panties has his nostrils flaring. He grips the back of my head with his other hand. It's a rough hold. His nails scrape my scalp, and my mouth drops open from the sharp pain. "Answer me. Are you going to tell me no?"

"Right here, Patrick?" I ask, a bit dazed, as his wide fingers continue lazily slipping through my lips. I'm getting wetter and wetter with every stroke.

"Right here." He backs me up against the door, and with a rough shove, flips me around to my stomach. I think he must really love this position. I often find myself with my cheek pressed against a pillow, wall, or door when we have sex.

I'm not complaining.

It means he wants it rough.

I love it when he's unhinged and about to break. I come best that way.

He doesn't bother taking my underwear off. Patrick keeps them parted to the side, and just when I think he's about to plaster his body against mine, his warmth is gone.

"Wha—" I turn around to see him on the floor, licking his lips as he plays with the globes of my ass. "What are you doing? Fuck me, damn it," I complain. I'm too hot and bothered to wait much longer.

"All in good time, Sunshine." He parts my cheeks and blows onto my forbidden hole. "I want to fuck this ass. Not right now, but later." Patrick kisses my hole and then spears his tongue through my folds, the vibrations of his groans trembling my clit.

"Oh god," I moan a little too loud.

He chuckles. "Sunshine, you gotta be quiet. We don't want to get caught, do we?"

I shake my head, keeping my forehead against the door.

"Every sound you make, the longer you'll have to wait to come." He dives his tongue into my pussy, spearing it in and out like he'd do with his cock.

I dig my nails against the door and bite my lip. "I... I promise I'll be good. No noises." I have to shove my hand over my mouth to keep my promise while his tongue does magical, impossible things. Things that no man should be able to do.

The doorknob jiggles, and he stops feasting on me. I almost curse in protest. Almost.

"Hey, who's in there?" the janitor bangs against the door. "Fred, is it you?" he asks.

Patrick chuckles and muffles his mouth against my crease to hide his voice. "Something spilled in here. Just cleaning it up." He drags his nose as low as he can before stretching his tongue to roll against my clit.

"Oh, alright. See you around, man," the janitor says from behind the door.

"I don't think so. I'm blinded right now," Patrick hushes inside me.

I'm about to beg him to break my promise. My nipples rub against the door, and as my body temperature rises, a sheen of sweat begins to form.

"Such a perfect cunt." He stands and latches onto the side of my neck, fiddling with his pants between us to release his cock. "Can't fucking wait to slide inside and make it mine."

I nod because I don't know if I'm allowed to talk.

He settles his thick shaft between my ass cheeks and ruts, wishing we had time for him to fuck me there instead so I can really feel him all day when I sit. He yanks me back by my hair, and I hiss, licking the sweat off the top of my lip.

The tip of his cock is at my entrance. I'm dripping for him, getting the head slick.

"You're so fucking filthy, wanting to get fucked in a hospital closet. You a slut for my cock, Sunshine? Just like I am for this tight cunt?" he asks before taking my mouth in a savage kiss. Our teeth clink together, and our tongues duel while he slides to the hilt.

His heavy, swollen sack presses against my ass, and we both groan down each other's throat. I have to break away to catch my breath. My head bangs against the door as I inhale. He doesn't give me time for air; instead, he steals my ability to breathe. He slides out, and with a hard thrust, fills me back up, stretching me in the best way.

I hold onto the door, pressing my palms flat to push against Patrick's chest, so we aren't banging against it and giving away our location.

"Fuck, you feel so good." He grabs onto my hips and fucks me into oblivion.

Small, high-pitched whines escape my throat as he forces them out with every shove of his cock.

"I need to see you," he says breathlessly and flips on the light. "Oh fuck yes, I wish you could see what I see. Your panties are pushed to the side, grazing my cock every time I rock into you. Your ass shakes... goddamn it, you're going to make me come too fast." He spanks me out of nowhere. The slapping sound is so loud I know if anyone is outside the door, they'd hear it. My skin burns in the most delicious way, and then he gropes the stinging flesh, using the reddened cheeks to meet his long, thick cock with every stroke.

"Come. I need you to come, Sunshine. I'm not going to last."

I'm there. I'm right there. "Please, don't stop. I need more," I beg of him.

He reaches around and pinches my clit to the point of pain, and that's all it takes for me to throw my head back onto his shoulder, my climax tearing through me. Every part of my body quivers and quakes. My muscles clamp around him, trying to suck him deeper, trying to get him into the farthest part of my wicked depths.

He plants himself in one final, forceful thrust, orgasming with me. "Ah, damn it, Sunnie. Damn it," he whines, punctuating his hips with every word. "I'll never get enough. You have no idea how fucking hot you look right now." He's still rutting, using me while I flutter around him. "You have to walk around with me inside you now. Just think, later when we're in bed, you're still going to be wet with me," he drags his lips up the side of my ear. "I'm going to use it later to fuck your ass, so you have no choice but to be full of me." He flips me over and wraps his hand around my neck, squeezing tight, which has my eyes rolling back. I fucking love it when he gets like this.

Wild.

Alpha.

Obsessive.

I could come all over again.

"Who owns you, Sunshine?"

I tilt my chin in defiance for the hell of it, even as the warmth of his come dripping down my thighs tells me who I belong to, but I love this game.

"I do."

He cups my pussy, his fingers gliding along with the mixture of our juices. "Who. The. Fuck. Owns. You?" he repeats on a thunderous rumble.

I lean forward, touching my nose with his, and curl my lip at him. "I fucking do."

The displeased sound that leaves his mouth has me rocking onto his hand for friction.

"You like to test me..." he huffs. "Tell me, or I won't make you come for a month."

I gasp. "You wouldn't."

"Try me, Sunshine." His face softens. The hard edges of his lips fade, and his eyes dilate. "I need to hear it," he admits.

I know he does. I love it when he does. "You own me. I'm yours. I'm your property. Your ol' lady."

"Mmm, you're getting me hard again." His eyes drop to my lips. "Want to go for another round?"

"Want to go somewhere where... I don't know." I swirl my finger across his shirt. "Where it's a little riskier?"

"Babe... do you want to get caught?" he curls a brow up at me, but I can see the surprise written on his face.

"I mean... would it be so bad? It's kind of exhilarating, right? Maybe a patient room... or in the car on the side of the road... in a club? Unless you don't want to—" I sigh to make it obvious I'm bummed.

He pulls up my panties, then my jeans, and he rushes to tuck his cock back in his pants and hisses when he almost zips up his cock. "Fuck, let's do all those things. Now. Patient room. Oh, sneak into the bathroom while they are sleeping?"

"And then let our noise wake them up, and we'll run out of the hospital with security on our heels," I say excitedly.

"I fucking love you." He grabs my face and kisses me senselessly. I melt into it like I always do.

And then I remember why we're here.

"After we go see Sarah one last time and say goodbye to everyone because that's the right thing to do."

"Yeah, because that's the right thing to do, but after... you're mine, Sunshine."

How easily he forgets that I'm always his.

Always.

I think I can give up having kids if it means being this happy with Patrick for the rest of my life.

Yeah, I can do that.

Having these wonderful adventures with Patrick is all that matters.

He opens the door and checks the hall, and we walk out right in front of a nurse.

Oh my god, he just outed us.

While we walk hand in hand, I'm happier than I've been, and the urge to start a family isn't as strong. I'm happy.

I've made my decision.

So why is the voice in the back of my head asking, "Are you sure?"

I am. Sure.

I think.

CHAPTER TEN

Patrick

I WAKE UP TO THE SHARP TRILL OF MY PHONE GOING OFF. My body is stiff, and my cock is rubbed raw with how many times Sunnie and I fucked yesterday. Thinking about it has my cock trying to come to life, but it's way too sensitive right now. I reach for my phone on my nightstand and press the volume button once to silence the vibrations.

Turning over, I wrap my arms around Sunnie and tug her to my chest. Her bare ass rubs against my cock, and I'm tempted to fuck through the pain. I don't know what it is. Seeing her yesterday so sad, so vulnerable, so unlike herself set me off.

I don't get to see her like that often. In a fucked-up way, it turned me on because I got to know a side of her I didn't know existed. I kiss the middle of her neck and snuggle against her instead. If I'm sore, I know she has to be hurting too.

The ceiling fan whooshes and the chains dangling that control the lights and speed of the blades clink together. The sound has me closing my eyes. I'm drifting deeper into the soft down feathers of the pillow when my phone starts vibrating again.

Careful not to wake Sunnie, I pull my arm away, and she rolls over onto her stomach. I watch her for a few more seconds to make sure she isn't awake and then blindly reach for my phone. The blanket pools around my waist; even the soft thread count rubbing against my cock sends a stint of pain zinging through me.

I think I might have sex burn. If that's a thing. It has to be.

My phone stops ringing, then starts again, which has me rolling out of bed. I tug on a pair of sweatpants I keep on the floor for middle-of-the-night runs to the kitchen. Giving Sunnie one last glance, I rub my right eye to wake myself up and stare at the number I don't recognize flashing across my screen.

"Yeah? Who the hell is calling me at four in the damn morning?" I bite out, opening the cabinet for a glass to get some water. When I turn around, I slam my toe into the kitchen table. I suck in a deep breath, barely holding back an agitated curse.

"Pa—Patrick?"

My brows pinch when I recognize the voice, but I can't place it. It's a woman, young, but I haven't met anyone recently. "Yeah, this is him. What do you want?"

"It's Poppy."

I sit up straighter and place the glass in the sink. "Poppy, is everything okay? What's going on?"

"Can you please come get me? I'm sorry. I know it's late, but I'm scared, and I didn't know who else to call and—" she breaks off into a sob. The fear in her voice has me alert and awake, stuttering my heart.

There's music in the background, but she must be in a room of some kind because it's muted. "—Hey, it's okay. I'm sorry for snapping. I'm not used to anyone calling me so late." It's been a while. When the club whores were around, they would call me when they wanted to suck my cock, or I'd call them for a quick fuck, but things have changed around here.

Hell, Becks hasn't even come back around. She went to that massage conference, and fucking ghosted us without a postcard or a heads up.

I like the change. We have ol' ladies and kids in the house now. We have jobs to do, and things don't get clouded with free ass walking around. The fights that would happen if they were here…I'd bet Sarah and Ruby would kill a whore in a heartbeat.

"What's wrong, Poppy? What's going on? Are you safe?"

"I don't know," she whispers. "I don't think so. My ex-boyfriend won't let me leave and—" she begins to cry again. "He held me down and tried to give me heroin, but I fought him off. He locked me in his bedroom, and his windows are nailed shut. I can't get out. He has friends here… friends he threatened to let gang bang me if I didn't listen to him. I don't want to get high, Patrick. Please. I don't want to."

"Poppy, what's the address? Can you text it to me? I'll bring a few of my buddies, and we'll get you out of there."

"Your biker friends?" she asks, a note of hope in her voice.

"Yeah, Poppy. You're going to be okay, but I'm going to need you to hold on a little longer. Can you do that for me?"

"Yes, I think so."

God, she's terrified. She's too young to have to deal with this, but isn't that always the case?

Youth is never kind. That's when life likes to test the cruelty, test your strength and see if you can make it into this world.

You either sink from trying or swim, and if you make it to shore, there's no doubt you're going to be fucked up for the rest of your life.

"Do you have a weapon?"

"I... I can look for one." I hear drawers banging as she rustles through her ex's belongings.

"Okay, good. Text me the address. I'm going to get ready now. I just need you to hold tight. Text me every five minutes to let me know you're okay."

"I don't want to get off the phone. I don't want to be alone." Goddamn it, she sounds so desperate.

"I know. I know you don't. I know you're scared, but this is where you prove to yourself that you're better than your fear. You're stronger. I'll wake up a few of my friends. We'll take the truck, and I'll call you the moment I'm on my way, okay?"

"You'll hurry?" she sniffles.

"Like the rum that I used to pour down my throat, Poppy."

She snorts and then gasps. "I didn't mean to laugh—"

"It was supposed to make you laugh. Let's get off here and get ready, okay? Whatever you do, you fight like fucking hell, you hear me? I don't give a fuck if you kill the bastard. We'll take care of it."

"I will. I promise," she reassures me.

"Okay. I'll talk to you soon." I hang up the phone and rub my hands over my face.

"Sunnie know about this woman?"

I jump in my chair and look up to see Badge standing there with his arms crossed.

And he looks fucking pissed. He's been gone since the ladies had the babies. When he heard about Sarah, he immediately came back from wherever he went. I think he wanted to clear his head about Hope. That pairing would be a disaster, especially with how much he 'can't stand' kids.

"What? I'm not having an affair." I grind my teeth together that he would even think I'd do that to Sunnie. "She's from AA. She's eighteen, and I gave her my card with mine and Sunnie's numbers on it. She's in trouble, Badge. Locked in her ex's bedroom, windows are nailed shut, and he's threatening her with drugs and his friends."

He uncrosses his arms, and his stance becomes straighter. "Okay, I'm in. No woman needs to be in that situation. Who else are we bringing?"

"I really wish Tongue was here. He'd have a field day."

"I miss that crazy motherfucker."

My brows raise. If Badge is admitting a feeling, then he must really mean it.

"We can't ask Reaper, Bullseye, or Doc," I say, switching the subject from emotion to facts.

"Fucking kids," he grumbles. "Knives for sure then, and fucking Boomer. His crazy ass is here. Skirt. Not Poodle..." he says with a hint of sorrow. "And we can't have Tool leave the clubhouse. He has to stay here just in case. And Slingshot should probably stay, too, since we're taking most of the members."

"We should be fine. Me, you, Boomer, Knives, and Skirt. That will scare the hairs off their chests."

Badge knocks his fingers on the wood. "Better hope so. Alright. Meet out front in five? I'll wake Skirt and find Boomer. You deal with Knives."

No one likes waking Knives up. He always throws a ninja star from being startled, and plenty of us have gotten nicked a time or two.

"Fine, but if I die from a star to the head, that's on you," I say.

"The fuck it is. That's on his ass. I'm not taking the blame." Badge heads down the hall toward his room, leaving me all to my lonesome to deal with Knives.

Asshole.

I keep my phone close and head to the bedroom Knives hasn't stayed in since he met Mary. Everyone is piled in the clubhouse right now. Everyone needs to be close right now with everything happening with Sarah. It's an incredible sense of family.

His door next to the basement door. I knock carefully and try for the doorknob. It's locked. I breathe a sigh of relief. It means I won't get slammed with a ninja star. I lift my fist and bang louder. A loud thud hits the door a second later.

See? I would have died.

"What?" he sneers, opening the door naked, with his hair standing in every direction.

I look up at the ceiling. "I need your help. A friend of mine from AA called me. She's in trouble, and no, I'm not having a fucking affair. She's eighteen. A kid. I feel like I got to protect her."

"Eighteen never stopped some of us," he snickers, clearly pleased with his jab at Reaper. "Alright, give me a second to get dressed. Let me tell Hellraiser what I'm doing, so she doesn't worry."

"I'm doing the same," I say. "Meet out front and grab the truck keys."

He gives me a nod before slamming the door in my face.

My phone pings with the address Poppy is being held at and another text that says she's still safe. I puff out my cheeks while blowing out a breath and stride back to my room. My bare feet pat along the hardwood floor. The scent of lavender wafting from Poodle's bathroom tickles my nose as I pass it. I open my bedroom door, the knob cold in my palm. Sunnie is sprawled out on the bed like a starfish.

I take a quick picture because she's so goddamn cute.

"Sunnie," I whisper her name gently while stroking her cheek and neck, wanting to wake her as loving as possible. "Sunshine, wake up, baby. I gotta go."

"Mmm," she flips over to ignore me.

I can't help but laugh. "Sunshine, wake up for me. Come on." I urge her again by rubbing small circles on her back.

When she turns over again, she blinks up sleepily at me and gives me a lopsided smile. "Everything okay?" she asks, her voice hoarse from resting.

"My friend from AA called. She's in trouble at her ex's house. I gave her our numbers in case she needed us, as in you and I. She's just a kid, eighteen. It's a real bad situation. The guys and I are going there to get her, okay? I don't want you to worry. I'll be okay. I love you."

"Oh no, I'm sorry. Text me on your way back, and I'll try to have tea waiting for her."

I bend down and kiss the middle of her forehead. "You're the best. I love you, Sunshine. I'll be back."

"Be safe, okay?"

"I promise. Get a little more rest, beautiful." I rub my thumb across her bottom lip, and she presses a quick kiss to the pad of my finger.

She has no idea how much I'm addicted to her. If someone would make me choose, gun to my head, between her and a bottle of rum, two things I crave more than anything, I'd choose Sunnie every time. Maybe that isn't a big deal to some because it's the right thing to do, but no one knows what alcoholics are willing to give up for one more taste.

I'd give up everything, but I wouldn't give up Sunnie.

She's the soul I need to live every day.

I've been soulless once, and I never want to be that man again.

I get dressed and throw on my cut. It's the cut people always notice first. No one wants to fuck with a Ruthless King.

I shut the door quietly and pass Tyrant and Chaos on the way to the main room. It's sad not to see Lady with them. "We'll be back. Keep everyone safe, okay?"

Tyrant licks my hand in reply.

"Good boy," I tell him, and Chaos gets jealous, bumping his head against my hand to lick it too. "Aw, you know I love you too, buddy. Okay, I gotta go. I'll be back." I give him a scratch behind the ear and head out the door.

When I step onto the porch, Knives is laughing with Boomer, picking up his feet as Boomer throws those firework poppers that make a loud noise when they hit the ground.

"Dance monkey, dance!" Boomer shouts at Knives as he tosses them next to Knives' boots.

The truck is grumbling waiting for us to leave. Badge is leaning against it, completely unamused, with his ankles and arms crossed.

"Didn't know ye could move so fast, Knives," Skirt hollers with laughter.

I'm heading down the steps to join them when Braveheart and Tank come out onto the porch. "Hey, where are you guys going?"

Shit. They need to stay here too.

"Braveheart. Tank. We have an errand to run, but you need to stay here in case anything happens. Kids are here. Alright?"

"Do both of us need to stay?" Braveheart asks. "Come on, man. Let one of us come."

"I'll stay. I don't mind," Tank offers. "I gotta piss anyway."

I place a cigarette between my lips and light it, inhaling as hard as I can. "Fine.

Let's go. Tank, if anything happens, you fucking fight till you die. My Sunshine is inside."

He gives me a salute. "You can count on me, Patrick."

I clobber down the steps and blow out a cloud of smoke. "Boomer, it's good to see you." My eyes drop to his cut, especially that patch that says 'President.' "Looks good, man."

He tugs on the lapels and runs his fingers through his dirty blonde hair. "It does, don't it? I'm fuckin' good at it too."

"We can shake our dicks later. Let's ride." Badge hits the side of the truck with his palm and hurries around the tailgate to get to the driver's side.

"We'll follow on our bikes," Skirt says, throwing his leg over the seat.

Knives, Boomer, and Braveheart do the same, and I climb into the truck's passenger seat. Badge rolls down the window for me so I can blow the smoke outside. Classic rock and roll blares through the speakers as we head out of the parking lot and line up behind each other as we wait for the gate to swing open.

My phone vibrates again, and it's Poppy telling me she's still safe. I type out a quick message telling her we're on our way, then click on the address she sent to bring up the directions.

"She's only ten minutes out," I tell Badge, who takes a quick peek at my phone to see which way he has to turn.

The bikes behind us roar from the powerful horses stampeding through the engines. The Ford Raptor is just as loud, with a custom exhaust that bellows all the same with deep baritones. Badge curls his fingers around the leather steering wheel to the point that it creaks as he takes a turn.

I inhale the smoke again and blow it out of the corner of my mouth, hoping it makes its way out the window. "Okay, what?"

"Nothing," he lies.

"Bullshit. Tell me."

"You swear this girl is just some kid? Nothing more? You aren't cheating? 'Cause, you've been acting real squirrely lately, and I swear to god, Patrick, if you're cheating on sweet Sunnie, I'll fucking waterboard you with a bottle of rum."

I swallow at the threat. My fingers tremble when I think about how wonderful and awful that would be all at the same time. "I'm not cheating on Sunnie," I say with a deadly warning. "I'd never do that. I'm going to ask her to marry me. I wouldn't do that if I were fucking around, which I wouldn't do. We already talked about this, Badge. Do you not believe me?"

"I do. I just wanted to make sure. When are you thinking of asking the big question?"

"Soon. I hope." I'm trying not to relapse. Once I get through this itch, I'll get down on one knee and put a ring on her finger. She's already wearing my property patch. To a biker, that's everything, but I know marriage would mean a lot to Sunnie.

Plus, tying her to me in every way sounds pretty fucking good to me.

"Then what's been going on with you?" he asks.

Other than wanting to get drunk off every kind of alcohol there is? Nothing.

"I'm fine, Badge. If I need help, I'll ask for it." I won't ask, but there's nothing wrong with trying to believe I would.

"Fucking liar," he grumbles.

Yes, lies build a sense of false self, and I really need that right now.

I point out the window with the butt of the cigarette before tossing it outside to let the wind take it. "That looks like it."

"It's a trailer park."

"What the fuck is wrong with that? There's nothing wrong with trailer parking living Badge. Not everyone is trash."

"What the fuck? That's not what I meant. When I was a cop—" I don't miss the crack in his voice when he says the words. He misses it more than anything. "—I was called here a lot. It's known for drugs, assault, dog fighting rings, the works. It isn't a safe place."

He flips on his blinker and turns onto the gravel road that leads through the middle of the park. There are a few dozen trailers, but it seems most everyone is outside around a bonfire right now, drinking and dancing to music.

Plenty of guys have their shirts off, and couples are making out then switching partners. I couldn't imagine sharing Sunnie like that. Her lips, her touch, her body are all mine. Other men aren't allowed to watch or touch.

This leads me to wonder how Bullseye does it. There's a part of me that wonders if he and Skirt switch partners. I don't think so—but they're in that damn room a lot these days. I mean, one thing eventually leads to another, right? Someone pushes one boundary, then another, and then all of a sudden, what if you're in a big orgy and don't know how you got there?

"It's this one." I point to the trailer to our right. It's old. The outside has rust on the siding from the weather, and the porch is sagging. The steps are broken, and there's a screen door lying on the lawn. I wonder if it was ripped off from the hinges.

Badge slams the truck into park and turns off the engine, tucking the keys safely in his cut pocket. "Let's get this party started." We hop out of the Raptor and slam the doors while waiting for someone to come up and stop us.

I expected… violence.

The bikes stop grumbling, and all of us turn to see the people dancing around the fire, the music is blaring, and no one is paying us any mind.

"Well, this might be easier than we thought," Skirt comments, knocking his kickstand with his boot before dismounting his bike.

"Sorry, guys. She made it sound worse than it is."

"Damn, I really wanted to throw some stars. I'm out of practice," Knives says sadly.

"Not according to your bedroom door." I point out.

We climb the steps, bypassing the broken ones, and the porch groans from our added weight.

"That sounds ominous," Braveheart says as he looks around.

The first thing I notice is the front door. It's open. I press my fingers against it and push. The hinges squeak in need of oil or replacement, and a cloud of smoke that reeks of weed smacks us in the face.

Boomer whistles. "Damn, that's some strong shit. Wonder who their supplier is?"

"I know you aren't trying to network right now," I glare at him.

"A businessman is always looking for business, no matter the circumstances," Boomer shrugs.

I step inside first the guys follow behind me. Badge has a gun out, Knives has his stars out, Skirt is wearing his brass knuckles, and Braveheart... I don't know what he's doing. He's putting on his brave face, and that's why we like him.

The TV is playing static, and the rabbit ears on top are bent. The carpet is a puke green color and a shag material that reminds me of the '70s. The wallpaper in the kitchen is peeling, and the linoleum floor is chipped from age and wear. The recliner has stains on it, the couch sags in the middle, and the dark wood coffee table has various drugs on it.

Boomer snags the bag of pot and tucks it in his pocket. All of us deadpan him with a dirty look.

"What? Homer has rice crispy joints. This will help him."

What a sorry excuse. We all know Homer has more pot than a marijuana distribution center.

There's a spoon next to a white substance, along with a candle flickering and a needle. None of that is getting to me.

But the spilled bottle of vodka dripping onto the carpet? My mouth is fucking watering. I take a step toward it, but Skirt yanks me back by my cut, and Badge takes the bottle to the kitchen to get rid of it.

They always have my back.

"I'm okay."

"Ye sure?"

"I'm fine. Thanks." I take a deep breath and pat my pocket for the sobriety chip. I'm okay. I'll be fine. "Poppy!" I call out for her, but I don't hear a thing. "Poppy?" I begin to head down the hall.

The trailer moans with every step—the pictures lining the wall tilt to the side.

"Poppy? You here? Say something."

The door at the very end of the hall opens, and Badge is next to me, aiming his gun directly at the door. "Come out with your hands in the air," he shouts, cocking his weapon.

"Patrick?" Poppy whimpers as she comes out of the room. "I... I protected myself like you said, but... I think I went too far."

As I get closer, I notice the blood on her clothes and the splatter across her face. In her hand is a small handgun with a short barrel. She's shaking and in shock.

"I found a weapon like you said. They came back. They were starting to strip. I didn't know what else to do. I... I didn't know. I'm sorry."

I pull her in for a hug, not caring about the blood. I wonder if this kid is really eighteen or if she just told me that. She seems too... innocent. "It's okay. We're here now." I lean away and notice the black eye she's carrying. "Did they do that to you?"

She nods.

Badge and Skirt are the first to enter the room she was in. "Holy fucking hell," Skirt announces. "Did ye run out of bullets, Poppy?" he asks her.

"I kept shooting. It was all I had."

I gently take the gun away from her and tuck it in my waistband. "Don't ever apologize for protecting yourself. Ever. You understand me?"

She nods, and it has a tear break free. "Stay with Braveheart, okay? I'm going in the room."

"No, no, don't leave me, please. Don't go." She wraps her arms around me tight like a child clings to their father when they're afraid.

"I have to figure out what to do with the bodies, okay? We aren't going to let you get in trouble, okay?" The bass of the music takes that moment to pound the walls. No wonder people aren't running around freaking out, or the place isn't swarming with cops. No one could hear the gunshots. "Stay right here with Braveheart. He's a good guy. I promise."

"Okay," Poppy says softly, with a bit of resignation. She sags against the wall and slides down onto the floor, then lifts her knees to her chest and cries.

I hate leaving her, but I have to head into the room where the guys are. When I get there, what I see makes my eyes go wide. "Holy fuck."

"She shot them all in the chest and groin. Her aim is impeccable."

"That's what yer getting from this? We have three bodies here. What are we going to do with them?" Skirt asks.

"We take them back to the compound and burn them," I say.

"And then I blow this place to smithereens." Boomer takes out two sticks of dynamite from his cut and wiggles his brows. "No one will know."

"Everyone is going to know, Boomer. You can't exactly hide an explosion."

"No," he says. "But you can time it. We can get the truck to the back door, load the bodies in the back, I can set up a contraption, and with a press of a button with this burner, the place will go 'boom.' We can go out the back way and never look back. Everyone here is too fucking drunk—sorry, Patrick—to know what the hell is going on anyway. And no cop is going to put a lot of faith in this place," he adds.

"No offense taken," I say.

"He's right, unfortunately." Badge sounds disappointed, but there is nothing we can do about that right now.

I have to make a decision. We can't be here all fucking night. "Boomer, get your dynamite ready. Braveheart!" I call out.

He sticks his head in the crack of the door. He doesn't even blink at the carnage around our feet. "Yeah, Patrick?"

"Bring the truck around back and get Poppy settled too. She doesn't need to see us loading the bodies."

"You got it," he says, giving the wall a quick tap of his knuckles. Braveheart disappears and leaves us in the room that smells of blood and something else that I can't quite put my finger on. It reeks, whatever it is. The mattress is on the floor, and the bed is unmade. There are half-filled plastic water bottles everywhere and burnt ends of blunts in the ashtray.

"Well, they aren't going to get up and load themselves," Badge grunts, lifting one guy up and slinging him over his shoulder.

Skirt laughs. "Imagine if they did, though? Christ, I'd be shitting my damn kilt. I'd be so scared."

"Please don't. One mess to clean up at a time," I answer, somehow managing to smile during a time like this.

I must just be used to blood and bodies.

Each of us carries a body to the hallway and watch out the window. The taillights shine bright red as Braveheart reverses as close as he can to the back door. Boomer is whistling as he sets up his bomb, having the time of his life.

Badge kicks the door open, and Braveheart opens the tailgate. "Come on. Before someone comes." Braveheart gestures with his hand.

"We'd just kill them too," Badge states simply as if killing is the solution for everything.

I throw the body on the bed of the truck a bit harder than necessary, and the man's head smacks against it with a crunch. I cringe. Skirt follows suit, and Badge tosses his guy in next. I shut the tailgate and pull the cover over it next to hide the bodies.

The hinges of the door whining have me turning around to see Boomer coming out of the trailer with a post-orgasmic smile on his face.

The dude has issues when it comes to blowing shit up.

"Let's get out of here," I declare and climb into the truck. Poppy is crying in the front seat, mumbling how sorry she is over and over. Her hands are shaking as she tries to wipe the blood on her jeans.

I know nothing I say will make it better.

"Hey." Boomer pokes his head through the window from the passenger side. "You want to press this button right here?" He shows her a small remote-like device, tapping a button that's labeled number three. "And your worst nightmare will go up in smoke."

"Really?" she sniffles.

ORBITING MARS

"Really. Do it. You'll feel so much better." Boomer pats the door as he, Skirt, Knives, and Braveheart head to their bikes.

"Let's get out of here," Badge says, turning on the engine and throwing the truck in drive.

"Oh, you're going to want to wait until we're a safe distance," Boomer yells at the last minute before the roars of the motorcycles take over his voice.

The tires crunch against the gravel while we go out the back entrance. I turn around to make sure my brothers are behind us. Their headlights finally come to view as they round the corner from the trailer. We turn onto the road, and I double-check everyone is still behind us. When Knives is the last one to turn on the street, I tap Poppy's shoulder. "Now. Press it now."

Her hands continue to shake as she cradles the device. Her thumb presses the number three hard until her flesh turns white from the pressure. We all look out the window to see the trailer explode. Flames lick the sky in reds and oranges, and the ground mimics an earthquake. Poppy's eyes are and wide and full of tears—tears of relief.

"Alright, let's go before the cops show up," Badge states and presses his foot against the gas to get us home quicker.

The song "Bad Company" thumps through the speakers, and I smirk at the irony since we have bodies in the back and bikers behind us.

While one issue is taken care of, now we just have to burn the bodies.

My biggest concern—

What the hell am I going to do with Poppy?

CHAPTER ELEVEN

Sunnie

I'M IN THE KITCHEN FILLING THE KETTLE TO THE BRIM, THEN PLACE IT ON THE STOVE TO boil. I told Patrick I'd be up to make his friend tea, and I meant it. I rub my eyes to get the grit of sleep out and lean my hip against the counter as I wait for the kettle to whistle.

"No, I got it. We'll burn them. Go take care of Poppy."

I snap my head up when I hear Boomer's voice and the tea kettle whistles at that exact moment. I hurry to the cabinet that holds all the mugs and take three down, fill them with tea bags, and pour boiling hot water over them.

I'm nervous. Is that okay? I've never met anyone from Patrick's AA meetings except Wendy, his sponsor. I want to make a good impression on his friend, and by the sound of it, it seems like she's had a hell of a time.

Deep breaths. Everything will be fine.

I place the mugs on the table and sit. No, maybe I should stand. Maybe that's too intimidating? Sitting is best. No, then it will look like I'm waiting. I stand right as Patrick and a girl come into the kitchen. A very young girl.

Oh my god, the poor thing. She's skin and bone. Her hair is messy and bright blue, matted to her scalp, and she has dark circles under her eyes. She's flickering her eyes all around as if something is going to jump out of the corner and snatch her.

I study her and notice a very similar tic that I have.

She's scratching her inner arms.

Her eyes are red and swollen from tears, and the bruise on the right side of her face is nasty-looking. It's black and looks painful.

"Poppy, this is Sunnie. My ol' lady. Sunnie, this is Poppy."

"Hi Pop—" my words are cut short when she slams against me.

Poppy wraps her arms around my waist and buries her face against my chest. Her hot tears wet my skin, and I return her needy embrace.

"Thank you so much. Thank you both so much," she sobs. "I know you didn't have to let him help, but you did. Thank you."

"Of course. Any friend of Patrick's is a friend of mine. Take a seat. I made us some tea." I push against her shoulders, breaking the hug, and that's when her arms fall to her side. That's when I notice the blood. "How about we get you cleaned up first?" I walk her over to the sink and turn on the faucet. Hot and cold water at the same time, so it's comfortable. I guide her hands under the steady stream, squeeze soap on her hands, and take the rough bristle brush, and scrub across her hands. I make sure to get under the nails too.

"Doesn't it bother you?" she whispers, giving me a quick glance before looking away.

"Oh no. This isn't anything. You are in a place where everyone understands where you're coming from." The water that swirls down the drain turns pink as the blood rushes off her hands.

"Patrick said…" she licks her lips. "Never mind."

"What?"

"Patrick said you were a heroin addict?" she whispers even softer so Patrick can't hear her.

"That's correct." I glance at her track marks on her arm.

"Does it get easier?"

The question has me scrubbing her hands softer. "Everyone is different. I went to rehab, which is where I met Patrick. I don't have the urge for heroin anymore, but that doesn't mean someone else wouldn't." Once her hands are clean, I dry them off with a paper towel, then scrub the red splatter off her left cheek. "Come on, the tea will help you relax."

I pull out her chair, and she lowers herself to sit. Her eyes close for a second when she wraps her hands around the hot mug. I bet she's feeling that warmth through her entire body.

As I watch her sip her tea, I notice how young she really looks. "How old are you, Poppy? And don't say you're eighteen. You aren't, are you?"

She swallows the mouthful of chamomile tea and shakes her head. The greasy blue strands of her hair block her face as she curls in on herself.

"It's okay. You aren't in trouble." I reach for her hand and give it a light squeeze. "We just want to get to know you." The smell of the bonfire out front is stronger than usual, and I make a face to stop myself from throwing up. I know that smell.

It's burning flesh.

They're burning bodies. Whatever happened to Poppy, she had to protect herself.

"I'm sixteen." She lifts her eyes to Patrick. "I'm sorry. I thought saying I was eighteen would make you take me more seriously. Please, don't be mad at me." Poppy falls to her knees and rests her head against Patrick's leg. "Please, don't be mad. I won't lie again. I promise."

"Hey, none of that. I'm not mad. No one is mad, but how are you only sixteen with all this happening to you, kiddo? Addicted to drugs? I can't help you if you don't talk to me," Patrick says, keeping his voice level and calm.

He pets the side of her head, and that seems to calm her.

What in the world has this poor girl been through?

I scoot closer to Patrick and take his hand in mine. I know we have a lot to discuss. She's clearly attached to us somehow, him more than me, which makes sense. It seems she misses a dominant figure in her life.

"Talk to me, Poppy. I can't help you if you don't." He's stern, and I'm about to slap his arm for doing that. He's going to scare her. More fear and the girl will turn into a pumpkin before Halloween.

She stares up at him, eyes wide as she digs her fingers into his pant leg.

"Where are your parents? Do you have anyone we can call for you?"

She shakes her head. "My parents died last year, and it's just been my stepbrother and me. He's my ex. Please, I don't want to go back to the park. So many bad people there."

I can't help but watch her body language. She isn't pawing at Patrick, just clinging to him for safety. She wants to make him happy. She's clearly been abused. She has scars around her wrists, maybe from being tied up.

"Hey, no one is going to make you go anywhere you don't want to go. Okay? Finish your tea, and then Sunnie is going to get a room ready—"

"I can't stay with you guys in your room?" she whips her head so fast her hair flies around her shoulders. "I don't know this place or these people."

"I know we're big scary bikers, but I promise, we're good people. We'll protect you. And Sunnie and I will be right in the next room. Okay? I promise you won't be far and that you're in a safe place. No one can get onto this land."

"You swear?"

"On the bottle," Patrick says, and his choice of words has me falling in love with him a little more. "Now, finish your tea, shower, and then we'll talk more in the morning."

"Okay, Patrick." Poppy seems so eager, staring at Patrick as if she's a puppy waiting to be trained. She stands and goes back to her chair, curling in on herself again and holding the mug to her chest.

"I'll go get the room ready." I get up to leave, and Poppy drops her mug onto the kitchen floor. It shatters into a hundred bits. The liquid is still hot enough that it's steaming from the ground.

Poppy drops to her knees and begins to pick up the pieces, ignoring when her fingers bleed. "You can't go. You can't. I'm sorry for the mess. I'm so sorry."

Patrick and I are at her side instantly, and I yank the paper towels from the counter. "Poppy, it's okay. I didn't mean to scare you or for you to think I was leaving forever," I tell her. I didn't think she was that attached to me just yet, but it seems she has latched herself on to the both of us. "You're hurting yourself. Never do that. It's okay to drop things. It's just a mug." I pat her index finger with a towel to stop the bleeding. "Never pick up sharp objects. Always use a broom, okay?"

She nods numbly, staring into space as silent tears drip down her cheeks. Patrick is staring at the shattered ceramic, lost in thought.

"Come on, let's go shower and get you into clean clothes. Patrick, can you clean this up, please?" I ask him as I guide her to Poodle's bathroom.

She's shaking.

"It's okay. I'll give you some privacy."

"No!" she yells. "I mean," Poppy lowers her voice. "I don't want to be alone."

"Sure. I understand." I shut the door behind me and turn around to give her privacy to get undressed.

"I don't think I can lift my arms, Sunnie. I'm exhausted," she admits.

I turn around to witness her trying to take off her shirt, but she can't. Her muscles are trembling from the effort.

"I can help if you want," I offer.

She nods, and an embarrassed flush takes over her bruised cheek. "I'm so weak."

I grip her arms, but not too hard. She's so small that I'm afraid I'll do more harm than good. "You're not weak. Something bad happened to you. You lived through it. Now, we just have to get you healthy again, but you're not weak. Okay?" I help her take off her shirt. She's able to take off her own pants.

A lump lodges in my throat as tears sting my eyes when I see the state of her body. I don't mean to look, but it's too hard not to since I'm helping her bathe. I can count her ribs. Her hip bones protrude. Her stomach is sunk in, and she has faded bruises along her body, turning a faint yellow.

I muster the best smile I can before reaching in and turning on the shower. I wipe my cheek when a tear breaks free. I don't want her to see that I'm upset.

"Do I have to shower? Can I bathe? I don't want to stand. Everything hurts."

I can't imagine how tired she must be or how embarrassed she must feel to trust someone she hardly knows to take care of her like this.

"I think a shower would be easier. We'll be quick, okay? Then you can sleep for days."

She listens to me without argument, which concerns me, and steps inside the shower. She groans when the hot water hits her skin. "Oh, it's been so long since I've felt hot water. I never want to leave."

I watch the water turn from clear to a murky grey as the dirt is washed away from her body.

"Tilt your head back, and I'll wash your hair," I ask her while trying to slide my fingers through her tangled hair. I bend down to pick up the shampoo bottle and squeeze a generous amount in my hand. I'll have to buy Poodle a new bottle, which costs an arm and a leg. He's a fuckin' freak about his lavender shampoo.

I rub my palms together to get them nice and sudsy before scrubbing her hair. The blue dye turns the water into the color of the sky. Her shoulder blades are sharp from the lack of meat on her bones. The divots in her spine can be counted right along with her ribs.

I'm so happy she decided to trust us. I can't imagine what would happen to her if she didn't. Sixteen... god, just what was she doing at the AA meeting?

I rinse her hair out and hand her a loofah to wash her body. She's slow in her movements. Eventually, I shut the water off, wrap her in a towel, and then dry her hair with an extra one. She moves like a zombie as we head out the door. I guide her to my bedroom and open the dresser drawers to grab clean clothes.

She drops the towel to the ground and throws on the oversized shirt. She tugs the panties on, then the sweatpants. When she's dressed, she looks like she's about to fall over.

To break someone's spirit is cruel, but to break a child's, that's demonic and inhumane. People who do such horrible things deserve to die, be burned to ash, then get scattered in the desert.

Poppy is safe now. I'll protect her as if she were my own flesh and blood.

"Come on. Let's get you to bed." I take her hand and lead her to the door before the bathroom, right across from me and Patrick's room.

She drags her feet across the floor, and I flip on the fan to help circulate the air. I yank the fluffy green comforter back, and she crawls in, laying her head on the pillow while I tuck her in.

Sixteen. More like eight. The girl is so young mentally. Doc will need to examine her and make sure she's healthy.

Her eyes are already drooping as she fights to stay awake. "It's okay. Sleep. We'll see you in the morning."

"Can you leave the door cracked?" she slurs the question with exhaustion.

"Of course, Poppy."

"Thanks, Mom."

I hold my breath as I leave the room and head to mine. I know she didn't mean it. She's so tired, and when you get into that kind of state, it's hard to decipher dreams from reality. It only makes the decision I made not to have kids if Patrick didn't want, to wishing I never made that decision, to begin with.

She reminds me of how much I do want kids. My heart hurts again; even though Patrick didn't say he didn't want them when I tiptoed around it, he's never said he does. He also bypassed that detail.

"Crazy night, right?" Patrick shuts the bedroom door as I climb into bed, groaning with how good it feels.

I didn't realize how stressed I was until now.

"Yeah, very," I yawn.

Patrick crawls in beside me and wraps an arm around my shoulders, tucking my head into the nook of his arm. "I didn't know things were so bad with her." He breaks the new silence in the room that lasted all of two minutes. "If I did, I wouldn't have... I didn't know—"

"—Of course, you didn't. You gave her a safe place. That's what matters. Don't blame yourself, okay?"

I know he's going to. It's just the kind of man he is.

After another quiet beat passes, Patrick's deep voice cuts through the silence while I rub his chest. "When she was on the floor picking up broken pieces of that mug, it reminded me of the lowest time in my life. I dropped a liquor bottle. Then I got on my hands and knees, picking up the pieces and licking them. I needed every drop. When Reaper saw how bad I was, the shape I was in, that's when he forced me into rehab."

He rubs his fingers lazily up and down my back as I listen to him. My cheek is pressed against his chest, and I can feel his heartbeat pound against my ear.

It's beating a song of empathy and agony, love and hate, full of laughter and screams.

"We'll make sure she isn't us."

"That's the thing, Sunnie. She already is."

Yeah, but she has something that neither Patrick nor I had.

Us.

CHAPTER TWELVE

Patrick

I'M HAVING THE BEST DREAM.

There's a hot wet mouth wrapped around my cock, sucking me deep, humming around the thick meaty flesh until the crown tingles and my sack pulls tight to my body. I thrust my hips into the warm hole. Sunnie is sucking me like she's fucking starved.

The more the sensation continues, my eyes flutter open—and that's when it hits me that the sensation isn't a dream.

Sunnie's bright blonde head is bobbing up and down, sucking me like a fucking popsicle on a hot summer day. I blink the night away and place my hand on the back of her head, sifting my fingers through her hair while she sucks me down. Her hand wraps around the base while she gives me my morning delight, stroking me and licking the tip the way I like.

I groan when she lifts her big blue eyes to mine and nearly fill her mouth right then and there. I love it when she locks eyes with me while wrapping her tongue around the crown. She licks the pulsating vein on the underside, then palms my sack and gives it a quick tug.

I arch my back and bite my bottom lip. "Fuck, Sunnie. You know how to suck my cock. That fucking mouth," I snarl and growl at the same time while she bites down on the head. I bring my other hand from above me and grab her head with more force. "Enough teasing." I thrust my hips off the bed and ram my cock in the back of her throat. She gags and coughs, a string of spit coating my cock.

Her eyes water with the next thrust. Her beautiful swollen lips are puffy as they stretch around my girth to accommodate me.

Sunnie loves getting her face fucked.

I ram between her lips, using her silken mouth as my own fuck toy. She continues to cough and choke, which only makes me fuck her harder. I want her throat to be sore. I want her to feel me all day, every time she swallows or eats. I want her to remember whose cock was here, whose cock she sucks and only fucking sucks. I want her to taste my come on her tongue to remember whose seed she's only allowed to drink.

I want her to know who fucking owns her, just like this mouth owns me.

"You're going to make me come. Do you want to swallow it, or do I paint your face and feed it to you?" I don't give her a choice. I pull out and grab my cock to aim. Thick creamy streams pulsate from me, landing on her mouth, cheek, her hair, and the final one adds a necklace around her neck.

"Mmmm, look at you. You look so fucking pretty wearing pearls, Sunshine." I rake my finger through the come on her face and shove it into her mouth. "Lick it clean," I order. Her tongue circles around the digit, and when I'm satisfied, I gather the seed across her neck and have her drink that down too.

When she's clean, I flip her onto her back, yank her panties down and shove my face between her legs, feasting on her soaking wet cunt and swollen clit. I roll my tongue through her delicate petals. They are so soft, sweet, dripping with honey.

She's worked up from sucking my cock, so it doesn't take many licks to her center to have her tugging on my hair as she comes. "Patrick," she cries out my name as she floods my mouth with her honey. Her thighs shake around my head while she enjoys the ecstasy of the safest high she can get.

"Good morning," she sighs, throwing her arm across her eyes while she catches her breath.

I chuckle and kiss her folds before climbing up her body. "Now that is the way we should wake up every morning."

If you aren't orgasming before you start your day, are you even starting it right?

Once the haze clears, she sits up on her elbows and cups my face gently. "What are we going to do with Poppy?"

I lay my head on her chest and sigh. "I don't know, Sunshine. I wish I knew. I didn't know things were so bad with her. If she doesn't have another place to go, then does she stay here? What about social services?"

"Honestly, I don't think it would be good for her to leave. She has trust issuues. Foster care would ruin her, and she already needs so much help," she says, running her fingers through my hair as I lay my head in the middle of her chest. "She couldn't even wash her own hair, Patrick. She was so weak, and she trusts you. She's attached. If you take that small amount of security away from her, who knows what will happen?"

She isn't a baby; she's nearly grown, but am I ready for the responsibility? I don't know. The thought terrifies me and makes me want to drink.

The sound of a baby crying has me rolling to the side and sighing. "I don't know how they do it," I admit as I listen to the entire house wake up due to the babies crying. Once one baby starts crying, all of them join in.

"What do you mean?" Sunnie asks.

"The babies. Everything changes when you have kids. I'm glad we aren't there yet." I don't know if I imagine it, but I think I feel her tense below me.

"Really? What makes you so hesitant?"

I don't think I like where this is going. "Come on, Sunshine." I roll to my side and prop myself up on my elbows and place my chin in my hands. "You're doing better than me, but what do addicts know about raising kids? Poppy is kind of different. She isn't a baby."

"I think us being in recovery gives us an edge to parenting. We would be great parents because we know what our child needs from us."

I narrow my eyes. "You've thought about this. Sunnie, do you want kids?"

She glances away from me to stare at the wall and shrugs.

"Sunnie. Look at me. Do you want kids?" I'm waiting for her to turn her head and tell me no because I don't know what I would do if she told me yes. I haven't thought that far ahead. I still think about drinking too damn much to even think about having kids. How does an alcoholic care for a baby when he can't even take care of himself?

"Sunnie, talk to me."

"Yes! Okay? Yes. I want kids. I want your children, Patrick. Is that so hard to believe that I want babies with you? I think about it all the time, and do you know how hard it is around everyone else moving on with their lives and starting families while we seem to be stuck? We're allowed to want more than this, Patrick. We're allowed to dream of what can be, instead of feeling like we aren't allowed happiness and love because of who we used to be."

Sunnie rolls out of bed, and I quickly run my eyes down her naked frame before she bends over to grab her robe off the floor. "It's all I've been thinking about. I want to get off birth control, Patrick. I want you. I want us. I want more for our lives than what we have allowed. That's fair, isn't it?"

I blink a few times and let her words set in while I sit up and hold the sheets around my hips. There aren't many times I feel exposed, but right now is one of them.

"Say something," she begs, her voice high-pitched with emotions.

I don't know what to say. I stand, heading toward the bathroom to take a shower, letting her words run over and over in my head. She wants kids. My kids.

My fucked-up DNA that's addicted to alcohol and who knows what else. What is she thinking, wanting my kids? Does she have any idea what she's asking?

"That's it? You're just going to walk away? We aren't even going to talk about this?"

"What's there to talk about?" I reply, pausing before the bathroom door. "How long have you been feeling like this? How long have you wanted kids?"

"I wasn't sure until a few weeks ago."

"Weeks?" I raise my voice and sound a bit hysterical. "You've known this for weeks, and you didn't talk to me sooner?"

"I didn't know how to bring it up, Patrick. You have to understand. I also thought you were having an affair. When would I bring up kids when you would stay out all hours of the night without telling me what you were doing or where you were going? Like I'd bring up kids when I thought you were fucking someone else."

I take a step toward and her and point toward the floor. "I would never fuck someone else. I would never do that to you. Ever. The fact that you thought I would makes me wonder just how low you think of me."

"Oh," she scoffs, tightening the belt attached to her robe around her waist. "Don't turn this around on me. Things were adding up. You pulled away," she begins to count on her fingers. "You stayed out late. You never answered your phone. When you talked to me, it seemed like you were keeping the truth from me. So while I knew you would never do that to me, I couldn't avoid the fucking facts staring at me in the face."

"Fuck the goddamn supposed facts you thought you saw. What about my love for you? What about your love for me? Isn't that fact enough to know I'd never fuck anyone? I don't want anyone else but you, Sunnie. Don't you get that? I only want you!" I shout.

"You want me enough to have kids?" she asks. "Do you want to have kids with me?"

"That's not fair, Sunnie, and you know it. I don't know. I don't know if I want kids. That's a big decision that I don't know if I'm ready for, but I know I love you. Why can't that be enough? Why can't I be enough? Why can't it just be you and me?"

"When has it been me and you?" she screams at the top of her lungs. "Here I am, all the time, giving every inch of myself to you. Do you do the same for me? Do you give me the same courtesy?"

"Yes. You know everything about me. You know my deepest, darkest secrets," I sneer. "You know everything."

"Then tell me if you want kids."

"I don't know," I say honestly. "That I can't answer."

"I think you know. Do you?"

"Sunnie..."

"Do you want kids?"

"I don't know."

"Do you want kids?"

I groan with the repeated question. "I said I don't know."

"Patrick, do you—"

"No!" I roar. "No, I don't want kids. I don't want them. I don't think I'm ever going to want them. They're going to require a part of me that I don't think I know how to give. I don't think I have room to love anyone else the way I love you. No." I shake my head. "I don't want kids."

She weeps, her wet cheeks shining under the light, breaking my fucking heart with my honesty. "Then where does that leave us?"

"What do you mean where does it leave us? It's us. Me and you. It's always going to be that way."

"Patrick, that's not fair to either of us. You don't want kids, yet I do want kids. Who sacrifices their wants? No one should." She looks away, and my heart begins to pump vigorously at her implication.

No.

We'll get through this. We get through everything together.

My eyes burn at the thought of being in this world without her. "I physically," I cough to try and catch my bearings. "I physically can't be without you. I mentally can't be without you. I need you."

"I need us to grow," she whimpers, pressing her hands against her eyes. "I need us to be more than the people we were when we met, Patrick."

I rub my hands down my face. "Maybe I'll want kids one day. I can't tell you right now that I do because I don't. People change. I might change."

"You won't if you're too scared to," she says. "I'm not saying we would be perfect parents, but I think we'd be amazing. You have so much love to give."

"The only love I want to give is to you, Sunshine."

"Maybe—"

I shake my head while putting my arms around her. I drop my head to her forehead. "Don't. Please, don't." I back her against the nearest wall and undo her robe. "Don't. No maybes. There are never any maybes with us."

"Patrick. It isn't fair to either of us," she sobs. "I don't want to force you to have children, and I know you wouldn't want me to give up what I want either."

I drop my forehead to her shoulder. The ends of the sheet unravel from my waist and fall to the floor. I'm so fucking scared right now.

It sounds like she's ending things with us. I haven't been this scared in a long time. Having her in my life has been the only thing that's kept me on the straight and narrow.

"We'll figure it out, baby. We always do," I say, wrapping her legs around my waist. "We always do. Don't talk like this." I keep my hand between us and push my cock against her entrance.

"Patrick." Her wet cheek rubs against my shoulder, and I thrust inside this beautiful body that I haven't been able to breathe without since the day I met her.

"Don't do this. Don't take my Sunshine away." I clutch onto her shoulders and drive into her, slow and hard. It's desperate. It's painful.

Why does it feel like the last time?

"I don't want to. I love you. I love you so much." Her words break with every stroke.

"I'll get there. I swear, I'll get there. Just give me time." I yank her head back, and we stare at one another, both of us hurt, sad, and torn. "I'll give you what you want. I'll give you anything."

She shakes her head and moans, but it's a moan full of pleasure and heartache wrapped in one. "Don't force yourself. The last thing I want is for you to regret me." She claws at my back, and a sob breaks free from her chest. "God, I'd never regret you, Patrick. You're the love of my life."

"Then marry me," I say desperately. "Marry me. Marry me. Marry me," I repeat, asking with every stroke.

"Don't," she begins to cry again. "Don't do that. Don't ask me that if you don't mean it."

"I mean it. I can't be without you, Sunnie."

"This isn't fair." She tosses her head back against the wall, her nails scratching across my shoulders, marking me. "This isn't fair. You know we can't. Not with this hanging between us."

I squeeze my hand around her neck, and a damn tear breaks free of my waterline as I choke her. "I can't fucking be without you, Sunnie. Do you hear me? Do you feel me? I can't." I thrust. "Be." *Thrust.* "Without." *Thrust.* "You."

I hang my head and angrily thrust into her, wanting to punish her for making me feel like this, making me feel like I'm losing her. The tears fall from my eyes onto the floor as I watch myself disappear inside her.

"You want kids?" I snap my head up and look at her in the eyes. "I'll give them to you. Starting right now. I'll give you all the kids you want. I won't lose us. I won't lose you because of this." The more I try to give her what she wants, the more my orgasm fades.

I haven't had this issue since rehab.

"Stop. Stop! Stop it. I can't," she cries, shoving at my shoulders.

I slip out of her and stumble back. My cock is half-hard, and she slides down the wall, sobbing into her hands. The sounds leaving her break apart the small amount of hold I have on myself. I drop to my knees and scoot closer to her.

"Sunnie," I rasp. "I know this is something we can get through. I know this is something we can work through. We've beaten the worst of the worst situations." I rub her legs with my hands.

"Patrick," she shakes her head. "We have to figure it out soon." Her blue eyes are neon lights from crying. "I took a test earlier this morning because I've been feeling more emotional than usual, and I'm pregnant, Patrick. I wanted to see how you felt, and I guess I know," she says.

She's pregnant.

I stand on shaky legs and jerk on my jeans. I need to go. "I need to get some air."

"Patrick, we need to talk about this. If you don't want this, I won't pressure you to stay with me and raise a child. I won't get rid of him or her, though. That's something I won't do."

"I just need time to think, okay? I just…" I tug on my shirt and throw my hair in a messy bun, sweeping the motorcycle keys off the dresser.

I'm not ready for this. I don't think I want kids. What am I going to do? The love of my life is pregnant, and all I can think about is how I'll ruin their lives, or what if they get kidnapped like Macy and I did?

I can't do this right now.

I need a drink.

CHAPTER THIRTEEN

Sunnie

"I DIDN'T THINK THE CONVERSATION WOULD BE THAT BAD," I SNIFFLE AS I TALK TO Sarah. I don't know if she can hear me, but I need to speak to someone. "Maybe I shouldn't have gone about it that way. Maybe I should have eased into it, but because I bottled it up, I let it get too far." I place my elbows on the mattress and cover my face with my hands as I sob. "I don't know what to do. I knew him not being happy was a possibility, but I didn't think it would be like this. I thought… I thought he'd be shocked, but I didn't think he'd be so against it. I don't know what to do, Sarah."

I drop my hands to the mattress and take her hand in mine. "I need you to wake up, okay? Please, I need my best friend. How do I fix this? I can't be without him. Now that I am, I want to do anything to keep him." My hand drops to my flat stomach. "But I want to keep him too."

"Hey," Reaper's deep voice comes into the room, and I drop her hand gently.

I cover her hand with the sheet, then wipe my eyes with my palms. "Hey, sorry. I'm sorry. I didn't mean to intrude on you. I just really needed to see her."

"You don't have to apologize to me, Sunnie. You can always come to see Sarah. Always."

"Thank you. I think I did something terrible." My lip quivers again, and the fat tears blur my vision. "I think Patrick and I are over."

"What? Why would you say that?" he rushes over to my side and takes the seat that's against the wall, dragging it beside me. "He loves you. There is no way in hell that man could live without you. I'm actually afraid he'd relapse." He places his hand on my knee and squeezes. "Talk to me. Anything that happens here stays here."

The door opens again, and the nurse wheels in the large incubator, and then another nurse is followed by a bunch of other machines—reaper grins. "There is my little bit. How did the doc say she was doing?" he asks the nurse, who is currently chewing on a piece of bubble gum too loudly.

It's grinding my fucking nerves.

"Oh, your little bit is strong. She is surpassing expectations and has a clean bill of health. I think she'll be ready to go home soon," the nurse adds.

Reaper's happiness slips from his face, and he eyes Sarah. "Without her, Mom?"

The nurse has a sympathetic smile on her while staring at him. "It's norma—"

"I'm not going anywhere without my wife. My daughter deserves to see her mother every day. I don't care what I have to do. I don't care if I have to sleep in this room every day on a cot and bring in the crib myself. We aren't leaving, and you can't force us to." Reaper's voice begins to rise, and the nurse takes his anger professionally, listening to him vent as if she's heard it a hundred times before.

"Sweetie, I was just about to suggest you could stay here. I'll make sure to always sign off on Hendrix's form saying she needs a little more oxygen or something. There is always a way around it."

He lets out a breath at the same time the door swings open again, and a woman dressed in fishnet stockings, a blue jean skirt, and red permed hair throws her arms in the hair. "Oh my god, have no fear, Auntie Trixie is here."

"Trixie? What the hell are you doing here? I thought you sold the lingerie store and moved to Belize or something?" Reaper hurries over to Trixie, who, if I remember correctly, is Hawk's sister. Hawk was Boomer's dad, and he died when Boomer was just a kid.

We never see Trixie around. Reaper said it was hard for her to be around everyone and not see Hawk, but maybe she's okay now.

She fluffs her hair before wrapping him up in a hug. "Ah, you know how it goes. I move to the Caribbean, date a hot man in too tight of a bathing suit, just to find out he had a wife."

I gasp. Oh my god, that's terrible.

"Tell me about it, but I took me and my fine ass self with my money and came back home. I figured I belonged here, you know? Maybe try to get to know the family I've been running away from, and I'm so sorry. I called Boomer, and he told me everything. He isn't ready to see me yet, understandably, but I wanted to see how you were doing. I hope that's okay."

"Of course," he says. "Trixie, the club is your home. You never have to ask. You want to meet my little girl?"

Trixie's eyes water as she nods her head. "Oh, I love that."

"Come here." He guides Trixie to the incubator as the nurses make sure the machines are all hooked up.

I give them their privacy and stare at Sarah. I sniffle again. The waterworks just won't seem to stop since Patrick is on my mind. I dig into my purse and pull out a blue hairbrush. I lean over her and gently comb the brush through her hair, which is in desperate need of some dry shampoo. I brought that too. "I miss you. I know you're in there. I know you're going to wake up, but don't leave us waiting too long. You don't want to miss Hendrix looking like a newborn." The bristles get caught on a tangle and hold the strands above the knot while I comb it out so it doesn't hurt her.

"Her name is Hendrix," Reaper says.

I smile when I hear the pride in his voice. "Sarah did so good. I really need her to wake up, Trixie. I can't do this alone. I can't do it without her."

It's hard not to get choked up while listening to him. He loves her so much.

A phone trills, and Trixie excuses herself. "Sorry, I need to take this. It's my realtor. She's beautiful, Reaper. I'll call you later, okay?"

Reaper kisses her on the cheek. "You bet. Glad you're home, Trix."

She gives me a friendly wave, and I tuck the brush back in my purse. The nurse opens the incubator, and Reaper dips down to pick her up. "I can't get over how small she is," he whispers in awe, staring at her as if she's the only thing in the world that matters.

It hurts seeing him so in love with his baby when Patrick would never look at his daughter or son like that. I don't think. Maybe. I don't know anymore. The one thing I do know, he doesn't want kids, and he only wants me.

Why can't that be enough for me? Why do I have the urge to have children?

"Now, hold her to make yourself feel better and tell ol' Reaper what happened." Reaper sits down in the seat beside me and transfers her to my arms.

And this is why I want kids. I want to be a mom. I want to be the mom I never had, and I know I can do it. My heart warms, and happiness overloads my system as I hold this bundle of joy. God, she's beautiful. She has big brown eyes and long dark lashes, and she stares up at me with a new wonder she has for the world.

"Oh, hello, sweet girl," I coo at her. "You are so pretty. Look at those chunky cheeks." I pinch them gently, and she grins, stretching her arms and legs in the air. "Reaper, she's perfect."

"I know." He tickles underneath her jaw. "It kills me that Sarah hasn't been able to hold her yet. I hope she does soon."

"Me too." I'm holding her, and everything makes sense to me. I know I can't wait to have a child of my own. If Patrick doesn't want that, it really isn't fair for us to be together. I won't judge him for it, and t doesn't make him less of a man. People want different things. People want kids, or they don't. "I'm pregnant, Reaper."

"What? Well, for the love of all things vile, I'm so damn happy for you guys. Gosh, the clubhouse is becoming a real family space. I love it."

His happiness has new tears forming. I try to hold them back, but it's no use. They fall down my raw cheeks, and I wipe them with my shoulders, so they don't fall onto Hendrix. "No, Reaper. Patrick doesn't want kids."

"I'm sure that's not true. A lot of guys get scared. It's a lot to process. Just give him time. He loves you so much, Sunnie. You'll see."

"No, Reaper, you don't understand. The fight was bad." Hendrix begins to get restless and starts fussing, making noises as if she's about to cry. "Oh, shhh, it's okay little one. It's okay." I lift her to my shoulder and close my eyes while I bounce her.

"What happened?" he asks.

"Well, he's been off the last few weeks. Going to more meetings."

He exhales and leans back, rubbing his palms on his jeans as he clicks his tongue. "I figured."

"I've been wondering how to bring it up to him, and this morning we stumbled upon the subject, and I decided to be honest. I said I wanted kids, and he said he didn't, and there was this heartbroken energy surrounding us, you know? The one that feels doomed. I said it wasn't fair for us to give up what we want. No one should sacrifice that. And he said we could figure it out, but then I said I was pregnant, and we had to figure it out soon. He left, Reaper. He just… left. And Poppy is at home, alone. Doc gave her a sedative to let her sleep, so she won't know for a while that we aren't there, but she needs us. He says Poppy is different because she's older and not a baby."

He stops me by holding up his hand. "Who is Poppy?"

"Oh, Tool hasn't told you? Poppy is Patrick's friend from AA. She's only sixteen, and she's in a really bad way, Reaper. She's addicted to heroin and alcohol. She called for help last night, and the guys rescued her. She needed Patrick because her ex trapped her in his room. She killed him and two others when they threatened to gang-rape her. And now she's attached to Patrick and me as if we're her parents."

"Christ. I'm gone one fucking day, and all goes to shit," Reaper says with exhaustion. He pinches the bridge of his nose. "So, where's Patrick?"

"I don't know. I wish I knew, but I have no idea. His phone is off."

"This isn't good. Patrick doesn't handle change like the rest of us do. He doesn't know how to accept it. He has to build up to it when he feels pressured. That's when he wants to drink the most."

"I know, and that's where I messed up. I pushed him to tell me if he truly wanted kids, and that's when he broke and yelled at me. He got dressed and left. I'm worried, Reaper. I'm scared."

"It'll be okay. He'll come around. He always does. He needs time. He probably has no idea how to handle this. I can guarantee you he's thinking of Macy."

"God." I close my eyes, hating myself for not thinking about Macy. "Oh my god, I can't believe I forgot, Reaper. Of course, he doesn't want kids. He's probably scared out of his mind. I'm such a bitch—" I wince when I realize I said that right into Hendrix's ear. "I mean, I'm such a bad woman," I correct myself, but it sounds more like a question.

"Eh, she doesn't know what the fuck you're saying, plus, if she's anything like Maizey, she'll be cursing and conning us out of money by the time she's five."

"I'm such a jerk." I feel terrible. I didn't expect us to get pregnant without trying. I know birth control isn't one-hundred percent effective, but it hasn't failed us until now. I would have preferred to talk to him about this, worked through it like he said. We could have talked about Macy together, and then we could try if all went well.

Of course, his fear is rooted in Macy. He feels like he didn't protect her when nothing he did was his fault. And then there's his problem with alcohol...

"Reaper, what did I do? What do I do?"

"You let him blow off some steam. Talk to him later. Let him wrap his head around having a kid. It's a beautiful thing. He'll see that."

"I was so heartless. I should have talked to him when I was ready weeks ago instead of thinking he was cheating on me."

He laughs. "I can't believe you'd think that. Listen, Sunnie, it's going to be alright. Sometimes, it takes us, men, to realize what we need in life is to take a step forward and move on to the next thing in our relationships. Patrick is comfortable. For the first time in his life, everything feels safe to him. He doesn't want to give that up—even if things could be so much better. It'll be alright. You and Patrick are going to be amazing parents, and you'll forgive him, and he'll forgive you."

He makes it sound so easy, but nothing about this situation is going to be easy. I'm not just going against the ghost of his past. I'm fighting the addiction that haunts his future.

Love is far from easy when the person who you're fighting to love is worth *more* than everything.

CHAPTER FOURTEEN

Patrick

HELL MUST BE EMPTY SINCE ALL THE DEVILS ARE HERE, DANCING IN BOTTLES.
"You look like hell, mate," Matty comments, setting my club soda down in front of me. "Want to talk about it?"

Of course, the first place I come to is a bar when I feel like I can't handle my fucking problems. How pathetic am I? My ol' lady is pregnant. She's pregnant! And I should be jumping off the walls with happiness, but instead, I'm halfway between drowning myself in rum and driving to Macy's grave. Both would be hell on my heart.

"Give me a shot of your top-shelf whiskey, rum, whatever," I state, slapping my sobriety coin on the bar table.

Electric Paradise better take me to a fucking island far away from here.

"I don't think so, mate." Matty tosses that damn bar rag over his shoulder and crosses his arms in defiance.

"Give me a fucking drink, or I'll go elsewhere." I toss my sobriety chip at him next, and it slaps against his chest before falling to the ground.

"Don't do this, Patrick."

"You don't get to decide what the hell I want to do."

"I can refuse to serve you and kick your ass out of my bar."

I slap a hundred-dollar bill on the bar and reach around to grab the closest bottle. I don't know what it is, and I don't care. "Fuck you, then. So much for being my friend."

"Give me the bottle, Patrick. Don't ruin your life for a drink."

I spread my arms out and toss my head back and laugh. "My life is fucking ruined," I sneer. I twist off the cap and take a big swig. My eyes roll to the back of my head, and my cock plumps when I feel the fucking burn slide down my throat, into my stomach, and set fire to the fear in the veins. "Ah, fuck yes, that's good," I groan and turn my head to the side to see what brand I'm drinking.

Vodka.

It's well, cheap, and will leave me with a nasty fucking hangover, but it feels so good to get lost in it again.

"Your life is good, mate. You have a girl, right? You have a family. It don't get better than that."

No, I went and ruined her life too. She's stuck with a fuck up like me for the rest of her life. I shake my head and take another long swig until my eyes burn.

Matty jumps over the bar and marches to me, planting himself directly in front of me. He yanks the bottle from my lips, vodka spilling from my mouth and down my chin. I lick it off to try and get every drop. Why did I stop drinking again? I love this feeling it gives me. I have no fucking worries. My head is already starting to swim.

Fuck, it's been so long since I've indulged that I can't handle a little taste. How sad. "Hey, I paid for that," I grumbled, reaching for it again.

"Will you talk to me instead of getting lost in something that nearly killed ya in the first place, mate?"

I swipe for the bottle again, and he brings it up out of my reach—big Australian bastard.

"Sit. Talk. Every time you say something, I'll fill a shot glass," he offers.

"That sounds like a deal, Matty." I blink away the haze and stumble to the barstool. Damn thing won't stay still. I figure out how to grab it and sit down. "You need new stools. This one is uneven." I rock back and forth on it, the legs tapping against the floor.

"Talk."

"Pour," I say, pointing to the shot glass in his hand.

"Not until you talk."

Oh yeah, that was the deal. I chuckle. How could I already forget? "Sunshine, my ol' lady, she's pregnant."

He keeps true to his word and pours me a glass. "That sounds like congratulations are in order."

"Yeah, you would say that. You're normal. I don't want kids."

"Should have thought about that before you fucked without a condom," he says without sympathy.

Rude.

"No, nothing between Sunnie and me. That's how it always has to be." I slam my finger into the table to make a point. "I mean, that's how it was." I pinch my brows together in thought, trying to remember what happened earlier. "I think... she broke up with me?" I snort and take the shot he poured. It doesn't feel as strong.

It doesn't burn as good as the other stuff unless my taste buds are already gone because I'm fucked up. "I sound like a fucking sad song on the radio, don't I?"

The shot glass hits the polished cherry wood top of the bar, and for a second, I think it might shatter. "We didn't break up. A couple like us don't break. We just... ah fuck, I don't know, Matty." I drop my head in my hands and run my fingers through the sides of my hair. "I don't know. I can't be a father, Matty." I sit up the shot glass and gesture for him to pour.

"Why can't you be a father? You'd be a good one."

I snort in disbelief. I lift the shot to my mouth and down it. Man, it's smooth. He must have changed it again. It doesn't even burn. "A good dad doesn't come to a bar."

Matty shakes his head. "I'll have to disagree with you, Patrick. I serve plenty of dads, and guess what? Not many are so bothered like you are. Plenty of good dads stop for a drink."

I peek up from under my hands. "You and I both know I'm not stopping for a drink; I'm here to swim in them."

"What's the problem, Patrick?" he asks, lifting a dark brow as he leans against his forearms on the bar. "The woman you love is pregnant with your baby. You love her, right?"

I stare at the inside of the shot glass, watching a drop of vodka flow down the side like a teardrop. "I love her more than I love myself." I hold my finger in the air and shake it. "No, that isn't a fair comparison. I don't love myself at all. I love her more than I love alcohol." I twist the shot glass in the air, and the neon signs hanging above the bar reflect through it.

"Then why are you here drinking it?"

"Because I don't love myself at all." I gesture him to fill the glass again, and the splash of liquid falls on top of my hand.

"So she's pregnant, and you're what, freaking out? You're relapsing out of fear about having a baby? Come on, man. Sack up."

"That's not it... not totally. It's deep-rooted, twisting around my soul like bent fucking metal." I toss the shot back, swallowing it down as if it's water. "How can I be a father when I couldn't be a brother? Being a father is much more difficult than being a brother. I couldn't do that."

Bubba.

I squeeze my eyes shut when I hear her voice.

"What's wrong?" Matty asks. "What's going on?"

I wait for a beat before speaking up again. When I don't hear her voice, I let out a breath. "Nothing."

Bubba. You left me.

"No, no, no," I beg her to stop. I can't be hearing her voice. Not again. Before, it was a fluke, but I hear it again. "Please, don't. Please."

Daddy. You don't love me.

A sob breaks free from my lips when I hear a child's voice I haven't heard before. I'm fucking going crazy. Fucking vodka. Goddamn it.

"Mate, what's going on?"

Daddy.

Bubba.

Daddy.

Bubba, you left your baby like you left me.

"No! No, I didn't. No!" I didn't. I swear I didn't. I just needed to clear my head. I wasn't going to walk away. I'd never walk away from Sunnie. She's everything. I needed to think. "I just needed to think."

"Okay, Patrick, I think it's time you go. Okay? Let me take you home. You've had enough. You can't drive your bike."

"Leave me the fuck alone, Matty. Just leave me alone." I spin the shot glass on the bar top, seeing Sunnie and Macy's reflection in the glass as it dances under the neon lights. I think about all the ways I've fucking disappointed the people that matter most to me.

And Wendy, shit, when she hears that I gave in, she's going to kick my ass.

I deserve it.

I deserve everything that's about to happen to me. I'm probably going to lose Sunnie now because of my thoughtless moment. I just left her there crying as she told me she was carrying our baby. Isn't that what I really wanted? I wanted to tie her to me in every way.

The song changes on the jukebox a hundred times, and Matty is filling my shot glass every time he walks by. I don't look at him. I can't. I'm too ashamed. What kind of man sits here drinking when he has everything a man could want at home?

I look at the time and raise my brows. Shit, I've been drinking for six hours. I scrub my hand over my face, the stubble scratching my palm as I think about how to sack up like Matty says and go face my issues. Not issues. Sunnie isn't an issue, but I am. I'm going to have to grovel.

I'm going to have to beg her to forgive me.

I'm not a boy anymore. I'm not the kid trapped in a basement that couldn't help his sister. I'm a man. If I try, I can be a good dad and a good husband to Sunnie. If she says yes when I ask her to marry me again. It wasn't fair how I asked her before. I am so screwed up in the head. I don't know how she loves me.

I can be what Sunnie needs me to be. I can be what that baby needs a father to be. I can be better. I'll go to more meetings, I'll go back to rehab. I won't stop fighting for my family. I won't give in to the easiest way to lose myself when I'm afraid or stressed or angry.

The shot glass falls from my hand when I let it go. It's like watching my past drop in slow motion and shatter when it hits the bar. Right where it belongs.

A thousand pieces of glass drenched in alcohol isn't enough to bring me to my knees now. Only Sunnie can. Only our baby can. And when I'm a praying man, Macy can.

I have to start over to reinvent myself, but I will.

"I'm going home, Matty. Do you have my chip?" I ask him even though he's at the other end of the bar, placing a martini in front of a woman with big hair and a fake tan.

"Yeah, I do. You want it back, mate?"

"Keep it safe for me until I deserve it again. I have to start all over, but I'm going to." I hiccup. "For Sunnie and my kid. They deserve more."

"That they do."

"How much longer do I need to wait to drive?"

"Anytime. I've been filling your shot glass with water and lime juice. You drank enough from those two swigs to get you tipsy. I've been trying to sober you up since."

"You're a good man, Matty. Thank you."

He bends down and flicks my chip in the air, and tucks it in his pocket. "You come to see me when you get your shit figured out."

I take the keys out of my pocket and give him a nod, running smack into a chest as I turn around.

"What the fuck, Patrick?" Mercy's voice holds judgment as he stares down at me. "What are you doing here?"

"What are you doing here?" I ask him instead to switch the attention off me.

"I'm here to see Matty about working for me. God, don't tell me you relapsed."

I hold my fingers together to show him the small space. "Just a little, but I'm done. Really, Matty has been pouring water down me after I stole his bottle of vodka. Don't tell Sunnie, okay? I want to."

Mercy eyes for me a minute before sucking his tongue over his teeth. "You good to drive?"

"Yeah, I'm good. I'll see you around, Mercy." I head out the door before Mercy can stop me. The breezy night hits me in my flushed face, and I breathe it in. There's a faint hint of vodka on my breath, and just the reminder has me disgusted with myself. My feet are a bit heavy, but I'm going to assume that's from exhaustion. I swing the keys around my finger and swing my leg over my bike.

The engine comes to life, shaking the muscles of my thighs. Nothing like this power throttling and waiting to be let go underneath you. I look up at the stars for a second to try and stop my head from spinning. It isn't often that when I drink, I'm coherent. Matty is a good guy, switching out my vice for water like that.

I don't bother to turn on my phone. I don't want Sunnie to worry until I'm home and talking to her. I don't even know where to begin to apologize to her, but now that I know what I want, I'm excited to get back to her and our baby.

Grinning, I shove the kickstand up and pull out the gravel parking lot, turning on the Loneliest Road. The streets are empty, the night blends into the pavement, and it's hard to see where I'm going. I swerve off to the side, and when my tire hits the sand, I turn the handlebars and right myself on the road.

What the hell is wrong with me?

The wind whips through my hair enthusiastically while I ride, reminding myself that I really need to get it cut. Maybe my beard too, but Sunnie likes the beard. It helps me fall asleep at night when she runs her fingers through it.

The ride back to the compound is quick and my eyes hood from the hum of the tires almost singing me to sleep. Pouring onto the road to help me see are bright lights casting into the night from Friday night lights, as Maizey calls them. I can see the turn for the driveway coming up on the left. Fuck, I don't think Matty gave me enough water. I should not be driving.

My vision is fuzzy, and my limbs are heavy. I bare down on the throttle, and the bike jerks forward to get me home quicker.

Just a few more seconds. I only have to last a few more seconds.

A car pulls out from the driveway, and the headlights blind me and send a pulsing pain through my head. A horn blares, but it's too late. My bike smashes into the car's front bumper, and I fly from my seat and over the car.

The smell of burnt rubber assaults me before my body hits the ground. My helmet smacks against the pavement, and I slide a few yards away. My cut and jeans are getting torn apart, and the flesh on my arms is peeling away.

My vision is growing darker. The last thing I see before the darkness takes me is the car running off the road and slamming into a tree. One of the fucking few we have around here. Unbelievable. I try to get up, but my body is sinking into the road. There is smoke coming from the hood of the car. The person might need my help. If I could just get up.

But the only thing I smell before I sink into darkness is the vodka burning on my tongue. It doesn't hurt as bad as the regret wrapping its arms around me to drag me to hell.

What have I done?

CHAPTER FIFTEEN

Patrick

"**N**o! Be careful. Set him down gently. Fuck. I can't believe this is happening.**"** My helmet is tugged from my head. I try to blink, but something wet and warm is stopping me from opening my left eye.

"Patrick, hey. Can you hear me?"

Not really. There's a high-pitched ringing in my ears. I shake my head and wince when pain shoots up my left side.

"Don't move, okay? I think you're banged up pretty good, but I need to get a scan of your spine. Thank god Moretti fucking bought us everything we needed, so we don't ever have to go to the hospital."

I close my eyes when the pain starts to set in. Fuck, my arms are killing me.

"Patrick, I need you to be honest with me. How much did you have to drink tonight?"

I grumble, unable to form words because I still can't decipher what he's saying. He's muted from the ringing in my ear.

"Damn it, his left eardrum is blown. Juliette, test his blood for alcohol."

"I'm already on it," I think she says.

"How is she?" the ringing in my ear lessens, and I'm able to hear him better.

"Sunnie is—"

I sit up and look around desperately when I hear her name. "Sunnie? Where's Sunnie? The person in the car. Who was it?"

"I need you to calm down, Patrick."

"He's been drinking," Juliette says. I hear the sadness in her voice. "His blood alcohol level is just at the legal limit."

"Damn it, Patrick. What were you thinking? You could have gotten yourself killed."

"I'm done with it. I swear. Sunnie? Where is Sunnie?" I ask again and wipe wetness off my forehead.

Blood.

"I need you to listen to me," Doc says.

"I need to find Sunnie," I yell over the ringing in my ear. "I need to apologize. "

"Patrick." Doc holds my shoulders, the one place that doesn't hurt. "You're injured, so I need you to remain focused."

I glance around to see a few members here. Tool is on the phone, probably talking to Reaper to update him on my fuck-up.

"The person in the other car is seriously injured. The bags didn't deploy. Patrick, the person in the car, was Sunnie. I have her in the separate room we kept Moretti in."

I shove him away from me. Fuck the road burn. I don't give a fuck about anything except Sunnie. "No! No, no, no. Please, not Sunnie. The baby. Is the baby okay? Sunnie!" I call out for her and sway when I stand from the bed.

"Lay down, Patrick—"

"Sunnie! Sunshine!" I call out for her. "It couldn't have been her. Not her, Doc. Please, not her. I fucked up, but I didn't mean it. I didn't mean to." I take his hands with my marred ones that are bleeding and dirty and let him see how sorry I am. "I didn't mean to. Is she okay?"

"She's pregnant?" he grinds his jaw. "Juliette, get an ultrasound on her now."

"My baby. Our baby. I didn't handle the news well." I stumble and hold onto the bed next to me. "I didn't mean it. It wasn't supposed to happen. Not my Sunnie. Oh, god." I fall to my knees when my eyes lock on the room Moretti was in for so many months. There are machines all around her, and her face is black and blue. I can see it from here with my blurred vision.

Blurred from the injury.

From the pain.

From vodka.

What if my irresponsibility kills her? "I didn't mean to," I mutter again, staggering as I walk over to the sealed-off room.

Doc reaches for me, but I pull away, limping to the love of my love.

"Let him go, Doc," Tool says. "Just let him go."

The door is open, and Juliette is preparing the ultrasound. I pause in the doorway and hop to the side of her bed. Everything clears now that I'm with her, and I can see the damage I've done. Her nose looks broken. Her eyes are swollen shut, and there is already a bruise forming on her chest from the seatbelt.

I did this.

My addiction did this.

Why was she on the road? Why?

I grip the edge of the bed as my knees crumble from under me and hit the floor.

The physical pain doesn't register because nothing's as agonizing as the pain I feel mentally and emotionally. I let out a broken, terrorizing roar that shakes my heart. It's so loud. "No! No, Sunnie." I place my head against the mattress. "I'm so sorry. I didn't mean to. God, I didn't mean it." I sob just like I did in rehab.

I break.

I fall apart.

I let every bit of progress I've made in my sobriety, all the building blocks, all the strength that took months to achieve—I let it go.

I don't deserve it. I deserve to have to start over.

No, I deserve death for what I've done to her.

"Sunshine." I pull myself to the chair closest to her side. My hands shake when I reach for hers. They are so still. So cold.

I did this.

I've ruined everything good in my life for a drink that can never love me in return. Sunnie was right. I did cheat on her.

With my addiction.

It was a one-sided love affair because of rum? Vodka?

They can never love me the way she does.

A hand touches my shoulder, and I look up to see Doc standing there. "We think she was on her way to find you." He hands over the stack of letters the club wrote me and lays them on the mattress. "She knew you were struggling, and now I know why you went to get that drink, Patrick."

"I wouldn't have if I knew this was the outcome." I'm still talking with my voice raised since I can't hear out of my left ear. "What's her prognosis?"

"She's knocked out. She has a little bit of swelling in her brain that I expect to go down soon. She has no broken bones, but she will be unconscious for a few days. We are mainly watching for clots, embolisms, or a sign of stroke. She's young and healthy, but her pregnancy makes everything a little more concerning."

I cry in front of everyone. I lose myself in front of my brothers, devastated. Absolutely devastated. "I deserve this," I whisper, running my ruined fingers across the tops of her smooth hand. "I deserve every bit of torture. I deserve to be in pain. I deserve to feel every scratch from this accident. I'm refusing treatment."

"Patrick, Sunnie wouldn't want that. I need to check you out."

"No." I grab the letters and trace my name over the envelope. "I could have killed her because of the need to drink instead of facing my issues head-on and realizing that being a father is exactly what I want, and losing either of them…" I press my palms against my eyes. "Losing either of them is something I can't handle, Doc. I deserve this."

"I can't treat you if you refuse."

"Good. And if the worst comes to worst and they die—"

"—Patrick, the chances of that happening—"

I silence him by continuing. "—If they die, I want Reaper to cut out my heart.

I want to watch the damned thing beat in his hands as I die. That's what I deserve." I lift my eyes to look at Doc. "I deserve to watch my own death happen."

A whoosh fills the room, and I hold my breath because it takes a second to realize it isn't anything bad. It's amazing. "Look at that," Juliette points to the screen. "She's pretty far along. I'm surprised she hasn't realized it. She's around nine weeks." She points to the screen, and I see something that looks like a blob or a bean, maybe a bat. "That's your bab—" she doesn't finish her sentence as she moves the wand across her stomach again, her brows knitted in concern.

"What? What is it? Is it the baby? What's wrong? I killed it, didn't I?" I begin to panic; I can't breathe. There's a million-ton weight on my chest. I'm a horrible person.

You killed them like you killed me.

My stomach lurches. I turn my head in time and puke onto the floor when I hear Macy's voice. The vodka burns my throat and my nostrils.

God, why can't she leave me alone?

"Whoa, okay. I think we need to get you to bed."

I shrug Doc's hand off me. "I'm not leaving her! You can fucking forget it. I left them once. I'm not leaving them again. They deserved more than what I gave them, but they are going to get the best of me from here on out." I wipe my mouth on the back of my hand, the sourness of bile rancid on my tongue.

The best of me might not be as good as someone else's, but I'm willing to learn. I'm willing to learn how to give my all.

"Patrick—"

"I said I'm not fucking going anywhere. Leave me the fuck alone!" I yell.

I'm in this war all by myself. This is a battle I have to learn how to fight on my own. People can't always be there to catch me when I fall, so right now, I'm fighting this. I'm fighting the mistake I made. The only thing I want to be addicted to is Sunnie and our baby.

Christ, even the thought of alcohol after this makes me sick. Before, I'd crave it, miss it, need it, but not now. I didn't care when it only affected me, but when it puts my family in danger, that's my fucking limit.

Fuck alcohol. It's done nothing but add extra burdens.

"Looks like you're having twins, Patrick."

I wait for the panic, the fear, the hesitation, and the urge to run away, but it isn't there. I'm excited. I know it's nearly a little too late to come to this realization. Sunnie needed this from me the first time, and I'll always live with that regret. "Twins? You're sure?" I ask.

"Yes. Identical. Their heartbeats are strong. Everything seems to be on track."

Almost everything. I hover over Sunnie's face, and tears prickle my eyes. "You hear that, Sunshine? Twins. We're having twins." I pet the side of her head, pushing her hair away from her face. She's black and blue. Her bottom lip is busted open, and I let my forehead drop to her chest. I weep for what I nearly lost—hell, for what I may have already lost. When she wakes up, she might not want anything to do with me.

I deserve that. I'll work hard, though, every day. Every minute. I want to prove that I can be the man she needs. I can be the father these babies need.

I'm so fucking lucky.

"I'm sorry I wasn't what you needed when you first told me, but I can be. I'll prove it to you, baby. I'll show you. For you and our twins. Twins, Sunshine. I can't believe it." I lean down and place a feather kiss on her lips, so I don't hurt her. "You're doing so good. You protected them in the accident. You didn't let my bad decisions hurt them. You took all the pain, all the abuse, all the trauma my addiction caused. And it's showing on you. My beautiful bright Sunshine, what did I do to you?" I hover my knuckles over her black and blue cheek and then drop my hand.

She's a canvas of what it's like being a spouse of an addict.

Every drink I had tonight is a bruise she earned in this car accident.

"I think it's time I read these letters, don't you?" I ask her. "You wanted me to read them. I bet you were going to go to every bar in a fifty-mile radius to find me because that's how good you are to me. And look how I repaid you. I relapsed."

And I regret every fucking drop I allowed in my body.

"I'll spend the rest of my life making it up to you, Sunshine. I don't blame you if, after this, you decide you don't want to be with me." The thought has me nearly throwing up again. I'll throw myself in rehab before I relapse again to prove to her I know how to handle life. I can't go to the bottle every time something happens.

Doc mops up the rest of the puke on the floor. Juliette prints out a picture of the ultrasound and hands it to me. "Congratulations, Patrick."

"Thank you," I say in a small voice as I look at the picture of my kids.

"Let's give them some privacy, Juliette. I'll be back every fifteen minutes to check in on her, okay?" Doc tells me.

"Wouldn't have it any other way." I rest my hand on her flat stomach where our babies are growing and hang my head.

I'm a fucking bastard.

Nothing I do will ever be good enough to make amends for what I've done.

Once we're alone and the door is shut, I tug the first envelope free from the rubber band and take a deep breath. I've been putting these letters off for some time now. I've been too afraid to see what they say.

Not surprising, right? Seems I'm a fucking coward when it comes to dealing with my emotions. Well, no more. It's time to face them. No more shoving them further away because it's just making matters worse.

I have to lift my hand away from her stomach, something I fucking hate, to tear open the first envelope. I unfold the paper, then set my hand on her belly again, trying to pour all the love I have for her and our kids through my touch.

Before I can start reading, there's a commotion outside the doors, and when I turn around, I see Poppy crying and trying to push the guys away to get to us. I get up and limp to the entryway, opening the door. "Poppy."

"Patrick!"

Doc finally lets her go, and she runs to me, throwing her arms around me. Well... I believe this is our first kid. Didn't mean for that to happen, but I'm glad it did.

"I was so scared. What happened?"

"I happened." I guide her into the room and give Doc a look that says, 'it's okay for her to be here,' and close the door. "I relapsed and ran right into her car."

Poppy inhales a sharp breath but doesn't say anything. She sits down on the other side of the bed and takes Sunnie's hand.

"I was about to read the letters the club wrote me back when I was in rehab. She was on her way to find me with these in her purse. So I'm going to read them like she wants me to." I hobble over to the chair again and plop down, groaning when pain shoots up my body to my head.

I'm not allowed to be in pain from the accident I caused.

"She's pregnant, too. Twins." My hand finds the spot where the wand that checked for my babies' heartbeats was, and I inhale a sharp breath. I'm so relieved everyone is alive.

"Oh, that's so exciting." Poppy places her hand on mine, and this moment of being complete for the first time in my life engulfs me.

This is my family, and it's time to be the man of the fucking house.

I clear my throat. "Okay, Sunshine. This first one is from Tongue. I'm reading it first like he asked me to do when I was in rehab." I grin when I see the first page. "Well, he drew something. It's me holding a bottle, and a cloth is tucked inside it and lit on fire. Below that is me throwing it, then below that is a liquor store on fire." I flip the page over, and my eyes are met with words. "Okay, Sunshine. Are you ready?"

The heart monitor beeps in a steady reply. I'm once against disgusted with myself when I see the letter begins with Pirate, my old road name.

"Pirate,

I have Sarah writing this for me because I don't know how to read or write, and since I'm admitting this to you, it means you're the first to know besides Sarah. So while I'm not addicted to alcohol, I know the struggle of what it's like not to be able to beat something. I try all the time to read good and speak good. My writing fucking sucks. I gave up on it. It looks like a child's handwriting. My vice is reading and writing while yours is booze.

"My issue isn't as dangerous as yours, but it's embarrassing. I'm not proud to be a grown man who doesn't know how to read, and I know it isn't easy for you to be a grown man and not be able to turn down a drink.

"I want to let you know that the clubhouse isn't the same without you now that you're gone to rehab. I know you probably won't agree because you were always busy with a cut-slut and drinking, but your presence made the clubhouse feel like home. When one of ours isn't here, it just doesn't feel right."

My voice begins to shake as I continue to read on.

"We all feel responsible for letting your alcoholic-ism? Sarah says it's alcoholism, but same thing, right? Anyway, we should have noticed your problem a long time ago, before it grew into something we couldn't change. It isn't an excuse, but things were different in the *club then. We had cut-sluts, and we did whatever the fuck we wanted, when we wanted, how we wanted. We didn't know just how bad it was until we saw you on your hands and knees picking up broken glass to lick the rum clean from it."*

The second-lowest point in my life. This is the first—hurting Sunnie.

"I think you can beat this. I know it's going to be a hard road, but we're here for you. We want you to get better. You're stronger than the alcohol pretends to make you feel. You don't need it. Whenever you're drowning, you don't have to. We are here. I'll listen. I probably won't say anything. I don't like to talk. This letter is actually getting really long, and I'm tired of talking. You are better than the demons on your tongue. I could always cut it out. Then you wouldn't taste a thing. Just think about it.

—Tongue"

I can't help but laugh at the last sentence. Typical Tongue, thinking everything can be solved with cutting a tongue out. "You're right, Sunnie. I should have read these a long time ago. Let's see who's next." I pull out the next envelope. I can't say I recognize the handwriting on the front that spells out 'Pirate.'

I unfold the next letter, the paper crinkling as I press it flat against the mattress, hoping that someway, my Sunshine can hear me through the coma she's in. Maybe these letters will help her find her way back to me.

CHAPTER SIXTEEN

Sunnie

I HEAR HIM.

I'm right here, my love.

I'm listening, Patrick. I'm listening to you.

"Alright, let's read this second letter together," he says.

His hand is on my stomach. Does that mean he accepts us?

"Pirate—"

I hate that they called him that. He was more than some peg-legged, day-drinking asshole.

He chuckles softly. "I can't believe he wrote this out on his accent. Alright, here we go.

"*Lad, I fucking hate this for ye. I hate that yer in rehab, a place we can't see ye often. It's driven me mad. I want to help ye on me own, ye know. I wanted to be able to take the problems away from ye. I don't think ye knew how it fucking tore me apart on the inside seeing ye fall to ye knees, making yer fingers bleed to get that glass.*

"*Gods help me, Pirate, I didn't want this for ye. Yer a good man with a big heart, and it's been too long since we've all since it. I blame meself, ye know. I saw it. I saw yer problems with the liquor, and yet I didn't do anything to help ye. It's just as much me fault that yer in rehab and addicted to alcohol as it is yers. I sat back and did nothing. It's me job as yer friend to help ye, protect ye, tell ye when ye got a problem, and I didn't do any of that. I blame meself. I always will.*

"*I want you to know while yer there and trying to get help, we're going to change things around the clubhouse, so it's safer for ye to come back home. We're taking yer sobriety* seriously. We want ye to be safe, and to do that, we have to change things around here. We can be badass and a notorious MC while keeping it safe for our members. We are family, Pirate. I want to say how sorry I am that I didn't help ye sooner. I'll never forgive meself, but I hope one day ye find it in yer heart to forgive me.

Yer friend,

Skirt."

Patrick sniffles and lets out a sad chuckle.

"I'll have to make sure to tell Skirt that it isn't his fault. It's no one's fault but my own. No one needs to take responsibility for my actions and choices. I knew deep down what I was doing to myself, and I didn't care."

I hear the folding of paper as he slides the letter back into the envelope, and then I hear the unfolding of another.

"No shit. This one has a stamp on it. It's from Boomer. I'll be damned. He didn't have to do that." He coughs to clear his throat and lets out an odd sound of annoyance when the emotional lump in his throat won't go anywhere.

"*Pirate, I hate to be writing this letter knowing it's because you're in rehab, but you know what, I'm glad you're there, and I'm proud of you for trying to deal with this. I know it isn't easy. I know you're only there because Reaper forced you to go, but you're still facing it, and I have no doubt you'll succeed because I remember growing up with you.*

"*I remember being the kid mad at the world because his dad was killed, and you were there when Reaper was dealing with club business. You weren't too heavy on the bottle then, or maybe you were, I can't remember. You taught me how to ride a bike, not a motorcycle after Dad died. He had just started to teach me when he was shot. You took over without a second thought. You don't know how much that meant to me. You probably never will, and that's okay. Thinking back on it now that I'm grown, I know that's how—*" his voice breaks when he can't hold the emotions in anymore "*—That's how I know you'd make a great dad one day. I know you probably think you wouldn't, but man, you taught me something I can pass down to my kids that I'll have one day.*

"*You helped me achieve something I thought I could only learn with my Dad. It changed my entire life. You spent your entire day with me after I fell and fell and fell, and then some kids were making fun of me, and you chased after them. I think you called them 'Fucking punks that deserve to get their asses kicked.' They were only around my age, but you didn't care. You were ready to fight them. You took care of me that day, and I don't remember you drinking a drop.*

"*Oh! And we never used training wheels. You said training wheels were for pussies. And Reaper didn't know you taught me, so when he was ready to teach me, I pretended like I didn't know how to ride. I didn't want to steal his thunder.*"

Patrick chuckles as he continues reading.

"*Anyway, I didn't mean to make this so long. You mean a lot to everyone, and I know whatever you're going through isn't easy. Whatever made you be the man you are today, it had to be really fucked up and twisted. Just know, I have all the faith in the world in you. You're the best uncle a kid could ask for. I love you lots, man. Get better for us. And then we'll go blow some shit up in celebration.*

—Boomer"

Patrick tries to control himself by taking deep breaths, but the more he tries, the more he loses control. *I'm here, Patrick. I love you. I'm listening.*

"How fucked up is it that I can't remember teaching him to ride a bike? Goddamn it. I hate my rotten, ruined brain. I want to remember that."

"It's okay, Patrick. He can remember for you."

Poppy. Oh, good. Poppy is here, and she's okay.

"Alright, who's next?" Patrick changes the subject.

I know he feels like he doesn't deserve kindness. He does. He's been terrible to himself long enough.

"Pirate,

I don't know what to say. I don't know what to do. I'm pretty new to the Kings, so it's hard to share a memory, but I know what I do see right now. I see a man struggling, a man who wakes up with a bottle and goes to bed with one. I see a man who stopped caring about himself a long time ago, but we care for you. I'm glad you're safe in rehab. You deserve a happy life. I wish you wouldn't be so hard on yourself. Bad shit happens. Life doesn't deserve to be lived in misery. All you can do is forgive yourself—and I know that's easier said than done, but just try.

I look forward to getting to know the real Pirate. Until then, you have my faith, man. I know you can do this.

—Tim (Just earned the name Braveheart)."

"Short and sweet and to the point. I like that," Patrick says. "Braveheart is a good kid. I appreciate him taking the time to write this. Maybe we save the rest for later."

No, I want to hear the rest. I need him to continue reading.

"I think if you stop now, you won't pick them back up," Poppy says.

Yes, listen to her. She's right. You like to avoid your emotions when you finally feel them. This is why I wanted you to read the letters, Patrick. You need to know how much people care about you.

"You sound a lot like Sunnie, Poppy. Alright, I'll keep going. Pick a letter, any letter," he kids with her.

"This one." She plucks one out of his hands.

"Pirate," he begins. "*I hate writing you like this, knowing what you're going through. As a doctor, I've researched and studied the effects of addiction. With alcoholism, things can be worse than people imagine. If you're reading this before detox, prepare yourself mentally, Pirate. You're going to hear things, see things—things that aren't real. Your mind is going to play tricks on you. Your guilt is going to manifest. It's going to make you wish you were dead, Patrick, but I need you to fight it. You're better than the alcohol. Don't give up on yourself.*

"*I realized what was happening to you over the years, and no matter how many times I tried, in private, to tell you to stop drinking, I feel like I didn't do enough. As your doctor, that was shameful of me. I should have my medical license suspended for not doing more for you. I didn't realize how bad you were hurting and how much you needed to overcome. I'm so sorry. When you come back, I'll make sure to be a better doctor to you, a better friend, and a better brother. Rehab is the first step into this long journey, but you aren't alone. We* are all here for you. I can't wait for you to return home. Stay strong, Pirate. Good things are waiting for you.

Best,

Doc."

"I think I'm done reading, for now, Poppy. I'm tired."

No, you can't stop now.

"I can't bear reading them knowing I failed them all over again. This fucking sucks. What kind of man am I to let this happen twice? I can still feel the aftereffects of the vodka. I'm lightheaded, my movements are lagged. How can I read their words knowing I've relapsed?"

Patrick, you're human. You're allowed to make mistakes. I made the mistake of not thinking about your fear of being becoming a parent. I should have handled things differently.

"How about I read them?" Poppy offers.

"I'd like that Poppy. Thank you." Patrick's thumb rubs across my stomach, and then something heavier takes his hand's place. His cheek.

"*Pirate*," Poppy starts. "Oh, hey, why did they call you Pirate? And not Patrick?"

"My road name was Pirate because I always had a bottle of rum in my hand," he explains, with a deep depression in his tone.

"Oh, that's not nice," Poppy states. "What's your road name now?"

"I don't have one. I haven't earned it."

"I think you have. I think you've earned more than you give yourself credit for."

"You're sweet, Poppy. Thank you."

"Now, let's read another beautiful letter."

Yes, Poppy. Don't make him stop. Make him face the love and support he has around him, and then maybe he'll learn to accept it.

"*Pirate*," she starts the letter over. "*I wish tacos could make this situation better for you. They make everything better for me. Maybe when you come home, I can treat you to a bunch, and then you'll see there are better things in life to put in your stomach besides alcohol. I'm sure all these letters are the same or sound the same, so I don't really know what to say other than I'm sorry. I'm sorry for not being better for you. I'm sorry for not kicking your ass and stealing the bottle from your hand to replace it with a taco. I bet if I did that, you wouldn't have needed to go to rehab.*"

Poppy pauses. "This guy is weird," she says.

"Slingshot relates everything to tacos. It's endearing. Go on."

I can hear the smile on his face, and it makes me relax.

Poppy reads, "*But I'm glad Reaper made you go. I was worried about you, and I didn't know how to help someone that didn't want to be helped. I know that sounds rude, but it's the truth. Seeing you drink, I didn't think you even wanted that help. I realize I should have been more aware, considering I had cancer as a kid, and I needed help. I know our diseases are different, but they do the same thing on the inside. They eat us alive until we're dead. Luckily, I survived, and I know you can too.*

"*The clubhouse feels empty without you. Come home. Get well. Have tacos with me.*

And we can have a good life. I can't wait to get to know the real Pirate without him slurring his words. I don't think you know how much you're loved around here. We're worried sick about you. And I haven't had a taco since you left for rehab. I feel too guilty enjoying myself when I know you're being tortured.

"Oh, okay, I'll tell you a secret I've never told anyone, so you aren't just reading about how sorry we all are and shit. One day, I think I want to own a taco truck. I want to drive around in neighborhoods and play a festive song out of the speakers like the ice cream man does. Only instead of ice cream, I'm serving the best fucking taco on four wheels!

"Don't tell anyone. It's a silly dream, but that's what so great about dreaming. They can be as silly as you want to make them. So get well, come home, dream, and let's live the rest of our lives disease-free. Including STDs—you might want to get checked for those while you're at rehab, by the way. You were with some nasty bitches, man. Get your burrito checked.

—*Slingshot.*"

Patrick is laughing so hard I know he's having issues breathing. He makes this weird high-pitched noise in the back of his throat, and he likes to slap his hand on the nearest hard surface as he cracks up.

"Slingshot never fails to bring a smile to my face."

It's been too long since I've seen that smile. It's beautiful. It's one of the many reasons I fell in love with my Patrick, the Pirate. I loved him through his worst, I loved him at his best, and I will love him through his worst again.

Because that's what love is.

It's trial and error.

And eventually, there is happiness.

CHAPTER SEVENTEEN

Patrick

"How many are left? It's about time for you to go to bed, Poppy."

"Aw, Patrick. I don't want to. I want to stay down here with you and Sunnie. Please?" she begs.

"You can stay down here, and when the letters are done, you take one of the beds out in the treatment room, okay?"

She nods happily and plucks another letter from the pile. There aren't many left. Four or five, I think.

Poppy tears the envelope happily, humming while she smiles. I will say she looks better than she did when we picked her up. She needs to gain plenty of weight, but she seems in better spirits, and that's all that matters. I'm hoping one day, I'll be in better spirits too. I'm never going to be able to forgive myself for hurting Sunnie and our children, though. No matter how much therapy, AA meetings, or rehab, that's just impossible.

Forgiveness is easier when it's about forgiving other people, but when it's about yourself? It seems out of reach.

"Pirate," Poppy rolls her eyes at the name. *"I want to throw a dart at you for pissing me off so much. I want to stab myself too. I'm mad at both of us. You've been with the Kings since the beginning, and I've watched you go downhill faster than I fucking go-cart. And I'm mad I didn't try to stop the destruction.*

"Here's the thing, Pirate. Most likely, one day, and I hope it is sooner rather than later, you're going to relapse. It's the good hard truth. It is hard to swallow, but you have something you didn't have before—the effort to get better and us at your back.

"And yes, we could have been better, but guess what? We weren't that educated on your issues, and now we are. So we're here. We're ready. When you relapse, we'll be here. We're prepared to help you. Just try not to, okay? You're better than this, and I sure as fuck don't feel like throwing a dart at you because I don't fucking miss, asshole. So, yeah. Words. Insert fluffy heart-filled shit I'm not good at.

—Bullseye."

I snort when I hear Bullseye's sweet, poetic letter. Wow. If I had only read it while I was in rehab, maybe I would have magically got better. Bullseye has always been a grumpy bastard, but I bet if I showed him this now since he is a different person, he'd crack up. You know what? This is one of my favorite letters because I can see how much he's changed as a person. I've changed too. He's made bigger strides than I have. I've had a significant setback, but I know I can be better. I can do better.

"Well, he isn't very nice," Poppy grumbles, displeased.

"Hey, we never judge someone, alright?" I try to be as stern as I can without hurting her. "He wasn't the same person he is now. He's been through a lot, like you, and he was a grump like I was a drunken asshole, but he had his reasons. And he always means well. Okay?" I lower my voice to be as gentle as possible now. Poppy is fragile, and she'll always have a lot to overcome, even if she doesn't realize it yet. Most of us don't realize how fucked up we really are until it's nearly too late.

"Okay, Patrick. I'm sorry. You're right. Can I read another?" she asks.

I rub my cheek against Sunnie's stomach and sigh, then clutch her hips, wishing I could squeeze, but I don't want to hurt her. For all I know, she's in pain everywhere.

Because of me.

How could I have walked away from her, knowing that inside her are two miracles? If I could rewind time, I'd tell her yes, I want kids. I'd give her anything. But time isn't a movie or a show; we can't rewind or press pause on the things we regret doing at that moment. All we can do is try to make the future better.

"I love you," I whisper to them, hoping my babies can hear me. "I love you so much, and I promise to be the father you need. I can't promise I'll be perfect, but I can try to be."

Poppy tears another envelope and flicks the letter, so it unfolds with a whipping sound. "Ready?" she asks.

No. I'm tired of hearing everyone saying how sorry they are. It isn't their fault. It's mine and mine alone. They need to stop trying to take the blame for my actions to make me feel better. "Go for it," I say, hoping I don't regret it.

"Pirate, Lady misses saving you."

I interrupt Poppy. "—Damn it, Lady. It's a dog, and she died recently."

"Aw," Poppy sticks out her bottom lip. "That's so sad." Poppy swallows, probably to coat her dry throat from reading so much. "*Lady misses saving you. She has been going to the couch where you usually passed out after a day and night of drinking and fucking whatever whore you could. I was worried about you. I still am, but I know you're in the place you need to be. I want to tell you this, don't be ashamed about rehab. It's the best damn thing that will happen to you. Be proud of it. Be proud you're getting the help you need. And* then, when you're out, be ready to move on with your life because the past has no place in the future. You can have a great one, too. I've never seen a guy who can take apart a motorcycle and put it back together as quick as you. I bet you could have your own custom bike shop if you wanted. You're talented, but that damn devil liquid you keep pouring down your throat is a paralytic. It's keeping you frozen in time, man. I can't wait for you to come back to reality.

"Don't tell anyone, but I think you might be Lady's favorite. She's got a thing for tortured souls. I'll be thinking of you, man. Can't wait to have you back home.

—Poodle."

Another one that's short, sweet, and to the point. I like that. They probably knew I wouldn't be in the headspace to read a fucking novel-length letter.

"Only a few left." Poppy is excited. She seems to be thrilled to help me. The next one isn't taped shut, so she peels the lip from inside the envelope and opens it. She frowns. "This one is only a few sentences."

"Pirate, my best wishes for you to get better. You're a nice guy. I'm pretty lost around here, and even on your drunkest day, you were nice to me. So, um, come back, because I don't know what I got myself into. I don't know if I'm cut out for this life. Braveheart is better at this life than I am. He fits in, which is funny, considering how much smaller he is than me. I'm too timid. Maybe it's best if I leave? I bet you don't want to hear about my problems. You have your own to deal with. I'm just afraid I'm not going to live up to the Ruthless Kings expectations. Anyway, kick this addiction's ass. I have faith in you, and I'm praying for you every night. I believe you will be better.

—Tank."

"Aw, damn. Let me see that." I snatch the letter from her and reread the letter from Tank. He's the only one that's gone on about himself instead of me, and I make a mental note to talk to him. He's the quiet type, a bit timid, strong as a fucking ox, and great with directions, which is why he's the Road Captain. He fits in. He just has to stop comparing himself to others here. Expectations are different for everyone, and Reaper knows it. Tank belongs here.

"Think she's listening?" Poppy questions while she tucks a piece of hair behind Sunnie's ear. It's so odd how Poppy just fits in with us. I think she was exactly what we needed and had no idea we needed it.

"I do. I hope she can hear us." I rub my knuckles down her cheek, and selfishly, when she wakes, I hope she forgives me easily.

But I doubt it will be.

Poppy sighs, "Me too. Sunnie is so sweet."

Sweeter than sweet fucking tea on a hot summer's day.

"Pirate," Poppy chirps. I didn't even see that she opened the next one. "I'm not sure what others said in these letters, but I'm here to give you the tough love and the truth. This happened because you let yourself get lost in the liquor. It wasn't about pain anymore. That was the excuse you used to keep drinking because you convinced yourself, 'Why want more when I have this?' Well, that mindset didn't work for me.

"You're going to have to understand one day why I did what I did. I realize you hate me for sending you to rehab, but you'll live with it because you'll live. You won't be dead from *choking from your own puke, which was inevitable. I know there were variables to attribute to your addiction, and I'm sorry for that, but to let it grow into what it was, that's on you. It's your responsibility to take ownership of your mistakes, and when you're out, it's going to be up to you to stay sober. If you relapse, you have to focus on the good things in life to heal again.*

"*We'll be here like we always are with support and love, but I'm here to tell you, no one can be coddled forever. Sometimes, for us to get better, we have to learn how to do things on our own. With that said, I love ya, Pirate. You're a good addition to the club. Bring your brilliance back.*

I believe in you.

—Reaper."

I cringe at his words. Brutal and honest. That's Reaper. He means really fucking well, though. He's right. He's always been right. This is on me. I could have picked another way to deal with my issues, but I didn't. Drowning in my sorrows was the easiest way to silence Macy's voice in my mind, but she's always been there whispering in my ear.

And she'll always be there if I don't do anything about it.

Poppy chuckles when she reads the next letter.

"What?"

"It's one sentence."

Oh, great. "Go on." I rub my temples and cringe when the dried blood from my head sheds from me onto the bed. I forgot about that little head injury. I glance at my arms and kick myself for not even letting Doc wash out the road rash. I could get an infection.

I deserve it. Nothing a few antibiotics can't fix, and I don't need them right now.

"*Pirate, I want to throw a ninja star at you for fucking making me worry about you. Love your dumb ass.*

—Knives."

"And he thinks I need help? He's dangerous when it comes to those fucking ninja stars. I'm surprised he hasn't taken out someone's eye from tossing them around so damn much." I like this letter too. Don't get me wrong, I like all of them, but Tank talking about himself and Knives being serious yet funny has me feeling lighter than the others.

"I think you should read this one." Poppy yawns, handing me the last letter. "I'm going to bed." She gives Sunnie a kiss on top of her head and walks around the bed to give me a gentle hug. "Night, Patrick."

"Night, sweetheart." I watch as she heads to the closest bed next to the isolated room we're in. She really doesn't like to be far away from us. As much as I should worry about that, right now, I don't mind it. I sigh and pinch my eyes with my thumbs. I'm exhausted and my head is killing me.

"Hey—"

"—Shit." I turn to see Doc standing in the doorway. "Fuck, you scared the hell out of me."

"Good. When you're done here, it's time to clean you up. I won't take no for an answer. Sunnie deserves to have the father of her children in tiptop shape."

I don't argue. I give him a salute. "I have one more letter, then I'll be out."

His eyes widen, and a faint blush takes over his cheeks. "I see." He tucks his hands in his pockets and rocks on his heels.

"I don't blame you, Doc. I don't blame anyone but myself. Don't be so hard on yourself."

He nods and rubs the stubble on his chin with his fingers. "I could say the same for you." With those words, he knocks on the wall before he leaves.

"Well, Sunnie, this is the last one. But I'll be back, okay? I'm never leaving you." I flip the envelope over in my hand and frown when I see how new it looks. The white of the paper is clean without age or crinkles from being tossed around over the months. My name—my real name—is written in beautiful cursive on the front.

It's Sunnie's handwriting. "Of course, you write me a letter." Since it's just her and me, I let the tears fall. "I don't fucking deserve you and your beautiful kindness when I've done nothing but be a burden to you, but I swear, baby, my sweet Sunshine, I'll be what you deserve from now on." I open the letter with shaky hands and unfold the paper.

It's one page. The words are evenly spaced out, and the cursive is gorgeous, fluid, and elegant, just like her.

"Patrick,

There are so many things I want to say to you right now. This is the only way I know how since I'm delivering the rest of the letters. I'm mad at you, but before you let those words get to your head, please know I'm mad at myself too. I'm mad at how I handled the situation. I should have understood your issues, your concerns, your fears. We should have sat down and talked about this. I shouldn't have blurted out I was pregnant like that. I was basically testing the waters by tiptoeing around the issue instead of being direct. That was unfair of me, and you deserved more than that. I deserved more than your reaction, but this is what life is about. We fight. We yell. We scream. We cry. We kiss. I wouldn't want to do that with anyone else but you, Patrick. I know having a baby will be challenging, but I do believe it will be worth it. So I'm going to write this letter, and then I'm going to go look in every bar and AA meeting that I know of and hope like hell you aren't in a bar.

"I'm worried. I'm scared. I can't lose you. I don't think you know just how much I'm in this, Patrick. You're more than some guy, you aren't temporary, you aren't this man I'm playing house with. You're this... necessity. You live inside me. You're in my heart. My mind. My soul. You've made yourself home in my bones. If you left, if something happened to you, that part of you that lives inside me would be ripped out from heartache, and I'd die.

"You're so worried about relapsing, you're so concerned about fucking up, but do you

ever think that I am, too? If something happened to you, I would relapse. You're the only thing keeping my feet on the ground and my head in the clouds.

"My love for you goes beyond fear and addiction and relapse. It goes beyond all the reasons why people say addicts like you and me can't work. It goes beyond this world. It's more than madness and chaos, understanding and kindness, love and loss. If what I felt for you was enough, it could cure the addictions between us if that were possible.

"I love you, Patrick. I love our baby.

"Now, let's talk about this and share how we feel without panic. I believe we can do this, but I can't do it without you.

"Now, kiss me and tell me you love me. Let's go home. —Your Sunshine."

A tear rolls down my cheek and drops from my jaw onto the letter, smearing the ink. "Damn it!" I shake the piece of paper, and that was the wrong thing to do because damn it, the water drips further down the page and makes it smear worse.

I set the letter on the dresser lean forward, bracing her head in my arms. I lower myself until I kiss her, letting my lips linger as long as I can. I take a breath and kiss her again, not getting enough of how she feels against me. "I love you, Sunshine. I love you so damn much. And I was at a bar. When we wake up, we can talk about it or whatever you want. I hope you can forgive me." I'm not the praying type of man, but I pray she can.

I pray I haven't lost her forever, but if I do, I deserve it. I vow never to be with anyone else for as long as I live. I'll work hard every day to earn her love back while loving our children.

"If I can't have you, then I don't want anyone, Sunshine." I watch her intently, waiting for her to blink those big blue eyes at me and tell me everything is going to be okay.

I wait.

The heart monitor beeps.

I wait.

And the longer I stare at her, the more still she becomes.

"Come on, Sunshine. Come back to me. You're scaring the hell out of me." I press my hand on her stomach and exhale, my breath full of hope and regret all at once. I'm a ticking fucking time bomb, and if she doesn't wake up, I'll explode.

I bend down and kiss her again, careful not to touch her nose since it's broken. "I'll be right back. Doc wants to fix me up. I swear, I'm going to be right back." I don't want to leave her. She'll be okay, right? She has to be. "I'll be right outside in the treatment room. Poppy is there too." I just hope making the decision not to leave... isn't too late.

The sound of those damn machines is going to haunt me. I steal one last look at her, memorizing the rhythm of her heartbeat, how still her form is, how black and blue her face is, how swollen her eyes are, and it takes all I have to shut the door behind me and head to Doc.

I head to Doc's office, and he's setting up the equipment and whatever else he needs to patch me up.

"How are you holding up, Patrick?" he asks without looking up.

His office is clean, neat, and organized. Some walls are just shelves filled with medical necessities. From cotton pads to scalpels, he has everything a doctor would need at the hospital. Reaper had to add on a separate room for the MRI, cat scan, and X-ray machines that Moretti bought Doc as a thank you for taking care of him so long.

"I'm at war, Doc. I don't know if I'll come out alive."

He lifts his head, and his blonde hair falls over his forehead as he nods. "The sun always ends up shining on the battlefield. Just keep faith. It'll work out."

Why do those feel like famous last words?

CHAPTER EIGHTEEN

Sunnie

I WAKE UP WITH A START AND INHALE A SHARP BREATH, DARTING MY EYES FROM LEFT TO right. Where am I? What happened? My entire body hurts.

Every time I blink, my eyes water from the pain.

The accident.

My hand flies to my stomach, and my chin quivers when I think about the baby. I hope he or she is okay. Oh god, I wouldn't know what to do. How would Patrick feel? I don't even want to think about it because what if he was relieved? There is no way I could be with him if he were.

"Well, hey there, Sunshine."

I slide my eyes to the left and see Doc replacing my IV bag, smiling down at me.

"Hi," I croak, sounding like a frog. My breath is horrible. Yuck.

"I'm sure glad you're awake. You gave us all quite the scare." He sits down in the seat closest to mine, and that's when I see the stack of letters sitting on the nightstand, opened, and read.

"Patrick? Where is he?"

"He made Poppy some breakfast. I made him go. He hasn't left your side, you know. He was worried sick, and he's riddled with so much guilt over what happened."

I stare at Doc as if he's speaking another language. "What do you mean? What happened? I know I was in an accident…" but I can't seem to remember why.

His smile disappears in the next second, and he shines a light in my eyes to check my pupils. His breath is heavy as it escapes him. "It's normal not to remember details. You had a serious concussion and still do by how your pupils are reacting."

He sits back down and takes my hand. "You and Patrick were in an accident. He relapsed, Sunnie. He hit you head-on. You swerved to miss, but he clipped you. You ran off the road and hit a tree. Your airbag didn't deploy, which is why you feel like shit. You took a nasty hit to the steering wheel. Patrick is okay. Bumps, bruises, and a whole lot of guilt. He wasn't wasted. I want to say that much. Just below the legal limit, but since he hasn't drunk in months, it hit him harder and quicker."

He relapsed. His decision put the baby and me in danger. I could easily forgive him if this were just me, but it isn't now. His choice negatively affected our child. What if he continues to relapse? What if… he regrets the child so much he ends up hurting him or her?

"The baby?" I ask through absolute devastation. It hurts so much to cry since my entire face is swollen, but I can't help it.

"I think you mean babies," he corrects me, reaching for a picture on the nightstand to give me. "You have twins. Right here—" he points to one blob. "—And then here—" he taps his finger on the other.

"Two?" I rub my fingers over their small, precious bodies. I'm so happy. Not one, but two. This is a dream come true. "Do we know the genders?"

"It's too soon to tell. We need to check when you're around twenty weeks. Sometimes it can be caught earlier if they aren't stubborn. You're around nine weeks right now."

"Wow, really? How did I not know?"

"Most women don't. I mean, sometimes you spot, which can be the excuse for having your menstrual cycle when really it's implantation. Then the next month, you're sensitive, and that can be PMS. I mean, the symptoms are similar, Sunnie."

"I have an IUD. Will that harm them?"

His face turns grim. "Yes. I'll need to remove that as soon as possible. As the babies grow, the IUD will still be there, and they can get harmed if it's in the way."

"Oh my god, take it out now. I don't want it to risk another second."

"Hey, shh, it's okay." He lays his hand on my shoulder when I begin to become hysterical. Nothing can happen to them, not after this. "I want to wait until you're a little more healed, okay? And…" he turns on the ultrasound machine, lifts my gown to mid-waist, and squirts cold jelly on my lower belly.

I hiss from the sudden quick freeze.

"Shit, sorry. I should have warned you. I'm not as thoughtful as Juliette. When she checked the babies—"

"—How did she know about the babies?" I haven't told anyone besides Patrick, and he doesn't seem to want to shout it from the rooftops right now.

"When Patrick woke up, and I told him what happened, to put it gently, he was frantic. When I told him who the other person in the car was, he lost it, and the first thing he asked about was the baby."

"He did?" Why am I so surprised? Patrick is the most loving man I've ever known, but I think his reaction to being pregnant is hitting me harder than I thought.

"Yep, and that's when we discovered..." he points to the screen as the wand swirls around my belly and a big whoosh fills the room. "Babies. Twins. And they are perfect."

I stare at the black and white screen and begin to get lost in dreams. Their first day of school, losing their first tooth, Santa Claus, the Easter Bunny, the Tooth Fairy, and then their first girlfriend or boyfriend, prom, a wedding...

So surreal.

"Wow." I'm not able to take my eyes away from the two beans filling the screen. "They're safe?"

"Like two peas in a pod," he laughs at his own joke, and it makes me grin. "Sorry, I've always wanted to say that to a pregnant woman carrying twins, 'cause they are literally two peas in a pod. Bad doctor joke."

"It's okay. I liked it."

"Sunnie!" Patrick bursts through the door, and his eyes water while he stands there assessing me. When he notices what Doc is doing, the relief clouding him disappears. "Are the babies okay? What's wrong?" he dashes to my side and takes my hand. "It's going to be okay, Sunnie. We'll get through it like we do everything else. I'm so glad you're awake. God, I'm fucking glad." He hangs his head, and he jerks it up a moment later to glare at Doc. "The babies?"

"Are fine. I was just showing Sunnie here the bundles of joy. I'll, uh... I'll give you two some privacy."

"Thanks, Doc." He wipes off the jelly from my stomach, and the closer he gets to leaving, the more nervous I become.

Patrick's touch doesn't feel comforting right now, and it's breaking my heart. It's taking all I have to keep my emotions in check. Doc rolls my gown back down, pulls the blanket to my hips, and leaves without a parting glance.

Yeah, even he knows how awkward it's going to be.

The door closes with a soft click. The air between Patrick and I becomes stifling and hard to breathe. I've never felt awkward with him. It's been natural, easy, effortless to be myself, and one hundred and ten percent happy.

"God, Sunshine. I've been so fucking scared you weren't going to wake up. You don't know how happy I am to see you and those gorgeous eyes staring back at me." He bends down to kiss me, and I do something I never thought I'd do.

I turn away.

I'm fucking mad at him, and maybe that's just my irrational emotions. If it were just me in that car, I know forgiving him would be easier, but I know I can't hand him forgiveness right now. He relapsed and drove drunk, slammed into me, and anything could have happened to our twins. He needs help. He's been struggling, and I don't know if this is something I can help with because I've been trying, and he's been turning me down left and right.

And now this.

"Sunnie, please... I know. I know I messed up. Can we talk about it? I want to make things right between us. I've been so worried about you, and I've been waiting for the day for you to wake up, and now you are. I can't take you being mad at me. I can't."

"Patrick—" I begin, but I'm interrupted again.

"—I read your letter." He picks it up from the top of the pile on the nightside, and the first thing I notice is that the ink is smeared. Did he cry? "I read it, and you said you would forgive me. You said we could work together on this. You were out to find me. You knew what I was doing—"

"—That was before, Patrick," I say with a shaken voice. "That was before you drove home drunk and crashed into me. Even then, I knew forgiving you would be as easy as breathing, but I can't do that right now. I can't forgive you right now. It could have been so much worse. What if something happened to the babies and me? Something did happen to me, and that isn't even my concern. I don't care about me—"

"—I care about you."

"—I care about our kids, Patrick. You need help. I don't know if you need meetings or rehab again, but right now, I don't know if I can trust you. I don't feel like I can trust you around me right now." I place my hand on my stomach. "I don't feel like I can trust you with us."

His forehead drops to my hand as he rocks it back and forth. "Don't say that, Sunnie. Don't. You know I'd do anything for you. Don't do this, please. I love you. I'll... I'll do anything. I won't ever hurt you again or put you and the kids at risk. I won't do it. The thought of having one drop now... it makes me sick. I'll never do it again. Sunnie, please... please..." he begs, squeezing my hand, so I don't let go.

I cover a sob that tries to escape me when I hear him plead. It kills me. I know he wouldn't succumb to that for anyone else besides me.

"Please, Sunnie. Please." He gets on his knees and holds my hand so tight I can't let go. I don't have a choice. "I'm begging you. I'll do anything. You want me to go to rehab? I'll... I'll go," he says through wet eyes and soaked cheeks. "I'll go to meetings every day. I'll talk to Wendy every day. I'll do everything, anything. Sky's the limit. I want to be a better man for you and for our babies. I know I need help. I want to be better."

"Patrick, get up," I urge him, keeping my tone light without anger.

He shakes his head. "Don't take your love away from me, Sunnie. Please. It's... it's the only reason why I'm here. I need it more than anything, more than the craving, more than the alcohol."

"Patrick." I cup my hand against his jaw, so sharp and defined even with his beard, and he finally looks up at me through spiked lashes.

"I'm so sorry. I fucked up. Give me a chance. Give me a chance to prove to you I can be who you need me to be, who I need me to be. I'm going to be a better man. I can do it, Sunnie. I've done it once; I know I can do it again."

He's speaking so fast I can hardly keep up with him. He has this dreadful, adorable, sad look on his face. God, he loves me just as much as I love him. I can see it in his eyes as he stares at me, his brown irises darting between mine.

"I know, and there isn't anyone in this world that believes in you more than me. I know you could rule this world if you wanted, Patrick. You're capable of anything. The strength in your spirit is one of the many reasons I fell in love with you. It's one of the reasons I love you."

"Then we're okay? We'll be okay? We'll get through it. I messed up bad, baby. I know, I know I did." He bites his bottom lip, and I can see how unwell he is. He's lost a bit of weight, and he has deep circles around his eyes. He's been worrying himself to the point of death.

He would, too. He'd die of worry for me.

"Come on, Sunshine." He drags himself up to his feet and sits next to me. "Tell me what you need, and I'll do it. I swear to god, I will."

His hand rubs over my stomach, and his breath hitches. "I love the three of you, and I know I didn't react well when you told me—"

I open my mouth to tell him how sorry I am again. I hate how selfish I was.

He places his fingers against my lips. "No, don't make excuses for me. How I reacted was wrong. I didn't take so many things into consideration. I bet you were so afraid to tell me, for good reason, considering I reacted like your fears predicted."

His lips tilt in a smile, and his eyes narrow as he thinks about his next words. "And then I saw what I did to you, and then I heard their heartbeats, and nothing felt more real to me. I couldn't lose you, and I couldn't lose them. It hit me that you were right; we were stuck. And that was on me, afraid to see what else the world had to offer. I was safe in my bubble, and anything different scared the hell out of me."

I stay quiet, not knowing what to say but wishing I did.

"I'm not saying tomorrow I can be perfect, but I can tell you tomorrow, I'll be working toward perfection. Just give me a chance." He brings my knuckles to his lips. "I'm many things, a drunk, but the one that means the most to me is being the man who gets to love you, Sunshine."

A hot drip of liquid rolls down my cheek, burning the cuts and scrapes along the way. "I love you too, Patrick. So much."

"Tell me what I can do."

The heat from his palm doesn't help settle my stomach. "I love you, but…"

He inhales a sharp breath. "But what, Sunshine?"

"But I need a little time, Patrick. That's all I need. I only need some time." It kills me to say the words out loud, but I have to stay strong. As easy as it is to forgive him, it isn't as easy to forget.

He kisses the tops of my hand again, and his tears glide against my skin. Even from here, I can see the lump lodging in his throat. He goes to get up, but he can't. He struggles for a moment, unable to let go of my hand. Patrick shakes his head again and kisses my fingertips as he stands.

"If that's what you need. I'll give my Sunshine anything." He gives me a tortured stare as he stops inside the doorway, the handle tight in his grasp.

As he leaves, I realize I have no idea what I want.

Wanting and needing are two different things.

I want time to think, but I need Patrick.

What I need to figure out is which one I need more.

CHAPTER NINETEEN

Patrick

"Thanks for meeting me, Wendy." It's been three days of not seeing Sunnie. She's moved out of our room and into one of the houses that are ready on the compound.

She needed time, and I've respected it. It hurts like fucking hell too. Poppy moved in with her as well to keep company and to make sure she's okay. I thought when I felt like this, I'd be down on the bottle again, wasted in my room for days, but when I said the thought of tasting alcohol makes me sick after what I did to Sunnie, I meant it.

I've wallowed and pined like a broken-hearted teenage boy for the better part of the last three days, feeling sorry for myself.

I'm a Ruthless King, but damn it, I'm human too. I'm a biker second and a goddamn human first. And right now, I feel like I can't breathe. The regret of what I've done has dug its nails into my heart. With every beat, the poisonous talons dig in more.

I sip on my club soda and lime, and Wendy crosses her arms at me, knowing that I've done something bad. Her brows are thin, and the way she draws them on darkens them. They remind me of curious spider legs twitching.

I'm at a local café Sunnie loves so much. Ironically, it's called 'Sunny Rays,' and Sunnie loves their mango orange alcohol-free mimosa. She refuses to drink, so I'm not in temptation. She thinks even if she kisses me while she has champagne on her tongue, I'll want to drink her down.

She shouldn't have to do that. If she wants a damn mimosa, she should be able to have one. I've trapped her in my bubble.

"Your food, sir," the waiter brings our food and sets it down in front of us. "Ma'am." He sets her eggs benedict in front of her, along with a plate of cut toast with butter.

My strawberry pancakes smell and look delicious. They are round and fluffy, with perfectly cut strawberries around the plate dashed with powdered sugar. He places a syrup jar next to me and gives me a curt grin.

I lift the fork to dig into the pancakes when Wendy smacks my wrist, "Son, what did you do?"

"I did what all of us don't want to do." I twist the fork on the table, and the sun reflects off it.

"Oh, you didn't, sweetheart. Tell me you didn't." Her hand grips mine, and the fork clatters onto the table.

The sweat from the glass cools my fingertips, and the lime is sour against my lips as I take a needy sip of water.

"Yeah, I thought I sobered up, but then I drove, and..." I don't want to admit this. "I ran head-on into Sunnie. She was coming outside of the clubhouse to look for me, and she ran off the road. She smacked her head against the steering wheel. Her airbag didn't go off, so she broke her nose, and she was unconscious for three days."

"Oh my god, Patrick." She squeezes my wrist. "Is she okay?"

"I think so. I mean, she will be. She's still black and blue in the face."

"What made you go off the deep end? You were doing so well."

"You know how I feel about my sister..."

"And that it wasn't your fault. You have to let that go, Patrick."

I laugh, and the sound lacks humor. "I know that now. Sunnie told me she was pregnant, but we were fighting before. She wanted kids. I didn't. She said it wasn't fair for us to be together if we wanted different things."

"She's right. Neither of you would have been in the wrong."

"But I didn't want to be without her. She's it for me. And she kept asking about kids until I finally blew up, and I said no. Then, she said she was pregnant, and I lost it, Wendy. I left her there, and I went to the bar. Matty wouldn't serve me, so I stole a bottle, and I think my two or three swigs took most of what was left. He tried to sober me up, but I guess it hit me harder than usual. I shouldn't have been driving."

"No, you shouldn't have." She wraps her wrinkled palm around her teacup. "Are congratulations in order?" she asks, lifting those black brows at me over the rim of her cup as she sips it.

I smile, a really excited kind of smile. "Yeah, Wendy. I'm fucking excited. I'm happy. As I can be. It's twins."

"Oh my, your hands are going to be full!" she chuckles, a sweet glimmer in her eyes. She plops her chin in her hand. "How are you and Sunnie doing? I know you two have a lot of history, but this couldn't have been easy on her or you."

The ache of separation from Sunnie has me rubbing my chest. "She said she needed time, so she moved into one of the houses on the compound."

"Oh, sweetie. I'm sorry. She loves you. I'm sure she just needs a little more time. She's scared. She has two people she needs to think about over herself. Give her time; she'll shake it off."

"This doesn't get shaken off. What I did was unforgivable. I'd understand if she never wanted anything to do with me again."

"Don't you dare talk like that. Don't you dare give up. The woman loves you. Time doesn't mean it's the end. It just means she needs time to decompress. She has been through much worse with you than a few bumps and bruises. I remember your rehab story. She was kidnapped. You killed for her, and you mean to tell me you don't think she won't forgive you for this?"

"This is different, Wendy. This is so different."

"The pain and the love felt are the same. Relapse is hard, but it isn't impossible to overcome. You will. I have faith. You won't have to prove yourself to her, honey. She knows your worth. Just give her a minute."

"I want to prove myself anyway. She deserves to see me make efforts to make sure I'm doing all that I can do to be the best I can be." I dig into my pancakes and take a bite. It's sweet, but it doesn't taste nearly as good as it does when I'm here with Sunnie.

Wendy places a sobriety chip on the table and slides it over to me. I stop chewing as I stare at it. "What's this?"

"It's your new sobriety chip."

"But how did you know?"

"Sweetheart, I've been a sponsor for a long time. I had hoped you weren't calling to tell me you relapsed instead of just asking me out to eat. I am always prepared. Come to the meetings three times a week, and next month you'll get your one-month chip."

I pick it up, rolling it across my knuckles. "I hate that I have to start over."

"I hate it for you too, sweetie, but we all start over at some point. I have. Some people hold strong for twenty years before they relapse. This is a journey, and it never ends. Stop trying to get to the finish line, honey. In this marathon, there isn't one. All we can do is keep going, falter, trip, and get back up. It's staying down that's the killer."

"Cheers to that," I say, lifting my water, and she clinks her teacup to mine.

We begin eating our food in comfortable silence, and I think about Wendy's words, letting them rattle around in my head. Before I know it, I'm taking the last bite of my pancakes, and the waiter comes just in time to give me the to-go order of chocolate chip waffles I got for Sunnie and Poppy. They're Sunnie's favorite.

"Here." I hand my debit card over to the waiter, and Wendy scoffs.

She digs into her purse. "Nonsense. Let me pay."

"No way. Your advice has to get paid for somehow." I pay and sign the bill, nearly forgetting the food I ordered for Sunnie.

Wendy and I walk out of the gate and onto the sidewalk. It's a lovely day, and that's why we ate outside. Plus, the truck is right here, parked on the side of the road.

"What's your plan for the rest of the day?" Wendy asks, pressing the fob to her own car that's directly behind mine.

"I'm going to walk to that new kid's store that just opened. I think it's called 'What happens in Vegas…'"

"Oh lord, what a name for a baby store. It's fitting, though." Wendy wraps her arms around me and gives me a tight hug. "Everything will be okay, Patrick. You'll see. Love doesn't come without hardships, that's what makes it love, and that's why it's so hard to come by."

"Thanks, Wendy."

"I'll see you tonight at the AA meeting?" she asks as she slides on her black sunglasses.

"I'll be there every Monday, Wednesday, Thursday."

"Good. Don't be so hard on yourself. It isn't healthy for you or for Sunnie and those babies." With those words, she opens her car door and slides inside, leaving me alone to come up with a plan to win my woman back.

I type in the name of the kid's place and notice it's only a five-minute walk from the café, so I use the opportunity to enjoy the day. The sun beams down on my neck. It's going to burn me if I stay out here much longer. Summers in Vegas, while beautiful, are fucking hot.

I pass King's Club, and for the first time, I don't have the urge to take a left and walk through the doors. It would be nice to say hi to Juliette or Tool, but I know going inside the Club isn't a good thing for me. And if word got back to Sunnie, I'd imagine she wouldn't be happy.

My shirt is sticking to my back by the time I make it to the store. I wipe my forehead off with the back of my arm and step inside, letting the breeze of air conditioning burst over me to cool the sweat against my skin.

All around me are baby clothes, cribs, strollers, everything baby-related. This is good. This is what I need. If I show her I'm serious about the babies, she'll have to see I am in this entirely and I care.

"Hi, Welcome to 'What Happens in Vegas…'" the salesperson giggles as she strolls up to me. She has a thick southern accent that reminds me of a southern belle talking to all the fine folks after church. I bet she has a lot of big hats at home. Southern women like big hats, right? "What can I help you with?" she asks me.

"Well, I don't know. My ol' lady is pregnant with twins. It's pretty early on, but I want to surprise her with a bunch of stuff. I want to show her I'm excited."

"Oh, you sweet thing. Congratulations. You've come to the right place. Is there something specific you're looking for?"

Uh, baby things? Is that too broad of a statement to make?

My eyes fall to her nametag. "MaryAnn, I'll be honest. I don't know what I'm looking for."

"Do you have your home baby-proofed?"

"Hmm?" I'm sorry, what did she say? How do you baby-proof a home?

"Diapers, clothes, bottles, stroller, car seats? Toys? Breast pumps?"

My head swims like it does when it's had a little too much to drink. "Yeah, all those things. I need them all."

Her eyes light up with dollar signs as if she has just landed the biggest schmuck in Vegas to buy out her entire store.

"If you're having twins," she shuffles over to the fancy stroller in the window, nearly tripping over her hot pink heels. "You need this bad boy." She spreads her arms out to showcase it. "It has all-terrain wheels and a cubby for the diaper bag. Two comfortable seats that clip in and out can be used as car seats as well, so you ain't luggin' around two separate things."

"That's convenient," I nod, feeling a bit overwhelmed. Maybe I shouldn't do this without Sunnie.

"Ain't it, though?" she smiles big, blowing a big bubble with the pink bubble gum in her mouth.

"Oh, and you're going to want this too. It's a Halo bassinet. As you can see, it's set up for twins. It helps calm them, so they have a restful night's sleep." She presses the button with her long, red-painted fingernail, and the bassinette begins to rock gently. "See?"

That seems like a good investment. "I'll take that and the stroller, and then I want two newborn onesies, but they have to be gender-neutral. We don't know the sex yet."

"Oh, aren't you just the cutest thing?" she gushes and then shuffles away again, keeping her hands in the hair as she walks. "These. We can put something special on them too. Like a little message from you? Daddy and Mommy love you? Maybe?"

I nod. She's good at her job. "Yeah, that. And cribs. I need a good one."

"Well, do you want a crib that can convert into a bed one day?"

"Uh," I say dumbly. "No?" I scratch the back of my head and think about how Sunnie will probably want to get the kiddos something special.

"Perfect, then I think this is the best one for you." She takes me over to a crib that's already set up. She has no idea, but my chest feels like it's about to explode.

In a good way.

I'm not panicking. I'm excited. I can't wait for her to see the things I'm about to get. "I'll take the best breast pumps and whatever else. Just load everything up you think I'll need and put it on this card." I slide my credit card across the counter, and she stares at it with big hearts in her eyes.

"Sir, you realize that's very expensive."

"I'm good for it." And I am. Since being in my own bubble, I've barely spent any money. Again, that's not fair to Sunnie.

She's deserved to go out dancing, dinner, dates, the works. Maybe I should pay for a girl's day or take her shopping myself. Make her feel wanted and loved again. I want her to know she's more to me than a body that warms my bed at night.

Sunnie is my everything, and I've done a shit job of showing it ever since we have gotten out of that hell hole of a rehab center.

"I'm going to go pull the truck in front. I'll be back. And don't rip me off, okay? I get I'm giving you the reins, but don't take advantage of me. That won't end well, got it?"

Her big hair bounces as she nods. "Oh yes, sir. I wouldn't ever do that. My Daddy raised me better. Goodness me. You don't need to worry about a thing."

She doesn't flinch at the undertone of my threat. "Okay, thank you."

I push the door open, and the bell jingles at the same time a fistful of head punches me in the face. Guess it could be worse.

It could always be Sunnie's fist instead.

CHAPTER TWENTY

Sunnie

I'M SAD.

Two long weeks without Patrick feels like two long years. I think maybe I was too hard on him. Was I harsh? I don't know. I don't know anymore. I have the right to be upset, right? I mean, I can work through his relapse, but I didn't think he'd drive.

My head is a mess.

"Are you going to get that?" Poppy asks me as she leans against the cabinets.

I blink out of my daze, and that's when I remember I put the kettle on, and it's whistling. "Yeah, yeah, I'm going to get it." I wipe my cheek when I realize I'm crying.

Again.

I'm always crying these days. Either because the bruises across my chest and face hurt or because I'm sad Patrick isn't here. I know it's what's best. Really, I just need some time to think. The problem is I haven't thought about anything other than how much I miss him. I haven't thought of the accident at all since moving into the house.

I haven't even talked to him.

How did things become so messy? I just want to know how he's doing, that's all. All I have to do is grab my phone and finally reply to the hundreds of texts, calls, and voicemails he's left me. The only updates I get are from Poppy when she heads into the Clubhouse.

"You still haven't turned off the kettle," Poppy says, stretching her arm out to flip the knob off. She pours hot water into two mugs, and then she sets the kettle on a burner that isn't hot. "Why can't you just invite Patrick back home?"

"It isn't that easy," I tell her, dipping the teabag into the cup. "He made a huge mistake."

"Yeah, but you're okay, right?" her brows dip in her sweet, oblivious naivety.

"Yeah, but what if something worse happened? It isn't just me; it's the babies. It wasn't just me in that car, Poppy."

"To be fair, I don't think he knew you were in it."

"It doesn't matter who was in it. He shouldn't have been driving after drinking. I knew…" I pinch the bridge of my nose to prepare myself for what I'm about to say. "I knew he'd relapse. I saw it in his eyes, in his struggle. I felt it. Relapsing is one thing. Driving drunk is another."

"So you're mad at him for driving drunk, which he shouldn't have done, then possibly almost hurting the kids, which aren't hurt. They're safe. You're safe. You look like hell, but you're safe." She blushes beet red. "Sorry."

"I know, it makes no sense to live on what-ifs, but I need to figure out my thoughts. I'm just as confused as you are. I love him, and I want to be with him. I just need a breather."

"A breather?" she repeats.

"Yep. A breather." I glance at the clock to see the time and then check my phone for the hundredth time to see if he texts.

Nothing.

It's late. It's around nine at night, and I haven't heard from him.

"He isn't drinking, Sunnie."

"I know that." But there's this voice in the back of my head that asks, 'what if he is?' What if he's drunk right now and needs help but is too afraid to call me because of the position I've put us in?

The doorbell rings, and I jerk my head up to look down the hall at the door to see if I can see who it is from here. It's too dark out. I can't tell. For the tenth time in thirty minutes, I brush off the tears and head to the front door.

The house has minimal furniture. Couch, tv, bedroom set, dresser, set of plates and cups in the kitchen. It's enough to get a family started.

The ground creaks with every step, and my heart pounds harder when I notice the tall man on the porch. How could I have forgotten how strong he is? His chest is broad, and his legs are thick. His long hair makes him look wild, and his beard gives him a lumberjack vibe.

God, I've missed him.

I throw the door open when I see him, and I step outside to be closer. The night air wraps around me, and the slight breeze carries his cologne to me. He smells so good. He must have just gotten out of the shower and used his body wash. It's pine and yet also smells like fresh laundry.

His hair is brushed and in gorgeous natural waves down his shoulders. Patrick is wearing a button-up shirt, and his jeans aren't torn. His boots are so polished, I'd swear, I can see the reflection of the stars twinkling in the leather.

In his hands is a bouquet of white lilies, the petals so bright they nearly glow in the night.

"Hi," he says lamely, not knowing what else to say.

I feel like we're dating all over again. Not that we ever really 'dated' in the first place. "Hi," I reply, glancing down at my feet and toeing the grooves of the porch with my feet.

"These are for you."

I reach out for the flowers, and when I grab the stems, our fingers brush together. The familiar spark zings through me and steals my breath. I want to reach out to him. I want to wrap my arms around him and tell him to come inside, to come to bed, to hold me.

I miss him. I need to tell him how I need him. *I regret everything. Come home.*

I don't know how.

"You look beautiful," he says, reaching a hand toward my face to tuck a wayward hair behind my ear. When he realizes what he's doing, he drops his hand. "Sorry. I'm sorry."

"Don't be. Thank you. I don't feel beautiful." I laugh, trying to make the conversation lighthearted. I mean, my face is black and blue, and I have a broken nose.

"You're always beautiful, Sunnie. Always."

My eyes burn from his compliment. Damn it, just tell him to come inside. Forget this misery and heartbreak. "You look really good too, Patrick. Very handsome, as always."

He runs his fingers through his hair, and even in the dark, I can see him blush since the living room light is on, casting a faint glow. "I wanted to look nice for you. I've been going to AA meetings every night for the last two weeks. I wanted to go and see how I'd do before coming back to you." He lifts up his sobriety coin and grins. "Wendy made me a second chip for going so often. Two and a half weeks sober. It's been good for me. I really don't miss drinking anymore because I miss you. Nothing can take that ache away like you can, Sunshine."

I go to reply, but he continues on.

"I looked into rehab too, but I'll be honest, I don't know if I'm there. I don't have the urge or want to drink another drop. What happened changed me forever, Sunnie. I'll check into rehab for you, but I'd prefer if I could try the meetings first? Maybe give me another month and go from there?"

He's going to do all this alone.

Because of me.

"I'm so proud of you, Patrick. I don't think you need rehab either. I can tell you're doing well." Really well. He has gained some weight. His muscles fill out his shirt, and I can't help roaming my eyes over his impressive body.

"I am, but I'm not doing well without you, Sunnie."

"Patrick—" I swallow the pain.

"—I know. I just wanted you to know. I'm not trying to rush you. I wanted to see you every day for the last two weeks, I know you got my messages, but it wasn't easy staying away. I wanted to give you the space you wanted."

"Thank you." I don't want any more space. How do I tell him that it's okay? I regret everything. I don't want us to be apart because we're supposed to get through this together.

"I... um... I bought some items for the babies I'd like to give to you. I've been waiting until I had a few meetings under my belt. I wanted to make sure you saw improvement. And I wanted to see myself get better before I came here."

"You didn't have to do that. I..."

He cuts me off. "—I wanted to. I'm excited. I know before I didn't seem like it, but I'm so happy to move forward with you, Sunnie. I want this. I'll prove it to you. I'm sorry it's so late, but the meetings were long with a few new members."

"It's okay. I wish I could have been there with you, for you. I wish... I wish I didn't push you away when you needed me most. I should have been there."

"Sunnie, you're always there. You've always been there. And I had to do this one on my own because I fucked up. I don't blame you. I hurt you. I physically caused you harm, and I could have done worse."

I shake my head and begin to cry. I can't hold it in anymore. I can't do it. "No! No, no more. Patrick, I'm so sorry. I should have been there. We do things together. We never leave each other alone, and we always have each other's backs. I meant what I said in my letter. I'm always here for you, and I haven't been. I didn't know how to be after everything. I love you. I miss you. I'm so sorry. I'll be better too, but please—"

He takes a step forward, invading my space as he tilts his chin down to look at me. "Please, what?"

"Please, come home to me." I take his hand and press it against my stomach. "Come home to us."

Tears well up in Patrick's eyes.

Poppy interrupts us by squeezing past us. "I'm heading to the clubhouse to hang out with the new babies. I'll stay there tonight." She gives Patrick a hug, and his eyes never leave me. "I'm glad you're home." Poppy bounces down the steps and heads across the desert to the clubhouse.

"Am I, Sunnie? Am I home?"

"I never want you to be anywhere else again."

"You're sure? I'm never leaving again. Things are going to be different with us because I'm different. No more living in a bubble."

"I'd live in a bubble with you for the rest of our lives if it meant being with you, Patrick. Come home. I need you."

Over the last two weeks, I've learned the difference between want and need. Wanting time doesn't fix the need to be with Patrick. It only makes it worse.

All this time, we could have worked through this together. No more time lost, no more time spent apart, no more thinking or having space.

Life is too short for this.

"I'm sure."

He backs me up and leads me inside the house. He kicks the door shut and slowly prowls toward me as if I'm prey.

I'm being hunted, and all I ask is that he kills me softly.

My back hits a wall, and his head turns left and right as he debates how or maybe if he wants to take me.

"I'm not going to leave. I'm going to be here every day," he says, cupping my stomach with his hands. "I'm going to either make love to you every day in every room or fuck you. Every." He rips my shirt over my head. "Damn." He hooks his thumb in the waistband of my pants and pulls them down my legs. "Day." Patrick's fingers play with the thin material of my panties.

I know he can feel how wet I am. I've wanted him since the moment I packed my bags in our bedroom.

"I'll take care of you like you deserve."

I wrap my arms around his neck, careful not to bump my sore nose against his. "And I'll take better care of you too. Like you deserve."

He traces the outline of the bruise the seatbelt left across my chest. It looks worse than it feels. It's a bunch of nasty yellow, grey, and light blues, but it doesn't hurt unless I stab it with my finger to test the pain level.

His brows crease in thought while he strokes my skin and his eyes become wishing wells, shining with coins that have been tossed and wishes that haven't come true. "I'm—"

"Shhh," I whisper, placing my fingers over his lips. "No more apologies. Just love, Patrick. Just love me."

His fingers slide through my hair as my jaw settles between the space of his thumb and index finger. "You'll never have to worry about me not loving you."

I expect him to bring his lips to crash down on me, but they don't. They inch forward slowly, and his beard touches me first by teasing my chin. My eyes flutter from the scratch. I love his beard, so I do what I always do. I sift my finger through the coarse hair, and a deep rumble vibrates his chest. His fingertips trickle down my shoulders, and I relish in his gentle touch.

We don't kiss yet; we just touch one another, enjoying one another's nearness for the first time in two weeks.

Two weeks too long.

"Bedroom," he growls, lifting me up by my ass.

I wrap my legs around his waist as he blindly finds the bedroom. I don't know how he did it while his lips are pressed against the side of my throat. He did help pick the floor plan of this house. It's a four-bedroom, four-and-a-half-bath ranch-style home. Luckily, we have lots of room for the twins now.

The door to the bedroom is already open, and the walk to the mattress is seamless. He lowers me carefully as if he's afraid to hurt me. He drags his lips from my neck to my cheek and pushes himself up higher so he can see me.

He's about to say something, and I'm about to ask him what it is, but he decides against it. He starts the journey to bring our lips together. It's slow, uncertain, and our breaths shake as if we're about to experience our first kiss.

When his lips finally reach mine, I sag against the bed with relief. Finally. We're home.

He sighs down my throat, and it's followed by a desperate moan as his hand cups my jaw and his thumb strokes along my cheek. His tongue is silk, twisting and flicking against mine, remembering what I like.

Like teenagers, we kiss and grope each other. It's followed by him parting my legs and thrusting his hips against mine. His hard cock finds my clit instantly, and the rough material of his jeans drags against my inner thighs. I whimper, wrapping my legs around his waist. I expect him to move faster or harder, but he doesn't.

He kisses me intensely, pouring every ounce of how he feels. I swallow it eagerly, needing it to coat the wounds in my heart from missing him. Without breaking the kiss, I begin to unbutton his shirt. One by one, the buttons come apart, and his chest is exposed. I slide my hands up and over his pecs and drag the shirt off his shoulders.

I toss it to the side and begin working on his jeans.

"You don't have to do this. I'm happy just kissing you, Sunshine," he says, stopping my hands from unzipping his jeans.

Every breath that leaves his mouth is hot, puffing against mine. I can feel how fast his heart is racing, and his cock is steel against my leg. I need him.

Not want.

Need.

"Make love to me, Patrick." I peck a quick kiss to his mouth again. "I missed you so much." I kiss him harder, frantic and afraid he's about to pull away from me.

He sits up, and I reach for him not to go. He can't leave. He just got here.

He sweeps down and claims my mouth before breaking away. "I'm not going anywhere." The sound of his zipper lowering is music to my ears, and I watch as his long, thick cock bobs free and smacks against his stomach.

He kicks his pants free, and before he settles in place, he yanks my panties down my legs and adds them to his pants on the floor.

I'm not wearing a bra right now. My breasts are too sore, and the constraint hurts.

"Fucking gorgeous," he praises, caressing my leg, sides and gently fondles my tits. "So much bigger, Sunshine. Do they hurt?"

I nod, knowing he's caught me in a trance.

"Aw, sweetheart, I'm so sorry," he says, bending down to press a kiss to each nipple. He doesn't suck them but licks them without using his hands to squeeze.

The attention feels so good. His tongue doesn't hurt. It's more like a soothing balm cooling the heated rage firing the tight peaks.

"Love how much your body has changed. I can't believe I didn't notice before." He drags his tongue down my chest and stops at the small swell of my stomach. I don't look pregnant as much as I look bloated—I'm probably bloated too, but that's not a sexy conversation topic.

He kisses me there, twice, one for each twin, as he stares at my swollen belly. "It's Daddy. I love you both so much." He lays his cheek down against them and wraps his hands around them in a makeshift hug.

"You're the dream I never knew I wanted or deserved. And I can't wait to show you how much I'm going to love you. We all deserve a happy life, don't we, Sunshine? And it all starts right here." He pats my belly, and his lips are on me twice like before.

I tear up to see the man below me, adoring me, adoring the kids, and in his eyes, I'm searching for the pain that always lived there. I'm looking for the ghost that haunted him. I'm digging to see the urge for a drink.

But I don't see any of that.

I see a new man.

I see a man ready to move on and live life the way he deserves to. He never had to prove anything to me. I knew the man hiding in the shadows of his pain could put the past behind him.

And the man I see now is beautiful and free.

Maybe the two weeks of space wasn't for me, after all. Patrick used that time to get to know himself again.

He slides up my body, and in a fluid, unexpected motion, his cock fills me too. My mouth drops open with the unexpected stretch.

"Oh god, you feel so good. Like mine. All mine. You are, aren't you, Sunshine?"

"Only yours," I gasp when he slides out and eases back in.

He intertwines our hands and pins them next to my head. "And I'm only yours."

His cock is big and wide, filling me to the brink with every timid stroke he gives me. He's taking his time, moving against me like lazy waves crashing onto the beach. He feels so good. It isn't some quick fuck or a desperate itch that needs to be scratched.

He's taking his time with me.

"Sunshine…" he says my name on a breath that is torn between pain and disbelief.

I understand.

How can something feel this good?

There's no more pain between us. It's different. The agony isn't there looming like it was before.

"Oh, Patrick." I hold onto his back, and those damn tears brim my eyes again as he takes me to new heights and new emotions.

He doesn't increase the pace. It's steady and strong, bringing me the same orgasmic high he always does, but the buildup is intense.

Patrick lifts me up into a sitting position, and I wrap my legs around his waist as he leans back onto his legs. We tremble as we ride together, his hand on my stomach every second we're joined, and it only makes me that much more unstable. I feel like I'm about to fall apart.

My eyes roll to the back of my head, and I throw my head back. He reaches a hand behind my neck to cradle my head. "Look at me. Look at me while we begin new again, Sunshine," he states, his voice smothered in pleasure, and it's enough to coax my eyes open.

"Eyes on me," he says. "Don't look away."

We move in perfect synchronization. Our skin slides against one another as we work up a sweat, and every few minutes, he groans and digs his fingers into my skin.

I kiss him and thrust down while he meets my move, pushing his hips ups so his cock is as deep as it can be.

"If you weren't pregnant, after this, you would be because it would have been my goal when the night is over."

"You've maxed me out. I'm already stuffed with two," I joke, loving how we can be serious and flip to having fun in a matter of seconds.

"You better get used to it then, cause after the twins are born—" he flips me onto my back and drives his cock as far as he can "—I'm going to make sure you're stuffed all over again."

"I'm always stuffed," I wink, talking about his big cock stretching and taking up every space in my depths.

"Damn right you are." He turns me to my side, spreading one of my legs straight out while the other is bent, as he slides in behind me.

I love this position.

He lets go of my hip and sinks back into my entrance. We groan in unison, and he tugs me to his chest, then cups my belly with one hand while keeping the other gripping my leg for leverage.

He begins another torturous slow motion, but in this position, the flared wide tip of his cock rubs against that spot inside me that always has me flying over the moon.

He hits it once, and I cry out.

Twice and my body shakes.

"Patrick!" I shout, my orgasm shattering my soul and putting it back together all at once. His cock becomes soaked from me, my orgasm never-ending as he continues to stroke through my trembling walls, only to brush against that spot again.

Oh, god, I'm going to die from pleasure.

"So sensitive, especially in this position," he marvels, pulling his hips back and pushing forward, so his pelvis is flush with the curve of my ass. His cock is impossibly deep. "I wonder how many times I could make you come." His hand drops to my clit, pinching the sensitive bud all the while massaging the button inside me too.

One stroke, I'm clutching the edge of the mattress.

Two strokes, I'm crying out, literally sobbing from the pleasure.

Stroke three and a hard rub of my clit, I explode again. Fireworks blind my vision, and sweat stings my eyes.

How long have we been doing this? Hours? Our bodies are slick with sweat, and our hair is damp, but I don't want to stop. I never want to stop this connection. It feels too good. I've never felt closer to him in this moment like I do right now.

"Such a good girl, coming for me. I can feel you milking my cock." He kisses my shoulder, and his hand leaves my clit to hold my stomach again. "So fucking wet. Do you hear it?"

When he thrusts a few times to let me hear how I flooded the space between us, my only reply is a moan. The squelching sounds are turning me on again.

God, what is wrong with me? I want to come again.

This time, I press against him and put him onto his back, then swivel on his cock to ride him. I plant my knees on either side of him, and we stare at one another. His chest rises and falls rapidly, and sweat drops are clinging to his hairline. We're wrung out, but we've only just begun.

And what's great about being so sensitive down there is that I come the easiest while I'm on top. It won't take long. I can always feel so much more in this position. I'm not going to be able to breathe.

I can't wait.

My hands slide across his chest, my right palm pressed against the sun tattooed on his pec while I rock back and forth. I ride him hard. His heavy sack slaps against my ass, and the hairs on his upper thighs tickle the sensitive flesh of the upper part of my legs.

My clit rubs against his pelvis, and that familiar pressure building in my body starts to rise. "I'm going to come again."

"Do it, Sunshine. Come all over me. Use me as many times as you want."

"Oh god, I'm going to. Patrick! I'm going to come. I'm… I'm—" I'm not able to finish my warning before the pleasurable waves zing through me. My muscles clench around his cock, milking him for his come. I want to be drenched in it.

He sits up and wraps his arms around me, flipping me to my back, and begins a hard, plummeting, unapologetic pace. Each thrust is hard. I don't have it in me to orgasm again, but I know I will. I'm on fire right now. I'm so sensitive. I'm primed and ready to come for the rest of the night if he wanted.

"Sunshine. Ah, Sunnie. You're going to make me come," he growls, and my hands drift to his firm ass, clutching the globes hard and pulling him against me so I can get every fat inch and every drop of his seed.

He groans, planting himself inside me, and I can feel every pulse of his cock spurting the fertile streams of come bathing my womb.

My womb he's already claimed.

Twice.

He has a firm grip on my stomach, and his body is trembling like mine. He lifts his head and stares at me through thick brown lashes framing his glowing honey eyes.

"You're shaking," he says, his voice quivering from exertion.

"So are you." I lick my lips as I hold onto him for dear life.

"That's what your love does to me," he answers, bringing his lips down on mine and dancing our tongues together in a tired kiss.

The best kiss we've ever shared, in my opinion.

I can't taste anything but sweat, but I don't care. It's the best taste in the world because it's love.

It's all love.

"Don't worry, baby," he begins to say. "I got you." He wraps his arms around me, and I bury my nose into his neck.

"I got you too, Patrick. Forever. It's us always. I'll always have your back."

"I don't want you to have my back."

I bring my head back until it hits the pillow, confused and worried about what he means.

"I want you at my side," he finishes, the thought.

And I'll always be there.

Love, like addiction, can relapse.

And sometimes, even love needs a little rehab.

EPILOGUE

Patrick
Mars

Twenty weeks into the pregnancy

THE RING IS BURNING A HOLE IN MY POCKET AS JULIETTE WAVES THE WAND OVER SUNNIE'S quickly growing belly. She thinks she looks fat. She's cried every day because her pants don't fit, and she's moved into maternity clothes. I've had to hold her every morning, crooning that she isn't fat while simultaneously feeding her pickles.

And I love it.

Every fucking minute of this pregnancy journey with her, I love it. I'm obsessed. I've made the nursery already. It's painted a pale green, and I hope Tongue comes back soon because I want him to paint a fun scene on the wall for the kids.

I'll have to observe, of course. His idea of a fun scene could be… graphic, but he's so talented. And deserves the opportunity for a larger canvas.

I have two recliners in the nursery, too—one for me and one for Sunnie. I want to pull my weight as a parent. We have books, diapers, clothes, cribs, the stroller, and the best part?

She hasn't seen it yet it. It's all a surprise.

"Let's see these babies!" Juliette says excitedly, and Doc chuckles with her enthusiasm.

I think Juliette is getting baby fever too.

At that moment, Tool bursts through the door.

Literally, he doesn't even open it. He shatters it.

"Fuck! Tool, are you okay?" Doc is in front of him in an instant, and Tool shakes his head, and bits of glass fly from his hair. "How many fingers am I holding up? Who is the President? When is your birthday?"

"Two. Reaper. Not telling you."

Everyone lets out a sigh, but Tool just shrugs.

"That really looked open. The clear glass thing really fucks with my eyes."

"Glass is clear," I tell him. "That's glass." I laugh, and everyone else joins in.

"Glass is clear…" Tool mocks me, then hisses as Juliette plucks a piece of glass from his arm.

"I love you," she says on a sigh. "Soooo much." She pats his head.

"Okay, assholes. I came to tell you Reaper called. Sarah gets to finally leave the hospital."

"Hey! That's great. We should set up a party," I offer.

Sarah finally woke up three weeks after she gave birth to Hendrix. Still, she had to do some physical therapy before she was discharged. She was out for so long that her muscles needed to retrain to normal functioning again. But now she's got a clean bill of health.

"After the appointment, we'll get started," Tool says.

"You're so dumb," Knives cackles to Tool. "Who runs through a door?"

"You're about to run into my fist," Tool sneers.

"A taco a day will keep the grumpiness away," Slingshot offers, pulling out a taco from his bag.

"Thank you, Slingshot. You're so kind." Tool narrows his eyes at Knives.

Tank begins to sweep up the glass, and Braveheart holds the pan on the ground for him.

"Okay, are we ready now? I really want to know if I'm going to have boys or girls," I say.

Juliette chuckles and picks up the wand again. "I'm so sorry. Don't mind my silly husband, Patrick." The whoosh of heartbeats fills the screen, and the pan holding all the glass falls to the ground as all the guys and their ol' ladies crowd around us, holding their breaths. "Your belly is growing faster than average," Juliette mutters to herself.

"Is that bad? It isn't bad, right?" I stumble, worried to death now. "I've been feeding her a ton of pickles. Is that why?"

Sunnie giggles. "No, but I could use a pickle right now. I'm starving."

"Healthy appetite is great." Juliette's brow bends as she stares at the screen, switching from heartbeat to heartbeat.

"What is it?" Doc asks, pushing his way to her side.

"Is something wrong?" Sunnie begins to sob. "Patrick, fix it," she wails.

"Can you guys please stop freaking us out?" I peck Sunnie's cheek while glaring at Doc.

"Yeah, sorry, um, it looks like you have a little surprise. You don't have twins. You have triplets. The little bugger must have been hiding behind his sister."

His.

Sister.

"Triplets?" Wow. I'm overwhelmed, but I'm so damn excited. "Triplets, Sunnie!" I jump up and down and kiss the hell out of her face. "Oh, thank you so much. Thank you."

She's smiling while she cries. "You said a girl and a boy, what's the other?"

"Another boy, it seems," Juliette says. "Congratulations, you two."

Everyone whistles and cheers. I'm becoming emotional because I wouldn't have wanted this, like a stupid idiot five months ago.

I pull out the ring from my pocket and drop to my knee. "Sunnie…"

"Oh shit!" Tool yells.

I chuckle.

"Patrick…"

"I need you as my wife, Sunshine. Marry me?"

The yellow diamond reminds me of Sunshine, bright and beautiful and warm just like her. Diamonds are surrounding the circular gem, twinkling in the light.

"Yes! Oh my god, yes! Give me, give me," she says eagerly while her belly is still exposed and wet with jelly. She gives me her hand, flickering her fingers in front of me.

"Stop moving," I chuckle, and she manages to calm down enough for me to put the ring on her finger.

Perfect fit. Just like us.

"Congratulations!" the guys cheer and clap.

I kiss Sunnie hard and quick. "Thanks for making me the happiest man in the world. Without you, I wouldn't be where I am." I go to meetings three times a week—not because I feel like I need to, but I'm there for Poppy now. She needs our support.

"Which reminds me," Tool says, brushing off the broken glass from his shoulder. "Reaper and I have something to give you, and we hope you like it." He fishes out a patch from his cut pocket. "This seems like the perfect time to give it to you." He hands it over, and I cock my head in confusion.

"Mars?" I frown as I read the new name on the patch.

"Your new road name. Mars is the God of war, but so many other things apply to it too. Mars can represent your willpower, your fight, your strength, and your impulsiveness. But there is something that balances Mars. The sun. The sun represents the soul, heart, and a pure source of energy for Mars. The sun makes Mars energetic and heroic. Fearless and warlike. You're always willing to fight because of the sun, and the sun reminds me of how good you are when you become stubborn, defiant, and cruel. The sun reminds you to claim your identity. There is no shame in who you are. The sun, Sunnie—" Tool points to her. "—Believes in you, Mars."

A lump in my throat forms as I trace the name with my fingers. It's the most thoughtful fucking road name I've ever heard of. Sunnie clutches my hand and gives me a watery smile.

"It's perfect," I whisper. "Thank you. So much." I throw my arms around Tool and pat his shoulders harder than necessary.

"Welcome back, brother."

I grab Sunnie's hand and press it against my cheek while I stare into her eyes.

It's a perfect fit.

Mars orbits the sun, but in this case, it's the sun that orbits me.

ALSO BY K.L. SAVAGE

RUTHLESS KINGS MC™ LAS VEGAS
PREQUEL—REAPER'S RISE
BOOK ONE—REAPER
BOOK TWO—BOOMER
BOOK THREE—TOOL
BOOK FOUR—POODLE
BOOK FIVE—SKIRT
BOOK SIX—PIRATE
BOOK 6.5—A RUTHLESS HALLOWEEN
BOOK SEVEN—DOC
BOOK EIGHT—TONGUE
BOOK NINE—A RUTHLESS CHRISTMAS BOOK
TEN—KNIVES
BOOK ELEVEN—TONGUE'S TARGET
BOOK TWELVE—BULLSEYE
BOOK THIRTEEN—ORBITING MARS
BOOK FOURTEEN—SLINGSHOT
BOOK FIFTEEN—TONGUE'S TASTE
BOOK SIXTEEN—BADGE
BOOK SEVENTEEN—HAWK

RUTHLESS KINGS MC™ ATLANTIC CITY
BOOK ONE—BOOMER'S RISE
BOOK TWO—KANSAS
BOOK THREE—ONE EYE

RUTHLESS KINGS MC™ BATON ROUGE
BOOK ONE—RAINBOW

RUTHLESS KINGS MC™ LA GRANGE, TX
BOOK ONE—TRIPLETS RISE
BOOK TWO—SAVAGE
BOOK THREE—JUST BROTHERS

RUTHLESS HELLHOUNDS MC
BOOK ONE—MERCY
BOOK TWO—WHISTLER

RUTHLESS ASYLUM
BOOK ONE—LUNATIC
BOOK TWO—CHAOTIC
BOOK THREE—EMPATHIC

MORETTI SYNDICATE
BOOK ONE—MATEO

ROYAL BASTARDS MC PORTLAND OREGON
BOOK ONE—THRASHER
BOOK TWO—RAVEN

RUTHLESS KINGS MC IS NOW ON AUDIBLE. ALREADY AN AUDIBLE SUBSCRIBER GO HERE TO WWW.AUDIBLE.COM/PD/REAPERS-RISE-AUDIOBOOK/B08FCPP2HQ TO LISTEN NOW. NON AUDIBLE SUBSCRIBERS GO TO WWW.AUDIBLE.COM/PD/REAPERS-RISE-AUDIOBOOK/B08FCPP2HQ TO ENJOY A MONTH NOW.

GO TO:
WWW.FACEBOOK.COM/GROUPS/RUTHLESSREADERS TO JOIN RUTHLESS READERS AND GET THE LATEST UPDATES BEFORE ANYONE ELSE. OR SIMPLY SCAN THE QR CODE TO VISIT AUTHORKLSAVAGE.COM OR STALK HER AT THE PLACES BELOW.

FACEBOOK | INSTAGRAM | RUTHLESS READERS
AMAZON | TWITTER | BOOKBUB | GOODREADS PINTEREST | WEBSITE
BOOK CLUB | AMAZON STORE | RADISH

Printed in Great Britain
by Amazon